1636
THE CHRONICLES OF
DOCTOR GRIBBLEFLOTZ

KERRYN OFFORD
RICK BOATRIGHT

1636: THE CHRONICLES OF DR. GRIBBLEFLOTZ

Copyright © 2016 by Kerryn Offord and Rick Boatright

A Baen Books Original

Baen Publishing Enterprises
P.O. Box 1403, Riverdale, NY 10471
www.baen.com

ISBN: 978-1-4814-8265-3

Cover art by Tom Kidd
Map by Gorg Huff

First Baen mass market paperback printing, June 2017

Library of Congress Control Number: 2016019603

Distributed by Simon & Schuster
1230 Avenue of the Americas
New York, NY 10020

Pages by Joy Freeman (www.pagesbyjoy.com)
Printed in the United States of America

To my friend Marina, who allowed me
to bounce ideas off her, even though she
often had no idea what I was talking about.
—Kerryn Offord

UNDER PRESSURE

Naturally, nobody bothered to check up on the work of a fourth-year apprentice when they were merely supervising distillations, so while he was gone no one noticed that the alembic's outlet had become completely clogged.

The moment the outlet clogged up, the pressure in the alembic started to grow. By the time Martin returned a few minutes later and started walking around the fire checking that condensate was flowing from all of the alembics, the pressure in the clogged alembic was climbing rapidly. The situation *might* have been saved if the clogged alembic hadn't been the last one he checked. By the time he got to it the pressure inside had reached critical levels.

The small beer Martin had gulped down had been too little too late, and consumed too quickly to alleviate his dehydration, so his thought processes weren't as good as they could have been. Instead of shouting out a warning and waiting for Herr Reihing, he tried to deal with the blocked alembic himself. He grabbed a couple of pads made from rags to protect his hands and reached for the container. The slight twisting action he applied as he tried to lift it rubbed the alembic against the firebrick circle in which it sat, creating a scratch. It wasn't much of a scratch, but it was too much for the now critically stressed vessel and it exploded in a spray of glass and a cloud of superheated sulphuric acid vapor. The acid cloud quickly enveloped Martin, condensing on his skin. As he inhaled to scream at the pain he dragged the blisteringly hot vapors into his lungs. . . .

Contents

Part One

The beginning

1606

Chapter 1

The World's Greatest Apprentice Alchemist

1606, Augsburg

Twelve-year-old Phillip Theophrastus Gribbleflotz held tightly to his mother's hand as she stopped in front of the Augsburg assay office of the Fugger banking family.

"This is the place," Maria Elisabeth Bombast said as she turned and crouched down so her eyes were at the same level as Phillip's. "Papa Johann didn't leave us much when he died." Maria scowled. "Your stepbrothers will not help. A place here is the best I can afford."

Phillip nodded. His stepfather had been a reasonably successful apothecary in Überkingen, but a condition of his marriage to Mama had been that most of his estate would go to his children by his first wife. Phillip suspected that Mama had not understood the details of the marriage contract. "I understand, Mama."

"The nice man at the assay office will see that you get the training you've always wanted." She stared into

3

his eyes. "Never forget who your great-grandfather was, Theophrastus, and do his memory proud."

Phillip wished his mother wouldn't use his middle name. It was such a silly name, and people made fun of him when they heard it. He stared at the building that was going to be his home for the next eight or so years while he served his apprenticeship. "I won't forget, Mama."

Maria laid a hand on Phillip's shoulder and pushed him towards the door. "On you go, Theophrastus. Mama has to go now. I'll write to let you know where I'm living when I'm settled."

Phillip glanced up at his mother. Even at thirty-four her painted beauty still attracted the attention of men. He knew it wouldn't be long before she married again. "Goodbye, Mama."

"Be good for mother, dearest."

Phillip glanced back one last time just before he entered the building. His mother was still there, watching. He waved one last time before stepping across the threshold.

Senior journeyman Jakob Reihing led Phillip first to the housekeeper, where he was supplied with more bedding than he'd ever had before, then past his laboratory before leading him to the dormitory where he would be living for the next six to eight years while he served his apprenticeship. "This is where you'll be sleeping," Jakob said.

"This" was a standard wood-framed bed with a canvas mattress cover. Phillip nodded his acceptance and laid his bedding and bags down on the trunk at the foot of the bed.

Jakob gave Phillip a padlock and key. "That's for the bed trunk. Don't lose the key. I have a spare, but you'll have to pay for any replacement."

The ability to secure his private possessions was something new for Phillip. The only way he'd been able to protect his possessions from his stepsiblings had been to hide them. With a lockable trunk, he would no longer have to hope people wouldn't find his hiding places. Phillip held the padlock and key tightly to his chest. "Thank you, Herr Reihing."

"Right. Report back to me when you're made your bed and put your things away."

After Jakob left the room Phillip got to work. First he found a bundle of herbs from his bag, and then he opened the canvas cover of the mattress. The straw smelled fresh, but Phillip had learned that that didn't always mean it was free of vermin. He sprinkled some of his herbs over the straw before closing the cover and making his bed. Then he put his clothes away in the bed trunk. The final things he put in his trunk were the journals he'd been keeping. They recorded all that he'd so far learned about alchemy and the apothecary's art. He used the padlock he'd been given to secure the trunk and hurried to Herr Reihing's laboratory.

That evening

"Hey, what's the smell?" Christoph Baer asked as he followed Phillip into their room.

Phillip was still ruminating over the very good dinner he'd just eaten and didn't immediately hear his roommate's comment.

"Hey, Gribbleflotz, Baer asked you a question!" Heinrich Weidemann said as he thumped Phillip.

That caught Phillip's attention. "What?" he asked, rubbing his arm where Heinrich had hit him.

"What's the smell?" Heinrich asked.

Phillip sniffed. He didn't smell anything unusual, and he said so.

"There's something different about the smell of the room, and you're the only change, so what is it?" Frederik Bechler, the third apprentice sharing the room with Phillip asked.

Phillip became immediately defensive. He sniffed the air again. "Do you mean the herbs I spread over the straw in my mattress?" he asked.

Christoph approached Phillip's bed and sniffed. "That's it. Why did you spread herbs over the straw?" he asked.

"They keep away vermin." Phillip was afraid the older apprentices would hurt him, so he resorted to a technique he'd used in his stepfather's household. "I've got some more if you'd like to spread it over your own mattresses, and I've got another mixture that promotes good sleep," he offered as he opened his trunk and produced a couple of bags of herbs.

"How would you know about herbs and vermin?" Heinrich asked. "And what are you doing with bags of them?"

"My stepfather was an apothecary. These are his herbal mixtures for bedding." Phillip said. "They're very effective."

Christoph and Frederik immediately accepted the offer. Heinrich looked from the cloth bags in Phillip's hand to his bed. His face went through all sorts of contortions before he finally added his acceptance.

The next morning

Phillip woke suddenly. There had been a strange sound. Then he remembered where he was, and relaxed.

"Hey, sleepyhead, it's time to get up," Christoph said as he shook Phillip.

"I'm awake," Phillip said as he pulled the covers aside so he could get out of bed. "What do I do now?"

"Just follow us," Christoph said. "Do you know where you'll be working today?"

"With Herr Reihing," Phillip said.

Heinrich snorted. "A green boy like you won't be working with Herr Reihing."

"Give over, Heinrich," Frederik said. "Phillip means he'll be working in Herr Reihing's laboratory." He turned to Phillip. "That's right, isn't it?"

Phillip nodded.

"Most of the apprentices in his laboratory are all right, but you'll want to watch out for Bernhard Bimmel," Christoph said. "He can be nasty."

"He's not that bad," Heinrich muttered.

"Just because he's your friend doesn't mean he's not a bully," Christoph said. He turned to Phillip. "That was the best night's sleep I've had in ages. What's in those little bags you gave us to put under our pillows?"

"It's just a mixture my stepfather used to make. He was an apothecary. I have the recipe."

"Well, I'm with Christoph," Frederik said. "Thanks to your herbal mixture, I had a really good night's sleep. See you later," he said as he headed off to breakfast.

Heinrich was the last of Phillip's roommates to leave. He paused beside Phillip long enough to mutter his thanks for the sleep-promoting herbs before he too disappeared. Phillip watched him walk off, surprised at the reaction of his roommates to such a simple thing. He was brought back to the real world when his stomach rumbled, reminding him that he was missing valuable eating time, and he hurried off after his roommates.

Herr Reihing's laboratory, the Assay Office

Except for its size, the laboratory where Phillip was to work wasn't too different from his late stepfather's work room. He was able to recognize many of the apparatus from his years helping his stepfather as Jakob Reihing led him around the laboratory, explaining what things were and what they were used for.

Jakob stopped by a couple of beer barrels sitting on a bench with taps installed. "Working in the laboratory, you're going to get thirsty. Don't try drinking from these barrels. They contain stale beer that we are distilling to make aqua vitae. If you want a drink, there are barrels of small beer over there."

Phillip followed the direction Jakob was pointing and located the barrels tucked away in a corner by the door to the outhouse. "I understand, Herr Reihing."

Phillip was then led past the brick furnaces with their circular openings on the top into which alembic were placed to a work bench where there was a range of different sized pestles and mortars. Jakob tapped on the shoulder of the journeyman working there. "Wilhelm, this is Phillip Gribbleflotz. He'll be helping you." He turned to Phillip. "Wilhelm will look after you. Just do whatever he tells you to do, and don't worry. There's not a lot that can go wrong with a mortar and pestle."

The moment Jakob left, Wilhelm Neuffer put Phillip to work grinding up green vitriol. It was work Phillip had done before, although he'd usually ground dried herbs and seeds rather than minerals, so he didn't need a lot of instruction or supervision. After a few minutes of watching to check Phillip knew what he was supposed to be doing, Wilhelm returned his attention to his own pestle and mortar.

Several days later

As the new boy, Phillip was starting at the bottom. It was his job at the end of each day to sweep the laboratory and clean out the furnace. The ashes had to be collected in metal buckets and dumped into a stone pit in the yard and dampened down with water until they were safe enough to leave. Then he had to bring in kindling to set the fires in the furnace ready for the next day. All of this was done under the watchful eye of Wilhelm. At the beginning of each day, while Wilhelm got the fire started, it was Phillip's job to ensure the wood baskets were full and haul in the buckets of water that some of the jobs performed in the laboratory required. It was hard work, not helped by the fact that he had to put in a full day grinding green vitriol as well.

A combination of a hot and windless summer's day and the heat radiating from the furnace meant that it was stiflingly hot in the laboratory. Phillip dragged his shirtsleeve across his sweaty forehead and glanced across to his supervisor. At least Wilhelm looked just as hot and bothered as Phillip. Unfortunately, he didn't look like he was slowing down, so Phillip shook out his tiring right arm to relieve the muscles and got back to grinding.

They weren't the only ones feeling the effects of a long day in the hot laboratory. One apprentice in particular was suffering more than everyone else. Martin Brenner was a fourth-year apprentice, and as such he should have known better than to let himself dehydrate while watching over the retort furnace where temperatures ranged from barely hot enough to distill aqua vitae at one end to hot enough to decompose green vitriol at the other. He had a headache coming on, and he was losing his ability to concentrate. Because of this he missed the first signs that the outlet from an alembic hood was clogging up on one of the retorts being used to make oil of vitriol.

Several minutes later Martin felt an urge to go to the toilet, and after a quick, superficial glance at the retorts, he hurried off. The close proximity of the casks of small beer to the door leading to the outhouse reminded him that he hadn't had anything to drink since noon, so he quickly filled a mug and gulped it down before heading for the privy.

Naturally, nobody bothered to check up on the work of a fourth-year apprentice when they were only supervising distillations, so while he was gone no one noticed that the alembic's outlet had become completely clogged.

The moment the outlet clogged up, the pressure in the alembic started to grow. By the time Martin returned a few minutes later and started walking around the fire checking that condensate was flowing from all of the alembics, the pressure in the clogged alembic was climbing rapidly. The situation might have been saved if the clogged alembic hadn't been the last one he checked. By the time he got to it the pressure inside had reached critical levels.

The small beer Martin had gulped down had been too little too late, and consumed too quickly to alleviate his dehydration, so his thought processes weren't as good as they could have been. Instead of shouting out a warning and waiting for Herr Reihing, he tried to deal with the blocked alembic himself. He grabbed a couple of pads made from rags to protect his hands and reached for the alembic. The slight twisting action he applied as he tried to lift it rubbed the alembic against the firebrick circle in which it sat, creating a scratch in the glass vessel. It wasn't much of a scratch, but it was too much for the now critically stressed vessel and it exploded in a spray of glass and a cloud of superheated sulphuric acid vapor. The acid cloud quickly enveloped Martin, condensing on his skin. As he inhaled to scream at the pain he dragged the blisteringly hot vapors into his lungs.

Nobody in the laboratory could miss the explosion of the alembic. Phillip's shaking hands barely managed to hold onto the pestle he was using long enough to bump it onto the bench as he stared in horror at what was happening. It would have been bad enough if the exploding alembic had contained aqua vitae, as the apprentice would probably have caught fire, but what he was witnessing suggested something much worse.

A man splashed with burning alcohol might try to beat out the fire. He might also drop to the ground and writhe about as he struggled to put out the flames. Either way, one thing you could be sure of was that he wouldn't be quiet about it. This apprentice hadn't uttered a sound.

A hand grabbed Phillip by the shoulder. "Come on, I'll need your help," Wilhelm said as he dragged Phillip towards an apprentice who was screaming about his face burning.

"Take your hands away from your face, Bernhard," Wilhelm said as he tried to pull the apprentice's hands away from his face. "Shit!" Wilhelm muttered. "Gribbleflotz, we need water to wash away the acid."

Phillip was sufficiently over his shock by now that he was able to string a couple of thoughts together. Acid, given that he'd spent the last few days grinding green vitriol meant oil of vitriol, a particularly corrosive acid, especially in the concentrations it was likely to be straight from the distillation retort. From the few times his stepfather and stepbrothers had suffered acid splatters he knew they needed to dilute, and if possible wash the acid off as quickly as possible. He glanced around, hoping to locate one or other of the buckets he'd brought in during the course of the day, but there was none close. What he did see close by though, was the barrels of stale beer. Beer was mostly water, so surely that would be good enough. "The beer barrels," he said, tugging at Wilhelm's hand.

Wilhelm's eyes lit up. "Yes, beer. That'll neutralize the acid. Good thinking, Gribbleflotz." Wilhelm dragged Bernhard towards the barrels. The moment he reached them he opened the tap on one of them and thrust Bernhard's face under the flow of stale beer. "Herr Reihing's going to need my help with Martin," Wilhelm said as he grabbed Phillip's hands and set them to holding Bernhard's face under the flowing beer. "Make sure you flush the oil of vitriol from his eyes."

Phillip swallowed at the idea of being responsible for the older apprentice, but Wilhelm was already hurrying towards the now still body of the apprentice who'd been at the center of the explosion. Phillip stayed with Bernhard, washing his eyes and face with stale beer until a woman arrived to take over the task.

That night

The dining hall was filled with quiet conversation that evening. The death of Martin Brenner was all most wanted to talk about. Those who had been there were being interrogated by those who had missed it. Many of them were embellishing their roles, and then there were those like Phillip, who'd been close enough to see what the acid vapor had done to Martin and would rather forget what they'd seen.

Phillip was doing his best to appear just another interested bystander, eager to hear about the heroics of others, when a shadow was cast over the table.

"You Phillip Gribbleflotz?" Bernhard Bimmel asked.

There was a collective inhaling of breath, which confused Phillip. He recognized the large youth as the person he'd helped in the laboratory. "Yes. How are you feeling?"

"Very lucky. I'm told I have you to thank that I didn't lose my sight."

Phillip shook his head. "All I did was what Herr Neuffer told me to do."

"Herr Neuffer told me he thought to use water to wash off the oil of vitriol, and that it was your idea to use the stale beer. Herr Reihing says that the stale beer saved my sight. So thanks. If there's anything I can ever do for you, just ask."

Phillip muttered "You're welcome." and after a glance around the table, Bernhard walked back to his table.

There was a massive sigh of relief from the table as Bernhard walked away. "Do you know who that was?" Christoph demanded in a whisper.

"He's one of the apprentices who got splattered by oil of vitriol." The name Wilhelm had used popped into his head. "Herr Neuffer called him Bernhard."

"That was Bernhard all right." Christoph said. "I don't think you need to worry about him bullying you."

That was when Phillip recognized the name from the warnings his roommates had given him. He stared in silence in the direction Bernhard had gone.

"How'd you save Bernhard's sight? Have you been holding out on us?" Christoph asked.

Phillip looked at the interested faces looking his way and sighed. He had so hoped for his actions to go unnoticed. "I was in the laboratory when the alembic exploded. Herr Neuffer saw that Bernhard was in trouble and dragged me along to help look after him. I continued to wash away the oil of vitriol with stale beer from the barrels in the laboratory while Herr Neuffer joined Herr Reihing to help him tend to Herr Brenner."

"How did you know to wash away the oil of vitriol with stale beer?" Frederik asked. "Is that something you learned from your stepfather?"

Phillip was all ready to admit that he'd only proposed using the stale beer because he hadn't known where to find water to wash away the oil of vitriol, but one of the other apprentices at the table asked if he'd been burned and the opportunity to correct the misapprehension was lost. Phillip answered by showing a few red marks on the back of his hand. "Only a little bit when I was washing the oil of vitriol off Bernhard."

"Does it hurt?" Another apprentice asked.

"Not now. I've smeared a special burn ointment over it," Phillip said.

"Does it work on ordinary burns?" Christoph asked.

Phillip nodded. The apothecary who'd made it had used the same ointment on the burns a couple of the apprentices had suffered when they dropped or grabbed hot items in the shock of the exploding alembic.

"Can you get me some?" Frederik asked. "I'm always getting small burns from coming into contact with hot alembics."

Again Phillip nodded. He'd watched the apothecary very closely as he'd prepared the ointment and was sure he had or could get all the ingredients to make it. "I can make it."

"What else do you know how to prepare?" Christoph asked.

Phillip hesitated. After a moment he described some of the things he'd helped his stepfather make. The man would have been horrified if he'd realized Phillip had kept accurate records of everything he'd helped him make in the last few years of his life.

Some of the concoctions he'd prepared were extremely dangerous in the wrong hands, and hands didn't come much wronger than those of a not-quite teenage boy. It was fortunate that although Phillip had the recipes and knew how to make them, he didn't know what some of the more dangerous concoctions were supposed to treat.

Over the next month Phillip started to fit in. Compared to his experiences in his stepfather's household, life was good, but there was still a blight on his life—his clothes. An apprentice was usually given two "new" sets of clothes a year, and it was going to be another five months before Phillip saw the first of them. That meant he had to continue wearing the clothes he'd brought with him. There wasn't really much wrong with them, if one ignored the washed-out colors and poor fit. They were warm and well patched. One might even say "overly well patched," with one pair of pants being more patches than pants. But that was what one had to live with when your clothes were hand-me-downs. Unfortunately, everyone else seemed to have better clothes.

Things came to a head that morning as Phillip dressed. He was pushing an arm down a sleeve when suddenly his fingers went through the fabric at the elbow. He examined it to see if he could sew the edges together, but the fabric was too worn. He was going to have to sew on a patch. Reluctantly he pulled on another shirt and went in search of the housekeeper.

He ran the housekeeper to ground in her workroom. "Frau Kilian, do you have any scraps of fabric I can use to patch my shirt?" he asked, showing the elbow he needed to patch.

Veronika Kilian lowered what she was working on and held out her hand for the shirt. After fingering it for a few seconds she nodded. "The girl is busy at the moment, but she should be able to have it done by Friday."

"Oh, no, Frau Kilian," Phillip protested. "I can repair it myself, but I need some fabric to use as a patch."

"You can sew?" Veronika asked.

Phillip nodded and gestured to some of the repairs on his shirt.

"Hmmm. Someone has obviously tried to teach you how to sew."

"My mother," Phillip said proudly.

Veronika's brow lifted for a moment in response to that statement. "If you're willing to do your own sewing, I can ask Sofia to supply you. Come along, and we'll make the arrangements now."

The next day

Phillip was sitting on his bed sewing when Christoph and Frederik entered the bedroom. "What're you doing?" Christoph asked.

Phillip was prepared for the question. There was no way he was going to admit to having to repair his clothes, so he lied. "Adding some color and style to my wardrobe." He held a shirt up to show them how he'd revamped its look by sewing matching scarlet patches over the elbows of the washed-out blue shirt.

Frederik pointed at a large strip of fabric in a vivid green. "What are you going to do with that piece?"

"I thought I'd use it to line the collar," Phillip said,

making sure his grip on his shirt hid the worn areas the green strip was going to cover.

"Where did you get the material?" Christoph asked.

"From Frau Kilian. She's letting me have some scraps." Phillip didn't mention that he was paying for the scraps by helping with the sewing.

"Can you sew patches like those on the elbows of my shirt?" Frederik asked.

Phillip didn't immediately answer. He didn't want to say no, but there was the small matter of getting the necessary cloth from Frau Kilian.

"I can pay," Frederik said, fumbling for his purse.

That changed things. "If you'd like to tell me what colors and type of cloth you'd like the patches made out of, I'll see if I can get some suitable material."

"Thanks, Phillip."

A couple of days later Phillip stole a few minutes during the noon break to see if he could find some suitable material for Frederik's patches. Being a logical youth, he'd asked Frau Kilian for advice and she'd given him the direction of a local rag collector, where he struck gold.

The rag collector usually sold his linens and cottons to the paper makers, but papermakers preferred white or near white rags, and didn't pay much for dyed cloth, whereas Phillip was looking for strong colors. The deal was mutually satisfactory. Phillip got good pieces of material in a variety of colors, and the rag collector got a little more than he would have got from the paper makers.

The next Sunday Frederik made an entrance to the dining room in his newly revamped shirt. All credit for the work was directed to Phillip, who immediately received half a dozen new requests to revamp clothes. It was to become a regular little earner for Phillip. He was never going to get rich dressing up shirts and pants for his fellow apprentices, but the few pfennigs they could afford to pay him allowed him to feed his growing addiction to color.

April 1607

Phillip had been an apprentice for nearly a year, and his mother hadn't written to him once. He had hoped that she would at least remember his birthday, but that had been and gone without a word. He kicked out at a stone on the road and idly watched it careen down the road as he continued to plod along beside the Fuggerei's new apothecary.

The Fuggerei was a social housing complex founded by and supported by the Fugger family for the needy citizens of Augsburg, and Herr Reihing had ordered him to assist Thomas Schmidt while he collected various materials—herbs, fungi, and bits of plants, including a lot of willow branches—to be used in the preparation of remedies for the residents of the Fuggerei. It had turned out to be much more interesting than he'd expected, because Herr Schmidt was a bit of a natural teacher. Either that or he liked the sound of his own voice so much he was happy to talk about anything. Whatever, deliberately or otherwise, Phillip had learned a lot about the various plants they'd collected and what they were used for. And maybe, if he was lucky, Phillip hoped he'd be asked to help prepare the various treatments Herr Schmidt intended to make.

"I hear that your stepfather was an apothecary in Überkingen," Thomas said as they walked back to the assay office facility. "With that and your own interest in *materia medica* I'm surprised you didn't apprentice to an apothecary."

Phillip turned to look at Thomas. "My great-grandfather was Philippus Aureolus Theophrastus Bombastus, and I want to be the world's greatest alchemist, just like he was."

"Paracelsus?" Thomas asked.

Phillip nodded.

"Are you sure he's your great-grandfather?" Thomas asked.

Phillip realized Herr Schmidt had obviously heard that Paracelsus never married and supposedly never had any children. "Mama says that her father, my maternal grandfather, is the illegitimate son of Paracelsus, and that the family passed him off as the son of Paracelsus' cousin in order to secure an inheritance."

"That's an interesting story," Thomas said.

"It's not a story. It's the truth. My mama wouldn't lie," Phillip protested.

"Yes, yes, I'm sure your mother wouldn't lie to you," Thomas said. "So you want to be like Paracelsus? Are you planning on going to university?"

"One day," Phillip muttered. "But I need to improve my Latin first. My stepfather insisted that I help him in his shop rather than go to a specialist Latin school."

"Well, if you like, I can have a word with Master Paler. Maybe he can arrange for you to take lessons."

Phillip's eyes lit up. "Oh, thank you, Herr Schmidt."

That evening

Thomas Schmidt placed his glass carefully on the little table beside the chair before collapsing into the chair opposite the assay office's senior chemist. Once there he picked up his glass of wine and sipped it. "That Phillip Gribbleflotz is an interesting character. Did you know he wants to learn Latin so he can go to university one day?"

Paul Paler looked over his wineglass. "Why would he want to go to university?"

Thomas sniggered. "He wants to follow in his great-grandfather's footsteps."

"What's so funny about that? Lots of boys Gribbleflotz's age want to follow in the footsteps of a famous ancestor. Who's he hoping to emulate?"

"Philippus Aureolus Theophrastus Bombastus von Hohenheim."

Paul was caught with a mouthful of wine, which he managed to spray everywhere as he tried vainly to smother a laugh. While he mopped up the wine he looked at Thomas. "Paracelsus never married."

Thomas nodded. "But that doesn't mean he never had any children."

"I don't remember ever reading about any bastard children."

Again Thomas nodded. "But just because you didn't hear about them doesn't mean they didn't exist."

"Come off it, Thomas. Paracelsus himself was the bastard son of a bastard son. It's not likely the Bombastus family would let a little thing like illegitimacy stop them laying claim to Paracelsus' son."

"Unless they had a better reason to keep it quiet."

"What possible reason could the Bombastus family have for keeping yet another bastard a secret?"

"What if they wanted to pass off the child as the son of Paracelsus' childless cousin in order to secure an inheritance?"

Paul whistled. From everything he'd ever heard about the family he could see them doing that. "Is that what young Gribbleflotz claims happened?"

"That's the gist of the story his mother told him, and just in case there is an element of truth to it, we should keep it between ourselves. His grandfather is still alive, and you know what families are like when it comes to inheritances."

Paul nodded his agreement, but such a story just begged to be told to one's trusted confidants—on the strict understanding that it wasn't to be passed on. In less than a week everyone at the assay office knew that Phillip Theophrastus Gribbleflotz believed himself to be the great-grandson of Philippus Aureolus Theophrastus Bombastus von Hohenheim, also known as Paracelsus, one of the renaissance's greatest scientists.

A lot of people hearing the story didn't believe it, and a few of the apprentices expressed the intention of confronting Phillip over the issue. However, they were actively discouraged from doing this when Bernhard Bimmel stood up. He didn't say he believed Phillip's story, but he made it clear in his own inimitable way that he supported Phillip's right to believe that he was the great-grandson of Paracelsus.

June 1608

At least one of the apprentices in the little classroom listened attentively as the teacher went over the lesson. Phillip had been attending Latin classes ever since that plant-gathering expedition with Thomas Schmidt, and he was sure he was making progress. The teacher left the homework on the blackboard for the students to copy down in their books and then they were free to report to their supervising journeymen.

Phillip was intercepted by Wilhelm Neuffer the moment he appeared outside Jakob Reihing's laboratory. "Ah, good. You're here. How's the Latin going?" Wilhelm asked as he walked with Phillip to the local equivalent of a cloakroom.

"Very well, Herr Neuffer."

"Good. Well, put your books away and grab your apron. We'll be doing something new today."

"What?" Phillip asked eagerly as he hastily donned his heavy leather protective apron.

"Today we start you making oil of vitriol."

Phillip didn't miss a step even as the words generated an image of Martin Brenner being enveloped in a cloud of acidic vapor in his mind. "I used to help my stepfather make oil of vitriol."

"And do you think that means you're qualified to make oil of vitriol?" Wilhelm asked.

Phillip shook his head. "No, Herr Neuffer."

"Good. There are only two ways to make anything here—the way I teach you to do it and the wrong way. Remember that. Now, are you ready to start?"

"Yes, Herr Neuffer."

Wilhelm took Phillip through the whole process,

from heating the ground green vitriol, or copperas as it was also called, until it lost its green and blue color, to the roasting in a glass retort and collecting the vapors—although as the laboratory was still experiencing a period of safety consciousness after the accident that killed Martin Brenner, Phillip's role was mostly limited to watching and keeping the fire stoked so that it burned as hot as possible.

The resulting condensate had a slightly yellow color. Of course, the roasting of the green vitriol took a long time, so it was sometime the next day before he got to watch Wilhelm test the strength of the acid they'd produced. The way the hole appeared in the rag where he'd dripped a little oil of vitriol was suitably impressive. It was as if he'd held a flame to the rag, although it didn't catch alight. It was certainly a timely reminder to always wear his heavy leather apron to protect not only his clothes, but also his skin.

Over the next few months Phillip learned to make oil of vitriol, aqua fortis, aqua regia, acidum salis, and even high-strength aqua vitae—which was not intended for human consumption, not even if diluted with fruit juice.

December 1608

"Come on, Gribbleflotz. Everyone knows you're virtually left to run the distilling furnace on your own," Bernhard Bimmel said.

Phillip had been quietly sitting on his bed sewing lime green cuffs to a shirt when the deputation of senior apprentices appeared with their simple request.

"But making illicit aqua vitae—what if I'm caught?" Phillip protested. There had been cases of apprentices being caught running illicit stills, and he didn't want to risk their punishment. He said so.

"But that's what's so good about you doing it using the laboratory furnace. Who's going to notice if you were to run a few extra alembic?" Heinrich Weidemann asked.

That was getting too close to home for Phillip. He had to share a room with Heinrich, and he could so easily make Phillip's life hell. But still Phillip resisted.

"We'll make it worth your while," Bartholomäus Kellner added.

Bartholomäus' involvement almost rolled up Phillip's resistance there and then. He was the assay office's best hope of victory over the Goldsmiths' guild in the next Schützenfest. They were unlikely to punish him for possession of illicit alcohol, and if they didn't punish Bartholomäus, then it was highly unlikely that they would punish his co-offenders.

"You're the best there is, Phillip," Christoph said. "Just look at how long they've left you on making acids. Nobody else has been stuck with that job as long as you have." Frederik and Heinrich chimed in with their agreement.

"That just means I'm a slower learner than everyone else," Phillip protested.

"Right," Frederik said with more than a hint of sarcasm. "You're such a slow learner that Herr Reihing and Herr Neuffer are happy to leave you running the distilling apparatus without supervision." He stared intently at Phillip. "When I had my turn on the stills, I had both of them constantly breathing down my neck."

"They only did that because they don't want a repeat of what happened with Martin," Christoph said. There were murmurs of agreement from the other apprentices.

"Herr Neuffer regularly checks up on me," Phillip said.

Christoph nodded. "Sure he does. But I bet it's only to check that you're drinking enough. I've been watching him, and he barely gives the retorts and receivers more than a cursory glance when you're running them." He looked imploringly at Phillip. "They trust you, Phillip. They trust you to work on your own like they trust nobody else. You're perfect for the job."

Phillip searched the hopeful faces gathered around him. He didn't know why they wanted the aqua vitae for their Twelfth Night party—well, actually he did know, but he didn't understand why they wanted it triple distilled. That was much too strong to drink.

They were so earnest, and they were saying such flattering things about his capabilities. It would be nice to prove them correct, but Phillip wasn't prepared to burn all of his bridges. "How about I try to sneak in an extra retort tomorrow and see how that goes? If that doesn't raise any suspicions, then I'll make as much as I can for your party."

That offer was gratefully accepted, and most of the apprentices left, leaving Phillip with just his roommates.

"It's going to be a great party," Frederik said.

"I haven't made any aqua vitae yet," Phillip pointed out.

"But you will. We're counting on you."

And that, as far as Phillip was concerned, was the

problem. Now he had to make the illicit aqua vitae, without getting caught.

Friday, January 9, 1609

Ulrich Hechstetter, the head of the Augsburg assay office, sipped from the glass of strong liquor and sighed. "It's a very good tipple, with not a hint of where they got the aqua vitae." He looked across the senior staff lounge towards Master Paul Paler and his senior journeyman Jakob Reihing. "That means they must have triple distilled it. Do you have any idea where they hid the still?"

Paul shook his head. "We looked in all the usual places, but they hid it well this year."

Ulrich thought back to his days as an apprentice. "And none of the senior staff realized they had a still running? Surely they had to have someone attending to it constantly?"

"You'd think so," Paul agreed. "But none of the journeymen reported unusual absences." He snorted. "They made it look like they weren't going to try to produce some strong alcohol for their Twelfth Night party this year."

"Which should have started the alarm bells ringing." Ulrich followed another sip with another sign of contentment. "Well, we'll know better next year."

Jacob chuckled and took a sip from his own glass. "It was nice of the apprentices to give the senior staff a couple of bottles."

"It was cursed impertinent," Ulrich muttered before taking another sip. "They were rubbing our noses in the fact that they were able to make more than enough for their party without us catching them."

April 1609

Paul Paler was deep in thought as he read a report when there was a perfunctory knock on his door and the head of the assay office walked in. "Herr Hechstetter," Paler said as he dropped the report and shot to his feet.

"Sit down, Paul," Ulrich said as he pulled over a chair and sat down. "There's something I want you to do for me."

Paul fell back into his seat. "Yes, Herr Hechstetter?"

"Bartholomäus Kellner has complained about inconsistencies between different barrels of gunpowder. I want you to do something about it."

"Powder? Barrels?" Paul stared at Ulrich in confusion for a few seconds before a light dawned. "Oh, you're talking about gunpowder for the Schützenfest."

"Of course I'm talking about the Schützenfest. And this year we are not going to be beaten by the Goldsmiths' guild."

Paul winced. The annual festival was supposed to be a demonstration of the readiness of the guilds to do their part to defend the city, but with no war threatening the city, the competitions had become a matter of bragging rights. Unfortunately, in the Augsburg inter-guild shooting competition, the Goldsmiths' guild had placed higher than the assay office for each of the last ten years. To say it was getting embarrassing didn't really convey the weight of feeling in the assay office. "I'll see about checking the powder and get back to you."

"I want a bit more from you than just confirmation that there is a problem, Paul. I want a solution." Ulrich stared at Paul for a few seconds before leaving.

Paul looked at the papers he'd laid on his desk and sighed. They were important, but not as important as keeping his boss happy. He got to his feet and went in search of his senior journeyman.

Paul glanced around the laboratory, taking in the various apprentices hard at work. His gaze settled for a few seconds on the only apprentice who hadn't turned to see who'd come in, before continuing the search for the senior journeyman who ran the laboratory. He located Jakob Reihing off in one corner and gestured for him to join him. It took only a few minutes to explain to Jakob what Ulrich Hechstetter wanted.

"Phillip Gribbleflotz can do the testing," Jakob said. "It's well within his capabilities, and you only have to show him how to do something once."

"Gribbleflotz? Isn't that the boy who claims to be the great-grandson of Paracelsus?"

Jakob nodded. "That's him over there." He gestured towards the youth Paul had noticed earlier. He was still diligently checking some distillation vessels.

"Is he deaf or something?" Paul asked. "He's the only apprentice that didn't look around when I walked in."

"Or something," Jakob said. "He's not easily distracted from whatever it is he's working on."

"And what's he working on?"

"Right now, he's making aqua fortis."

The mention of the strong acid reminded Paul of

a message he'd been asked to pass on. "That reminds me. The assayers asked me to thank you for the high quality of the acids you've been producing lately. They really appreciate how consistently pure they've been over the last few months."

"That's mostly because of Phillip. He's got a knack for producing very pure acids and such."

"A knack?" Paul asked.

Jacob shrugged. "He's certainly very capable for his age and training. Maybe he really is the great-grandson of Paracelsus."

Paul responded to that suggestion with a derisive snort. "Just do whatever you have to do to attract his attention so we can tell him what he's going to be doing for the rest of the day."

Phillip was deeply involved in controlling the distillation of the aqua fortis from the mixture of green vitriol and saltpetre when he felt a tap on his shoulder. He kept his eyes on what he was doing. "Yes?"

"I need to talk to you, Phillip."

Phillip recognized his supervisor's voice. He also recognized from the tone that he should stop what he was doing immediately. Reluctantly he raked away the coals heating the vessel and turned to face Jakob. The man beside him came as a shock. "Master Paler."

"Phillip, Jakob here says that you are just the person to run some tests for me."

Phillip didn't know how to reply, so he turned to his supervisor in mute appeal.

"Master Paler wants you to check the various barrels of gunpowder used by the shooting team for consistency."

That sounded interesting, but there was one major difficulty. "I don't know how to do that, Herr Reihing."

"That's all right. I'll show you what has to be done, and then leave you to get on with it."

Although he was proud that Herr Reihing thought he could perform this new task, he knew it wouldn't make him any friends with the other apprentices. He could already feel their eyes boring into his back. "When do I start?"

"Report to me as soon as you've finished your current distillations," Jakob said.

That evening the other apprentices crowed around Phillip when he returned to the dormitory.

"What were you doing with Herr Reihing today?" Heinrich asked.

"He wanted me to help him test some gunpowder for consistency."

"And why would Herr Reihing want you to help him do that, instead of someone with more training?"

"Such as yourself, Heinrich?" Christoph suggested.

"Yes, me. After all, I've only got another year to go in my apprenticeship." Heinrich turned his attention back to Phillip. "So, why did he drag you away from the production of acids, Gribbleflotz?"

"You're only complaining because they moved you to the furnace while Phillip was away," Christoph said.

Heinrich sent Christoph a quelling glare before turning back to Phillip.

Phillip shrugged. He had no idea why he'd been singled out. But that wasn't going to appease his current audience. However, Herr Reihing had told him why the powder was being tested. "He said Herr Kellner thought the quality of the powder the shooting team was using wasn't consistent between the barrels."

"So you had to check to the quality of the powder," Christoph said. "Go on; tell us how you did that."

Christoph's plea was seconded by the rest of the apprentices; even Heinrich indicated he was interested.

"Well, first we did a simple visual test," Phillip explained. "Herr Reihing said that over time gunpowder could separate into its component parts. So we looked for signs of that. Then we did a flash test."

"What's that?" Heinrich asked.

"You fill a small copper thimble with gunpowder and invert it onto a piece of clean parchment. Then you use a red-hot iron probe to ignite it. You can determine the quality of the powder by the marks it leaves on the parchment."

"I bet you can't do that," Heinrich muttered.

"Leave off, Heinrich," Frederik said. "Even if you aren't interested, I am." He turned to Phillip. "Why do you use a copper thimble?"

"It doesn't have to be a copper thimble. That's just what Herr Reihing used. Any small container will do. The idea is to use exactly the same amount of gunpowder every time so you can compare the results," Phillip explained.

"And I suppose you invert the thimble over the parchment rather than just pour it out so the shape of the mound of gunpowder is the same in each experiment?" Frederik asked.

Phillip nodded. He wasn't surprised at the sudden drop-off in hostility. Gunpowder was something dear to all their hearts. Most, if not all of them, had tried to make some with varying degrees of success at some stage, and Phillip was no exception. There was something about gunpowder that appealed to teenage boys.

"And that's what you've been doing all afternoon, igniting gunpowder?" Christoph asked.

"No, but the other tests aren't so much fun." Phillip wasn't being entirely honest, because he'd actually enjoyed doing the other tests, but he knew his audience would consider them boring.

"Let us decide if it's fun or not," Heinrich said.

"Well, what I had to do was take a sample from each barrel of gunpowder, wash each in warm water, and then I had to filter each solution and weigh the residues. The difference between the weight of the initial samples and the residue is the amount of saltpetre in the original sample."

"I've had to do something like that before," Heinrich muttered, "and it's so finicky to do that you're welcome to it."

Jakob passed on Phillip's results to Paul Paler, who in turn passed them on to Ulrich Hechstetter.

"Here are the results from the gunpowder tests," Paul said as he handed over Phillip's report. "The gunpowder in the store can be divided into two groups with different levels of saltpetre. I've marked the barrels as being either batch one or batch two."

"So that's the end of it. Thanks, Paul. I'll pass the news onto Bartholomäus Kellner."

"There is something else," Paul said hesitantly.

"Yes?"

"It's just a suggestion," Paul muttered.

"Yes?" Ulrich prompted.

"Jakob seems to think that there were a lot of

impurities in the gunpowder, and that we could make better gunpowder than we're getting from Master Böcklin by using purer ingredients," Paul said.

Ulrich shook his head. "Master Böcklin would never stand for us making gunpowder."

"That's what I told Jakob," Paul said. "But he pointed out that Phillip Gribbleflotz has a proven ability to make really pure acids, and that it wouldn't hurt to let him try to do the same with saltpetre and sulphur. If he can deliver purer saltpetre and sulphur, then you could ask Master Böcklin to use it to make a special batch of gunpowder for the shooting team."

Ulrich had heard about the high quality of the distillates young Gribbleflotz was making, and the idea that he might be able to work his special magic over the ingredients for gunpowder had a certain appeal. "That could give us the edge we need to beat the Goldsmiths this year. I'll have a word with Georg and see if he's amenable."

A couple of days later Ulrich dropped in on Paul with the news. "Master Böcklin is happy to make a special order for us, especially if we provide him with the raw materials. So I want you to get Gribbleflotz started refining the saltpetre and sulphur as soon as possible."

Paul passed on the instruction to Jakob Reihing, who took charge of teaching Phillip how to refine saltpetre and sulphur. The first step was to provide him with a copy of Lazarus Ercker's 1580 *Treatise on Ores and Assaying* to read. It was in Latin, and Phillip spent the next week fighting his way through the long section on saltpetre. In addition to learning the theory of making saltpetre, it did wonders for his Latin skills.

With the theory in place Jakob took Phillip through the various stages of preparing saltpetre, from the collection of the earths, through the treatment with lye and washing in warm water, and ending with the boiling away of the resulting filtered saltpetre solution to give the desired white powder. In comparison, the production of very pure sulphur was easy.

Once he was sufficiently sure that Phillip knew what he was supposed to be doing, Jakob left him to it. As he poured his first samples of wash water through the cloth filter into the evaporating pan Phillip couldn't help but think about the opportunity to make more triple distilled aqua vitae that was going to waste. The high proof alcohol was a valuable trade commodity amongst the apprentices, but Herr Reihing was paying too much attention to his progress for him to risk running any retorts on the furnace.

July 1609, the day of the Schützenfest

Phillip shaded his eyes as he tried to look through the window of the local bookstore. There were a couple of interesting looking titles on display. Unfortunately, as a mere apprentice, there was no way he could afford them.

"Stop drooling, Phillip," Christoph Baer said.

"Yes," Frederik Bechler said in agreement. "The Fuggers are good employers, but even they don't give their apprentices enough to buy books."

Phillip gave the practical alchemy books a last regretful look before pushing himself away for the window. "I can dream," he said.

"Sure. How much money do you have?" Frederik asked.

"Nearly two gulden."

"And how much were the books you were drooling over?"

Phillip sighed. "Four gulden."

"You could always try betting on the shooting contests," Christoph suggested. "Last year our team was four to one to finish ahead of the Goldsmiths. That would've given you enough to buy two of those books."

"They finished behind the Goldsmiths' guild last year," Phillip pointed out.

"Right, but this year things are going to be different," Frederik said.

Phillip shook his head. "The new gunpowder isn't enough to guarantee our team will beat the Goldsmiths' guild."

"But if they do, think of the payout. Come on, I want to see what odds the bookmakers are offering."

Christoph was willing, so Phillip made it unanimous. After all, they were just going to check the odds. He didn't have to lay a wager.

Phillip studied the bookmaker's odds board and was happy to see that he wasn't going to be asked to risk his hard-earned money. Beside him, his companions weren't quite so happy.

"Five to four? What kind of odds are those?" Frederik complained. "Last year you were offering four to one for the assay office to beat the Goldsmiths' guild."

The bookmaker gave the Frederik an enigmatic smile. "That was last year."

Frederik continued grumbling as he handed over

some coins and received a betting slip in return. Christoph followed suit, then both of them turned to look inquiringly at Phillip.

He shook his head. "It's not worth it. Even if I bet all my money I wouldn't win enough to buy one of those books."

Lucas Ehinger, ever the professional bookmaker, smiled at Phillip. "Perhaps I could interest you in a wager on the *Schützenkönig*? The odds are very attractive."

Phillip shook his head. "No thanks." The competition for the *Schützenkönig* required that shooters take turns shooting at a bird on a pole. There were prizes for the shooter who shot off a wing, a leg, and the head, but the big prize—being crowned *Schützenkönig*—went to whoever shot the last piece of the bird off the wooden pole on which it was mounted. That might sound like a test of accuracy, but no single shot was going to sever a limb or head, and it could take more than forty hits to reduce the bird to the point there was none of it left on the pole. As each competitor was allowed only one shot per turn at the shooting line, the shot that finally destroyed the bird, and it was a real bird, not a wooden or stuffed dummy, could come at any time. It was, as far as Phillip was concerned, more a matter of luck than ability, and the almost flat thirty to one odds the bookmaker was offering on the thirty approved competitors suggested he agreed.

"If you're not going to bet we might as well see if we can get a good spot to watch the shooting," Frederik said.

Christoph agreed and they set off. They hadn't gone far before Frederik started muttering about the snake in the grass who'd shortened the odds so much by betting heavily on the assay team to beat the Goldsmiths. Christoph joined in, making suggestions of who he thought might have been responsible. Phillip's contributions were halfhearted. He wasn't particularly angry at the people who had shortened the odds. In fact, he was somewhat fond of them. However, he was glad neither Christoph nor Frederik had thought to wonder how a third-year apprentice, who wasn't paid a wage, happened to have nearly two gulden. Phillip might not like to risk his money by gambling, but that didn't mean he wasn't prepared to sell information to people who did.

The crowds had returned to the range ahead of them, and Phillip and his friends were forced to stand near the back of the crowd as the three-man teams competing in the inter-guild competition marched with all due pomp and ceremony onto the range. There was a delay while the team captains introduced their teams to the referees, and then the referees broke up into two groups. A group of three walked the hundred yards down range to where the target stood while the rest of them took their places at the shooting line.

Phillip could barely make out the circle of painted wood in the distance. Beside it was the referees' hut, where the three scorers would shelter when a competitor was firing. He knew from the practice shots he'd been permitted to take with one of the handcrafted wheel-lock target rifles the assay office owned that the competitors would be aiming at something little bigger than a pinhead above the foresight of their rifles. How anybody could hit such a small target he couldn't understand. Certainly he'd missed it with all ten shots Bartholomäus had allowed him.

Over the course of the competition each shooter would take five shots from a standing position. If he hit the target a referee would wave a flag across the target. Another would plug the hole the bullet made with a wooden peg and write an identifying number beside the peg. The third referee kept a record of who was shooting and where their shots went.

At the shooting line, when a shooter scored a hit a referee would present him with a small flag. The successful shooter would then walk over to another referee, who would record the hit. The flags would then be placed somewhere prominent so the spectators could see who was winning. The maximum score a team could get was fifteen hits, but that almost never happened. Any ties would be decided based on which team had their hits closest to the bull's eye.

"You were lucky," Otto Hofbauer of the Goldsmiths' guild said as he begrudgingly shook Ulrich's hand.

Ulrich's smile was bright enough to blind a man as he accepted Otto's acknowledgment of defeat. "Luck had nothing to do with it. It was our team's superior shooting that beat your team."

"And a special production run of gunpowder," Otto muttered.

Ulrich allowed his smile to drop down to a mere grin. "Sour grapes, Otto. All we did was buy the best gunpowder Georg could make."

"Gunpowder that Georg refused to sell to anyone else."

"Of course he refused to sell to anyone else. He made it using super pure saltpetre and sulphur we supplied him just for our order."

"It gave you an unfair advantage."

Ulrich's smile blossomed again in the face of Otto's disgruntled expression. "But I'm sure Georg offered to make you a special batch of powder if you could provide him with the ingredients."

"He did," Otto said.

"There you are then. You have only yourselves to blame for not taking Georg up on his offer."

Otto gave Ulrich a sour look. "We did take him up on his offer. Unfortunately, the powder Georg made from our ingredients wasn't as good as yours."

"Oh dear, that means your ingredients can't have been as pure as ours." Ulrich put on his best fake sympathetic face. "That doesn't say much for the quality of your training. The training we provide is so good we were able to leave the task of purifying the ingredients to a mere third-year apprentice."

Otto snarled a response before storming off, leaving Ulrich almost purring.

"That wasn't very nice," his wife told him.

"But it felt so good." He glanced down at his wife. "We finally beat the Goldsmiths' guild, and not by just a few points. We beat them by the biggest margin there has ever been between us."

"And all because a third-year apprentice thought he could make better gunpowder using pure ingredients," Magdalena said.

Ulrich shook his head. "Georg has always known that the purer the ingredients the better the powder."

"So why doesn't he always use purer ingredients?"

"Because it's not that easy to make purer ingredients, and the small improvement in performance doesn't usually justify the extra costs."

"Except when it means the assay office can beat the Goldsmiths' guild?"

Ulrich felt the heat rising and knew he was blushing. "Except when it means we can beat the Goldsmiths' guild," he agreed.

Magdalena was about to say something more when Georg Böcklin and his wife intercepted them. While his wife distracted Magdalena, Georg pulled Ulrich to one side. "Someone has inquired about getting some of the special powder I made for you. Can you give me a price to supply me with the high-purity saltpetre and sulphur?"

Ulrich was immediately suspicious. "Would that someone be Otto Hofbauer?" he asked.

"No, it was Wolfgang Manlich."

"From the Brewers' guild? What does he need better powder for?" Ulrich asked. "He won two of his events."

"He might be by and far the best shot in Augsburg, but the competition in the intercity competitions is fierce, and he wants every advantage he can get. And seeing how Bartholomäus Kellner, using the special powder I made for you, leapt up five places compared with his score last year in the open one-hundred-yard competition, Herr Manlich seems to think that powder might be just the edge he needs."

Ulrich had absolutely no idea how much it had cost to produce the super pure saltpetre and sulphur, so he resorted to the old standby. "It's going to be expensive," he said.

"Of course it's going to be expensive," Georg agreed. "I've bought supposedly super pure ingredients before. But I've never used anything as good as the saltpetre and sulphur you provided me with. If the price isn't too much more than I've paid previously, I'm interested in buying as much as you can get me." He looked at Ulrich expectantly. "So, how much is it going to cost per pound?"

In the face of Georg's determination Ulrich had no choice but to admit he didn't know. "But I'm sure I can get you a price soon."

"How soon?" Georg asked. "Herr Manlich wants to start practicing with the new powder before he leaves for the next Schützenfest."

"I'll see that you have a price by Wednesday."

"Thank you." Georg collected his wife and they walked off.

Ulrich was still watching Georg and his wife walk away when he felt a jab in the ribs. That was a signal from Magdalena that he'd been ignoring her. He hastened to remedy the situation before she jabbed him again. "Yes?"

"I asked you what Herr Böcklin wanted," she said.

"He just wanted to know how much it would cost to buy a supply of our new super pure saltpetre and sulphur."

"But the assay office doesn't sell super pure saltpetre and sulphur," Magdalena said.

"We do now." Ulrich noticed Paul Paler and his wife were close by. He changed direction and headed towards them. "Paul," he called out.

Paul reacted to his name being called out by turning towards Ulrich. "Yes, Herr Hechstetter?"

"I promised Georg Böcklin that I would give him a price for super pure saltpetre and sulphur by Wednesday. See to it."

"Yes, Herr Hechstetter."

❖   ❖   ❖

Paul Paler muttered into his beard as he glared after his boss. It was just like Herr Hechstetter to offload a job like that onto him and expect an answer in a couple of days.

"What did you say?" Elisabeth Welser asked.

Paul smiled at his wife. "Nothing you want to hear. Herr Hechstetter wants me to calculate a price to supply Herr Böcklin with super pure saltpetre and sulphur by Wednesday."

"You won't have time to do that. We're going round to Mother's tomorrow."

That was a good enough reason to insist he had to do it himself, but using that excuse to avoid his mother-in-law probably wasn't worth the domestic strife it was bound to cause. "Don't worry, dear. I'm sure Jakob Reihing will be able to assemble the necessary figures before Wednesday."

"Good!" There was a certain something in the way Elisabeth said the word that told Paul he'd made a wise decision. "And there's Anna Maria and Jakob. Why not ask him now?"

Paul glanced in the direction Elisabeth was pointing and easily identified Jakob and his wife. They looked happy, and he really didn't want to break the mood, as he knew the news he had to impart would surely do.

"Come on," Elisabeth said as she tugged at his arm. "Anna Maria, Jakob," she called. "Wait a moment."

Paul saw that Jakob and his wife had heard and had stopped so they could catch up. Reluctantly he let Anna Maria drag him towards them.

"How can we help you?" Jakob asked.

"Herr Hechstetter just promised Herr Böcklin that he would give him a price for super pure saltpetre and sulphur by Wednesday, and I need you to collect the necessary information so I can work out a price."

"Oh, that's easily done," Jakob said.

"It is?" Paul was surprised at how happy Jakob appeared to be at having such a task dumped on him at such short notice.

Jakob nodded his head. "Phillip Gribbleflotz is a compulsive note-taker. I'm sure he'll have all the information you need to calculate a price in his notes. I should be able to get you all the information you need by lunch time tomorrow."

The next day Paul presented himself in Ulrich's office. "Herr Hechstetter, I have the pricing estimates for the super pure saltpetre and sulphur you requested."

"Already? That was quick work." Ulrich held out a hand for the piece of paper Paul was holding. "I hope they're accurate."

"The apprentice charged with purifying the saltpetre and sulphur kept very detailed notes on everything to do with the task. From his notes it was a simple task to calculate how much it cost to produce the saltpetre and sulphur, and therefore how much we would have to sell it for to make a profit."

"That'll be young Phillip Gribbleflotz again?"

Paul nodded. "I've already set him to making more saltpetre and sulphur."

Ulrich glanced up for the estimate he was reading. "Good, good. We really must do something for the young man to demonstrate our appreciation for his good work."

"Well, he's an apprentice, and they're always short of money," Paul suggested.

A few days later

Phillip laid down his pen and flexed his hands. He'd used the money Master Paler had given him to buy writing paper, and he was now was slowly copying a collection of treatises on alchemy by his great-grandfather that he'd found in the assay office's library. This handwritten copy would be the beginning of his own library.

August 1609

The parcel arrived for Phillip in the post. Mail of any kind for the apprentices was rare, and parcels, especially anything the size of the parcel Phillip received, were doubly rare. So there was a lot of interest in the parcel, and his fellow apprentices gathered around Phillip as he examined it.

"Who's it from, Phillip?" Frederik asked.

Phillip pointed to the return address written on the parcel. "It's from my mother." He stared at the address. Last time he'd heard from his mother she'd been in Stuttgart, living in the household of her father, his grandfather. But the parcel had been posted in Neuburg. It was possible that his grandfather, who was a surgeon in the service of the duke of Württemberg, had been sent to Neuburg, but according to the only other letter he'd received from his mother since he started his apprenticeship he'd been firmly settled in Stuttgart.

Phillip untied the string that was holding the parcel together and carefully opened the wrapping to expose a number of worn journals and a letter. He opened the letter and quickly read it before shoving it under his shirt. Then he turned his attention to the journals. He picked the top one up reverently and opened it.

"What'd she send you?" Frederik asked.

Phillip lowered the journal. "These are some of my great-grandfather's diaries. My grandfather left them to Mama, but she had to wait for probate to be granted before she could take possession of them and send them to me."

"I'm sorry to hear your grandfather died," Christoph said.

Phillip could only nod in acceptance of Christoph's sympathy. He certainly couldn't tell him that his grandfather had died a year ago and his mother hadn't bothered to let him know until now.

"Those are really the diaries of Paracelsus?" Frederik asked.

Phillip held one of them open on the front page and pointed to the name written there.

"Philippus Aureolus Theophrastus Bombastus von Hohenheim," Frederik read. "That must be a diary from before he adopted the name of Paracelsus."

Phillip checked the dates in the half dozen diaries he'd received. "That one is from his time at the University of Ferrara, and the others cover his subsequent travels."

"And your mother had them? You really are the great-grandson of Paracelsus," Heinrich Weidemann said with a touch of awe intermixed with disbelief.

"Was there ever any doubt?" Christoph asked.

Chapter 2

Dr. Phil's Journey

Saturday, January 5, 1613, Augsburg

The smoke was making Paulus Rauner's eyes water as he forced the sack stuffed with damp straw taken from the local stable down as far as he could into the chimney. Finally he was satisfied it was in place and turned his attention to getting down off the roof before it started to have an effect. The roof was slate, and it was wet, so he had to be very careful. But even being careful he still managed to slip, catching his leg against the roof of a protruding dormer window as he desperately fought to keep his balance. He managed not to fall, and a few minutes later he was safely on the ground.

"Did you do it?" Claus Schorer asked.

Paulus nodded. "It shouldn't be long before they're smoked out. That'll teach them to insult my sister."

"Then let's get out of here. I don't want to be around when they come out the doors."

Paulus sent the house of Master Fleckhammer a satisfied smirk before loping off after his friend.

They covered several hundred yards before Paulus' leg started bothering him. He ran a hand over where it was sore and it came up covered in something sticky. He sniffed his hand. It didn't smell yucky, so he touched it with the tip of his tongue. It was salty. "Hang on, Claus. I think I cut myself."

Claus joined him and they slipped into the moonlight to have a look at the injury. Paulus couldn't see much, but Claus was able to crouch down and peer at it closely. "Ouch! That hurt," Paulus protested as Claus poked the injury.

"It's bleeding a lot. Do you have a handkerchief?" Claus asked as he dug his out of a shirt sleeve.

Paulus passed him a linen handkerchief and watched and winced as Claus tied it to his injury. Their respite was disturbed by the sounds of activity coming from the direction they'd come. "What's that?" he asked.

Claus cocked his head and listened for a moment before shooting to his feet. "I've no idea, and I have no intention of hanging around to find out. Can you run?"

Paulus wasn't sure, but he was equally unwilling to hang around and risk getting caught. "I think so."

"Then what are we waiting for?"

They covered almost two blocks before Paulus had to stop.

"What's the matter?" Claus asked.

"It hurts," Paulus protested.

"It'll hurt a lot more if we're caught."

Paulus felt the pad covering his injury. It was tacky. "I'm still bleeding."

Claus adjusted the pad and tied it tighter to the leg. "Just keep going. We can't afford to be caught on the streets at this time of night."

Paulus answered by starting moving again. If the night watch were to discover them they would be in big trouble. Not just for being out without permission, but also because they would immediately become suspects to what he hoped was happening at Master Fleckhammer's house.

Ten minutes later they slipped almost unnoticed into their dormitory—almost, because their roommate was in the room.

"Where have you two been?" Dietrich Besserer demanded in a loud whisper.

"Out," Claus said as he struggled to light a candle.

"I can see that you've been out. I want to know where you've been and what you've been up to. And what's wrong with Paulus?"

"He cut himself." Claus took his lit candle and moved closer to Paulus.

"You haven't been fighting I hope?" Dietrich demanded. "You know they take a dim view of fighting."

"Of course I haven't been fighting," Paulus said. It came out with distinct pauses as even the slightest movement was shooting excruciating pain through his leg, causing him to suck in air each time.

"Let me have a look at what you've done," Dietrich said as he rolled out of his bed and stepped into the circle of light around Paulus' leg. "That doesn't look good."

"Tell me about it," Paulus muttered between sharp intakes of breath.

Dietrich took a closer look. He was the youngest

of six brothers in a family of carpenters and woods-
men, and he'd often seen the results of axes and saws
making contact with human flesh. This cut looked bad.
"That's going to need to be sewn shut. Claus, go and
get Frau Kilian."

Claus and Paulus glanced at each other before shaking their heads. "We can't do that," Claus said. "Frau
Kilian would report it, and then we'd be in trouble."

"What have you two been up to?" Dietrich asked.
Then quickly he waved his hands at them. "Never
mind, it's not important. We need someone who can
sew your cut and won't tell tales." He himself wasn't
a candidate. One reason he wasn't following the rest
of his family was because he was squeamish. Contrary
to what his brothers might say he did not faint at
the sight of blood, nor was he afraid of the sight of
blood. He just found the sight of someone's lifeblood
pumping out of their body uncomfortable, and he preferred not to look when an injury was being treated.
As a result, he'd never actually seen his mother sew
anybody up. And then there was the fact his sewing
skills were so bad he didn't even own a needle and
thread. However, there was one apprentice known
throughout the assay office for his sewing skills, and
not only that, he was also known for his knowledge
of the apothecary's arts. Dietrich took another look
at Paulus' cut. Yes, they were going to need both of
those skills if this little accident was to be kept quiet.
"Do you know Phillip Gribbleflotz?" he asked Claus.

"I know who he is."

"That's close enough," Dietrich said. "I want you
to find him and bring him here."

"Why?" Claus asked.

"Because his father was an apothecary and he knows how to sew. Now get a move on."

"I know how to sew," Paulus said.

"Do you want to sew up your wound?" Dietrich asked. Paulus shook his head. "Then we need Phillip." Dietrich found his eyes watching a drop of blood form on the bottom of Paulus' foot. The spell was broken when it grew too big and splattered onto the floor. His mind drifted to the fact someone was going to have to clean that up, and then he noticed Claus was still standing by the door. "I told you to go. Now get. The sooner Phillip gets here the sooner we can forget this ever happened."

Claus stared pleadingly at Dietrich. "I don't know where his room is."

Dietrich raised his eyes to the heavens. He was sure he hadn't been this bad when he started his apprenticeship. "He won't be in his room. Try Herr Neuffer's laboratory first. You do know where that is?" Claus gave a single nod. "If he's not in there he's probably in the library. Now go." The final instruction was reinforced with a foot in the behind.

As a senior apprentice, who had also made a significant contribution to the assay office shooting team beating the Goldsmiths' guild in the Augsburg inter-guild shooting competition for the last four years, Phillip Gribbleflotz had special privileges not granted to lesser beings, such as being permitted to conduct his own experiments in the laboratory after work. There were some things he was not supposed to do, and being a conscientious youth, Phillip abided by these restrictions, most of the time.

This winter's evening he was shivering in the cold as he studied the latest of his experiments. Ink and quill would have been unreliable in these conditions, so he was recording his observations with a pencil. Not that there had been much to observe so far.

"Herr Gribbleflotz, thank the lord that I have found you. Please, come quickly. Paulus has hurt himself badly and needs a cut in his leg stitched closed."

Phillip didn't like having his experiments disturbed. That was one reason he conducted them late into the night. Which reminded him, he glanced at the candle he was using to record time. It had to be after ten o'clock. He turned round to face the intruder. It was one of the new apprentices, a boy all of twelve years of age. "What do you want?"

Claus managed to choke out his message in the face of Phillip's hostility.

"Why are you bothering me with this? It's Frau Kilian's job to care for the junior apprentices."

"Herr Besserer said to get you, Herr Gribbleflotz."

"Why on earth would he do that?" Even as he said it Phillip realized there was probably a good reason why Dietrich hadn't immediately taken the boy to Frau Kilian. "What have you been up to?" Phillip reconsidered the merits of that question the moment he'd uttered it and held up his hands. "No, don't tell me. I'm sure that Dietrich has a very good reason. This Paulus is in Dietrich's room?" Claus nodded.

Phillip surveyed his current experiment. There was nothing that needed to be cleaned and put away other than the reaction vessel with its precious sample. However, nothing had happened in the last hour and a half, and it was becoming more and more obvious that nothing was going to happen. With the immediate problem dealt with he started thinking about his new problem. He turned to Claus. "I have to get some things from my room. I want you to get a bucket of water, as hot as possible, and some soap. I'll meet you in your room."

"Why do you want soap and hot water, Herr Gribbleflotz?" Claus asked.

"So I can wash my hands of course," Phillip said. "Now get moving."

Phillip watched the youth sprint out of the laboratory and wondered if he had ever been that young.

He managed to get to Dietrich's room without being noticed. Not that there would have been any questions asked about him being up and around at this hour, but he preferred not to take any risks. He slipped into the room and saw the reassuring sight of Dietrich and his new acquaintance watching over a second young apprentice. Sitting on the floor was the requested bucket of water. Phillip was happy to notice the steam coming off of it.

"Hi, Dietrich. Who's the patient?"

"Thanks for coming, Phillip." Dietrich gestured towards the boy lying on the bed. "Paulus here managed to cut open his leg rather badly. And I think it needs to be stitched up."

"I hope you're wrong," Phillip said as he removed his jacket and rolled up his sleeves. "I've never sewn human flesh before."

"My mother has insisted on sewing up cuts that weren't half as bad as Paulus'."

"What? You mean you know how to sew up cuts?

If you know how to do that, why do you need me?" Phillip demanded.

"I said my mother did the sewing. I didn't say I ever watched her doing it," Dietrich said.

That was different. "Squeamish?" Phillip asked.

Dietrich nodded. "You would be too if you'd ever seen what a saw can do."

Phillip didn't even want to think about the damage a woodsman's saw could do to human flesh. In an effort to rid his mind of that thought he picked up the candle holder and dropped to his knees so he could examine the injury. Fortunately, this wound had not been made by a saw. "It seems like a clean cut," he said as he ran his little finger the length of the wound. In fact it was too clean a cut. He turned and looked straight at Dietrich. "Was it a knife?"

Dietrich shook his head. "From what Paulus told me, it was probably a piece of copper guttering."

Phillip raised his brows at that. Copper guttering was usually found on roofs. Which raised the question, what had the boy been doing on a roof at this time of night. He thought about asking, but with a gentle shake of his head reconsidered. It was probably better that he didn't know. "Just as long as it wasn't a fight," he said, making it clear that he was not going to be a party to keeping quiet about a fight where knives had been used.

"It was copper spouting," Dietrich affirmed.

Phillip studied Dietrich for a few seconds. It seemed he honestly believed the cut wasn't from a knife. That was good enough for him. He felt in his satchel for his clothes repair kit and a small pot of ointment. He selected a curved needle that he used to sew lightweight leather and threaded it with some of his coarsest thread before sticking it point-first into the wood of the bucket so he could find it again easily. Then he opened the pot of ointment and took a big dab on his index finger and smeared it into the full length of the wound. There was an intake of breath followed by a yip of pain and the muscles of Paulus' leg tensed, reminding Phillip that he'd forgotten something. He rolled up one of the handkerchiefs that had been used to bind the wound and told Paulus to bite on it.

The impossible happened and Paulus turned even paler as he tried to focus on the bloodied handkerchief. "Why?" he muttered as he tried to push it away from his mouth.

"So your screams don't wake everyone up and get us all into trouble." Phillip punctuated the word trouble by shoving the handkerchief into Paulus' mouth and got to work.

The first thing he did was use the other bloodied handkerchief to wipe the skin around the wound so his hand wouldn't slip and grabbed the flesh on both sides of the injury with his left hand. With the edges of the wound held together he reached for his needle with his right hand, and froze. Just because he knew how to sew didn't mean he knew how to sew flesh together. The only sewing of flesh he'd ever seen was when cook sewed the belly of a chicken or goose closed after filling them with stuffing.

The room around him was so quiet you could hear a pin drop. Phillip looked up at the terrified face of Paulus. Well, that made two of them. He swallowed and stuck the needle into Paulus' flesh. It was much harder to force it through the flesh than he'd expected, and his ointment smeared fingers slipped on the needle. He wiped his hand on a rag and tried again, this time managing to get the point of the curved needle to come out the other side of the wound. He left enough thread to tie off later and selected a spot a quarter inch along for his next stitch. With the thread held reasonably firmly by the flesh it had been forced through Phillip was able to make a knot. He continued along the wound, using a modified blanket-stitch, until he had the whole wound sewn closed. With a sigh of relief he wiped his sweaty brow on his shirt sleeve and sat back to admire his handiwork. It was very neat and tidy. He smiled at Paulus. "Almost finished."

Paulus didn't respond, but then he wouldn't, having fainted shortly after Phillip started pushing a needle into his flesh. Phillip hadn't noticed that Paulus' muscles had stopped tensing with every jab of the needle because he'd been so intent on his task that the rest of the world might as well not have existed.

He tied he last stitch and cut the thread with the candle before using its light to examine the stitched wound. There didn't seem to be any leakage, so he smeared another finger's worth of his special ointment over the wound. "There you are," he said as he got back to his feet. "As good as new." At this point he noticed Paulus had fainted and turned to Dietrich. "The stitches need to be removed sometime, but I don't know when," he said as he washed his arms and hands.

"My mother usually left them in for a week," Dietrich said.

"You'll remove them?" Phillip asked. "Good," he replied when Dietrich nodded. He made a final check that he hadn't forgotten anything and noticed the needle sticking out of the bucket. He didn't remember sticking it there, but he must have. He grabbed it and returned it to its slot in his clothes repair kit. "Well, if that's everything. I'll leave you to clean up in here and be on my way, and remember..."

"You were never here," Dietrich said.

Phillip met and matched Dietrich's smile before checking out the two junior apprentices. Paulus looked like he'd fallen asleep, while Claus looked like he would soon follow him. Satisfied he'd done all he could, Phillip pulled on his jacket and left.

The next day Phillip got into the laboratory early so he could clean up last night's experiment before one of the apprentices could get to it and throw out his precious flecks of nobilis auri. He carefully washed and dried the flecks before brushing them onto a clean glass. He was so intent on getting every last particle that he didn't notice his supervising journeyman come up behind him. Fortunately, instead of disturbing his concentration, which could have resulted in his losing some of his flecks, Wilhelm Neuffer waited until he'd finished before speaking.

"Are you still trying to prove those bits of dust from the cupels are some new wonder element?"

Phillip jerked in surprise, but he managed not to drop anything. "Don't sneak up on me like that."

"I didn't sneak up. I walked right up to you as noisily as I could. You were just so intent of saving every last fleck of worthless dirt that you didn't notice."

Phillip smiled at his supervisor. There was a difference of opinion as to what the remnants were that were sometimes found at the end of a fire assay after they dissolved the small buttons of gold with aqua regia. "It isn't just dirt, and one day I'll make you eat your words."

Wilhelm snorted good-naturedly. "In the meantime, we need to get started on today's assays."

"I'm ready," Phillip said eagerly. The remnants he was trying to test weren't present after every assay, and even when they were, they never amounted to more than a few flecks. After a hundred and twenty-seven assays his total sample of nobilis auri weighed no more than three grains by the apothecaries' system of weights. Every assay he did was an opportunity to add to his sample.

"You just want more of your bits of dirt," Wilhelm said.

"They aren't dirt," Phillip insisted. "The more I have the easier it will be to test it. What I really need is a chance to do a fire assay on a sample of a hundred grains of gold, or better yet, a thousand grains." He looked hopefully at Wilhelm. "I don't suppose . . ."

"You haven't got a hope," Wilhelm said. "It's one thing to let you keep the remnants of an assay. After all, it's just worthless dust. But if you want to experiment with gold, you're going to have to use your own."

Phillip sighed. A hundred grains of gold cost about six gulden, and he just didn't have that kind of money. It wasn't that the gold would be lost, because it wouldn't. There were ways of precipitating the gold out of the solution. It was just that he couldn't afford the gold in the first place.

Dinner

Phillip was late arriving to dinner, as usual. He grabbed his dinner and hurried to his seat beside two of his oldest friends at the assay office.

"What kept you this time?" Christoph Baer asked.

"Just collecting more nobilis auri from an assay," Phillip explained as he sat down.

"You're wasting your time, Phillip," Frederik Bechler said. "Those flecks are just bits of dirt. If they were anything special someone would have found that out by now."

Phillip begged to differ, and he said so. "If the flecks are just dirt, then surely something would dissolve them. I've tried my best oil of vitriol, aqua fortis, acidum salis, and fresh aqua regia, all without success."

"What's 'nobilis auri'?" Dietrich asked.

Phillip and the others turned their attention to the fourth person at their table. "You haven't started doing fire assays yet, have you?" Frederik asked.

Dietrich shook his head. "We've just started doing touchstone assaying."

"Well, when you start doing fire assays, you'll discover that after you dissolve the resulting little bead of gold with aqua regia you're sometimes left with a few flecks of something in the beaker. Those flecks are Phillip's nobilis auri."

"Of course," Christoph said, "anybody with any sense knows that they are just flecks of dirt, but Phillip thinks they're something special."

"Of course they're something special," Phillip protested. "Everyone knows that only precious metals remain after cupellation. That means nobilis auri must be a precious metal. And as even aqua regia can't dissolve it, it must be more noble than gold."

"Hence the name, nobilis auri," Christoph said as an aside to Dietrich.

"It's just a pretty name for dirt," Frederick said.

"I'm right," Phillip insisted. "And one day I'll prove it."

"Well that day isn't today." Christoph leaned closer to the others. "Is everything set up for the Twelfth Night party?"

"I've got the food lined up," Dietrich said. He glanced Phillip's way. "Have you been able to make enough you-know-what?"

"A dozen bottles," Phillip confirmed.

"How'd you manage that?" Christoph asked. "You haven't been on the distilling furnace for months."

"That happens when you're about to be elevated to journeyman," Frederik said.

Phillip struggled not to blush. Rumors had been circulating since July last year that they were going to elevate him to journeyman status early this year. It wasn't unheard of for someone to achieve journeyman status as an assayist and metallurgist in just over six years, but it was rare. Most apprentices took closer to eight years. "I made it when I made the high purity saltpetre for the Schützenfest."

"But that was back in July," Christoph said. "Do you mean you've had a dozen bottles of you-know-what sitting around all this time?"

Phillip's smile was smug. Keeping a dozen bottles of high proof alcohol hidden not just from the staff at the assay office, but also the apprentices for over six months had to rank as a major achievement.

Friday evening, January 11, 1613

Ulrich Hechstetter, the head of the Augsburg assay office, sipped from the glass of strong liquor and sighed. "Another good tipple." He looked around the gathered staff. "I thought we found the still this time."

"We found a still," Wilhelm Neuffer confirmed. He sipped his drink and licked his lips. "But they must have had others."

"But where?" Master Paul Paler asked. "We looked everywhere."

Ulrich took another sip. "Well, we'll just have to do better next year. Now, to the real reason for this meeting. Do I hear any objections to elevating Phillip Theophrastus Gribbleflotz to the rank of journeyman?"

"He's a very gifted technician," Jakob Reihing said. "And he makes a good teacher."

"You've been letting an apprentice teach fellow apprentices?" Hieronymus Kiffhaber demanded.

Ulrich studied the assay office's newest journeyman over the top of his glass. He hadn't been trained in-house, so he probably hadn't come across Gribbleflotz yet. "As Jakob said, Hieronymus, Phillip Gribbleflotz is a very gifted technician. We would be failing in our duty to the other apprentices not to afford them the best possible teachers. If that means letting an apprentice teach them certain techniques, under proper supervision naturally, then we are quite prepared to do that."

"Hieronymus," Paul called out. "Phillip Gribbleflotz taught me how he makes such good acids. I'm quite happy to teach you, but surely you'd rather learn from my teacher?"

"But you're a master. What can an apprentice teach you?" Hieronymus asked, his voice shooting up several octaves.

"Quite a lot," Paul said. "I'm now able to make acids almost as good as Phillip's, which is considerably better than the best I used to make. With practice, I expect I could match his level of competence."

Hieronymus looked bewildered. "But how is that possible?" he asked.

"Speaking for myself," Wilhelm said, "I was never taught to be half as finicky and meticulous as Phillip is naturally."

"Unfortunately," Jakob said. "Although we can teach people what small changes to look for during a distillation, we can't teach them how to monitor a whole furnace worth of distillations the way Phillip can. That's a natural talent."

Hieronymus slowly nodded his head. "But how long will Herr Gribbleflotz stay here if he is elevated to the rank of journeyman?"

"I'm sure he'll stay on as a journeyman for a while," Ulrich said.

"This is Gribbleflotz we're talking about," Jakob warned. "You know, the boy who wants to follow in his great-grandfather's footsteps."

"Ahhh!" Ulrich had forgotten about Phillip's claim to be the great-grandson of the great Paracelsus. He took another sip of his drink, savoring the bite of the strong alcohol as it hit his tongue. "We could always delay his elevation to the rank of journeyman," he suggested. He didn't expect the idea to get any traction among the others, and it didn't.

"We can't do that," Paul insisted. "Everyone is

in hourly expectation of the announcement of his elevation."

"It was just a suggestion," Ulrich said. "If Hieronymus here wants to learn the subtleties of distilling acids, then we have to hold onto him for a while."

"Phillip hasn't finished copying Ercker's treatise on ores and assaying," Wilhelm said. "I think it'll take him another couple of months to finish it."

That made Ulrich happy. "There you are, Paul. Hieronymus will have until early spring to learn from the master how we make our high quality acids." He glanced around the room. "So, there having been no objections, I will advise Phillip Theophrastus Gribbleflotz that he may consider himself to be a journeyman Assayist and Metallurgist. Are we all in agreement?"

"When do you plan to make the announcement?" Paul asked.

Ulrich brought up a mental image of his schedule. "Wednesday," he said.

"That'll hardly give the apprentices time to arrange the party," Wilhelm said.

"That shouldn't be a problem," Ulrich said. "We will be providing the alcohol for this party."

Late April 1613, Neuburg

It had taken two days to walk from Augsburg to Neuburg, and Phillip was feeling the strain of the long walk with a heavy pack on his back. He had made the trip to Neuburg to visit his mother, whom he hadn't seen for over six years, and he was in the middle of the main street trying to decide where to start looking for her when he spotted a woman who painted her face with white lead just like his mother did. He watched her for a while, until it dawned on him that the woman was his mother. He walked towards her.

"Mother, is that you?"

His mother stared at him with dawning horror. "Who are you? I don't know you."

"It's me, Phillip, your son."

Maria Elisabeth Bombast von Neuburg looked nervously to her left and to her right. "You shouldn't be here, Theophrastus. You'll ruin everything."

"Ruin what?" Phillip demanded even as he ignored her use of his hated middle name.

"My life, just like you ruined it when you were born." Maria Elisabeth was growing more agitated the longer the meeting with Phillip went on. "You have to leave." She dipped into her bag and pulled out a drawstring purse. She shook out a handful of coins into her hand and thrust them at Phillip. "Here, this is what you want. Take it and go. Go away."

Phillip caught the coins in his hands without thinking. He was so dumbfounded at what had happened that he just stood there while his mother hurried away. What had brought on that reaction? All he'd wanted to do was say hello and ask how she was doing. He watched his mother until she disappeared around a street corner. Only then did he think to look at the coins she'd trust into his hands. It was a mixture of copper and silver which, as he discovered when he quickly added it up, came to just over three gulden. That was the better part of a week's wages, which seemed a lot to pay just to get rid of him.

Phillip felt very disillusioned with his mother. For

some reason she didn't want him in Neuburg. He wondered about that. What possible reason could she have for not wanting to acknowledge him? He thought about chasing after her, but she was already long gone. He decided to find a tavern and have something to eat and drink while he took the weight off his feet and considered his options.

He decided over a meal of sausage, cheese, bread, and raw onion that his options were limited. His mother had made it abundantly clear that she wanted nothing to do with him. He could force the issue, but he wasn't sure he wanted to risk alienating the only real family he had. It was probably better left alone, he decided. Besides, he had more important things to worry about. Like how to get to Padua where, like his great-grandfather before him, he hoped to study medicine. The great university was in the Republic of Venice, which was on the other side of the Alps. He was going to have to cross them, but April was not a good time to attempt the journey. It was time to find employment until the season was more favorable.

It took Phillip eight days to get to Innsbruck, but less than an hour to secure employment as an assayer with the local branch of Fugger's bank once he got there. The job was ideal. Innsbruck was the last major town before the Brenner Pass, and he was doing what he'd been trained to do. Over the next three weeks he not only earned more than enough money to cover his expenses for the nearly two hundred and thirty mile trip to Padua, he also added over forty flecks to his collection of nobilis auri. Phillip was feeling good when on a bright May morning he set off south.

May 1613, the Brenner Pass

Phillip was cold, wet, and miserable. His brain had shut down all but the most essential operations, like dreaming of the hot food and warm bed waiting for him at the travelers' inn on the other side of the Brenner Pass. Like a mindless automaton, he continued to put one foot in front of the other on the muddy road.

He was brought back to the real world only when he crested the saddle of the pass and felt the full force of the southerly wind blowing up the valley for the first time. It had been cold before, but as long as he'd kept moving he'd felt quite warm in his heavy woolen coat and oilskin outer layer. The strong southerly changed that immediately. It was as if it was going straight through him, chilling him almost instantly. He stared into the distance. Somewhere farther down the road was the next travelers' inn. He set off again, one foot in front of the other.

He didn't see the accident. In fact he was so blind to anything other than where he was placing his feet that he all but bumped into the group of men gathered around something on the ground. That was when he became aware of men trying to prevent an ox-drawn wagon slipping off the road. Any student of human behavior would immediately recognize the tight grouping of men as the sign that something interesting or gruesome was lying at the center of the group. Phillip, quite naturally, stopped to have a look.

One man was trying to comfort a youth who was writhing on the ground with a pretty selection of injuries. Starting at the top, there were multiple lacerations to the head and face. Naturally, these were bleeding spectacularly, but Phillip didn't think they were too bad—probably nothing worse than a few minor cuts. Then there was the right arm. The youth's oilskin was torn, so there were probably lacerations to the arm. Phillip couldn't be sure about the .hand, because it was covered in mud and blood, just like the youth's right thigh. Judging by the way he was grimacing and holding the thigh with both hands, that injury was probably quite serious. What disturbed Phillip was the fact no one was attending to the youth's injuries. "Isn't someone going to do something about his injuries?" he demanded. He got a ring of blank stares in response.

It looked like no one was going to do anything, which meant Phillip had to act. "Let me through," he demanded as he used his hiking stave to force a way inside the circle. There were a few protests about his pushing, but soon he was beside the youth. He dropped his backpack to the ground and knelt down to examine him. He quickly determined that in spite of all the blood, the head wounds were as superficial as he'd suspected, and while the scratches in his arm were deep, none of them needed immediate attention. That left the thigh.

Phillip had to force the youth's hands away from the injury they were trying to protect, and he could see why. It looked nasty. This was no nice and simple clean cut from a knife or sheet of copper such as Paulus Rauner had suffered. It was a messy tear caused by who knew what. Phillip just knew this was going to go bad no matter what he did. Still, it wasn't going to get better if he didn't do anything. He searched the surrounding faces for someone who might be able to enforce authority, finally coming to rest on the man supporting the injured youth. "I need a bucket of water."

The man stared blankly at Phillip. "Who are you?" he demanded.

"Never mind who I am. If I'm to be any help here I need to wash this man's injury before I can treat it."

He thrust his face close to Phillip's. "Are you a barber-surgeon?" he demanded.

"No, but I know what to do," Phillip said. It wasn't really a lie. He knew he'd been very lucky with Paulus Rauner's injury, so while he was in Innsbruck he'd found someone willing to show him how it was supposed to be done. He hadn't worked on a human since Paulus, but he had practiced on numerous pork bellies.

Phillip's apparent confidence seemed to satisfy the man, who started screaming out instructions in a language that seemed similar to Latin, but which Phillip couldn't follow. "Make sure it's clean water," Phillip called out.

The man sent out another batch of instructions before turning back to Phillip. "How can I help?" he asked.

Phillip thought back to when he treated Paulus who had only been a twelve-year-old boy and until he fainted it'd still taken Claus and Dietrich to hold him. The youth on the other hand was probably about his own age, and a lot bigger. He paused in the act of removing his medical kit from his pack. "Just keep a firm hold on him. I don't want him thrashing about."

"Babbo," the patient said, reaching out a beseeching hand.

"Everything will be all right, Carlo." The man glanced at Phillip. "He will be all right?" he asked.

Phillip was saved having to answer by a bucket being sat down beside him. "Thank you," he said before dipping a finger into the water. It was cold. He hadn't expected hot water, but this water was only a short step away from ice. He scooped up a handful and splashed it over Carlo's leg. He reacted to the icy cold water by trying to jerk his leg away. "Can someone hold Carlo's leg for me?" he asked.

His helper called out to a man who dropped down and took a firm grip on Carlo's leg. With the leg held securely Phillip was able to splash water over the gash with one hand while he wiped away the mud and blood with the other, giving him his first real glimpse of the injury. It was worse than he'd feared.

He looked up. "Babbo, Carlo's injury needs to be stitched, but I can't do it here. If I bandage it, can he be carried to the nearest shelter?"

There were giggles and smiles all round. Even Babbo allowed a smile to form momentarily. "Did I say something wrong?" Phillip asked.

Babbo shook his head. "My name is Alberto. Alberto Rovarini. Carlo is my son, and I am his babbo, his father. And yes, Carlo can ride on one of the wagons."

"Right." Phillip felt a proper fool, but he couldn't let his mind linger on that. The wind was getting up and the rain wasn't getting any lighter. He grabbed a roll of linen from his medical kit and wrapped it tightly around Carlo's thigh.

Even in the protective circle of the Rovarinis the wind had been able to reach Phillip. His whole body was chilled and he needed the help of one of Rovarinis to get back to his feet. He was handed his hiking stave, but when he bent to retrieve his pack he was pushed away as another picked it up and carried to one of the wagons. Phillip must have looked dumbfounded, because Alberto came up beside him. "You have helped Carlo, so we help you."

"I haven't done anything," Phillip protested.

"You stopped and did your best while everyone else just looked on or walked past," Alberto said. He bowed his head. "I am ashamed that I didn't immediately attend to Carlo's injuries. My only excuse is my relief that he was still alive."

The moment the Rovarinis arrived at the travelers' inn, an unconscious Carlo was unloaded from the wagon and carried in. A table was cleared and he was laid down on it. He'd barely been laid out on the table before someone deposited Phillip's pack at his feet.

Phillip started to take off his oilskins and winter coat. It was a struggle until helping hands divested him of his oilskins and coat and carried them away. It was clear that he was going to be provided with any assistance he required, so he put the situation to good use. "I need good light, and hot water."

Within minutes he had a good candle, a jug of steaming hot water, and a wash basin. He'd spent the time while waiting for the hot water removing his jacket and rolling up his shirt sleeves. When the water arrived he indicated that he'd like some of it poured into the basin and when that was done he lowered his hands into it. It was painful, but it was the quickest way to warm them.

With his hands functioning again Phillip unwound the bandage and used it to wipe the inside of the wound clean. Then, under the light of a candle, he made a close examination of the injury. It was bad. The first thing he had to do was tidy up the edges. He had a chunk of obsidian in his medical kit and a large flake from that served as an excellent scalpel, which he used to cut away the torn and ragged skin. He checked how well the two edges met and discovered that he'd cut away too much skin. He needed to cut away some of the tissue under the skin to ensure the edges of the skin met.

Once the wound was trimmed to his satisfaction Phillip smeared his special honey-based ointment liberally into the cut. Now he was ready to close the wound. Unlike when he stitched up Paulus' injury, this time Phillip had some idea what he was supposed to be doing and better yet, he now had a couple of more suitable needles, a palm guard to help force the needle through flesh, and some better thread.

Phillip pushed the needle through the skin and deep into the flesh, so that it was barely visible at the bottom of the wound when it emerged, and then back out through the skin. That formed the basis of the first stitch. He tied the ends together and repeated the procedure as he worked his way along the length of the wound. When he got to the end he wiped the wound clean before smearing it with some of his ointment. Then he reached for the bandage and started to roll it up so that it could easily be wound around Carlo's thigh once more.

At this point he was interrupted by the innkeeper's wife. She grabbed the dirty bandages from Phillip's hands while berating him for thinking to do something so foolish as use them to bind Carlo's injury. She pushed Phillip away so she could examine his handiwork. She touched a finger to the traces of ointment and tasted it, rewarding him with a grudging nod of approval before she pulled Carlo's pants down and efficiently wrapped his injury with a clean bandage.

"You did well," Alberto said, offering Phillip a mug of hot spiced wine. "Here, drink this."

"Thank you," Phillip said as he wrapped his hands around the steaming mug. He gestured with his head towards the innkeeper's wife. "She looks like she thinks she could have done better."

Alberto glanced in the woman's direction. "She has a lot of experience. And you..." He paused. "I don't even know your name."

"Phillip. Phillip Theophrastus Gribbleflotz." He held out a hand, noticed that it was blood covered, and quickly withdrew it.

"Wash your hands and come and join us for supper."

Supper was an enlightening meal. Over a hot, mostly vegetable, stew Phillip and the Rovarinis exchanged their stories, although most of Phillip's conversation had to go through Alberto. He realized that Padua was going to be full of foreigners who didn't speak German or Latin and that he was going to have to learn the local vernacular if he was going to live in the city any length of time. He admitted as much to Alberto.

"How can we be foreigners in our own country?" Alberto demanded good-naturedly.

Phillip apologized for the way it must have sound, and asked about the availability of Venetian lessons, and most importantly, how much did Alberto think they would cost.

"You are a student?" Alberto asked.

"Of medicine."

"Doctors are worthless," one of the Rovarinis said. "Give me a good apothecary or barber-surgeon any day. They are both safer and cheaper."

"Let the lad alone, Pietro," Alberto said. "If he wants to be a doctor, it's his choice." He looked over to Phillip. "University is expensive. How will you fund your studies?"

"I trained as an assayist and metallurgist at Fugger's assay office in Augsburg. If necessary I can earn a living doing assays and making acids."

"For an assayist and metallurgist, you seem to know a thing or two about treating injuries."

Phillip nodded. "My stepfather was an apothecary and I used to help him compound remedies."

"And the sewing together of the gash in Carlo's leg, did he teach you to do that too?"

Phillip related the story of Paulus and his cut, and how he'd realized how lucky he'd been and found someone willing to teach him how to do it properly.

"It was lucky for Carlo that you are here, Phillip," Alberto said.

Phillip blushed. "I haven't done anything the innkeeper's wife couldn't have done."

Alberto smiled. "True, but you are the one who did it, and for that you have my eternal gratitude. How are you getting to Padua?"

"I was planning on following the road to Verona, then heading for Padua."

"We are headed for Mestre, with cargo for Venice, but we stop at Padua." Alberto reached out and rested a hand on one of Phillip's. "You are welcome to join us."

That was seconded by Pietro, who added that their route was some fifty miles shorter than the route Phillip had been thinking of following. It was an offer Phillip would have been a fool to refuse. Not only was their route shorter, but he would no longer be a vulnerable lone traveler. Phillip paused to consider the possibility that Alberto and his men might rob him and leave him for dead, but it was only a momentary thought. They seemed truly thankful for what he'd done for Carlo. There was only one possible answer. "Thank you very much. I'd like to join you."

Phillip had been keeping an eye on Carlo for a couple of days now, and he was starting to get worried. Carlo was limping more and more, and although he was insisting that there was nothing wrong with him, Phillip couldn't miss the signs of a developing fever. He hurried ahead to warn Alberto that he needed to check the injury.

"There's a good spot near the river just ahead where we can get off the road," Alberto suggested.

Less than fifteen minutes later they turned off the road onto a meadow beside the River Talvera. While the Rovarinis checked the oxen and wagons Phillip got Carlo to pull down his pants so he could remove the bandage.

The wound was a mess. A wide area around the gash was inflamed, but worse than that was the swelling. The stitches were almost enveloped by the expanding skin. Phillip dug into his medical kit for a flake of obsidian and used it to cut the stitches. The wound started to open and pus seeped out even as he cut the stitches, and it oozed out after he removed them. That was what

Phillip's reading had warned him could happen, but it didn't make it any more pleasant to encounter. Still, he'd read his great-grandfather's dairies and knew what he had to do. He called out for some help to hold Carlo still before smiling apologetically at him and handing him a piece of wood. "I'm sorry, Carlo, but this is going to hurt. Put this between your teeth and bite down onto it." Carlo swallowed and inserted the piece of wood.

Phillip waited until he had a couple of Rovarinis holding Carlo before he wrapped a finger in bandage and poked it into the wound. Carlo let out a muffled scream as he fought against the restraining men. Phillip saw the distressed looks on their faces and knew he had to do something to sedate Carlo.

"Do you have any brandy?" He called out. That got a positive nod from Alberto who hurried over to a wagon, returning with a bottle of grappa. He offered it to Phillip, who shook his head and pointed to Carlo.

"You want Carlo to drink it?" Alberto asked.

Phillip nodded. "I want him drunk enough not to notice anything I might do."

Alberto raised a brow Phillip's way, looked at the label on the bottle and sighed heavily before forcing Carlo's mouth open. It took over half the bottle before Carlo became sufficiently insensitive to Phillip's jabbing of his wound that he could continue.

With Carlo no longer struggling Phillip was able to progress much faster. Finally the wound appeared as clean as he could get it. He could see blood seeping through some of the exposed flesh. That was supposed to be a good sign. But there were areas where blood wasn't seeping. That was a bad sign as it suggested the flesh there was dead.

According to his great-grandfather's dairies, there was only one thing to do with dead flesh in a wound, and that was to cut it out. Phillip knapped a large flake from his lump of obsidian and used that to slice small pieces from the wound until he was sure he'd removed all the dead flesh. Then he smeared some of his honey-based ointment into the wound and sewed it closed again. Only then did he turn away and throw up.

"Are you all right?" A worried Alberto asked.

Phillip wiped his mouth against his forearm and nodded. "I've never done that before."

"Have you finished doing what you have to do?" Alberto asked.

"I still have to bandage it."

Alberto thrust the bottle of grappa into Phillip's hands. "I can do that. Have some of this to steady your stomach."

A *week later, Padua*

No one had thought to tell Phillip that Padua was Alberto's base, so he was surprised when they pulled into a large property and a woman and four children ran up to Alberto.

"His wife," Pietro informed Phillip. "She will look after you while we go on to Mestre."

"Does Frau Rovarini speak German?" Phillip asked.

"Nope," Pietro said. "You'll just have to learn Venetian."

Phillip was spared an immediate introduction to Frau Rovarini because she'd moved her welcome on to Carlo. In sharp contrast to his last encounter with his own mother, Carlo's mother gave every impression of being pleased to see him. And that was after only a few weeks separation, not like the years Phillip and his mother had been apart. It was a sign, if Phillip really needed one, that his mother's behavior wasn't normal.

The surprises continued when he was introduced to Carlo's mother. She made it clear that he was welcome in her house, and even gently pinched his cheek and said something.

"Paola says that you're too thin and need a proper home cooked meal," Alberto translated.

Phillip smiled at Paola and expended most of the limited vocabulary he'd picked up traveling with Alberto's teams thanking her. Then he turned to Alberto and held out his hand. "Thank you for letting me travel with you. I don't suppose you could direct me to suitable lodgings?"

"But you will be staying here!" Alberto said. The tone of his voice suggested outrage that Phillip should think otherwise. "You didn't think we'd do anything less after what you did for Carlo?"

"Did what for Carlo?" Paola demanded.

Phillip didn't actually understand what Paola had said, but he recognized the "for Carlo" bit, so he wasn't surprised when after a brief exchange with Alberto Paola ran over to Carlo and, ignoring his protests, pulled his pants down. There was a wail of anguish when she saw the stitched injury, followed almost immediately by a flood of instructions.

"What's going on?" Phillip asked Alberto as Carlo was carried into the house.

"Please don't take offense, but my wife has called for her cousin to check Carlo's injury."

"I'm not offended," Phillip said. "In fact I'm glad

someone better qualified than me is going to check what I've done. Is your wife's cousin a doctor?"

"No," a cheeky Pietro said. "He's much better than a doctor. He looks after horses."

June 1613, Padua

Even with Alberto Rovarini vouching for him Phillip had been finding it difficult to find work in Padua that fitted around his university lectures. Today however there was a renewed skip to his footsteps as he hurried home. He stopped in his tracks while he digested that thought. Since when had he started calling his lodgings with Paola's cousin home?

He reached the house at the run, almost running down Giacomo's wife. "My most humble apologies," Phillip said as he stepped aside to let Francesca Sedazzari past.

"What's the rush?" Francesca asked. "You look happy. Have you found a job?"

"Sort of," Phillip said the pleasure at what had happened obvious in his voice. "Leonardo di ser Martino da Vinci isn't happy with the quality of cupels he's been getting. I told him I could make excellent cupels, and he's agreed to let me share his laboratory if my cupels are as good as I claim."

"Is that good?" Francesca asked. "I thought you wanted a job. What good is sharing his laboratory?"

"I can make acids. My acids were some of the best the Augsburg assay laboratory ever produced. I should find a ready market for them here in Padua." Phillip wanted to throw his arms around Francesca and hug her, he was so happy.

"So all you need to do is make some cupels?"

Phillip nodded.

"What are cupels?"

"They are small vessels that you use in a fire assay. They're usually made out of ash from bones, antlers, or wood. I'll need a few other things, but do you know where I might be able to get some bones? Preferably the skulls?"

"There's Giovanni. He has a knacker's yard by the river." Francesca smiled. "I'm sure Giacomo will be happy to introduce you to him."

Later that day a very impatient Phillip accompanied Giacomo at what he considered a snail's pace down to the river. Phillip looked around, not sure what he should be looking for. "Are we there yet?" he asked.

"Not far now," Giacomo said.

Not far turned out to be another half mile—the good people of Padua wanted trades such as the knackers as far away as possible from where they lived. When they stepped into the knacker's yard Phillip saw a horse strung up on a butcher's scaffold and a man hard at work disemboweling the carcass.

"Hey, Giovanni. Can you spare a moment?" Giacomo called out as they approached.

Giovanni looked around at the interruption. "Hi, Giacomo. How can I help you?" he asked as he ran his knife a couple of times against a honing steel.

Giacomo tapped Phillip's shoulder. "Phillip here wants some bones, preferably skulls."

Giovanni turned to Phillip. "What do you want the bones for?"

"To make cupels."

Giovanni nodded. "So you'll want fully rendered ones then, follow me." He led Phillip to a pile of clean white skull from a wide variety of animals. "How many do you want?"

Phillip told Giovanni how much he wanted to pay and between them they filled a basket with a number of sheep skulls. They returned to the yard to find Giacomo examining the carcass.

"I hope you weren't intending to use the guts for anything," Giacomo said.

"Why, what's wrong?" Giovanni demanded.

"Come and have a look at the mouth. Tell me what you see." Giovanni had a look and stepped back cursing.

"What's the problem?" Phillip asked.

"Have you heard of Spanish Fly?" Giacomo asked. Phillip shook his head. "It's an insect that can be found in hay. It can be poisonous if eaten."

"And this horse died after eating an insect?" Phillip asked.

"That or its eggs." Giacomo turned to Giovanni. "Give me your butchering knife for a minute, would you."

"What're you planning on doing?" Giovanni asked as he handed Giacomo his knife.

"Show Phillip why he never wants to try Spanish Fly," Giacomo said as he carefully cut out a chunk from the horse's kidney. With the chunk speared on the knife Giacomo walked towards Phillip.

"What are you going to do with that?" Phillip asked warily.

"Some people think Spanish Fly is an aphrodisiac," Giacomo said conversationally as he wiped the bit of kidney along Phillip's forearm. "They don't realize that it's really a dangerous poison."

"They will when they start pissing blood the next day," Giovanni said.

Phillip looked at the smear of blood on his arm and went to wipe it with his right hand.

"No, don't touch it!" Giacomo said. He turned to Giovanni. "Do you have some soap and water?"

"Over there," Giovanni said, pointing to a bucket and towel a short distance from the butchering scaffold.

Giacomo scraped the bit of kidney off the knife and stabbed the knife into a wood block before he dragged Phillip over to the water and washed his arm with soap and water.

"What was that all about?" Phillip asked.

Giacomo smiled at Phillip. "As I said, there are people who would use Spanish Fly as an aphrodisiac. It makes you hard and can keep you hard all night, but the next day, if it hasn't killed you, you'll find it painful to piss, and as Giovanni said, sometimes you piss blood."

"How do you know all this?" Phillip asked.

Giacomo grinned. "I too was young and foolish once. Have you got what we came for?"

Phillip gestured to the basket full of skulls.

"Right, let's get home." Giacomo turned to Giovanni. "The red meat should be safe enough, but I don't want to hear that you sold any of the guts for consumption," Giacomo warned Giovanni.

"Yes, yes, I understand. I'm not a fool, Giacomo. Now you and your young friend can leave me alone to complete butchering the animal."

Later that day Phillip was breaking up skulls so they could be reduced to ash on Giacomo's forge when he noticed there were blisters on his arm. He ran out to find Giacomo to ask what was going on.

"Those blisters are caused by bits of Spanish Fly in the kidney of the dead horse." Giacomo smiled grimly at Phillip. "Imagine what it would be like inside your body if you were to take some of the crushed beetle as an aphrodisiac?"

Phillip looked at the blisters on his arm and did what Giacomo told him to do, he imagined those same blisters forming inside his body. It wasn't a pretty picture. "I don't think I'll try Spanish Fly."

"Good. That's a smart choice."

"But how will I know if someone is offering me Spanish Fly? They might call it something else. What does it look like?"

Giacomo stared intently at Phillip before coming to a decision. "I've got some I can show you."

"Why do you have it?" Phillip asked.

Giacomo sighed. "Sometimes a client demands that I use it to excite a stallion they want to breed from."

"But you don't like doing it?"

"No I don't," Giacomo said. "It's a poison that can so easily kill the horse. But if I don't do as they ask, the owner will just find someone else who will."

Phillip understood Giacomo's position. "You feel it is better that you administer the dose rather than let someone who probably doesn't know what they are doing do it and end up poisoning the animal."

In order to make the best cupels, all the impurities have to be removed from the ashes. They can be removed by floating off the lighter impurities such as charcoal dust and anything else that floats, while the heavier impurities such as fine sand and stones will settle in the bottom of the container. It was a relatively easy matter to pour off the light impurities, but the heavy ones needed someone extremely meticulous to remove them all.

Phillip was naturally extremely meticulous in his procedures, so it came as no surprise to him when Leonardo da Vinci proclaimed his satisfaction with his cupels. With somewhere to work Phillip was able to start making acids for sale to the local alchemists—acids that were significantly purer than anything anyone else was selling, and therefore could command a premium price. Phillip was well set to continue his studies at Padua.

Friday, January 10, 1614, the assay office, Augsburg

Ulrich Hechstetter sipped from the glass of strong liquor and pulled a face. "It's not as good as last year," he said.

The other senior staff at the assay office sipped their drinks made from the bottles given to them by the apprentices in a tradition started only five years ago. "It's not bad," Wilhelm Neuffer said, "but I can almost taste the base alcohol they made it from."

"I wonder who made it," Paul Paler said.

"It can't be Phillip Gribbleflotz. Not this year," Jakob Reihing said.

"You think it was Gribbleflotz last year?" Ulrich asked.

Jakob nodded. "And the year before that, and the year before that, and the year before that."

"That's impossible," Wilhelm Neuffer said. "I admit he has the skills to do it, but he has never been out of sight long enough to do it. When he wasn't working he was either sleeping, in the library, or working on his experiments."

Ulrich studied Jakob. He had the look of a particularly proud teacher who knew one of his students had managed to put one over the school. "How could he do it, Jakob? Wilhelm has said he was always around."

"That's when I think he did it."

"That doesn't make sense," Wilhelm said, shaking his head.

"I think I understand what Jakob's getting at," Paul said. He looked at Jakob. "You think he slipped some extra retorts onto the distilling furnace."

Jakob nodded. "It's the only way Gribbleflotz could have pulled it off."

Wilhelm whistled. "I wouldn't have thought Gribbleflotz had it in him, at least not four years ago."

"Remember that as soon as it was obvious Gribbleflotz knew what he was doing on the distillation furnace we practically left him alone to get on with the task of distilling things?" Jakob asked. "Well, I bet the other apprentices noticed that and suggested he might slip in an extra retort or two."

In his mind's eye Ulrich could easily visualize the scene. Phillip Gribbleflotz had quickly gained a well-deserved reputation for the care and attention he put into running the distillation furnace. With plenty of other work to do and other apprentices who really needed to be watched it was no surprise that Gribbleflotz had been left to get on with his tasks. "And he wants to be a doctor," he complained. "What a waste of talent."

Chapter 3

The Quinta Essentia

December 8, 1615, Padua

Phillip stepped up to the dissection table in the public anatomical theater in the Palazzo Bo off the southwest courtyard at the University of Padua. He looked up at the six tiers of galleries, all of them packed, except for a little space either side of a man on the second tier. The observers and students around him were, quite naturally, not pushing up against Professor Giulio Casseri, holder of the chair of surgery at Padua.

The theater was expectant as Phillip bowed his head in honor of his mentor and then pulled back the draping to reveal the cadaver. There were cheers around the theater as students recognized the late and unlamented Professor Hieronymus Fabricius ab Aquapendente, Giulio's former mentor, and for the last thirty years his most bitter rival, on the dissection table. Not that the rivalry had been Giulio's fault. He could hardly be blamed for being a much better teacher, but Fabrictus, as Fabricius was known to Giulio's most devoted admirers for his rigid opposition to innovation, had resented Giulio's success and popularity and used all the power at his disposal to stifle Giulio's career. It was therefore fitting that Giulio's greatest apprentice would be the man to dissect his body.

Phillip held out a hand for the scalpel he would use to make the first incision . . .

"Phillip. Wake up!"

Phillip blinked a few times and looked around. He was no longer in the public anatomical theater, unfortunately. It had only been a dream, which was equally unfortunate. He was in his room in Giacomo Sedazzari's house in Padua. He turned his attention to the person who'd woken him. "I was having the most beautiful dream, I was . . ."

"There's no time for that," Francesca Sedazzari said. "We need you to amuse the children."

Phillip cocked an ear. There were only the faintest sounds of children playing. "They don't sound so noisy."

"That's because I told them that if they were good you would read to them." Francesca stood with her hands on her hips and stared expectantly at Phillip.

He knew what she was doing. She was trying to intimidate him, and as was usual, succeeding. He hauled himself off his bed and staggered over to the bookshelf. "How long do you want me to entertain them for?" he asked.

"The feast will be served at noon."

Phillip looked outside to see if he could estimate the time. Unfortunately, and he was using that word a lot right now, it looked like it was barely after eight. That meant he had to read for four hours. Still, the

Feast of the Immaculate Conception, as celebrated by the extended Rovarini family, would be more than adequate compensation. He selected a number of books that he hoped would take at least four hours to read and headed for the door.

"I'll see that refreshments are sent over soon," Francesca called.

Phillip was mobbed by the children the moment he stepped into the front room. Eager hands relieved him of the books while equally eager, but smaller, hands took hold of his and led him away. It was almost a tradition now when the Rovarini families gathered that Phillip would read to the children to keep them out from underfoot while the womenfolk got on with preparing the meals and the men got everything else ready. Not that Phillip minded. It was a completely new experience for him to be so much a part of a family.

A space in Giacomo's barn had been prepared. There was a lamp so Phillip had enough light to read, and the straw and hay around Phillip's seat were festooned with children wrapped up in blankets to keep warm. Phillip sat down on an oversized blanket and wrapped it around himself before he picked up the first book. He snuggled down on his chair of straw and made himself comfortable. The sense of anticipation in the barn was almost palpable.

Phillip had been forced by children constantly complaining that they couldn't hear to develop a speaking voice that could fill the barn. Once he'd mastered that he'd gone on to develop the ability to give identity and personality to the characters so the children could keep track of who was who. It wasn't a quiet reading, because Phillip didn't encourage silence. He changed his voice to suit the characters and changed his tempo to reflect events in the story. He interacted with the children, making them part of the experience, and they responded by hanging onto his every word. He loved the feeling it gave him. He imagined that this must be something like what Professor Casseri felt when he gave a lecture.

The end came as a bit of a shock to Phillip. He finished one book and automatically reached out for another, only to feel nothing but an empty space where the books should have been. He looked apologetically to the children, and realized they'd been joined by most of the adults. "Is it time for supper?" he asked.

Standing close to the main door, Francesca nodded.

Phillip glanced down at the plate of refreshments that he had been provided, and discovered it to be empty. He must have eaten everything without noticing, which was a shame, because Paola Rovarini's panettone was something to be savored. He fought his way out of his blankets and got to his feet. "Well, children, it seems dinner is about to be served, so story time is over."

There was a satisfying heartfelt sea of moans as the children got to their feet and packed up their blankets before walking off. Phillip was amongst the last to leave, with Francesca and her husband waiting for him at the door.

"Thank you for keeping then amused," Francesca said as Phillip joined them.

"No, thank you for treating me as one of the family," Phillip said. "I enjoy reading to them, and they certainly enjoy being read to." He glanced back to check his lamp and blanket had been collected before stepping out into the cold with his landlady and her husband.

A *few days later*

The lecture on theoretical medicine was exploring how to treat a fever and Phillip had to hold onto his seat to prevent himself shooting to his feet and protesting loudly when Dr. Francesco Piazzono started to talk about the virtues of bloodletting.

"The objective is to remove only enough blood to induce syncope, at which point the ..."

"... patient is almost dead," Phillip muttered his own ending to the sentence. Unfortunately, his utterance fell into an untimely silence and was heard by most of the room. There was a collective, and noisy, intake of breath as the audience waited to see how Dr. Piazzono would react.

He reacted by singling out Phillip. "What was that you said, Signor Gribbleflotz?"

"Nothing, Dr. Piazzono," he said, hoping that the pontificating Paduan hadn't heard him.

"I'm sure I heard you say something while I was describing the proper way to bleed a patient, Signor Gribbleflotz."

Phillip made eye contact with Dr. Piazzono. "All I said was that bloodletting to syncope can kill the patient."

Dr. Piazzono folded his arms and glared at Phillip. "It is not the bloodletting that kills the patient, Signor Gribbleflotz. It is the gross imbalance of the humors that causes the blood to overheat that kills.

One bleeds a feverish patient to purge their body of the feverous blood. Health will be restored as the liver produces new blood."

Phillip shook his head. "I board with an animal doctor, and he never bleeds an animal, no matter how feverish it might be. And they always recover." In truth some of them died, but Phillip knew that bleeding them wouldn't have helped, so they didn't really count.

"I am not impressed by whatever a common farrier may or may not do, Gribbleflotz. Man is more complex than a beast."

Phillip wanted to protest that Giacomo Sedazzari was more than a common farrier, but to the left of Dr. Piazzono he caught his mentor's eye. Professor Giulio Casseri's almost undetectable shake of his head told Phillip to stop arguing. But he couldn't resist one final salvo. "Paracelsus held that bloodletting drains the life essence from the patient, and that you should be treating the disease with drugs."

Silence greeted that sally. Everyone turned to Dr. Piazzono to see how he would react. He reacted with quiet fury. He straightened, keeping his eyes on Phillip, and pointed towards the door. "Get out of my lecture theatre and never return." It was growled out, leaving no one in any doubt that he was angry.

A faint nod from his mentor was enough for Phillip to grab his things and leave. He waited for Giulio in the courtyard just outside the Palazzo Bo. Unfortunately, Giulio walked out in the company of Dr. Piazzono. They were involved in a heated discussion that Phillip felt might be about him, so he kept his distance as he followed them. Eventually the two men separated and Phillip was able to approach Giulio.

Giulio turned at Phillip's footfalls on the paved courtyard. "That was not very well done, Phillip."

"But bloodletting is wrong," Phillip protested. "You've said so yourself."

"Maybe I have, and I thank you for not bringing that up during your little spat with Dr. Piazzono. But you shouldn't have compared the actions of a physician to those of an animal doctor."

"I bet Giacomo Sedazzari loses fewer patients than Dr. Piazzono," Phillip protested.

"It is not a competition, Phillip," Giulio said. "And it was very bad of you to bring Paracelsus into the discussion."

"But he was right," Phillip protested. "A physician should rid the body of the disease that causes the fever by treating it with the right drugs, not by draining it of blood."

Phillip was so intent on defending himself that he didn't notice another member of the teaching staff heading towards them until he realized Giulio was looking behind him. He turned and saw Professor Prospero Alpini, the University of Padua's head botanist, and director of the Botanical Garden of Padua approaching.

"Prospero, just the person I wanted to talk to. Could you just wait a moment?" Giulio glanced back to Phillip. "How are you going with the specimens for my course on anatomy?"

"I've managed to secure the animals you wanted, but there aren't enough executions scheduled." Phillip smiled. "Still, it's winter. We shouldn't have to wait long."

"That's not a very nice attitude, Phillip," Prospero said.

"Unfortunately though, it is very true," Giulio said. "Where would we be without the poor who are willing to lend us their dead in return for a fitting burial?"

"Rather short of cadavers," Prospero admitted. "I hear you're going to present your next course on anatomy in the public anatomical theater. I never thought I'd see the day that you stepped foot into Fabricius' anatomy theater." He turned to Phillip. "What do you think?"

Phillip understood why Prospero was so surprised. It was a remarkable about-face on Giulio's part. The public anatomical theater in the Palazzo Bo owed its very existence to Professor Fabricius, and in the twelve years since he took over the chair of surgery Giulio had refused to teach in what he considered his rival's territory. Still, there was a perfectly rational explanation. "There's been so much advance interest in Professor Casseri's next anatomy course that there just isn't enough room in his private theater for them all."

Giulio smiled at Phillip. "I've reserved a place on the second tier with an excellent view for you."

"Thank you, Professore," Phillip said. And he was thankful, because he'd been worried that he might miss out.

"You're not assisting?" Prospero asked.

"Not this time." Giulio reached out and patted Phillip on the shoulder. "Because the course is being held on university grounds the rector has control over who get to assist."

"Fabricius strikes again," Prospero muttered. "He's never going to give up on his feud with you, Giulio."

"He's old, Prospero. Now, I've finished the draft of my *Tabulae Anatomicae*, and I was wondering if you'd be so good as to have a look at it."

"Of course I'd be happy to look at it for you," Prospero said. "Shall we go to your office now?"

"Before you go, Professor Prospero," Phillip interrupted. "Have you had a chance to try the evaporated essence of coffee I gave you?"

"Not yet, Phillip, but I will. I promise."

Giulio turned to Phillip. "I won't see you again until we prepare for my anatomy course, until then, do please try to keep out of trouble."

"Trouble," Phillip muttered to himself as he walked off. He didn't get into trouble.

Prospero glanced back to check that Phillip was out of earshot before speaking. "What did he do this time?" he asked.

Giulio released a heavy sigh. "He spoke out during a lecture by Francesco."

"Speaking out isn't exactly discouraged," Prospero pointed out.

"In Phillip's case, it should be actively discouraged."

"Oh dear," Prospero sighed. Sometimes Phillip was his own worst enemy. "Do I want to know the details?"

Giulio shook his head. "Francesco was talking about the virtues of bloodletting, and Phillip countered with Paracelsus."

Prospero winced. Francesco wasn't a rabid Galenist, but he certainly wasn't a great fan of Paracelsus. "Enough said. You do realize, Giulio, that if you do manage to see Phillip through the examinations, it'll be considered amongst your greatest achievements."

"He's not that bad," Giulio protested.

"No, of course not," Prospero said. "But neither is he a William Harvey or a Giulio Cesare Casseri.

Anyone could get men of their ability through the Padua examinations, but one such as Phillip, now that will take a truly great teacher."

"It will be one in the eye for Hieronymus, won't it?" A smile lit up Giulio's face for a few seconds before he turned back to Prospero. "What's the story with Phillip's evaporated essence of coffee?"

Prospero smiled at the memory of Phillip's enthusiasm when he brought it to him. "He found an untouched cup of coffee I left in the laboratory a few days ago and..."

Giulio waved a hand. "No need to continue. Being Phillip, he will have extracted the soluble essence of the coffee and turned it into a powder."

"He didn't simply reduce it to a powder," Prospero said, a little of the outrage he felt entering his voice. "He went one better. He made it into pills." Prospero shuddered. "One no longer has to suffer the ecstasy of a properly brewed cup of coffee to experience the benefits it can bring. No, all you have to do is take a pill."

Giulio snorted. "Phillip still hasn't developed a taste for coffee the way you learned to drink it in Cairo?"

"No he hasn't. Now, about this book..."

Three months later, March 9, 1616, Padua

Things had been going so well. Between Giulio's mentoring and the Sedazzari family's acceptance of him, Phillip had felt that his goal was within sight. But now...

Phillip staggered into the house and collapsed into

the first chair he came across. The noise he made attracted the attention of his landlady, who arrived in the room seconds after he landed in the chair.

"What's happened?" Francesca Sedazzari asked as she entered the room.

Phillip looked up, the tears falling down his cheeks. "Giulio's dead."

"Your mentor at the university? What happened?" Francesca asked as she put her arms around Phillip.

"He died last night, of a fever."

Phillip felt arms around him. He put his arms around Francesca, buried his face in her shoulder, and let the tears fall.

A *few days later*

Phillip sat in Giulio's old office facing the new holder of the recently vacated chair of surgery. He was dressed in his best clothes, and had come with his portfolio of drawings and notes from the various medical lectures he had attended.

"I'm sorry, Signor Gribbleflotz, but any arrangement you had with my esteemed colleague was extinguished by his death," Adrianus Spigelius said. "If you wish to study medicine at the University of Padua you must first demonstrate your academic credentials, and to date you have not done this."

Phillip sighed. It wasn't unheard of for someone to earn a doctorate without first earning a Baccalaureus Artium, but all the cases he'd heard of had something else going for them, such as family connections, or as was the case with Giulio, apprentice themselves to a suitable mentor. Unfortunately, Giulio had been his mentor. To prove his academic credentials Phillip was going to have to earn a Baccalaureus Artium. It would take him at least three years to learn the material needed to pass the exams, and in the meantime he wouldn't have time to attend lectures on the things that really interested him, such as medical botany and iatrochemistry. He got to his feet. "Thank you for your time, Professor Spigelius."

Adrianus stood also and walked Phillip to the door. "You're still welcome to attend the open lectures," he said.

"Thank you, Professor Spigelius, I will do that," he said. Unfortunately, without his mentor's support Phillip knew he would struggle to get into the lecture theaters for some of the more interesting courses. He'd certainly never have got into Giulio's three-week course of anatomy back in January if the Professore hadn't arranged a spot for him.

Phillip stepped out of the room and shut the door behind him. He paused for a few moments to think, but he was distracted by a sound. He looked down the corridor and saw two men step out of the shadows. One of them was Dr. Piazzono, but the other was old Fabrictus himself—Hieronymus Fabricius. And judging by the sly smiles he and Dr. Piazzono were exchanging, they knew exactly what had happened in Professor Spigelius' office. Phillip nodded his head in an informal bow to his mentor's great rival and hurried off in the other direction.

Professor Prospero Alpini stood at the door to the courtyard and waited. The man he wanted to talk to had to pass through this way. Right on schedule Phillip Gribbleflotz entered the courtyard. Prospero left his doorway and moved to intercept him.

"Phillip, just the man I was looking for. How did your interview with the new chair of surgery go?"

Phillip grimaced and glanced back the way he'd come. "I think Professor Fabrictus gave Professor Spigelius orders that I was no longer to be admitted into any medical classes."

"You should be careful about the names you use to describe important members of the faculty, Phillip," Prospero said. Then he did an about face. "How did you work out the name?"

"Did you ever see the way he smiled when someone complimented Giulio?"

"Oh yes." Prospero sniggered. "Yes I have, and yes, the nickname fits Hieronymus. Now, what are you planning to do with yourself?" he asked.

Phillip shrugged. "I don't know. It's clear that as long as Fabrictus is around no one of stature will take me on as their apprentice, but everything has happened so suddenly that I haven't had time to think."

As a member of the faculty, Prospero knew that Phillip faced an uphill task completing his medical training at Padua. It wasn't just Hieronymus having it in for him as Giulio's last apprentice. There was also the enmity of the many people Phillip had managed to offend with his loose tongue. Prospero studied the young man. His paranoia over Hieronymus could make it so much easier to carry out his plan.

"Why don't we go to my office and talk about your options?" Prospero asked. He didn't give Phillip a chance to decline the offer. Instead he put a hand behind his shoulder and steered him towards the exit he'd been waiting by.

It was a leisurely walk of little more than ten minutes from the university to Prospero's office at the botanical gardens. Once there Prospero gently pushed Phillip toward some chairs. "Please, take a seat," he said before slipping into his favorite chair. "Would you like a cup of coffee?"

Phillip hesitated, and Prospero smiled. "Don't worry. Battista knows how you like it."

"Thank you very much. I would like coffee, please."

"Battista," Prospero called out. "Coffee for me, and colored water for Phillip." He turned back to Phillip. "Now, you're probably wondering why I wanted to talk to you..."

Prospero was interrupted by the entry of a matronly woman bearing a tray. She set a cup and a plate with a piece of cake beside Phillip before doing the same for Prospero, except he only got cookies, and plain ones at that. "Why does he get panpepato and I don't?" he demanded.

Battista ruffled Phillip's hair. "He's a growing boy, and you know it's not good for you," she said before leaving.

"Would you like the cake, Professore?"

Prospero turned back to see Phillip offering him his plate. He was tempted. In fact he was sorely tempted. Unfortunately, he knew that even though he might enjoy it while eating it, it would come back to haunt him later. It was better that he stuck to the plain cookies, which wouldn't disagree with his stomach. "No, no," he said, waving away the plate. "You have it." He sighed again. "What did you do to deserve such favored treatment?" he asked. "Battista only serves her special panpepato to especially favored people."

"It was nothing," Phillip said. "One of her cousins had an ox with bad sores from a badly fitted harness. All we did was let it get flyblown and left the maggots to clean up the wound."

Prospero realized that the "we" Phillip was talking about were him and the animal doctor he boarded with. "Yes, one does tend to forget that you sometimes help your landlord in his animal practice." He smiled at Phillip. "That just makes you even more suitable as the replacement physician for the botanical expedition to Dalmatia that Michael Weitnauer is leading. Are you interested? I need an answer quickly, because they're already in Venice."

"But I'm not a qualified physician," Phillip said.

"I know, but you are more than adequately qualified for the job, Phillip. The expedition doesn't need a fully qualified doctor. It only needs someone capable of dealing with common complaints, and someone who can help Michael cataloging specimens. The fact you know a little about the care of livestock is a valuable extra. So, are you interested?"

"Could you tell me more about what will be expected of me?" Phillip asked.

Phillip stood in preparation to taking his leave. He and Prospero had hammered out the details and he had to make arrangements to leave Padua as soon as possible, so as not to delay any longer than necessary the already delayed expedition.

Prospero also stood. He looked at Phillip for a few

seconds. "There is something I want you to take with you." He pulled a folder from his bookshelf and laid it in Phillip's hands.

Phillip opened the folder and quickly came to understand what it was he held. "But this is the manuscript for Professor Casseri's last book, his *Tabulae anatomicae*," he said. "I can't take this." He tried to give it back to Prospero.

Prospero refused to take it back. "But you must, Hieronymus is already looking for it. I expect he wants to include the plates in his own book on anatomy."

Phillip froze. The sometimes bitter rivalry between his mentor and Hieronymus Fabricius had lasted over thirty years and Prospero obviously didn't think that Fabricius was going to let the little matter of Giulio's death get in the way of him carrying on the feud. He flipped open the folder again and leafed through the pages. "These are just proof copies of the plates," he said. "Even if I take this, Professor Fabrictus will still have access to the plates."

"But he won't have access to the text, Phillip," Prospero shook the manuscript. "This is the only copy of Guilio's text. It will take Fabricius years to create a text to go with the plates."

The implication was obvious to Phillip. Professor Fabricius was eighty-three years old and he might not have the years in which to write a new text. It would be something he could do to protect the memory of his mentor. "I'll take it." He slid the manuscript into the student's satchel he always carried. "Thank you for thinking of me for a place on the expedition to Dalmatia, Professore."

"You are a natural for the expedition, Phillip."

May 1616, Near Lake Vrana, Dalmatia

The expedition was in a small village about twenty miles north northwest of Vodice, their port of entry, in the south of Dalmatia. The three teamsters responsible for the expedition's pack animals were gathered around a table drinking and eating. Michael Weitnauer, the expedition leader and botanist, was checking his notes for today's destination at another table, and Phillip was sitting on a log weaving together long-stemmed white flowers.

One of the teamsters had been watching Phillip for a while. He turned back to his companions. "That Gribbleflotz is such a waste of space. We should have a proper physician," Gasparo Luzzatto said. "Not some failed medical student."

"We did have one, until he broke a leg falling down the stairs in a brothel," Leon said. "And be fair, Gasparo, Gribbleflotz seems competent enough. After all, he did get Francis through that bout of fever when we first landed at Vodice."

"He was just lucky," Gasparo said. "I mean, he didn't even bleed Francis. What kind of physician doesn't bleed a man when he's feverish?"

"As the interested party here," Francis Scocco said. "Might I suggest that Signor Gribbleflotz is the kind of physician who has his patient's best interests at heart?"

"But everyone knows you have to bleed a man when he has a fever, how else can balance the humors?" Gasparo said.

Leon looked at Gasparo over his mug. "You seem to know a lot about bloodletting."

"I have a booklet that tells all about how to do

it," Gasparo admitted. He turned to Francis. "You were lucky to recover from your fever, and it was no thanks to Gribbleflotz and his silly infusion of herbs."

"Willow bark tea, actually," Francis said. He grinned at the looks of disbelief on his companions' faces and shrugged. "I asked him what he had given me."

"My grandmother used to give us willow bark tea when we were ill when I was young," Leon said.

"There you are then," Gasparo said, a smile of victory on his face. "What kind of physician prescribes remedies your grandmother would give you?" He turned back to watch Phillip again. "Do any of you have any idea what he's doing?"

"No," Francis said. "Why don't you walk over and ask him?"

"Not likely," Gasparo said.

Phillip tried on one of the wreaths he'd made from some of the flowers he'd picked. It took a little adjustment before it felt comfortable. Then he threaded his arm through the rest of the wreaths he'd made and walked across to the other members of the expedition. He dropped a wreath on the table in front of each of the teamsters.

Gasparo looked up at him. "What is it?"

"It's a wreath of insect repelling flowers. The locals use them and I thought we could copy them and wear these to keep the flies from bothering us."

"Not likely," Gasparo said as he tossed his wreath back towards Phillip. Leon and Francis followed suit.

Phillip hid a smile as picked up the unwanted wreaths. He didn't think the time making the wreaths had been wasted because, if what he'd heard about the area they were exploring today was correct, they would soon be begging him for a wreath. With that to look forward to he walked over to the team's botanist. "Hi, Michael, would you like a wreath of *Tanacetum cinerariifolium*?"

"I'd like that very much, thank you," the team botanist said. He accepted the wreath from Phillip and put it on. "How do I look?" he asked.

Phillip reached over and twitched it around a little. "Probably at least as silly as I do," he said.

Michael jerked his head towards the others. "I see none of the others wanted to wear one of your wreaths."

"They'll change their minds soon enough."

"They're teamsters, Phillip. You don't really expect them to change their minds do you?"

"I do," Phillip said. "In my experience, teamsters aren't totally stupid, and according to the locals I talked to, the marsh area you want to explore has some nasty insects." A small grin emerged on Phillip's face.

Michael shook his head ruefully. "You're all heart, Phillip."

"I made wreaths for them. All they have to do is come and ask me for them. I won't even say a word."

"Yeah, right," Michael snorted. "As if you'd ever be able to do that." He gestured to the bunch of wreaths Phillip still had on his arm. "You appear to have gone a bit overboard making the wreaths..."

Phillip shook his head. "No. I'm such a nice guy that I made one each for the animals as well. There's no reason they should have to put up with the flies if they don't have to."

A few hours later

Francis waved a hand at the flies buzzing around his head. They were persistent and annoying. Some of them also bit. He looked at the team of pack animals they were leading. Their tails were twitching regularly to stop the insects settling on their bodies, but they weren't shaking their heads around anywhere near as much as they usually did. Maybe, he thought, the flowers set around their ears were actually keeping away the flies. He stared at them enviously for a few seconds before making a decision. He hurried to catch up with Leon, who was leading the team.

"Those flower wreaths Signor Gribbleflotz made seem to keep the flies from bothering the ponies," he said.

"Yes," Leon agreed.

"I was thinking . . ."

"That you might ask Signor Gribbleflotz if the offer of the flower wreaths still stands?"

"Yes," Francis said.

"Get one for me while you're at it," Leon said. Francis responded with a savage glare, but Leon gestured to the string of pack ponies he was leading. "I can't leave the ponies."

Francis released a sigh as he conceded defeat. It looked like he would have to approach Signor Gribbleflotz to ask for a couple of wreaths. He trudged after Phillip and his donkey. Although why he'd insisted on having a donkey to carry his gear Francis couldn't understand. Ponies were much easier to manage. A minute or two later he came up beside Phillip. "Signor Gribbleflotz, I was just wondering if the offer of the daisy wreaths still stands."

Phillip responded by pulling three wreaths out of a sack on his donkey's back and handing them to him. He didn't say a word, but he did have an amused smile on his face. Francis thanked him and hurried back to Leon.

"Here you are," he said as he handed a wreath to him.

Leon took the wreath and pulled it on immediately. "What did he say?" he asked as he adjusted the wreath.

"Nothing," Francis said. "He just gave me three wreaths."

"One for you, one for me, and one for Gasparo?"

"It looks that way. You wouldn't want to take it to him, would you?"

Leon reached out and gently slapped the withers of the nearest pony. "Sorry, but I can't leave the ponies."

"That excuse is getting a bit old," Francis muttered, much to Leon's amusement. He glared at Leon's smiling face and stomped off after Gasparo.

"Here, you'll probably want this," he said when he caught up with him.

Gasparo looked from Francis to the wreath of flowers in his hand. "Where did you get them?"

"I asked Signor Gribbleflotz for them."

Gasparo looked from the wreath in his hands to the one around Francis' head. "Do they work?"

Francis nodded. Since he'd put on his wreath he hadn't been bothered by flies trying to land on his face. "It seems to."

Gasparo plopped on his wreath. "Where do you suppose Signor Gribbleflotz learned the trick?"

"Didn't he say the locals used the flowers to keep away insects?"

"Yes," Gasparo agreed, "but have you seen any of the locals wearing bunches of flowers on their heads?"

Francis thought about it. "No."

"So how did Signor Gribbleflotz know that wearing the flowers would work?"

Francis shrugged. "You could ask him," he suggested.

Gasparo shook his head. "I'd look like a fool," he protested.

Phillip hid a smile. A quirk of the terrain meant that he'd overheard Francis and Gasparo talking. The answer to Gasparo's question was that he'd learned about the flower wreaths from some of the locals. The reason Gasparo and Francis hadn't seen any of them wearing similar flower wreaths was because they hadn't seen any of the locals working in areas where flies and other insects were that big a problem. Things were different for the expedition. They were looking for botanical specimens, and that meant they were entering areas the locals would normally avoid at this time of year, such as the marsh Michael was currently exploring, which seemed to be a breeding ground for all sorts of flying insects.

He looked around to see where Michael was. As usual the botanist had his head buried in amongst the grasses. He walked over to see if he could help.

Slap! "Bastard!"

"What's the matter, Michael?" Phillip asked as he approached.

Michael held up his hand so Phillip could see the splat of blood on it. "An insect bit me."

Slap! Slap! Michael looked at the new splats of dead insects on his hands with grim satisfaction before turning his attention back to Phillip. His eyes widened and he pointed an accusing finger at Phillip. "Why aren't they biting you?" he demanded.

Phillip looked down at his hands. They were clear of insects and insect bites. As an experiment he moved his right hand towards the cloud of insects flying around the hand Michael was pointing at him. Rather than land on his hand they avoided it.

Michael had been watching with interest. "They must scent the flower essence on your hands from when you made the wreaths."

"Let's try something," Phillip said. He reached up and snapped a flower head from the wreath of flowers around Michael's head and grabbed Michael's left hand.

"The right hand, please, Phillip," Michael said as he pulled his left hand free and proffered his right hand to him.

Phillip held Michael's right hand and firmly rubbed the flower head over the back of it. The results were astonishing. Almost immediately the insects abandoned that hand in favor of the other.

Michael grabbed the flower head from Phillip and rubbed it over the back of his left hand. Then he rubbed it around his neck.

Phillip felt something on his neck and slapped it. He didn't bother confirming that it was a biting insect. Instead he retreated from the edge of the marsh to the relative safety of the track around the lake so he could rub a daisy on his exposed flesh. When he was finished he stared at the remains of the flower head in his hand. There had to be an easier way, and he made a note in his notebook to ask the next local they came across.

Later that day

Gasparo, Francis, Leon, and Michael were sitting at a table. Michael was carefully drawing a flower from a sample he had beside him while the others were relaxing over a mug of ale. The flower wreaths Phillip had made for them had wilted and now sat in the middle of the table. Off at another table they could see Phillip pounding away with a pestle and mortar.

Gasparo turned to Michael. "Do you know what Signor Gribbleflotz is doing?"

Michael glanced at Phillip. "It looks like he's grinding something."

Gasparo grimaced at Michael. "I can see that he is using a pestle and mortar. I was wondering if you knew what he was preparing."

Michael studied Phillip for a while before answering. "We had a few words with some of the locals. Apparently they sometimes use a lotion of water and powdered flower heads to ward off insects. I assume Signor Gribbleflotz purchased some dried flower heads and is now grinding them to make an insect repellent."

Francis ran a hand lightly over the bite marks on the back of his neck as he stared at Michael. "Do you think it'll work?"

Michael nodded. "Signor Gribbleflotz and I discovered in the marsh today that if you rubbed the flowers into your skin the insects would avoid that area, so I see no reason why splashing a solution containing traces of the flower over your skin shouldn't work at least as well."

"That's good to hear," Leon said. "I don't suppose you have anything with which to treat insect bites?" he asked.

"There's a broad-leafed plant that can be rubbed over the bites," Michael said. "I can look for some tomorrow."

"That's going to make for an uncomfortable night," Gasparo muttered. "Hang on. Here comes Signor Gribbleflotz. Maybe he has something to hand."

The group watched Phillip approach. He had a small pot of something that he placed on the table in front of them.

"What's that?" Gasparo asked.

Phillip looked fondly at the pot. "It's a paste made from the leaves of *Plantago major*. You should find it soothes the insect bites."

"That's the broad-leafed plant I was thinking of," Michael said. He looked up at Phillip. "Did you learn about it from Professor Alpini?"

Phillip nodded. "He mentioned it in his medical botany lectures, but I first met it when I was helping my stepfather. He was an apothecary."

Francis gestured towards Michael. "Dr. Weitnauer here thought that you were grinding up flower heads to make an insect repellent."

Gasparo turned to Phillip. He gestured towards the pot. "That's right. Does that mean you haven't made any insect repellent?"

"Don't worry. I've bought some powdered flower head. All I have to do is mix it with water. Now, who would like me to smear some of my soothing paste over their insect bites?"

The next few days progressed without any drama. Michael continued to bring the expedition to a halt whenever he found an interesting plant. Gasparo, Francis, and Leon continued to look after the animals and provide security. Meanwhile Phillip continued to help Michael and collect his own plant samples.

They were camped in the open tonight. The sun was still up, but it was late and all of them were tired. They gathered around the campfire close to Phillip as he pulled a book out of his pack and carefully opened it and started to read aloud. The book was an Italian edition of Spanish author Miguel de Cervantes Saavedra's *The Ingenious Gentleman Don Quixote of La Mancha*, and Phillip had been reading a few pages to the group every evening. Tonight he was reading chapter twenty-three, "Of What Befell Don Quixote in the Sierra Morena."

"You'd like the shirts," Michael said as Phillip read the description of what was in the valise Don Quixote and Sancho Panza found.

Phillip pointedly examined the sad state of his current shirt. "Four shirts of fine Holland wouldn't go amiss," he confirmed.

"And neither would the gold," Leon said.

Phillip grinned. "Gold never goes amiss. Now, can I continue?" All heads nodded and Phillip continued.

". . . and he said what will be told farther on." Phillip carefully marked the page with a ribbon and closed the book.

"You can't stop there," Leon protested.

"It's the end of the chapter," Phillip said.

"But it doesn't feel complete," Leon protested.

Phillip just grinned. "I'll read the next chapter tomorrow."

"There's still plenty of light," Leon said hopefully.

"No," Phillip said shaking his head.

On that note Phillip wrapped the book in an oilskin cover before putting it back into his pack. Then he laid out his blankets and made himself comfortable. He glanced around the campsite one last time before laying down his head. Leon was standing guard while everyone else went to bed.

The next night they exchanged the discomforts of the great outdoors for the more common discomforts of a small inn.

Phillip deposited the inn-supplied blankets in a corner and sprinkled powdered *Tanacetum cinerariifolium* over them. He was liberally sprinkling the powder over the canvas-covered straw pallets that were their beds for the night when Francis entered the room with one of the packs.

Francis stopped when he saw what Phillip was doing. "I thought you had herbs to keep down the bed bugs?"

Phillip stopped in mid sprinkle and turned to Francis. "The powdered flower is much more powerful than anything I've used before."

"Is it safe?" Francis asked as he dropped the pack he was carrying against the wall.

Phillip looked at the powder in his hand before smiling at Francis. "I wouldn't recommend eating it by the handful, but Dapple didn't have any trouble eating the flowers."

"But he's a donkey, and donkeys don't care what they eat."

Phillip wiped his hands clean of the dust on his thighs and shook his head. "Goats will eat anything because they think everything should be food. Horses and ponies will eat almost anything they find in the hope that it is food, but a donkey will only eat what it is sure is food." He grinned. "If Dapple thinks it is safe to eat the flowers, then it should be safe to sleep in the powdered remains of the flowers."

Francis looked a bit dubious at Phillip's explanation. "Should be?" he asked.

"We all applied a lotion of the same powder mixed with water this morning, and I don't know about you, but I don't feel any the worse for the experience."

Francis smiled in relief. "And it did keep the insects away today," he admitted. "Will you be reading the next chapter to us tonight?"

Phillip's brows shot up. "Yes, and thanks for reminding me. I have to let the innkeeper know."

"Are you angling for better victuals again, Signor Gribbleflotz?"

Phillip grinned. That had been the result of his reading in inn common rooms previously. "That and because it is a sure way of getting most of the village together so Dr. Weitnauer can talk to them."

"I could warn the innkeeper that you will be reading aloud in his common room this evening," Francis suggested.

Phillip thought about the offer but shook his head. "He might want to see what I'll be reading to his customers, so it's probably best that I speak to him."

That evening Phillip sat down to read to a packed house. He checked the small table beside him. There was a mug and a jug of the local cider to keep his throat lubricated. He poured a mug full and took a sip. There was shuffling about in the room as people got comfortable, and drinks were ordered. Phillip opened his book and adjusted the position of the lamps until he was comfortable with the light. Finally he was ready. A glance with a raised brow towards the innkeeper produced a nod of the head. He too was ready for the reading to begin.

Phillip inhaled the rarified air of expectation and started to speak. He gave a brief synopsis of the story so far before he started to read.

"Chapter twenty-four, 'In Which Is Continued the Adventure of the Sierra Morenaí.' The history relates that it was with the greatest attention Don Quixote listened to the ragged knight of the Sierra, who began by saying," Phillip read. His strong voice was able to be heard in even the most distant spots in the inn—the long hours reading to his landlord's extended family in the barn had unexpected benefits.

After only a few sentences he knew he had the audience's complete attention, the sound of the crackling fire being his only competition. It brought a sense of satisfaction, but also an obligation to deliver.

With each character he changed his voice, giving them different personalities so his listeners could more easily keep track of who was supposed to be speaking. Just like the children of the Rovarini in Padua this audience lapped it up.

Phillip lost track of time as the thrill of all those people hanging onto his every word took over. Eventually he had to stop, and he closed the book to absolute silence. He'd held everyone's attention all that time. With a sense of intense satisfaction Phillip stood and took his bows. "That's all for tonight, good people. You have been a wonderful audience, and for that I thank you. Now I must leave you to get on with your own business."

He left the floor to Michael and found a quiet corner where he could rest. His thumb rubbed against a wart that had emerged on his finger recently. It had been annoying him for a couple of days now, but for various reasons he hadn't got around doing anything about it. He knew a proper way to remove it, but it was bothering him right now. So he tried chewing on it. It was inefficient, but it did at least alleviate the itching.

He was checking his progress in the light of the fire when an older woman captured his hand and looked at it. "That's the wrong way to get rid of it," she said.

Phillip smiled at the gray-haired woman. "It's annoying me. Its right where my thumb rubs against the finger and it itches whenever I touch it."

"There are better ways of making them go away than trying to chew them off," the woman said.

"I know," Phillip said. "Apply a slice of garlic that has been left to soak in vinegar."

"I know a better way," the woman said. "Come to my cottage tomorrow morning and I'll show you how to get rid of it."

Phillip realized he might have made contact with the village wise woman. Such women existed in most villages. They knew the local herbal lore and cared for the health of the community. His great-grandfather had written in his journals about how such women could be fonts of knowledge. He would be careful.

Phillip bowed his head. "Thank you, madam. I am Phillip Gribbleflotz. And you would be?" he asked.

"You may call me Eufemia. The innkeeper knows me."

"Then tomorrow I will come and be schooled, and lose a wart. Which is your cottage?" he asked.

"You can't miss it. It's the third on your left when you leave the inn heading north."

Phillip thanked the woman, watched her leave and settled down to wait for Michael.

Next morning

Phillip asked the innkeeper about the woman, and was reassured by his answer. Eufemia was not only the village wise woman, but also happened to be his mother. Phillip thanked the man for the information and left the inn heading north.

Eufemia had been right; her house, which was a riot of color, was impossible to miss. He opened the rickety gate and walked up to the door and knocked.

"Come in Signor Gribbleflotz," Eufemia called.

Phillip entered the dark cottage and followed the sounds of a knife on a chopping board to find Eufemia pouring chopped vegetables into a kettle. A large gray and white cat was entwining itself around her legs.

"Take a seat in the sunlight," Eufemia directed. "I'll be with you in a minute."

The moment Phillip sat down the cat stopped twining itself around Eufemia's legs and walked over to where he was sitting, leaped onto the arm of the chair and sniffed Phillip before stepping onto him.

"Don't mind the cat," Eufemia said as she put the kettle to one side and grabbed a clay pot and a couple of twigs. "Now let's have a look at your wart," she said as she turned Phillip's hand in the sunlight.

Eufemia took his hand in her left hand, and with her right she opened the pot and used the twigs to pick up a dead iridescent green insect about as long as her thumbnail was wide.

"That's a Cantharis beetle," Phillip said, recognizing the insect from an example his landlord in Padua had shown him.

Eufemia shook her head. "No, it's a blister beetle."

"Right, sorry, different places, different names," Phillip apologized. "What are you going to do with it?"

"I am going to rub it against the skin around the wart."

Phillip instinctively tried to jerk his hand back, but Eufemia had a firm grip on it. "Don't be such a baby," she said as she carefully rubbed the dead beetle against Phillip's finger.

Moments later she released Phillip's hand and he drew it protectively close to him.

"Don't touch the area I brushed with the beetle," Eufemia warned. "Anything that touches it will also blister."

Phillip immediately moved his hand clear of his body and stared at his finger. "I can't continue to avoid touching my finger," he protested.

"Just leave it a little longer and then we'll wash it with soap and water."

"Then what happens?" Phillip asked.

"A blister will rise where I rubbed the blister beetle. When the blister bursts you should check to see if the wart is still in your finger. If it is, then you repeat the treatment."

"And this will work?" Phillip asked.

Eufemia nodded. "Yes. And even better, it doesn't leave a scar. Unlike what would happen if you managed to bite out the wart."

That evening the skin around the wart on Phillip's finger started to itch even as it ballooned out. He examined the blister. The wart was right there on the surface. He played with the blister a little. Surely, if the wart was rooted in his flesh the fluid in the blister wouldn't have lifted the skin away from the flesh? It was a thought, which he immediately wanted to enter in his journal.

When he opened his journal Phillip's eyes fell on the last entry. It was about the effect of the *Plantago major* paste he'd used to treat the teams' insect bites. He thought about it. The blister wasn't a bite, but maybe some of that paste would soothe it. It certainly couldn't make it worse. Phillip wrote up his thoughts about the wart being lifted off the flesh by the blister before hunting out the pot. It wasn't immediately soothing, but over time he ceased noticing the finger.

The next day Phillip stopped off at Eufemia's cottage to show her his finger, and to hopefully talk to her about the local plants she used. His finger turned out to be a bit of an ice breaker for that discussion.

"What have you done to your finger?" she asked pointing to the bandage Phillip had wrapped around it.

"It was itching, so I applied a simple balm to it, and wrapped it in a bandage to insure it stayed in contact with the blistered area."

Eufemia started to undo the bandage. "What did you use?" she asked.

"A paste made of *Plantago major*." Phillip didn't expect Eufemia to know plants by their Latin names so he showed her a few leaves he'd brought with him.

Eufemia took a leaf from Phillip and crushed it and sniffed. "Plantain. That's a wise choice. Did you know that a tea from plantain leaves can be used to treat someone with the runs?"

Phillip leaned closer. "No I didn't, could you describe the treatment?"

That evening

Phillip was late returning to the team's lodgings. He'd ended up spending all day with Eufemia, following her around her garden learning how to identify plants and what they could or shouldn't be used for. He was happily contemplating going over what he'd recorded in his journal as he entered the inn.

"Where've you been all day?" Michael demanded the moment he entered.

Phillip was a little taken aback at the aggression Michael was displaying and took a couple of steps away from him. "I've been talking to the village wise woman about the local plants."

The anger in Michael's face dropped immediately and he reached out a hand and dragged Phillip over to a table. "What did you learn?" he demanded.

"Well, did you know an infusion made from *Plantago major* can be used to treat diarrhea?"

Michael shook his head. "Anything else?"

Phillip laid down his journal where Michael could see it and they spent the next hour before supper going over the bits of information he had gleaned from Eufemia.

July 1616

They were still working their way around Lake Vrana a week later. Progress as measured in distance was slow, as they'd barely moved two miles in six days, but in terms of specimens they were doing very well. Michael had so many of them that he'd called a halt and they'd set course for the nearest civilization. The port city of Biograd na Moru beckoned, and now, while the teamsters checked the animals and Michael wrapped up his specimens, Phillip took care of Dapple before collecting his satchel and finding a quiet place where he could check the condition of his finger.

He sat down in the grass and opened his satchel. In addition to anything else he might need at a moment's notice, such as his latest journal, writing instruments, or food, it also contained a small medical kit. He pulled the kit out and opened it beside him. There was a scalpel made from a shaped piece of wood with a shard of obsidian mounted into it. He used that to trim back the loose skin that had been lifted by the blister before using a lens to check his finger. The wart was still there, but much smaller. That meant he had to rub it again with a blister beetle. Fortunately he'd prepared for this eventuality and he had a dozen or so dead beetles in a small pot. He opened that and used a couple of twigs to pick up a beetle and rub it against his finger.

He was putting the used beetle back when he heard a bit of a commotion. He sealed the pot and pushed the twigs he'd been using to hold it into the ground, so nobody could accidently touch them, before looking up. In the distance, maybe fifty yards away, a group of children were running around screaming. In his time living in the midst of the Rovarini family Phillip had learned that this was perfectly normal behavior with children, so he ignored it and concentrated on his finger.

He was just putting everything back into his satchel when the primeval scream of a mother in distress

rent the air. Phillip, like everyone else within earshot, turned in the direction the scream came from.
He saw a woman kneeling on the ground holding a
small child who was obviously in some distress. Phillip
jumped to his feet, thrusting the medical kit into his
satchel, and ran toward the woman, where a crowd
was already gathering.

The woman was holding a boy about the same
size as Giacomo and Francesca Sedazzari's ten-year-
old daughter. But this was a boy, meaning he was
probably anything between eight and eleven. She
was wailing over the child, holding him in her arms
and crying out for something. Phillip knew enough to
recognize the language as Yiddish, but after that he
would only have been guessing. He turned his attention to the child, and froze. The boy's face was badly
swollen, and the lips were turning blue. Phillip took
a deep breath and pushed his way forward. "Let me
through!" he said. "I'm a physician," he added as he
fumbled in his satchel.

That cleared a way, and moments later Phillip bent
down over the child. He forced open the child's mouth
and looked to see if he could force a cannula down
the airway, but the tongue was swollen, suggesting
that the throat might also be swollen.

The woman said something to him. He didn't understand her, but he assumed she was pleading with him
to save her son. Phillip swallowed. He could think of
only one way that he could save the boy's life. He
would have to cut an opening into the trachea. Both
Professor Fabricius and his mentor, Giulio, had written
descriptions of how they felt the operation should be
performed. Both of them had also recommended that

it only be performed as a last resort. Phillip looked down at the boy. He was still struggling to breathe, but his struggles were weakening. The face that should have been pink was pale and his lips were turning blue. That was enough to convince Phillip that a tracheotomy was the only way to save the child.

Phillip shoved his satchel under the boy's shoulders so his head naturally fell back, extending the neck. He opened his medical kit and grabbed the smallest of the curved brass cannula he'd had made according to his mentor's specification just in case he had to perform this operation. Giulio had actually specified silver in his writings, but that was beyond Phillip's purse. He also picked up his obsidian scalpel and felt for the cricoid cartilage just below the larynx with his free hand.

The only warning was the renewed screaming of the woman, but Phillip didn't realize the screams were directed at him until she started to strike him. He held up his arms defensively as the boy's mother continued to scream and lash out at him. "Someone hold her," he screamed.

Two shadows grabbed the woman and pulled her away. Meanwhile Michael dropped down beside Phillip and took hold of the boy. "You're going to do a tracheotomy?" he asked.

"It's his only hope," Phillip said as he relocated his target on the boy's throat and spread his fingers to tighten the skin.

Michael whistled. "I've only heard of the operation. Have you done one before?"

"No," Phillip whispered as he made a vertical incision about an inch long. "But I've watched Professor

Casseri demonstrate how to do it on cadavers and animals many times." He sliced at the tissue under the skin until he reached the cartilage of the tracheal rings. He pushed the tissue aside with the fingers of his left hand as he tried to locate the cricothyroid membrane. Once he found it he made a horizontal incision in the membrane between the tracheal rings. Air tried to whistle through the hole he'd made, telling him he'd made an opening into the trachea. He enlarged the hole enough to slip in the curved cannula into the hole and pushed it in a good inch, until the wings on the cannula, which were there to stop it being pushed in too far, came into contact with the boy's throat. Almost immediately the boy's struggles eased. But Phillip couldn't rest yet. He needed to tie the cannula in place so it wouldn't slip out. He threaded a ribbon through the hole on one wing of the cannula and passed it under the boy's neck. He then threaded the other end through the hole on the other wing and pulled the ribbon tight before tying a knot to hold it securely in place. He'd done it. Now he could rest.

Phillip was feeling almost faint. He collapsed onto his buttocks in relief. It was one thing to watch someone of Professor Casseri's caliber demonstrate the operation, it was something else do it oneself. Phillip wiped the sweat from his brow and looked up. He was surrounded by interested faces, not least of which was the woman who'd been hitting him. She was being held by Gasparo and Leon, whom he assumed had come to his aid. "Thanks for holding her, but you can let her go now," he told them as he laid his shaking hands on his knees.

The moment she was released the woman collapsed beside her child, kissing him and cooing over him.

"He's still in a bad way," Phillip warned the woman. She laid a hand on her son's forehead and spoke. Phillip couldn't follow what she was saying, but guessed that because she was looking at him that she was thanking him for saving her son. He waved that away as being of little importance, the achievement being sufficient reward in itself. Still, he had a problem. The cannula in the boy's trachea was only a short-term solution to an unknown problem. He needed more information, but he couldn't communicate with the mother. He looked around the crowd that had gathered. "Can anyone tell me what happened?" He asked. It didn't draw a reply in Venetian, so he tried again in his native German. That also failed to elicit a satisfactory response. In desperation he tried his last remaining language, classical Latin.

A man approached and laid a gentle hand on the shoulder of the woman. "My name is Isaac, and I would like to know the name of the man who saved my son's life."

"Phillip Theophrastus Gribbleflotz." They were speaking in classical Latin, the language of instruction, so Phillip knew he was dealing with an educated man. "Do you have any idea what might have caused the swelling?" he asked.

Isaac nodded. "I believe the swelling is caused by the stings of bees. Jusufio and the other children were playing near the trees when they disturbed a bees' nest."

Phillip turned back to the boy and studied his face and neck. Now he knew to look for them he could make out little dots that were the sites where he'd been stung. He did a quick count, finding thirty-four possible bee sting sites. He had little doubt that there were more, and even less doubt that they were the cause of the swelling. He turned back Jusufio's father. "Your son won't be able to breathe without the cannula until the swelling goes down."

"I understand, Phillip Theophrastus Gribbleflotz. I too am a physician, and I know it will be many days before the swelling reduces enough so that Jusufio can breathe normally. I lack a tube such as you used, can I buy it from you?"

"It's one of a set, and I'd rather not sell it, as I might need it again. Where are you headed? If it's the same way we are going we can leave it in place a while longer. We're bound for Biograd na Moru."

"We too are bound for Biograd na Moru. Mayhap we can travel together, and you can tell me about what you did? Galen and Aretaeus both wrote about such an operation, but that's the first time I have ever seen it performed."

Phillip wasn't sure this was the right time to say he'd never seen it performed on a live human before, but he was happy to talk to the man.

Biograd na Moru

Phillip spent the morning talking to Isaac on the trip to Biograd na Moru, and once the expedition was settled he hurried over to the table where Michael was sitting to beg permission to follow him to his lodgings where they could continue their conversation.

"You have to let me spend some more time with him, Michael," he pleaded. "His theories about the Quinta Essentia of the human humors could be important."

"The what?" Michael asked.

Phillip ran his hands lightly over the table top as he tried to assemble his thoughts. "Are you familiar with *De Secretis Naturae Sive Quinta Essentia*?"

"The book by Ramon Llull? I've heard of it."

Phillip nodded. "Yes, that one. Well, whereas Signor Lull talks mostly of using the fifth essence, the Quinta Essentia, of things as a cure, Isaac sees it as more of a solvent for the medicines, making them a hundred times more powerful."

Michael responded by slowly shaking his head. "I can imagine using the fifth essence of *Plantago major* as a basis for an infusion made out of the leaves rather than using water, but I can't see any logical reason why the resulting medicine should be any stronger. And certainly not a hundred times stronger."

"A hundred times stronger might be a slight exaggeration on Isaac's part," Phillip admitted. "But imagine if mixing a drug with the right Quinta Essentia could even just double its strength..."

"I'm trying to imagine it, Phillip." Michael shook his head. "Nope. I can't see it happening. It sounds too much like witchcraft."

"But you must have seen it happen. Think of how neither acidum salis nor aqua fortis can dissolve gold on their own, but if you mix them together in the right proportions you create aqua regia, which can dissolve gold."

"You've got me there," Michael said. "I've seen

aqua regia at work. Why do you suppose it works?" he asked.

"Ah, well, that's a good question."

Michael's lips twitched. "Do I get a good answer though?"

"Of course." Phillip planted his elbows on the table and steepled his fingers so he could rest his chin on his fingertips. "Consider Adam. God created man, but on his own Adam cannot produce children. So God took of Adam a rib and created Eve. On her own Eve can't conceive a child, but together Adam and Eve produced Cain. So as with Adam and Eve, who alone can't produce a child, neither acid on its own can dissolve the noble gold. But together they make aqua regia, which can dissolve gold." He looked expectantly at Michael. "Do you understand now?"

"What happened to Abel and Seth?"

"It's just an analogy for illustrative purposes, Michael. For now imagine that Adam and Eve only had one child."

"But..."

Phillip exhaled noisily through his nose. It was more of a sigh than a snort. He was sure Michael was just trying to be difficult. "Michael. Surprisingly enough you still seem to have most of your teeth. Would you like me to remedy the situation?"

Michael smiled in the face of Phillip's threat, displaying his teeth in all their glory. "I still don't see the connection between Adam and Eve and the Quinta Essentia of something being able to double or more the power of a medicine."

Phillip paused to think about his explanation. "Okay, how about this. Acidum salis is the acid of salt. Salt is ultimately derived from the sea, which is the all-mother. It's dried and heated and put through extensive complex processes to make the acid, so acidum salis is the acidic essence of the all-mother."

"So acidum salis is feminine?"

"Yes. Think of it as being Eve," Phillip said. "Now..."

"So aqua fortis is supposed to be Adam?" Michael asked. "Why do you say that?"

"Because aqua fortis enables the violent masculine explosions in gunpowder. Therefore it is male."

"But you don't use aqua fortis to make gunpowder," Michael said. "You use saltpetre, sulphur, and charcoal. Everyone knows that."

"And aqua fortis is the acidic essence of saltpetre," Phillip said a little more forcefully than was possibly necessary. "You do know how to make aqua fortis, don't you?" he asked.

Michael bit his lower lip and shook his head.

"And you consider yourself an educated man." Phillip gave rein to a set-upon sigh before continuing. "You make aqua fortis the same way you make acidum salis, only instead of using the feminine salt of the sea, you use the masculine saltpetre."

"So aqua fortis is Adam, acidum salis is Eve, and aqua regia is Cain?" Michael asked.

"For the purposes of this explanation, yes." He stared hard at Michael. Was it possible he was laughing at him?

"I don't remember. Was Cain more powerful than Adam or Eve?"

That tilted Phillip's suspicions heavily towards being laughed at. Still, he was going to finish this explanation even if he ended up killing Michael. "The Adam and

Eve analogy is purely to show that two parts, which can't achieve something on their own, can achieve that same something when they are combined.

"So, aqua fortis and acidum salis come together to form aqua regia, which unlike its parent acids, can dissolve gold, thus proving that the power of a mixture can be greater than the power of the individual ingredients. Of course, like Cain, aqua regia changes as it ages, transforming into other states and natures, which is why only fresh aqua regia can dissolve gold." At last Michael was nodding, raising Phillip's hopes. They were dashed only moments later.

"So how does the Quinta Essentia of anything increase the power of a drug?"

Phillip admitted his lack of knowledge with a well-practiced Italian shrug. "Perhaps the extracted Quinta Essentia pulls out more of the masculine essence of the medicine than a lesser solution. Who knows? And that is why I need time to talk to Isaac, so I can find out."

"How long do you want?"

"I'd like as long as you can give me."

"I can give you five days. I expect it'll take me that long to clear my backlog of specimens."

That was much better than Phillip had hoped for. "I can do that." He grabbed Michael and hugged him. "Thank you," he said before running off.

A week later

Phillip was trying to pack, but Michael was walking along the bench checking everything he'd been doing over the last few days. "Do you mind?" Phillip demanded as he edged Michael away so he could plant a basket of horse manure on the bench.

Michael took one look at the contents of the basket and jumped clear, pinching his nose. "What is that?" he asked, pointing at the basket.

"It's exactly what it looks like," Phillip said as he carved a hole in the manure.

"What do you want that for?"

Phillip held up a flask of a clear liquid. "This is fivefold distilled waters of wine. According to Isaac, if I bury it in horse manure for four months, then decant it into a clean flask, and bury it for another four months, and then decant it into another clean flask and bury it for another four months, I will be left with a flask of the Quinta Essentia of the waters of wine." He thrust the flask into the hole and covered it with manure, firmly patting down the top layer.

"A year!" Michael repeated. "That's a long time. I hope it's worth it."

Phillip walked over to a bucket of water and started washing his hands. "According to Isaac, if you mix the distillate of any item with the Quinta Essentia of the waters of wine you'll have a medicine that can cure any malady."

Michael's eyes screwed up and he stared at Phillip. "If I drank a medicine mixed with fivefold distilled waters of wine I'm pretty sure I'd feel cured, for a while."

Phillip grinned. "Maybe I misunderstood Isaac. We did have a bit of a communication problem, with him thinking in Yiddish but trying to explain in Latin."

Michael nodded. "That's possible. So, what are you

going to do now?" his gaze settled on a number of glass jars on the bench awaiting packing. "What are these?"

"Those are the Quinta Essentia of such things as *Plantago major*, willow bark, *Tanacetum cinerariifolium*, and Cantharis beetle."

"And they were all collected by the destructive distillation of the parent?"

"Of course. How else can one extract the Quinta Essentia?" Phillip demanded.

"Phillip, I have this vague recollection that the whole idea of this Quinta Essentia of whatever is so you can do something with the Quinta Essentia of the human humors."

"That's right."

"Well," Michael said with some emphasis. "I can't help but think you're going to run into a bit of resistance when you use destructive distillation to extract the Quinta Essentia of the human humors."

"You don't extract it," Phillip said. "The idea is to invigorate it while it's still in the body," Phillip sighed. "At least that's what I'll be trying to do in a year's time when my Quinta Essentia of the waters of wine are ready."

Michael looked dubiously at Phillip. "Do you really think burying a flask of fivefold distilled waters of wine in horse manure for a year is going to somehow give it special powers?"

"But Michael, according to Isaac, his people have been preparing the Quinta Essentia of the waters of wine in this way for hundreds of years. Why would they continue doing it if there was no benefit?"

May 1617, Zadar, Dalmatia

Phillip was in his natural habitat, an alchemical laboratory. He was hard at work producing pure acids, which were to be his payment to Davitt Tapiero for the use of his laboratory. At the door Davitt was watching on in awe when Michael turned up.

"He is absolutely magnificent," Davitt said with a very Italian flourish of his arms.

"How do you mean?" Michael asked.

"Look at him," Davit instructed with a wave of his arm. "Look at the way he has a dozen retorts working at once."

"Running a dozen retorts on a distilling furnace isn't anything special. I've seen plenty of people do the same," Michael said.

"Yes, but no doubt they are all distilling the same thing. Signore Gribbleflotz is distilling three different acids, aqua vitae, and water, all at the same time."

Michael whistled. "That's impressive. But I still need to talk to him." He walked over to the bench where Phillip was working on something. "Phillip. I've got some bad news for you."

Phillip carefully laid down the pen he was holding and turned to Michael. "What's happened?"

"Professor Alpini died on the sixth of February." Michael held up a letter. "This was waiting for me when I checked with our shipping agent."

Phillip was shaken by the news. "How did it happen?"

Michael checked the letter. "They think an imbalance of the humors caused his kidneys to fail."

Phillip slumped into a chair. He'd lost the second of his great mentors. He'd learned a lot about the various medical qualities of plants from the man who had been the director of Padua's botanical garden. And now he was dead. "There's nothing left for me in Padua now."

"So what will you do now that our plant gathering expedition is over?"

Phillip shrugged. "I don't know."

"Are you still interested in being a military surgeon?"

Phillip nodded. It was something he'd mentioned during one of the many discussions they'd had around a campfire over the last few months.

"Well, the Republic is fighting the archduke of Styria. I'm sure they'd welcome someone of your talents."

"I'll think about it," Phillip said. He turned his back on Michael to hide the tears that were starting to fall. His tear-filled eyes settled on the jars of Quinta Essentia. One day he'd learn how to invigorate the Quinta Essentia of the Human Humors. It would be too late to save Giulio and Prospero, but he would do it. It was personal now.

Chapter 4

Dr. Gribbleflotz, I Presume

July 1622, Basel

Phillip was footsore and sweaty as he made his way up to the main gate on the northeastern wall of the city of Basel. He stopped short of the moat and stared at the walls. They were impressive, and this was only the bit of the city protecting the bridge across the Rhine.

A tug on the lead he was holding brought him back to his need to get into the city before they shut the gates. "Come on, Dapple. Let's get a move on," he told his pack-donkey. This wasn't the same donkey he'd had in Dalmatia. He'd sold that Dapple before he left the country, but he liked the name.

With a gentle tug on the lead rope Dapple reluctantly gave up on snatching at any grass that was within reach and fell in beside Phillip. Ahead of them was the Riehen-Tor, and standing waiting for them, and any other travelers, were the gate's guards.

As they got close, one of the guards stepped out in

front of Phillip holding up his hand. "Halt. Who are you, and what is your business in the city of Basel?"

Phillip had expected to be challenged, so he pulled out his papers and offered them to the guard. "I am Phillip Gribbleflotz, and I am a physician and surgeon."

The first guard passed Phillip's papers to the other guard, who was either of higher rank, or more able to read. That man skimmed the documents Phillip had handed over.

"You served as a physician and surgeon in the army of Count Wilhelm of Nassau-Siegen for four years?" the sergeant asked.

Phillip nodded. It was after all, what the documents said.

The sergeant handed the papers back to Phillip. "Where have you been since you left the count's service?"

"I stopped over in Leiden to attend some lectures at the medical school there." Phillip shuddered at the memory. It hadn't been a good idea. "Leiden was full of Galenists, while I'm a Paracelsian We had a few disagreements on medical theory, so I decided to head here, to Basel."

"What are Galenists and Paracelsians?" the first guard asked.

"Galen was a famous Classical Roman physician, while Paracelsus died less than a hundred years ago..." Phillip warmed to his subject and spent the next ten minutes explaining the differences between the two medical movements to the guards without them even hinting that they wanted him to stop.

"So what makes you think the professors at the university here in Basel will be any more likely to accept the ideas of the Paracelsian movement?" the sergeant asked when Phillip finished his explanation.

"But didn't I say?" Phillip asked, shocked that he might have missed out such an important piece of information. "Many years ago the University of Basel gave the great Paracelsus the Chair of Medicine, and surely they would only do that if they were amenable to the ideas of the Paracelsian movement."

The guards conceded the point. "You may find it difficult setting up a medical practice in Basel," the sergeant said.

"I know," Phillip said. "Any city with a medical school usually has a surplus of physicians. However, I'm more interested in setting up a laboratory to continue my studies in iatrochemistry than creating a practice."

"If you're not planning on setting up a practice, how do you intend earning a living?" the sergeant asked.

"I expect to make alchemical and apothecary supplies. Would you have any idea where I might secure a suitable laboratory?"

The guards stepped back from Phillip and a conversation involving a lot of arm waving and pointing took place. A couple of minutes later the sergeant provided Phillip with directions to somewhere that might be suitable. Phillip gave them a gratuity for their help, and entered the city.

December 1622

Phillip wanted to keep up with the latest medical developments, so he had cleared his schedule in order to attend a private dissection. Unfortunately, the course he bought a place in was being presented by Dr. Ambrosius Laurent.

Over the last hour Phillip had been grinding his teeth at the atrocious medical advice Dr. Laurent was giving. He'd managed to hold his tongue, if only barely, all that time, but when Dr. Laurent went on to describe how he thought an amputation should be performed, Phillip lost it. His comment wasn't very loud, but the voice he'd developed over the years of reading aloud in inns and barns easily carried throughout the dissection theater.

Dr. Laurent turned a baleful glare onto Phillip. "The peacock dares suggest I don't know what I'm doing?" he said to his companion in a carrying voice.

The slur was aimed at Phillip's taste for colorful clothes. It was obviously envy, Phillip decided. "I wear colors because they feed the essence of my spirit. I could wear black, but people who wear black are usually intent on showing off how much money they can afford to waste on their clothes." He looked Dr. Laurent up and down. "And then there are those people who can't quite afford real black, who instead settle for a merely good dark blue." Phillip added a smile, just to ensure Dr. Laurent knew he'd been insulted.

There were hastily muffled twitters around the theater and Dr. Laurent's face grew fiery red as he stroked the fine cloth of his merely good dark blue jacket. He glared angrily at Phillip. "If you think you're so good, why don't you come down here and take over?"

Phillip thought about it. The problem was, any surgery could get blood or gore on his fine clothes. Of course the dog being dissected had been well bled, so . . .

Dr. Laurent must have taken Phillip's hesitation to mean he lacked conviction in his ability, because he said something to the man beside him and they both started laughing. That was the last straw for Phillip. Any gore or blood on his clothes would be a small price to pay for putting Dr. Laurent in his place. He swung down from the gallery onto the stage and walked towards the dissection table where the carcass of a dog was substituting for the cadaver Dr. Laurent had failed to provide.

"What do you think you're doing?" Dr. Laurent demanded as Phillip paused beside the table where surgical instruments were laid out.

"You asked me to take over," Phillip said as he selected the instruments he knew he would need for an amputation.

"I most certainly did not," Dr. Laurent insisted.

Phillip ignored Dr. Laurent, which he knew would really annoy the older man, and turned to face the now very interested audience. "You really need to witness an amputation on a living beast to truly understand the difficulties involved," he explained. "There is a lot of difference between an amputation on a dead animal and a live one," he said. "For a start, the live ones feel pain." He cracked a smile. "They tend to wriggle when you start to cut." With that Phillip started to demonstrate on the front right leg of the dog how to perform an amputation.

It took him less than a minute to take the leg off. He could have done it faster, he explained, but he was demonstrating the process, not his speed. He went on to demonstrate the proper way to close an amputation. That too could have been done faster, but he let the audience closest to the dissection table help him.

When he finished Phillip stepped back from the dog and waved his hands. "And that is how an amputation should be done," he announced to the students who'd followed his every move.

There was a resounding round of applause, to which Phillip bowed, before climbing back to his spot in the galleries. Behind him Dr. Laurent was seething. "I don't know who you think you are, or what gives you the right to try to make a fool of me, but I will not stand for it!"

Phillip stared straight back. "I am Phillip Theophrastus Gribbleflotz, and I don't have to try to make a fool of you, you're doing a more than adequate job of that yourself, which is more than I can say for your demonstration so far." That sally was received with roars of laughter, which didn't go down well with Dr. Laurent.

"As for what gives me the right?" Phillip continued. "I studied at Padua under the great Professor Casseri. After I left the university I gained real world experience as a military physician and surgeon in the service of the counts of Nassau-Siegen." Phillip stared right into Dr. Laurent's eyes. "How many real amputations have you ever performed?" he challenged.

Dr. Laurent's face was red. He pointed a trembling finger at Phillip. "I want you out of my theater, now!"

Phillip stood his ground. "I'm not leaving," he said. "I've paid to attend a series of lectures, and even though I'm not particularly impressed by what I've seen and heard so far, I insist on getting my money's worth."

Dr. Laurent turned to one of his assistants. "Repay Dr. Gribbleflotz's entry fee and see that he is not allowed back in."

A few minutes later Phillip was back outside the building, his purse recharged with the refunded entry fee. A rumbling stomach and coin in his purse decided for him where he would go next.

Around noon the lecture broke up for lunch and a chance to warm up—the private anatomy theater being quite cold, because the low temperature helped slow the decomposition of the bodies.

"Did you see Dr. Laurent's face when Dr. Gribbleflotz took over his lecture?" Martin Stoler asked the two students he was walking with.

"I thought he was going to have an apoplexy," Georg Plannter said with a snigger. "He certainly didn't expect Dr. Gribbleflotz to take him up on his challenge."

"And serves him right, too," Daniel Schreyber said. "Dr. Gribbleflotz sure showed him how an amputation should be done. And the way he described what he was doing and why was almost as good as Professor Bauhin."

"I wonder if he gives lessons," Georg said.

"It'd be wonderful if he did," Martin said. "He certainly appeared to know more about what he was doing than Dr. Laurent."

"How do you think he learned to take off a limb that quickly?" Daniel asked as they stepped into a local inn.

"He said he served as a military surgeon," Martin said. "No doubt he got plenty of practice." He looked around, searching for a free table, and discovered the man who'd made such an impression in Dr. Laurent's lecture sitting at a table. He gestured in Phillip's direction. "Why don't we ask if he gives lessons?"

Daniel looked in the direction Martin was gesturing, and froze on the spot. "But we can't just walk up to him, he's a doctor."

"Of course we can," Georg said as he started towards Phillip. "What's the worst he can do, say no?"

Martin and Daniel hurried to catch up with Georg and the three of them arrived at Phillip's table at the same time. Martin, as the eldest of the three, assumed responsibility for disturbing the doctor. "Herr Dr. Gribbleflotz, could we have a word with you?" he asked.

Phillip looked up from the book he was reading. He was momentarily confused by the honorific, but for now he let that slide. "How can I help you?"

Georg gestured to his two companions. "We were in Dr. Laurent's anatomy class when you took over the amputation demonstration."

"You were fantastic," Daniel said. "Where did you learn to give a demonstration like that?"

"Ouch!" Daniel glared at Martin. "That hurt," he said as he rubbed the spot Georg's elbow had struck.

"It was supposed to," Martin muttered as he raised his eyes heavenward.

Phillip managed to smother a grin. He now knew why the man had addressed him as Dr. Gribbleflotz. He'd heard Dr. Laurent granting him that honorific, and no doubt believed he was truly a doctor. He was surprised at how good being addressed as Dr. Gribbleflotz made him feel. If things had been different, and Professor Casseri hadn't died so inconveniently, he would have graduated from Padua with an M.D. years ago.

Georg glared at Daniel and Martin before turning back to Phillip. "Daniel is right though. You were fantastic. You knew exactly what you were doing and your explanation as you did it was fascinating. Where did you learn to give a demonstration like that?"

"I learned at the feet of the great Professor Casseri," Phillip said. He didn't mention Padua, because everyone should know Professor Casseri had taught at Padua.

"Professor Casseri," Martin mumbled in awe. "He was one of the greatest teachers ever. I've read the reports of that anatomy course he gave in Padua's public anatomy theater just before he died."

"I was there," Phillip said.

Martin's eyes lit up. "Really?"

"Really," Phillip agreed. "I stood just behind Professor Casseri on the first tier and saw and heard everything."

"Herr Dr. Gribbleflotz, could you teach us to do surgery like you do?"

Phillip straightened. It was all he could do not to preen at being called Dr. Gribbleflotz again. He really should tell them that he wasn't a doctor, but maybe not yet. "It took me years of practice to get as good as I am."

"We understand that, Dr. Gribbleflotz," Martin said. "But until Professor Bauhin gives his annual anatomy course we're dependent on what people like Dr. Laurent can teach us."

"Which isn't much," Phillip muttered.

"Exactly," Daniel said. "So we were wondering if you were planning on putting on a proper teaching demonstration, where we might actually learn how to do surgery."

Phillip licked his lips. That sounded like an interesting idea. He would certainly be better than that bumbling fool, Dr. Laurent. "I wasn't planning to, but having seen Dr. Laurent at work, maybe I should consider it. Do you know where I might find a suitable place to hold a demonstration?"

"The theater Dr. Laurent is using will be free at the end of the week," Daniel said.

Phillip thought back to the small anatomy theater erected in a warehouse that Dr. Laurent had been using. "If I was to charge the same fee as Dr. Laurent and attract the same number of people, I could afford to give a week-long course," he suggested. "Of course, I'd first have to secure a supply of suitable cadavers."

Martin's head jerked up. "You think you could get real cadavers?"

"Of course," Phillip said. "It's a bit difficult to teach anatomy without suitable bodies."

"Dr. Laurent only has dogs," Daniel said.

"Yes, well, Dr. Laurent hasn't exactly impressed me," Phillip said. "Suitable cadavers are more expensive than animals. I wouldn't be surprised if his failure to secure cadavers was merely him trying to maximize his income."

"You really think you can get cadavers?" Martin asked.

Phillip nodded. "It's the right time of year." He smiled at the blank looks of the young students. "Winter is when a lot of the poor die, and Basel's climate is even less forgiving than Padua's, where I helped secure cadavers for Professor Casseri's dissections. How about you check that there are enough people interested in a private anatomy course while I check to see if I can get the cadavers and a suitable place to hold the demonstration?"

Martin got to his feet. "Thank you, Herr Dr. Gribbleflotz. We'll get onto that right away." He dragged Georg and Daniel to their feet. "How will we get in touch with you," he asked.

"I have a place near the St. Alban cloister," Phillip said as he wrote the address on a scrap of paper and offered it to Martin.

"Out by the paper mill?" Daniel screwed up his nose. "Why would you want to stay there? It stinks."

"I dabble in alchemy and the apothecary's arts," Phillip said. "And I have managed to lease a laboratory out that way."

Martin carefully folded the scrap of paper and put it away in his belt purse. "Thank you, Herr Dr. Gribbleflotz. You won't regret this."

"If I do decide to present a short course on anatomy, I'll need some assistants. Would you three be interested?"

"Oh, yes," Daniel answered. Martin and Georg quickly added their agreement.

"Then I look forward to hearing from you soon."

Phillip smiled as he watched the three students leave. The money from giving a course on anatomy would certainly be welcome. But that was secondary to the glow he'd felt when they called him Dr. Gribbleflotz. He was going to have to see about arranging to teach a course on anatomy. That raised a smile. Doctor was Latin for teacher. He'd be teaching, so he'd be fully entitled to call himself a doctor.

With the smile still on his face Phillip rose from his seat and walked over to the innkeeper. He needed information, and innkeepers were usually a good source of that.

Later that afternoon Phillip was at a bit of a loose end. By the time he got back to his laboratory it had been too late to start up the distillation furnace, so he couldn't distill anything. He'd cleared his schedule so that he could attend Dr. Laurent's series of lectures, so none of his regulars were going to expect him to be in his laboratory. That meant there was little likelihood that anybody would drop by for any reason. And it was going to take a couple of days at least before the man the innkeeper recommended to him was free. All in all, he was going to have a boring afternoon.

He was gloomily staring at the report he'd written on Professor Casseri's last anatomy course, trying to generate the enthusiasm to reread it, when he heard the rapid beat of someone running on cobblestones. He closed the report and concentrated on the sound. It sounded like wood on cobblestones. Most of the people living or working in this part of Basel wore wooden clogs, but few of them would choose to run in them except in an emergency. Phillip started to feel hopeful. An emergency could mean someone needed his services. He laid down the report and got to his feet. Maybe it was wishful thinking, but . . . Phillip's musings were interrupted by someone hammering on his door. He smiled. Maybe he wasn't being so wishful after all.

"Dr. Gribbleflotz, are you in?" a breathless voice called. "There's been an accident at the Aeschen-Tor and Sergeant Schweitzer says can you please come."

"Coming," Phillip called out as he hastily dressed for the outdoors and grabbed his medical bag. A quick glance round the room confirmed there were no candles burning, and he hurried over to the door. The messenger was pounding on it again as he opened it.

"I said I was coming," Phillip said as he opened the door. "Well, are you going to lead the way?" he asked after he'd locked the door.

The boy took off, only to stop and wait when he realized he was leaving Phillip behind. The boy took a side street, and Phillip followed as quickly as he could with his heavy doctor's bag banging against his legs. They hurried past houses and then market gardens as they came within sight of the gate tower. They made it to the gate a couple of minutes later; the boy was hardly breathing heavily while Phillip was huffing and puffing.

"Good job, Peter," Heinrich Schweitzer said as he paid the boy. Then he turned to Phillip. "This way, Dr. Gribbleflotz, Private Stohler managed to tear open his thigh on a passing cart."

Phillip stumbled to a halt and turned to stare at Heinrich. "Again? I patched him up barely a month ago."

"It's the left leg this time," Heinrich said as he led the way upstairs to the gatehouse guard quarters.

Ulrich Schmidlin was sitting beside Leonard Stohler feeding him cheap pear brandy. He turned as Phillip stepped into the room and his eyes lit up. "Dr. Gribbleflotz, am I pleased to see you. Leonard seemed to think you were attending some dissection demonstration this week."

"I was supposed to be attending Dr. Laurent's demonstration," Phillip said as he set his medical bag down beside Leonard and started to examine the injury. "Fortunately for Leonard here, I was invited to leave, and so I was at home when Sergeant Schweitzer's messenger arrived."

"What did you say to upset Dr. Laurent?" Heinrich asked. He and the others grinned.

Phillip matched their smiles. He'd become the unofficial physician to the city guard soon after he arrived and he'd got to know quite a few of the guardsmen, and they'd got to know him. "The silly fool had no idea about the realities of performing an amputation."

"And you called him out on it," Heinrich said.

"Naturally," Phillip said, happy that Leonard was being distracted by the banter while he cleaned his wound. "Then he challenged me to show everyone how I thought it should be done."

"You took Dr. Laurent up on it, I hope," Ulrich said.

"Of course," Phillip said. That set all three guardsmen off, and Phillip joined in. "You should have seen his face," he said as he struggled to control his laughter. He pulled out a scalpel to trim off some of the more damaged flesh.

"Are you going to take Leonard's leg off?" Ulrich asked.

Leonard jerked his leg out of Phillip's hand, wincing at the pain. "You're not going to cut it off, are you?" he asked.

"No," Phillip said. "But I do need to trim off the worst of the damaged skin before I pack the wound and bandage it tightly." He looked questioningly at Leonard. "Unless of course you'd rather I sewed it closed?"

"No, no," Leonard said, waving his hands. "If you think it doesn't need stitches, then I'm happy."

"It will leave a bigger scar if I don't stitch it," Phillip warned.

"But last time you said not stitching the wound closed would speed up healing," Leonard said. "So, what are you doing now you're not attending Dr. Laurent's course?"

Phillip gestured for Ulrich to feed Leonard some more of the brandy before he set to trimming the worst of the damaged skin and flesh from the wound. While he worked he talked, mostly to distract Leonard. "A group of students attending the course have asked me to give my own course."

"What does that involve?" Heinrich asked, getting into the spirit of distracting Leonard.

"I need to confirm with the owner of the warehouse where Dr. Laurent has set up a theater that I can use it, and then I have to see about obtaining some suitable cadavers."

"How do you get suitable cadavers?" Ulrich asked. "I thought they used condemned prisoners for the public anatomy course?"

Phillip nodded as he finished trimming the damaged flesh from Leonard's wound. "That's one source, but back in Padua we used to look for poor families who might be willing to let us dissect the bodies of their family members in return for a proper burial. Unfortunately, I don't have the contacts in Basel that I had in Padua."

"I could help you," Peter Hebenstreit said.

Phillip had completely forgotten about the teenage boy who had brought him Heinrich's message. The boy had the look of the urban poor, which meant he might have the contacts. "The funeral expenses are paid directly to the priest or pastor," he warned, knowing that a child of the streets like Peter would be looking for every opportunity to make money.

"But you'll pay a fee for someone to find the bodies and talk the family into letting you cut them up, right?"

Phillip nodded and mentioned a sum.

Peter's eyes lit up. "I'll do it for you," he said. "I'll find you some dead people."

Phillip smeared some of his special formula ointment into the wound before bandaging it closed. He looked up at Heinrich. "Is he reliable?"

"He hasn't let me down yet," Heinrich said.

Phillip turned back to Peter. "Here's the situation.

I'm waiting on confirmation that there will be enough interest to warrant running a course. When I get confirmation, I'll need to confirm a location, and a supply of ice to preserve the bodies until they can be used. If you report to my laboratory in three days' time, I should know whether or not I will need you to find me some bodies."

Peter ran his tongue over his lips. "It's a deal." He spat on his hand and held it out.

Phillip, who'd met this method of closing an agreement before, spat on his own hand and shook hands with Peter. Then he turned to Leonard. "Don't use that leg more than you have to for the next three days. I'll drop by then to check on how it's healing, and if necessary, put in some stitches."

Heinrich escorted Phillip out of the gate tower. "Thank you for coming, Dr. Gribbleflotz. The men really appreciate your willingness to help," he said as he placed a couple of coins into Phillip's hand.

"Don't mention it," Phillip said as he dropped the coins into his purse. The payment would barely cover his costs, but his willingness to help wasn't born from a pursuit of wealth. It was born of his experience in the service of the counts of Nassau-Siegen. Too often he'd seen common soldiers suffering unnecessarily because their leaders didn't care enough about them to provide proper medical care. Soon after he'd settled in Basel he'd made a point of cultivating the sergeants of the guard and offered them his professional services for a fraction of what a doctor might charge. There had been some skepticism at his apparent altruism, but once he'd explained his motivation, they'd been much more receptive. The fact that his professional services were superior to what the local doctors provided had sold them on the idea.

"Oh, and Dr. Gribbleflotz," Heinrich said. "Basel isn't Padua. The local religious authorities might not look so favorably on dissections of human bodies."

"But if the families agree," Phillip protested. He hadn't thought of this problem, because it hadn't been a problem in Padua.

"Even if the families agree, and it is a private demonstration." Heinrich smiled and clapped a hand on Phillip's shoulder. "But don't worry. If you let me know where and when you intend holding your demonstration, the guard will do what it can to see that you aren't bothered."

Phillip was almost at a loss for words. He muttered a disjointed thanks before heading back to his laboratory.

That evening, the home of Professor Gaspard Bauhin

"It was absolutely hilarious, Papa," sixteen year-old Jean Gaspard said as he dashed into his father's study.

Gaspard Bauhin, professor of the practice of medicine and professor of anatomy and botany at Basel, was ensconced in a comfortable armchair with a drink in one hand and a book in the other. He raised his eyes from his book at the interruption. His eyes lit up he recognized his son. "Hilarious? Are you sure you went to Ambrosius' lecture?"

Jean sniggered at the sally. "It was as boring as you warned me it would be, until one of the audience made a comment about Dr. Laurent's surgical technique."

He giggled at the memory, his eyes sparkling. "You'll never guess what happened."

Gaspard lowered his book to his lap and set his drink on the table beside his chair. "Ambrosius told your man that if he thought he could do better, that he could come down and show everyone how it should be done," he suggested.

Jean pouted his lips. "Someone's already told you."

Gaspard shook his head. "No, but I do know Ambrosius. Who was it and was he any good?"

Jean quickly recovered his good humor. "Someone I've never seen before. A Dr. Phillip Theophrastus Gribbleflotz, and he was almost as good as you, Papa. But that wasn't what was so funny."

"I've heard of him," Gaspard said. "So if Dr. Gribbleflotz showing Ambrosius up for the fool he is wasn't so funny, what was?"

"That." Jean struggled to speak though his laughter. It took a few attempts before he could explain without bursting out laughing. "Dr. Laurent's accused Dr. Gribbleflotz of trying to make a fool of him, but Dr. Gribbleflotz said to Dr. Laurent that he didn't have to try to make a fool out of him, because he was doing a good enough job of that himself."

Gaspard joined in the laughter. They managed to stop laughing, several times, but every time they made eye contact they started again. Eventually they were all laughed out. With tears still streaming from his eyes he looked at his son. "I haven't laughed like that in years."

Jean was glad his father was in such a good mood, because there was something he wanted. "Papa..."

"No."

"But I didn't ask for anything," Jean protested.

"I'm your father, and I knew you were going to ask for something."

"But I only want to attend a private anatomy course," Jean pleaded.

Gaspard raised a brow. "I thought you weren't impressed with Ambrosius' course."

"I'm not," Jean admitted. He started pacing around his father's study, glancing at his father every now and again. "Three of the students happened to bump into Dr. Gribbleflotz during a break in Dr. Laurent's course. They say that if there's enough interest, he's prepared to deliver a short course on anatomy." He paused to give the next statement added emphasis. "With real cadavers."

"Ambrosius still economizing by only using animal carcasses?"

Jean nodded. "Not that I think Dr. Gribbleflotz would be against using animals, Papa. I think that if he were to demonstrate an amputation, he would use a live animal, just to show how difficult it could be in reality."

"This Dr. Gribbleflotz sounds very interesting," Gaspard said. "Yes, you may attend, and I might drop in and watch myself."

*A few days later: the first day of
Dr. Gribbleflotz's anatomy course*

Professor Bauhin stood in the gallery beside his son and watched as Dr. Gribbleflotz cleared up from the morning session of his public dissection. He was impressed. The man certainly knew what he was doing, but more impressive than his obvious knowledge of anatomy and surgery was the way he managed to involve the audience. Not just the half dozen young hopefuls who, he was sure, were pleasantly surprised at just how much of the actual dissection they were doing, but also the people who were just watching.

He felt an aggressive tug on his hand and looked down into the pleading eyes of his son. With a rueful smile he let Jean lead him onto the dissection floor where Dr. Gribbleflotz was taking off his surgical apron.

"A most impressive display, Herr Dr. Gribbleflotz," Gaspard said. He smiled at the startled look in the eyes of Martin Stoler before the youngster hastily whispered into Dr. Gribbleflotz's ear.

"A pleasure to meet you, Herr Professor Bauhin," Phillip said as he wiped his hand clean on the folds of his still relatively clean surgical apron before reaching out to grasp the hand Gaspard held out. "I hope my poor efforts haven't bored you."

"No. I wasn't bored. You're a credit to your teachers."

"Thank you, Professor Bauhin. I studied for three years under Professor Casseri," Phillip said, "and he would be pleased to know his efforts weren't in vain."

"Ah, Professor Casseri. He was merely Giulio Casseri when I was studying at Padua under Professor Fabricius. Were you there when Giulio gave his anatomy course in the public anatomy theater?" Gaspard had read reviews of that course and was envious of those who had been there.

Phillip nodded. "I took comprehensive notes, which you are welcome to borrow, Professor."

"I might take you up on that offer. Meanwhile, you

may not be aware that human dissections are supposed to only be done with the approval of the university." Gaspard held up his hands to silence Phillip's immediate response. "However, having seen you at work, I'm sure that I can persuade the university to backdate its approval of your demonstration."

Phillip's jaw dropped. He hadn't expected that kind of support. "Thank you, Professor Bauhin," he managed to mutter.

Gaspard clapped his hand on Phillip's shoulder. "Come, let's have lunch together."

Next day

Peter Hebenstreit was a survivor. Chronologically he was fifteen, but his soul was much older. Right now he was cursing his lack of forethought. He'd heard Professor Bauhin invite Dr. Gribbleflotz to lunch. He'd seen the two men, with Professor Bauhin's son trailing behind, leave the anatomy theater together the previous day. He should have realized that after his performance that first day, and with the apparent endorsement of Dr. Gribbleflotz by Professor Bauhin, that places on the anatomy course would be in high demand. Foolishly, instead of raising the price for the remaining spaces in the audience, he'd actually sold them at a discount, thinking that no one would pay full price for a five day course after missing the first day.

Two men with entry tokens hanging from strings around their necks approached. Peter checked off the numbers written on the wooden tokens and let them into the theater. That was everyone. He then turned to the group of hopefuls who had turned up hoping to attend the lectures. "I'm sorry, but there are no vacancies. Maybe there will be some no-shows tomorrow," he told them.

"But I have money," one of them protested.

"There is no more space in the theater," Peter apologized. And that really annoyed him. He could have sold another twenty places if they'd been available. "I'm sure Dr. Gribbleflotz will put on another series of lectures soon." Certainly he would be doing so if Peter had anything to do with it, and in a much larger theater. Peter backed through the door and bolted it before heading over to the preparation room where Dr. Gribbleflotz was tying on a clean apron. "You have a full house, Herr Dr. Gribbleflotz."

"Very good, Peter. You may occupy yourself as you will until the noon break," Phillip said as he waved for his assistants to carry the body into the theater.

Now the dissection was starting Peter took his position at the entrance to the dissection level. The previous day Dr. Gribbleflotz had only had one stoppage during his lecture, for lunch. Members of the audience had got hungry and sent him out to buy snacks. They'd also needed the chamber pot, and rather than miss any of the demonstration they might have relieved themselves in a convenient corner. Dr. Gribbleflotz had provided Peter with some buckets and told him to see that the audience used them.

A hand waved and Peter made eye contact with the man who'd waved—his first customer of the day. Peter slipped back through the entrance and made his way up to the gallery.

Three days later

Johann Rudolf Glauber walked up to the Riehen-Tor, where he was stopped by one of the gate's guards.

"Name and purpose for entering the city?" Hans Keisser asked.

Johann leaned on his hiking stave as he answered. "I am a student looking for teachers."

"What kind of student?" Sergeant Niklaus Heffelfinger asked as he walked over to join Hans and Johann.

"I'm a student of the alchemical arts. Would you know where I might find a suitable teacher?"

"You might try Dr. Gribbleflotz," Hans suggested.

"No." Niklaus shook his head. "You're forgetting that he is running an anatomy course this week."

"But today was the last day, Sergeant," Hans said. "Dr. Gribbleflotz should be in his laboratory tomorrow morning."

Niklaus turned to Johann. "There you are, Herr Glauber. Dr. Gribbleflotz might be willing to provide the training you seek. Otherwise you could ask around over by the paper mill."

At only eighteen Johann didn't have much experience of doctors, but the ones he'd met so far hadn't known anything about practical alchemy. Too many of them were, as Paracelsus had written, lazy and insolent. Too idle and given to displays of wealth to actually dirty their hands in the pursuit of alchemical knowledge. So he had no intention of contacting this Dr. Gribbleflotz, but the other suggestion had merit "Where might I find this paper mill?" he asked.

Niklaus pointed vaguely to an area on the other side of the Rhine. "You cross the bridge and turn left. Keep walking past the St. Alban cloister. You can't miss it."

Johann thanked the guards and entered the city.

"You want alchemical training?" the man at the paper mill asked.

Johann nodded. "That's right. The guards at the north gate said you might know where I can find a suitable teacher."

The man chewed on his mustache and looked around. Seeing another worker he called out. "Hey, Kuntz. This youngster wants to find someone who can teach him alchemy," Tobias Brunner said.

Kuntz Hegler wandered over to join his colleague. "There's Herr Ackermann. I heard he was looking for a new laborant."

Johann was suspicious of the grins on his new acquaintances' faces. "What happened to his last one?" he asked.

"Now that's a good question," Tobias said.

"And deserving of a good answer," Kuntz added.

"So?" Johann asked.

"Herr Ackermann threw a flask of oil of vitriol at him," Tobias said.

"Missed him, of course, but it sure scared Young Fritz," Kuntz said. "He's probably still running."

Johann could well imagine Young Fritz running. Oil of vitriol was a very strong acid. If the youth had been hit by it he would have, at best, been horribly scarred. At the worst, it could have killed him. "Why did Herr Ackermann throw a flask of oil of vitriol at this Fritz?" he asked.

"He was probably upset that his oil of vitriol isn't as good as the new guy's," Tobias said.

"What new guy?" Johann asked.

"Dr. Gribbleflotz," Kuntz said. "He leased Old Man Steiner's laboratory from his widow back in July and he's been showing up the local alchemists ever since."

"Seriously?" Johann demanded. "The guards at the north gate suggested that Dr. Gribbleflotz might be suitable, but they also said he was giving an anatomy course. What would such a man know about alchemy?"

"Quite a lot," Tobias said. "He's an iatrochemist in the Paracelsian mold. He makes a lot of his own medicines, and his acids sell at a premium because they're so much better than anyone else's."

"The Paracelsian mold?" That wasn't the kind of thing Johann would expect a paper maker to say. "What do you know of Paracelsus?"

Kuntz and Tobias exchanged grins. "More than you're likely to believe. Dr. Gribbleflotz will talk about his great ancestor and his school of thought at the drop of a hat," Kuntz said.

"He really doesn't think much of the Galenists," Tobias added.

This was so much in line with Johann's own beliefs that he knew he was going to have to at least talk to the man. "How might I find Dr. Gribbleflotz?"

"His laboratory is just down the road." Tobias pointed in the general direction of some buildings opposite the St. Alban's cloister. "Of course, you might do better to wait until tomorrow, because I don't know when he'll be getting home tonight."

Next day

Johann presented himself at the door of Dr. Gribbleflotz's laboratory at the crack of dawn. He knocked on the door and waited. Five minutes later he knocked again, only harder. He knew there was someone awake inside because he could see the light of a candle through the window.

"Coming!" a voice from within called.

The door opened to reveal a man in his late twenties with a candlestick in his hand. "I'm looking for Dr. Gribbleflotz," Johann said.

"You've found him," Phillip said as he held up the candle to get a better look at Johann. "How can I help you?"

Johann stared at Dr. Gribbleflotz. He'd always imagined alchemists as being wizened old men.

"Well? I don't have all day," Phillip said.

Johann recovered himself. "I have heard that you are a noted iatrochemist and alchemist, and I am hoping that you will take me on as a student."

"Are you looking to take up an apprenticeship? Because I can tell you here and now, I don't expect to be in Basel long enough to train an apprentice."

Johann held up his hands. "Oh, no, Dr. Gribbleflotz. I am traveling around learning new techniques from different alchemists."

Phillip glanced back over his shoulder into his laboratory. "I do have need of an assistant. Are you willing to commit to working for me for the next two years?"

"Two years?" That was a little more than Johann had planned. "I was thinking more along the lines of a year," he said.

"A year's not worth my time," Phillip pointed out. "I'll have just got you trained and you'll be off."

"But I'm trained," Johann protested. "I've worked for alchemists before. Could we have a trial of, say, a week in which I can prove myself?" Johann asked.

"Only if you can start now. I have orders to fill and an able assistant might be useful."

"I can start now, Dr. Gribbleflotz."

"Good, come on in." Phillip shut the door after Johann and led the way into his laboratory. "There should be a spare apron over there."

Johann followed Phillip's pointing hand to a number of leather aprons hanging from a peg in the wall. He hurried over to them, dropped his bag in the corner, and grabbed the top apron and put it on. "Now what?" he asked.

Phillip pointed to a shelf full of carboys in wickerwork. "I want two of those bottles on the bottom shelf carried over to the bench where I'm working."

Johann walked towards the large carboys. In passing he noticed a large clear crystal on a higher shelf and paused to examine it. "What's this?" he asked, pointing at the crystal.

"Just something a grateful officer gave me many years ago after I saved his leg, and probably his life, using maggot therapy."

"What's maggot therapy?" Johann asked.

"It's nothing you need to worry yourself about unless you want to study surgery."

"I don't want to study surgery," Johann said. The crystal still fascinated him. He leaned closer for a better look.

"Are you going to bring me those bottles any time soon?" Phillip asked.

Johann looked up guiltily. "I'm sorry, Herr Dr.

Gribbleflotz." He used the wicker handles to pull the first carboy off the shelf. It was surprisingly heavy. "What's in it?" he asked as he lifted the first carboy.

From the other side of the laboratory Phillip answered. "Just how much alchemy did you say you've learned?"

That put Johann on his mettle. He considered the possibilities as he carried the carboy over to the bench where Phillip was working. The way it sloshed around when he moved suggested it definitely wasn't water, or even aqua vitae. The weight of the full carboy, being nearly twice what he'd expected, was another clue. "Is it oil of vitriol?" he asked as he put it down.

"Yes. Now, get the other bottle."

Johann did as he was told. "What are you making?" he asked as he lowered the second carboy of acid onto the bench.

"I have an order for acidum salis," Phillip said as he measured what looked like salt into a retort.

"But you don't make acidum salis with oil of vitriol," Johann protested.

"Are you sure about that?" Phillip smiled. Anybody who'd attended his recent anatomy course would have recognized the look on Phillip's face. He was entering his teaching mode.

"You make acidum salis by distilling a mixture of salt and green vitriol," Johann insisted.

"That is one way," Phillip agreed. "However, think just a moment. How do we make oil of vitriol?"

"You distill green vitriol."

"And how do we make aqua fortis?" Phillip asked. Johann had no idea where this was leading, but he answered anyway. "You distill a mixture of saltpetre and green vitriol."

"Correct," Phillip said. "Now, do you see a pattern here?"

Johann stared blankly at Phillip and shook his head.

"What is common to the production of all three acids?"

Johann's eyes widened as slowly he started to understand. "The green vitriol," he said. "But alchemists have been making the acids by distilling salt or saltpetre with green vitriol for centuries. Surely if there were an easier way, someone would have discovered it before now?"

"Maybe they did," Phillip said. "And maybe somehow their knowledge was lost. Of course, it's not just a simple matter of mixing oil of vitriol with salt and suddenly your oil of vitriol is turned into acidum salis. If that was all it took, everyone would be doing it."

Johann surveyed the retorts Phillip had arranged. "It seems a lot of work for something that could just as easily be done the old-fashioned way. All you're doing is adding an extra step to the production of acidum salis and aqua fortis."

"It makes sound economic sense," Phillip said. "Oil of vitriol is obviously the Quinta Essentia of acids. And as long as you have a supply of oil of vitriol, you can make any acid you like."

"But the Quinta Essentia only applies to distillates of living things," Johann protested.

"That is quite true, but in the case of oil of vitriol, it's a good analogy," Phillip said as he loaded a number of retorts with a mixture of salt and oil of vitriol. With the last of a dozen retorts loaded he stretched his back and turned to Johann. "Now you can help me set these up on the furnace."

Johann helped set the retorts up on the furnace and then he watched in surprise as Phillip carefully weighed some wood before adding it to the furnace. "Why are you doing that?" he asked.

"Being an alchemist is a business. By keeping track of how much fuel I use, I can accurately price my products." Phillip waved his notebook at the furnace. "I have to be very careful. This furnace is one of the least efficient I've ever used. It's because of the distressing economics of distilling green vitriol on this furnace that I first explored using oil of vitriol to make acidum salis and aqua fortis."

Johann hoped he didn't look half as confused as he felt. "I'm sorry, Dr. Gribbleflotz, but I don't see the connection."

Phillip grinned. "It is obvious you've never had to concern yourself with the economics of running a laboratory. Because if you had, you would know that the price of fuel goes up in the winter."

"How does the price of fuel going up in winter lead to you making acidum salis and aqua fortis from oil of vitriol?"

"It takes as much fuel to make oil of vitriol from green vitriol as it does to make acidum salis or aqua fortis from green vitriol. But you can never be sure how much of any acid you need or can sell. With my new process, as long as I have oil of vitriol, I can make aqua fortis and acidum salis on demand. And I'll never be left with surplus stock." Phillip paused to glare at the furnace. "Of course, it still wouldn't hurt for the furnace to be a little more efficient."

Johann looked at the furnace. It didn't look any different from the half-dozen or so other furnaces he'd seen. "Why haven't you done something about improving it?"

"I've been busy," Phillip said defensively before going on to explain what he was doing with his retorts.

Johann was interested in the idea that furnaces could have different efficiencies, but he didn't have any time to think about that as he tried to keep up with Dr. Gribbleflotz. The doctor was everywhere as he monitored the numerous retorts while also managing the fire in the furnace and preparing other compounds on his bench.

"Why are you doing that?" Johann found himself asking later in the day as he watched Dr. Gribbleflotz dissolving saltpetre in warm water.

"The secret of purer acids is purer ingredients," Phillip said. "By purifying my saltpetre before I mix it with the oil of vitriol, I get a much purer aqua fortis."

"Does purer saltpetre make better gunpowder?" Johann wondered aloud.

"It does," Phillip answered. "Any variation from the standard seventy-five to fifteen to ten formulation is usually due to impurities in the ingredients, especially of the saltpetre. Usually the improvement in performance doesn't justify the effort to make the saltpetre purer."

"You sound as if you've tested that theory," Johann said.

"I have." Phillip related his experiences in Augsburg during his apprenticeship, much to Johann's delight.

"Could you make some gunpowder?" Johann asked.

"Gunpowder isn't something to fool around with,"

Phillip warned. "I've seen men torn apart by explosions, and I have nightmares imagining what it must have been like at Wimpfen last May when that cannon shot blew up the magazine of the forces of the margrave of Baden-Durlach."

Johann was more interested in the practicalities of the situation rather than the physical injuries sustained. "How does that work?" he protested. "Surely a cannon shot can't set off a barrel of gunpowder."

"No, it can't," Phillip agreed. "It isn't hot enough. However, a sufficiently large cannonball hitting a barrel of gunpowder can easily turn it into a cloud of dust and stave pieces."

"How does a cloud of dust cause an explosion?"

Phillip looked around his laboratory. "Get that stool and place it in the middle of the room."

While Johann was moving the stool, Phillip opened a clay pot and measured some fine black powder onto a sheet of paper. "Light the candle and stand the candlestick on the stool," Phillip directed as he approached the stool.

With the lit candle standing on the stool Phillip stepped closer to the flame and blew on the paper in his hands. The fine black powder was dispersed in a cloud of fine particles, until the first one hit the flame, then the whole lot erupted in a ball of fire. He dusted off the piece of paper and collected the candlestick. "That's what a cloud of gunpowder can do, and all it needs to set it off is a single smoldering ember. Please put away the stool and sweep the floor," he instructed as he returned them to the bench.

Johann was so stunned by what he'd seen that he didn't move. "Could I try that?" he begged.

Phillip sighed and held out the candlestick. "Put that back on the stool."

Johann took the candlestick and Phillip set about placing a small amount of fine gunpowder on the sheet of paper. By the time he'd finished and put the gunpowder away Johann was back. He handed him the sheet of paper with the small measure of gunpowder on it. "The paper needs to be about a foot away from the candle and level with the top of the flame before you blow," Phillip said as he handed it over.

Johann set himself up relative to the candle and blew. The resulting fireball wasn't as impressive as Phillip's but it still brought a gleam to Johann's eyes.

"No, you can't do that again," Phillip said. He ignored Johann's protests. "Put the candlestick and stool away and sweep the floor."

Phillip knew that nothing he said would discourage Johann from playing around with gunpowder. He'd have to discover the realities of just how dangerous it was himself. So while Johann swept the laboratory, Phillip wrote down clear and concise instructions of how to make gunpowder. He handed it to Johann when he finished sweeping.

"What's this?" Johann asked as he skimmed over the list of instructions.

"*That* is the *safe* way to make gunpowder." Phillip put a lot of emphasis on the word "safe." "Not that making gunpowder can ever be considered safe."

"You're down on gunpowder because of your experiences in the war?" Johann asked as he carefully folded the sheet of paper and put it away.

Phillip nodded. He wasn't willing to go into the

details, but any enthusiasm he'd ever had for gunpowder had well and truly been lost during his time in the service of the counts of Nassau-Siegen. "I gave you those instructions because I know that the first chance you get, you'll try to make some. And I'd rather you didn't blow yourself or anybody else up whilst doing so."

"I'll be careful," Johann promised.

"Good, now let's get back to work. Those retorts won't monitor themselves."

A *few days later*

Phillip walked around the distillation furnace, carefully checking the various retorts. He was paying special attention to the retorts at the cooler end of the furnace. Johann followed him like a shadow, and stood just about as close.

"Why are you redistilling the aqua vitae so often?" Johann asked.

Phillip turned and looked down his nose at Johann, his disappointment in his student evident on his face.

Johann looked around the laboratory. His eyes darted to the bench where retorts of aqua vitae were awaiting their turns on the furnace before returning to Phillip. "What did I do wrong this time?" he demanded.

Phillip sighed loudly, which caused Johann to blush. "What have I told you about the need for accuracy?" he asked.

Johann's eyes darted back to the bench. "Oh," he said as he turned back to face Phillip. "You mean I should have asked why you are distilling the aqua vitae four times?"

"That would have been much better," Phillip said, "although you should really have asked why I am distilling it for the fourth time." He smiled to show he wasn't too upset. "We will actually be distilling it one more time, to give fivefold distilled waters of wine. Then I will pour it into clean containers, seal them, and bury them in baskets full of horse manure."

"But you started with beer, not wine," Johann pointed out.

Phillip elected to just glare at Johann before continuing as if he hadn't spoken. "I distill it five times so as to make it as pure, and therefore as strong, as possible."

"But you insist on accuracy, Dr. Gribbleflotz," Johann protested.

Phillip settled his clenched fists on his hips and glared at Johann. "Johann, by the time it has been distilled five times, the distillate of beer is indistinguishable from the distillate of wine." He continued to glare at Johann, daring him to say anything. When Johann broke eye contact Phillip continued speaking. "And besides, 'waters of wine' sounds much more impressive than beer, or aqua vitae." Johann's head shot up at the sudden levity. Their eyes met and he saw the smile in Phillip's eyes as he continued to speak. "Now, you will no doubt be curious to know why it must be buried in horse manure for four months before being decanted into a clean flask and buried for another four months, and when that time is over, it needs to be decanted into yet another clean flask before being buried for a final four months, after which it will be decanted one last time?"

"Now that you mention it, Dr. Gribbleflotz, I would like to know why you have to do that."

Phillip hadn't been idle since his first attempt to explain to Dr. Michael Weitnauer back in Dalmatia why it had to be buried for a year. "Obviously the first consideration is protecting it from light while any sediment in the liquid settles. The removal of sediment is of course why it is decanted at four-monthly intervals, and we repeat the decanting to ensure all sediments are removed."

"But why horse manure?" Johann asked.

"You could probably use anything that can keep the light out, but the spongy nature of horse manure provides an added measure of protection to the flask, and when one is investing a year in the production of the liquid, you really do want to minimize the chances of accidents breaking the vessels."

Johann nodded. "So what is this fivefold distilled waters of wine good for?"

Phillip stood up straight and all schoolmastery. "Fivefold distillate of the waters of wine that has been purified by keeping it buried in horse manure and decanted thrice is no longer mere fivefold distillate of the waters of wine. If it has survived that treatment it has become the Quinta Essentia of the waters of wine."

"And?" Johann prompted.

"If you mix the Quinta Essentia of any item with the Quinta Essentia of the waters of wine you'll have a medicine that can cure any malady, maybe."

"Maybe?"

Phillip gave a self-conscious shrug. "I haven't been able to test it yet, but that's what I was told."

"How does this Quinta Essentia of the waters of wine fit in with the Paracelsian school of thought?"

"Ah, well," Phillip said. "That's the thing about the Quinta Essentia of any living thing. It's what is left when you remove the four elements." He walked along the racks of flasks and selected two, one in each hand. He showed the flask in his right hand to Johann. "This contains the Quinta Essentia of *Plantago major*, and this," He held up the second flask. "Contains the Quinta Essentia of willow bark. If you test either of these you will find no trace of mercury, sulphur, or salt."

Johann reached out for the flask of the Quinta Essentia of willow bark. "Can I test it?"

"Be my guest," Phillip said as he passed the flask over.

Johann removed the stopper and sniffed the clear liquid. Then he poured a little into a watch glass and dipped a wooden splint in it and held that over a candle. Finally he turned back to Phillip. "It certainly doesn't contain sulphur."

"Of course not, and if you taste it you'll discover that it doesn't contain salt either."

"Is it safe?" Johann asked.

Phillip nodded. "Consider what it is, Johann. It's merely the result of the destructive distillation of willow bark. Why shouldn't it be safe?"

Johann dipped a finger into the liquid and licked his finger. "It's tasteless."

"It's as I said, no salt, no sulphur, and no mercury. It's nothing more than the pure nonputrefying essence of willow bark."

"But Paracelsus says that all created things consist of sulphur, mercury, and salt. How is it possible that willow bark is deficient in all three?"

"No, no, no!" Phillip shook a finger at Johann. "You misunderstand. Of course the willow bark contains sulphur, mercury, and salt. However, all of that is left behind when we destructively distill the bark to produce its Quinta Essentia."

Johann nodded. "And this," he shook the flask of the Quinta Essentia of willow bark, "when mixed with the Quinta Essentia of the waters of wine will give a medicine that can treat any malady?"

Phillip gave a gentle snort as he smiled. "I consider that very doubtful. However, if an infusion of willow bark is made using the Quinta Essentia of willow bark and the Quinta Essentia of the waters of wine, you will produce a medicine for the treatment of fevers that is much stronger than mere willow bark tea."

"You seem very sure of that, Dr. Gribbleflotz."

"I have run some tests," Phillip said in a self-complimentary way. "From a measured amount of willow bark, an infusion prepared with ordinary water, when filtered and evaporated, leaves less white powder than the same amount of willow bark in an infusion made from a mixture of the Quinta Essentia of willow bark and the Quinta Essentia of the waters of wine."

"What is the white powder?" Johann asked.

"The essence of willow bark, of course." Phillip smiled. "It's a very useful powder. When bulked out with wheat flour, gum arabic, and chalk it can be turned into pills."

"How do the pills compare with willow bark tea?"

"Well, willow bark tea is usually used to cool the heated blood to reduce a fever. An infusion isn't inherently cooling, so the essence of the willow bark has to work extra hard. Therefore I include a natural substance that turns the pills blue, a naturally cool color, to enhance its performance. Because of this, my blue Sal Vin Betula pills are more effective than the equivalent dose of willow bark tea."

"Do you sell those pills?" Johann asked.

"Not very often," Phillip said. "The cost of a single Sal Vin Betula pill is greater than the cost of a similar dosage supplied as an infusion of willow bark tea, so few people ask for them."

"But do people know about your Sal Vin Betula pills, Dr. Gribbleflotz? I'm sure that people who would happily pay extra for the convenience of a pill if only they knew that it was available."

Phillip wasn't so sure about that. In his experience people wanted cheap over convenience. "Maybe when fuel prices come down we can look into it."

Early January 1623

Johann was happily working on his latest attempt at an improved distillation furnace when there was yet another knock on the door to Dr. Gribbleflotz's laboratory. With a resentful sigh at yet another interruption he put down the firebricks he'd been carrying and made his way to the door.

"How may I help you?" he said as he opened the door.

"I'm looking for my brother."

Johann did a double take. The normal run of people knocking at Dr. Gribbleflotz's door were older men— either fellow alchemists looking to procure some of his excellent acids, or ordinary men looking to purchase treatments for their various ailments. The few women who'd knocked at his door since Johann had been working for him had been mature women looking to sell Dr. Gribbleflotz various herbs and plant cuttings. Young women, especially attractive young women like the one he was currently staring at, just didn't knock at the doctor's door. "Brother?" he managed to mumble.

She smiled, and what he'd thought merely a pretty face became a beautiful one as the smile lit up her face and brought a sparkle to her eyes. "Peter Hebenstreit. I understand he's currently working for Dr. Gribbleflotz."

Johann released a breath he hadn't realized he was holding. "Oh, him. Peter's your brother?" he asked, just to confirm the relationship.

The girl nodded.

"Do you have a name, Peter's sister?"

Again she smiled. "Katarina, and you'll be Dr. Gribbleflotz's new laborant, Johann Glauber."

Johann preened at the thought that such a pretty girl had heard of him. "That's right."

"Do you know where Peter is?" she asked.

Johann nodded. He noticed she was still waiting for an answer and quickly provided it. "He's working all day at the university's public anatomy theater."

"Oh." She nibbled at her lip before looking pleadingly at Johann. "I thought he was just sourcing dead bodies for that."

"No," Johann said. "He also runs errands for the audience during the demonstrations."

"Oh, bother!" She looked appealingly at Johann. "I don't suppose you could take him a message? I'd do it myself, but I have to get back to work, as my mistress is getting married in the spring and we're extremely busy with preparations."

Johann sighed regretfully. "I'd like to help, but I can't leave the laboratory." He shrugged. "I don't have a key with which to lock the door."

Katarina tossed back her head and laughed.

"I don't see what's so funny," Johann said.

"What's so funny, Young Man, is the idea that anyone with any sense would steal from Dr. Gribbleflotz," Frau Bader from next door said. "Now, lad, let the young woman give you her message and get back to work. I'll keep an eye out on the doctor's laboratory while you're gone."

Johann turned to the older woman. She was a laundry woman, with the arms and shoulders of someone used to physical labor. He could easily believe that would-be thieves could be scared off by her. "Thank you, Frau Bader." He turned expectantly to Katarina.

"Tell Peter that Elisabeth Brotbeck died less than an hour ago."

"That's it? That's the message?" Johann asked.

Katarina nodded. "Peter'll understand. Please hurry. I have to go now."

Johann stood and watched Katarina hurry away. He was still staring down the street long after she'd turned a corner when something jabbed him under the ribs.

"That's not getting a message to her brother," Frau Bader said, a smirk on her face.

Johann took the hint. He removed his leather apron and hung it up before shutting the door and hurrying off towards the public anatomy theater. He arrived in good time—no place in Basel being more than a few minutes' walk away—and knocked on the door of the theater.

It opened a little and a head poked out. "What do you want?" the guard asked.

"I need to get a message to Peter Hebenstreit. He came with Dr. Gribbleflotz." Johann wasn't deliberately name dropping, he was just stating a fact in the hope that it would help the guard identify Peter.

"Wait here," the man said before closing and locking the door.

A few minutes later Peter turned up. "I hope it's important," he said by way of greeting. "I'm losing money just talking to you."

"Your sister came round to the laboratory with a message . . ."

"Katarina's all right?" Peter demanded.

Johann held up his hands. "She's fine. She just wanted me to pass on the message that Elisabeth Brotbeck died an hour ago."

"Brotbeck?" Peter looked skyward as he repeated the name a couple of times. Then suddenly he looked back at Johann. "Yes!" he said as he shot a fisted hand into the air. "I have to tell Professor Bauhin this." Peter pushed past the door guard and disappeared into the darkened building.

Johann followed, ignoring the halfhearted protest of the man at the door. "What's so important about someone dying?" he asked once he caught up with Peter.

Peter shot a glance at Johann. "Professor Bauhin needs bodies for his anatomy course," he said.

Johann nodded. He knew that. "But I thought you already had as many bodies as he needed."

"We do, but Elisabeth Brotbeck was with child." Peter smiled smugly. "Professor Bauhin will pay well for such a cadaver. Wait here," he said when they arrived at the curtained-off entrance to the anatomy theater.

Johann twitched the curtain aside so he could watch Peter. First he slipped up beside one of Professor Bauhin's assistants and spoke to him, and then the assistant attracted the attention of the older man leading the dissection. A few words were exchanged before the older man made his apologies to the audience and left an older assistant in charge while he followed Peter back behind the curtain.

"The woman still carries the child?" Professor Bauhin asked Peter the moment they were behind the curtain.

"Frau Brotbeck was over three months pregnant, Professor Bauhin. My sister would have said if she'd lost the child."

Professor Bauhin licked his lips. He paused for a few seconds before nodding vigorously. "It'll have to be a private demonstration," he muttered aloud. "Stay here a moment while I get Jean," he told Peter before disappearing through the curtain.

Less than a minute later Professor Bauhin returned with his son. "Jean, I want you to go with Peter to check out the body. You know what to look for?"

"That the body still contains the unborn child," Jean said.

Professor Bauhin nodded. "Now, don't pay too much for the body," he said as he handed Jean a purse.

The three of them stepped out of the chilly dead room attached to St. Ulrich's Church and into the sunlight. Peter turned to Jean. "Do you think your father and Dr. Gribbleflotz could determine what killed her?"

"Of course," Jean said. "Why do you want to know?"

"There's no of course about it. Your father and Dr.

Gribbleflotz were unable to work out how Hans the Boatman died."

"That's hardly fair," Jean protested. "When Dr. Gribbleflotz failed to find river water in his lungs it opened a whole world of possibilities."

Johann hurried ahead a few paces and turned to face his companions. "Hold it. Who's Hans the Boatman, and what's so important about water in his lungs?"

Peter and Jean stopped, and Peter took a deep breath. "Hans the Boatman was the cadaver Dr. Gribbleflotz dissected in his anatomy course back in December."

"His body had been pulled out of the Rhine, so everyone assumed he'd fallen into the river and drowned," Jean said.

"Except there was no water in his lungs, so Dr. Gribbleflotz and Jean's father thought he must have been dead before he hit the water," Peter said. "And over the next three days they failed to determine how he died."

"Hans' body had been in the river for several days before it was discovered, so a lot of the important clues were lost," Jean said. He waved back towards St. Ulrich's. "Frau Brotbeck's body is so fresh it's still warm, so the clues should still be there."

"Why are you so interested in how the woman died?" Johann asked.

"The families like to know," Peter answered.

A week later

Johann was enjoying walking around with a delightful companion on his arm when he noticed Peter accepting money from a couple of guys. He turned to Katarina. "What sort of thing would Peter do for guys like those two?" he asked.

Katarina looked in the direction Johann was indicating and snorted. "He's not getting paid for any work he might have done, he's collecting his winnings."

"Peter gambles?" Johann asked. That didn't fit his image of the youth. He seemed too concerned with money to risk losing any on a game of chance.

"Only on sure things," Katarina muttered. She looked at her brother for a few seconds more before tugging at Johann's arm. "Let's keep moving. I need to get some ribbon for Maria."

Maria was Katarina's mistress, and Johann had the impression they were good friends for all that Katarina was her maid. He let her lead him away from Peter, only glancing back once, to see Peter collecting money from someone else. "What kind of sure things?" he asked.

"The latest was that Dr. Gribbleflotz and Professor Bauhin would be able to determine what killed Elisabeth Brotbeck."

"What kind of sick individual bets on things like that?" Johann muttered.

"Sick people like my brother and his friends," Katarina said. "Look, there. They have ribbon just the right color for Maria's wedding dress." She tightened her grip on Johann's hand and surged through the crowd.

Johann let himself be dragged along. Visiting haberdashery shops was part of the price of walking out with Katarina, but her company more than made up for any embarrassment he might have felt being seen in such a store.

Early April 1623

Phillip emptied the maggots into the large glass bowl of warm water and gently swished them around. A quick glance Johann's way caught him watching what he was doing. "Shouldn't you be watching your retorts?" Phillip asked.

Johann nodded guiltily, but continued to stare at the bowl in front of Phillip. "What're you doing?" he asked.

"Do you remember we talked once about 'maggot therapy'?" Phillip asked.

Johann nodded. "You said that maggot therapy was surgical, and that if I wanted to learn about surgery, I should enroll at the university."

"That's true. However, what I'm doing now is more iatrochemical than surgical. While I was serving in the Low Countries I noticed that in patients having their wounds treated with maggots the wounds became flooded with a clear—"

"Treated with maggots?" Johann's voice was high pitched. "What are you treating with maggots?"

"Battle wounds," Phillip said. "While I was serving as a military surgeon and physician, I discovered, like many military surgeons and physicians before me, that soldiers who have been left for days on the battlefield with flyblown wounds often had a better chance of surviving than soldiers who receive timely treatment from a surgeon or physician.

"Well, if you were to inspect a wound that is full of maggots, you would see that they are immersed in a clear, thick, liquid. I looked at that clear liquid, and wondered at its properties."

"What properties?" Johann asked.

"Well, why is it that maggots can live in rotten flesh?" Phillip asked. "Could it be because they live in a liquid that somehow protects them?

"Naturally, I conducted some tests," Phillip said.

"Of course you did," Johann muttered.

Phillip ignored Johann's muttered comment and continued as if he hadn't spoken. "I discovered that a wound, when the liquor was introduced into one not being treated with maggots, healed a lot faster than ones where it was not used. So I hypothesized that there was something in the liquor that is medically beneficial." Phillip carefully siphoned off the slime from the surface of the water and poured it into an apothecary's mixing bowl. "I now use it in my special wound ointment."

Johann pointed to the maggots still struggling in the bowl of water. "What do you do with the maggots after washing off the slime?"

Phillip smiled. "*You* will now fish them out of the water and destructively distill them to produce the Quinta Essentia of maggots."

Johann reluctantly collected the maggots and loaded them into retorts before setting them over the furnace. It wasn't long before the Quinta Essentia of the maggots was dripping into the collection vessels.

"What do you want me to do with the remnants?" Johann asked sometime later as he removed the first of the spent retorts form the furnace.

"Empty the powder into a jar and seal it for later. I've got some fresh Quinta Essentia of the waters of wine due to mature in three months' time, and I'll see what I can extract from the remnants..." Phillip stopped speaking to listen. Yes, he had heard the clatter of wooden shoes on cobblestones coming down the street. He didn't have much of a medical practice, preferring to work in his laboratory rather than treat patients, but he was still on call for the guard. Maybe one of them had injured themselves. He just hoped it wasn't Leonard Stohler again.

The footfalls slowed just outside, and then the door burst open.

"Please, Dr. Gribbleflotz, you must come," Peter said between gasps for breath. "They think Katarina murdered Ludwig Schaub."

"Is Katarina all right?" Johann demanded as he grabbed Peter.

"Settle down!" Phillip ordered as he pulled Johann from Peter. "Now, Peter, can you tell me what has happened?"

Peter took a deep breath and slowly released it. "Katarina's mistress married Herr Ludwig Schaub yesterday, and the bridegroom died before the marriage could be consummated. Herr Schaub's family is insisting that he was poisoned, and they're claiming that Katarina and Frau Beck did it."

"Calm down, Peter," Phillip said, "the guard isn't going do anything to your sister just because someone claims she poisoned someone. They need evidence."

Peter nodded. "That's why you have to come. I told Captain Brückner how you and Professor Bauhin determined what killed Elisabeth Brotbeck. Both the Becks and the Schaubs have agreed to let you examine Herr Schaub, and Captain Brückner sent me to get you." He paused for a moment. "The Beck family will pay for your time," Peter added as an afterthought.

"I don't have the reputation in Basel to carry enough weight with the courts," Phillip said. "We need someone with a higher public profile." He turned to Peter. "I want you to find Professor Bauhin and tell him what you've told me. No." Phillip stopped speaking and shook his head. "That won't work. I need you to lead me to Herr Schaub's house."

"I know where it is," Johann said.

Phillip looked questioningly at Johann.

Johann blushed under Phillip's gaze. "I've been walking out with Peter's sister, and she showed me where she would be living after her mistress married."

That was good enough for Phillip. He turned back to Peter. "Quick as you can, find Professor Bauhin and give him the message. Johann will lead me to Herr Schaub's house."

Peter nodded and made for the door. Seconds later his wooden shoes could be heard clattering along on the cobblestones.

Phillip turned to Johann. "Help me collect my medical bags. We'd best take a bit of everything."

Even though it was bigger than most bedrooms, Ludwig Schaub's room felt crowded. Captain Daniel Brückner of the city guard was there with Sergeant Heinrich Schweitzer. Katarina and Maria were sitting huddled together on a settee as far away from the bed where the body was lying as they could get. A man Phillip assumed was the dead man's personal servant stood by the bed, and members of the Beck and Schaub families lined opposite sides of the room with their respective lawyers in attendance.

"What are we waiting for?" Professor Dr. Johannes

Thomas Cludius, counsel for the Schaub family, demanded. "Herr Dr. Gribbleflotz is here. Let him get to work."

"A woman's life may be at stake, so I've asked that Professor Bauhin join me," Phillip said.

Professor Dr. Kaspar Bitsch's eyes lit up. The counselor for the Beck family obviously appreciated the inclusion of the professor of the practice of medicine. "I'm happy to wait for Professor Bauhin to arrive."

So wait they did. No more than ten minutes later Professor Gaspard Bauhin, his son, and Peter entered the room.

"It's a bit crowded in here," Gaspard said to Phillip.

"Maybe some of them will leave when we start the autopsy," Phillip said.

"Where were you proposing to hold it?" Gaspard asked. He waved towards the bed. "If nothing else, that's an awkward height."

"There should be a big table in the kitchen. Failing that, there's always the dining room," Phillip said.

"You can't cut open Ludwig in his own dining room," one of Ludwig's relatives protested.

"I hardly think he's going to mind," Phillip said. "Still, I'm sure his widow will allow us to do whatever is necessary to discover what killed her husband."

"She killed him," one of the Schaub wives said, pointing an accusing finger at Maria.

"Maria didn't kill Ludwig," one of Maria's family countered.

It quickly degenerated into a yelling match between the two families, which Phillip tried to ignore as he looked around the room looking for clues.

Gaspard joined him as Captain Brückner and Sergeant Schweitzer separated the two families. "What are you looking for?" he asked.

Phillip nodded towards Ludwig's personal manservant. "He said that his master complained of abdominal cramps, and burning pain in his stomach and throat before he went into convulsions," Phillip whispered.

"That's consistent with poisoning," Gaspard whispered back.

"I know. I'm hoping that if it was poison, it was self-administered, and somewhere there should be a pill box of some description." Phillip crouched to look under the bed. The stink of urine hit him as he lifted the cover. He reached out for the chamber pot and pulled it out from under the bed. Phillip smiled at the sight and glanced at Gaspard. "Blood in the urine."

Gaspard examined the chamber pot. "That certainly had to have happened before the real pain set in."

"What are you two whispering about?" Dr. Cludius demanded.

"Let me handle this," Gaspard whispered to Phillip. He got back to his feet and faced Dr. Cludius. "It's very simple, Johannes. We noticed the smell of urine and were looking to find the source." Gaspard lifted up the chamber pot so everyone could see. His innocent sounding statement calmed everyone down. "Now, can we get the body moved to the kitchen? I'd like to get started on the autopsy."

Chamber pots were such innocuous devices that no one noticed that after Gaspard passed the pot to Phillip he poured the contents into a flask from his medical kit. Meanwhile footmen carried the body down to the kitchen where it was laid out on the kitchen table.

Ludwig Schaub's bed gown was removed to reveal a corpulent and hairy body. Phillip handed the flask to Johann and told him to put it away before he joined Gaspard in examining the now naked body. They walked around it, taking turns to poke at the fat belly.

"Where would you suggest we start?" Gaspard asked.

Ever since he'd seen the bloody urine Phillip had been thinking about the combination of blood in the urine and a brand new, and young, wife. He had an idea of what might have killed Ludwig Schaub; now he just had to collect the confirming evidence. "The stomach."

Gaspard turned to the people encroaching on the space around the table. "I'd appreciate it if everyone would give us some room," he said as he attempted to shoo them away from the table.

Everyone took at most half a step back, until Gaspard started unrolling his autopsy equipment. Not to be outdone, Phillip found room on a work bench to lay out his own tools of his trade. The sight of the various saws and blades had the onlookers stepping well clear of the two surgeons.

"After you?" Phillip suggested to Gaspard, gesturing to the naked belly of Ludwig Schaub.

"No, after you, Phillip. Today I'll assist."

To have Professor Bauhin assisting him was a great honor, and Phillip had no intention of declining his offer. He selected a scalpel and made a long incision from Ludwig's groin right up to his neck. He followed the vertical incision with a couple of horizontal incisions at rib level to form a cross and the two surgeons started to peel back the skin.

Finding the stomach took a little time, but soon

afterwards Phillip was able to cut it out and drop it onto a silver platter that had been requisitioned for the purpose. Together Phillip and Gaspard opened it and examined the contents.

"Look at those flecks," Phillip said.

Gaspard scraped some small iridescent flecks from the stomach lining. "What do you think it is?" he asked.

Phillip examined them under a lens. With everything else he had seen he was pretty sure he knew what had killed Ludwig, but there was one sure way of confirming it. "I think it's what killed Ludwig," he whispered. "I need to conduct a test. Let's find a kidney."

The kidney was a little harder to find in amongst the fatty tissues, but eventually Gaspard was able to cut one free. He dropped it into a bowl. "Now what?" he asked.

Phillip looked at the fat-encrusted kidney. "If what I think is right, if we cut that open and rub it on skin, it should raise blisters."

Gaspard glanced at the interested onlookers. "Well, we can't use any of these people. Would a rabbit do?"

Phillip nodded. "Although it would probably be better to have two—one for the Becks and one for the Schaubs."

Gaspard grinned before turning to the onlookers and requesting a couple of live rabbits, with large patches of their fur shaved off.

While Gaspard gave instructions, Phillip cut open the kidney and proceeded to mash up some of it, while being careful not to touch it with his bare skin. He was finished well before a kitchen hand returned with a couple of rabbits.

While Gaspard described what was happening, Phillip used a pair of metal tongs to take some of the mashed kidney and smear it on the shaved flanks of the rabbits. Then they sat down to watch.

"What are we looking for?" Dr. Bitsch asked.

"I believe Herr Schaub died of poisoning," Phillip said. He had intended qualifying the statement, but the man who'd since been identified as the dead man's younger brother exploded.

"You agree that she poisoned Ludwig," Heinrich Schaub shouted, waving an accusing finger towards a white-faced Maria.

"You're supposed to be proving that my daughter didn't poison Ludwig," Maria's father shouted at Phillip.

Phillip hastened to reclaim the situation. He held up his hands and called on everyone to "please calm down."

Naturally, in such a charged environment, such a plea went unheeded, until Professor Bauhin added his weight to the request.

"Please, I'm sure Dr. Gribbleflotz will explain if only everyone would calm down." Gaspard cast speaking looks at the counselors for the families, who took the hint. A couple of minutes later the room was silent and everyone was looking intently at Phillip.

"As I was saying," Phillip reiterated. "I suspect that Herr Schaub died from the ingestion of poison." Members of the Schaub family started smiling while the Beck family frowned. "However," Phillip continued, "rather than being poisoned by his wife, I believe he died of a self-administered overdose..."

"My brother did not commit suicide," Heinrich shouted.

Phillip winced at the volume Heinrich was directing at him. "I didn't mean to imply that it was suicide, Herr Schaub. If we can just wait to see what happens with the rabbits, I will be able to explain everything."

The combined parties settled down to watch the two rabbits. Initially not much happened, but after about a quarter of an hour the rabbits started to display signs that they were suffering pain. Then, as more time passed, blisters started to appear on their shaved flanks.

"Professor Bauhin, if you would please examine the rabbits and tell everyone what you see," Phillip said.

Gaspard picked up each rabbit in turn, displaying the shaved and blistering flanks to the audience. "I see blisters in the areas where Dr. Gribbleflotz smeared tissue from Ludwig's kidney." He turned to the two counselors. "Wouldn't you agree?" he asked them. Both men nodded.

"Thank you," Phillip said as he rubbed his hands together. He smiled benevolently at his audience—he so loved being proven right. "With this evidence, I am confident that Herr Schaub died after ingesting powdered Cantharis beetle," Phillip saw the blank looks being sent his way and quickly elaborated, "more commonly known as Spanish Fly."

"But that's not a poison. Ludwig's been taking that for years," Heinrich protested.

"Then he has been very lucky for years, Herr Schaub," Phillip said. "I've seen horses that have died after eating feed that has been contaminated with the Cantharis beetle." That was a slight exaggeration. In his life he'd seen exactly one horse that had died from eating contaminated feed, but they didn't need to know that. "The powder of the Cantharis beetle is actually a poison. However, as Paracelsus himself said, a little poison can be good for you." He gave a wry smile. "There are a number of conditions where a little of the powder is supposed to be beneficial; unfortunately, a little too much can kill you."

Phillip turned to Captain Brückner. "I expect that somewhere in his rooms is Herr Schaub's supply of 'Spanish Fly.' Could you see if you can find it?"

Captain Brückner nodded.

"Do you know what you're looking for?" Phillip asked.

"A sort of brown powder with iridescent reflections," Captain Brückner said as he gestured to Sergeant Schweitzer. The two of them, with the two counselors and members of both families in tow, headed back to Ludwig's bedroom.

"What made you think Ludwig died of Cantharis poisoning?" Gaspard asked after the procession had left, leaving only a handful of people in the kitchen.

Phillip gestured towards the body still lying on the kitchen table. "A man of his age and constitution is likely to feel the need for an aphrodisiac when marrying a much younger woman. If we add that situation to the presence of blood in his urine, I was sure we were looking at Cantharis poisoning."

"But Heinrich insists his brother has taken Spanish Fly for years with no ill effect," Gaspard said.

Phillip shrugged. "As I said before, he's been extremely lucky. I've extracted the essence of Cantharis from a variety of Cantharis beetles over time, and one thing I have discovered is, the amount of the essence present in a sample can vary from as little as half a part per hundred by weight in older female beetles to up to six parts per hundred in males. And if you are selective in what parts of the beetle you take, the legs and thorax can contain up to twelve parts per hundred."

"So that's why you want Ludwig's supply of Spanish Fly. You want to check to see how strong it is."

Phillip nodded. "Usually the powder is a random mixture of male and female beetles. If the ratio is about equal, the active essence of Cantharis makes up less than two parts per hundred."

"But if the ratio starts to favor the male beetles, that particular dose of Spanish Fly can be stronger than normal."

"Or if there is a surplus of the larger female beetles it can drop. The amount of essence of Cantharis in any given dose of Spanish Fly can vary from as little as one part per hundred to as much as six parts per hundred."

Gaspard whistled. "And the person buying it has absolutely no idea how strong it's going to be!"

Phillip nodded. "Like I said, Herr Schaub's been extremely lucky."

"Up until now," Gaspard added with a smile.

"Yes, up until now," Phillip agreed. "He probably purchased a fresh supply so he could be sure of performing for his new bride and, just to be doubly sure, exceeded his normal dosage."

"Resulting in the overdose that killed him. Congratulations," Gaspard said as he held out his hand. "It's been a pleasure working with you, Phillip."

"We haven't checked the strength of Herr Schaub's supply of Spanish Fly yet," Phillip protested.

"I'm sure we'll find it is somewhat over two parts per hundred," Gaspard said.

✧　　✧　　✧

Phillip was still in the kitchen in Ludwig Schaub's house, but now he was carefully weighing the amount of essence of Cantharis he'd extracted from a one-hundred-grain sample of the Spanish Fly they'd found in Ludwig's room.

He gently brushed the white powder he'd isolated into the pan of his apothecary's scales and weighed it. "Just over five grains," he announced to his audience.

"What does that mean?" Dr. Cludius asked.

"It means that the Spanish Fly Ludwig took in preparation for his wedding night was more than double the normal strength one would expect," Gaspard said. He turned to Captain Brückner. "You need to contact Ludwig's supplier and warn him that his powdered Spanish Fly is stronger than normal."

"I will do that," Captain Brückner said. He turned to Phillip. "Would you be willing to conduct a similar test on any Spanish Fly powder the man might have?"

Phillip nodded.

"That's it?" Heinrich protested. He pointed at Phillip. "That man produces some white powder and claims that it's what killed my brother, and you just believe him?"

Captain Brückner turned to Phillip. "Can you prove that white powder is poisonous?" he asked.

"Sure," Phillip said. "Just let me mix it with some water and Herr Schaub here can drink it."

Captain Bruckner smothered a grin. "Maybe you could feed it to one of the rabbits?"

Phillip looked at rabbits in the basket. "They aren't stupid enough to eat or drink enough of it to kill them."

"Are you calling my brother stupid?" Heinrich demanded.

Phillip really wanted to say yes, but warning glances from both Captain Brückner and Gaspard stopped him. Instead he considered the problem of getting a rabbit to ingest the poison. "I could try pouring it down its throat."

"Please do that," Captain Brückner said.

Phillip dissolved a quarter of the powder in a little warm water and with the assistance of one of the kitchen hands, poured it down the rabbit's throat. He put it back in the basket and stood back to watch.

Naturally, the rabbit died, and as a result, the death of Ludwig Schaub was recorded as an accidental death. That allowed Maria Beck to collect her full entitlement as Ludwig Schaub's widow, much to the distress of his family. Maria took her inheritance and moved out of Basel, taking Katarina and Peter with her. Katarina's departure left Johann distraught for a while, but he soon found a new target for his affections.

Captain Brückner warned the apothecary that his Spanish Fly was unusually strong, and quite naturally, the apothecary used that information to promote sales of his especially strong aphrodisiac. Public announcements were made about the risks of using Spanish Fly, and demand for the aphrodisiac jumped, as did the number of deaths associated with its use.

Phillip also suffered as a result of the case. Previously a bit of a nonentity in Basel outside the small community of alchemists, Phillip suddenly found himself the center of attention amongst a certain stratum of society—the middle level merchant class—and had more requests for his professional services as a physician than he wanted to handle.

Chapter 5

Dr. Phil's Piles

Saturday, December 7, 1624, Basel

Phillip chewed at his mustache as he read the letter from his landlord's lawyer. Bad news came in threes. On Thursday his friend Professor Gaspard Bauhin died. Today he had been served notice that his lease would not be renewed. He didn't want to imagine what the third event would be.

He slowly turned, staring at the various aspects of the laboratory he'd been using for the last thirty months. It had started to feel like home, and had collected the detritus of living a home usually accumulated. Did he really want to go through the experience of moving everything to a new laboratory, or should he take this as a sign that it was time to leave Basel?

He was busy contemplating his future when, after a perfunctory knock on the door, Jean Bauhin walked in. The sight of the youth in his laboratory so soon after his father's death didn't bode well. "How are you?" Phillip asked.

"Surviving," Jean said. He stood back and looked at Phillip, his eyes failing to maintain eye contact.

"Do you have more bad news?" Phillip asked.

"More? Oh, you mean in addition to Papa?" Tears started to form in Jean's eyes, and he let them fall.

Phillip passed him a clean handkerchief and pulled out the letter from his landlord and offered it to Jean. "I've been given notice that my lease won't be renewed."

Jean snorted vigorously into the handkerchief. "That didn't take them long," he said as he wiped his nose.

"What didn't take who long?" Phillip asked.

Jean gave Phillip a grim smile. "There are people at the university who are scared of you."

Phillip's brows shot up. "Scared? Of me?" he asked, pointing to his chest. "Why would anyone be scared of me?"

"Because you manage to show them up," Jean said.

Phillip still didn't understand. "Show who up?"

"Doctors like Dr. Laurent."

Phillip blew a snort of contempt. "Who worries about a man of his poor talent?" he asked.

"There are people who respect Dr. Laurent, Dr. Gribbleflotz, and they remember what you did to him a couple of years ago."

"All I did was show his paying customers the correct way to conduct an amputation." Phillip started pacing. "It's just like Padua. People like Professor Fabricius would hold demonstrations where they pontificated on their favorite topic, which had little to do with the knowledge the examiners were going to test the students on." Phillip smiled at Jean. "Really, I was doing the university a favor."

Jean nodded, but there was still a sign of worry on his face. "Dr. Laurent and his followers have managed to engage Professor Stupanus in the proposal to ban all private dissections."

That was bad news. Professor Emmanuel Stupanus' inaugural lecture when he joined the University of Basel faculty had been entitled *De fraudibus Paracelsistarum*, and from what Phillip had heard, the man's opinion of anyone who claimed to follow the Paracelsian school of thought hadn't improved. "Maybe it is time for me to move on," he mumbled.

"Are you thinking of leaving?" Jean asked.

Phillip nodded. "I miss your father and our discussions, especially his ideas of how to classify botanical discoveries. There's nothing here for me now."

"Where will you go?"

Phillip smiled. "Give me a chance. I've only just now decided to leave. For now I think I'll take a barge down the Rhine."

February 1625

The trip down the Rhine turned into a trip down the Waal and eventually Phillip found himself in Dordrecht, in the United Provinces. He'd barely landed his baggage when a colleague from his days in the service of the counts of Nassau-Siegen discovered him.

"Phillip, how have you been?" Wilhelm Dorschner asked as he approached and hugged Phillip.

"All right. And yourself?"

"I can't complain." Wilhelm put on a smile. "After Gradisca I went north and joined the forces of Ernst von Mansfeld. I'm still with him."

Phillip recognized the name and winced. "Were you at Wimpfen?" he asked, naming the 1622 battle which von Mansfeld had lost.

Wilhelm nodded. "We were holding our ground," he sighed and dropped his head, "until a cannon shot hit the magazine and . . ." He shook his head again. "I was lucky to get away unhurt."

"So you've been in the United Provinces since then?" Phillip asked.

"Sort of," Wilhelm said. "We've just recently crossed from Dover with an army to relieve Breda, which has been besieged since August. If you're looking for a position, I'm sure they'll be happy to take you on."

Phillip hesitated. He had a supply of maggot extract that he was simply dying to try out, and a siege would be an ideal situation in which to test his new treatments. One tended to stay in one place, and few if any of the casualties that passed through his hands would have family who were likely to interfere with his experiments.

"We need you, Phillip. We are almost seven thousand soldiers, and only a handful of physicians."

Phillip had to smile. It seemed his opportunities to experiment would be even greater than he'd thought.

The campaign produced a lot of work for Phillip and his colleagues. The only way for Sir Horace Vere and his seven thousand Englishmen to approach the siege lines was along a network of causeways. After a short engagement they managed to capture a redoubt, but the resulting Spanish counterattack forced Sir Horace to retreat, taking heavy casualties.

His work didn't end there as, with Sir Horace's attempt to break the siege failing, the siege lasted another four months. When in June of 1625 Breda finally surrendered, only about half the original seven thousand man garrison survived, including about six hundred Englishmen. Phillip accompanied the English wounded when they were repatriated back to England, where he stayed with them for a year while he improved his English before taking to the road and working his way north, stopping in villages as he passed to offer his professional services or to learn medical uses of plants from the locals. It was thus that he finally ended up near Kingston upon Hull, known locally simply as Hull.

May 1630, Anlaby, three miles west of Kingston upon Hull, England

Phillip paid the messenger from the bookshop he patronized in Hull for the letter and package he'd delivered and retired back into his laboratory to inspect them. He laid the post on his workbench and washed the grease from the spit-roasted duck he had been eating from his hands before hunting out his letter opener.

The letter was from his old colleague from the Dalmatian expedition. Michael Weitnauer was in Jena, working at the university's botanical gardens, and he wrote that he had hopes of being put in charge of the facility. His letter went on to describe some of the changes he wanted to make. Phillip could only feel that Jena would be well served by employing Michael as the director of the botanical garden.

He laid down Michael's letter and picked up the package. It was wrapped in brown paper and tied with string. Phillip carefully untied the string and added it to the ball of string he was creating from short lengths he saved. Then he carefully opened the brown paper wrapping to reveal a brand new copy of Dr. William Harvey's *De Motu Cordis*. It was bound in human skin, just like his copy of Andreas Vesalius' *De humani corporis fabrica libri septem*, which probably explained why it had taken so long to arrive. He placed the manuscript to one side while he folded up the wrapping paper and put it into a drawer for use at some later date. Only then did he turn his eyes to his new book.

As it was a mere seventy-two pages, including illustrations, Phillip didn't think it would take him long to skim through the manuscript. That meant he could probably afford to look at it while his laborant ground green vitriol, because, he thought, not even Robert could get into trouble doing that.

He was wrong. It wasn't that he was wrong thinking Robert couldn't get into trouble grinding green vitriol, he was wrong in assuming that he could afford to read the manuscript instead of closely monitoring what Robert got up to. The youngster was the latest of a line of hopefuls he'd tried as assistants, and Phillip was having trouble repressing his delusions of grandeur.

What this meant was that while Phillip was distracted with his book, Robert finished grinding up the green vitriol and, having time on his hands, did a little experimenting of his own. Phillip was deeply into Dr. Harvey's discussion of the evidence for his new theory that rather than being made in the liver, that blood actually circulated through the body, when a panic-laden scream from Robert burst through his reader's trance. He looked up in time to see Robert grabbing a flask emitting a red vapor and dashing outside with it. Phillip dropped the book onto the bench top and gave chase.

By the time he caught up with Robert he'd already thrown the glass flask away. It shattered on the stone wall, splashing whatever the liquid was all over some willow branches from which the bark had been removed. Almost immediately the willow branches started to blacken. "What did you do that for?" Phillip demanded. Unfortunately he didn't stop there and wait for an answer. He exploded with more questions. "What did you do? What was in the flask?"

Robert stammered that he didn't know and Phillip went bombastic. "What do you mean you don't know?" he demanded. He glanced at the smoking wood. He had to know what had caused that. "Haven't I told you to record everything?" he shouted.

Phillip was normally mild mannered, but right now he was overly excited and coming over as aggressive. Robert panicked and ran, leaving Phillip to shout curses at his rapidly disappearing back. When Robert disappeared from view Phillip walked over to where the flask had broken and examined the damage. The burns on the wood suggested the liquid had probably been acidic. He hurried back into the laboratory for some Litmus Paper.

The liquid tested positive for acid, leaving Phillip with a problem. He'd never seen any of his acids affect a piece of willow wood quite like that. He broke off a few lengths and retired into his laboratory. At the bench where Robert had been working he laid down the wood and studied the flasks Robert could have used. Nothing leapt out at him, so he carefully tested a little of each container on a piece of wood.

All that managed to confirm was that none of the acids he made was as strong as the acid Robert had created. That meant it had probably been a combination, just like how aqua regia, a combination of aqua fortis and acidum salis, was much stronger than the individual acids used to create it.

While he experimented Phillip went back to chewing on his roast duck. It was cold now, but he was used to eating cold food.

It was late, and his candles had burned low before Phillip discovered a combination that yielded a red vapor such as he'd seen coming from Robert's flask. The beaker was hot to the touch, which might explain why Robert had thrown his flask once he got outside. Phillip dripped a few drops onto a piece of willow and waited to see what happened.

Phillip stared at the black marks that appeared where the drops had fallen in disbelief. A quick reexamination of his notes confirmed that all he'd done was add concentrated oil of vitriol to concentrated aqua fortis. Neither of the acids individually was as strong as the new combination, but aqua fortis was just oil of vitriol and saltpetre. How was it possible to make something stronger than aqua fortis by simply adding more oil of vitriol?

It was a question that Phillip decided would have to wait for another day as the candles started spluttering. He added his latest thoughts to his notes of his experiments before pinching the wicks out and falling into his bed, his mind awhirl as he tried to explain what he'd seen.

The next day Phillip returned to reading Dr. Harvey's book. The mathematical argument was compelling. If a heart did pump about one and a quarter drachm of blood with each beat of the heart, and if a heart were to beat two thousand times an hour, then, in the course of a day the heart would pump sixty thousand drachm of blood a day. That was, as Dr. Harvey claimed, more than five hundred pounds of blood that the liver would have to produce every day. Phillip nodded his agreement with Dr. Harvey's conclusion. There was certainly no way his liver was producing five hundred pounds of anything—he was sure he would have noticed if it did.

He laid down the book. It was all very well reading about Dr. Harvey's theory, but Phillip liked to see his own proofs. The first thing to do was check the claimed volumes for a heart. Phillip dressed for a visit to the local butcher.

Phillip's initial tests with human-sized animal hearts tended to confirm Dr. Harvey's numbers, so he moved on to the next stage. He could have tied off veins and arteries, like Dr. Harvey had, to show that veins flowed into the heart while arteries flowed out, but he preferred a much more direct approach. He bought a live pig.

It wasn't a very large pig—because Phillip was operating alone he'd settled for an animal of less than thirty pounds—but he still dosed it with laudanum to calm it down before he tied it down to a heavy work table. Even after a heavy dose of laudanum it still struggled and squealed when he cut it open. Phillip bound the pig's snout with rags to quieten it before going on to cut through the ribs to gain access to the animal's beating heart.

He stared at the beating heart in wonder for a while before using his thumb and forefinger to pinch off in turn the veins and arteries leading in and out of the organ. By this simple expedient he was able to confirm Dr. Harvey's contention that veins let blood into the heart while arteries let the blood out. His final test was to cut the pulmonary artery and measure the blood being pumped out.

He counted off ten heartbeats as blood squirted into a small flask. He put that to one side before slicing through the remaining veins and arteries connected to the heart so he could remove the organ. He held it in the sunlight streaming in through the window so he could examine the still beating heart more closely. It was a suitable size for the pig, which meant it was considerably smaller than the other hearts he'd examined, so he was going to have to measure the volume of blood it could hold. He set to doing that.

A couple of days later

As a trained surgeon Phillip had the skills and the tools to butcher the pig, but it would have taken time he could better spend on his research, so he'd had the dead pig collected by the local butcher, who had cut it up and was now in the process of making ham, sausage, and bacon from it. He'd already delivered some pork chops and Phillip was chewing on one of them when there was a knock at the door. "Coming," he called. He grabbed a cloth and wiped his hands clean as he hurried to the door. He pulled it open to reveal not one, but both local vicars—Reverend Edmund Garwood from the parish of Hessle and Reverend William Wilkinson from the parish of Kirk Ella.

"Mr. Garwood, Mr. Wilkinson, how can I be of assistance?" he asked.

Edmund turned to William. Their eyes met before they turned Phillip. "There is a story going around the parishes that you have been engaging in witchcraft and devil worship," Edmund said.

"That's preposterous!" Phillip said.

"We're sure it is, Dr. Gribbleflotz," William said, "but you have been observed cutting the still-beating heart out of a living animal, and in the eyes of some of the locals, that signifies devil worship."

"Who could have seen that?" Phillip demanded. Someone would have had to been looking through the windows of his laboratory to do that.

"You admit it?" Edmund asked.

"Of course," Phillip said. He noticed the wide-eyed looks he was getting and remembered the claim of devil worship. "But it's not devil worship," he said. "I was merely conducting a scientific experiment."

"A scientific experiment that involved cutting a still beating heart out of an animal?" William asked.

Phillip took a deep breath and let it out slowly. "You're both educated men," Phillip said. Both William and Edmund smiled. One could say they straightened and put on airs in response to being called educated men by the very learned Dr. Gribbleflotz. Phillip barely managed to hold back a smile. "Please, come in and I'll explain."

Phillip led the two country vicars into his laboratory and guided them to his work bench where he had a number of drawings of hearts laid out on its surface. He located Dr. Harvey's book and added that to the papers on the bench. "It's really quite simple," he started.

Edmund laid down the remains of the pork chop he'd been chewing. "So what you're saying," he said as he wiped his greasy hands on his thighs, "is that your experiment confirmed Dr. Harvey's contention that blood circulates around the body?"

Phillip nodded.

"But why has no one discovered this earlier?" William asked between nibbles at his own pork chop.

Phillip shrugged. "That's a very good question, and my only answer is that medical science has been blinkered by its blind adherence to the writings of Galen and his followers. It's only by experimentation that we can improve our knowledge of how the body works."

"That's all very well and good, Dr. Gribbleflotz, but why did you have to cut the still-beating heart out of the pig?" Edmund asked.

"That wasn't intentional," Phillip said a little red-faced. "I'd just taken a sample of arterial blood from the heart, and I wanted to measure how much blood the heart could hold. To do that I needed to cut the heart out. It just so happened that the pig was still alive when I started to cut the heart free." He shrugged nonchalantly. "It did come as a bit of a surprise how long it continued to beat."

"Why did it continue to beat?" William asked.

Phillip shook his head ruefully. "You really like asking the easy questions, don't you?"

"So you don't have any idea?" Edmund asked.

"Not yet." Phillip smiled at Edmund and William. "Maybe both of you gentlemen would like to assist me next time I operate on a living animal and we could investigate the problem together."

"I'd like that," Edmund said as he struggled to his feet. "I'd better be getting on my way then." He turned to William. "Are we satisfied that Dr. Gribbleflotz is not engaged in devil worship?"

William got to his feet as well. "Quite satisfied." He turned to Phillip. "It's been most interesting talking to you, Dr. Gribbleflotz, and I too would be interested in assisting you next time you operate on a living animal."

Phillip walked with the two men to the door and watched them walk through the village. They waved and stopped to talk to Phillip's neighbors, no doubt reassuring them that Phillip wasn't a devil worshiper.

A *few days later*

Phillip made a mad dash for the chamber pot, barely getting his pants down before he emptied his bowels, again. He wiped his bottom clean. That activity was starting to hurt. He gently felt around, and realized he had hemorrhoids forming. He'd met them in the past, on patients, so he knew how to treat them.

He carefully made his way to his workbench where he had some chopped *Plantago major* in hot water. The infusion was a treatment for people with diarrhea.

It didn't actually treat the diarrhea, but he'd found time and again that patients suffering from diarrhea who were given the infusion to drink did a lot better than those who just drank water or small beer. If it was good enough for the people he treated, Phillip felt it was good enough for him. He emptied the infusion through a cloth filter into a mug and stirred in the usual spoonful of honey he'd learned to add to improve the taste so patients would drink it. He sipped the infusion while he checked his journals to find a treatment for hemorrhoids, finishing his drink just in time to make another emergency call of nature.

He was getting better. Phillip reminded himself of this fact as he sat on the chamber pot. The first three days had been the worst. He'd only left his bed to use the chamber pot, or to get a drink. Food had been the last thing on his mind, then. But now that he was getting better, Phillip was able to think about the cause of his discomfort. He'd met diarrhea often enough before—only in a professional capacity of course—to know the probable cause.

Usually, when he'd tried to track down the cause of an outbreak of diarrhea in the military, he'd traced it back to a common issue of food that the initial batch of afflicted men had all eaten. Phillip considered what he'd eaten in the last week. There had been the duck. He'd eaten that over a couple of days, but he hadn't fallen ill for days after eating that. This left the pig. He'd been eating that right up until the time he fell ill. He spared a thought for Reverend Garwood and Reverend Wilkinson, who'd also eaten some of the pork and sausage, and hoped, for their sakes, that they weren't similarly afflicted.

The wiping of his bottom was again a painful act, so the first thing he had to do was make up a soothing ointment. He compared the ingredients he had on hand with the recipes he'd collected and made up an ointment, which he promptly applied.

That evening

It was getting late, but the sun was still well above the horizon, when a child ran into Phillip's laboratory calling out in a panicky voice. "Dr. Gribbleflotz, Dr. Gribbleflotz."

Phillip recognized the son of a former patient. "What's the matter, John, is someone ill?"

"Papa says the village is ill," John said.

That response lacked clarity. "Who needs my professional services?" Phillip asked.

John stared at Phillip. "No, no, Dr. Gribbleflotz. No one needs your professional services. Papa says you need to escape before the angry villagers get here. A dozen people in the village have been ill these last few days, and Mr. Sissons, the butcher, is claiming that you, the devil worshiper, are the cause. Right now he's trying to rouse the village to march on your laboratory and burn you as a witch." John paused to stare at Phillip. "Are you a devil worshiper?" he asked.

"What? No, of course I'm not a devil worshiper." Phillip swallowed a couple of times. "Are you sure about this?"

John nodded. "I was there with Papa. Mr. Spofford and Mr. Craike both spoke up in your defense, but Mr. Sissons pointed out that both Reverend Garwood and Reverend Wilkinson fell ill soon after visiting you. Papa says 'things are going to get nasty,' so he sent me to warn you."

Phillip wanted to protest his innocence, but John wasn't interested in his guilt or innocence. It was the crowd he had to worry about, and no doubt they would be all fired up and unwilling to listen. "What can I do?" he asked. "Where can I hide?"

"Papa says you should take what you can and hide in one of Mr. Legard's barns. He told me to guide you."

Phillip started grabbing things. "What is your father doing?"

"He said he would try and delay the crowd, to give you time to escape." John hurried over to the window and looked outside. "They're coming."

Phillip hurried to his bedroom to grab some clothes and his valuables. He paused in front of his library. His and his great-grandfather's journals were irreplaceable, so he added those to the bundle he was creating with a blanket from his bed. He ran a finger along the leather-bound books in his library, and sighed over their size and weight. He had to make a choice between taking his books or taking the medical kit and apothecary's box that contained his livelihood.

"Hurry!" John called out. "They're almost at the corner."

It was with great reluctance Phillip abandoned his library in favor of the tools of his trade and ran back into the laboratory. John had raided Phillip's sadly depleted larder and had a stale loaf of heavy rye-bread in his hands. He hand it to Phillip. "We have to go now, otherwise they'll catch us!"

Phillip added the bread to the clothes and journals

he'd already bundled into the blanket and thrust it into John's hands and grabbed his medical kit and apothecary's box. "I'm ready. Let's go."

Phillip sat at the loading hatch of Mr. Legard's barn idly rubbing his fingers over his lucky crystal while he watched the flames claim his laboratory. He stared at the crowd gathered around his former home, trying to identify them, but it was too far, the light was bad, and his eyes weren't the best. Still, his eyes were good enough to count individuals, and by his calculations, over half the adult population of the village were gathered there. That didn't bode well for his continued safety in Anlaby.

Phillip sat down in the moonlight to check what he'd managed to save. It wasn't much. In addition to his own and his great-grandfather's journals, he'd managed to save a summer-weight coat, a hat, a couple of changes of clothes, a spare pair of leather boots, and the woolen blanket they were all laid out upon. He also had his medical kit and his apothecary's kit, and finally, a very stale loaf of rye-bread. He hacked off a bit with his belt knife and manfully chewed on it. It wasn't much, but it quietened his grumbling stomach. With his stomach settled, Phillip gathered his possessions together and set out for Hull.

Phillip entered Hull early the next morning. His mind was set on getting out of the city before the stories of him being a devil worshiper could catch up with him, but his first order of business was to get a proper meal. Only after he'd eaten did he walk over to the Holy Trinity Church where he explained to

Reverend Richard Perrott why he was leaving and to ask him to pass on some money to young John's father.

"I'll ride over to check on William and Edmund tomorrow. Then, if they're fit, we'll drop in on Anlaby to talk to the villagers," Richard said. "Will you hang around in Hull long enough for me to get back, just in case we're able to salvage anything from the ruins?"

Reluctantly, Phillip nodded. "I'll wait." He dug some coins from his meager supply and handed them to Richard. "Could you pass this on to John Beecroft, a shepherd in the employ of Robert Legard Esq. as thanks for sending his son to warn me what was happening? I owe him my life."

Richard counted the coins. "A pound?"

"Is it too little?" Phillip asked, concerned that he might not be adequately rewarding John Beecroft for his help. Unfortunately, he couldn't afford much more, not after losing most of his possessions in the fire.

Richard hastily closed his fist around the coins and shook his head. "No, no. Dr. Gribbleflotz. A pound is more than adequate recompense for the service Beecroft performed for you."

Phillip released a sigh of relief. "Thank you."

Phillip had time while Reverend Perrot was gone to think about where he should go next. It had helped that amongst the few things he'd saved had been Michael Weitnauer's letter. The Danes had recently signed a peace treaty with the emperor, so it should be relatively safe to travel from Hamburg to Jena; Jena was where he would go.

Reverend Richard Perrot was only gone a day, and when he returned he had a few of Phillip's possessions.

There was his portable fire assay kit. That had probably survived the fire because it and the cupels were supposed to operate at temperatures hot enough to melt gold. Unfortunately, the same couldn't be said for any of his fine clothes or books. They'd all been lost.

Richard made apologies on behalf of the good people of Anlaby, and asked that he reconsider leaving, but Phillip's mind was made up.

"I have a friend I haven't seen for over ten years who has recently taken a position in Jena. I think it's time I dropped by to see how he is doing."

Richard nodded his acceptance of Phillip's departure. "The good people of the parishes of Hessle and Kirk Ella will miss your medical services."

Phillip wanted to shout that they should have thought about that before they burned him out of house and home, but you couldn't say things like that to a minister of a church, so instead he settled for a silent smile. Reverend Perrot seemed to understand the silent message and took his leave of Phillip.

Phillip bought a donkey in Hamburg and set off along the main trade route south to Erfurt, a distance of some two hundred and thirty miles. A teamster moving cargo by pack animal would normally make the trip in ten or eleven days, but Phillip wasn't in any hurry. Instead he followed his usual practice of stopping at every village to talk to the locals, discovering uses for local plants and providing his professional services in exchange for food and lodgings.

It was August, some two months after he left Hamburg, before he reached Erfurt. He found stabling for Dapple (the third of that name) and a room for himself.

After washing off the dirt of the road Phillip went for a walk around the city. He didn't need the exercise, but he was desperately in need of intelligent conversation.

He found the conversation in an inn, naturally. A group of people were talking when one of their number, a wine merchant by the name of Casparus Menius, announced that he'd been offered the chance to buy land in which a magical plant grew. The plant was magical because pollen gathered from the plant in the light of a full moon on the evening of the summer solstice could be turned into gold.

That caught Phillip's attention and he responded without thinking. "That's impossible."

Casparus turned to glare at Phillip. "I have seen it," he said.

Phillip did some rapid mental calculations. "What did you see? Did you see them harvesting the pollen?" he asked. "The last full moon on the evening of the summer solstice happened sixteen years ago."

"No," Casparus admitted reluctantly, "but I watched as they showed me the pollen they'd collected being turned into gold." Casparus smiled at his colleagues before returning his attention to Phillip. He pulled out his purse and extracted a small bead of gold. "Tell me that's not gold," Casparus said as he placed the bead on the table.

Phillip looked at the bead. It certainly looked like gold. He pointed to it. "May I handle it?"

Casparus nodded and Phillip picked up the bead. It certainly felt heavy enough to be gold, "I'm a trained assayist and I have a touchstone with me. May I test this 'gold' on it?"

"Of course," Casparus said.

Phillip pulled his portable assay kit out of his satchel and proceeded to test the bead. "It's pure gold," he declared, handing the bead back to Casparus.

"See," Casparus said with a meaningful look at one of his more vocal colleagues. "I told you it was gold, Jacob."

"But I doubt that was made from some wondrous magical pollen," Phillip said.

Casparus turned to glare at Phillip. "How can you say that?" he protested. "You weren't there. I saw them with my own two eyes use their magic pollen to make gold." Casparus stared suspiciously at Phillip. "You just want to beat me to the gold."

Phillip shook his head. "Sometimes something is just too good to be true," he said. "Tell me, why would these people be willing to sell you this 'gold mine'?"

"That's simple," Casparus explained. "Their father didn't know what he had when he collected the pollen sixteen years ago, so he didn't collect very much, and it took years to discover how to turn it into gold." Casparus smiled smugly. "Now they find themselves in need of money and unable to wait until the next full moon falls on the evening of the summer solstice."

"They can't wait three years? Just how much are they asking for this land?" Phillip asked.

"They tried to sell it to me for ten thousand thaler, but I've beaten them down to five thousand," Casparus said smugly.

Phillip could only whistle in admiration at the audacity of the individuals. "So you've paid these people five thousand thaler for a bit of marshland you don't even know exists?"

"Of course not," Casparus protested. "I'm not stupid.

Five thousand thaler is a lot of money you know. I have deposited the money with my lawyer while he checks the legal title on the land."

Phillip did know it was a lot of money. Whoever these people were, they'd picked out their mark with care. "I think you should inform your lawyer you are no longer interested in buying the land and get your money back."

"Why?" Casparus demanded. "I could be sued for breach of contract."

Phillip shook his head. "I really doubt these people will want to take the matter to court."

"You seem very sure of this," one of Casparus' colleagues said.

"All Herr Menius' lawyer would have to do is insist the sellers demonstrate that they can make gold from pollen gathered on the land in question."

"Which they can do," Casparus said. "I've seen them do it."

"But have you?" Phillip asked. "If you'd like to follow me back to my lodgings, I'm sure I can replicate what they showed you."

"You can make gold from pollen?" Casparus asked.

Phillip smiled. "Wait and see."

Half a dozen people followed Phillip back to his lodgings. He dug out his portable assay furnace and some cupels, and his apothecary's box and took it out to the inn's courtyard, where he set everything up. By the time he was ready to start, quite a crowd had gathered.

"Prepared to be amazed as I, Dr. Phillip Theophrastus Gribbleflotz, The World's Greatest Alchemist, demonstrates to you, this day, the alchemical wonders of my magic pollen."

That introduction caught the interest of his audience as Phillip removed a jar containing a yellowy-brown powder. He held it up so everyone could see. "This jar contains magical pollen I collected from rushes in a marsh near Augsburg in the light of the full moon of the evening of the summer solstice sixteen years ago."

"Where is this marsh?" Casparus asked.

Phillip shook a silencing hand at Casparus. "Please don't interrupt, Herr Menius." Phillip paused to take a deep breath to get his thoughts back into line before continuing. "I will carefully measure out ten grains of my magic pollen and place it into a cupel."

Phillip emptied the powder into a cupel. "To this I add some quicksilver, to give weight, as everyone knows gold is heavy while pollen is light." He added a small spoonful of mercury to the yellow powder. "Now some sulphur, because everyone knows gold is yellow, and born of fire, just like sulphur." Phillip smiled at his audience. It felt wonderful to have everyone waiting on his every word. He really should do this sort of demonstration more often, he thought.

"To this I shall also add a little salt, because according to Paracelsus, all matter is made up of quicksilver, sulphur, and salt." Phillip smiled at his audience while he gently stirred the mixture. "Now we must add a special elixir, without which nothing will happen—the sacred Quinta Essentia of the waters of wine—the secret of which I was taught by a Jewish alchemist as a reward for saving the life of his son." Phillip poured a couple of spoonfuls of alcohol over his mixture and continued to stir it. "I must expose my mixture to fire, for only fire can combine the ingredients to form the noble metal that is gold."

Phillip placed the cupel in his portable assay furnace and shut the door. "We must now wait for the furnace to get hot enough."

"Are you really making gold?" a man dressed like a farm laborer asked.

"Wait and see," Phillip said as he used a small bellows to boost the temperature of the fire in his portable furnace.

Phillip checked the progress of his sample regularly, until he was sure it was ready, he then used metal tongs to lift the red-hot cupel out of the furnace and poured the contents into a large iron kettle full of water. The water spat as the red-hot gold hit the water.

Phillip placed the still glowing cupel on the ground before fishing around in the kettle with his fingers for the gold. He collected several beads of gold, which he displayed to his audience. "Now to see how much gold we have made."

Phillip was aware of the intense interest of the crowd, but he was enjoying the attention, so he drew out the weighing of the gold. "And there we have it, a grand total of ten grains of gold."

"But you started with ten grains of pollen," Casparus said.

There were murmurings of agreement from Phillip's audience. "Fancy that," he said with a smile. He picked up his jar of "pollen." "Of course, this isn't really pollen. It is in fact pure gold, as I will now demonstrate."

Phillip measured out ten grains of his gold powder into a fresh cupel and placed it in the furnace. Minutes later he was picking beads of gold out of the kettle again. And again he had ten grains of gold.

"But he didn't use the magic elixir," a stable hand protested loudly.

"That's because he didn't need it," one of his companions said. "The powder was always gold."

Casparus walked up to Phillip and looked at his jar of gold powder. "But it doesn't look like gold," he said.

"It is gold, Herr Menius. Lift the jar and feel how heavy it is," Phillip suggested. While Casparus hefted the jar, Phillip continued speaking. "It is gold in a very fine powdery form. For some reason it lacks the sheen of larger particles of gold."

Casparus laid down the jar of gold powder and looked at Phillip. "They lied to me. There is no magic pollen," he said.

"I'm afraid not," Phillip said. "But hopefully your money is safe."

Casparus sighed and looked from Phillip to his colleagues. "Nothing can save me from having made a fool of myself in front of my colleagues, but at least you have saved me five thousand thaler. For that I thank you. What is your name again?"

"Dr. Phillip Theophrastus Gribbleflotz."

"And where are you headed?"

"To Jena," Phillip said. "An old friend of mine wrote that he was applying for the position of director of the university's botanical garden."

"You're an old friend of Professor Werner Rolfinck?" Casparus asked.

"Who?" Phillip looked at Casparus in surprise. "No, my friend is Dr. Michael Weitnauer."

"Then I'm sorry to have to tell you that your friend failed to get the position. Professor Rolfinck is the director of the botanical gardens."

Phillip was taken aback for a moment. Then he shrugged. "I've come this far, I might as well continue on to Jena."

"Then I must give you my direction, for I am heading there shortly," Casparus said.

"Just as soon as he's found a doctor to treat his piles," one of Casparus' colleagues called out.

Phillip could only feel sympathy for a fellow sufferer. "I have a most excellent ointment for piles," he said.

"Every quack has an excellent cream or ointment for any ailment," Casparus' noisy colleague said.

Phillip had to concede that point. His natural father had been one such person. "However, I have personal experience of the ability of my ointment to treat piles." He smiled ruefully. "I suffered a bout of diarrhea, which resulted in painful hemorrhoids. I couldn't sit down for days, until I stumbled upon a formulation which relieved the pain and reduced the swelling."

"I'm willing to try it," Casparus said.

October 1630, Jena

Phillip swirled the wine in the glass and inhaled the bouquet. With a smile on his face he took a sip. Having a wine supplier as your patron had certain advantages, he thought to himself.

A knock on the door disturbed his moment of peace. With a heavy sigh Phillip put down his glass and hurried to the door of his laboratory. He opened the door to none other than his patron. "Herr Menius, how nice it is to see you," he said. Right now he was remembering why he preferred not to have a patron—they thought they could interrupt you at any time. "How can I help you?"

"I would like some more of your pile ointment."

Phillip bit his lip as he quickly ran his eyes over Casparus. "They still haven't gone down?" he asked.

Casparus threw up his hands. "Oh, no, it's not for me. One of my colleagues is in need of some, and as I was dropping by, I offered to get him some."

And, Phillip thought, naturally I'm expected to drop everything and make up a fresh batch just for his colleague. This kind of interruption was why Phillip preferred not to have a medical practice. At least his fellow alchemists knew to place an order that could be picked up at a later time. Unfortunately, patients, and more especially patrons, expected to be served immediately. "Please, come into my laboratory while I mix up the ointment."

Casparus followed Phillip, his eyes darting around the laboratory as he followed Phillip. "You're finding the laboratory satisfactory?" he asked.

"Yes," Phillip answered. What else could he say? Casparus had purchased the lease on the building and presented it to Phillip as a gift. To be fair, Phillip admitted, it was a very good laboratory, by most standards.

"You don't seem too sure, Herr Dr. Gribbleflotz."

Phillip waved towards the distillation furnace. "While I was in Basel my assistant, Johann Glauber, and I developed some designs for superior furnaces."

Casparus' brows shot up. "Johann Glauber? Not Johann Rudolf Glauber? The man who discovered Glauber's Salt?"

Phillip hid a smile as he nodded. Johann had done

very well for himself in the years since he served as his laborant. Putting his name to a product was exactly the kind of self-promotion he would have expected of Johann, who had constantly said that Phillip would never amount to anything while he refused to promote himself.

Then Phillip saw the look on Casparus' face. He wasn't sure how to interpret it, but there was a hint of prideful ownership in his eyes that worried him. He'd heard horror stories from other alchemists about being treated as little more than a performing animal for a patron, so he leapt into describing his preferred topic of research. "I have recommenced my studies into the invigoration of the Quinta Essentia of the human humors," he said.

Casparus' reaction was a bit of a surprise. He listened to all Phillip had to say and even asked intelligent questions. When, a little over an hour later, Phillip waved Casparus goodbye, it was with an invitation to make a presentation of his research to a handful of Casparus' friends.

November 1630

Phillip watched the last of Casparus' guests leave the room. He was feeling quite kindly towards his patron as he cleaned up the remains of his seminar on the invigoration of the Quinta Essentia of the human humors. The seminar had been well received, and some of Casparus' colleagues had even asked intelligent questions. Now, as became the evening's entertainment, it was time for Phillip to leave, by the tradesmen's entrance of course.

Phillip passed his traveling apothecary's box to a menial, who swung it up onto his shoulder, and after graciously accepting a small leather drawstring purse from Casparus' majordomo, they left.

It would have been uncouth to have examined the contents of the purse in front of Casparus' majordomo, even if the man probably already knew what was in it, so Phillip waited until they were a reasonable distance down the street before opening the purse to assess how much his patron considered his time was worth. He was pleasantly surprised to find the contents totaled five thaler, which was about five times what a doctor might charge for a consultation. It seemed his patron had plenty of money he was willing to spend. Phillip walked home thinking about what projects he might be able to persuade Casparus to fund.

December 1630

Phillip was hard at work in his laboratory keeping up with orders for his high purity acids when Casparus walked in with a man in his late thirties.

"Ah, Dr. Gribbleflotz," he said as he led his companion into the laboratory. "My friend here has voiced an interest in meeting you."

Phillip quickly checked on the state of the various retorts before approaching Casparus and his friend. He held out a hand to Casparus' friend. "A pleasure to meet you," he said.

"I'm Dr. Zacharias Brendel," Zacharias said. "I'm a professor of iatrochemistry at the university, and I've been hearing a lot about the quality of your acids."

Phillip positively beamed at the compliment. "Would you care for a demonstration?" he asked. "I make the purest and the strongest acids you'll ever see."

"Yes, thank you," Zacharias said.

"I'll leave you to show Professor Brendel anything he wants to see then, Dr. Gribbleflotz," Casparus said.

Phillip had completely forgotten about his patron. He hastily said all that was needed and saw him out before returning to Zacharias, who was staring at the line of retorts on the distillation furnace.

Zacharias pointed to the lineup of retorts. "I see you're distilling oil of vitriol," he observed.

Phillip looked at the lineup. "There are a couple of retorts of acidum salis being concentrated as well."

"As well?" Zacharias made a more detailed examination of the retorts around the distillery furnace. "So you are." He shook his head in gentle disbelief. "You say that as if it is normal to concentrate acidum salis while also distilling oil of vitriol."

"Depending on what I need to produce I've had oil of vitriol, aqua fortis, acidum salis, aqua vitae, and water all on the furnace at the same time," Phillip said with a touch of smug pride. He'd never met anyone with even half his ability on the distillation furnace.

"You're a real master of the distillery furnace!" Zacharias said. Suddenly his brows shot up and he stared at Phillip. "Professor Casseri's last apprentice was supposed to have been a master of laboratory techniques. Was that you? Were you Professor Casseri's last apprentice?" he asked excitedly.

Phillip nodded warily.

Zacharias clapped his hands on Phillip's shoulders.

"It's an honor to meet you, Dr. Gribbleflotz," he said. "I understand you were making some of the best acids the university had ever seen? And now you're in Jena?"

"That's right."

"And already you're making an impression on the local market for alchemical supplies I hear," Zacharias said with a smile. "Now I know exactly who you are, I'm no longer surprised at how quickly you have managed to dominate the market for premium quality acids.

"What have you been doing since you left Padua?" Zacharias asked.

Phillip gave him the short version of his adventures, concentrating on his time as a military physician and surgeon and finishing with his being burned out of house and home in England.

"But what were you doing to bring such an action upon you?" Zacharias asked.

"I'd just read Dr. Harvey's *De Motu Cordis*, and I wanted to test his theory for myself," Phillip said. He related how he'd been seen holding a still beating heart in his hands.

"That was most unfortunate," Zacharias said. He stared into the distance for a while before speaking again. "I wonder how long a human heart could continue to beat."

"I'd like to know the answer to that myself," Phillip said, "but I can't imagine being permitted to conduct the experiment, not even on a condemned criminal."

Zacharias released a heartfelt sigh. "There are so many rules that seem to have no other purpose than to limit our ability to understand our world." He shook his head gently before looking back at Phillip. "And what are you experimenting with now?"

Phillip couldn't resist an opportunity to talk about his long time interest. "I'm looking for a way to invigorate the Quinta Essentia of the human humors," he said, and from there he went on to describe the current state of his investigations.

Zacharias walked away from Phillip's laboratory in a bit of a quandary. Phillip was known in Jena as Dr. Gribbleflotz, and it had crossed his mind that maybe Phillip wasn't entitled to the title. Some things were just accepted, such as the idea that people who claimed doctorates had them, unless someone had good reason to doubt it. Zacharias didn't exactly doubt Phillip's doctorate, but he did know that Professor Casseri's last apprentice hadn't earned his doctorate before his, Professor Casseri's, death.

That in and of itself didn't mean Phillip didn't have a doctorate. All it really meant was that he hadn't been awarded one by Padua before Professor Casseri's death. It was possible, he thought, that Phillip had earned his degree at some other university, such as Basel or Leiden, which raised another point. Phillip's lack of proper academic training was obvious. So how did he find a school willing to let him take their exams? Without a bachelor's degree no reputable medical school would accept him. Unless, that is, he found himself a new sponsor. Zacharias smiled. He'd seen with his own two eyes Phillip's ability to attract sponsors. Happy that it was possible Phillip had in fact been awarded a doctorate, the proof of which had unfortunately been lost when his home and laboratory had been burned down, Zacharias turned his mind to other things, such as the experiments he could conduct with Phillip's new, super strong yellow aqua fortis.

Winter 1630-31

The public anatomy demonstration was running night and day so as to maximize the learning opportunities before the stench of the decomposing body being dissected became too strong, so it was near midnight when Phillip stumbled out of the anatomy theater at Jena and joined the flow of spectators leaving after the last session of the day.

"Is it always like this?" Casparus asked Phillip.

Phillip raised a brow to his patron. "The long hours?" he asked.

"That, and the stench," Casparus said.

"There's not a lot you can do about the long hours," Phillip said with a smile. "Once it's been cut open a cadaver might last three days before the stench becomes intolerable. So it's normal practice to continue night and day until the stench is unbearable."

"This cadaver is into the fourth day," Casparus pointed out.

"And it smells like it too," Phillip agreed. "Professor Rolfinck's problem is he only has two cadavers to dissect over the duration of his anatomy course compared with the up to nine Professor Casseri had for his anatomy courses in Padua. He's obviously trying to get as much teaching time out of each of them as he can, but I think he's going to have to accept that he can't continue with this cadaver and dissect some animals until the other convict is executed."

"Ah, yes, that reminds me." Casparus smiled at Phillip. "I'm putting together a party to attend the execution. Would you care to join us? I have a table with a good view of the scaffold."

Phillip managed not to cringe. Death was no stranger to him, but watching a man being led to his death amidst a cheering and jeering crowd turned his stomach. "Thank you for the offer, Herr Menius, but if you don't mind, I don't want to miss any of Professor Rolfinck's lectures."

"You'll be missing a fine spectacle," Casparus said.

"Yes," Phillip agreed, "but unfortunately, I need to attend all of Professor Rolfinck's lectures if I want to keep abreast of discoveries and developments in our understanding of the human body."

"Ah, you think you might learn something new to help in your investigations into the invigoration of the Quinta Essentia of the human humors?"

"Yes!" Phillip said. It wasn't exactly a lie. There had already been Dr. Harvey's theory of the circulatory system since he left Basel, and surgeons had been bleeding patients for centuries in an attempt to balance the human humors. No doubt there were plenty of other, less well publicized, advances that had passed him by in the five years he'd been in the relative backwater of Anlaby, England.

"Well, I guess I'll see you in the theater again first thing tomorrow morning," Casparus said.

Phillip waved Casparus away before setting off for his lodgings.

A week later

Phillip should have gone to the execution with Casparus. It wasn't that Casparus deliberately set out to cause trouble, but his memory of what Phillip had actually said when he compared dissections in Padua with those in Jena wasn't the best, and if Phillip had been there, he could have provided corrections or clarifications. But he hadn't been there, and comments attributed to him took on a life of their own as each person repeated what they thought they'd heard to the next person in the chain. Thus, what finally reached Professor Werner Rolfinck's ears bore little resemblance to Phillip's original comments. Of course, Werner didn't know that. As a result, instead of entering the medical faculty staff room buoyed by a successful public anatomy course, he entered the staffroom fuming at the insult he believed had been leveled at him.

"What do any of you know about this Dr. Phillip Theophrastus Gribbleflotz?" Werner demanded of his senior teaching staff.

"I've heard that in Erfurt he claimed to be able to make gold from pollen," Conrad "Kunz" Herbers, a lecturer in iatrochemistry and theories of medicine, said.

"That's impossible," Werner said. "You can't make gold, and anyone who claims that they can is a fake and a charlatan."

"My informant was most insistent that he saw Dr. Gribbleflotz make gold from nothing more than some magic pollen, quicksilver, sulphur, salt, and some mystical elixir, the secret of which he learned from a Jewish scholar," Kunz said.

"That only convinces me he's a charlatan," Werner said. "He should be chased out of Jena."

"I've heard that he makes a most excellent ointment for hemorrhoids," Wilhelm "Willi" Hofacker, a senior lecturer in iatrochemistry and medical botany, offered.

"Really?" Kunz asked. "How well does it work?"

"Kunz!" Werner roared.

Kunz jumped back in surprise. "I'm sorry, Professor Rolfinck."

"And so you should be. We have a charlatan in our midst, and all you can think about are your hemorrhoids."

"You have hemorrhoids, Kunz?" Willi asked.

Kunz nodded. "They've been bothering me for over a week now, and nothing I've tried has..."

"Dr. Herbers!" Werner roared. "I said we were not interested in your hemorrhoids. I wish to discuss how we can get rid of this charlatan."

"Ah, Werner," Zacharias said.

Werner spun round to face Zacharias. "What? Are you suffering from hemorrhoids too?"

Zacharias shook his head. "I think you should know that Dr. Gribbleflotz was apprenticed to Professor Giulio Casseri, and studied medical botany under Professor Prospero Alpini. He also spent a couple of years with Professor Gaspard Bauhin in Basel."

Werner stared hard at Zacharias. "And how do you know this?"

"Dr. Gribbleflotz told me," Zacharias admitted.

Werner snorted. "All three men are dead," he pointed out. "We have only the charlatan's word that he knew them."

Zacharias shook his head. "Dr. Gribbleflotz matches the descriptions I've heard of Professor Casseri's last apprentice, and Professor Alpini's son is still in Padua," he said. "And," he added, "Dr. Gribbleflotz said he got to know Professor Bauhin's son in Basel."

"He's a charlatan," Werner insisted. "And I want him run out of Jena."

"I wouldn't be so fast, Werner. Dr. Gribbleflotz has a patron," Zacharias warned.

"A patron?" Werner scoffed. "Who cares if the charlatan has a patron? I'll soon have this Dr. Gribbleflotz out of Jena, and his patron will be thanking me for saving him from the charlatan."

"Casparus Ludovicus Menius," Zacharias said in the middle of Werner's tirade.

Werner froze. "Our Casparus Ludovicus Menius?" he asked.

"Yes," Zacharias agreed, "the wine merchant responsible for the high prices the Winzerla vintages have been receiving lately. Oh, and who is also a close friend of Jacob Berger in Erfurt."

Werner swallowed. The income from the Winzerla vintages was one of the major sources of the university's financial support, and both Casparus Menius and Jacob Berger were major players in the trade. If he went after that charlatan Gribbleflotz, they could put pressure on the university, and he could lose his position. "Then I shall have to collect evidence that this Dr. Gribbleflotz is nothing but a charlatan. Then the university's governors will have no choice but to deal with the charlatan."

Willi looked up smiling. "Does that mean I can buy some of Dr. Gribbleflotz's hemorrhoid ointment?"

Werner glared at Willi. "Do what you want," he said before stalking out of the room.

Part Two

The Start of HDG Enterprises
1631

Chapter 6

Calling Dr. Phil

October 1631, Jena

"Unless you are matriculated as a student or a member of staff, you are not welcome on university grounds," Werner Rolfinck said to Dr. Phillip Gribbleflotz.

It was like having a door slammed in his face, Phillip thought, but without the actual slamming of the door. He looked from Professor Rolfinck to the other members of the University of Jena faculty who'd witnessed his expulsion. There were a number of smug smirks visible. They didn't even care that he saw them.

Phillip struggled to maintain his dignity as he turned and strode out of the university grounds. He held himself together all the way back to his laboratory, where he was greeted by his landlord. The perfect end to the perfect day, except it wasn't even noon yet.

✧   ✧   ✧

Phillip collapsed onto his bed. His landlord wanted the next quarter's rent, which he didn't have, and it was all his former patron's fault.

Casparus Menius had been paying Phillip to research the Quinta Essentia of the human humors, which had been nice, because that was what he wanted to research. Unfortunately, Casparus had died while on a business trip to Erfurt. The nature of the establishment where he'd died hadn't impressed his wife, who'd somehow managed to blame Phillip for not just his death, but also for where he'd died. That had resulted in his funding being cut off immediately. That wouldn't have been so bad if he hadn't been doing his research into the Quinta Essentia of the human humors at the expense of producing acids for his usual customers. He had very little stock and was facing imminent eviction from his laboratory and bankruptcy.

None of it was his fault, of course. Phillip didn't think he could be blamed for taking on a little debt to replace the clothes and books he'd lost in the fire at Anlaby. After all, his patron had been happily paying him a stipend and paying his bills. And with the bills being paid, it had seemed sensible to concentrate on doing the research Casparus wanted him to do rather than waste valuable research time producing acids for sale.

Unfortunately, with Casparus dead and his funding cut off, Phillip needed money fast. He did a mental checklist of his assets, and didn't like the results. He could pawn enough clothing and footwear to buy in supplies or pay the next quarter's rent, but not both. That just left his lucky crystal. He walked over to the little niche above his writing desk where it lived and took it in his hands. It was a nondescript clear crystal no bigger than a chicken's egg. The local pawnbroker had admired it when he saw it and offered Phillip a ridiculous price for it. He'd turned the man down of course—one didn't sell one's luck, but maybe the man would be willing to advance a small loan with the crystal as security? Phillip resolved to find out.

A couple of days later

Phillip had a well-deserved reputation for the quality of his acids, so he wasn't surprised to find the orders coming in once word got out he was back producing them. He took the pile of orders and started to sort them out on one of his work benches. It didn't take him long to realize that many of the orders had been placed by members of the University of Jena's faculty. He swore as he quickly checked through them. Professor Rolfinck's name wasn't there, but of course he wouldn't sign his own name to an order; he'd have someone else do it for him.

"So," he said to himself, "I'm good enough to make their acids for them, but not good enough to darken the halls of their university."

That was wrong. He should be welcome at the university. He was definitely better qualified than most, if not all of the medical faculty. They might have their degrees, but he'd been trained by Professor Giulio Casseri, one of the best teachers of anatomy and surgery there had ever been, for three years and followed that up with years of practical experience as a military physician and surgeon.

Even Professor Rolfinck couldn't match Phillip's training. He'd been taught by a lesser man, the man who inherited the chairs of anatomy and surgery upon Professor Casseri's death, Dr. Adrianus Spigelius. A man who'd had the misfortune to be taught by none other than Professor Hieronymus Fabricius ab Aquapendente rather than Professor Casseri.

And now this pretender, and the rest of the medical faculty, were treating him, Phillip Theophrastus Gribbleflotz, the great-grandson of the great Paracelsus, the world's greatest alchemist of his time, as a mere technician.

Well, that was wrong. Phillip slammed his hands on the bench hard enough to smart. There was nothing mere about his skills around the distillation furnace. He was a great technician, no, he was a great alchemist.

Phillip nodded to himself. He'd show those imbeciles at the university that he wasn't just a mere technician. He'd show them that he wasn't just a great alchemist. He would show them that he was the world's greatest alchemist. Not just in his time, but ever. He would show them that he was even better than his great-grandfather.

Phillip's eyes fell on the empty niche where his lucky crystal usually lived, and he qualified that last thought. He'd start proving he was the world's greatest alchemist ever, just as soon as he earned enough money to redeem his lucky crystal.

October 1631, Sunday, Grantville

Tracy Kubiak counted out the last ten jackets that needed button holes and placed them on the work table with the other four piles. There was a lot of work to do before she could turn this latest order over to the government, but she knew some people who would be only too happy to help her finish them off.

She stretched muscles that were still protesting from the last few days spent over her heavy-duty sewing machines as she worked to complete the order and surveyed her domain. She had turned the oversized basement into a workroom when she first went into business making and repairing camping and outdoor equipment soon after she married Ted Kubiak. A smug smile grew on her face at the thought of her husband of four years.

"Are you ready yet? We're running late."

Speak of the devil. Tracy cast one last glance over the piles of jackets waiting to be finished and hurried over to join her husband. "Just have to lock the cat flap and I'm ready." So saying, she locked the flap that allowed Toby, the family cat, and Ratter, Ted's Jack Russell terrier, access to the workroom.

Upstairs in the house proper, Tracy discovered that Ted had everything ready. All she had to do was load the baby into the push chair. "You have been busy," she said.

"Someone has to be. You can lose yourself once you step into your workroom."

She reached up to drop a kiss on Ted's lips. Ted tried to make more of it, but after a few seconds she pushed him away. "I thought we were running late?"

Ted sighed dramatically. "I'm married to a cruel woman. You get the kids while I load Fred."

"Are we taking the girls as well?" Tracy asked. Fred was their male llama gelding, originally purchased to mind the few sheep they ran on their land. The girls were a couple of llamas that had joined the menagerie after their original 4H owners had been left up-time.

"They insisted," Ted said. "They can hear the crowd over the road and don't want to miss out."

By the time Tracy had collected three-year-old Justin and eight-month-old Terrie, Ted had the panniers on Fred and was waiting for her. She locked up and joined him for the short walk to Belle and Ivan Drahuta's place, which was just across the road from their property.

Every Sunday after church the extended Kubiak clan gathered at the home of one of the families for Sunday lunch. Today was Belle and Ivan Drahuta's turn to be hosts. Grown men and women were messing about playing touch football in the yard with some of the children. Others congregated around the grill chatting and talking while Ivan and Tommy Barancek attended to burning the meat on the grill. Children of all ages were running around underfoot, and of course, Fred and the girls were hanging their heads over a fence gobbling up any treat the children cared to offer them.

Tracy lounged back on the sheltered veranda with a group of Kubiak clan women watching the activities, relaxing after finally getting their assorted babies settled.

Erin Zaleski, one of Ted's cousins, turned to Tracy. "How's the military outfitting business going, Tracy?"

Tracy dragged her eyes from Ted, who was playing in the yard. "I'm still being run off my feet." Tracy looked around the assembled women. They were all, like Ted, direct descendants of Jan and Mary Kubiak, the original owners of the land known locally as Kubiak Country. "I've got a pile of jackets that need buttonholing if anybody wants a job."

There was a smattering of "I'm in" and "Yes, please"

from the other four women. Tracy gloried in the easy camaraderie and supportive nature of the Kubiak women. It was so different from her own family, left up-time in Seattle. "If you come over the road after lunch I'll show you what needs to be done and give you the necessary thread and buttons."

There were murmurings of agreement before the women turned back to watching the activities going on in the yard. Their quiet contemplations were disturbed only when Tasha Kubiak set a covered tray of steaming biscuits on the table. "Tuck in while they're still warm, girls. After this batch, there are no more."

Mary Rose Onofrio turned away from watching Jana Barancek and a couple of other cousins trying to get everyone to sit down at a couple of food-laden tables set out by the grill. "What do you mean, Tasha?"

"This batch used the last of my baking powder," Tasha replied.

Belle Drahuta waved a hand. "I've still got some if you need it."

"Same here," Tracy said. "I haven't had time for much baking lately, but I think I've still got an unopened can in the pantry."

"Thanks Belle, Tracy. You'd think there would be a way to get more baking powder wouldn't you?" Tasha shook her head.

Mary Rose snorted. "Get real, Tasha. If it doesn't go boom, none of the guys are interested. I can just imagine going up to Cousin Greg and asking him to please make some baking powder so we can do some baking. He'd laugh his head off."

"You really think Cousin Greg would know how to make baking powder, Mary Rose?" Tasha asked.

"If he can make his boom toys and rockets I don't see why he can't make baking powder. I mean, how hard can it be? Baking powder has been around for I don't know how long. It's probably written up in one of his books somewhere and all he needs to do is look it up."

"But, Mary Rose, that doesn't get us any baking powder."

"No," Mary Rose agreed, "but it would get us some instructions on how to make it. Maybe Cousin Greg can write out a recipe. Something easy to follow. Then we could make our own baking powder." She looked around the table at the other women, an excited look in her eyes. "That would be great wouldn't it? We'd never have to worry about running out of baking powder ever again."

"So when can you ask Cousin Greg for an easy to follow recipe for making baking powder?" Belle asked.

Mary Rose looked from Belle to Tasha. "I was kinda thinking, maybe Tasha might like to ask Amy to ask Cousin Greg. After all, she is a chemistry teacher in training."

Nodding her head, her mouth full of biscuit, Tasha agreed to ask her daughter to pass on the request.

"Michael. How many times have I told you not to feed that dog from your plate," Belle bellowed before launching herself from her chair and making her way to her son.

The ladies watched Belle put a strong restraining hand on her five-year-old son while giving her husband, who should have been watching him, a sharp talking to.

"Situation normal," muttered Erin with a giggle.

A week later, Sunday lunch, Tasha's place

"Guys, Amy here has come through. Come on, Amy. Show them the recipe," Tasha said pushing her daughter towards the seated mothers. A little self-consciously Amy placed a single sheet of paper on the coffee table in front of the ladies and stood back to let them read it.

"Uh, yuk. Do you see that?" Mary Rose pointed to the first instruction. "Imagine carefully fermenting urine. Does that mean we have to, you know, ask people to fill a bottle? And why add honey? Is that to sweeten its taste?"

"Ha ha, Mary Rose. Obviously the honey is there to help fermentation," Tasha said, continuing to run her eye down the directions. "How do you cook off limestone?" She looked up at her daughter, a question in her eyes.

With a heavy sigh Amy looked at her mother and her friends. "I think this is going to be a bit like the time Dad tried to do some baking. You remember how he couldn't understand how you got cream from butter and sugar?" Smiling at the memory Tasha nodded her head. "I think you might want to find someone who knows a little chemistry and see if they'll make the stuff for you."

"But we know somebody who knows something about chemistry," Tasha pointed out, giving her daughter a significant look.

In horror Amy took a sudden step back, getting some separation between her and her mother. "No way. Sorry, but no way. I'm much too busy at school." She held her hands out defensively and shook her head. "Really. I think you should find yourselves a friendly alchemist and pay them to make the stuff."

"And how are we going to find one of them?" asked Mary Rose.

"Well, Jena is a university town. There must be tons of them there."

"So you think we should go knocking on doors in Jena asking alchemists, 'Please sir, can you make baking powder for us?'"

"Baking soda. If you'll read the recipe again you'll see it's for making baking soda, not powder," Tracy pointed out, her finger pointing to the top of the sheet.

"Amy?" Tasha turned to her daughter. "I thought you were going to ask about making baking powder?"

"I did, Mom. I asked Mrs. Penzey. She said you have to make baking soda before you can have baking powder. If you look near the bottom," she pointed to the bottom of the sheet of paper, "you'll see she's included how to make baking powder. The problem is getting the cream of tartar. Mrs. Penzey says that it's a by-product of wine making, but she's never seen it in its raw state, and has no idea how to get any. And that's another reason why I think you should contact an alchemist. They know about things like cream of tartar, except they probably call it something different."

Mary Rose looked at Amy. "What you're saying is, we can get baking soda easily, but if we want baking powder, that's going to take a little experimentation?"

Amy nodded. "Yes."

"That's not so bad," Belle said. "We can make biscuits using baking soda. I'm sure we all have some recipes that'll work. Besides, there are tons of uses for baking soda. There's toothpaste substitute for a start. And soon enough we should be able to get baking powder."

Amy slipped away while the ladies sat silently digesting their thoughts.

"Tracy, are you planning on a buying trip to Jena anytime soon?" asked Tasha.

"Ted and I were planning on going down river in another week or so. I guess we can ask around. We should see if Danielle and Steve can go as well. It's a pity we don't have more people able to speak German. The more people searching the faster things will go." Turning to Belle, Tracy continued, "Will you be able to look after Danielle and Steve's two little monsters if they go?"

"Sure. They aren't that bad, and they are closer in age to Louis and Michael than your mob. It'll keep all of them out of my hair if they can entertain each other."

Jena, ten days later

Ted Kubiak had lucked out. He'd managed to get an appointment with the professor of medicine at Jena. He'd actually been hoping to talk to a professor of chemistry, but there was no such thing, yet. Instead he had to settle for a lecturer in iatrochemistry, Professor Zacharias Brendel.

Zacharias waved the sheet of paper Ted had handed him. "You want to know if I can make this?"

Ted smiled at the man in his white ruffed-collar and black coat and said, quite seriously, "I'm pretty sure you could, if you wanted to. What I really want to know is if you are willing to make a lot of it for us."

Zacharias nodded. "You're right. I could make it, but

to make it in any volume would take me away from my students and my research. Have you considered asking one of the alchemists in the city?"

Ted frowned and nodded. "None of them are interested. They think making a cooking powder is beneath them."

Zacharias nodded. "That might be a problem." His face pursed in thought for a while. "Have you tried Dr. Gribbleflotz?" he asked.

"A doctor?" Ted laughed. "If the alchemists aren't interested, what chance is there that a doctor will be interested in helping us?"

Zacharias hemmed and hawed for a while before explaining. "Dr. Gribbleflotz isn't a practicing doctor. He's sort of an experimental alchemist with pretensions to being an iatrochemist, but he lacks the proper academic training."

"But you called him Dr. Gribbleflotz," Ted said.

"There are some who question his right to the title. However, he is a gifted laboratory technician. His acids are the envy of every other alchemist and even the university iatrochemists. Anybody who can afford them buys their acids from him."

"And you seriously think someone with all that going for him is going to make us our cooking powder when everyone else has said no?"

Zacharias nodded. "I'm sure he will. Dr. Gribbleflotz's patron died recently, and he is in the unfortunate position of being financially embarrassed. If you can afford to cover his needs, he will be beholden to you."

Ted nodded. This man sounded interesting. "You're sure Dr. Gribbleflotz can make our baking soda?"

Zacharias nodded. "He originally trained as an

assayist and metallurgist at Fugger's in Augsburg. There's probably no one in Jena more able to make it for you. He has no experimental flair, but I know no one better able to follow a recipe without deviating from what is written down." He pulled a piece of paper out of a drawer and wrote on it. After sanding the paper he handed it to Ted. "That is Dr. Gribbleflotz's direction."

"Thank you," Ted said. "And thank you for your time."

Tracy slumped down with her elbows on the table while she waited for her order to be delivered and looked across the table to Danielle and Steve Kowach. "It's as if they don't want our money," she said. "As soon as I say I want someone to make baking powder for cooking they get all uptight and condescending. Their holier than you 'I am an alchemist, not a cook' line is really getting to me. Have you two had any better luck?"

Danielle shook her head and looked at her husband, who shook his head in negation. "We've been getting the same story, 'Alchemists are not cooks. Please go away and stop bothering me. My work is important.'" She mimicked the condescending attitude that Tracy had run into with so accurately that Tracy started to giggle.

"Here comes Ted. I wonder if he's had any luck." Steve waited for Ted to sit down beside Tracy. "Any luck?" he asked.

"Well, I've ordered a heap of canvas. A few hundred yards of cord of varying diameter, and some oils for waterproof—ouch!" Ted grabbed Tracy's hands to stop her pummeling him.

"Edward Robert Justinian Kubiak, you know that's not what Steve meant," Tracy said, struggling to pull her hands from Ted's grip.

"Has anybody ever told you you're beautiful when you're riled?" Ted asked, a smile in his eyes. They both fell silent as their eyes locked.

"Hey, you two. None of that in public," Danielle said. "So Ted, have you found us an alchemist?"

Ted broke eye contact with Tracy and turned to Danielle. "First thing I learned is we don't want an alchemist."

"What?" Danielle and Tracy asked in unison. "Of course we do," Danielle continued. Tracy nodded in agreement.

"That's where you're wrong. No." Ted held up his hands to silence their protests. "No alchemist will lower themselves to do what you are asking. What you need . . ." he paused dramatically, "is a technician. Some suitably trained plodder who can follow directions without making any spontaneous additions just to see what happens."

"And how do we find this suitably trained plodder?" Tracy asked.

Ted theatrically drew a piece of paper from a pocket. "By pure chance I have here the directions to one Phillip Theophrastus Gribbleflotz, who was originally trained at the Fugger's in Augsburg. Apparently he lacks the proper scholastic and academic attitude to be an alchemist, but in some quarters he is a highly regarded technician."

"What's the significance of him training at Fugger's?" Seeing Ted's blank look Danielle hurried on. "Never mind. He has to be better than those supercilious morons from the university."

"I wouldn't bet on that, Danielle. He styles himself as Herr Dr. Phillip Theophrastus Gribbleflotz. His clientele humor him. He's good at what he does, and it's a fairly harmless conceit. But it does mean you'll need a lever to persuade him to make your baking soda."

"Will money talk?" asked Tracy.

"Ah, the Evil West Coast Businesswoman strikes. Yep. My informant indicates that the good doctor has a massive ego, only eclipsed by his vanity. His major expenses are his continuing experiments and flashy clothes. Currently he's financially overextended and he struggled to make this quarter's rent. I'd say he's the perfect mark for what you want."

Tracy smiled and rubbed her hands together in anticipation. If he was desperate, then he couldn't afford to knock them back. He would probably offer token resistance as a matter of pride, but to Tracy's mind, they already had him in the palms of their hands. It was always better to negotiate from a position of strength.

Jena, later that same day

Phillip pulled his hand out of the bucket of cold water and examined the burn. It was going to blister. He sighed and looked around his laboratory. He'd had the misfortune of burning his hand when a glass retort broke. It was the latest of a string of silly accidents caused by his overtiredness, but there wasn't anything he could do about that. He had to work sixteen-hour days if he was going to pay off his debts and redeem his lucky crystal before the pawnbroker could sell it.

It was only the fact that his creditors knew he was back producing acids that was keeping them from his door. Unfortunately, he was now one retort down, which he couldn't afford to replace. That meant he was going to have to work even longer hours just to keep volumes up.

Phillip was in a pain-induced foul mood when he opened the door to a couple who, based on their styles of dress, he knew immediately were two of the infamous up-timers. "What do you want?" he asked them in his native German.

"I'm Tracy Kubiak and this is my husband Ted," Tracy said, "and we've been informed that you might be willing to make some of this for us." She held out the recipe for baking soda.

"Informed by whom?" he asked as he accepted the paper. The movement aggravated the tender flesh of his burned hand.

"Professor Brendel," Ted said.

Phillip raised a brow at that before skimming through the contents of the paper. "What is it?" he asked.

"It's a rising agent for baking."

Pain made Phillip more irascible than normal and he took it out on Tracy. "Let me see if I understand you correctly, Frau Kubiak. You wish me, Herr Dr. Phillip Theophrastus Gribbleflotz, great-grandson of the Great Paracelsus, to make this 'baking powder.'" At Tracy's nod, he continued. "I. I am not a cook. I, do not follow a recipe. I, am an Alchemist. A Great Alchemist. A Great Alchemist does not make funny white powder so people can bake." It came out stilted, growing in volume as he spoke, until he was almost roaring.

It was a strategic cough from Ted that drew Phillip's fire from Tracy. The six-foot, two-hundred-plus-pound frame of Ted towered above Phillip's thin, short frame. With his pronounced Adam's apple bobbing, Phillip swallowed his words and turned his attention back to Tracy.

"But you could make the powder if you wanted to, couldn't you, Herr Dr. Gribbleflotz?"

Phillip flashed his eyes over the recipe again, then looked back at Tracy. "Of course. Any marginally competent student of alchemy could easily make this 'baking soda.' The 'baking powder'...a little time in the laboratory, and that too can be made."

"Well, can you at least help us find someone to make it?"

"I am not a procurer. If you wish someone to make this baking powder you must find them yourself. Now, please. I wish to get back to real work. Do not bother me with 'cooking.'"

"Herr Dr. Gribbleflotz, we can pay, and pay well for this baking soda. Won't you please reconsider?"

Phillip stared at Tracy. There was no way he could afford the time it would take to research how to make their cooking powder while also keeping up his acid volumes. And he couldn't see them compensating him for the income he'd have to forgo. "No. It's impossible. I'm too busy..." He moved suggestively, trying to usher his visitors out of his laboratory.

"What about a couple of sets of clothes? Tailored to fit. With pockets, zippers, and buttons. In the fabric and color of your choice." Tracy was almost desperate.

Phillip stopped midstride and turned to look at the up-timers. He'd heard stories about the new colors coming out of Grantville. His eyes traveled up and down Ted, examining the denim trousers, plaid linen shirt and leather jacket. Then they moved onto the woman. Again the denim trousers, a bright yellow-green shirt with a canary yellow chemise. Her jacket was a fabric he didn't recognize but the color was a bright blue he had never seen. The styles weren't anything he particularly admired, but the colors were amazing. Yes, the offer was appealing. With a couple of sets of clothes in the new colors, he could afford to sell some of his other clothes. That would be enough to justify the research, and if they really were prepared to pay him well for the cooking powder, then he'd come out ahead, and he'd be able to redeem his lucky crystal sooner. Still, he couldn't tell them that, nor could he allow them to think he'd caved in too easily. His eyes settled on the wedged heeled shoes Frau Kubiak was wearing. "I want shoes like yours, Frau Kubiak, with the elevated heels."

"Yes, even shoes with elevated heels."

His ego firmly stroked by Tracy's complete capitulation, Phillip held out his hand. "Give me another look at that recipe. I believe we can talk business."

Phillip watched the American man and woman walk away. He ran his fingers through his goatee beard as he looked into the distance, seeing himself in his new clothes. A fine figure of a man, commanding, dignified, the target of envy from less fortunate beings. Drawing his attention back into his rooms, he looked about his suddenly shabby quarters and laboratory. Maybe, if the Americans were as good as their words, he could move into accommodations more befitting Herr Dr.

Phillip Theophrastus Gribbleflotz, the World's Greatest Alchemist. With the advance payment they had promised he could obtain supplies, employ laborants to do the dull repetitive tasks, and even keep his creditors at bay. Yes. If the Americans came through he could purchase some of that new glassware Herr Geissler was making after his visit to Grantville. With the areas of investigation the new glassware opened, soon those narrow-minded imbeciles of the university would kneel before Herr Dr. Phillip Theophrastus Gribbleflotz, the World's Greatest Alchemist, begging him to accept one of their diplomas. Begging him to join the staff of their university. One day…

Sunday lunch, Tracy and Ted's place

"Well?" Tasha asked significantly, staring inquiringly at her cousin by marriage. "Did you find us an alchemist to make baking soda?"

Holding her mug in both hands, Tracy took a sip of tea before looking over the lip of the mug at the expectant faces surrounding her. "No." She paused, teasing them. The quiet groans of disappointment were interrupted by Danielle breaking into a fit of the giggles. "We found someone better." With that Danielle started to roar with laughter. Tracy limited herself to a broad smile as she too tried to imagine Herr Dr. Phillip Theophrastus Gribbleflotz as being "someone better." "The guy is a bit of a pompous ass. But at least he's willing to make our baking soda."

"When can he have it ready?" asked Mary Rose.

"At the moment he's only making a test sample. He

said he needs at least a week for the urine to properly mature so as to produce the best spirits of hartshorn."

"Gross." Erin shook her head in disgust. "What are spirits of hartshorn?"

"Ammonia. Spirits of hartshorn is what it's called here and now. And quite frankly, I think it will be less trouble if we learn to use whatever names Herr Dr. Phillip Theophrastus Gribbleflotz wants to use."

Belle's forehead creased. "Hang on. He's a doctor? But you said you couldn't find an alchemist."

"He's not an alchemist. For that matter, Ted says there is some doubt that he's a doctor, at least not from any reputable university. Anyway, he said he could deliver a couple of pounds in about two weeks' time."

Two weeks later, Sunday lunch at Belle's

"Now for the big test. Everybody take a bite and let's see what we think." Belle passed a plate of steaming biscuits around the table.

"Mmmm, nice. Different from baking powder biscuits, but still very good," Tasha volunteered. The other women nodded and agreed that the biscuits were good.

Tracy looked over her friends, "So we are agreed that Dr. Phil . . ."

"Dr. Phil?" Belle's raised eyebrows were duplicated by the rest of the girls.

"That's just Ted's name for Herr Dr. Phillip Theophrastus Gribbleflotz," Tracy replied.

"I thought he claimed he never watched Oprah?"

Tracy smiled at Belle. Ted had often made that claim. However, it seemed he had been a little economical with the truth. "Anyway, are we agreed that we should look at getting Dr. Phil to make lots of baking soda?" At the nods of agreement, Tracy continued. "Then we have to think about raising capital. I've made enquiries. Dr. Phil will need to rent new facilities, buy additional hardware and supplies. He will also need to employ some people he can teach to do the work. We will also need to supply someone to manage everything when Dr. Phil loses interest and goes back to his pet projects. I'm thinking that if all the family can contribute maybe a thousand dollars per household to the project we can raise at least twenty thousand dollars. That should be enough to get him started, and running for at least three months."

"Hang on, Tracy. What are we going to get for our investment?" Mary Rose frowned. "A thousand dollars is a bit steep for a few pounds of baking soda." The other ladies looked at Tracy, nodding agreement.

"I'm suggesting that we set up a manufacturing company with Dr. Phil as the head or consulting chemist. He gets paid a retainer, a share of any profits, and access to the company's supply of chemicals and facilities for his experiments. In exchange, he's responsible for ensuring the processes work, the staff he trains are capable of doing the work they are paid for, and," Tracy paused dramatically, "the company owns anything he develops on company time, or using company facilities or chemicals."

"Nasty." Belle licked her lips in anticipation. "Can you enforce that last condition?"

"Herr Hardegg of the law firm of Hardegg, Selfisch, and Krapp seems to think so. He doesn't expect any problems dealing with Dr. Phil. He did, however, suggest that Dr. Phil have a large share of the company. Something like fifty percent. Although he did agree that forty-nine percent would do."

"Are you saying your Dr. Phil is worth twenty thousand dollars, Tracy?" Erin asked.

"I think so. Certainly there's nobody else offering to make baking soda. You do realize that there's a potentially big market out there, and whoever gets in first could dominate the market? I just think we should get in first."

"That recipe Amy got. You think someone else could get one?" a thoughtful Tasha asked.

"Yes," replied Tracy. "And there are plenty of bright people in Grantville capable of following the recipe. However, if we get in fast we can lock in a lot of the local suppliers of urine. That's where some of the start-up capital will go. We also need an ice-making machine—something that will work in Jena."

Mary Rose blushed. "If we lock in the local suppliers of urine? Hold it. How do we do that? And who are the local suppliers of urine?"

Tracy grinned. "Ted claims that the various drinking houses produce buckets full every day. Currently a lot of it is being dumped via the sewage system. He reckons he and a couple of the cousins can modify the urinals so that the urine is diverted into some barrels rather than the sewer. If we offer to make the modification at no cost in return for the urine, he thinks we could lock in most of the taverns. They'll save on the toilet tax since they won't be pumping so much into the sewerage system."

"Those years with O'Keefe's are good for something then," Belle commented with a grin.

"Don't forget the papers in waste engineering Ted's done at college. But yes, he's happy to be able to make a useful contribution to this project."

Late November 1631, Jena

Maria Anna Siebenhorn sat on the blanket-wrapped bundles of the worldly goods of her, her brother, and their friend, leaned against the exterior wall of the bakery and tried to absorb a bit of warmth from the oven's chimney. Across her body was a stick she could use to defend herself and the bundles, although to use it she would first have to free her hands. She was cold, as one would expect in Jena in November during the Little Ice Age, and she was hungry. Both problems had their origin in her current situation—she was a refugee. It wasn't that the good citizens didn't care about the refugees from the wars who had looked to their city for aid, but there were too many of them for the available alms.

Maria, her older brother Michael, and his friend Kurt had found shelter in the city. They'd also managed to find work, but now that the grape harvest was almost over the vineyards no longer needed so many pickers. The three of them had been without work for three days, which was about the limit the city authorities allowed, and things were strained.

Across the street Maria Anna watched a man approach a young woman who'd been standing in a doorway flashing her wares all the time Maria Anna had been sitting against the wall. They talked, and then, after striking an agreement, they entered the building, the man's hand clamped firmly to the buttocks of the young woman. Maria Anna knew what was going on, and she shuddered at the idea of doing it herself. She knew that if she and Michael didn't find work soon, she might be forced into selling her body.

"Maria Anna!"

The shout, almost in her ear, freed Maria Anna from her nightmare. She looked up at her brother. He looked excited. "You've found work?" she asked.

Michael nodded. "But we have to be quick." He hauled Maria Anna to her feet and thrust one of the bundles she'd been sitting on into her arms before grabbing the other two and setting off.

"What sort of work?" Maria Anna demanded as she hurried to catch up with her brother.

"An alchemist is looking for people he can train to produce something for the Americans."

Maria Anna rushed in front of her brother and turned to confront him. "An alchemist?"

"Yes," Michael said, "an alchemist. But it's honest work, with meals and accommodation provided."

Maria Anna stood aside to let Michael past and walked along beside him. Michael had just said the magic words. She was cold, tired, and hungry, and this job addressed all three of her problems, overcoming any fears she might have about working for an alchemist.

A few days later, Jena, the shop floor
of Dr. Phil's new laboratory

Phillip passed his eyes over the hard-working young urchins he had recruited as laborants to make the "baking soda" for the American women. He smiled to himself as he remembered his victory over naming of the product. Who would want to be known as the man who makes "baking soda?" Sal Aer Fixus, now there was a product to be proud of. Any alchemist worth the title would immediately respect the abilities of the man who can produce Sal Aer Fixus. Baking soda was for cooks.

"Hans." His high-pitched squeal penetrated the noise of the laboratory. "Did I tell you to stop grinding the ice maker?" All eyes turned to Hans Saltzman, who had hastily returned to grinding the icemaker.

Phillip walked up and down the production line checking on his workers. For a pack of illiterate street refuse, they had taken to the work well. Most of them didn't understand what they were doing, but they were all capable of following his clear and concise instructions. At the ringing of a bell, everybody concentrated on finishing the current batch. As the batch passed from station to station, the youths cleaned down their work stations before helping other workers clean up. Soon, the batch was finished and ready for packaging in the fancy new paper bags the Grantville ladies had supplied. Waving his workers off to the noon meal, Phillip ran a finger over the image printed on some of the bags, a woodcut portrait, with "Gribbleflotz's Sal Aer Fixus" written around the border. The image was very good, if he did say so himself. The artist had managed to catch his true essence. He appeared suitably regal and dignified. On the back of the bag there was more printing. There was a list of several uses for Gribbleflotz's Sal Aer Fixus, including a recipe for the America culinary atrocity they called "biscuits."

He gave the workroom one last sweep with his eyes. What he saw filled him with pleasure. The workroom and his personal laboratory had been fitted out to his specifications, with a few suggestions from the Americans, at considerable expense. The Americans themselves had come in and done much of the work setting up the laboratories. They now boasted "fume cupboards," something that was especially valuable when dealing with fermented urine and spirits of hartshorn, and easy to drain hot and cold baths. There was even running water, as long as the tanks were kept topped up.

Passing into the dining room, Phillip waved the laborants back to the important task of eating. He well remembered the times when he had lacked sufficient food to eat, and had insisted to the Grantville ladies that the laborants should eat as well as he and Frau Mittelhausen. His eye caught on a couple of the laborants. They were some of his best workers, in spite of being female. If they caused any trouble it would be up to Frau Mittelhausen to deal with it. After all, that was what she was paid to do.

He walked into his study. A cloth-covered tray sat on the table where he wrote up his research and did his accounts. Not that he had to do many accounts since the ladies from Grantville had encouraged him to join them in a company. Frau Mittelhausen did all that, and ran the household. All he had to do was ensure the baking soda was prepared according to the recipe, and that sufficient quantities were being made. He relaxed in his chair before removing the cloth covering his lunch. The steam rising from his simple meal reminded Phillip of the meals he had been eating only a few weeks ago. Those meals had been anything he could buy cheaply and eat quickly before returning to his laboratory where he did assays and other work to pay off his debts. He cast an eye to the shelf where his lucky crystal now sat. He would be a lot more careful with his money in future.

He had recently started training a couple of the better laborants to do assays. Soon he would be able to leave them to conduct the rote aspects of the assay work while he concentrated on more important things. Meanwhile, he was receiving a good income from the company just for supervising its production of Sal Aer Fixus. He smiled, remembering the contract the Grantville ladies had had him sign. He received a salary, and a share of any profits, all without having to pay a pfennig towards the costs of the wretched baking soda.

Chapter 7

Dr. Phil's Amazing Lightning Crystal

November 1631, Jena, Freedom Arches

Tasha Kubiak tried to tune out the pompous ass who was still pontificating. Somehow both Tracy Kubiak and Danielle Kowach, the two other members of the Kubiak Country partnership who could speak competent German, had managed to be needed elsewhere when this trip had come up. It was now two weeks since Dr. Gribbleflotz had commenced deliveries of Gribbleflotz Sal Aer Fixus, also known as baking soda. But there had been no word from the good doctor about when he would commence production of baking powder. Someone had to travel to Jena to find out what the holdup was and do whatever it took to get Dr. Gribbleflotz making baking powder. Tasha had hoped her boss, Sebastian Mora of Mora's Café, would refuse to give her the time off to travel to Jena. However, as soon as Sebastian had heard she was going to ask about baking powder, he had all but packed her bags for her.

So here she sat, letting the drone issuing from the good doctor pass over her head. Growing restless while she waited for Dr. Gribbleflotz to finish, Tasha tried to relax. It wouldn't do to aggravate the good doctor by interrupting. In an effort to give her restless hands something to do she reached for her purse. Well-drilled hands felt inside for the cigarettes and lighter. Still looking attentively at Dr. Gribbleflotz, Tasha expertly felt for a cigarette. There were only a few left. Did she really need the comfort a precious cigarette would offer? Yes.

It was the action of a moment to remove a cigarette and place it in her mouth. For a brief moment, just the time it took to put the flame to the end of the cigarette and to inhale that first blissful lungful of nicotine-laden smoke, she took her eyes off the doctor.

"What is that you have there?"

Tasha looked up. The change in tone and volume had penetrated her best efforts to shut out his drone. She waved her left hand, the one with the smoldering cigarette in it. But Dr. Gribbleflotz's eyes didn't follow it. They were locked on her right hand. Looking down she couldn't see what was holding the good doctor's attention. It was just an ordinary cigarette lighter.

"It's a cigarette lighter." Tasha offered it for inspection. "You pull that jewel down and a spark ignites the gas."

Dr. Gribbleflotz looked at Tasha. Then, his eyes alight with interest, he carefully examined the lighter. He flicked it several times. Each time a flame issued from the hole on the top. "How does it work?"

Tasha stumbled mentally, trying to remember anything she had ever heard about cigarette lighters. "It uses a flammable gas for fuel. When you pull down the jewel the gas is turned on. At the same time, a spark lights the

gas. It says lit as long as you hold the jewel down." Tasha
felt quite proud of herself for remembering all of that. It
was almost word for word the explanation her daughter
Amy had given when Tasha had asked the same question.

"But what makes the spark?" Dr. Gribbleflotz asked,
a little too controlled.

"Oh." Tasha looked back at the lighter Dr. Gribbleflotz held. This was getting too deep for her. "It's an
electric spark. Pulling down the jewel completes a circuit
which creates an electric spark which lights the gas."

"Electric spark?"

"Yes, like . . ." Tasha struggled for a synonym, something Dr. Gribbleflotz might be familiar with. Her
eyes reached out, searching for something. And there
it was. A pole towering above a building. A lightning
conductor. "Like lightning, only much smaller."

Eyes wide, brows lifted almost to the back of his
balding head Dr. Gribbleflotz looked back at Tasha,
hastily dropping the lighter. "Lightning? You carry a
lightning maker on your person?"

"No, silly." Tasha rescued her cigarette lighter, shaking her head gently. "Lightning is much more powerful. The electric sparks in my lighter can only jump
a tiny distance." She held her thumb and forefinger
a hair's breadth apart.

Carefully, Dr. Gribbleflotz reached out again for
the lighter. Holding it once again, he tried to light
it. "How does it store the lightning?"

"Oh, that type of lighter doesn't use a battery. It
uses some fancy crystal that emits a spark when you
pull down the jewel."

"The 'fancy crystal' stores the lightning and releases
the spark when you pull the jewel?"

"Something like that. I do know it doesn't ever need batteries, though. We have one of the same kind of thingies to light the gas range. It must be more than ten years old, and neither I or my husband has ever replaced any batteries."

Dr. Gribbleflotz looked carefully from the lighter to Tasha. Each time he glanced at the lighter he flicked it on. "Do you know how to make these crystals?"

"Oh, no. They're way beyond me. My daughter, though. She grew all kinds of crystals when she was at school. Why, if I remember correctly, she even grew some pezzi . . . piezo . . . ah . . . pezeyletric crystals for a science project once."

Eyes beaming brightly, Dr. Gribbleflotz took a deep breath. He carefully placed the lighter on the table in front of him. Releasing his breath, he looked Tasha in the eyes. "What . . . are . . . pezeyletric crystals?"

"They're crystals just like the one in the lighter. If you do something to them they throw out an electric spark."

"Can you obtain a 'cheat sheet' to make these pezeyletric crystals, Frau Kubiak?"

"Oh, yes. My daughter, Amy. She made a wonderful display for her science project. It had pictures and even a working model that would spark."

"How long would it take to get a cheat sheet?"

"Oh, I don't have to get a cheat sheet. My Amy had all the details on her science project. With pictures and everything." Tasha looked up at Dr. Gribbleflotz, her eyes brimming with pride. "She got an 'A' for it and a certificate as well."

"Frau Kubiak. What does your daughter's 'science project' have to do with these pezeyletric crystals?"

Confused, Tasha looked at him. Surely it was obvious? "My daughter did a science project on pezeyletric crystals. All I have to do is dig it out of the back shed. I kept all her school projects you know." Tasha smiled to herself. She knew she had Dr. Gribbleflotz hooked. "I'll let you borrow my daughter's science project if you will start making us baking powder. Only as a loan, though. I want it back. Do we have a deal?" Tasha held out her right hand.

With one final look at the cigarette lighter, Dr. Gribbleflotz carefully reached over and dropped it lightly into Tasha's waiting hand. "Only if I can follow the directions. If I cannot make any of these pezeyletric crystals, then there is no deal."

Tasha thought about it. If her daughter could make pezeyletric crystals using household items, then surely he could. "It's a deal." Tasha stood and collected her coat and handbag. A sudden thought sent her hand into her coat pocket. Pulling out an envelope, she waved it before passing it over to Dr. Gribbleflotz. "There's a bank draft in there for your share of the profits so far. Oh, and by the way, could you increase production of the baking soda? Please? More and more people in Grantville want to buy our baking soda."

"Sal Aer Fixus!"

"What?"

"Sal Aer Fixus. Not baking soda. Sal Aer Fixus. Baking soda is not a proper product for a great alchemist. I do not make baking soda. I make Sal Aer Fixus. Gribbleflotz Sal Aer Fixus. Remember that, Frau Kubiak." With that final utterance Dr. Gribbleflotz exploded to his feet and stomped off.

Tasha shook her head in amused disgust and watched

the figure of Dr. Gribbleflotz disappear down the street. *It's a wonder he can stand upright with an ego that size.* Tasha turned to leave and was confronted by a waitress holding a tray. There was only a single piece of paper on it. Flicking her eyes to the face of the waitress, Tasha smiled. The good doctor had stiffed her with the bill for lunch. With a rueful grin, Tasha reached in her purse and dropped some money onto the tray. She waved off any change and left. Mission almost accomplished. Now, where did she put that science project?

Sunday, the fellowship hall, after Mass

Patrolling the fellowship hall with the large teapot, Erin Zaleski came across the widow, Mary Anna Abruzzo. "Mrs. Abruzzo, would you like me to top up your cup?"

Mrs. Mary Anna Abruzzo took another sip of her tea and grimaced as she looked up at Erin. "No thank you, Erin. I have my own special tea." With a sour look at the contents of her cup, she took another small sip.

"Is there anything wrong with your tea, Mrs. Abruzzo?" Erin gave Mrs. Abruzzo a worried look. She was sitting at a table near a radiator in the fellowship hall and she had fair screwed up her face when she took that last sip.

"No, Erin. There's nothing wrong with the tea. If you like willow bark tea, that is."

"If you don't like it, why are you drinking it?"

"It's my arthritis, Dear. It helps relieve the pain."

"Isn't aspirin supposed to be good for arthritis

Mrs. Abruzzo? Surely aspirin would be better than that willow bark tea?"

"Young lady, it's quite clear you aren't familiar with the price of things these days. Do you realize what aspirin costs these days? Twenty dollars a tablet, if you can get them. That's the black-market rate, mind. If the doctors will prescribe them you can get them cheaper, but not much cheaper. And me living on a pittance and dependent on the charity of my children."

Erin, a little lost for words, backed away, keeping an eye on Mrs. Abruzzo, who grimaced over another sip of her tea.

Sunday lunch, Belle's place

"Hey guys, what do you think of the new baking powder?" Belle Drahuta looked around at the rest of the Kubiak Country Industries directors. "Three cheers for Tasha. Hey, Tasha. How did you get the geek to make baking powder?"

Tasha Kubiak blushed. "I lent him some of Amy's old school science projects. He seemed fascinated by my cigarette lighter and wanted to make some of those funny electric crystals. I threw in a couple of simple electricity experiments, as well. You know. The lemon battery, and bubbling off hydrogen and oxygen. I was wondering if we could get one of those machines that generate electricity. You know what I mean, the ones where someone stands on a wooden stool and puts a hand on the top shiny dome while someone turns a handle, and their hair goes all funny."

Tracy Kubiak shook her head. "You mean a Van

de Graaff generator. I don't like our chances. It's not the sort of thing anybody around here would buy. The schools are probably the only places with them, and I doubt they're going to sell them for any price."

"Maybe some of the guys can make one. Tracy, you've still got a lot of your up-time stock haven't you?" asked Mary Rose Onofrio.

Tracy sneaked a quick look around. "Well, yes, but don't talk too loud. I don't want the wrong people suspecting what I might have stashed away for a rainy day."

Erin looked around the table. "Speaking of things stashed away... how is everybody for aspirin? I was chatting with Mrs. Abruzzo after mass. Did you know aspirin is going for twenty dollars a tablet?" Erin targeted her question at Belle's sister-in-law, Katie Jackson, a pharmacy clerk at Nobili's Pharmacy.

"I had heard that there was a black market in aspirin. The boss has been saying he should look into making his own pills. But, he just hasn't found the time," Katie replied.

There was a communal "Oh" and "arhhh" as an idea simultaneously dawned around the room. The Kubiak Country ladies looked at each other, then turned to stare at Tasha Kubiak.

"*No.* Absolutely *no.* No way. I am not going back and begging the geek to make aspirin. It's somebody else's turn. Tracy. He doesn't scare you. Why don't you go and ask him?"

Tracy gave a little shiver. "I had Ted riding shotgun last time."

"Well, there you go. Take Ted with you again. Believe me, you're going to need all the support you can get. I bet he's elbows deep in that electricity stuff. He really hates spending time away from his precious experiments."

Tracy looked at her family. She wasn't actually related by blood to any of the ladies, but they were more family than anybody but her brother, Terry, had ever been. "Okay, if it's what everyone wants?" Everyone nodded. "Then Katie, could you ask your boss about a cheat sheet for aspirin? We'll have to arrange some kind of deal so he gets a royalty payment. Probably something similar to what we have with Christie Penzey for the baking soda and baking powder. Meanwhile, I'd like everyone else to hunt around at home to see what they have on experiments in electricity. Any old children's science books or home laboratory sets. I'd like to go visit Dr. Phil with something to trade."

Jena, Dr. Gribbleflotz's study

"Now, when I pump away at the foot pedal, the two discs spin. When they spin they collect a static charge. Those bottles, the Leyden Jars, store the charge, and eventually, we have . . ." *Crack.* A spark leapt across the two terminals set above the Wimshurst generator.

Phillip's eyes lit up when he saw the spark. His new Lightning Crystals, even the biggest he had been able to grow, had only cast a spark barely a finger's breadth. This new machine the American was demonstrating had sent a spark more than a foot through the air.

Ted Kubiak carefully discharged the Wimshurst generator and the Leyden Jars before removing the jars. "And, if we could have a willing volunteer to stand on this stool, and touch this wand to the globe. Tracy, would you care to volunteer?"

"Ted, aren't you forgetting something?" Tracy asked.

"But this is important, dear." Ted tried to placate his wife. "I'm sure Dr. Gribbleflotz will be really impressed by the hair-raising experiment."

With a sigh sufficiently loud so that her husband could be in no doubt she was less than impressed, Tracy removed her coat and jewelry, took the wand in her right hand, and stepped onto the stool before shaking out her shoulder-length hair. "Well, what are we waiting for? Let's get this show on the road."

With Tracy in place, Ted started his foot pumping at the modified spinning wheel assembly that provided rotational force to the Wimshurst generator. After a few moments, Tracy's hair started to stand out. After a couple of minutes all of her hair was standing on end.

Fascinated, Phillip reached out towards her hair. "*No!*" Tracy screamed. But too late. Phillip leapt backward shaking his hand. Quickly, Ted discharged the generator and his wife before going to check on Dr. Gribbleflotz.

"Are you all right, Doctor? I should have warned you. That was a big charge you took there. You should never try to touch the generator or anybody being charged by it."

Phillip looked from his stinging hand to the American and his woman. The spark that had flown as he reached to touch the woman's hair had bitten him, but there appeared to be no real injury. Waving off the American's attentions, he approached the "Wimshurst generator."

"This is for me?" he asked. "Why?" Phillip was getting used to the way these Americans operated.

They wouldn't have come bearing gifts unless they wanted something.

"We would like you to make some of these." Tracy passed over a sheet of paper and a small glass bottle.

Sparing a glance from his new lightning generator, Phillip spent a moment reading the paper. Even at a quick glance he realized he had already made this . . . he did a quick re-reading of the title of the sheet . . . ASPIRIN. Except he'd called his willow bark extract pills Sal Vin Betula, and they'd been a proper cooling blue, not white like the pills in the bottle. He knew how much effort went into making Sal Vin Betula. He would have to spend time away from his latest line of research. And a very promising line of research it was. Electricity was simply fascinating. That Lightning Generator. In his mind's eye, he could already see people coming to his private salon to see it demonstrated. And there were the other electricity experiments. People in Jena had heard about the Americans' electricity. His salon would be the first place those people would be able to see it. Phillip looked back to his still-stinging hand. And feel it. Better to discourage these Americans before they got too enthusiastic. "The price will be ten dollars per dose."

The American woman smiled. Smiled. She should have been outraged. Ten of those American dollars for a pill that cost less than a few pfennigs to make, and she was smiling.

"When can you start making them, Dr. Gribbleflotz? I don't think we should try for more than five thousand a week, to start with. At least until we can properly judge the demand."

Phillip was horrified. Thousands a week. The time

away from his precious experiments. He would need to buy more cauldrons, more alembics, more retorts, and he would have to find and train more peasant children to do the work. And he would have to shop for the materials. Phillip sank into his chair and watched the American man and woman leave his study. Idly, he reattached the Leyden Jars to his new lightning generator and started pumping the foot pedal. He sat in contemplation, absently watching the sparks of lightning leap through the air between the terminals.

Phillip didn't hear the knock on his study door, or the sound of it opening. It was the stifled cry of amazement from Frau Mittelhausen that brought him out of his thoughts. Looking up he saw the look of wonder on his housekeeper's face. "Frau Mittelhausen? Frau Mittelhausen? Is there a problem?"

"What? No. No problem, Herr Dr. Gribbleflotz. The Americans said that you would require me to make some purchases." Frau Mittelhausen looked back at the still-sparking lightning generator. "What is this wondrous machine? How does it produce lightning from thin air?"

"A better question might have been 'what do the Americans expect in exchange for this wondrous lightning generator?'" Phillip picked up the small glass bottle. Inside it were a few white tablets. Up-time aspirin, the woman had said. Phillip shook his head and moved to his desk to start doing some calculations. It took only moments to write a list of what he would need. He handed it to her. "Frau Mittelhausen, I need you to go out and purchase these items. Also, I will need more workers. Can you handle more apprentices?"

She glanced at the list and nodded. "I will need to employ an assistant. Do you wish for me to find the additional workers? I'm sure your current group of laborants have family and friends who would be interested in employment in your new manufactory."

"Frau Mittelhausen, I am *not* a manufacturer. I am an *alchemist*. Just because I train street refuse to make the products the Americans want does not make me a *manufacturer*. Do you understand me, Frau Mittelhausen?"

"Yes, Herr Doctor." Frau Mittelhausen gazed longingly at the lightning generator. Gently, she reached out a hand towards it.

"*No!* Do not touch it."

Frau Mittelhausen leapt backward, her hands wrapping themselves around her body, the sheet of requirements crushed in her hand. She looked at Dr. Gribbleflotz, shock showing on her face. Dr. Gribbleflotz had never used that tone before.

"The machine bites if you are not careful, Frau Mittelhausen." He waved his hand so she could see the red mark on his fingers. "I have already been bitten. Nobody is to touch the lightning generator. Please ensure that the rest of the staff know. Meanwhile . . ." He ran a hand over the books the Americans had delivered with the lightning generator. "I need to do a little reading to understand what is happening."

"I will get onto the purchases and recruitment of new workers immediately, Herr Doctor." Her eyes alternating between Dr. Gribbleflotz and the wondrous lightning machine, Frau Mittelhausen backed out of the study. She closed the door after one last look at the wondrous lightning generator.

Chapter 8

Dr. Phil Takes the Piss out of Grantville

November 1631, Grantville

Tracy sat at the kitchen table of her home and idly played with some small pale blue pills.

"What's that you've got there?" Ted asked as he walked over to the table.

"It's a test sample of Dr. Phil's version of aspirin."

Ted picked up one of the pills. "Why're they blue?" he asked as he examined it.

"He insisted that they had to be blue, because blue is a calming and cooling color."

Ted raised a brow suggestively.

Tracy smiled in response. "Yeah, I know. It's a load of crock, and the color is going to make it hard to get Americans to buy them."

"Nah, if they want their aspirin, they'll buy them. Anyway, I just need to collect my bike and I'll be off."

"Off?" Tracy asked.

"Yeah, Jonathan Fortney's got to deliver one of

the APCs up north, and he's agreed to take me and a load of urine as far as Jena."

It was Tracy's turn to raise a brow this time. "He's allowed to do that?"

Ted shrugged. "He seems to think so."

Tracy shook her head slowly. "What time do you think you'll be home?"

Ted shrugged. "Late afternoon probably. I want to check about that canvas you ordered. What are your plans for the day?"

"After breakfast Belle's coming round to collect Justin and Terrie, then I'll drop by Nobili's Pharmacy and see what Tino thinks about Dr. Phil's blue aspirin . . ."

"He'll agree with me," Ted said.

Tracy glared at Ted. "And then I'll finish off the last of the order for tents for the Refugee Commission."

From the road a truck horn sounded.

Ted hurried to the window and looked out. "That's my ride," he said as he kissed Tracy goodbye. "See you this afternoon. And in the meantime, stay out of trouble."

Tracy swatted Ted on the buttocks. "I won't have time to get into trouble."

She handed Ted his coat and followed him to the door, where she stood watching as he loaded his bike and cycled down to the waiting modified coal truck. She waved until the truck was out of sight, then turned and returned to the kitchen. She had to get things ready for when Belle arrived to pick up Justin and Terrie.

Jonathan Fortney was a tall and lanky twenty-one-year-old West Virginian male. Like a lot of West Virginian males, he'd been a bit of a shade tree mechanic back up-time, but unlike most of his contemporaries, he'd worked mostly on diesels. That was the influence of his father, who'd had a lifelong love affair with diesel engines. His experience with diesel engines had proved a godsend when it came to finding employment after the ROF.

Back up-time he'd been training to be a collision repair specialist, but post ROF there wasn't enough demand, and certainly the Army wasn't employing any collision repair specialists, but they did need diesel mechanics. So he became a mechanic with the Mechanical Support Division.

Today he was taking an APC—actually a 1986 Mack RD688S tandem rear axle coal truck with steel plate welded onto it in strategic areas to provide protection from down-time muskets while the back was enclosed with quarter-inch plate—back to its parent unit. The armor added a lot of weight, but not enough to be a problem for a vehicle designed to haul up to twenty tons, so, naturally, he'd asked around for anyone needing to move a bit of cargo north. Ted Kubiak had made the best offer—a full cargo as far as Jena.

Jonathan pulled up outside the entrance to Ted's place and sounded the horn. While he waited for Ted to arrive he gazed at the house. If he remembered correctly the property had belonged to a coal company executive who'd sold up when the coal mine on Dent's run was mothballed, and it looked it. He had to wonder how the Kubiak's had been able to afford such a flash new house. He shrugged. It was none of his business, but it was an impressive house, nestled as it was into the hillside like that.

He saw Ted cycling down the drive and called out to him when he got to the road. "Tie your bike to the rack at the front."

A short time later the door opened and Ted Kubiak hauled himself up and in. "Morning, Jonathan. Do you know where to go?" he asked as he laid a scabbarded rifle on the seat and dropped a saddlebag at his feet.

Jonathan nodded. "Though I can't imagine why you'd want to ship urine to Jena," he said as he got the truck moving.

"Dr. Gribbleflotz uses it to make spirits of hartshorn."

Jonathan turned to look at Ted. "What's that?"

"Ammonia. He needs it to make baking soda and baking powder."

"But urine's not all ammonia, is it?" Jonathan asked. "So why don't you turn it into ammonia here before shipping it to Jena? Surely that would reduce the volume you have to send."

"By at least ninety percent," Ted agreed. "Unfortunately, Dr. Gribbleflotz doesn't have anybody trained to do that, yet."

"Ah, so you plan to do it eventually?"

Ted nodded. "We'd be silly not to."

They picked up the full barrels of urine from a warehouse close to the Freedom Arches and headed for Jena, arriving there just over an hour later. They could have made the trip a lot quicker, but speeds in excess of thirty miles per hour consumed considerably more fuel and, more importantly, increased wear and tear on the truck tires, the supply of which was extremely limited.

While the barrels of urine were being unloaded Jonathan wandered around the facility. To his surprise he found himself on his own in what was obviously a private laboratory—the fume cupboard and racks of laboratory apparatus gave that away—looking at the containers of chemicals arranged along a wall, "Hey, cooool!" he said when he spotted a jar of iodine. He checked out the rest of the rack, occasionally touching a marked jar in fond memory of the experiments he'd done with the home chemistry set his father had assembled for him.

It was only when he saw Dr. Gribbleflotz's reflection in the fume cupboard's sash window that he realized he probably shouldn't be here. He turned quickly. "I'm dreadfully sorry, Herr Dr. Gribbleflotz. I know I shouldn't be in here without your permission, but I noticed the jars of chemicals and was curious to see what you have." He smiled. "You can do a lot of cool experiments with what you have."

"How did you know that I understand English? Did Herr Kubiak tell you?"

Jonathan did a quick double take. Firstly, he realized he'd spoken to Dr. Gribbleflotz in English, which given the quality of his German didn't come as a surprise. But the second question raised the possibility that Dr. Gribbleflotz had been hoping to keep his knowledge of English from the Kubiaks. "No, Mr. Kubiak didn't tell me. Does he know you understand English?"

"I was hoping that he and his wife were in ignorance of my English skills," Phillip said.

"They might still be," Jonathan said.

"Then why did you address me in English?"

Jonathan dropped his head momentarily in shame, then looked up and gave Phillip a rueful smile. "My German isn't very good."

"Herr Kubiak and his wife speak acceptable German," Phillip pointed out.

"Yeah, but they get to practice it more often."

Jonathan shrugged. "Most of the guys in my department are Americans, and the few down-timers are all trying to learn English, so I don't get to say much more than hello and goodbye in German."

"I understand." Phillip smiled at Jonathan. "So, you like my laboratory?" Phillip asked.

"What's not to like?" Jonathan asked as he waved an all-encompassing hand around the laboratory, "especially when you've got iodine and ammonia."

Phillip asked. "Don't you mean spirits of hartshorn?"

"Yeah, probably," Jonathan said with a smile. "Where did you learn? You know, to speak English?"

"I spent a number of years in England," Phillip said as he wandered over to the rack of chemicals and lifted up the jar of iodine. "So, what can you do with this and spirits of hartshorn."

"It makes a cool contact explosive," Jonathan said.

Phillip hastily put the iodine back. "There is nothing *cool* about explosives," he said.

"Oh, it's not a real explosive," Jonathan protested. "Mr. Morrison wouldn't have been allowed to do such a cool demonstration with it in class if it was dangerous. It's more sound than substance, rather like a kid's cap gun, except that when it goes off there's a big cloud of purple vapor."

"So, describe this *cool* demonstration!"

"Well, Mr. Morrison had one of those stands," he pointed to a chemical apparatus ring stand, "with half a dozen of those round beaker supports arranged along its length. He placed filter papers on each of the beaker rings and put a little bit of wet triiodide onto each filter paper. Then he taped a feather to a pole and waited for the triiodide to dry. Then he touched one of the piles of triiodide with the feather." Jonathan had grown more and more excited as he described the demonstration. "They all seemed to go off at once and there was a big purple cloud."

"Do you know how to make this triiodide?" Phillip asked.

Jonathan combed his fingers through his hair as he procrastinated. "Not really," he finally admitted. "But I know where to find instructions."

"When you find them, please drop by," Phillip said, "meanwhile, why don't I show you around my laboratory?"

"Sure," Jonathan said.

Phillip laid a hand on the sash window of his fume cupboard. "This is my fume cupboard, in German I call it my abzugschrank, it uses..."

Grantville

Tracy walked into Nobili's Pharmacy and waved to Tino, who was chatting at the till with Katie Jackson. "Could I have a word?" she asked.

"Sure, come on out back," Tino said.

Tracy followed Tino into the back. "I've got Dr. Gribbleflotz's test run of aspirin, except he calls it Sal Vin Betula."

"That's not a problem," Tino said as he craned his neck trying to look into Tracy's bag.

"And he insists on dying them blue," Tracy said as she hauled a large jar out of her bag. "Is that going to be a problem?" she asked as she held up the jar of Dr. Gribbleflotz's Sal Vin Betula.

Tino opened the jar and picked out a pill so he could examine it. "That shouldn't be a problem." Suddenly Tino sniggered.

"What's the problem?" Tracy asked.

Tino popped the pill back in with the rest and closed the lid. "I was just thinking that we could advertise them as Dr. Gribbleflotz's little blue pills of happiness."

She stared blankly at Tino. "I'm sorry, but I think I'm missing something here."

Tino grinned. "They're almost the same color as Viagra."

Tracy stared at the pills. She vaguely remembered seeing advertisements on TV, but couldn't remember what the pills had looked like. "I'll have to take your word for that. Is it going to be a problem?"

Tino shook his head. "We identify different pills and tablets by their size, shape, and color, and although the color is close, the shape is completely different. Now these," he said as he tapped the jar, "are going to cost ten dollars a pill?"

Tracy nodded. "It's steep, but that's the price Dr. Gribbleflotz insisted on charging, and it is half the current black-market price."

"I know," Tino said. "But such a high price will just encourage others to get in on the act." He frowned. "The problem there is, they won't be able to get fresh supplies of suitable willow bark until next spring. But once the spring growth arrives, everyone will be jumping on the bandwagon, and if your pet alchemist wants to keep selling his aspirin, he's going to have to drop his price to remain competitive." He shook the jar carefully. "How many are in here?" he asked.

"A thousand," Tracy said.

Tino whistled. "I hope you don't expect me to pay for it all right now."

"No, you can take them on consignment."

Tino nodded. "Thanks. Have you thought about packaging for across the counter sales?"

Tracy had to shake her head. "No. I thought the pharmacies would just fill glass bottles with the pills."

"At ten dollars a pill?" Tino asked archly. He shook his head. "That's not going to happen. At that price people are going to be pushing it to buy more than ten at a time, and that'd cost a fortune in glass bottles."

Tracy wanted to kick herself. Of course glass bottles were going to be expensive. "What do you suggest?"

"You could try a casein-plastic pill box." Tino smiled. "You could even dye the plastic the same color as the pills."

"Plastic? How are we going to make that?"

"You've never made casein plastic?" Tino shook his head ruefully. "Give me a couple of minutes and I'll write down some instructions."

"What's it going to cost?" Tracy asked, thinking of the royalty they were paying Tino for the cheat sheet to make aspirin.

"This one's on me," Tino said with a beaming smile.

Jena

"Hey, Jonathan, where are you? The truck's unloaded and cleaned," Ted's call from the courtyard was easily heard in Dr. Gribbleflotz's private laboratory.

"I'd better be going," Jonathan said. He held out his hand to Phillip. "Should I call at any particular time when I have the cheat sheet for the triiodide?"

Phillip shook Jonathan's hand. "No, you can call any time. I'm usually in my laboratory or checking up on the laborants."

"Lab rats?" Jonathan asked, unsure if he'd heard correctly.

"No." Phillip smiled. "Laborants. It's a name for laboratory assistants, although lab rat fits some of the current crop of workers better."

"Jonathan!" Ted called out again.

"I'd better be going."

Phillip nodded. "And please, don't tell anyone that I understand English."

Jonathan drew a finger across his lips. "My lips are sealed," he declared. Then with a friendly wave to Dr. Gribbleflotz he hurried off.

"Where have you been?" Ted demanded when he got back to the truck.

"Oh, you know, just having a look around," Jonathan said.

"Just as long as you didn't do anything to upset Dr. Gribbleflotz," Ted said. "I've got my bike and things, so you can go now."

Jonathan grinned. "You're eager to get rid of me."

"Yeah, well Dr. Gribbleflotz is the sensitive type, and I don't want you upsetting him."

"He seemed okay showing me around his laboratory," Jonathan said.

"What were you doing in his laboratory?" Ted demanded. "No, never mind that." He looked at Jonathan earnestly. "Dr. Gribbleflotz really showed you around his laboratory? How did you manage that with your German?"

"My German's not that bad," Jonathan protested. That got a wry grin from Ted, and Jonathan realized Ted didn't know that Dr. Gribbleflotz understood English. Dr. Gribbleflotz's secret was still safe and it was his duty to keep it that way. "As he showed me around he'd point to things and say their names in German, and I told him the English name in return."

"You and Dr. Gribbleflotz got on well together then?" Ted asked.

Jonathan nodded. "He's invited me to visit any time I'm in Jena." He smiled. "I'd better be off before someone starts asking where their APC is. See you around," he said before hurrying back to the APC.

Later that afternoon, Grantville

Tracy placed her mug of chicory coffee on a heat mat and collapsed on the window seat, exhausted from several hours bent over her industrial sewing machine putting the finishing touches to the latest order of tents. Toby, the household cat, ruler of all he surveyed, lifted his head and looked at her.

"You poor thing, did I disturb you?" she asked as she rubbed the base of his ear. Toby answered by purring and nudging his head into her hand. "It's so nice and peaceful without the kids, isn't it?" She read Toby's "mrrroww" as agreement. "Unfortunately," she continued, "their Auntie Belle will be bringing them back soon."

"Yip, yip, yip, yip."

"Ratter!" Tracy called as she shot to her feet, spilling a disgruntled Toby from her lap. She looked out the window and could see Ratter barking at something in the bush just above the garden. This was unusual behavior for the little Jack Russell, so she hurried over to the ammo drawer and grabbed a handful of cartridges for the .410 before unlocking the kitchen gun cabinet. With the single-barreled shotgun loaded but the action still broken, she relocked the gun cabinet before setting off to see what had Ratter so excited.

As she approached she heard the wailing of a baby, quickly muffled, coming from the bush Ratter was excited about. With Ratter holding the front, she worked her way around the back. Sneaking up on whoever Ratter had found.

She almost stepped on them. The woman—more of a girl, really—was huddled up, with the baby in her arms, staring at Ratter. The girl looked as if she hadn't had a meal, let alone a good one, in many days.

"Hello, can I help you?" Tracy bent down and offered her a hand up, but the girl drew back in terror.

"If you come with me I'll feed you and your baby," Tracy said as calmly as she could. But it can't have been calmly enough because the girl just sat there, on the ground, staring at her with her big blue eyes.

Tracy reached out and gently pulled the girl to her feet. "Come on, there's food in the house." She was talking to calm the girl down, and it seemed to be working. Or it would have if Ratter hadn't kept making a noise.

"Ratter, shut up." That didn't work too well, so Tracy called him to her. When he arrived she picked him up and introduced him to the girl. "This is Ratter," she said.

Fortunately, from his position of safety in Tracy's arms Ratter didn't feel he had to be so protective of his territory, and he tried to lick tears that were running down the girl's cheeks. That got a giggle from her. It wasn't much, but as far as Tracy was concerned, it was real progress.

Tracy led the girl into the house and sat her down on the bench seat by the table, then she put Ratter down beside the girl and stood back to take stock. She didn't have much basis to estimate the age of the girl, but she looked way too young to be the child's mother. But there was a war going on, and Tracy knew that it wasn't beyond the bounds of possibility. Unfortunately, those possibilities included rape, and she wasn't really sure she knew how to deal with the ramifications if that was how the baby had been conceived. There was, however, one thing she could do right now, and that was feed the pair.

Keeping an eye on her guests, Tracy put the shotgun away before microwaving a watery bowl of stew and slicing and buttering some bread. The girl, her eyes darting between Tracy and Ratter, was ever watchful. The moment Tracy put the food down the girl dived in.

Tracy stood back and watched. She was worried that the girl might be eating so fast that she'd be sick. Now, what to do? After a moment's thought Tracy went to the phone and called the police.

It was getting late. Soon the sun would be hidden behind the surrounding hills. Tracy was waiting at the door as the police vehicle pulled up. Officer Ralph Onofrio stepped out of the driver's seat while a young uniformed woman stepped out from the passenger seat. While Ralph approached Tracy, the young woman helped an older woman from the back seat before letting a large dog out of the back. It looked like a gray, long-haired German Shepherd, its long ears standing erect, and with a heavily furred neck and shoulders.

"Tracy, this is Police Recruit Erika Fleischer and her mother. We understand you need someone to help with a young German woman and baby?"

Before Tracy could answer, Ratter charged through the door, his fur puffed up, and a sound that could only be called a growl issued from his mouth. The woman's dog, actually little more than a puppy, advanced sniffing.

"Pluto, no!"

"Pluto?" Tracy turned to Ralph. "You called that monstrosity Pluto?"

"Hey, blame television," Ralph said with a shrug. "Erika was watching a Disney video when her boyfriend turned up with the little fellow."

"Little, that animal was never little. Just look at the size of those paws. He's going to be enormous when he grows up." Pausing for breath Tracy reached forward to restrain the excited Ratter. "Can you please keep your dog outside? We don't need a territorial squabble just now." With Pluto left waiting just outside the door, occasionally pushing his snout through the "cat flap." Tracy led Ralph and the two women to her guests.

Tracy watched Ted cycle up the drive. He disappeared for a couple of minutes into the garage before reappearing with the saddlebag slung over a shoulder and his rifle, still in its scabbard, in his hand. Behind her Erika joined them. She appeared upset.

"Her name is Richelle," Erika said. "She's almost fifteen, and the child is hers, a girl. The father was her stepfather; they executed him for incest. It's only because she was pregnant they didn't execute her. She managed to escape before her baby was born." She wiped the tears that were starting to fall from her eyes before continuing. "The bastard didn't touch her until she was fourteen." With the last comment Erika stormed out of the house, to be shortly seen crying into Pluto's neck.

Tracy looked to Ralph. "What did she mean?"

"The bastard bit? Under fourteen, and she's under the age of responsibility, and the guy gets all the blame. Over fourteen, she's a willing party, and also liable for the death penalty. What Erika probably means is, the bastard deliberately waited before he raped her, until his stepdaughter stood to suffer the death penalty for incest if she complained."

Ted was just coming through the door as Tracy barged past him out into the yard. He turned to follow her.

"Don't." Ralph laid a restraining hand on Ted's shoulder. "Let her go."

Ted looked to Ralph. "What the hell's going on?"

"She's experiencing what my wife calls a 'men are utter bastards' moment. Give her a bit of time to cool down. She's just had a rather brutal introduction to the local customs."

Erika was peering through the windows trying to see into the basement workshop when Tracy joined her.

"Do you want to come in for a better look?"

She nodded and followed Tracy as she unlocked the

door and turned on the lights. Erika found herself in a workroom. "What do you make in here?"

"Lately it's been tents, and more tents."

"Those marvelous canvas houses for the refugee center? You made those? Here?"

"Yes, I sent the last lot off earlier today. Until I get more canvas, I'm a lady of leisure."

"Lady of leisure? What is that?"

"It's an expression. It means that I won't be working, in here at least. With two young children, the household chores never end."

Erika's ears pricked at the mention of children. Her eyes casting around the workshop, she could see a cordoned-off area where children could play without getting underfoot. Before she could voice her thoughts there was a clatter and whine from the door. Looking at it, she could see a long gray snout poking through the little flap near the bottom of the door. Turning to Tracy, she started to speak, only for Tracy to interrupt.

"Oh, let him in. We'll never have any peace if you leave him out there."

"Is he going to be a police dog?" Tracy asked, while Erika let Pluto into the workshop.

Erika turned her head, leaving herself exposed to a lick on the other side of the face. She pushed Pluto's snout away. "Chief Frost has talked of it. He thinks Pluto would have much to offer the police department if he were properly trained."

Erika, closely followed by Pluto, walked round the workroom. Stopping, she gestured at the machines. "Do you have anybody to help you?"

"Ted, my husband, used to help, but now he's needed to help with the building program. Why do you ask?"

"I have a widowed sister, and a sister-in-law. Both have young children, so their work options are limited. Maybe they could work for you?"

The idea of having someone over the age of five to talk to appealed to Tracy. "I don't suppose they know anything about using a sewing machine?"

Erika smiled. "No, but that means they won't have any bad habits to unlearn."

A few days later, Jena

Phillip held the directions close to his eyes so he could focus on the words, then he laid the paper down and proceeded to the next step in making nitrogen triiodide.

"Do you need glasses?" Jonathan asked.

"Glasses?" Phillip asked.

"Spectacles. You know." Jonathan used the thumbs and forefingers of both hands to make spectacle frames and held them to his eyes. "They improve your eyesight."

Phillip snorted and waved to a drawer under one of the benches. "Over there. They are useless."

Jonathan sent Phillip a shocked look before he hurried over to the drawer in question and pulled out a pair of down-time spectacles. The moment he had them in his hands he held them in front of his eyes and smiled. "I'm not surprised you think these things are useless, but what about proper up-time ones. There's an optometrist in Grantville. He can test your eyes and make you a pair of glasses that'll give you twenty-twenty or better vision."

"Twenty-twenty vision?" Phillip asked, not having any idea what it meant.

"It means you can read a line of type of a certain size at twenty feet that a normal person can read at twenty feet." Jonathan waved towards the paper Phillip had been reading. "The way you were squinting at that, your vision might be something like twenty-thirty or twenty-forty."

"How much would this cost?" Phillip asked.

Jonathan laughed. "You're worried about being able to afford new glasses? You must be raking in a fortune with your little blue pills of happiness."

Phillip winced a little at the name they were using for his Sal Vin Betula in Grantville. More important though, was the idea of getting spectacles. "How long would it take?"

"Well, the actual examination shouldn't take more than an hour. Making up your prescription will depend on what they have in stock. You might be able to walk out of Grantville on the same day with a new pair of spectacles, or it could take a week or so if they have to grind some new lenses."

"I will instruct Frau Mittelhausen to make an appointment for me. Who should she make it with?" Phillip asked Jonathan.

"Dr. Shipley, but make sure you ask for the optometrist, otherwise you'll end up with an appointment to see his wife, the doctor of osteopathy."

"Doctor," Phillip said.

"Well, yes. Is that a problem?" Jonathan asked.

"No, no, of course not."

Jonathan didn't look convinced. "Dr. Gribbleflotz, I've heard a rumor that you don't actually hold a doctorate."

"Rumors, who believes rumors?" Phillip said with

a shaky voice. "There is also a rumor that Professor Rolfinck would like to have me run out of Jena."

"We can't have that," Jonathan said.

Phillip shook his head regretfully. "No one can stop him."

"Well, I'm sure Mr. and Mrs. Kubiak can do something."

"What can they do against the dean of medicine at the University of Jena?"

"Would it make a difference if you held a doctorate?" Jonathan asked.

"Of course it would, but unfortunately, I don't. Almost, but I don't."

"Does it matter where you get your doctorate from?" Jonathan asked.

"Of course it matters," Phillip said. "A medical degree from Padua is the top medical degree. Jena has a good reputation for law, and . . ."

"No," Jonathan said. "I meant does it matter where your doctorate comes from when it comes to dealing with Professor Rolfinck?"

Phillip shook his head. "But it doesn't matter, because I don't have a doctorate, and I am unlikely to ever earn one."

Jonathan nodded sympathetically. "There might be a way to get around your problem, Dr. Gribbleflotz."

"Oh!"

Jonathan nodded. "Back up-time there were institutions that awarded degrees, including doctorates, based on what they called relevant life experience. All we have to do is find a suitable down-time institution."

"No reputable university will award a degree based merely on *relevant life experience*," Phillip said.

"They might," Jonathan said, "if they were offered enough money."

Phillip snorted his disbelief. "Impossible."

"You wait," Jonathan said, waving a finger at Phillip. "I'll talk to Mr. and Mrs. Kubiak and see what they think."

"It would be easier for me to leave Jena," Phillip said.

"But you'd be leaving under a cloud, and it would damage your brand," Jonathan protested.

"My brand?" Phillip asked.

"Sure. Gribbleflotz Sal Vin Betula, Gribbleflotz Sal Aer Fixus, and Gribbleflotz's little blue pills of happiness." Jonathan waved his hands. "The Kubiaks can't afford to have you kicked out of Jena."

Phillip glanced around his laboratory. It was a nice space, built according to his specifications, with a few up-time improvements. He didn't want to leave it. "You're welcome to talk to the Kubiaks about a, what do you call the kind of institution that sells degrees?"

"A diploma mill," Jonathan said. "You won't regret this," he said.

Whooooomp!

Jonathan leapt over to the fume cupboard and hauled down the sash. He turned and smiled at Phillip. "I guess we forgot about something. Do you want to have another go?"

Phillip looked at the purple cloud being drawn up the fume cupboard chimney. He'd forgotten all about the experiment. "That is supposed to be safe?"

"Hey," Jonathan protested. "It's not like we're chasing mercury around the bench tops with our bare hands."

Phillip looked askance at Jonathan. "What is wrong with mercury?"

"It's considered too dangerous to use in the class-room," Jonathan explained. "Dad calls it health and safety gone mad, because when he was at school they used to be allowed to play with it. On the other hand," Jonathan admitted, "there are the stories about mad hatters."

"Pardon?" Phillip asked.

"Hat makers used to use mercury, and it drove them mad. Hence the phrase 'mad as a hatter,' like in *Alice in Wonderland*."

"Alice in Wonderland?" Phillip asked. He was getting very confused.

"It's the name of a famous up-time book. One of the characters was called the Mad Hatter."

Phillip shook his head. "Mercury is perfectly safe," he said as he wandered over to a bookshelf and pulled out a book. "My great-grandfather, the Great Paracelsus himself, wrote this book about using mercury to treat syphilis."

"But did it work?" Jonathan asked. "Back up-time we were regularly bombarded with reports on the dangers of mercury."

"Of course it worked!" Phillip said with some heat. "My great-grandfather wouldn't have promoted a treatment that didn't work."

Jonathan held his hands up defensively. "Keep your shirt on. I know they tried and failed to ban its use in dentistry." That reminded Jonathan of something else. "While you're getting your eyes tested, it might be an idea to have one of the dentists check out your teeth."

"There's nothing wrong with my teeth," Phillip insisted, even as he tried to look at them in the reflection of the fume cupboard's sash window.

"It's just a suggestion," Jonathan said. "Now, back to our experiment."

Phillip touched the feather to the nitrogen triiodide on the middle paper. He'd thought that he'd been ready for it, but the reaction happened so fast. Fortunately he'd had the sash of the fume cupboard almost closed, so only a little of the purple vapor entered his laboratory. A few minutes later the vapor dissipated to reveal the tower of samples of nitrogen triiodide on sheets of paper had all exploded. He looked at the result with interest. He'd only touched one sample, but all of them had detonated, and so quickly. It would definitely be an interesting addition to his public demonstrations.

He walked over to his chemicals rack and pulled out the jar of iodine. It was nearly half full, or for someone intending to use the contents in important public seminars, half empty. He turned to Jonathan. "Next time you're in Grantville, could you order some more iodine for me?"

"Are you planning on repeating the experiment?"

Phillip nodded. "I hold regular seminars and demonstrations of various things of interest. I'm sure my regulars would be interested in seeing your contact explosive."

Jonathan stopped off at the Kubiak residence on the way home. Actually, the house on Mahan Run was quite a way out of the way home, but he thought that the sooner something was done about finding a diploma mill for Dr. Gribbleflotz the better.

There was a new face it the house when he arrived.

A young girl grabbed a baby and bolted the moment she saw Jonathan at the door.

"Who was that?" he asked when Ted let him into the house.

"Richelle. She's a refugee we've decided to adopt."

Refugee, female, plus baby all went together to give Jonathan an idea why she might have bolted at the sight of a strange male. It made him sick to think of what might have happened to the girl, but there was little he could do about it, so he turned to the reason for his visit. "I stopped by to visit Dr. Gribbleflotz today and..."

"You did what?" Tracy demanded from the kitchen door.

"I had to pass through Jena today, so I stopped by to see Dr. Gribbleflotz," he explained.

"You sound awfully familiar with Dr. Gribbleflotz," Tracy said.

"Didn't your husband tell you that Dr. Gribbleflotz invited me to visit him?" Jonathan asked. With the high ground firmly in his possession he continued with the reason why he'd dropped by. "I'd heard a rumor that he didn't have a doctorate, and well, the long and short of it is, I asked him, and he admitted that he didn't."

"He admitted to you that he doesn't hold a doctorate?" Tracy demanded. "Why would he do that?"

Jonathan thought it better not to try and answer that question, so he hurried on. "And he said that the dean of medicine at the university was trying to get him run out of Jena."

"Run out of Jena? But we've invested a fortune in him," Tracy wailed.

"Yes, well, apparently all Dr. Gribbleflotz needs to stymie Professor Rolfinck is a duly awarded doctorate, and I was wondering if there mightn't be an institution somewhere in Europe willing to award him a doctorate based on *relevant life experience*."

Off to the side a loud choking sound came from Ted. "You mean a diploma mill?" he asked.

"Or something like that," Jonathan said. "I mean, Dr. Gribbleflotz is earning you a fortune with his little blue pills. So surely you owe him something." He shrugged. "What can it hurt to at least make inquiries?"

Next day

Jonathan stopped by his local pharmacy to ask about iodine for Dr. Gribbleflotz, and about using mercury to treat syphilis. He entered and walked up to the counter.

"Hi, Jonathan, how can we help you today?" Susan Little asked.

"I've just got a couple of questions. First, can I buy iodine?" Jonathan asked.

Susan shrugged and called out to her colleague. "Hey, Bibi, Jonathan here wants to know if he can buy some iodine."

"What do you want it for?" Bibi Blackwood called back.

"It's for Dr. Gribbleflotz. He needs it for some experiments."

The two pharmacy clerks exchanged looks. "I'll ask Lasso," Bibi said before disappearing out the back.

"How do you know Dr. Gribbleflotz?" Susan asked.

"Ted Kubiak introduced me to him."

Susan nodded knowingly. "You delivered a load of urine for them in one of the army's trucks?"

Jonathan nodded. It wasn't as if he had received any money for that trip. It had gone straight to the army.

"I understand you want to buy some iodine," Lasso Trelli said as he entered the shop front.

"I don't actually want to buy it, Mr. Trelli. It's for Dr. Gribbleflotz. I just want to know if you have any available for sale."

"You're in luck," Lasso said. "The Sanitation Commission deemed a reliable supply of iodine sufficiently important to make getting it a matter of urgency. You can extract iodine from seaweed ash, and we recently received our first shipment from the Baltic, so we have a reasonable supply on hand."

"Why's it so important?" Jonathan asked.

"It's important because it's so useful. Iodine can be used to sanitize drinking water, and as an antiseptic. Also, your body needs iodine. Iodine deficiency can cause goiter and intellectual disability, and that can be prevented by adding iodine to the salt supply." Lasso paused. "Is that all you needed?"

"Yes. No." Jonathan said.

Lasso grinned. "Make up your mind."

"It's about mercury. I was talking to Dr. Gribbleflotz, and I said how they didn't allow it in schools back up-time because of how dangerous it is, and he insisted that it was safe, and that his great-grandfather, the Great Paracelsus, used it to successfully treat syphilis." He looked earnestly at Lasso. "Can it treat syphilis? I always thought it was a dangerous poison."

Lasso nodded. "That's the modern view, but mercury has been used as a topical antiseptic for centuries. They only stopped distributing Mercurochrome in the U.S. in October of 1998, and even then, that was done purely on the fears of potential mercury poisoning rather than because of any evidence. It was still available in Europe in 2000."

"So Dr. Gribbleflotz was right, it is safe. Can it be used to treat syphilis?"

Lasso sort of shook his head. "It's mercury, so I'm not sure I'd go so far as to say it's totally safe, but it could be applied to genital ulcers as a topical antiseptic. But I doubt it would be much use beyond the primary stage."

"Thanks," Jonathan said. "I'll tell Mrs. Kubiak that Dr. Gribbleflotz wants some iodine and that you can provide it."

Lasso snorted. "Tracy'll probably place the order with Tino." He shook his head ruefully.

Jonathan dropped his head. He'd forgotten about Mrs. Kubiak's connection with Nobili's Pharmacy. "I'm sorry, Mr. Trelli."

"Don't worry about it, Jonathan. We're making enough off Dr. Gribbleflotz's little blue pills of happiness that missing the sale of a little iodine won't hurt us."

"Thanks for the information," Jonathan said as he left. He was going to have to apologize to Dr. Gribbleflotz for doubting him, he thought. Maybe he'd better check what the encyclopedias had to say about the medical uses of mercury.

December 1631, Amsterdam

Casper Barlaeus sat at the table with the other members of the recently created Athenaeum Illustre. He looked around at his colleagues. "Can anyone tell me why this meeting has been called?"

His question was met with blank faces and shaking heads.

There was a perfunctory knock on the heavy wooden door before it was pulled open. Casper shot to his feet, all ready to protest, but then he recognized who were standing at the door—Jacob Dircksz de Graeff and his nephew Andries Bicker. Together the two men controlled the city's politics. There was a third man, a colorless functionary of some sort. Judging by the quality of his clothing he was probably a lawyer, though why Jacob and Andries would turn up at a meeting of the faculty with a lawyer in tow he had no idea.

"Please be seated," Jacob said, as if he was in charge. "I have wondrous news for the Athenaeum Illustre." He gestured for the lawyer, who walked around the table placing some papers before each person.

Casper glanced down, meaning to just have a glance, but the title on the top page caught his eye and he started reading in earnest. He only looked up after reading the first couple of paragraphs. When he did he saw his colleagues were equally shocked. "How can the Athenaeum Illustre suddenly be turned into a university?" he demanded. "It's only just been formed as a school of higher learning."

Jacob turned to his nephew and raised a brow, inviting him to answer the question.

"It's not a done deed, yet," Andries said, "but with my uncle and me supporting the petition, I am sure the city council will sign off on it and present it to the Stadtholder for confirmation."

Casper could readily believe that these two men could force anything they wanted through the city council, but that didn't explain why they would do it. "That's not what I meant. I'm sure you and your uncle are capable of having the Athenaeum Illustre suddenly turned into the University of Amsterdam, but why would you do it?" he demanded.

Andries gestured for the lawyer to speak.

"My esteemed colleagues in Jena have a client who wishes to have a doctorate awarded to a man in their employ," Johannes Rutgers said.

Casper didn't like the implications of that, but he had a ready solution that wouldn't put the school in an invidious position. "Our charter doesn't allow us to award degrees, let alone doctorates," he said.

"Your current charter may not permit you to award degrees or doctorates," Johannes corrected, "but the new charter, which would be in force if the Athenaeum Illustre were to become the University of Amsterdam, would allow it."

"You can't just suddenly turn an advanced school into a university," Casper protested.

Jacob Dircksz de Graeff just smiled. Casper understood what that smile meant. When you were as rich and powerful as he was, you could do just about anything you wanted.

One of the men at the table stood up. "Even if we were a university able to award degrees you can't just walk in here and expect us to give a doctorate to someone to suit yourselves," Wilhelm Dorschner protested. "It violates every principle one has as a teacher. Why can't this client of your colleagues do the proper thing and pass the requisite exams?"

All eyes turned to the lawyer in response to what Casper could only consider a very good question.

"For reasons which I have not been made aware, there is a matter of urgency surrounding my esteemed colleagues' client's requirement to secure a doctorate from a reputable institution," Johannes said. "My esteemed colleagues hope that you will consider awarding their client a doctorate based on *relevant life experience*."

Casper snorted. "And what relevant life experience does this man—" he checked the name on one of the papers in front of him, "this Phillip Theophrastus Gribbleflotz—have that should cause us to award him a doctorate?" he asked.

"Phillip!" Wilhelm said in surprise before flicking through the pages to find the page Casper had read from.

"Do you know this man?" Casper asked, waving the page in question from his pile of papers in front of Wilhelm.

"If it's the same man I knew," Wilhelm said as he finally found the page in question, "then he was apprenticed to Professor Casseri in Padua for three years, and studied medical botany under Professor Alpini at the same time."

"He studied at Padua?" Casper asked. "Then why does he need us to award him a doctorate?"

"Professor Casseri died before he was ready to sit the exams," Wilhelm said, "and for reasons he never went into, he left Padua without a degree."

Casper did some rapid calculations. "Professor Casseri died nearly sixteen years ago. What's he been doing since then?" he asked.

"He served in the army of the counts of Nassau-Siegen as a physician and surgeon between 1618 and 1623," Johannes said.

"That's when I met him. We worked together most of that time," Wilhelm said.

"And that is when he saved the leg and life of my niece's son," Jacob added.

Casper glanced at Jacob. That bit of information went some way towards answering the unasked question of why Jacob and Andries were willing to see Mijnheer Gribbleflotz awarded a doctorate. He checked the paper in front of him. "It says here that he worked with Professor Bauhin for two years while he was in Basel." Casper looked at the lawyer. "Why didn't he take the exams in Basel? With three years study under Professor Casseri and four years as a military physician and surgeon, he should have had little trouble passing the exams."

"I'm sorry, but I can't answer that question," Johannes said. "However, is what is laid out before you a satisfactory collection of relevant life experiences?" he asked.

Casper was still hesitant. He trusted that Wilhelm had actually worked with the man, but why, he wondered, had Mijnheer Gribbleflotz, in all that time, not taken his medical exams at some institution? He glanced at Jacob and Andries, wondering what was in it for those two for them to be so willing to push for the Athenaeum Illustre to become a university.

"Of course the Collegium Chirurgicum will also become a part of the new University of Amsterdam," Jacob said into the silence that permeated the meeting room.

That, Casper was aware, was both a promise and a

threat. If the Athenaeum Illustre promised to award Phillip Theophrastus Gribbleflotz a doctorate, then the medical school would be the senior department in the new university, and if they didn't, the Collegium Chirurgicum would be given the option. He glared at Jacob. "We would like some time alone to discuss this," he said.

Jacob nodded affably. "Of course you do." But then he ruined it by adding, "but don't take too long," before leaving the meeting room with his nephew and the lawyer.

Early January 1632, Jena

"This is outrageous," Professor Rolfinck said as he slammed the newspaper down on the table.

Willi, Kunz, and Zacharias all jumped at the noise the paper made. "What's outrageous?" Willi asked.

"Haven't you read the newspaper?" Werner demanded.

Willi pursed his lips and shook his head.

"Well look at it now," Werner told him.

Willi unfolded the four-page newspaper and skimmed through it from front to back. "What am I looking for?" he asked after his first pass.

"It's on the front page," Werner said. "That charlatan!"

"What's Dr. Gribbleflotz done this time?" Zacharias asked.

Werner turned to glare at Zacharias. "You call him doctor as if he's entitled to the title," he accused.

"I've seen no evidence to the contrary," he answered.

"No evidence?" Werner demanded. "What about his claim that he can make gold?"

"Hearsay," Zacharias said. "No one I've spoken to can verify that he ever made such a claim."

"And his hemorrhoid ointment works," Willi said.

Werner turned to glare at Willi. Meanwhile Kunz had been scrutinizing the newspaper. "It says that the Grantville papers are calling him the Aspirin King." Kunz turned to Werner. "What's aspirin?"

"It's the name the Americans gave to a pill made from the powder left when you evaporate willow bark tea," Zacharias said.

Kunz continued reading. "Sales of Dr. Gribbleflotz's little blue pills of happiness are rumored to exceed ten thousand a week, at ten dollars each." He whistled and looked at his colleagues. "That's a fortune."

"For a pill that costs less than a dollar to make," Werner said. "That proves he's a swindler."

"There's a shortage of suitable willow bark, Werner," Zacharias said. "I believe Dr. Gribbleflotz has had to buy his supplies from as far afield as Dresden."

"That would certainly add to the price," Willi said.

"But not enough to justify charging ten dollars a pill," Werner said.

"A simple article in a newspaper doesn't explain your anger, Werner. Why're you so upset?" he asked. "What else has happened?"

"That happened," Werner said, pointing at the newspaper. He looked up at Zacharias. "This morning I had a visit from Johann Selfisch, of the respected Rudolstadt law firm of Hardegg, Selfisch, and Krapp. He informed me that if I did not immediately cease and desist making defamatory comments about his client, he would be forced to bring an action against me."

"I don't see the connection," Willi said.

"Don't be silly, Willi," Kunz said. "It's obvious that with his income from the sale of Gribbleflotz Sal Vin Betula he can afford the best legal representation."

"And that's another thing," Werner muttered. "The names he gives his products; Sal Aer Fixus, Vin Sal Aer Fixus, and now Sal Vin Betula. The man has no sense of what is right and wrong."

"Well," Zacharias said, "you'll just have to be careful what you say about Dr. Gribbleflotz in the future."

Werner shook his head. "The threat of legal action is the sign of a worried and desperate man. As soon as I get responses to my letters to Padua and Basel I'll have the proof I need that he has no right to call himself a doctor and I'll be able to run him out of Jena no matter how many lawyers he employs."

Phillip stood in front of the mirror and frowned. He turned to the left, then to the right. "No," he sighed, "it doesn't work." He turned to the young laborant as he struggled out of the jacket. "I need the green shirt, Hans."

Hans Saltzman dashed over to the open wardrobe and carefully removed the lime green linen shirt and hurried back to Phillip, who'd been distracted by a sight out the window.

While he changed his shirt Phillip watched the men unloading the barge from Grantville. Another load of urine for the American's silly cooking powder, he thought. Still, it did pay for his fine clothes. He glanced at his image in the mirror. "That's better," he declared. The lime green of the shirt perfectly set off the puce lining of his dark blue, almost black, jacket. He turned to the waiting Hans. "Off you go. I'll catch up with you in the laboratory."

With his personal laborant gone, Phillip returned to the window. Nine-tenths of every barrel was little more than water, and it made no sense to pay to transport water when there was plenty of perfectly adequate water in the river. That money could be better spent elsewhere, such as on some new trousers to complement the new boots he'd ordered. The problem, Phillip reminded himself, was that there was no one he trusted to turn urine into spirits of hartshorn without his supervision. He was going to have to pick out someone from his best laborants and train them especially. The question was who?

With the question of who to train bringing a frown to his face, Phillip left his room and headed for the laboratory.

Chapter 9

Dr. Phil's Portrait

January 1632, Amsterdam

Dr. Nicolaes Tulp was just leaving the dissection theater when Casper Barlaeus fell into step beside him.

"The dissection is going well," Casper said.

Nicolaes shot Casper a speculative glance. "Spit it out, Casper. What is it you really want to talk about?"

"I hear the Guild commissioned a new group portrait to celebrate your appointment as the new praelector..."

Nicolaes snorted. "I was appointed *Praelector Anatomiae* nearly four years ago, and it is only now the Guild of Surgeons is getting round to commissioning a portrait, and they insist I pay for it." He studied Casper. "But you already know that, don't you, Casper?"

Casper nodded. "They're given the commission to that new man, van Rijn." He drew a folded paper from under his doublet. "These people are willing to share the cost of the painting."

Nicolaes snatched the paper out of Casper's hands

and opened it. "Jacob Dircksz de Graeff and his nephew, Andries Bicker." He released a short laugh. "Why am I not surprised that they want to be included? Wait a moment." He looked up. "Phillip Theophrastus Gribbleflotz? Isn't that the same man you want to award a doctorate?"

Casper nodded. "It is only fitting that the first person to be awarded a doctorate by the University of Amsterdam be included in the painting."

"Aren't you getting ahead of yourself?" Nicolaes asked. "The charter hasn't been granted yet."

"*Yet,*" Casper said with emphasis. "Besides, paintings as large as van Rijn intends to paint take time. The Athenaeum Illustre should be a full university and able to award doctorates before he finishes his masterpiece."

"Masterpiece?" Nicolaes asked. "It's just another group portrait for the guild hall."

Casper smiled. "According to the information I have received, this painting will make van Rijn so famous he'll still be remembered as a master painter three hundred and seventy years into the future."

"You've been in contact with the people from the future?" Nicolaes demanded. "Do you have..."

Casper held up his hands. "I haven't personally had dealings with the people from the future, but I have spoken to someone who has."

"Oh." Nicolaes tried to hold back his disappointment.

"But," Casper said, "awarding a doctorate to Mijnheer Gribbleflotz should help open doors."

"Almost you convince me to go along with this fraud," Nicolaes said, "but not even for direct access to the medical profession in the city from the future can I condone awarding a degree to someone who is not worthy of it."

Casper nodded in an understanding and sympathetic way. "Of course, Nicolaes, and of course no one is expecting you to condone awarding a degree to someone who is not worthy."

Nicolaes snorted with laughter. "I've had Bicker on my back to support doing so since the idea was first mooted."

"Oh, I agree, Bicker is carrying on like an elephant in a glass store, but I have reason to believe Mijnheer Gribbleflotz is worthy. Did you know he was apprenticed to Professor Casseri and helped him perform a number of dissections?" Casper didn't wait for a reaction to that little piece of information before continuing. "I also understand he helped Professor Bauhin, in Basel, dissect a pregnant woman's body."

"What? Dissect a pregnant woman's body?" Nicolaes shook his head in disbelief. "How is that possible?"

Casper shrugged. "I have no idea how he did it, but I am reliably informed that he did do it."

"What do you call reliable?" Nicolaes asked, still not prepared to believe what he was hearing.

"One of our lecturers, Dr. Wilhelm Dorschner, has worked with Mijnheer Gribbleflotz, and he has seen the man's personal journal account of the dissection."

"I know Wilhelm. He's a good surgeon." Nicolaes nodded.

"He worked with Mijnheer Gribbleflotz in the service of von Mansfeld for over four years."

"That doesn't prove anything. There were plenty of incompetent butchers serving as military surgeons."

"But was he incompetent?" Casper asked. "He's the

man who saved Major Jan Bicker's leg." He paused for effect before continuing. "The major, then only a captain, suffered a compound fracture of the femur."

Nicolaes whistled. "How's that possible?" he asked. "That kind of injury is usually fatal. Yet I've seen Jan just this week, walking around the city with Catharina." He shook his head in negation. "It can't have been a fracture. Maybe he just broke it."

"Don't take my word for it, Casper. Talk to Major Bicker."

Major Bicker's house, Amsterdam

Jan Bicker stood up to greet Nicolaes as he was led into the morning room. "Dr. Tulp. How can I help you?" he asked.

Nicolaes waved away the attentions of the maid and pulled an A4 ink-jet printout of a photograph of Phillip Gribbleflotz from the satchel the maid had been trying to take away. "Do you know this man?" he asked.

"That's Dr. Gribbleflotz," Catharina said. "That's a very good painting. Where did you get it from?" she asked. "Look at the colors he's wearing. I wonder where he got them."

"You know this man?" Nicolaes asked.

"Of course," Catharina said. "He operated on Jan. He saved my Jan's life," she said growing teary eyed. Suddenly she smiled. "Is he in town?"

"I'm afraid not." Nicolaes tried to think of how to broach the subject of Jan's leg. After a silence that was growing uncomfortably long, he blurted out the question that had been bothering him. "I've heard he treated you for a compound fracture of the femur."

Jan smiled. "That's right. The other surgeons wanted to amputate, but Dr. Gribbleflotz said he knew a way of possibly saving my leg if I was willing to take a risk."

"Did he tell you how big a risk you were taking?" Nicolaes demanded. "A compound fracture of the femur is usually fatal, even after amputation." A gasp from Catharina had Nicolaes cursing his loose tongue. He smiled reassuringly at Catharina. "But it seems Jan was one of the lucky ones."

Catharina turned to Jan. "And we rewarded him by giving him that cursed lump of crystal."

"Cursed crystal?" Nicolaes asked.

Catharina pointed an accusing finger at her husband. "He stole it from a Jew, who cursed him for robbing him. We had nothing but bad luck for years, until we gave it to Dr. Gribbleflotz as a token of *thanks* for saving Jan." She looked from Jan to Nicolaes before returning to look at her husband. "He saved your life, and that's how we thanked him," she muttered bitterly.

"We didn't have much left to give him, Catharina, and he took it gratefully," Jan said.

"Because he didn't know it was cursed," Catharina said.

As a man married recently for the second time, Nicolaes knew better than to get involved in a marital spat; however, this one he felt he could settle amicably. He coughed loudly enough to attract Jan and Catharina's attention. "I think that you broke the curse when you freely gave the crystal to Dr. Gribbleflotz."

"How can you say that?" Catharina demanded.

Nicolaes held up the picture of Phillip again.

"Because this is the image of the man who wishes to be included in the group portrait the Guild of Surgeons has commissioned to celebrate my appointment as the *Praelector Anatomiae.*"

"And that sort of thing doesn't come cheap," Jan said, a look of relief on his face.

Catharina looked at the picture of Phillip again. "Surely a man wearing such colors has to be lucky," she said.

"So, Dr. Tulp. You didn't say how I could help you," Jan said.

"You have helped me," Nicolaes said. "I just wanted to confirm the pictures I've been provided are of the right man." He smiled. "It wouldn't do for the artist to paint the wrong person, would it?" That elicited a smile from Jan and Catharina. "Thank you for your time," Nicolas said.

"Will we be able to see the finished painting?" Catharina asked.

Nicolaes shook his head slowly. "I'm afraid not, Mevrouw Bicker. It will be hung in the Guild hall. Now, I'm sorry, but I must take my leave."

Nicolaes was escorted to the door by Jan and Catharina, and he couldn't help but notice that Jan walked with no sign of a limp. He really needed to ask Wilhelm if he knew how Gribbleflotz had done it.

Casper Barlaeus' office

Nicolaes pushed his way into Casper's office after a perfunctory knock. "Okay," he announced. "I will support your awarding a doctorate to Mijnheer Gribbleflotz."

"Good, good, and am I to take it that you also have no objection to him appearing in the portrait Mijnheer van Rijn will be painting?"

Nicolaes waved his hand at Casper. "You've won. There's no need to rub it in. I'll support the awarding of a doctorate to Mijnheer Gribbleflotz if the Stadtholder approves the university."

Van Rijn's studio

Casper stood in van Rijn's studio and couldn't help but stare at the size of the portrait the artist was working on. "Are you sure your canvas is big enough, Rembrandt?" he asked.

"It has to be this big to contain the self-importance of all the subjects," Rembrandt said.

Casper grinned. "Dr. Gribbleflotz will not be able to sit for his portrait."

The charcoal in Rembrandt's hand snapped. "How am I to paint a man when I don't know what he looks like?" he demanded.

Casper pulled a folder of A4 papers from his satchel and handed it over to the artist. "I was given these."

Rembrandt snatched the folder of color photographs from Casper. "Such colors, and so realistic." He looked up at Casper. "How is it done?" he demanded.

Casper had to shrug his shoulders. "If you want to learn, you'll have to visit the city from the future, but please, not until after you finish the painting."

Rembrandt sighed and returned to his canvas, comparing the half-dozen color photographs of Phillip Gribbleflotz with his canvas. "I think I will put him here," he said, making a lightning sketch of Phillip. "I do hope you won't mind if I use the colors he has chosen for his clothes. It makes such a change from the normal black."

"You're the artist," Casper said.

"Of course I am, and whose face would you like me to use on the cadaver?" Rembrandt asked.

Several inappropriate options flashed through Casper's mind, but good sense prevailed. "Phillip of Spain?" he suggested.

Rembrandt stood back to look at his canvas. "Yes, I can do that."

Grantville

Phillip stood in front of the mirror in his room and admired the way the lime green shirt played off the barely visible puce lining of his dark blue jacket with the yellow lace collar. He slowly turned around, taking in the full magnificence of his outfit, properly set off by the tasteful orange-colored Western boots. A gentle tug at his sleeves ensured that a bit of the lime green was visible below the cuffs of the jacket. Yes, perfect. With a smile on his face Phillip gave his lucky crystal a rub before he left his hotel room and went for a walk around Grantville.

Chapter 10

Dr. Phil's Aeolian Transformers

March 1632, Jena

It had been a hard day of almost wasted discussions with the scholars at the university. John Grover and Ken Butcher, accompanied by Derrick Mason, a young radio operator on loan from the army, had been trying to identify the materials and skills available down-time for the manufacture of earphones for crystal radios. They had hoped that it would be an easy matter to find people capable of making the wire-wound headsets at a sufficiently low price that affordable crystal radios could be made, allowing anybody to listen in to the broadcasts of the Voice of America. As things stood, there were about ten thousand up-time radios that could receive the signal. However, they were expensive. What was needed was a crystal radio set that anybody could make or buy extremely cheaply. That way, the Voice of America radio broadcasts would be able to reach everybody, not just those who could afford an up-time radio and a power supply.

Father Gus, who had been pressed into service as an interpreter, sat with the Americans while they continued to discuss the problems surrounding cheap earphones with a couple of members of the Jena faculty. Listening in, interpreting as needed, Father Gus considered the problems. They needed to wind thin copper wire around "magnetic" iron to somehow convert their "electric signals" into sound. The concept sounded extremely interesting, if such a thing was really possible.

That had been part of the problem. The Americans had come into Jena with a certain reputation for outlandish ideas and inventions. People, however disbelieving, had been prepared to listen. However, sound from the air? If it hadn't been for the *two-way radios* they had brought with them, nobody would have believed them. Even with the two-way radios as proof, many were still unconvinced that they could be made.

"Hello, Dear. Have you been having fun?" asked John Grover's wife, Leota.

Father Gus had to smile. John's wife, Leota, Ken's wife, Sarah, and Ken's sister-in-law, Esther Sloan, presented quite a sight with all their bundles and baskets. They were settling down and displaying their booty from a lightning raid on the unsuspecting shops of Jena.

"You'll never guess what I managed to get," Esther said. She pointed to a heavily laden basket. "It's almost impossible to get in Grantville. But here in Jena, I managed to pick up a whole ten pounds of Gribbleflotz Vin Sal Aer Fixus, and the price was less than in Grantville."

"That's marvelous, Esther. Can I buy some off you?" asked her sister, Sarah.

"There's still some left in the shop. Most of this lot is destined for the school cafeteria. We've been forced to feed the students sourdough bread, but with the Gribbleflotz Vin Sal Aer Fixus, we can do biscuits again. The students have almost been up in arms having to go without biscuits."

A rustle of paper drew all eyes to Leota and the flyer she was spreading out on the table. "What's that, Leota?" Esther struggled to read the upside-down flyer.

Leota looked up at Esther, then placed the flyer down where her husband could read it. "When you mentioned the name Gribbleflotz, I suddenly remembered this. It's a flyer advertising seminars on the 'Philosophy of the Essence of Lightning,' which are being given in the private salon of a Dr. Gribbleflotz. Apparently, the man gives demonstrations of 'The Wondrous Lightning Generator,' 'The Amazing Lightning Crystals,' 'Storing the Essence of Lightning,' and 'Continuous Lightning.' It sounds a lot like the kind of things the early scientists used to do. John, maybe you can drop by and see what the man has. It could be interesting."

Father Gus had been translating as best he could for Dr. Werner Rolfinck and Dr. Willi Hofacker of the University of Jena. When he mentioned Dr. Gribbleflotz though, both men started to go red. Frau Grover had barely finished speaking when Dr. Rolfinck exploded. Father Gus struggled to keep up as the invective flowed from the good doctor.

"Dr. Rolfinck says that this Dr. Gribbleflotz is little better than a charlatan. These philosophical seminars are little more than cheap demonstrations of lesser technology with an unscholarly commentary pretending to explain what is being shown."

There was a pause while Father Gus listened to a quick discussion between Dr. Rolfinck and Dr. Hofacker. "Apparently, this Dr. Gribbleflotz has no true credentials. He has failed miserably in the university courses on iatrochemistry. The man claims to be related to the Great Paracelsus, father of modern medicine. But the doctors doubt it. He is totally lacking in scholarly skills. He was little better than a self-employed laborant until he started making cooking powders for the American women. That was about his level, they claim. Though, I do wonder why the invective. I wonder what they have against the doctor?"

Sarah wrinkled her forehead. "Yes. If they don't think he has credentials, why are they even letting him call himself 'Doctor'? I thought that was a protected title?"

Father Gus smiled at Sarah before turning to talk to the doctors. Moments later he had an answer. "They say they dare not challenge him on his doctorate. Apparently, he is doing quite well with his little 'blue balls of happiness,' his Gribbleflotz Sal Vin Betula. With the money from that he has retained the services of Herr Hardegg of Hardegg, Selfisch, and Krapp, a Rudolstadt legal firm with a certain reputation. The good doctors are not rich men. They cannot afford to defend an action of slander."

Dr. Rolfinck had been trying to calm down while Father Gus translated for the Americans. But when Father Gus mentioned Sal Vin Betula, he again exploded. Father Gus tried to calm Dr. Rolfinck.

After a moment, Father Gus explained. "The dean is a little upset at the unscholarly name Dr. Gribbleflotz has given his little blue pills."

Later that same day, Jena, outside
Herr Dr. Gribbleflotz's Private Salon

"Well. That was a complete screw up. What did you have to go and laugh at his 'Wondrous Lightning Generator' for anyway, Derrick?" John Grover asked.

Derrick Mason smiled apologetically "It wasn't the generator I was laughing at, Mr. Grover. Whoever made it used a couple of old 78s for the rotating discs. I was just laughing at their choice of titles."

"Well, it was pretty unfortunate timing. He'd just demonstrated his Amazing Lightning Crystal. It was a piezoelectric crystal. I'm not sure what type, but apparently he grew it himself. I was at the point of asking him about making some more for us when you cracked up." John looked at Derrick. "He was not impressed when you started laughing." John turned to Father Gus. "Father, what do you think?"

"Herr Grover, I am very much afraid the good doctor took deep offense. I cannot be sure, but the way he immediately called upon his housekeeper to have us shown out...I think he may have felt your man was laughing at his lightning generator." Father Gus gave Derrick a penetrating look. "Also, I believe Herr Dr. Gribbleflotz's English may be a little better than he lets on. I noticed he paid attention when Herr Mason commented on how all of his experiments were really simple. I think he was ready to take offense."

Father Gus turned to John Grover and Ken Butcher. "I do hope you do not need the good doctor's services. I do not think Herr Dr. Gribbleflotz will forgive easily."

❖   ❖   ❖

"John, how did your visit to the electricity man go?"

John sighed. "A bit of a mixed bag, Leota. Dr. Gribbleflotz has an interesting range of electrical toys, and his amazing lightning crystal is a piezoelectric crystal. I was talking to him about sourcing some of the crystals when the comedian here," he waved at Derrick, "decided to laugh at the good doctor's lightning generator. From the manner in which we were invited to leave, I don't think the doctor is going to be too enthusiastic about helping us."

"What do you want the crystals for, John?" asked Esther.

It was Ken Butcher who responded. "If they're piezoelectric crystals and he can make more, well... depending on the price, we might have an answer to our headset problem. Rather than use wire coils, we can use fine piezoelectric crystals. John and I are trying to remember recipes for piezoelectric crystals, but we're coming up blank. If this Dr. Gribbleflotz can make them, then, based on the opinion of Doctors Rolfinck and Hofacker, I reckon we should be able to make them as well. I sure would like to know what he's making and where he heard about them, though."

Esther grinned. "Where is easy. He probably heard about them from one of the Kubiak Country people."

"The who?"

"The Kubiak Country people. Look, here." Esther passed over a bag of Gribbleflotz Vin Sal Aer Fixus and pointed to the printing on the package. "See. It says 'Made by HDG Enterprises (Jena), a branch of Kubiak's Country Industries (Grantville).' The address is up Mahan Run, which isn't surprising if the Kubiak clan is behind it. Anyway, if you talk to one of the

Kubiaks up on the Run, I'm sure you'll find someone who can help you."

Head Office, Grantville Canvas and Outdoor, Mahan Run, Grantville

John Grover turned to his wife. "Are you sure this is the right place?" He was sitting on his horse, outside the front gate of Ted and Tracy Kubiak's home.

Leota nodded. "Yes, dear, this is the right place. Careful how you cross the cattle guard now."

With a sour "teach your grandmother to suck eggs" look, John carefully guided his horse over the cattle guard and waited for Leota. They could hear the yipping of a dog while they rode up the drive to the house, so they tightened their reins and halted their horses until the source of the noise came into view. It was a small dog—a Jack Russell terrier. Before it could get under the horses' feet there was a loud whistle. The dog stopped in its tracks. Shortly afterwards, a man walked up, bent down and lifted the excited animal up to his chest.

"Hi, John, Leota. Can I help you?" Ted Kubiak waved a greeting while struggling to keep a firm hold on his dog.

"My wife and I are looking for the Head Office of Kubiak Country Industries. We were directed here. I was just wondering if we've come to the right place."

Ted smiled up at the mounted couple. "Yep. You've come to the right place. Tracy's working up in the house. If you'd like to tie your horses to the corral by the shed, I'll lead you to her."

Ted waited while John and Leota loosened the cinches and tied their mounts to the corral. When they finished tending to their horses he released Ratter, who immediately ran up to John and Leota. The dog sniffed around them for a moment, then turned and trotted off. When John and Leota joined him, Ted asked, "So, what's your poison? Gribbleflotz Vin Sal Aer Fixus, Sal Aer Fixus, or Sal Vin Betula?"

John stared at Ted, a grin appearing, "None of the above. I was wondering if you know anything about Dr. Gribbleflotz's Amazing Lightning Crystals, though. We were in Jena and Leota here picked up a flyer advertising seminars on the 'Philosophy of the Essence of Lightning.' So me, Ken Butcher and a couple of other guys went visiting. I was just watching him demonstrate his lightning crystal when Derrick Mason, one of the other guys, started laughing around the doctor's lightning generator. Before we knew what was happening we were out the door."

Ted stopped so suddenly that John and Leota bumped into each other as they attempted to avoid running into Ted. "You have had a run-in with Dr. Gribbleflotz?" Ted's voice was stilted.

John nodded. "Unfortunately. We were in Jena hoping to find out about affordable ways of making headphones for the new crystal radios. When I saw the flyer, I wondered if the lightning crystal might not be a piezoelectric crystal, because if it was, that might be a solution to our problem. Anyway, as I said. Derrick cut loose a belly laugh and we were all but thrown out before I could ask any questions."

About then they made their way into the study. Tracy was crouched over a computer, working. She kept working until Ted spoke. "Tracy, a couple of people to see you."

Tracy jumped. "Huh? What?" She turned away from the computer. "Oh. Hi, Leota, John. Did you want to speak to me?"

"Yes, Tracy. John was wondering if you know anything about a Dr. Gribbleflotz and his Amazing Lightning Crystal?" Leota asked.

Tracy looked at John. "What is it you want to know, John?"

"Well. We were in Jena when we heard about him and his Amazing Lightning Crystal. I was wondering what he was using. We need something like his piezoelectric crystal if we want to spread the radio service. Without a cheap piezoelectric crystal, we won't be able to make affordable radios for the masses."

"Why didn't you ask Dr. Gribbleflotz?" Tracy was a little confused.

"Err." John paused and turned to look to his wife for support.

"What John is trying to say is; they tried to speak to Dr. Gribbleflotz and screwed up. They were just about thrown out of his house. He's hoping you, Kubiak Country Industries, might know something about the crystals, and if you could get us some."

"Oh, Leota. John. I hope you didn't upset him." Tracy looked toward John. "John, just how did you 'screw up'?"

"Derrick Mason was looking over something the doctor called his lightning generator . . ."

"The Wimshurst generator," Tracy muttered, identifying the offending article.

"The what? Oh, yes, a Wimshurst generator. I remember using one years ago. Anyway, Derrick was looking at it when suddenly he started laughing. Dr. Gribbleflotz took offense and had us shown out." John held up his hand halting the obvious question, "Derrick says he was laughing at the titles on the records being used as the static generating discs."

Tracy looked over at Ted. "Do you have anything to say?"

Ted shrugged his shoulders, a guilty grin on his face. "Do you know which one he laughed at? There was 'That Old Black Magic' by Spike Jones and his City Slickers, and 'Stormy Weather' by Carmen Cavallaro. I'm quite proud of the Spike Jones one. Given how Spike liked to use expedient materials as instruments. Somewhere, we should have a recording where he used a selection of carefully tuned revolvers. And for a static generator, I thought 'Stormy Weather' was a good pick. But I wouldn't think Dr. Gribbleflotz would take offense at a harmless joke like that."

Leota sighed. "If only that was all. Apparently Derrick made a few innocent comments about how he had done things just like all of Dr. Gribbleflotz's demonstrations while he was at school. John and Ken took Father Gus with them to help translate. He thinks the guy understands more English than he lets on. Anyway, Dr. Gribbleflotz took offense, and that was that. Which reminds me, why do you call him Doctor? My understanding is that he doesn't have a doctorate."

Ted and Tracy grinned at each other. "Oh, he has a doctorate all right. Not from one of the best institutions, of course." Tracy gave her husband a harmless slap when he started to laugh and turned to give Leota a "what can you do with the man" look.

"But Dr. Rolfinck was absolutely sure that Dr. Gribbleflotz wasn't entitled to the title," John said.

A smile lit Ted's eyes. "If this Dr. Rolfinck is so sure Dr. Gribbleflotz is not entitled to be called Doctor, why doesn't he do something about it?"

"Because Dr. Gribbleflotz can apparently afford a good lawyer...Oh." Wide-eyed, John turned to stare at Ted and Tracy. "'Not one of the best institutions?' You don't mean a diploma mill? An honest-to-goodness Mail Order Diploma?"

Straight-faced, Tracy spoke, "Dr. Gribbleflotz is a prima facie Doctor of Medicine. I've seen the diploma. It's real sheepskin, with a fancy embossed wax seal."

"Wow." John shook his head and slumped into a nearby seat. "Are you sure? The scholars at Jena could contest the diploma. Will it stand up in court?"

"Our lawyers have the utmost confidence in the stature of the issuing institution."

John licked his dry lips. "I'll take your word for it. But that doesn't help me. What will help is getting some of the doctor's lightning crystals. Do you know what it is?"

Ted and Tracy exchanged a glance. Ted gave a slight nod of his head. Tracy turned back to John and Leota. "Rochelle salt."

"Oh," A light started to dawn for Leota. "Gribbleflotz Vin Sal Aer Fixus," she pronounced. Seeing the question in her husband's eyes, she elaborated. "Dr. Gribbleflotz is making baking powder. Baking soda and cream of tartar are needed for baking powder. You can also make Rochelle salts from the same ingredients."

John tried to suppress his excitement. "Is this right? Your Dr. Gribbleflotz is making Rochelle salts?"

"Gribbleflotz Amazing Lightning Crystals, please." Ted held up his hand to silence John. "Just a moment. I have something you should see." Ted turned to the door and called. "Richelle, could you bring in one of the GribbleZippos please?"

Ted grinned at John. "This you have to see."

A teenage schoolgirl with a baby in her arms walked into the study and passed a small object over to Ted. She passed curious eyes over the guests. Then, she gave a gentle wave before leaving. "That was Richelle, our adopted daughter," Ted said. "Anyway, John, have a look at this lighter."

John took the lighter in his hands. It was shaped like an oversized up-time Zippo. He opened it and looked at the mechanism. Instead of a flick wheel, there was a simple lever. John pushed the lever. There was a spark and the wick lit.

John looked from the lit lighter to Ted and Tracy, then back at the lighter. He gave it a closer examination. "A piezoelectric lighter? You're making piezoelectric lighters?" At Ted's nod, John smiled. "Do you have a supply of Rochelle..." Seeing Ted's reaction, John hastily changed what he was saying, "a supply of Gribbleflotz Amazing Lightning Crystal?"

Ted nodded. John let out a long sigh of relief. "I don't suppose you could sell me a pound or so?"

"Sure. Not all at once, though. But if you can afford to wait, I have a few ounces to spare, and I can ask Dr. Gribbleflotz to make some more. There'll be a price though."

"Hell, at the moment I'm prepared to pay just about anything. How much?"

"I wasn't thinking about money, John. Dr. Gribbleflotz

is doing quite well as it is. The few dollars for a few ounces of his Amazing Lightning Crystal is neither here nor there. What he will really want is something money can't buy."

Jena, an inn

Dr. Werner Rolfinck was quietly seething. Beside him, Doctors Conrad "Kunz" Herbers and Wilhelm "Willi" Hofacker were keeping their mouths shut and a careful eye on their boss, because there, in pride of place in one of the best inns in Jena, the man Werner insisted was a charlatan was describing his philosophies to an enthralled audience.

"This up-time 'chemic,'" Dr. Gribbleflotz was saying, "is fine for technicians, cooks, and industrial processes. It certainly allows unlettered peasants to tend my caldrons and alembics and produce their powders and potions, but it completely *ignores* the spiritual component of alchemy." Phillip looked over his attentive audience. "Did you know that the up-timers produced Sal Vin Betula pills which were *white*?" At his audience's collective shaking of heads, Phillip nodded. "Yes, it is true. White. For a pill that is supposed to reduce pain and reduce fever. When every competent alchemist knows it should be blue, because blue is a soothing and cooling color that reduces pain and fever. They are such children in the Great Art. As my Great-grandfather Paracelsus—whose namesake I am—said: it isn't enough to treat the body, one must treat the spirit. Which is why *my* amazing headache pills are superior to what the up-timers have, for my

Sal Vin Betula pills are pale blue. Yes, Dr. Gribble-flotz's Little Blue Pill is your friend."

Phillip paused for breath. He looked up, made eye contact with Doctors Rolfinck, Herbers, and Hofacker. He raised a hand in silent greeting before continuing his discourse.

"The nerve of the man. Did you see that? He waved to us as if we were his colleagues," muttered Werner. "We are going to have to do something about the man. His conceit is beyond words. We have to do something about him."

Willi shook his head. "Our hands are tied, Werner. The radio people passed on the news that Dr. Gribbleflotz holds a doctorate from an institution of some stature. It's best we ignore him."

While Werner drank to drown his sorrows, and Willi and Kunz drank to keep him company, on the other side of the common room Phillip continued to talk to his audience. He was getting into his stride talking about the topic dearest to him. Dr. Phillip Theophrastus Gribbleflotz.

"Of course there are some up-timers that have a clue. I have been pursuing references in their library's collection about pyramids, and crystal power. While much of it is obviously in conflict with well-established systems, some of their points are most amazing." Phillip removed his spectacles and drew a special up-time cleaning cloth from a pocket in his up-time style jacket. He exhaled onto the lenses and wiped them. After he slid the spectacles on, he smiled at his audience. "I am particularly interested in the combination of gems with the new metal, aluminum. My careful calculations, corroborated by a most interesting tome in the Grantville Public Library, suggests that a pyramid composed of aluminum members with the appropriate colors and cuts of gems at the strategic points, especially these new faceted gems Herr Roth is producing, could result in the invigoration of the Quinta Essentia of the human humors. I am *most* anxious to pursue it. But as always, funding is problematic. Perhaps the new Aeolian Crystals will assist in it."

Phillip looked over his audience again. He had them in the palm of his hand. Tonight's crowd would be happy to go home and spread the words of Dr. Phillip Theophrastus Gribbleflotz, the World's Greatest Alchemist.

"You have heard of the Gribbleflotz Aeolian Crystals I am supplying the up-time radio technicians?" It was a rhetorical question. Aeolian Crystals were too new for any of the audience to have heard of them yet. "They allow the conversion of the Essences of Lightning the technicians have captured in their singing wires to be converted into sensible sounds. The crystals themselves sing. The up-timers insist on referring to them as 'Rochelle salts,' but I can assure you that they have *no* parallel in Rochelle, or any other part of France. No, the singing Aeolian Crystals are a purely German product of German alchemy and up-time technology." Dr. Gribbleflotz paused dramatically. "We are calling the 'earphones' Gribbleflotz's Aeolian Transformers. They are *much* better than those simplistic mechanical earphones produced by the Jewelers' guild. Wire and bits of Iron! Ha! Cold Iron can never compete for the Spirits of Sound with Salts of Sound Itself!"

Chapter 11

Dr. Phil's Friends

May 1632, Grantville

The owners of Grantville's three pharmacies had gathered together to share out the latest shipment of Dr. Gribbleflotz's Sal Vin Betula, or as it was known colloquially, Dr. Gribbleflotz's Blue Pills of Happiness. Tino Nobili, by virtue of his connection with the Kubiaks and HDG Enterprises, was in charge of sharing out the pills.

Lasso Trelli trusted Tino not to take more than his fair share, so he let his mind wander a bit. His eyes wandered around Tino's office, and came to a shuddering stop when they fell on the old ceramic chemical jars Tino had lined up on a shelf. A light-bulb moment followed. "You know, guys," he said as he tried to suppress his excitement.

Tino and John Moss turned to Lasso. "What?" John asked.

"Yeah, what's got you so excited?" Tino asked.

"I just had a great idea for something we can sell," Lasso said.

"What?" Tino asked.

"Chemistry sets," Lasso said. He saw Tino and John's eyes light up. "Yeah, children's chemistry sets. Not the silly politically correct things they were making back up-time, but the proper ones, like the ones that got us interested in chemistry in the first place."

John grinned. "Did you make stink bombs?"

"Of course," Lasso said. "Didn't everyone?"

John and Tino nodded. "There'll be resistance from the mothers," Tino warned.

"So we offer them in junior, intermediate and senior levels," Lasso said, "with each level adding more chemicals and experiments."

"Anyway," John added, "it'll only be the American mothers that want to keep their babies in leading strings. The down-timers will see the fortunes Tom Stone and Dr. Gribbleflotz are making and decide they want their children to be just like them."

Lasso stared at John. "You know," he said before stumbling to a halt.

"I know what?" John asked.

"If we could get Dr. Gribbleflotz to lend his name to the chemistry sets..."

Tino whistled. "That'd be great. We could have a line of Dr. Gribbleflotz chemistry sets, suitable for different ages and levels of ability, why..."

"So how do we go about approaching him?" John asked.

"I could ask Tracy, I suppose," Tino said with an obvious lack of enthusiasm.

"Jonathan Fortney might be a better bet," Lasso said.

"What makes you say that?" Tino asked. "Tracy has a direct line to Dr. Gribbleflotz."

"So does Jonathan," Lasso said. He smiled conspiratorially at John and Tino. "Late last year he asked me about getting some iodine for Dr. Gribbleflotz. I told him I could get it, but that Tracy would probably buy it from you."

Tino nodded. "That's right. I sold Tracy a couple of pounds, though what he wants to do with it . . ."

Lasso snorted in disbelief. "Can't you guess?" he asked. Tino looked back at him blankly. "Spirits of hartshorn," he said, giving him a clue.

"Triiodide!" Tino's eyes lit up. "You think Dr. Gribbleflotz is making ammonia triiodide?"

"I know he is," Lasso said. "Jonathan told me that Dr. Gribbleflotz has included a simple demonstration of triiodide in his regular public seminars."

"So you think Jonathan might be able to persuade Dr. Gribbleflotz to lend his name to a line of chemistry sets?" Johan asked.

Lasso shrugged. "It won't hurt to ask."

"Before we ask him to talk to Dr. Gribbleflotz, it might be a good idea to find out what chemicals we can get, and what sorts of things can be done with them," John said.

A couple of weeks later, Grantville

Jonathan lined up the stone on the drive and kicked it. It shot away a satisfying distance. He should have known better than to volunteer to do anything. Of course, he wouldn't have felt half so disgruntled if he hadn't punctured halfway up Mahan Run and discovered he didn't have a tire lever. A few minutes later he turned up the drive to Ted and Tracy Kubiak's home. He wheeled his bicycle up to the house and leaned it against the wall.

"Hi, Jonathan. You got a problem?"

Jonathan looked up and saw Ted leaning against the deck's railing. "A puncture. I don't suppose you have a tire lever? I've got a repair kit, but I seem to have left the tire lever at home."

"There're a couple of forks I use in the kitchen," Ted said as he pushed himself off from the railing. He glanced back to Jonathan and waved for him to take the stairs onto the deck. "Truth be told, I was actually wondering what brings you out this way. We're a bit off your beaten track."

"Mr. Trelli and the other pharmacy owners have an idea they wanted to put to Dr. Gribbleflotz."

"That doesn't explain why you're here?" Ted said.

Jonathan grinned. "I'm here because, although I think it's a great idea, I'm pretty sure Dr. Gribbleflotz won't be interested," he said as he collected the promotional material Mr. Trelli had given him and started up the stairs.

Ted stood aside to let Jonathan past. "Interested in what?"

"In lending his name to a line of chemistry sets." Jonathan pulled out a roughed out sketch of a possible box cover and handed it to Ted. "Mr. Trelli and the other pharmacy owners want to launch a range of chemistry sets, and they'd like to use Dr. Gribbleflotz's name."

Ted held the paper up and looked at it. "A 'Dr.

Gribbleflotz Junior Chemist'?" He grinned at Jonathan. "What makes you think Dr. Gribbleflotz won't be interested?"

"It's not that I think he'd object," Jonathan hastened to say, "but I don't think he cares about anything other than his research." He shrugged. "If it was presented to him in the right way, and he didn't have to do anything, then I'm pretty sure he'd agree to let his name be used."

"What's in it for you?" Ted asked.

"For me?" Jonathan stared at Ted. He hadn't thought of asking for anything. "I'm just doing Mr. Trelli a favor."

"You'll never make a businessman," Ted said as he guided Jonathan into the house. "Tracy, Jonathan's here," he called out as he led Jonathan through the house. "What else is in the box?" he asked.

Jonathan readjusted his hold on the box. "Mr. Trelli and the other owners collected what equipment they could and made up some sample chemistry sets."

"Well," Ted said as he guided Jonathan into the lounge, "I'm sure Dr. Gribbleflotz will appreciate the extra chemicals."

Jonathan had time to see that Mrs. Kubiak was comforting a tearful Richelle before her adopted teenage daughter looked up, saw him, and bolted. "Was that because of me?" he asked, hurt that anyone would run away from him like that.

"Sort of," Tracy said. "Some boys at school are giving her a hard time."

"So I got tarred with the same brush," Jonathan muttered.

A heavy hand landed on his shoulder. "Don't take

it too much to heart, Jonathan." Ted turned to Tracy. "Tell me who they are and I'll sort them out."

"I'd rather it didn't come to that," Tracy said, "but they're pestering her while she waits for the bus to Mahan Run." She sighed heavily before turning to Jonathan. "What brings you here?"

Jonathan licked his lips. Now was probably not a good time to make his sales pitch. He glanced at Ted, who nodded. Taking that as an indication to go on, Jonathan laid the wooden box he'd been carrying on the floor and grabbed the various promotional sketches the pharmacy owners had put together and offered them to Tracy. "Mr. Trelli and the other pharmacy owners would like to start selling a range of children's chemistry sets."

Tracy shot a glance in the direction Richelle had bolted, sighed, and then turned back to Jonathan. "What's that got to do with us?" she asked as she accepted the papers.

"Look at the advertising Jonathan handed you, Tracy," Ted said. "They want to use Dr. Gribbleflotz's name on their chemistry sets."

Tracy looked at the various proposed box covers and other advertising she'd been handed for a while, then handed it back, shaking her head. "I can't see Dr. Phil being interested."

"Dr. Phil?" Jonathan asked.

Tracy blushed.

"It's a pet name for Dr. Gribbleflotz," Ted said. "We'd prefer that you don't use it, especially not around him."

"No problem," Jonathan said with a cheeky grin. "I don't fancy trying to explain Oprah to Dr. Gribbleflotz."

He turned back to Tracy. "I agree that he probably won't be interested, Mrs. Kubiak, but I don't think he'll mind if you were to approve the licensing agreement. It's not as if Mr. Trelli and the others expect him to actually make and market the chemistry sets."

Tracy nodded absently. Jonathan could see that most of her attention was still on the door Richelle had run through. He shot the door a quick glance, and thought he caught a glimpse of the girl before she drew her head back. He didn't like to think that she was being victimized by some kids at school and offered a possible solution to the problem. "My sister's attending some dance classes Miz Bitty is giving to her old students after school. I could ask Lynette to keep an eye on Richelle while she's waiting for the bus."

"Dance class?" Richelle appeared in the doorway. "I could dance?"

The life in Richelle's face was a revelation to Jonathan. She looked like a completely different girl. "It's ballet," he warned.

"Dancing," Richelle said with a distracted look on her face. "I loved to dance."

"Then that's settled," Tracy said. "I'll call Bitty and arrange for you to join her after-school classes."

Richelle ran across the room and hugged Tracy. She shot Jonathan a wary look before dashing out of the room.

Jonathan had been watching the girl all the time, and now, with her out of the room, his eyes drifted back to Ted and Tracy Kubiak, whom he discovered were both looking at him.

"Thank you," Tracy said.

It was a simple statement, but Jonathan knew

it came from the heart. "I didn't do anything," he protested. Still, seeing the tension leaving Tracy's body, he resolved to ask his sister to keep an eye on Richelle anyway.

"You did more than you can imagine," Ted said. "That's the most animated I've seen Richelle since we took her in."

A couple of days later, Jena

Phillip was busy writing up his latest experiment in his journal when Hans called from over by the window. "Herr Dr. Gribbleflotz, Herr Fortney has just arrived on his bicycle, and he's got a big box tied to the carrier."

Phillip thrust his dip pen into the holder and rushed over to the window, just managing to catch a glimpse of Jonathan before he passed through the door into the main office. He was carrying a large wooden box in his arms. Phillip turned to look at Hans, who'd turned to look at him. Both then looked over at the fume cupboard, which Hans had only recently cleaned after their last experiment. Their eyes then checked the work benches. Everything was tidy. Their eyes met again, and as one they started for the door. Hans, being the subordinate, paused long enough for Phillip to go first. Within minutes they were in the kitchen, which tended to double as the place where everyone congregated when they weren't working, or as in this case, when someone interesting turned up.

"Hello, Jonathan," Phillip said as he gently pushed his way through the laborants who were eagerly looking at the smaller boxes Jonathan was removing from the larger box. Phillip got close enough to identify the boxes. "Chemistry sets? I already have chemistry sets."

"Not like these, Dr. Gribbleflotz," Jonathan said as he laid some sheets of paper out on the kitchen table.

Intrigued, Phillip wiped clean the new spectacles Dr. Shipley, the Grantville optometrist, had made for him, before having a good look at the papers. They looked like the covers of some of the up-time chemistry sets the Kubiaks had given him a few months ago, except these were slightly different. "The Dr. Gribbleflotz Junior Alchemist Set?" he asked after looking at the first one.

Jonathan nodded. "The Grantville pharmacies want to sell a range of chemistry sets, and Frau Kubiak is agreeable to licensing the use of your name, if you're willing."

Phillip caught the "range of chemistry sets" and checked out the other papers. In addition to the junior set there were also intermediate and advanced versions. "Why do they want to use my name?" he asked.

Jonathan smiled. "Brand awareness. To most people in and around Grantville your name's synonymous with alchemy. Anyone who hasn't heard of your blue pills of happiness must have been asleep the last six months. And then there's the Gribbleflotz jingle."

Phillip winced at the mention of the jingle. He cringed every time he heard it. It was tacky, and it reeked of advertising. Still, according to Frau Mittelhausen, sales of all of their products had jumped since they started sponsoring some program on the radio. "What would I have to do if I agree to them using my name?"

"Nothing, Dr. Gribbleflotz. Although they might want you to record a few advertisements, sort of like you do for the *'and now a few words from our sponsor'* segment before each episode of 'Robin of the Committees of Correspondence.'"

Phillip realized he was nodding and hastily stopped. He didn't enjoy recording those messages, but Frau Mittelhausen insisted. No doubt she would insist on him making some sort of speech about the alchemy sets. He sighed. Women were so bossy and managing. "Very well," he said, "you may tell Frau Kubiak that I'm agreeable."

"That's great," Jonathan said. "Herr Trelli'll be pleased."

Phillip tried to fit the name to a face, but he couldn't imagine the Herr Trelli he knew having anything to do with selling chemistry sets. "Herr Trelli at the Vo-tech?" he asked, just to be sure.

"No, Herr Lasso Trelli of Trelli's GoodCare Pharmacy. He owns my local pharmacy, and he asked me if I thought you'd license them the use your name to sell chemistry sets." Jonathan sent Phillip a wry smile. "He's the guy I asked about iodine and the medical uses of mercury."

"Ah, yes, that's right." Phillip smiled at Jonathan. "You doubted that mercury could be used to treat the great pox because you understood that it was too dangerous. What did your Herr Trelli have to say about that?"

"He said that that right up until a year or so before the Ring of Fire you could buy a mercury-based paint-on antiseptic, and that topical use—that means applied to the surface of the skin—might be able to treat the ulcers you see in stage one syphilis."

"So my great-grandfather was right?" Phillip asked.

Jonathan glanced around at the interested faces of the laborants and sighed. "Yes, Dr. Gribbleflotz, your great-grandfather was right."

"Naturally," Phillip said, trying not to appear too smug. Of course he'd known that his great-grandfather, the great Paracelsus, would never have prescribed a treatment that damaged a patient's health, but it was nice to know up-time medicine agreed with the treatment. "Now, what should we do with these alchemy sets?"

"I think you should let your laborants try them out, Dr. Gribbleflotz, just to see if you think the instructions are adequate."

Phillip was aware of a sudden change in the room. He glanced along the surrounding laborants. A few of them had practiced begging faces on. Others were merely looking at the alchemy sets like starving children around a table of food. He picked out his three best laborants, Hans, his personal laborant, and Michael Siebenhorn and Kurt Stoltz, the two eldest and best educated of his laborants. "Hans, Kurt, and Michael, I want the three of you to each take one of the alchemy sets and supervise a small group of laborants as they try the experiments provided."

Phillip would have said more, but the laborants were making too much noise as they quickly formed themselves into three groups. He glanced at Jonathan, who was looking enviously at the laborants. "You can join them if you wish," he said.

"Thanks, Dr. Gribbleflotz," Jonathan said before joining the throng.

Monday night, Grantville

Tracy was on edge as she waited for Richelle to get home from dance class. Her adopted daughter had never been out alone this late before, and if Ivan hadn't offered to pick her up after dance class, she wouldn't have let her go. She leapt to her feet, disturbing Toby, who'd been sleeping peacefully on the window seat, and started pacing.

"Stop worrying," Ted said from the safety of the kitchen. "Richelle'll be okay."

Tracy stopped her pacing to shoot her husband a glare. "She's never been out this late, and you know how strangers scare her."

"She's attending ballet class," Ted said. "What could possibly go wrong?"

Tracy shuddered as she started to imagine what could go wrong, but her imaginings were interrupted by the sound of a pickup truck coming down Mahan Run. Moments later light from the vehicle's headlamps passed across the windows, and Tracy rushed out onto the deck.

Richelle climbed out of Ivan's pickup and with Lenya in her arms, danced across the drive and up the steps onto the deck. "It was wonderful, Mama Tracy." She stopped dancing long enough to kiss Tracy before dancing to the railing and calling down to Ivan. "Thank you for the ride, Herr Drahuta."

Tracy watched her adopted daughter dance into the house with her baby in her arms before walking down the steps to her husband's cousin, who was unloading Lenya's baby buggy from his truck. "Thanks for picking up Richelle and Lenya," she called.

"Hey, no trouble," Ivan said as he passed the collapsed baby buggy to Tracy. "I have to go past the school on the way home from the station." He shot a look in the direction Richelle had taken. "If that's what happens to a girl who attends one of Bitty's ballet classes, I'm glad our girl is only three."

"Did you talk to Bitty?" Tracy asked as she accepted the baby buggy.

Ivan shook his head. "No, but I wouldn't worry about Richelle. I had to tear her away from her new friends."

Tracy read the grin that accompanied Ivan's comment to indicate that he wasn't really serious. "Who was she with?"

"Lynette Fortney, Bitty's Melanie," Ivan paused for a moment before continuing, "and Cathy McNally."

Tracy sniggered. "You do realize Cathy took up ballet before she was five?"

"Noooo."

Tracy nodded. "Lolly told me that Cathy was so hyperactive that it was a choice of ballet, karate, or medication, and the local karate school didn't take students that young." She smiled at the anxious glances Ivan was sending across the road. "Has Caecilia stopped running around everywhere yet?" she asked.

Ivan shook his head. "Do you think we should enroll her in a ballet class?"

"Talk to Lolly," Tracy said. "Well, thanks again for looking after Richelle. We owe you."

Ivan shook his head. "Nah. Richelle's already got that covered." He shot Tracy a grin. "She's agreed to babysit the horde this weekend."

Tracy shook her head ruefully. "You're taking unfair advantage of the poor girl. There's no way picking

Richelle up on the way home from the fire station is worth taking on your mob for a weekend."

"But you will let her stay at our place all weekend?"

Tracy hesitated to answer. There were lots of good reasons why she should object, but...

"The boys like her," Ivan offered, "and you are just across the road."

That was true, but... Tracy was still hesitant.

"And there are plenty of guns in the house."

That was probably meant to reassure Tracy, but it failed. "She doesn't know how to shoot."

"What?" Ivan protested. "Why not? If you don't have something suitable, I'm sure I can dig something up."

"It's not that," Tracy said. She sighed. "Richelle's got issues..."

"Something to do with Lenya's father?"

Tracy nodded. "And now some boys at school are giving her a hard time over being an unwed teenage mother."

"You think she might pull a gun on them if she knew how to use one?" Ivan grinned. "It'd probably scare some manners into them."

"I'm not worried about her pulling the gun. I'm worried about her using it on them."

Ivan whistled. "That might be going a bit too far. What about running her through one of your ladies' self-defense courses?"

"I'll think about it," Tracy said, "but I'll need a couple of male training dummies; are you volunteering?"

"Jeez, Tracy, you could at least pretend that the guys aren't there to get beaten to a pulp." He shook his head. "Sorry, you're going to have to find some other poor sucker. Meanwhile, you should teach Richelle to shoot." He held up his hands. "She's too young to have a carry piece, but with so many guns in the house, she needs to know how to handle them safely."

Tracy sighed. "You're right. I'll get on to it."

"Right. See you same time tomorrow."

Tracy waited for Ivan to start down the drive before going back into the house, where the first person she saw was Ted.

"Richelle seems to have enjoyed her dance class," he said.

Tracy nodded. "She enjoyed it so much that she volunteered to look after Ivan and Belle's mob this weekend as payment for bringing her home."

Ted whistled and shook his head. "Still, it'll do her confidence a world of good to be given the responsibility."

Saturday morning, a couple of weeks later

Richelle noticed Jonathan Fortney the moment she stepped into the Middle School gymnasium. She couldn't really miss him, because he and another young man were sparring on some mats in the middle of the floor with most of the women and girls enrolled in the self-defense class standing around watching. "What's he doing here?" Richelle muttered. She winced at just how petulant she sounded. A glance to the woman beside her told her that Mama Tracy had heard, and was amused.

"Tommy Karickhoff is probably the highest ranked martial artist in Grantville. He used to be an instructor at a dojo in Fairmont, and he's helped me with the self-defense courses before," Tracy Kubiak said.

Richelle rolled her eyes. "I mean Herr Fortney."

Tracy's lips twitched. "I told Tommy I needed an extra warm body and he said he knew someone who might be suitable." She smiled innocently at Richelle. "It seems Jonathan was that someone."

Richelle turned her attention back to Jonathan and Herr Karickhoff just in time to see Jonathan lunge forward with a knife. What followed happened so quickly that Richelle wasn't sure what she'd seen. But it looked like Herr Karickhoff grabbed Jonathan's knife hand in both of his hands, ducked under the arm, and somehow stabbed Jonathan with the knife Jonathan was holding. It was only when both of them stood up and Jonathan handed the knife to Herr Karickhoff that she realized he hadn't been hurt. She turned to Mama Tracy. "Isn't that dangerous?" she asked.

Tracy shook her head and waved the combatants over. "Hi, Tommy, Jonathan. Richelle wants to know if the knife counter you were doing is dangerous."

Tommy tossed the knife he was carrying to Richelle, who had a panicky moment before she caught it and realized it wasn't a real knife.

"It takes a real effort to actually stick it into someone with that move," Tommy said.

Richelle handed back the rubber knife. "Will you be teaching us moves like you were doing, Herr Karickhoff?"

He shook his head. "The best thing to do when someone starts waving a knife around is be somewhere else."

Richelle's brow screwed up as she considered what she'd just heard.

"Tommy means you should run," Tracy said. "I'll cover what else you should do later in the program."

Richelle nodded her acceptance of Mama Tracy's dictate, but something still bothered her. "If your best advice is to run, why practice fighting someone with a knife?"

"Because sometimes running away isn't an option," Tracy said. "Enough of this. Are you two ready to get started?" she asked Tommy and Jonathan.

"Any time you are," Tommy said. Jonathan nodded in agreement.

Richelle gave the two men one last glance before hurrying off with Mama Tracy to join the other women assembled for the ladies' self-defense class.

Four hours later Richelle stumbled out of the gymnasium with Tracy for the lunch break. "He's horrible," she said.

"Who?" Tracy asked.

"Jonathan. He was always grabbing me."

Tracy grinned. "He's only supposed to be trying to grab you. It's not his fault you haven't been able to avoid his attempts."

Richelle glared at Tracy. "He hurt me." He hadn't really hurt her, but she hadn't liked being grabbed.

"And you hurt him back."

A smile flittered across Richelle's face as she remembered some of the things she'd done to Jonathan. There had been the kicking and punching, which hadn't been quite as satisfying as she would have liked because of the protective padding he was wearing. Although she had managed to drop him with one knee attack to the groin even with the protection he was wearing. Then there had been the grappling. She'd had him writhing on the floor with one particular finger hold.

"Don't get too cocky, Richelle. Jonathan could have countered any of your attacks."

Richelle snorted her disbelief.

A hand grabbed her shoulder and spun her round until she faced Tracy. "I mean it, Richelle. After lunch you can pad up and run through the same drills, but this time Jonathan will be allowed to use any counter he knows. It'll be a whole new ballgame."

"Bring it on!" Richelle said, using an Americanism Papa Ted often used.

That afternoon

Richelle was grabbed from behind. Immediately she grabbed for Jonathan's right hand. Her right hand clamped his against her body while she ran her knuckles across the tendons on the back of the hand. When it released its grip she grabbed a couple of fingers and pushed them back. Her hand clamping Jonathan's hand against her body formed a fulcrum against which she could apply pressure on Jonathan's fingers. She smiled at him, confident she had control of him.

Then something hit her in the midriff and she folded up. A moment later Jonathan wasn't just free, he had her in an unfamiliar hold. One arm was levering her bent right arm so that she wanted to bend forward, while his other hand was pushing back at her shoulder. He wasn't even really holding her, and he was still able to make her stand on tip-toes.

"Okay, you can let her go now, Jonathan," Tracy said.

"Only if you grab hold of her so she doesn't try and hurt me," Jonathan said.

Richelle glared at Jonathan. He'd guessed that she was just waiting for him to let her go before retaliating.

Tracy grabbed her hand and Jonathan released his hold and jumped back a safe distance. Richelle made a move to attack him, but Mama Tracy had a firm grip on her.

"I told you not to be so cocky," Tracy said.

"He hit me," Richelle protested as she took in the interested expressions on the women who'd gathered around to watch the demonstration. "That wasn't in the drill."

"What did you expect him to do when you just stood there like that?" Tracy asked. She turned to Jonathan. "Would you like to demonstrate how Richelle should have reacted?

"Richelle, I want you to play the aggressor and grab Jonathan like he's been grabbing you," Tracy said.

Richelle ran her eyes up and down Jonathan's nearly six foot frame, stopping when she met his eyes. He was smiling, and she just knew he was going to make her look foolish. "Do I have to?"

"The best way to learn is by experiencing the hold being applied to you," Jonathan said before turning his back on Richelle and just standing there, waiting for her to start.

Richelle glanced around the gymnasium. Everyone but Jonathan was watching her. She swallowed and stepped up behind Jonathan and swung her arms around him. The next thing she knew she was yelping in pain because of the tension on her fingers.

"Okay, you can let her go now," Tracy said.

Richelle settled her sore fingers safely under her arms and stared hard at Jonathan. He couldn't have seen the daggers she was shooting at him, because he just smiled at her.

"You were too tentative," Tracy said. "Now try again, but with a little more aggression."

"Do I have to?" Richelle asked.

"Could I have a go?" Melanie Matowski asked.

Melanie was Miz Bitty's youngest daughter, and she attended the same dance classes as Richelle. She was also one of a number of girls in the dance class that considered Jonathan Fortney *cute*. Richelle didn't agree. Kittens and puppies were cute, not men like Jonathan.

"Okay," Tracy said. "Are you ready, Jonathan?"

"Yes."

"Okay, Melanie, in your own time."

Richelle watched as Melanie swung her arms around Jonathan and hugged him. The thought that she seemed to be enjoying the contact flashed though her mind and she missed how Jonathan broke Melanie's hold and skipped to one side while maintaining the finger lock. Melanie tried to lash out at him, but Jonathan was able to manipulate his hold so Melanie was unable to strike him no matter how much she tried.

"Okay, you can stop now!" Tracy said.

"How are we supposed to do that?" Richelle said. She waved at Jonathan. "He's probably had years of training."

"*He* has a name," Tracy said pointedly, "And yes, Jonathan has had years of training." She turned to Jonathan. "Do you have your black belt yet?"

Jonathan shook his head. "Sensei has invited me to grade this year."

Tracy nodded before turning to the class. "Obviously

none of you have the training to control someone like Jonathan was controlling Melanie, but then, I don't expect you to." She smiled. "No, if you are ever attacked and you get a finger lock like Jonathan just demonstrated, what you should do is immediately apply maximum force to dislocate the fingers."

Richelle winced. Her fingers were sore enough as it was, she didn't want to even imagine what they would feel like if Jonathan had dislocated them. She saw Mama Tracy was still talking and tuned back into what she was saying.

"Your demonstrated ability to hurt your assailant may cause him to cut and run, but if he does stick around, not only will the dislocated fingers make it difficult for him to grab you, the damaged hand will be extremely sensitive to being struck. If you are ever in that situation, don't hesitate to attack that hand." Tracy glanced around the class. "Okay, girls, pair off and take turns trying the counter you've just seen. Tommy, Jonathan, and I will roam around helping."

Late June, Jena

Phillip was frowning at the letter he'd just received when he noticed Jonathan Fortney at the door of his study. Hastily he dropped the letter on the little occasional table beside his armchair. "Come on in and sit. Pull up a chair. How have you been?"

"Bad news?" Jonathan asked, gesturing to the letter Phillip had been reading as he limped over to one of the spare armchairs and collapsed into it.

Phillip glanced down at the letter he'd been reading

and shook his head. "Just an inquiry from an old student of mine."

"Anyone I might have heard of?"

"Johann Rudolf Glauber."

Jonathan's brows shot up. "The Johann Rudolf Glauber? The man who discovered Glauber's salts?"

Phillip nodded reluctantly.

"And discovered how to make hydrochloric acid by adding common salt to sulphuric acid, and nitric acid by adding saltpetre to sulphuric acid?"

Phillip shot to his feet. "Johann Glauber did not discover how to make acidum salis by the action of oil of vitriol on common salt, nor did he discover how to make aqua fortis from oil of vitriol and saltpetre."

"The encyclopedia I read seemed pretty sure, Dr. Gribbleflotz."

Phillip started pacing. "I discovered those methods for myself more than ten years ago." He stopped pacing to turn and glare at Jonathan. "Johann was my laborant for a year back then, and I taught him how to make acidum salis and aqua fortis using oil of vitriol."

"Oh!"

Phillip nodded. "Yes, oh! Like everyone else with access to Grantville's encyclopedias, I too searched them for my name . . ."

"And didn't find it," Jonathan chipped in.

Phillip nodded. "And didn't find it. But I did find my former student's name, and that he was laying claim to *my* discoveries."

"But not until 1648," Jonathan said. "Why would he wait so long before claiming the methods as his own?"

Phillip shrugged. "Who knows? For that matter, who cares? In your history I was forgotten while

Johann was remembered. Why? Because he was a self-promoter while I wasn't. But this time I will beat him. I've learned from my mistakes. This time I've grasped the idea of self-promotion. This time I shall be remembered as the man who discovered how to make acidum salis and aqua fortis using oil of vitriol. Not some self-taught technician."

"Didn't you say he was your student for a year?"

Phillip glared at Jonathan for picking up on that little detail. He might have held his gaze long enough to force Jonathan to drop his eyes, or maybe that should have been eye, if he hadn't suddenly noticed that Jonathan had a rather impressive black eye. "What happened to you?" he asked, gesturing towards the eye.

Jonathan brushed a finger lightly over the swelling that was trying to close his right eye. "I helped out at Frau Kubiak's latest ladies' self-defense course, and one of the girls accidently hit me in the eye."

Phillip studied the eye and winced in sympathy. "I have an ointment that might help. Let me get you some."

Jonathan held up a hand. "There's no need, Dr. Gribbleflotz. I'll be okay. I'm more interested in knowing why you wanted me to stop by?"

Phillip held up a single finger. "One moment," he said before hurrying over to his desk and extracting three files from a drawer. "Have a look at these while I get the ointment."

"What are they?" Jonathan asked as her accepted the folders.

"The laborants kept asking about the science behind the experiments in those sample alchemy sets you brought over, so Hans, Michael, and Kurt got together to prepare a booklet for each set that explains the science behind the experiments. We have them in three languages. I'm confident that the German and Latin versions are correct, but the manuscripts you have are the English translations, and while I can read and understand the language very well, things go wrong when I try to speak or write in English."

Jonathan flipped through the pages of one of the booklets, pausing to skim over what was written a couple of times. He looked up at Phillip. "But why do you want an English version? Hardly any of your laborants know more than a few words of English."

Phillip nodded. "That's true, but English is still a language of instruction in some technical subjects."

"Only because the teachers aren't sufficiently fluent in German or Latin yet."

"Of course, but it means people are learning English, and that means that there is a market for an English translation, and best of all, with the three versions in the same booklet, the booklets can double as a language-learning aid." Phillip gestured to the file. "You have a look at them. I won't be a moment." He left Jonathan reading one of the manuscripts and hurried off to the store room and grabbed a jar of his special cure-all ointment with the added extracts of maggot. Jonathan was well into the first manuscript when he returned.

"How does it look?" Phillip asked as he opened the jar and placed it on the work table beside Jonathan.

Jonathan smiled at Phillip. "You were right. Things go wrong when you try to write in English." He waved the manuscript. "Someone's going to have to go through this and mark all the corrections that need to be made."

"That's the task for which I asked you to come." Phillip smiled as he tilted Jonathan's head back so he could study the swelling around Jonathan's eye. "Hold still a moment." He dug a finger into the ointment and applied it liberally to the swollen area before gently massaging it in.

"Ouch!" Jonathan's cry of pain had Phillip backing off for a moment. "You want me to check the English in those manuscripts? Why?"

"Because you're a native English speaker," Phillip said as he started to gently massage in the ointment again, "and you don't need to ask who wrote the original English translation."

"Ah." Jonathan tried to nod, but Phillip's hold on his head prevented him from doing so. "You still haven't told the Kubiaks that you understand English."

"No. And I'd like to keep it a secret a little longer." Phillip used a rag to gently wipe the excess ointment from Jonathan's face before stepping back to inspect his handiwork. He nodded in satisfaction as he put the lid back on the jar and handed it to Jonathan. "I want you to gently massage a liberal coating of the ointment into the swelling twice a day for a week."

"Thanks, Dr. Gribbleflotz," Jonathan said as he accepted the jar.

Phillip waved away Jonathan's thanks. "So, will you check my translation? I will pay you."

"I'll be happy to look at them, Dr. Gribbleflotz," Jonathan said, "and there's no need to pay me."

"I insist."

Jonathan held up the jar of ointment. "Then consider this payment."

"It's a lot of work," Phillip said.

Jonathan shook his head. "I'll type it all up on the computer at home and run it through the grammar and spell checker. It'll hardly take any time at all. Then I can print everything out and pass it on to Herr Trelli to check the science."

"If you're sure," Phillip said. He'd heard about the wondrous computers, but he'd never seen one working yet.

Jonathan nodded. "I'll get onto it the moment I get home."

Phillip walked Jonathan to the door and watched him put the folders and jar of ointment into one of his bicycle's saddlebags. Then, with a quick wave Jonathan was on his bike and pedaling away. Phillip waved him off and turned round, to find the expectant faces of Hans, Michael, and Kurt watching him.

"Jonathan has agreed to check the English translations before passing them on to Herr Trelli to check the explanations you wrote," he told them.

"Herr Trelli won't find anything wrong with the explanations," Kurt said.

Phillip was in total agreement. A lot of the booklets were taken straight out of a selection of up-time chemistry textbooks. The only way the booklets could be wrong was if the textbooks were wrong, and that was unlikely, because surely the textbooks had been written by knowledgeable up-timers.

A few days later, Grantville

It was a fine Saturday afternoon when Jonathan walked over to Trelli's GoodCare Pharmacy with the printouts.

As he entered the pharmacy he looked around. Not seeing Mr. Trelli anywhere he headed for the counter. "Hi, Mrs. Little. Is Mr. Trelli around? I've got something I want to show him."

"Lasso's..." Susan Little looked up, and whistled. "What happened to your eye?"

Jonathan sighed. The bruising around his eye couldn't go down soon enough. "I was helping out with Tracy Kubiak's ladies' self-defense course and I caught a swinging arm," he explained for what felt like the thousandth time.

Susan winced and leaned closer to have a better look at Jonathan's eye. "Are you using anything for the bruising?"

"Dr. Gribbleflotz gave me something that seems to be working."

"Oh? What?"

Jonathan shrugged. "Just some ointment."

Susan looked skyward for a few second before shaking her head and looking at Jonathan. "I haven't heard of any Dr. Gribbleflotz ointment. How long has he been making it? We'd be happy to sell yet another Dr. Gribbleflotz product."

"I don't know," Jonathan said. "I guess I can ask him next time I see him."

Susan nodded. "You do that. Just remember though, that Lasso will want to know what goes into it before he's willing to sell it."

"Willing to sell what?" Lasso Trelli asked as he appeared at his office door. "Hi, Jonathan. What brings you here today?" Lasso's eyes locked onto Jonathan's eye. "Who hit you?"

"One of the girls at Mrs. Kubiak's ladies' self-defense

class accidently hit me," Jonathan explained for the one thousand and first time. "But that's not why I'm here."

Jonathan pulled the printouts from the satchel he had across his shoulder and offered them to Lasso. "Some of Dr. Gribbleflotz's laborants have got together to prepare a multilingual booklet for each of the Dr. Gribbleflotz alchemy sets that explains the science behind each of the experiments, and I offered to ask you to check out their chemistry."

Lasso had a quick skim through the pages. "Did you type these up?" he asked.

Jonathan nodded.

"You used a spellchecker, didn't you?"

Jonathan nodded.

"It shows," Lasso said. He waved the printouts. "What're they planning on doing with these?"

"They want to sell booklets to accompany the chemistry sets."

Lasso nodded. "I'll have a look at them. If they're any good, we might cut a deal to include them in the chemistry sets."

"Thanks, Mr. Trelli."

"No, thank you, Jonathan." He studied Jonathan's eye for a few seconds. "I've got an ointment that'll help with the swelling," he offered.

Jonathan shook his head. "Thanks, Mr. Trelli, but Dr. Gribbleflotz has already given me something for my eye."

"Really? Is it any good?"

Jonathan nodded. "You should have seen my eye before I started using it."

"Do you have some I can run some tests on?"

Jonathan shook his head. "I'd rather you talked

to Dr. Gribbleflotz before doing anything like that, Mr. Trelli."

Lasso nodded. "Fair enough." He shook the printouts. "I'll have a look at these and get back to you."

"Thanks, Mr. Trelli," Jonathan said. He waved to Susan as he walked out of the store. He paused outside the door to consider his options. He was feeling hungry, but he didn't like paying for food when there was plenty waiting back home. With the thought of saving a couple of dollars he turned to head home. A short distance away he thought he recognized Richelle Kubiak pushing a Baby Jogger. He let his eyes follow her as she walked away from him.

Richelle was obviously enjoying a walk in the sun, waving to people she knew, and Jonathan was just about to turn the other way and head home when he saw her do a double take and speed up. Where previously her progress had been carefree, now there was a sense of urgency as she took the side street that led to the shortcut over the hill to Mahan Run.

Jonathan searched for what had scared her, and saw a heavyset man staring after her. That wasn't unexpected. Lots of men stared at attractive young women as they walked past. But then the man started walking purposefully in Richelle's wake. It could just be nothing, but Jonathan felt sure something about that man had scared Richelle. He started after them.

Richelle was desperately trying not to panic. Had that really been her stepfather's brother? Had he recognized her? How had he found her? Was it just an accident that he'd been visiting Grantville and seen her, or had he come to Grantville because he knew she was living there? She glanced back over her shoulder, but the trees meant visibility along the dirt track she was following was limited to twenty or so yards. She increased speed.

Jonathan didn't like the idea of Richelle being followed up the shortcut by a man who scared her and the sooner he caught up with her the better. He started jogging. A few hundred yards later he heard screaming and started running.

He rounded a corner in time to see Richelle swing a branch at the man. It broke, leaving her weaponless and off balance. The man threw her to the ground and pulled a knife.

"Hey, what do you think you're doing?" Jonathan shouted. It was a silly question, but it served the purpose of distracting the man's attention. He continued to approach, breathing heavily as he struggled to recover his breath.

"This is none of your business," the man said. "This harlot has been condemned to death for the crime of incest." He turned his head to spit in Richelle's direction. "She entrapped my brother, and they were both convicted and sentenced to death. My brother was executed immediately while the whore's execution was delayed until after she gave birth to my niece. But she escaped." He turned to glare at Richelle. "You will tell me who helped you before I execute you."

Jonathan was scared. The man was shorter than him but probably had thirty pounds on him, and none of it looked like fat. He was also armed with a knife. The man didn't look particularly skilled with the knife, but it still gave him an advantage. "Drop the knife," he said. "Your laws don't apply here in Grantville."

"God's law applies everywhere," the man said as he turned to face Jonathan. "She's entrapped you too, has she? Just like she entrapped my brother."

There was a religious fervor in the man's eyes that told Jonathan he wouldn't listen to reason. Not that Jonathan was particularly interested in getting him to listen to reason. He'd heard enough to know that the man constituted a risk to Richelle's continued safety. The law in Grantville might not condemn a victim of incest to death, but he wasn't sure where Grantville's law stood on extradition. That left him with only one possible course of action. Jonathan licked his dry lips and advanced on the man. "I'm not going to let you hurt Richelle."

"Then I will kill you first," the man said as he came at Jonathan, swinging the knife in front of him in an arc.

Jonathan kept his eye on the knife as he slowly closed the distance.

A backhanded swing of the knife forced Jonathan to skip back out of reach, but when the man swung the knife back the other way Jonathan's long hours of training took over. His left hand swung, grabbing the man's knife hand. Moments later his right hand joined his left hand. With a double-hand grip on the knife hand Jonathan twisted the wrist as he swung his arms up and spun under the swinging arm. This caused the man's arm to bend so that the knife was now pointed at his gut. At this point Jonathan's brain caught up with what his body was doing—a number four knife counter. He pushed hard, trying to drive the knife into the man, but he lacked momentum to stick more than the point into the man's body. It was a conscious decision to slam his knee into the pommel of the knife, driving it into the man's body.

The man screamed and crumpled. Jonathan released his grip on the knife hand and stood there, staring at the man whimpering on the ground, clutching at the knife wedged into his body just below his ribs.

Jonathan staggered back a few steps, almost stepping on Richelle as he fixated on the handle of the knife moving as the man breathed. The look on the man's face as he struggled to remove the knife was just as distressing. "Don't remove the knife!" he called, to no avail.

After a struggle the man managed to pull out the knife and tried to sit up. The bloodstain on his jacket grew, and then he fell backwards.

Jonathan swallowed the bile trying to rise from his stomach as he gingerly approached the man and felt for a pulse. It was there, barely. He stared at the still-growing bloodstain on the man's abdomen. He knew the theory. A knife left in place could stem the flow of blood from severed veins and arteries, but if you removed it, the blood could flow. The man had only minutes before he would be beyond help.

Jonathan turned his mind back to the living. Richelle was just getting back to her feet and appeared deeply shocked. He thought about offering her his jacket, but he caught sight of Lenya with her blanket lightly covering her. Under the circumstances, he thought, that would probably be better. He quickly exchanged his jacket for the blanket and draped the blanket around Richelle's shoulders. She pulled it tight and inhaled. Jonathan saw her shoulders relax and mentally complimented himself on his good sense. He wasn't sure how she would have reacted if she'd smelled the sweat on his jacket.

"We have to go back to town and report this," Jonathan told Richelle.

She stared at him blankly, so Jonathan wheeled the baby buggy around to face the way they'd come and gently nudged Richelle along until they were both heading back to town. Jonathan glanced over his shoulder. The man was in shadow, so he couldn't tell if he was still bleeding. He might have a better chance of survival if Jonathan ran back for help, but that would have meant leaving Richelle and Lenya alone.

Grantville Police Station

"Hold that position," Fred Sebastian said.

Jonathan did the best he could to do what he was told as the flash illuminated him.

"That's it. I don't think there are any more angles I can take," Fred said. He turned to Jonathan. "Do you have any injuries that I haven't photographed?"

Jonathan shook his head. "No, you've got them all, and I don't understand why you're bothering." He touched his black eye. "This wasn't caused by the guy I fought today. He didn't touch me. I got the shiner from Richelle."

"During Tracy Kubiak's latest ladies' self-defense class," Officer Estes Frost hastened to say.

Fred looked up from winding back the spool of film he'd just shot. "You volunteered to help out at one of those blood fests?"

"Sensei said I had to prove my temperament if I want to go for my black belt this year," Jonathan said.

"Was it worth it?" Fred asked.

Jonathan thought of how Richelle had fought back today. "Yes," he said.

Fred shrugged. "Well, if you think a black belt is worth getting beaten up by a bunch of dangerous females..." He turned to Estes. "How soon do you want the prints?"

"Any time in the next couple of days," Estes said. He turned to Jonathan. "Now, let's get your statement."

Jonathan watched Fred Sebastian, who had to be at least seventy, walk away. "Why did you make him walk up the hill to photograph the body?" he asked.

"Because he's the guy with the camera and the dark room. Until someone starts making more photographic supplies, Fred's the best we have."

Jonathan was feeling ill. He'd just killed a man, and now he was sitting in an interview room at the police station opposite Officer Estes Frost describing what had happened. He looked up when the door opened. An attractive American woman in her late twenties entered.

Estes looked up. "Hi, Dita. I'm just about finished with Jonathan." He turned back to Jonathan. "This is Dita Petrini, licensed professional counselor."

"A shrink?" Jonathan asked. He felt able to smile, even if only slightly. Surely they wouldn't be calling in a counselor if they were going to arrest him.

"You've just experienced something very traumatic, Jonathan, and Chief Frost asked me to have a little talk with you before you were released."

"I'm free to go?" Jonathan asked.

"Sure," Estes said, "just as soon as you sign your statement." He smiled at Jonathan. "Hey, you're a hero, and we don't arrest heroes."

Jonathan knew he was going to be sick. He held a hand over his mouth, shot to his feet, and made for the door.

"To your left, three doors down," Estes called out as Jonathan passed through the door.

Dita turned to Estes. "What's to the left three doors down?" she asked.

"The men's toilets."

Dita nodded. "I guess Jonathan's going to be otherwise engaged for a while, so I might as well drop into the other interview room and check on Richelle."

"You do that. I'll let you know when Jonathan comes back."

Sitting at the desk in the interview room, Richelle had both arms around Lenya, who was still wrapped in Jonathan's jacket, while Richelle still had Lenya's blanket draped around her. Across the table from her sat Officer Erika Fleischer, whom she'd met when she first arrived in Grantville, and one of the female dispatchers, who'd been called in to record the interview.

While Officer Fleisher and Frau Carson conferred over the interview notes, Richelle mentally reviewed the fight. In her mind's eye, she could see Jonathan perform the knife counter she'd first seen Tommy Karickhoff demonstrate at the self-defense course, and she remembered Herr Karickhoff saying that it wasn't easy to stick a knife into someone with that move. In her mind the action slowed down until she could see the deliberate effort Jonathan made, driving his knee into the pommel of the knife to drive it home. She'd seen the look in Jonathan's eyes, and she knew he'd been trying to kill her stepfather's brother. "Is Jonathan in trouble?"

Erika looked up from the interview transcript. "From what you've said, and the evidence at the scene, it appears to be a clear case of self-defense."

Mimi Carson nodded in agreement. "Jonathan was protecting a young mother attacked by a knife-wielding man. He could have emptied a gun into him and there still wouldn't be a jury that would convict him."

Richelle relaxed. Jonathan wasn't going to get into trouble for saving her.

The door to the interview room opened and Dita stepped in. "How are you holding up, Richelle?" she asked as she stepped into the room.

"Okay," Richelle said. She'd had a number of counseling sessions with Frau Petrini, and knew her reasonably well.

"She was worried about Jonathan being in trouble," Mimi said.

Dita turned and smiled at Richelle. "Chief Frost is treating it as a straight case of self-defense."

"Can I see him?" Richelle asked.

"He's not feeling very well at the moment," Dita warned. "Last I saw of him, he was making a mad dash for the men's toilet."

"What's wrong with him?" Richelle demanded as she shot to her feet.

"I think it's started to hit him that he's just killed a man," Dita said. "I'll be scheduling some counseling sessions with him when he's feeling more himself."

Most of what Dita said was said to Richelle's back as she ran out of the interview room.

She found Jonathan kneeling in front of a toilet, crying and shaking. She adjusted Lenya's blanket until it covered both of them and held Jonathan tightly. "You saved me, Jonathan. You did what you had to do to save me."

Erika, Mimi, and Dita were still looking at the door when Tracy Kubiak turned up.

"Where's Richelle? How is she?" she demanded.

"Richelle's okay," Erika said. "She's a little shaken, but basically unharmed."

Tracy slumped and swayed. She had to plant her hands on the interview table to maintain her balance until Dita could maneuver her into the chair Richelle had recently vacated. "Where is she?"

Erika, Mimi and Dita exchanged looks. "I think she went looking for Jonathan," Mimi said.

"That's good," Tracy said, a smug smile appearing on her face.

"I hope you aren't imagining a romance, Tracy," Dita said.

"Of course not. Jonathan's six years older than Richelle, but that doesn't mean she can't have a crush on him," Tracy said.

Dita pursed her lips and shook her head. "He's still a guy, Tracy, and Richelle still has issues."

"I thought she was getting better," Tracy said. "Under the circumstances, you'd expect her to hate Lenya, but she absolutely loves her daughter."

"She does," Dita agreed, "and for a very good reason. Her stepfather's abuse stopped when the community discovered that Richelle was pregnant. Then, her pregnancy kept her alive when they executed her abuser. In Richelle's mind, Lenya saved her."

"Oh!" Tracy mumbled.

"Yes, oh," Dita agreed. "Richelle's got a long way to go before she recovers from what happened to her, if she ever does."

July 4, Grantville

Richelle stood beside Jonathan watching the Fourth of July parade march past. Perched on Jonathan's shoulders, a happy Lenya followed the beat with her hands on his head.

Suddenly Jonathan hunched his shoulders and reached up for Lenya. "Someone, who shall remain nameless," he told Richelle, "needs her diaper changed."

Richelle glanced at the back of Jonathan's T-shirt as he lifted Lenya. Yes, there was a damp patch around the neck. She felt a grin coming and tried desperately to smother it as she reached out to take Lenya. Then she saw the look on Jonathan's face and lost it. She pulled Lenya close before turning and running, laughter ringing out as she ran.

Jonathan caught up with her a short distance down Market Street from Main Street. "It's not that funny," he said as he caught up.

Richelle struggled to stop laughing. "You should have seen your face."

"It's a bit awkward to see your own face," Jonathan said.

Richelle wiped the tears of laughter from her eyes

and smiled at Jonathan. Surprisingly enough she'd enjoyed the day in town with him. He was fun to be with, and he was safe. A movement to the side attracted her attention and she stopped laughing as she recognized a couple of the boys who'd been pestering her. They stared at her for a while before bolting.

"Who were they?" Jonathan asked.

A quick glance confirmed that Jonathan had seen the boys, which probably explained their hasty departure. They didn't want to mess with Killer Fortney. "I don't think I need to worry about any of the boys at school pestering me again."

"Were they a couple of the guys who'd been pestering you?"

"Yes."

"Then it looks like your mother's plan worked."

"Yes, but I've really enjoyed today. Thanks for agreeing to walk out with me."

"Hey, no trouble," Jonathan said. "I've enjoyed today too."

They fell into step as they headed towards Trelli's GoodCare Pharmacy, where they'd stashed Lenya's baby buggy rather than struggle with it in the crowd. "I still want a gun," Richelle said.

"You can't have one. The law's pretty clear on that. You're what, sixteen?" Jonathan asked.

"In September."

"Right, and the legal minimum age to openly carry a gun is eighteen."

Richelle skipped around in front of Jonathan and looked imploringly at him. "You're twenty-one. We could get married."

"What?" Jonathan roared. "People don't get married just so they can carry a gun."

Laughter rippled from Richelle as she stepped up beside Jonathan again. "And you call yourself a West Virginian."

"Yes I do, and I can just imagine your Mama Tracy's reaction if we told her we wanted to get married."

Richelle grinned back. "The explosion would be impressive."

"Which is why it's not going to happen."

"Of course it isn't," Richelle agreed, although she would have preferred that Jonathan not be quite so empathic about it not happening.

They walked in companionable silence towards Trelli's GoodCare Pharmacy. Richelle noticed the signs advertising the new Dr. Gribbleflotz alchemy sets in the window. "Why are they pushing the alchemy sets now? I would have thought they'd wait for Christmas, or at least until Halloween."

"They couldn't possibly miss the Fourth of July," Jonathan said.

"What's so special about the fourth of July?" Richelle asked. "I know it's your independence day, but what does that have to do with selling alchemy sets?"

"This is your first Fourth of July, isn't it?"

Richelle nodded.

"Thought so," Jonathan said. "Well, they end the day with a fireworks display."

Richelle nodded. "So Mama said. We're supposed to be going to the Fair Grounds to watch the fireworks tonight." She looked up at him. "Will you be there?"

"I hadn't planned on it."

"Oh." Richelle wasn't aware of how disappointed

she must have sounded until a hand landed lightly on her shoulder. She just barely managed not to try to shrug it off.

"I'll call and arrange a time and place to meet you."

She smiled at Jonathan, and stepped away just enough that his hand slipped from her shoulder. "That'd be nice." Both of them stared at each other as Jonathan shoved his hands into his pockets. She was happy to see that he hadn't taken offense at her maneuver. Maybe he understood that she hadn't felt comfortable with him touching her. "You were explaining why Herr Trelli is pushing the alchemy sets."

"Fireworks use gunpowder, and the alchemy sets all have the ingredients needed to make your own fireworks. There are going to be a lot of kids making their own fireworks for their own fireworks displays this evening."

Richelle stopped to stare at Jonathan. "Are you telling me those alchemy sets give instructions on how to make gunpowder?"

"In excruciating detail," Jonathan confirmed.

"Isn't that dangerous?"

"Sure, but it's a lot safer than leaving the kids to make gunpowder based on what they can find from sources like *The Anarchist Cookbook*. At least Dr. Gribbleflotz's instructions contain safety warnings."

Inside Trelli's GoodCare Pharmacy

"I don't think it's a good idea to buy Troy a chemistry set for his birthday," Phebe Morton said. "He'll only be twelve."

"Elisabeth Hockenjoss got a Dr. Gribbleflotz Junior Alchemist set for her birthday, and she's only ten," Tracy Morton said.

Phebe glared at her ten-year-old daughter. "But she's a down-timer," she said.

Tracy looked questioningly at her mother. "Why does Elisabeth being a down-timer mean she can have a junior alchemist set for her birthday and Troy can't?"

"Can I help you?" Susan Little asked.

Phebe grasped the lifeline she'd just been thrown. "It's Troy's birthday soon, and he's got his heart set on a Dr. Gribbleflotz Junior Alchemist set, and I'm worried that it might be dangerous."

Susan nodded her head. "That is a reasonable fear. Of course there is an element of danger. That's why the boxes are marked 'parental supervision recommended.' However, the instructions for all of the experiments have been carefully written by Herr Dr. Gribbleflotz himself. They explain in great detail how to perform each experiment, and come with warnings of what to look out for."

"But I've heard that it is possible to make gunpowder and other explosives from the chemicals in the chemistry sets."

"You're right about the gunpowder. There's not much we can do about not including charcoal, sulphur, and potassium nitrate. However, that's the only 'explosive' you can make from the chemicals in the Junior Alchemist set. You need the intermediate set for the triiodide, and the advanced set for fulminates and guncotton."

"You can make triiodide from an Intermediate Alchemist set?" Truman Morton asked.

"Truman, you're not helping," Phebe said.

"Sorry, dear."

Phebe glared at her husband, who she could see was reading the advertising for the Dr. Gribbleflotz Advanced Alchemist set. "We are not buying one of those for Troy."

Morton grinned at Phebe. "I was thinking of getting an advanced set for me. Come on, Phebe. You know Troy's got his heart set on a Dr. Gribbleflotz Junior Alchemist set."

Phebe released a heavy sigh. "Okay, but you better supervise him when he's using it."

"Of course, dear."

Chapter 12

Making Waves

August 1632, HDG Enterprises, Jena

"Quiet!"

Fourteen-year-old Magdalena Rutilius was oblivious to the stunned looks directed her way as she huddled down in the suddenly silent room listening intently to the broadcast she was hearing through the earpiece of her crystal radio set.

A gentle tap on her nose had her looking up and seeing Maria Anna Siebenhorn, the nineteen-year-old sister of Michael Siebenhorn, one of Dr. Gribbleflotz's top laborants. Magdalena guessed that the question Maria Anna was mouthing had to do with what she was listening to. "Croat cavalry is attacking Grantville," she answered.

Maria Anna reared back a couple of steps, a look of horror on her face. Magdalena looked around. There were similar looks of horror growing on the faces of all the laborants as the news spread around the room.

Grantville was an unwalled city. That meant it was defenseless against the Croats. Those that had them rushed out to listen to their own crystal sets while those without hung onto any news they passed on. Not a lot of work was done for the rest of the day as the laborants listened in on the latest news broadcasts.

A *few days later*

Dr. Phillip Gribbleflotz walked around the storage yard just outside Schwarza where barrels of urine bound for his laboratory in Jena had been stored. Keeping pace with him as he inspected the damage were Ted and Tracy Kubiak. The smell of stale urine permeated the air.

"Our best guess is that some of the Croats thought the barrels contained beer and tried to drink it," Ted said.

"And they reacted badly when they discovered they were wrong," Tracy added. "Hence the rampant destruction."

"We have sufficient spirits of hartshorn at my laboratory in Jena for another week's production of Sal Aer Fixus and Vin Sal Aer Fixus," Phillip said.

"Yes, I've been meaning to speak about that," Tracy said.

Phillip had a feeling of foreboding. "Speak to me about what? The spirits of hartshorn?" he asked.

"Sort of," Tracy said. She gestured to the broken barrels. "Ninety percent of what was in these barrels was water, and it's ridiculous to pay a small fortune to ship water to Jena."

"You want me to set up a facility in Grantville to process the urine so only the spirits of hartshorn is sent to Jena." Phillip nodded. "Unfortunately, I don't really have anyone suitable to run such a facility."

"But you've had nearly a year to train someone," Tracy said. "What about whoever is in charge of making the spirits of hartshorn in Jena? Can't he do it?"

Phillip shoved his hands into the pockets of his new jacket—in a rather fetching emerald green color made possible by the new dyes being produced by Lothlorien Farbenwerke—so Frau Kubiak couldn't see his tight fists of frustration, which she was probably in no doubt of anyway when he kicked savagely at a fragment of barrel stave, sending it bouncing across the yard.

"Is that a no?" Tracy asked.

Phillip turned to Tracy. "Michael Siebenhorn is one of my top laborants. Moving him to Grantville just to run a facility making spirits of hartshorn would be a complete waste of his talents."

"Siebenhorn?" Ted asked. "Any relation to the M. Siebenhorn of Saltzman, Siebenhorn, and Stoltz fame?"

Phillip nodded. "Michael is one of the coauthors of the 'Expert's guide' range of booklets that complement the Dr. Gribbleflotz Alchemy sets."

"Smart fellow," Ted said.

"Yes. Too smart to waste running a facility that turns urine into spirits of hartshorn," Phillip said.

"Would he be smart enough to benefit from classes at the high school?" Tracy asked.

Phillip's jaw dropped. He hadn't thought of sending Michael to school. "That's a marvelous idea. I'm sure he'd..." Phillip frowned. "No, he'd never willingly leave his sister alone in Jena."

Ted and Tracy exchanged looks. Ted shrugged and turned to Phillip. "Why not send her here as well?"

"And what would she do here?" Phillip asked.

"Can't she work at the new facility?" Tracy asked.

"She could," Phillip said, "Maria Anna has nearly a year of training as a laborant. However, she would be over qualified for the work, and she would know this."

"Then, what about sending her to school?" Tracy asked.

"I'm sure she would like to attend school, but she would not want to be a burden upon her brother," Phillip said.

"She wouldn't be a burden on her brother. We could pay her way," Tracy said.

Phillip shook his head. "Some of my laborants might snatch at such an offer, but Maria Anna isn't one of them." He released a heavy sigh. "I'll speak with Frau Mittelhausen and see if she can suggest anything."

Meanwhile, back in Jena

"I'm sorry, Maria Anna. I know Magdalena is a friend of yours, but her heart isn't really in her work, and it shows," Ursula Mittelhausen said as she paced the floor on the other side of the kitchen table

Maria Anna sighed and slumped down further on her chair. "She's more interested in electricity and radio," she agreed.

"And Herr Dr. Gribbleflotz doesn't work with electricity," Ursula said. "We're going to have to let her go."

"But you can't throw her out," Maria Anna protested. "Magdalena would never survive on her own."

"We are not a charity," Ursula said. "But I will help her find a suitable position."

Maria Anna shook her head. "No. If Magdalena goes, then I go too!"

Ursula stopped pacing and stared at Maria Anna. "Don't be so ridiculous. What would you do if you left Dr. Gribbleflotz?"

"I'd find a job, and I'd support Magdalena while she does that electrician's course she wants to do."

"And what kind of work are you going to do to support both of you while she spends the next few years studying?"

Maria Anna had been expecting this meeting for days, so she'd come prepared. She pulled a folded piece of newspaper out from her top and passed it to Ursula. "I saw this in the paper and thought it might be interesting."

Ursula read the advertisement and stared at Maria Anna. "You do know what Brennerei und Chemiefabrik Schwarza do?"

Maria Anna nodded. "They make explosives and primers. But the pay is more than enough money to support me and Magdalena, and they offer full board."

"Of course they do. How else do they expect to get staff?" Ursula muttered. "Your brother will never allow it."

"Michael can't stop me," Maria Anna insisted.

"If you go, he will insist on following you," Ursula warned.

Maria Anna winced. That was the truth, and the fly in the ointment. Michael was a success for the first time in his life. With Dr. Gribbleflotz training him, the sky was the limit. "I don't want Michael to leave Dr. Gribbleflotz."

"You're not going to have much choice if you insist

on leaving," Ursula said. "We both know he'll follow you." Ursula walked round the table and hugged Maria Anna, "and we don't want that, do we?"

That evening, Jena

Phillip paced around his study, occasionally flicking Frau Mittelhausen a glance as he described his problem. "I need to get Michael to Grantville to run the new spirits of hartshorn facility Frau Kubiak wants to build there, but there is no way he'll go without his sister, but there will be nothing for her to do at the facility once it's up and running."

He glanced to see that Frau Mittelhausen understood the gravity of the situation before continuing. "Frau Kubiak suggested that the business could pay for Maria Anna to attend school, but..." He left the sentence floating. Frau Mittelhausen knew the girl even better than he did, so there was no need to say anything more.

"I might have a solution," Ursula said.

Phillip froze in his pacing and turned to look at Ursula. "Explain!"

"Today I warned Maria Anna that we were going to have to let Magdalena Rutilius go."

Phillip nodded. They'd discussed the girl a couple of days ago.

"Well, Maria Anna said that if Magdalena went, she'd go too." Ursula shrugged. "I hadn't thought they were that close. Still, I asked Maria Anna what she would do, and she replied that she would find work in Grantville to support both of them while

Magdalena took the electricity and electronics course she's apparently set her heart on."

"If Maria Anna left with Magdalena, Michael would insist on going with her," Phillip muttered, seeing where Frau Mittelhausen might be headed. "So all we have to do is dismiss Magdalena. Maria Anna will insist on leaving with her, and Michael will insist on following his sister."

"All the way to Grantville," Ursula said was a smug smile on her face. "It'll be a good idea for you to sound Michael out about taking charge of the new spirits of hartshorn facility in Grantville before we dismiss Magdalena, Dr. Gribbleflotz," Ursula said. "We wouldn't want him to think he had to leave the company to keep an eye on his sister."

The grin that had been growing on Phillip's face died. "How is Maria Anna supposed to support herself and Magdalena?" he asked.

"She is thinking of applying for work at Brennerei und Chemiefabrik Schwarza."

Phillip shivered at the name of the company Maria Anna planned on working for. It wasn't that the company used unsafe practices, because it didn't. His problem with the company was what they made—something called Fulminate of Mercury. Hans and Kurt had eagerly demonstrated its explosive qualities to him. It was less sensitive than ammonia triiodide, but much more powerful. He shuddered at the thought. Triiodide was as powerful as he wanted to go. "What will she do if they won't employ her?"

Ursula snorted. "Maria Anna has been trained by you, Dr. Gribbleflotz. They'll employ her in an instant; especially with the reference I intend writing for her."

Phillip walked over to a chair, slumped down into it, and sighed contently. It looked like Maria Anna's future was assured, which meant Michael would be heading for Grantville to set up and run the spirits of hartshorn facility that Frau Kubiak wanted, which in turn meant that Frau Kubiak would stop nagging him about the money being wasted shipping raw urine all the way to Jena. Today had started badly, but was ending beautifully.

Late September, Grantville

Magdalena had her face glued to the window, looking out as the world whizzed by. This was her first ever trip in a *bus*, and she was enjoying every second of it. She turned to say as much to Maria Anna. "Isn't this fun?"

Maria Anna nodded and smiled at Magdalena, but the smile was forced, as the sight of her hands holding onto the seat with a white-knuckled grip shouted out.

"There's nothing to worry about," Magdalena said in her most reassuring voice. "The driver is an experienced up-timer."

Just then Barton Dobbs called over his shoulder. "Frau Siebenhorn, your stop's just ahead," he called out.

Magdalena felt Maria Anna tense and wanted to laugh. She waved to the driver, who waved back before turning his attention back to the road ahead. The moment he was looking at the road ahead again Maria Anna's body relaxed, a little.

"Next time, I'll walk," Maria Anna muttered.

Magdalena smiled at Maria Anna. The older girl

had been her fearless protector back in Jena. "I'll be using the bus to get to and from school every day."

That statement was greeted by a shudder from Maria Anna. "You're welcome to it."

Magdalena reached out an arm and hugged her friend. "I'll protect you." As she said it she felt her body being thrown gently forward and hastily braced herself while keeping her hold on Maria Anna. She knew that her friend was getting used to this motion every time the bus slowed, but she also knew it was one of the things that upset her about traveling in the bus.

When the bus came to a halt Barton turned round. "This is your stop Frau Siebenhorn, and it looks like Carl's here to meet you."

Magdalena and Maria Anna gathered their things and made their way off the bus. When it drove off they could see a man standing beside a handcart. Magdalena smiled. She hadn't been looking forward to carrying all her things who knew how far. "It looks like we won't have to carry our bags," she told Maria Anna.

The man who stood watching them was strange. His skin was darker than any other up-timers Magdalena had seen, which wasn't saying much, because she'd only seen a few people she was sure were up-timers. This man was definitely an up-timer. It wasn't just the clothes; there was something about the way he held himself. "Are you waiting for us?" she asked.

"Maria Anna Siebenhorn?" Carl Schockley asked.

Magdalena shook her head and nudged Maria Anna forward. "I'm Magdalena Rutilius, this is Maria Anna."

"I'm Carl Schockley. I own the property where you'll be living. So which of you two is hoping to study for the Electrical Trades Certificate?" he asked as he started loading their luggage onto the cart.

"Me," Magdalena said as she carefully placed the wooden box containing her precious crystal radio on the cart.

"When it comes to doing your on-the-job-training, Kelly Construction will be happy to take you on."

Magdalena stared at Herr Schockley. "How can you promise that, and why would they do that?" she asked.

"I'm a part owner, but even if I wasn't, we'd still need electricians. Hopefully you'll enjoy your time with us so much you'll take a full time job with us when you complete your apprenticeship."

"Thank you. I'll keep Kelly Construction in mind."

"What do you do at Brennerei und Chemiefabrik Schwarza?" a previously silent Maria Anna asked.

Carl got the cart moving before answering. "I just live there these days; although I did help Jakob and Catharina get the company started."

"Are you a chemist?" Maria Anna asked.

Carl shook his head. "No, I'm into construction and destruction."

"So how did you help get Brennerei und Chemiefabrik Schwarza started?" Maria Anna asked.

"I was in the army up-time."

"And they trained you to make explosives?" Magdalena asked.

Carl grinned. "Not all the courses were official, but we made fulminate of mercury primers and detonators as well as a few military grade explosives."

Magdalena knew all about courses that weren't official. She exchanged a smile with Maria Anna. Her brother Michael, Kurt Stoltz, and even Dr. Gribbleflotz's personal laborant, Hans Saltzman, had run demonstrations for the other laborants where they performed all of the experiments in the Dr. Gribbleflotz Alchemist sets, and a few that *weren't* included in the instruction sets.

Brennerei und Chemiefabrik Schwarza,
Grays Run, Grantville

The house was enormous, or at least it appeared that way to Magdalena. It was set on what Herr Schockley called a hobby farm, which seemed to consist of a few acres of pasture and a few acres of woods. Around the main house there was a number of other structures. Magdalena spun around, taking in everything. "You own all this?" she asked Carl.

"Me and the bank," Carl said as he wheeled the cart up to the front door.

Magdalena skipped along beside him while Maria Anna walked normally, her head swinging from side to side as she took in everything. "You have a lot of horses."

"They're all survivors from the Croat attack." Carl stopped to point to a group in a corral. "Those ones are ours, the rest belong to people who've leased grazing." He smiled down at Magdalena. "If you're interested in learning, I'm sure someone will be happy to teach you how to ride."

"Really?" Magdalena asked. She licked her lips in anticipation. "I'd like that."

"Well, it's something for another day. Let's just get you settled and introduced to everyone first." With that, Carl pushed the cart up to the front door and started unloading it.

A few days later

Magdalena literally danced all the way from where the bus dropped her off on Route 250 to her new home. She skipped up to the front door and pushed it open before skipping into the kitchen.

"Someone seems pleased with themselves," Tom Frost said from the kitchen table where he had some sheets of paper spread out in front of him.

Magdalena smiled brightly at the husband of the Brennerei und Chemiefabrik Schwarza senior chemist. "I got the results of my admittance tests today, and I've been exempt the first year."

"Congratulations. How did you manage that?" Tom asked.

"Frau Mittelhausen insisted that everyone had to learn to read and write properly," Magdalena said as she explored the pantry for something to eat before grabbing a plate and moved to look over Tom's shoulder. "What're you working on?" she asked.

"It's a basic proof of concept Birkeland-Eyde reactor."

Magdalena filled a glass with small beer and sat down beside Tom. "What does it do?"

Tom released a set-upon sigh and turned to Magdalena. "I hope you're not planning on eating that," he said, pointing to the raw onion on her plate.

"I am," she said as she started to peel the skin.

"Well please eat it somewhere else. I can't stand onion breath."

Magdalena froze in the act of removing yet another layer of onion skin.

"Either it goes or you go," Tom said, pointing at the offending onion.

She fought a short mental battle before getting to her feet and putting the onion back in the pantry, wiping the plate she'd used and putting it back in the rack, and washing her hands. "Happy now?" she asked.

Tom nodded and gestured for her to sit down beside him. "It's a machine that uses high voltage electric arcs to produce nitric acid from air."

Those words were magic to Magdalena. Now she was very glad she'd given in to Herr Frost's demands. She leaned closer for a better view of the schematics. "Can I help?"

Tom laughed. "Mags, you haven't even started your electrical training."

That reminded Magdalena of the bad news she'd been given. "And they're insisting that I have to take an arts class." She stared at Tom, a disgusted look on her face. "Can you imagine? They think it'll make me a more rounded person."

Tom looked her up and down and nodded. "You could do with a few more curves."

Magdalena folded her arms and glared at Tom. Yes, she knew that even by up-timer standards she was thin, but he didn't have to rub it in. "That is not what Frau Warner meant," she said.

The grin didn't leave Tom's face as he nodded. "So, what subject are you thinking of doing?"

"The only class that fits in with my schedule is music," she said, outraged that she had to take the class.

"Hey, you never know, you might enjoy it."

Magdalena snorted. "Music has nothing to do with electricity."

"That's kind of the point, Mags, although electricity is often used to amplify the sound."

Magdalena grabbed the schematic Tom had been working on. She shot him a glare. "At least you didn't say electricity is needed to play tapes and records." That had been Frau Warner's response when she protested. She turned her attention to the equipment Tom had drawn. "Herr Dr. Gribbleflotz has a glass maker who can make some of this," she said.

"Oh? Does he have a name?"

"I don't know it. You'll have to ask Maria Anna. She used to help Frau Mittelhausen keep the books, so maybe she'll know."

Tom spun a pencil idly around his fingers. "Maria Anna knows something about keeping accounts?"

Magdalena nodded. "Her brother learned a lot about arithmetic at Latin school." She sighed. "I wish I'd had a big brother to teach me mathematics." She set her elbows onto the table and dropped her jaw into the palms of her hands. "Because I'm starting late, I'm weeks behind the other students, and I'll never catch up without a tutor," she muttered distractedly.

"So find yourself a tutor."

She slapped her hands down on the table. "Frau Warner has already given me the name of a suitable tutor, but he costs money." She stared pointedly at Tom, just to make sure he got the message. "I can't ask Maria Anna to pay for a tutor on top of everything else she's paying for."

"Hey, there's work here you can do."

Magdalena looked carefully at Herr Frost. Yes, there was definitely a smug smile hidden there. "You just want someone else to work on the .22 line."

Tom had the gall to nod. "Loading the cases with primer needs a steady hand," he said.

One thing Magdalena did have was steady hands. It was one of the primary skills Dr. Gribbleflotz insisted his laborants had to have, and she wouldn't have lasted as long as she did at HDG Enterprises if her hands hadn't been amongst the steadiest. Still, she resented being offered one of the worst jobs at Brennerei und Chemiefabrik Schwarza, even if a single hour loading .22 cartridges with primer paid more than the tutor Frau Warner had recommended charged for fifty minutes of tutoring. She released a set-upon sigh. "Okay, it's a deal. But I'm only going to do enough hours loading primer to pay for my tutor."

Saturday

Magdalena checked the address. Yes, the number was right. She stepped out onto the road to check the sign over the door—Pastorius Auctions. Well, the name of the tutor Frau Warner had recommended was Daniel Pastorius, so maybe the family lived on the premises. She walked up to the door and tried it. It was unlocked and opened as she pushed it, ringing a bell set just above the door.

A down-time woman appeared almost immediately, a dust cloth in her hands. "Can I help you?" Elisabeth Sultzner asked as she twisted and untwisted the dust cloth.

Magdalena wiped her sweaty palms before answering. "I'm looking for Daniel Pastorius. Do you know where I might find him?"

Elisabeth nodded. "Can I ask what business you have with my son?" she asked.

Magdalena smiled. It seemed she'd come to the right place. "Frau Warner, one of the guidance counselors at the high school, suggested I get in touch with him about tutoring me in mathematics."

"Another one," Elisabeth muttered before pointing to a door. "He's out the back, through there with his brothers and some of their friends," she said. "You should have no difficulty finding them. They're making enough noise."

Magdalena took the door Daniel's mother had pointed to and walked down the corridor. She could hear a weird sound. Maybe that was the noise Daniel's mother had been talking about. As she approached she realized the weird sound was some kind of musical instrument. This was confirmed when she got to an open door and could see a youth of about her own age, with yellowish-brown skin like Herr Schockley's, waving his hands over a small box with a pole sticking out of the top and a bent wire out one end. It was curious, because the sound and volume changed as he moved his hands, even though he didn't touch anything. She walked straight up to the instrument. "What is it?" she asked, her original purpose totally forgotten.

The up-timer boy who was playing the instrument, and she used the term *playing* very loosely, stepped back from the instrument. "It's a Moog Etherwave Theremin," Jason Cheng said. "Would you like to have a go?"

Magdalena didn't have to be asked twice. "What do I have to do?" she asked.

"Come round this side," Jason said. "Stand in front of it, and move your hands through the electromagnetic field."

"She's not going to know what an electromagnetic field is," David Kitt said.

Magdalena stepped back from the theremin, right into Jason. A tingle shot up her body and she hastily broke contact. "I do too know what an electromagnetic field is," she told the boy, who she guessed was about her age also. She'd been exposed to the concept while working with Tom Frost on the design of the bench test version of his continuous flow Birkeland-Eyde reactor. She just hoped no one asked her to explain what they were. "When you wave your hands inside the electromagnetic field you interfere with the force lines of the electromagnetic field of the pole, which causes the sound to change." She proved her statement by waving her hand through the pole's electromagnetic field.

Jason turned to David. "She's got you there, Dave."

David snorted. "Sure. So what's she doing here?"

That question had Magdalena tearing her attention away from the theremin. "I'm looking for Daniel Pastorius."

The four youths glanced towards another youth hidden near a window, quietly working away on a large slate, before returning to look at Magdalena. "What do you want with Daniel?" Michael Pastorius asked.

"I'm starting the electrical trades course a month late and the guidance counselor told me that he might be willing to tutor me in mathematics."

"He doesn't work for free you know," David said.

The boy was trying to be offensive, but you didn't survive in the rough and tumble of HDG Enterprises without learning how to deal with boys. Magdalena chose to treat the statement as a question and not the implication that she was looking for free help. "I know." She produced her most innocent and disarming smile. "I've negotiated to work a few hours a week at Brennerei und Chemiefabrik Schwarza to earn enough to pay even his exorbitant rates."

"Brennerei und Chemiefabrik Schwarza?" David choked out. "You make explosives?"

"Not personally," Magdalena said. "But Herr Frost often tests the quality of the detonators we make." A smile blossomed across her face at the envious looks being cast her way. Boys could be so predictable. She'd seen the same looks back in Jena when she bragged about attending demonstrations by Hans, Kurt, or Michael. Sometimes it had helped to be friends with the sister of one of Dr. Gribbleflotz's top laborants.

"Can we watch next time?" Jason asked.

"I could ask," Magdalena said. She glanced once more at the theremin. "What's going to happen with that?" she asked.

Jason patted the wooden box gently. "Now I've fixed it, it's destined for the high school music department."

Magdalena's tongue traced her dry lips. She noticed Jason staring, blushed, and hastily drew it back. "Frau McDougal?" she asked hopefully.

"You want me to put a word in for you when I turn it over?" Jason asked.

Magdalena nodded. "Please."

"It'll cost you," Jason said with a smile.

She checked the attentive faces of the other three. They were waiting on her next words. She smiled. "I'll talk to Herr Frost about letting you all watch next time he does a quality control check if you'll tell Frau McDougal that Magdalena Rutilius wants to learn how to play the theremin."

Jason held out his right hand. "It's a deal."

Magdalena grasped the warm palm and shook it. "I'll need some names."

"Jason Cheng," Jason said before using his free hand to single out the others. "That guy is David Kitt, and the two big guys are Michael and Johan Pastorius." He waved to the youth over by the window. "And that's Daniel over there."

Magdalena tugged her hand free and turned her hot face away. She studied Daniel. There was an aura of innocence about him. "Is he deaf or something?" she asked.

"Or something," Johan said. "When he's solving mathematics problems the rest of the world might as well not exist."

"And he does it for fun," David muttered.

She shot David a glance. "He does what for fun?" she asked.

"He solves mathematics problems," Jason answered. "The only other person I've ever met like him is my mom." He tried to catch Magdalena's hand again before settling for placing a hand at her waist to guide her towards Daniel.

Jason reached out and tapped Daniel a couple of times. "Daniel, someone to see you."

Magdalena was suspicious the moment she saw the hastily hidden twinkle in Daniel's eye. The sly so-and-so had been listening. She glanced at the slate he'd been writing on, and swallowed. It looked like he was using half the Greek alphabet. "Hi, I'm Magdalena Rutilius and I'm been exempt the first year of the electrical trades certificate, but because I've missed the first few weeks of year two, Frau Warner suggested I should ask you to help me catch up."

Daniel stood up clumsily, as if he was still growing into a growth spurt, and Magdalena only then realized he couldn't be any older than her. "How old are you?" she demanded.

"Fourteen."

"And a half," Jason said. "Don't let his age fool you, Magdalena. Daniel was supposed to start at the University of Jena a couple of years ago, but a family friend advised them he should come to Grantville to study."

"Come along," Daniel said to Magdalena. "We need to sort out where and when we can get together."

Magdalena paused at the door for one last glance back. She was distracted for a moment by a waving Jason, but then her eyes settled on the theremin until a less than subtle cough from Daniel told her that he was waiting. "Sorry," she said before hurrying through the door.

"Jason is a member of the computer club," Daniel said.

Magdalena shot him a look. There was no sly grin or anything in his demeanor. It was like he was simply stating a fact. Still, Magdalena chose to deny she had any interest in the up-timer. "I was actually saying farewell to the theremin."

"Of course you were."

"I don't know what you're trying to suggest, but I want to learn how to play that instrument."

"Keep telling yourself that," Daniel said. "I've got an older sister, and . . ." He grinned. "I can't promise that Frau McDougal will issue the theremin to you, but I can arrange for you to get the first chance to prove you deserve to learn how to play it."

"How can you do that?" Magdalena demanded.

"Some of her best students need help keeping up their grade average, and I'm the best mathematics tutor there is."

"And so modest too," Magdalena muttered.

Thursday

"Magdalena, please stay after class," Elizabeth "Bitsy" McDougal said before dismissing the class.

Magdalena gathered her papers and presented herself at Frau McDougal's desk. As the other students filed past they gave her sympathetic smiles and pats on the shoulder. The last student left and the room fell silent. "Is everything all right, Frau McDougal?" she asked.

"You have some interesting friends," Bitsy said.

Hope built up in Magdalena. It had been days since Daniel had promised to have words with Frau McDougal about the theremin. "Yes," she said hopefully.

"I hope you don't have anything else planned over the lunch break," Bitsy said as she pulled a familiar box out of a supply cupboard.

"I can learn to play the theremin?" she asked, her excitement betrayed by the way the pitch of her voice shot up.

Bitsy took a step backwards, clutching to her chest the box the theremin was packed in. "Do you have access to power where you live?"

"Yes. I live in a house on Grays Run Road," Magdalena said, barely restraining her urge to snatch the theremin from the teacher. "There's a small shed where I can practice without disturbing anyone."

She didn't have to tell Frau McDougal that she'd made those arrangements the moment she got back from the Pastorius Auction Rooms.

Bitsy relented and laid the box on her desk. "Then let's get it assembled and I'll try to teach you how to play it."

Magdalena shot Frau McDougal a look. "Try to teach me? Do you think I can't learn?"

Bitsy shook her head. "Until this week I've never had more than a minute or two on a theremin."

"Oh! You don't know how to play it?"

Bitsy smiled at Magdalena. "We'll just have to learn together. Now, let's put it together and get started."

Magdalena didn't dance home that day. Neither did she skip. Instead, she walked quickly, but carefully, fully aware of the irreplaceable instrument she carried on her back. When she got home she stopped by the house to drop off her school bag and tell people she was home before hurrying over to the shed she'd been allocated. It took her only minutes to assemble the theremin and plug it in. Then she started playing it.

She was still working on her scales an hour later when Tom Frost stopped by.

"So that's the magic machine, is it?" he asked as he walked up to the theremin.

Magdalena nodded. "It's fun," she said as she randomly poked her hands into the machine's electromagnetic field.

"Nice. Is it enough fun to justify inviting your boyfriends around to watch me and Carl blow things up?"

"They're not my boyfriends," Magdalena protested. "Will you let them set anything off?"

"Maybe, but it'll cost you," Tom warned.

Magdalena looked at Tom suspiciously. "What do you want now?" she asked.

"Right now, I just want to know if you have some headphones for your new toy."

"It's not a toy," Magdalena protested. She saw the grin on Tom's face and shot daggers at him. "Yes, it comes with headphones. Why, is the noise disturbing you? I'm sorry, but I'll only learn how to find the right notes with practice."

"No," Tom said, "it's not disturbing me, yet, but I've got a couple of guys coming round to have a look at the Birkeland-Eyde reactor." He started moving boxes away from the reactor to allow easy access to it.

"Is there something wrong with it?" she asked. They'd run it just the previous evening, and it had seemed to work correctly then.

"No. It's working great. But Sam Haygood and Erwin O'Keefe have agreed to help design an industrial model," Tom said as he dragged a heavy box to one side, "and they want to see the bench test version running."

"Can I watch?" Magdalena begged. "Herr Haygood's my electrical technology teacher, and I'd like to see how he solves a real world problem."

Tom shrugged. "It'll cut into your practice time," he warned.

"I think it'll be worth it."

"If that's what you want," Tom said. "I'm off to the house. You get back to your practice and I'll bring Sam and Erwin around when they get here."

Magdalena waited until Tom left the shed before turning the theremin back on and starting her scales again.

❖　　　❖　　　❖

Magdalena had been expecting Tom to return with Herr Haygood and Herr O'Keefe at any moment for the last fifteen minutes, so she was a little on edge when Tom finally opened the door. Her eyes lit up when she saw her favorite teacher, and faded when she saw Herr O'Keefe, the head of the apprentice training program. "Herr O'Keefe, Herr Haygood."

"Hi, Magdalena. Tom's been telling us that you helped him build a Birkeland-Eyde reactor," Sam said.

She giggled. "I was his *gofer*, Herr Haygood," she said, using one of Sam's favorite loan words.

"But it's all good practice," Erwin said as he swept his eyes over the instrument she'd been playing. "That a theremin?" he asked.

"Yes. Frau McDougal allocated it to me," she said defensively.

Erwin seemed to miss her discomfort. "You got a circuit diagram for it?" he asked.

Magdalena nodded.

Erwin nodded. "I know you're only just started your trade certificate, but Tom seems to think you might like to make the creation of your own theremin your graduating project."

Magdalena's eyes flicked from a smiling Tom Frost to the theremin. Graduating projects were usually undertaken in one's final year and contributed to your final grade. They could be based on just about anything electrical, with the strict proviso that they had to be constructed solely from down-time sourced components, using only down-time sourced tools and instruments. She looked back up. "I wouldn't know where to start," she admitted.

"If you can get me a copy of the circuit diagram,

I'll see about putting together a reading list for you," Sam said.

"It's never too soon to start thinking about your project, Frau Rutilius," Erwin said. "That way, if for any reason your first choice is considered unsuitable, you'll have time to start something else."

"But why might a theremin be considered unsuitable, Herr O'Keefe? You've just suggested that I make one as my graduating project."

Erwin nodded. "True, but I don't know if it'll be possible with the available technology. It'll be your job to prove that it is possible before the project can be approved."

"It won't hurt to do a little reading, Mags, and you might walk out of it with your very own theremin," Tom said. He turned to Sam and Erwin. "If you'll just come over here, I'll demonstrate how the reactor works."

Magdalena stared unseeing at the backs of the three men. Herr Frost had hit on a sore point. The theremin she was using belonged to the high school. When she left school, she'd have to give it back. She reached out and patted it gently before checking that it was turned off. Then she walked over to listen as the men talked about the problems associated with turning a bench test reactor into an industrial reactor capable of continuous operation.

Saturday, the old quarry

Magdalena was lying back against a tree enjoying the warmth of the autumn sun as she watched Tom Frost and Carl Schockley set up their latest series of tests. Hanging on their every word were Jason, David, Michael, and Johan. Daniel had been invited, but he was sitting against the next tree industriously scribbling away on his oversize portable slate.

In the distance a bell was rung. Magdalena switched her attention to the bell-ringer. It was a warning that they were ready to detonate. She grabbed her earmuffs and stood, waving to show the flag waver, Jason, that she'd heard the warning. She walked over to Daniel, picked up the earmuffs dropped carelessly beside him, and waved them under his nose. "They're ready," she told him.

With both of them wearing ear protection she raised two fists with upraised thumbs to Jason and stood and waited.

She didn't have to wait long, as almost immediately after Jason ducked down behind a protective berm the charge was detonated. She saw dirt kicked up and she felt the shock wave before she heard the sound, much muffled by her hearing protection.

Beside her Daniel took off his earmuffs. "I hope these results are better," he muttered.

"Better?" Magdalena asked.

"The results so far don't correlate well with my predictions." He shook his head in frustration. "There's something wrong with my force calculations for the charges they're using," he muttered.

"How do you mean?" Magdalena asked as she crouched down beside Daniel and looked at the slate he was scribbling on.

He turned despairing eyes to Magdalena. "The force generated is much greater than I calculated."

The Pastorius family affectionately referred to Daniel

as the Puppy, mostly because he had about as much control of his growing body as a puppy. Right now Magdalena could see another explanation for the name. His soulful eyes gave him the appearance of a beaten puppy. She tried to think of how she might reassure him, but this was Daniel. If he was miscalculating something, what chance did she have to help him? She settled for what she had to offer, a hug. "Maybe you missed something," she suggested.

Daniel pulled away from her. "But what?" he demanded as he crushed the chalk he was holding into the slate in frustration. "I've got the amount of powder used, the composition, and the rate of combustion." He ran a hand through his hair. "What am I missing?"

Magdalena struggled to think of something to remove the despairing look on Daniel's face. She found it in a vague memory of something she'd heard. "Gunpowder has to be confined before it can explode," she said.

Daniel's head jerked round. "What was that?"

Magdalena gave him a wry smile. "Just something Maria Anna's brother said once. If you pour a sample of gunpowder onto a piece of paper and ignite it, it'll flare off, but if you roll that same sample tightly in the paper and insert a fuse, the gunpowder will explode."

A smile grew on Daniel's face. He glanced from his workings back to Magdalena. "That's it. Time. I missed out the amount of time the expanding gases were confined." He threw his arms around Magdalena and hugged her.

"Hey, are you messing around with my girl?" Jason asked.

Magdalena sighed happily as she went from Daniel's arms to Jason's. She gave him a little kiss. "Have you been having fun?"

"Yes, but maybe not as much fun as you two," Jason said.

A quick glance reassured Magdalena that Jason wasn't serious. "I think I just helped Daniel solve a problem," she informed him.

Jason whistled. "You helped Daniel solve a problem?" She giggled at the mock disbelief.

"Yes," Daniel said. "She made me realize I'd failed to consider how long it would take for the pressure in the barrels to grow to breaking point." He looked earnestly at Jason. "Would your father know the pressure limits on the barrels Herr Frost and Herr Schockley are using?" he asked.

Jason laughed and hugged Magdalena. "I have absolutely no idea. I can ask, but what good will it do you?"

Daniel looked horrified. "What good? It'll help me calculate the effects of a gunpowder explosion," he said.

Magdalena broke away from Jason and hugged Daniel. "It's okay, Daniel, he didn't really mean it the way it sounded." She shot Jason a condemning glare for his insensitivity. "I think he meant to ask what is the practical use of the knowledge."

"Oh!" Daniel grinned at Jason. "If I know the maximum pressure of a container, I can calculate the minimum amount of gunpowder needed to shatter it."

"Thereby saving on the amount of gunpowder being used," Carl Schockley said. "Can you really calculate that?"

Carl's question was greeted by disapproving glares

from Jason, David, Michael, Johan, and Magdalena. Daniel just said "yes."

"And he'll work it all out using just his slate," Jason added for good measure.

Carl held up his hands defensively. "Hey, no offense intended. I'm just surprised, and amazed. That's pretty advanced engineering."

Daniel shook his head. "It's not engineering, it's mathematics."

"At least he didn't say 'simply mathematics,'" Jason muttered into Magdalena's ear.

"Let's everyone go over to the pit and measure up Daniel another data point," Michael said, defusing the situation nicely.

*A week later, the back room at
Pastorius Auction Rooms*

Magdalena was enjoying some quality time with Jason. He was running tests on the latest collection of electrical goods the Pastorius brothers had collected for auction while she worked on a new and improved crystal radio. With Jason's help she'd designed a better holder for the cat's whisker signal detector—one that was less susceptible to misalignment caused by the radio being moved. She was just running a wire against the coil trying to locate the Voice of America when a girl, who could only be a relative of Jason's, entered.

"I see the lovebirds are hard at work," Diana Cheng said as she waltzed up beside her brother to check what he was doing. "Any hair dryers?" she asked hopefully.

"Not a chance," Jason said. "Why don't you ask dad to make one for you?"

"Because all I want is a simple hair dryer, not something with a hundred and one features I'll never use."

Jason turned to Magdalena. "This, in case you're wondering, is my elder sister Diana."

Magdalena lowered the earpiece she was holding and waved. "Hi."

"Hi, I'm Diana. The scumbag might have mentioned me." She glared at Jason. "And that's older sister. I'm the only one you've got."

"For which I'm eternally grateful."

Magdalena grinned. It was clear to her that these siblings actually liked each other. "Not by name."

"I can imagine what he did call me." She glanced at Jason. "Mom sent me round to ask if Magdalena wants to join us for lunch. So, are you free?" she asked Magdalena.

Magdalena swallowed and nodded hesitantly. Being invited to meet your boyfriend's family was a significant step, even if you were only fourteen.

"Hey, don't worry," Diana said. "Mom's just going to ask if you can cook, can you keep a household, do you like children, how many children you'd like to have. You know, just the usual things a mother asks her son's girlfriend."

"Sis!" Jason roared.

Magdalena looked from an outraged Jason to a grinning Diana. Their eyes met, and they both broke down. A disgruntled Jason stalked off long before they managed to stop laughing.

Chapter 13

Dr. Phil's Amazing Essence of Fire Tablets

March, 1633, Grays Run, Grantville

Catharina Gerber placed herself right in front of Celeste Frost. "Why do we have to invite this woman into our house?" she demanded. "She has her own house, and a very good one from what I've seen."

"Lettie's just lost her husband," Celeste said. "She keeps seeing him everywhere she looks around their old home."

Catharina gave a graceless nod of acknowledgment. "If she has to leave her own home, why can't she stay with her family?" She paused for a moment. "She does have family here in Grantville, doesn't she?"

Here Celeste felt she was on safe ground. She nodded, and before Catharina could take advantage of the admission, she told her who Lettie's family was.

"A Methodist minister?" Catharina shook her head at the idea.

"Both her daughter and son-in-law." Celeste smiled

at the look of horror on Catharina's face. "Yes, double trouble, and besides, Lettie knows about photography."

Catharina's brows shot up. Celeste felt as if she should be seeing cartoon dollar signs in her eyes. "Yes, and all she wants for her help recreating photography is sanctuary from her daughter."

Catharina's tongue dashed out and wet her lips. Celeste could only guess at the calculations going on in that mind.

"What does she know about photography that makes you so interested in her?" she asked.

Celeste gestured to some of the boxes that filled the room. "Her husband was a real enthusiast. He didn't just have his own regular darkroom, he also reenacted as a photographer."

"What does that have to do with helping us recreate photography?"

"During the American Civil War, photography was wet plate. That means Fred, and by long association, Lettie, had to learn to make their own photographic paper and plates. That knowledge can save us years of trial and error research."

"Right," Catharina said, rubbing her hands together briskly. "Let's go and make sure our new resident feels welcome."

Dr. Gribbleflotz's office, Jena

Phillip took another look at the bill. He was spending *that* much on candles? Surely not. "Frau Mittelhausen. This bill for candles. Who's been using wax candles so wastefully?"

Ursula Mittelhausen sighed heavily before looking Phillip straight in the eye. "You have been, Herr Dr. Gribbleflotz. You use the good wax candles to heat your beakers. Why you can't use that alcohol burner the up-timers provided, I don't know."

Phillip paused to digest Frau Mittelhausen's statement. Well, yes, he did use candles to heat the beakers sometimes. Especially when he didn't want a big fire. The problem was that the tallow candles didn't give anything like the same heat. And they produced too much soot. Even wax candles, which burned cleaner and hotter, made a lot of soot. He often needed to use several candles at once.

He knew what he needed. Something like the "Bunsen burners" at the up-timer high school. However, that would have to wait until he had access to gas. He knew there had been talk of producing "propane," but for now that was as far off as his much-needed aluminum. As for the alcohol burner the Kubiak Country people had given him, it was very clever. But he could never see the flame, and the alcohol was always evaporating, and it always ran out at the most inconvenient moment. At least with candles he could easily add more, and the heat from several candles was greater than that of the single alcohol burner.

He returned to checking the bills. "There must be a better way."

Grays Run, Grantville

"No, not there. Would you mind moving it against the other wall?" Lettie Sebastian was having the time of her life ordering two able-bodied men about as she arranged her new room to her complete satisfaction.

"How's everything going?" Celeste asked from the door.

"Everything's just peachy," Tom said. He turned to Lettie. "Are we just about finished?"

Lettie contemplated asking them to move her bed again, but decided she actually liked where it was at the moment. "There are just a couple of boxes of clothes and things. If a couple of you big strong men would like to bring them in, I'll sort them out."

Lettie waited for Tom and Carl to leave before grabbing a magazine from the bed. "I know it's in here somewhere," she muttered as she flipped through the pages.

"What?" Celeste asked.

"Fred took some photographs of this property years ago, and I'm sure they printed them in this magazine." She flipped through a few more pages, then back one. "Yes, here they are." She held it out for Celeste. "The place has changed a lot since then."

"Coming through," Tom called before entering with a stack of cardboard boxes. "Where do you want them?" he asked.

Lettie dropped the magazine on the bed and quickly cleared a space for the boxes. "Just here will do."

Tom set his cartons on the bed and then Carl added the ones he was carrying. The top box from his stack slid off, onto the bedspread, sending the magazine onto the floor.

"I'll get that," Carl said as Lettie moved to recover the magazine.

His hand paused just before picking it up. Then he grabbed it and started reading. "I'd like to borrow this for a moment," he told Lettie before heading for the door.

"Where're you going, Carl?" Tom called after him.

Carl paused by the door and waved the magazine. "I need to make a telephone call."

"What was that about?" Lettie asked after Carl disappeared.

"No idea," Tom said. "What magazine was that?"

"Just a local promotional guide," Lettie said. "I only kept it because there are several of Fred's photographs in it."

A few minutes later Carl returned. "Thanks," he said to Lettie as he returned the magazine. "Is it okay if I borrow the cart?" he asked Celeste. "I want to head over to Tracy Kubiak's to pick up something."

"We're finished with it for today," Celeste said.

"Right, thanks, I shouldn't be too long."

Celeste, Tom, and Lettie stared at each other after Carl left. Then Lettie started flicking through the pages of the magazine until she came to a page with an advertisement for *Grantville Canvas and Outdoor*, the mostly online business Tracy Kubiak had started in the basement of her home shortly after she married Ted Kubiak and settled in Grantville. "I'm sure that's the page Mr. Schockley was so interested in, but it's just advertising canvas goods and military surplus supplies." She passed the open magazine to Celeste.

"Military surplus can cover a multiple of sins," Tom suggested.

"And we know it has to be bulky or heavy," Celeste said, "otherwise Carl wouldn't need the handcart."

"Which doesn't help us in the slightest," Tom said. "I wonder what Tracy has that Carl's so excited about."

Grantville Canvas and Outdoor,
Mahan Run

Tracy Kubiak was removing a photograph from her 'Me Wall' when her husband Ted returned from helping Carl carry out his purchases.

"Well, that was all very cloak and dagger," Ted said, "Any idea what Carl wants with those cases of fuel tablets?"

"He said he had a recipe to turn it into a precursor for C-4," she said as she moved other photographs around to fill in the gap she'd made.

Ted whistled. "I wonder where he dug up that recipe," he said as he joined Tracy. "Hey, what are you doing? Culling your Me Wall?"

"Carl asked me to remove this photograph." She wondered how quickly Ted would catch on as she offered it to him.

"Carl asked you?" He looked dubiously at the large corkboard decorated with the photographs and other memorabilia of Tracy's life held in place by crisscrossed elastic, shook his head, and then looked at the photograph. "Hey, is that Carl?" he asked, pointing to a uniformed man in a group photograph.

She edged over to check Ted had located Carl in the photograph. "Yes."

"What was he doing at Yuma?"

Tracy raised a brow at the silliness of the question. Carl was in a photograph with her and other personnel at the Military Free Fall School at the Yuma Proving Ground in Arizona, where she'd served as a Rigger. "What do you think?"

"But freefall training was reserved for . . . Oh." Ted

nodded knowingly. "That's where he learned how to make C-4 from fuel tablets. He was a Green Beret."

"Engineering sergeant and Military Free Fall specialist," Tracy agreed.

Ted handed the photograph back. "Shouldn't he be in the army? All that special training has to be good for something."

Tracy accepted the photograph and dropped it into a drawer. "He's making a lot more money with Kelly Construction. Still, he told me he's currently helping train the Thuringian Rifles."

"The snipers?" Ted asked. "Are you saying that on top of being able to cook up explosives from things he finds lying around like MacGyver, Carl's also a trained sniper?"

"No, but he is a trained trainer, and he said he'd helped the weapons sergeants run sniper courses for foreign forces abroad often enough to remember most of the drills."

"So the C-4 is for the Thuringian Rifles?" Ted asked.

"That's the plan," Tracy said. "At least until Greg Ferrara discovers how to make hexamine."

April 1633, the new HDG Laboratories facility, Jena

Phillip walked around the site of what would soon be the head office and main manufactory of HDG Enterprises. The new facility, hence the new name, was a large compound with buildings for the various production lines, accommodations for laborants and other employees who lived on site, the head office, and the new apartment for himself and his household.

Finally, there was the set of rooms that were his personal office and laboratory.

The current area of interest was the large water-wheel, or more precisely, the area where the water-wheel would be installed. Phillip could see the men clambering around the heavy structure that would eventually support the wheel. He joined the small crowd watching an older man slapping clay around the joints in the steel. Confused, he continued to watch.

"You might want to step back, Dr. Gribbleflotz."

Phillip turned and looked up to see Ted Kubiak. "What's he doing?" He pointed to Erwin O'Keefe.

Ted followed Phillip's pointing arm. "We want to weld the steel frame together so Erwin is going to use thermite to do it. Right now he's slapping on clay to contain the molten steel until it cools."

"Molten steel? How can you melt steel without a furnace?"

"Thermite burns really hot, Dr. Gribbleflotz. I can ask Erwin to explain if you like, but for now, just watch. This is going to be really cool."

Phillip watched as the man he assumed was Erwin set an odd package over one of the clay-covered joints, lit a fuse and jogged back a considerable distance. After a few moments, the brightest light Phillip had ever seen burst from the package. White-hot droplets leaked from the bottom of the clay seals.

Ted pointed. "Those droplets are molten iron from the thermite. The clay holds it in, and the iron cools in place to make a weld. It's really neat to watch."

Phillip stared, awestruck. "Yes, please, Herr Kubiak. Do ask Erwin to explain."

A *few days later*

Phillip idly fondled a crude iron ingot while he read the letter from Erwin O'Keefe. The ingot was the product of a final demonstration of the thermite reaction that Herr O'Keefe had conducted with one of the remaining thermite kits he had brought with him. The demonstration had so impressed Phillip that he had asked for a "cheat sheet." Herr O'Keefe's letter described the thermite reaction in such detail that he was sure he could easily duplicate it. Herr O'Keefe had even included a couple of alternative methods of initiating the reaction.

Phillip looked over at his cabinet of chemicals in their jars and bottles. He selected a jar and a bottle and walked to his fume cupboard where he placed a watch glass on a dished firebrick and carefully measured out a small amount of the purple crystals from the jar. Then he added just a drop of the oily liquid from the bottle and started the stopwatch function of his repackaged up-time digital watch.

While he waited, Phillip admired the "Buick" logo on the sash window of the fume cupboard. He watched through the safety glass as the purple powder ignited. With the first signs of ignition Phillip stopped his watch. After observing the whole pile of crystals burn, he retreated to his desk where he made notes in his journal. The observed time for the reaction to occur was within the range Herr O'Keefe had written. It was a most interesting experiment, but not as interesting as melting iron in a ceramic pot would be.

As he read Erwin O'Keefe's directions, Phillip could see a potential problem. The thermite reaction used aluminum. Aluminum was a rare and strategic resource. The Kubiak people had indicated he was lucky to get the few pounds they had been able to provide.

Unlike his aluminum pyramid, the thermite reaction could use any aluminum. Minor impurities did not matter. Phillip looked along his bookshelf, toward the model pyramid with its faceted gems. He sighed. He had had such hopes when the Kubiak Country people had provided him with the ingots of aluminum. However, his tests with the scale model had failed to invigorate the Quinta Essentia of the humors of the small rodents he had tested it on. He had concluded that it was the aluminum that was at fault. He'd postulated that it wasn't pure. The Kubiak Country people had later admitted that the aluminum they'd provided him had in fact been an alloy, and not the pure metal.

Phillip already knew that pure aluminum would not be available until the up-timers were able to mine the ore. Well, they had admitted that there might be a way to purify the aluminum. However, it required a chemical he wanted nothing to do with. After reading the up-timer handling instructions and warnings, he was happy to let others play with hydrofluoric acid.

He walked over to his store cupboard. Once there, he picked up the few remaining ingots of aluminum. At a guess he had half a pound left. Biting his lip, he turned his gaze to his dysfunctional model pyramid. Make that two pounds.

Seated back at his desk he caressed the iron ingot while he re-read Herr O'Keefe's letter. An image appeared in his mind. He could see it vividly. He, Dr. Phillip Theophrastus Gribbleflotz, the World's Greatest Alchemist, giving one of his justly famous seminars, and as the pièce de resistance, a demonstration of thermite with... Phillip looked down at the iron ingot in his hand... a specially molded shape. Something special. Something of distinction.

Thinking of distinction, he looked down at Erwin O'Keefe's letter. No. "Thermite Reaction" didn't have the right ring to it. It needed something more. A real name. Phillip allowed his mind to wander as he searched for inspiration. The molten iron could obviously be molded into any shape. It would take a little experimentation to get it right, but imagine, in a haze of the brightest light, forming an ingot of pure iron from the dross of rust. Phillip shivered. It was almost a holy event. Then it struck him. The "Gribbleflotz Candles of the Essence of Light." Nobody in Jena would be able to duplicate the demonstration, and if people should want to buy the iron ingot... Maybe if it was formed into some significant shape? The ideas ran through his mind while he visualized the demand for his demonstrations.

With a sigh he came back to reality. He didn't have enough aluminum to demonstrate the Gribbleflotz Candles of the Essence of Light at all of his regular seminars. It was a pity, but he would just have to limit the demonstration to maybe one a month. Maybe by the time he used up his small store of aluminum the up-timers would be mining the ore for more. But first things first. Before he could do any demonstrations he had to be sure he could make the Gribbleflotz Candles of the Essence of Light work reliably. To have one fail would be humiliating. He walked over to the door of his personal laboratory, opened it and called out for his laborant. "Hans. We have work to do."

August 1633, HDG Laboratories, Jena

The first demonstrations had gone well. The audiences had been most impressed by his Gribbleflotz Candles of the Essence of Light. The molds his personal laborant, Hans Saltzman, had prepared had produced finely detailed animals. The rabbit, the lamb, even a ram. Phillip smiled at the memories of his success and turned back to watch Hans preparing for his next lesson in alchemy.

With the electricity from the water-driven generator, Phillip had been able to experiment with electrolysis. His first experiments had duplicated the work he had seen demonstrated at the water works in Grantville. Since then he had been adding things to the basic "bleach" to see what he could make.

Phillip withdrew the jar containing his latest creation. So far he hadn't had time to examine the white powder Hans had scraped from the wash filters. This was . . . he looked at his notes again . . . this was the twenty-third result from mixing something with "bleach." Bleach was such an ugly word. It did nothing to describe the substance. "The Ethereal Essence of Common Salt." Much more satisfying.

"Light the candle, Hans." Phillip stood just behind his laborant while he instructed him on laboratory procedures.

"Now, using the wood split like a spoon, scoop a small amount of the compound onto the splint." Hans held the loaded splint just above the jar. "That's a little too much. Tap it gently on the jar to reduce the amount. Yes. That's enough. Now hold the tip of the splint over the flame."

Their eyes followed the loaded tip of the wood splint as it was placed over the flame. Phillip waited to see what would happen.

"What!" Hans dropped the suddenly flaring splint. He slammed the sash of the fume cupboard down, sealing the still burning chemical inside. He was shaking a little.

"What happened, Hans?" Phillip's voice was remarkably calm.

Hans' voice shook. "I was holding the compound over the flame when suddenly it burst into a violent flame. I am sorry I dropped the splint, Herr Dr. Gribbleflotz. Should I repeat the experiment?"

"No, Hans. You did well. Even I, with my years of experience, was surprised at the vigor with which the compound burnt. I compliment you on your quick thinking in closing the safety door so promptly. I want you to write up what you did, what happened, and your conclusions. We'll compare our observations and conclusions over dinner."

"Thank you, Herr Dr. Gribbleflotz." Hans grabbed his notes before making his escape.

Phillip smiled at the retreating back. Hans was proving himself a suitable student of alchemy. He certainly had the right reflexes. Shutting the safety door of the fume cupboard and letting the splint burn rather than try to pick it up again had been the right thing to do.

He made his way over to his desk and sat down to consider the experiment they had just conducted. It had been a most vigorous reaction. Excepting the candles of the essence of light reaction, and the self-ignition of the flowers of hartshorn, it was one of the most vigorous he had ever seen. He wrote up his observations and conclusions.

The noise in the courtyard attracted Phillip's attention. Looking through the window he was in time to see Frau Mittelhausen greeting the up-timer, Ted Kubiak. A couple of men helped Ted unload the wagon. There were a number of large bottles of something. Ted took one handle of a large basket that contained a bottle, and, with Hans Saltzman, carried the bottle into the building.

Moments later he could hear them in the corridor outside his laboratory. Quickly he hurried over to open the door for them.

"Where do you want it?" Ted asked. "This sucker is pretty heavy."

"Over there on that table, please, Herr Kubiak." Phillip waved towards a table set against a wall. "What's in the bottle?"

Ted smiled and patted the five-gallon bottle. "This is some of the new waters of formalin you were asking about when you visited the gas works."

Phillip looked at the size of the container. "That is much more than I usually deal with in my experiments, Herr Kubiak."

"Sorry about that." Ted shrugged. "But the gas works were going to charge about the same price to fill the big bottle as they would if we filled a little bottle. So I went for the big one. You never know, you might find a use for it all."

Phillip smiled in return. Yes, if the price was much the same it would have been silly to buy just a small bottle.

Ted had been looking around the laboratory. Right

at the moment he was sniffing the air around the fume cupboard. "What are you working on at the moment, Dr. Gribbleflotz? If you don't mind me asking."

Phillip looked from the fume cupboard to his notes. "Nothing much. Just before you arrived, I was supervising Hans as he tested a new compound. It was something I created using the new electrolysis equipment, 'The Salt of the Ethereal Essence of Common Salt and Ash.' However, it was most disappointing. All it did was increase the rate at which a splint of wood burnt."

"Oh, well. Not everything you discover has an immediate use. Maybe sometime in the future you'll find something it's good for."

Phillip smiled at the up-timer's attempt to raise his spirits. He rested his eyes on the bottle of waters of formalin. "I now have something new to experiment with. Thank you for bringing me the waters of formalin, Herr Kubiak. To make a special trip to Jena just to make the delivery was most kind."

Ted's ears showed a red tinge. "Actually, Dr. Gribbleflotz, I'm on my way to Magdeburg and points north on a buying and selling trip. I had to stop by anyway, to stock up here before I left." Ted shot a gaze at his wristwatch. "Is that the time? I really must get on my way. Your people should have filled the wagon by now."

Phillip smiled broadly while the tall up-timer made his hasty escape. Then, with a contented sigh, he turned his attention back to his laboratory. That fume cupboard needed to be cleaned out first. "Hans, please clean the fume cupboard while I gather my notes from the gas works. We will both have to do some reading."

Hans, who had been hanging back while Phillip talked to Ted, hastened to clean up the fume cupboard.

"What do you intend doing with the new waters of formalin, Herr Dr. Gribbleflotz?" he asked.

"We will decide that after I have read my notes."

A *few days later*

In accordance with the recommendation of his up-timer contacts they had spent the first few days concentrating the waters of formalin. Now, at last, they could begin experimenting with it. Phillip stood just behind and to one side of Hans and took notes while the laborant carefully released spirits of hartshorn from the titration tube into the beaker of concentrated formalin with his left hand while his right hand constantly stirred the solution in the beaker.

"Stop!" Phillip had seen the first signs that something was precipitating out of the solution. Stepping forward, he read the level from the titration tube and recorded the information.

"Notice, Hans, how something is 'precipitating out' of the solution. Under the up-timer chemistry, we should be able to calculate something about the nature of the product. That will be an assignment for you."

"Thank you, Herr Dr. Gribbleflotz."

Phillip smiled at Hans' less than enthusiastic response. Even as a coauthor of the Expert's guide range of booklets that complemented the Dr. Gribbleflotz alchemy sets, Hans was finding some aspects of the up-timer chemistry difficult. "Continue to add the spirits of hartshorn until you are sure there will be no more precipitate produced. Then run it through a filter paper and we'll see what we have."

Phillip stood back and observed while Hans added some more spirits of hartshorn. When his laborant thought the reaction was complete, he selected a piece of filter paper from a drawer, folded it, and placed it into a funnel. He then poured the contents of the beaker through the funnel. Then he placed the filter paper on a clean watch glass. He glanced in Phillip's direction, and he nodded to indicate that Hans should continue. Hans then opened the folds of the filter paper to expose the precipitate. Then he used his fingers to squeeze it.

"It is waxy, Herr Dr. Gribbleflotz. And..." Hans touched his fingers to his tongue. "It is sweet."

"Hans!" Phillip almost roared at Hans in disappointment. "What is the first rule of safe alchemy?"

Sucking his finger still, Hans looked at Phillip. "Everything is considered dangerous until proven to be safe?"

"Yes. And do you know that compound is safe?" Phillip was pretty sure it was, but he wanted to use this opportunity to drive home to Hans the need to be more careful in the laboratory. The next thing he tasted might not be so benign.

Hans took his finger from his mouth and looked at it. The implication of what Phillip was saying had clearly just hit him. "No, Herr Dr. Gribbleflotz."

"Then why did you use your bare finger to test the texture of the compound, and then put it into your mouth?"

"But it should be safe, Herr Dr. Gribbleflotz. The waters of formalin and the spirits of hartshorn are not poisonous." Hans hesitated a moment. "Are they?"

Phillip looked pointedly at his watch, a Frankensteinish creation combining an up-time digital watch and a down-time produced battery all shoehorned into something no bigger than a standard pocket-watch. "It's only been a couple of minutes since you first introduced the substance to your mouth. That's much too soon to be sure of anything. We will need to wait a little longer to be sure." He deliberately took his time pretending to carefully study Hans. "How do you feel?" He had to bite down hard on his teeth to stop himself laughing at Hans, who was starting to sweat.

Hans used the front of his lab apron to mop the sweat from his brow. "I don't feel unwell, Herr Dr. Gribbleflotz."

"That's a good sign." A few minutes later Phillip touched a hand to Hans' forehead. "You are still with us, Hans?"

"Yes, Herr Dr. Gribbleflotz. I still do not feel unwell."

"And you show no signs of fever, so I believe we can conclude that, in the dosage you took, the compound is not poisonous." Phillip paused to consider the obvious relief on Hans' face. "But let that be a lesson to you, Hans. Never take an unnecessary risk in the laboratory." Phillip paused and looked from Hans to the compound sitting on the watch glass. "Sweet, you said?"

Hans nodded.

"Could it be 'sugar'?"

After a period of deliberation Hans shook his head. "No, Herr Dr. Gribbleflotz, it's not that sweet."

"A pity, a great pity, Hans. To have been able to make sugar by mixing chemicals would have ranked as a glorious discovery, especially given the cost of sugar. Now, I guess I must taste it myself."

Phillip stood behind Hans while they tested their new compound. Hans had loaded the tip of a wood splint and was about to place it over the burning candle.

Both of them paid close attention. The reaction, when it occurred, was most interesting. The compound, whatever it was, caught fire before the thin splint of wood.

Hans took some of the remaining precipitate and rolled it in his fingers. Then, holding it between two splints, he held it over the candle until it caught fire. He then passed his left hand above the burning compound. "It gives off a good heat, Herr Dr. Gribbleflotz."

"Drop in onto a clean watch glass and see how cleanly it burns."

Hans dropped the burning compound onto a clean watch glass and held a second clean watch glass over the burning compound. He had to put it down quickly because of the heat, but by placing it on a clean piece of paper they were better able to see any soot collecting on the glass.

"It is less soot than from even a wax candle, Herr Dr. Gribbleflotz." Hans turned excited eyes to Phillip. "Could it be a wickless candle?"

Phillip thought for a moment, then shook his head slowly. "No, Hans. It doesn't give off the light of a true candle. However, you say it gives off heat. Maybe we have discovered a replacement for the expensive candles we currently use in our experiments. Come. Let us make a bigger batch. We have many more tests to conduct."

December 1633, Magdeburg

"Hi, Mike. We've got something for you." Greg Ferrara and Christie Penzey slipped into Mike Stearns' office.

Greg delved into a paper bag and extracted a package from it. He slid it across Mike's desk.

Mike poked suspiciously at the waxed-paper bundle. "So, what is it?"

"Cyclotrimethylenetrinitramine."

Mike looked to Christie. "Could you translate that, please?"

"It's RDX, or Cylonite. One of the main ingredients in military C-4 high explosive," Christie said.

Mike turned to Greg. "I thought you said you couldn't make anything other than nitro or dynamite without benzene from the coal tar process?"

Greg grinned a bit sheepishly. "We did. We were wrong. Not about getting benzene from the coal tar process of course, but we were wrong about needing benzene to make high explosive."

"So when did you start making this RDX?"

"We aren't making it, Mike. There's a small company that's been making small lots for the Thuringian Rifles." Greg nodded to the package on the desk. "That's where we got that package."

"Well, how much more can they make? And how come the Thuringen Rifles got it first?"

Greg shrugged. "I've no idea why they were getting it. As for the people making it, they're currently only set up to make pounds per week. The RDX is a sideline from their main product." Greg shuddered as he remembered the main product of Brennerei und Chemiefabrik Schwarza, or the Distillery and Chemical Factory of Schwarza. "Percussion caps."

Mike pulled back from his desk and stood up. "I thought you said we couldn't make percussion caps," he said as he walked around his office. "Wasn't that the reason we went for flintlock over caplock?" Greg nodded. "So how is it that some backwoods down-timer operation can make percussion caps when you say you can't?"

Greg shuddered. "You have to understand, Mike. They're using *mercury*. They're making fulminate of mercury percussion caps, for God's sake. Believe me. That stuff is lethal. It's not that we can't make percussion caps, Mike. We could easily make fulminate of mercury percussion caps. Just tell me how many lives I can budget for. What's my death quota?"

Mike glared at him. "What's with this 'death quota' and 'lives budget' nonsense?"

Christie spoke up. "What Greg is trying to say, Mike, is that people are literally dying to make percussion caps. Sure, we could make percussion caps. But we would have accidents, and probably deaths. Neither Greg nor I want to be responsible for people dying while they make percussion caps. Fulminates are very sensitive. If they're less than pure they become unstable. Hell, copper fulminate will explode as soon as look at you. That's the problem. To make fulminates you need pure ingredients. Trouble is, we can't just call up our friendly chemicals supplier and ask for a few hundred gallons of pure nitric acid. We have to triple distill everything, even the water we use."

Greg took over. "Then there's the matter of volumes. The best of the backwoods outfits is making maybe a couple of ounces of fulminate of mercury a day. That's enough for about a thousand caps. The army needs millions. There's just no way we can safely make the numbers of caps the army needs using fulminate of mercury."

Mike collapsed into his chair. "Okay. I think I understand. We can make caps, but not safely. Certainly not as many caps as the army would need." At Greg and Christie's nods, he settled and returned his gaze to the RDX. "So, how did these folks make this RDX before anybody else?"

"Fuel tablets." At Mike's raised eyebrows Greg smiled. "Yep. Initially they developed the technique using fuel tablets from Tracy Kubiak's old stock from before the Ring of Fire. Apparently, she still had a few cases left. Anyway, they picked up a cheat sheet for RDX from somewhere and started making it. The real break, though . . . that came from Jena." Greg grinned and drew another packet from his bag and presented it to Mike.

Mike nudged the package round so he could better read the labeling. "Gribbleflotz Essence of Fire Tablets?" He looked up at Greg. "Are you telling me that the Kubiaks' pet alchemist is making fuel tablets that can be turned into high explosives?"

"It came as a bit of a shock to me and Christie too, Mike."

"How the . . ." Mike shook his head in frustration. "How does some tin-pot alchemist succeed where you two failed?"

Greg and Christie shrugged. "We don't know," Christie admitted.

"Anyway," Greg continued, "Ted Kubiak knew that the supply of up-time fuel tablets was pretty limited, so the moment he learned Dr. Gribbleflotz had developed a fuel tablet of his own, he passed some on to Brennerei und Chemiefabrik Schwarza to see if they could be turned into RDX."

"And obviously they can," Mike said, picking up the packet of fuel tablets. "So when can you start volume production of RDX?"

"It depends on what you call volume, Mike. Dr. Gribbleflotz has built a facility just across the road from his ammonia facility to make the fuel tablets. They're following his normal model of mass production—if you want more product, just add more workers."

"How much they make will depend a bit on how much demand there is for fuel tablets," Christie said. "Ted seems to think that there should be good demand from the soldiers wanting something that they can use to cook or start fires with. But for high explosives, the problem is still the pure acid needed to convert it from fuel tablet to explosive."

Greg had gained his second wind and took over talking. "Neither Dr. Gribbleflotz nor Brennerei und Chemiefabrik Schwarza want to touch volume production of high explosives. The Chemiefabrik guys are happy to license their methods to anybody who is interested." Greg paused to collect his thoughts, "The question then is, what's the government's priority here? Do we buy a license, set up a plant, and set money aside for widow's benefits? Or we can pay a premium and convince Brennerei und Chemiefabrik Schwarza to up their production. The miners could certainly use it. So could the military. This decision is, as Frank says 'above my pay grade.' So, what do you want us to do?"

Chapter 14

Dr. Phil Zinkens a Bundle

August 1633, HDG Laboratories, Jena

Phillip smiled at the dim light being emitted by the small light bulb. The electricity was coming from his new chemical "battery," and the theory behind what he was seeing was most interesting. Who would have thought that just by hanging two bits of metal in a glass container of weak oil of vitriol one would do anything, let alone produce a little bit of tamed lightning?

He turned back to check the up-time science book. The large printing and colorful pictures gave clear directions on the process and explained everything in the simplest of English. Just what was needed for someone who was just learning English. Not that he, the World's Greatest Alchemist, was just learning. He'd spent over five years in England and could read, write, and speak the language reasonably well. Actually, his ability with the language had improved considerably since he'd started taking lessons from the young up-timer. Speaking of whom ... Phillip headed over to the window and looked out. Yes, there was the bicycle Jonathan Fortney used when he traveled to Jena to see him. So where was the boy?

"It's almost all gone!" Hans Saltzman called out.

Phillip turned his attention from outside the window and back to the experiment he'd been conducting. The zinc electrode was wasting away before his very eyes. He had been warned about this. He pulled the electrodes from the oil of vitriol and wiped them with a rag. Then he turned to the collection of chemicals the Grantville females had given him when they presented him with the up-time science books. One jar caught his eye. It was labeled "Zinc Zn." There was less than half a jar of the precious metal left.

With a heavy heart he turned back to survey his laboratory. There were a number of electricity experiments that really needed zinc. However, zinc was not available in Europe except as an expensive import from the distant East Indies.

Dragging his feet, Phillip made his way to his study. In there were all of his reference books. Maybe there was something in there about zinc.

There was nothing on sources of zinc in his library. He sighed heavily. He had been afraid that would be the case. He moved over to the window and looked out, across the moat that surrounded Jena towards the university. No. That would never do. He would not go begging those people for help. Phillip conceded defeat. He collapsed into his chair and reached for his pen and ink. He removed a clean sheet of paper from a drawer and sat and chewed the end of the iron-tipped pen while he debated how to start the letter to Frau Kubiak. If any of the up-timers knew how to get zinc, he was sure Frau Kubiak would be able to obtain the necessary information. His only worry was what the dratted woman would ask in return.

Grantville Canvas and Outdoor, Mahan Run

Tracy Kubiak carefully placed the letter from Dr. Gribbleflotz on the kitchen table. She stepped back from it and walked around the kitchen. All the while, she kept an eye on the letter, expecting it to get up and bite her, or try to escape. She had had sufficient dealings with Dr. Gribbleflotz to know just how hard he must have found it to write that letter. The fact that there were no errors or blots suggested that it wasn't a first draft. A lot of care and attention had been invested in it.

Tracy searched high and low for her husband, calling out as she searched. She finally ran him to ground in his workshop. "Ted. There you are. Why didn't you answer when I called?"

Ted very carefully didn't say that he had answered. "What's the problem, Trace?"

"I just got a letter from Dr. Phil. He wants to know about zinc. What do we know about zinc?"

Ted smiled at his wife and shrugged his shoulders. "Somewhere between nothing and not a lot. What does he want to know?"

"He says he's afraid of running out of zinc for his electricity experiments. I think he wants us to find him some more."

"That's not going to happen. Every bit of spare zinc, even up-time coins, is being melted down for use in industry. They don't make it in Europe yet. They import it from the Far East, as far as I know. Do you want me to check out the library?"

"Please. If there's nothing else you need to do, I'd like you to see what you can find."

Ted smiled wryly. "So, what is it you want from Dr. Phil this time?"

"Actually..." She smiled back. "Nothing. I can't think of a thing, but it won't hurt to have Dr. Phil owe us. You never know. Maybe one day we'll get something really good out of him."

"Yeah, right." There was only a hint of skepticism in his voice. "I'll finish cleaning up in here, then head over to the library. While I'm out that way, I might as well drop in on the ammonia plant and see how Dr. Phil's crew is doing."

A few days later, HDG Laboratories, Jena

Dr. Gribbleflotz and his personal laborant, Hans Saltzman, carefully worked their way through the large bundle of notes Tracy Kubiak had sent. They described zinc and the extraction process, but the notes created more questions than they answered.

"I shall have to journey to Grantville and examine the research material myself, Hans. Please see that everything is made ready."

"Of course, Herr Doctor. Will you be visiting the spirits of hartshorn facility?"

Phillip paused to think for a moment. "Yes. If I

include an inspection of the facility, I will be able to claim the cost of the trip against the company."

"Very reasonable, Herr Doctor. Will you be requiring my presence on this journey?"

"No." Phillip shook his head. "Not unless you wish to come. You could visit some of the up-time facilities if you wish. I am sure Michael Siebenhorn will be only too happy to make arrangements."

Once in Grantville, his duty visit to the spirits of hartshorn plant complete, Phillip had set out to complete his real mission. Michael Siebenhorn, the ex-laborant in charge of the facility, had introduced Phillip to a most excellent specialist library researcher and a copyist to do the hard work of the actual library search and the taking of notes. While the two specialists visited the various libraries around Grantville, Phillip, with time heavy on his hands, had taken the opportunity to investigate the clothing and shoe stores of Grantville. Hans was left to amuse himself touring some of the up-time facilities.

HDG Laboratories, Jena

The copious notes assembled by the researcher and copyist sat in piles on Dr. Gribbleflotz's desk. Both Phillip and Hans worked away in silence, reading and taking notes.

"'Both sphalerite and calamine are ores of zinc.' Well, that is old news." Phillip looked across to Hans, a look of disgust on his face. "You'd think, for the exorbitant fees those leeches charged, that they would tell me something I didn't already know. Why, I've made brass using both of those selfsame ores many a time."

"But, Herr Dr. Gribbleflotz, read this." Hans waved the sheet he had just finished reading. "It says here that it is from the vapors of those ores that one can obtain the zinc."

"What? Let me see that." Phillip grabbed the sheet and quickly read it. He dropped his head into his hands. "So close." He looked up at Hans. "So many times I have been so close to discovering zinc. If only I had thought to trap the vapors. I would have earned my rightful place beside my great-grandfather, the great Paracelsus."

"Herr Dr. Gribbleflotz, one of the notes says that the great Paracelsus named the metal zinken." Hans hurriedly flicked through the researcher's notes. "Yes, here it is."

Phillip read the note. "Then in honor of my great-grandfather, from now on, I shall call the metal zinken."

Phillip started to walk around his study. "We will need to prove that we can isolate the zinken. Either of the ores will do for that. However..." Phillip paused to read from the sheet he held. "It appears that 'pure' oil of vitriol can be made by catching the vapors from the zinken ore sphalerite. As the process to isolate zinken is the same for both ores, we shall experiment with sphalerite."

Phillip stopped to read further. "I believe ten thousand *Pfennige* should be enough. According to this paper, that is sufficient to produce four thousand *Pfennige* of metallic zinken and two gallons of strong oil of vitriol."

Phillip made for the door. "Hans, start making a list of what else we will need while I instruct Frau

Mittelhausen to place an order for some sphalerite. We will start designing the new retorts we will need when I return."

Phillip found his housekeeper-cum-business-manager in the kitchen. After stopping to slip a couple of cookies out of the cookie barrel, he approached her. "Frau Mittelhausen."

"Yes, Herr Doctor?"

"Frau Mittelhausen, please place an order of ten thousand *Pfennige* of sphalerite ore. I believe it should come from the Harz region. Please be sure to insist on only the best quality ore, and ask that it be delivered as soon as possible. For such a trifling amount the transport cost should not be excessive."

"I will pass on the order to Herr Ostermann when I collect the bread and pies from the bakery, Herr Dr. Gribbleflotz." Frau Mittelhausen added a note to her shopping list.

Ostermann Transport, Jena

"Good afternoon, Frau Mittelhausen. What can we do for you today?" Joachim Ostermann asked.

"Herr Dr. Gribbleflotz wishes to purchase some material from Harz." Frau Mittelhausen checked her shopping list. "Ten thousand *Pfennige* of sphalerite."

"Sphalerite, ten thousand *Pfennige*?" Herr Ostermann checked to confirm he had heard correctly.

"Yes. Only the best premium grade ore, mind, Herr Ostermann."

"Of course, Frau. For the good Herr Dr. Gribbleflotz,

only the best of the best. For such a small amount, the supplier might charge a premium price. Will that be agreeable?"

"Yes, Herr Ostermann. If you would prepare a contract, I will sign it when I return from the bakery."

December 1633, Ostermann Transport, Jena

Joachim Ostermann passed a horrified gaze along lines of pack mules carrying what the mule skinner leading them claimed was Dr. Gribbleflotz's order of sphalerite. "How did it happen?" he demanded of the world.

Hans Ostermann, his son, checked the bill of lading the skinner had presented. Confused, he looked at his father. "What is the problem, Papa? The order was for ten thousand *Pfund* of premium ore, to be delivered as soon as possible. That is exactly what we have here."

"Let me see that." Joachim grabbed the bill of lading from his son's hand. A quick glance confirmed what his son had said. Someone, somewhere, had converted the order from *Pfennige* to *Pfund*.

"How did you pay for the ore, Hans?"

"I sent a signed money order, Papa. Just like we always do. You saw me collect Frau Mittelhausen's signature before I took the authorization to the banker."

Joachim slumped against the first of the more than fifty pack mules that carried the premium quality ore and sighed. "Hans, my son. We have a problem. We could be bankrupted over this error."

"Bankrupted? But the Frau signed for it. We have a signed contract." Hans took time to have another look at the bill of lading. He waved it like a talisman towards his father. "Yes, Dieter correctly calculated the estimated cost of freight. So even the freight has been mostly paid. How can we be bankrupted?"

Joachim mopped his sweating forehead. "Hans..." He paused as he struggled to find the words. "Hans, the order should have been for ten thousand *Pfennige*, a little less than twenty *Pfund*. Not ten thousand *Pfund*. We have over-ordered by a factor of more than five hundred, and the freight is inflated more than a thousand fold. I do not know that Herr Dr. Gribbleflotz will accept the mistake."

"But Frau Mittelhausen signed confirming the order, Papa."

"Yes." Joachim shook his head. "Someone made a mistake. Somehow the order was prepared using *Pfund* rather than *Pfennige*." Suddenly Joachim jerked upright. His eyes opened wide. "That fool Beyer. It must have been him. Dr. Gribbleflotz's order was the last one he processed before he became so ill he had to be taken to St. Jakob's infirmary. Come, let's check his desk."

Hans passed a sheaf of papers towards his father. "Papa, I think this explains what happened."

Joachim read the notes taken by the late Dieter Beyer. He could only nod his head in agreement. "It is obvious what happened. There is a drop of something, I hope it is just water and not whatever killed Dieter, on the word *Pfennige*. It is smudged so badly that it could be read as either *Pfennige* or *Pfund*."

Hans nodded. "He hadn't been with us long enough to be aware of the small units Herr Dr. Gribbleflotz uses and read it as ten thousand *Pfund*."

Father and son exchanged grim looks. "Well, we

know how the mistake was made, but that doesn't get us any further forward. There is no way we can repay the cost of the ore and its priority transport."

"But, Papa! It was an honest mistake, and we have a signed contract."

"I know, son. But a signed contract will not save our reputation. I will have to go to him, cap in hand, and ask for understanding."

HDG Laboratories, Jena

"Ten thousand *Pfund*? How is this possible? What was the cost?" Ursula Mittelhausen all but roared.

Originally, when he discovered that Dr. Gribbleflotz was out of town, Joachim Ostermann had felt happily confident to be dealing with the housekeeper. However, that was before he felt the full force of an outraged Frau Mittelhausen. Anybody would have thought the money spent had been her own.

"Frau Mittelhausen, it was an honest mistake. My clerk was ill when he prepared the contract. However." Joachim was careful to emphasis this part, "the contract you signed clearly stated ten thousand *Pfund*. If you had read the contract before signing it, the problem would have been detected and easily corrected before the order was sent out."

Miffed at being blamed for someone else's mistake, Frau Mittelhausen looked down her nose at Joachim. "And where is this clerk who so conveniently made such a mistake?"

"Dead. Dead of fever at the infirmary that same night."

Stymied, Frau Mittelhausen sighed heavily. "Herr Dr. Gribbleflotz will not like this."

Joachim nodded his head in agreement. "No, he will not be happy. However, I am hoping that we may come to some kind of arrangement. If Dr. Gribbleflotz were to honor the contract, I am willing to refund some of the cost of transporting the ore. I am sorry, Frau, but that is the best I can do. The only other alternative is I try to sell the excess ore elsewhere. There have been rumors that the staff at the university might be interested."

Joachim sneaked a quick look at her when he said that last. There were no such rumors, yet. However, if necessary, he would start one himself. One never knew. The university faculty might even want to buy the ore. The animosity between Dr. Gribbleflotz and the faculty of the university was well known and a source of constant amusement to the good people of Jena.

"Humph!" Frau Mittelhausen eyed Joachim skeptically. "I will leave it for Herr Dr. Gribbleflotz to decide."

"That is all I ask, Frau. A fair hearing with Herr Dr. Gribbleflotz."

"Herr Dr. Gribbleflotz. Herr Ostermann has the sphalerite ore you ordered." Frau Mittelhausen had been waiting for Phillip to return to his office.

"At last. What took so long? I expected delivery weeks ago."

"There has been a slight mix up, Herr Doctor."

"What? A mix up? It is the ore I ordered?"

"I believe the ore is sphalerite, Herr Doctor, and all premium quality. The problem is the quantity. There is significantly more than you asked for."

"Where is it? Where is my ore? I wish to start my experiments immediately."

"Herr Doctor, Please listen to me. The ore is still at Herr Ostermann's. I have declined to take delivery of it."

"Declined to take delivery? Why ever not?"

Frau Mittelhausen sighed heavily. Getting through to Herr Dr. Gribbleflotz was often a trial. "Because it is significantly more than you asked for, Herr Doctor. I felt that only you could acknowledge delivery."

"Only I could acknowledge delivery?" Phillip paused, something of the sense of what Frau Mittelhausen was trying to say finally penetrating. "How much ore did Herr Ostermann try to deliver?"

"Enough to require some fifty pack mules, Herr Doctor. Ten thousand *Pfund*."

"But that's..." Phillip looked at Frau Mittelhausen in shock. If Herr Ostermann had tried to deliver that much ore... "You haven't already paid for the ore yet? Have you?"

"Yes, Herr Dr. Gribbleflotz. I signed the contract and the request for the banker's draft at Herr Ostermann's at the time of ordering. Apparently, they were correct for the amount of ore delivered."

"Didn't you..." Phillip started, only to stop. Of course Frau Mittelhausen hadn't checked the documents. If she had, she would have detected the mistake. He couldn't really blame her for not checking. He himself usually signed without really confirming that the amounts were correct. It wasn't as if Joachim would have deliberately inflated the order. His livelihood depended on his honesty.

"Someone at Herr Ostermann's made a mistake processing the order?"

His housekeeper nodded. "Herr Ostermann says it was a new clerk, ill with fever. The order form was smudged and the clerk calculated the order based on quantities he normally dealt with."

Phillip collapsed into a chair opposite Frau Mittelhausen and buried his head in his hands. "With a signed contract Herr Ostermann is legally entitled to keep our payment, unless..." Phillip looked up hopefully. "Unless Herr Ostermann can find an alternative buyer. Is there a chance that Herr Ostermann can find a buyer for the excess ore?"

"Herr Ostermann suggested that there were rumors that the Jena faculty might be interested, Herr Doctor."

Shocked, Phillip shot to his feet. "*No.* I will not let *them* get ahead of me in the discovery of zinken."

"Herr Doctor, I suspect your reaction is exactly what Herr Ostermann is hoping for."

Phillip nodded agreement and lowered himself back into his chair. "Yes. He is probably hoping that I will not take the risk." He slammed his fist onto the arm of his chair. "He is right. I am unwilling to risk that the university might be interested. If Herr Ostermann is willing to keep the mistake secret, I will accept the ore. Please confirm delivery with Herr Ostermann, Frau Mittelhausen."

Frau Mittelhausen issued a loud sniff of disgust. "You shouldn't let Herr Ostermann get away with his incompetence so easily, Herr Doctor."

"You may renegotiate a new price if that will make you feel better, Frau Mittelhausen. But please take delivery of the ore. My research is already much delayed. Why, there is the chance that someone else, maybe even from the university, might isolate the zinken before I do."

"If you insist, Herr Doctor. But what are you going to do about the drain on company finances? Frau Kubiak is sure to question the magnitude of the expenditure."

"How much did the ore cost, Frau?" Phillip had an idea that it was going to be a truly terrifying amount.

Frau Mittelhausen answered by passing over the statement from Ostermann transport. The long string of zeros had Phillip almost choking.

Defeated for the moment, Phillip pulled himself to his feet and stumbled up the stairs to his rooms. In the draft created by his departure, the statement gently floated to the floor. Frau Mittelhausen watched him struggle up the stairs. Then, with a sigh, she picked up the statement and filed it.

December 1633, HDG Laboratories, Jena

"I have called you all to meet here to address an emergency situation." Frau Mittelhausen looked around the collected faces of Herr Dr. Gribbleflotz's senior laborants. All of them had started with the original baking soda production line. These were the smart ones. Some of them were responsible for the production lines producing the various products of HDG Laboratories and Kubiak Country Industries.

"Recently, at considerable cost, Herr Dr. Gribbleflotz took delivery of ten thousand *Pfund* of premium quality sphalerite. That purchase has created an enormous hole in the accounts. Such a big hole that, unless something is done, we will not be receiving any bonus this year, and probably not next year either."

"Why would Dr. Gribbleflotz purchase so much ore, Frau Mittelhausen? That is much more than he would ever need for his experiments," Michael Siebenhorn asked.

Frau Mittelhausen looked everywhere but at Michael. "A trifling mistake was made in the preparation and confirmation of the order. But the how is no longer important. The Herr Doctor has barely left his laboratory for the last two weeks. Isn't that right, Hans?"

Hans Saltzman, Dr. Gribbleflotz's trusted personal laborant of nearly two years nodded. "Yes. Herr Dr. Gribbleflotz feels that he is responsible for the problem. Even as we speak he is driving himself hard making the zinken and oil of vitriol."

"Zinken?" Maria Anna Siebenhorn, Michael's younger sister, looked up with some excitement. "Chemical symbol Zn?" They were all aware of the way Dr. Gribbleflotz used his own naming methodology.

"Yes. 'Zn.' Why? Is it important?"

"Yes, Hans. It is important." Maria Anna looked around the dinner table. "You all do know that I'm working for a company making percussion caps?" The people at the table nodded. "What you might not know is that the company has up-timer partners."

Kurt Stoltz lifted his eyebrows in a scowl. "Some of us know, and are fully aware that the up-timers are happy to let down-timers risk their lives with fulminate of mercury. You don't see them risking their own lives."

"Kurt, settle down. They pay well and they provide the best safety equipment they can. I earn over a hundred dollars a day for less than five hours work. Where else can I earn that kind of money, plus free bed and board in an up-time house?" Maria Anna turned back to the group. "Anyway, the up-timers are really interested in zinc. Hans, can the Herr Doctor really make pure metallic zinc?"

"Zinken, Maria Anna. He calls it zinken. Apparently his great-grandfather Paracelsus first used that name for the metal. Yes, he has managed to make zinken and oil of vitriol. However, he will take years to convert all of the ore to zinken and oil of vitriol."

Frau Mittelhausen stood to attract attention. "That is why I asked you all to meet here. The Herr Doctor is good at what he does. However, he works only in small amounts. I have been following the progress of all of you and the facilities you are running. I have noticed that production volumes have increased while running costs have declined." Frau Mittelhausen looked almost fondly over the young faces. "I can only assume you have been able to modify the processes so as to increase batch sizes."

"We have introduced a few continuous processes, Frau Mittelhausen," Kurt admitted. Michael and a couple of others nodded. The up-timers had been very helpful when it came to improving the production techniques.

"My question of all of you is: can you take whatever process Herr Dr. Gribbleflotz has created and increase the volumes?"

"Will Herr Dr. Gribbleflotz let us help him?" Maria Anna asked.

In silence everybody waited for Frau Mittelhausen to respond. Herr Dr. Gribbleflotz was a proud man. Would he accept help from his students?

With a resigned sigh, Frau Mittelhausen looked up the stairs towards Herr Dr. Gribbleflotz's laboratory. "I will ask."

February 1634, Kubiak Country

"Hey, Tracy. Wasn't the geek working on zinc?"

"Tasha, please don't call him 'the geek.' Yes, Dr. Phil was interested in zinc. Why do you ask?"

"But he is a geek. Okay, I'll try not to call him a geek. Anyway, there's an article in the newspaper by one of those Jena doctor guys. He's written something about how to make zinc. Do you think he's beaten Dr. Phil to the punch?"

"Could you show me the article, Tasha?" Tracy looked over Tasha's shoulder.

"There, that one." Tasha pointed out the article before she passed the folded newspaper to Tracy.

It took only a few minutes to read the article. Tracy grimaced. Dr. Phil was not going to be happy. It was possible that the author had only been interpreting what he had found in up-time books, but the way the article read did suggest the he had actually tried the process.

"Oh, heck. I think a trip to Jena might be on the cards. Dr. Phil isn't going to be happy having a Jena academic alchemist beating him to produce zinc."

February 1634, HDG Laboratories, Jena

"Ted. Why do you suppose everyone is looking at us so guiltily?"

"I have no idea, dear. Do you suppose we could just ask Frau Mittelhausen how Dr. Phil is taking the publication of that article on the secrets of zinc?"

"But, Ted. Haven't you noticed the people? There are

too many laborants. I'm sure there weren't this many last time I visited. What about when you last visited?"

"Pardon? Oh, the new faces. Well, Dr. Phil was working on his fuel tablets. I'm sure he's just training up some more people to work on them."

"The fuel tablets..." Tracy nodded as if the information confirmed something, "Yes. That would explain why I saw Michael Siebenhorn and Kurt Stoltz."

"What?" Ted searched around the central compound of the HDG Laboratories facility. "Both Michael and Kurt?"

"Yes. Over by the west wing. Why? What's so special about those two being here? I thought they were two of the company's best production alchemists."

"They are. But converting Dr. Phil's test tube level production to volume production shouldn't need both of them. Besides, if they're here, who's minding the store back in Grantville? No. Something is going on. Come on. I want to talk to Dr. Phil and find out." Ted strode off toward Dr. Phil's office.

"Herr Kubiak, Frau Kubiak. How can I help you?" Frau Mittelhausen's not inconsiderable bulk blocked their way into the office.

"You can tell us what is going on, Frau Mittelhausen. Why are both Michael and Kurt here in Jena? What is so important that both of them had to be called in from Grantville? And why weren't we notified?" Tracy's voice was cross.

Frau Mittelhausen looked from Ted to Tracy. They were obviously after answers and wouldn't leave without them. With a heavy sigh of resignation, she guided them into the office.

"Frau Kubiak, if you will remember, Herr Dr. Gribbleflotz and I can sign for goods without limit..."

"Yes, yes. I know that. With you both in Jena, it was silly to require everything to go through Grantville. Please get to the point."

"Frau Kubiak, that is the point. If either the doctor or I sign a contract there is no further check. There is no bookkeeper to question any purchase..."

Ted frowned. "Hold it. Are you suggesting either you or Dr. Gribbleflotz have ordered something you shouldn't have?"

"No, Herr Kubiak. The order was for sphalerite ore for Dr. Gribbleflotz's zinken experiments. No. The problem was not what was ordered but, rather, how much was ordered."

Confused, Tracy searched Frau Mittelhausen's face. "But why would there be a problem? We have never complained about what Dr. Gribbleflotz has ordered yet."

Frau Mittelhausen went to a cabinet and removed a folder. Opening it she selected a sheet of paper and passed it to Tracy. Tracy took a while to read the invoice, finally reaching the bottom where the costs were tallied. Horrified, she looked at Frau Mittelhausen. "You paid that much for zinc ore?" She waved the invoice in the air. "Why?"

"There was a mistake, Frau. The doctor only asked for a fraction of the amount. Such a quantity, barely a small shopping basket full, should have been easily conveyed by the fastest method for only a few dollars. However, the mistake resulted in ten thousand *Pfund* being delivered by pack mule." Frau Mittelhausen stopped speaking, unable to convey in words the significant difference in cost of transporting a small basket of ore as part of someone else's cargo compared with the cost of more than fifty pack mules and their handlers.

"The actual cost of the ore, Frau, was a mere pittance compared with the cost of transporting it all the way from the Harz Mountains."

Tracy slapped the invoice onto a table. "How badly does this affect the books, Frau Mittelhausen? Are we in debt?"

"No, Frau Kubiak. We had sufficient reserves from the sales of Gribbleflotz Sal Vin Betula, although expenses have increased considerably."

Tracy winced. Sales of Dr. Gribbleflotz's Sal Vin Betula, better known as Dr. Gribbleflotz's Little Blue Pill of Happiness, had been very profitable. So profitable that others had started making aspirin in competition. Prices were stable at about a dollar a pill, but they had been forced to invest in advertising to maintain market growth.

Ted read the invoice, then turned to Frau Mittelhausen. "What is being done with the ore?"

Tracy stared at her husband. That was a very good question. Somewhere, there was something like five tons of sphalerite. If Dr. Gribbleflotz could extract the zinc, then maybe all was not lost. "Yes, Frau. What is Dr. Gribbleflotz doing with all that ore?"

"Please, follow me and I will show you."

Tracy and Ted followed Frau Mittelhausen to the wing where Tracy had seen Michael and Kurt.

They were greeted by silence when they entered the building. Young men and women lining the room turned and looked at them. Accusing looks were directed towards Frau Mittelhausen.

Michael Siebenhorn made his way towards them. "Frau Kubiak, Herr Kubiak. How can I help you?"

"We would like to know what is being done with the sphalerite that was delivered here late last year."

With a guilty look at both Ted and Tracy, Michael called for the laborants to return to work. "You know then? It wasn't Dr. Gribbleflotz's fault. It was an honest mistake."

"Michael, what have you been doing with the ore?" Ted asked impatiently.

"We have been refining it."

Tracy perked up. "All of it? You've refined all of that ore?"

"Nearly. We are on the last couple of bushel baskets now. Come, follow me and I will show you what we have."

Bubbling with hope, Tracy dragged Ted along as she followed Michael. Michael unlocked the door to the storeroom and stood back to let them look at the treasure within.

"What's in those big bottles?" Ted asked.

"Strong oil of vitriol. Actually, very strong oil of vitriol. We think it is over ninety percent pure. Herr Dr. Gribbleflotz is still testing it."

"How much do you have?"

"About fifteen hogsheads, Herr Kubiak."

"And the metallic zinc?"

"About four thousand *Pfund* of zinken, Herr Kubiak."

Ted laughed. "Zinken? Is that what Dr. Gribbleflotz is calling it?"

"Yes, Herr Kubiak. It is in memory of his great-grandfather, Paracelsus. Zinken is the name Paracelsus gave the metal."

Ted nodded. He drew out a pencil and paper and began recording the contents of the store room. "Anything else?"

Michael smiled. "Yes, Herr Kubiak. There is also some four hundred guilders worth of other metals and compounds."

Ted and Tracy tried to calculate the worth of the goods. "The value of everything you extracted from the ore is probably enough to cover the cost of it, with something left over. But, what about the cost of recovery? What were those costs?"

Michael shrugged. "Too much, I am sure, Frau Kubiak. We worked with great haste, and with considerable secrecy. Both of which added to our costs. However, we have been developing our technology. We now know how to recover the metals and compounds from sphalerite."

"And what good is this technology, Michael?" Tracy asked.

Smiling smugly, Michael guided them out of the storeroom. "Frau Kubiak. With our technology we can smelt zinken. Other people..." Michael paused to look at Ted and Tracy. "Did you read about the doctor on the Jena faculty who isolated the zinken?" They nodded. "Other people might know the secret of zinken, but they do not know how to recover not only the zinken, but the sulphur and the other metals and compounds. We at HDG Laboratories have developed the necessary technology. The more we can recover from the processing of the sphalerite, the more economic the process becomes. We have already sent out feelers for partners. We believe we can construct a smelter outside the city of Halle. There is ample coal near the city that can be used to smelt the ore, and transport of the sphalerite from the Harz Mountains should be affordable, because we can use barges to float the ore down the river to Halle."

"Nice. But why the secrecy? Why didn't you notify Tracy and me?"

"It is the Herr Doctor. We had to prove the technology first, otherwise Herr Dr. Gribbleflotz could have been a laughingstock. At least, that's how it all started." Michael smiled at the memory. "There is also the fact that we currently hold the largest supply of pure metallic zinken in Europe. We have an agent exploring the prospects of 'selling short.' We think we will be able to maintain the current high price as long as people don't know we are producing zinken locally."

Tracy snorted. "How do you hope to keep your activities quiet? Surely people will see your production facilities?"

Michael smiled. "That is the thing with the new technology, Frau Kubiak. That academic, he talked of calamine. We are using sphalerite. If we used calamine, then people might suspect we were making zinken. But sphalerite? From sphalerite people will see us making and selling oil of vitriol. It is an important and valuable chemical. If we are careful, we can keep the zinken processing secret." Michael's smile grew triumphant. "And, of course, that will keep the local price high. High enough for the maximum profit."

"What about those partners you were talking about?"

"Only a few of them know of the zinken. Most of the potential partners are either miners looking to sell their ore, or people interested in the oil of vitriol and other by-products. Only fifteen people, including you two, know of the zinken."

Ted and Tracy exchanged glances, then turned their attention back to Michael. "You really think you can make a going concern of a zinken smelter?" Michael nodded in answer. "Then . . ." Ted turned to check that Tracy agreed. She nodded. "How can we help?"

"Money." Michael rolled his eyes. "And if possible, Herr Kubiak, can you get some more of those 'catalytic converters'?"

"How much money?" Tracy asked.

"What do you want the catalytic converters for?" Ted asked.

"The converters improve the yield of the oil of vitriol, Herr Kubiak. Frau Kubiak, we don't know how much money, but it will be a lot. We may have to ask that you mortgage the HDG Laboratories facility and the ammonia facility. Mining and mineral processing is very expensive. However, the potential returns are enormous."

"You know, Trace, I wouldn't have thought Dr. Phil had it in him to build up that kind of personal loyalty."

Tracy looked back over her shoulder at the HDG Laboratories facility. "It was a bit of a surprise. Maybe there's more to our Dr. Phil than meets the eye."

Part Three

HDG Laboratories Later
1633

Chapter 15

Feng Shui for the Soul

October 1633, Grantville

Kurt Stoltz ignored the rumbling of his stomach and continued his careful scanning of the pages of the newspaper. He well knew that *they* censored everything. So one had to read everything to detect the tiny inconsistencies that hinted at what *they* had removed. He knew there were censors about, especially in Grantville. There was no way that they would allow easy access to all the information from the future, no matter what they claimed.

He turned the page and started reading the advertisements.

The ad in the "situations vacant" column practically leapt off the page. Kurt stared at it in disbelief. The Gribbleflotz spirits of hartshorn facility in Grantville was looking for multilingual people with fluent English (preferably up-timer English), Latin, and German to work in the research department. He could do that.

He was fluent in Latin and German, and had spent several years in England. As for up-timer English, he was a regular user of the various libraries around Grantville. Not that he was well known of course. Anybody growing up in the Stiefel-Meth sect learned the value of keeping his head down and being inconspicuous.

He placed a hand inside his satchel where his notebooks resided. His personal notebooks, with all his notes about the research being undertaken by the great Herr Dr. Gribbleflotz. The doctor was publishing information that Kurt couldn't find in Grantville's libraries. Did he have a source of information the censors hadn't gotten to? This advertisement suggested a way to find out.

A position as a researcher with his company, even if it was in Grantville rather than in Jena, was an opportunity not to be missed. Kurt copied the address for applications, then for the first time since he arrived in Grantville to see the truth of the *Corona Conflagrens* miracle nearly two years ago, he left a library early. He needed an early night if he was to get to the Gribbleflotz spirits of hartshorn facility before any other applicant tomorrow.

April 1634, HDG Laboratories, Jena

Dr. Phillip Theophrastus Gribbleflotz glared at his special aluminum pyramid with the strategically placed faceted gems. He picked up his pen and dipped it into the ink. The pyramid wasn't working, but the world's greatest alchemist couldn't just write "it isn't working" in his notebook. That kind of comment lacked any hint of scientific credibility.

Phillip paused in thought, idly chewing on the wooden shank of his pen. Then he remembered how the Americans would record the lack of results. He dipped his pen again and wrote "No invigoration of the Quinta Essentia of the human humors were observed." It was nice. It described the lack of observed results in suitable language, but then, why couldn't he see anything? Phillip started worrying his pen again.

The obvious answer was that there was nothing to see, but that couldn't be right. Maybe . . . Phillip sat up straight. Of course! The changes in the Quinta Essentia were invisible to the human eye. What he needed was some method of detecting the invisible forces.

A few days later

He'd found it. Photography. More specifically, Kirlian photography. With Kirlian photography one could record the image of a person's aura. All one needed was some simple electrical equipment . . . and some photographic equipment. That last brought Phillip back to earth. What was the availability of up-timer photographic equipment?

He went to the door of his office and called out. "Hans. I need you."

The normally reliable Hans Saltzman didn't answer. Phillip went searching. The first person he found was Ursula Mittelhausen, the housekeeper and bookkeeper for HDG Laboratories.

"Frau Mittelhausen, have you seen Hans?"

"He is in Halle helping set up the oil of vitriol facility, Doctor."

Phillip stifled an unsuitable exclamation. Just when he needed his personal assistant, Hans had to make himself unavailable. Well, when everyone else failed you, there was only one person left to do the work. "I need to make a trip to Grantville. Please book a seat on the train."

"Of course, Doctor. The evening train? Do you wish for me to also book accommodation?"

Phillip considered the work he had backing up, and the expense of accommodation in Grantville. "At the Higgins. I don't know how long I'll be. I need to ask about 'photography.'"

Ursula perked up. "Michael's sister, Maria Anna, sent a photograph of herself that one of the up-timers took. Are you going to be working on photography now, Doctor?"

"I wish to investigate the application of photography to the detection of the invisible forces of the invigoration of the Quinta Essentia of the human humors."

"So you'll be taking photographs, Doctor?"

"Purely for science, Frau Mittelhausen."

"Oh!" Ursula was crestfallen. "I was hoping that I could have my photograph taken so I could send it to my sister in Leipzig."

Grantville

Phillip had the choice of talking to the dreaded Frau Kubiak, or to Maria Anna. It wasn't that difficult a decision to make, so he caught the bus to Grays Run. He easily found the property where Frau Mittelhausen said Maria Anna worked. There was a sign declaring the house to be the head office of Brennerei und Chemiefabrik Schwarza. He looked around. It was vaguely similar to the property of Frau Kubiak—a large house on a few acres of land with a number of outbuildings. Obviously it was only a small company.

The door was answered by a little old lady, an up-timer.

"I am Dr. Phillip Gribbleflotz. I believe Maria Anna Siebenhorn works here?"

The little old lady shook her head. "Oh dear, I'm sorry, but Maria Anna's not in at the moment. She's in charge of the new explosives division at the *Schwarza Gewerbegebiet* and won't be home until late . . . Gribbleflotz did you say? The Aspirin King?"

Phillip grimaced. "The Aspirin King" was not something the world's greatest alchemist wished to be known as. They could at least get the name right. "Yes, I am the Gribbleflotz behind Gribbleflotz Sal Vin Betula."

"Do come in, Doctor. Your people were most helpful when Celeste and I wrote asking about photographic chemicals."

They were? Phillip hadn't seen a letter from this company. "You wrote asking about photographic chemicals?"

"Yes, and we got such a nice letter back from your Herr Saltzman."

Phillip made a mental note to remind Hans just who was in charge in Jena. So, the next question was, had they done anything with the information? "Did you take Maria Anna's photograph?"

"Oh, yes." The woman fluttered a bit. "Would you like me to take yours?"

Well, it seemed he'd come to the right place. "Yes please, Frau—"

"Sebastian, but everyone calls me Lettie. Come on in."

Several days later, the Spirits of Hartshorn Facility, Grantville

Dr. Gribbleflotz was doing what he did best, pontificating on his latest hobbyhorse. Michael Siebenhorn glanced over at his sister. She smiled back and shrugged. When one worked for the doctor, one learned to put up with his little foibles. He didn't force them on anybody, and the open disbelief of most of his senior laborants only made him work harder to prove his theories.

Michael shuddered. One of the consequences of the doctor's continued failure to invigorate the Quinta Essentia of the human humors in test subjects was Kurt Stoltz being authorized to work on artificial cryolite so he could make pure aluminum. Dr. Gribbleflotz had theorized that the impurity of the materials might be why his experiments weren't producing the results he expected. Well, Kurt was welcome to the task. Even the stink of ammonia that hung around the spirits of hartshorn facility was preferable to being around hydrofluoric acid.

"I have been unable to observe anything happening when I use my pyramid to invigorate the Quinta Essentia of the humors in test subjects. I believe the reason I can't see anything is because the actions taking place are not detectable by the human eye. However, a special photographic technique I have read about should allow me to observe the otherwise invisible forces at work and help me progress my research. The diagram you are looking at is taken from a reputable up-time source, and both Frau Sebastian and Frau Frost believe that such a device should produce the Kirlian images I desire."

Michael dragged his attention back to what Dr. Gribbleflotz was saying. At least this wasn't going to be anything as dangerous as hydrofluoric acid. The diagram was a simple electronic circuit, easily understood by anyone with knowledge of the up-timer science. Of course, actually making the device needed a level of expertise he knew the doctor lacked. For that matter, so did he. What was needed was a specialist, someone who knew how to make a transformer. Fortunately, such people were relatively easy to find in Grantville. "Where are you intending to use this..." Michael paused to think up a suitable name the doctor would enjoy. "Kirlian Imager, Doctor?"

"Kirlian Imager...I like that, Michael. Yes. I will of course use the 'Kirlian Imager' in my laboratory for my research, but also, I am running short of the aluminum for my Candles of the Essence of Light demonstrations, and I hope that I might be able to add the Kirlian Imager to my seminars."

Michael grimaced. He suddenly had an idea where this meeting was heading, and an explanation for his sister's presence. It wasn't going to be a simple request to make a Kirlian Imager. No, nothing that easy. "That will require a lot of the new photographic materials. Can Brennerei und Chemiefabrik Schwarza supply your needs?"

Maria Anna, Michael's little sister, answered. "Lettie Sebastian knows a lot about photography, but not a lot about chemistry, and while Celeste Frost knows a lot about chemistry, she doesn't know a lot about photography. Together they make a competent photographic chemist, but neither of them understands production on the scale Dr. Gribbleflotz requires."

Michael sighed. He'd guessed right. "So you want me to develop the information your friends have into procedures to produce photographic chemicals?"

"Yes." Phillip smiled. "I've already talked to the Frau Kubiak, and she is happy to make the necessary funds available. I'm sure you'll have no trouble recruiting additional workers for a new production line."

Michael struggled not to swear. He shot his sister another look. She was smirking quietly in her corner. The little witch. He knew why she was smirking. She'd been trying to get him to produce the chemicals her friends needed for their photography project for weeks. Well, it looked like she'd succeeded this time. One didn't turn down Dr. Gribbleflotz. Not when he had taken you, starving and desperate, off the streets and then trained you in the new alchemy. It wasn't even as if the doctor was interested in the potential fortune Maria Anna insisted photography could bring in either. For someone who must be one of the richest men in Thuringia, the doctor displayed a sometimes distressing disinterest in making money.

Michael tried a last desperate rearguard action. "Doctor, I am currently running not only the spirits of hartshorn facility, but also the facility producing the new fuel tablets. Couldn't you find someone else?"

Phillip shook his head. "There is no one else, Michael. Hans and Kurt are both occupied getting the Halle facility up and running. With Hans in Halle I've been forced to not only waste my valuable time supervising operations in Jena, but I've also been forced to endure the illiterate fool who is Hans' temporary replacement."

Well, that hadn't worked. Michael could well imagine how his boss might be suffering in Hans Saltzman's absence. Hans had developed from a scared teenager into one of the four best alchemists at HDG Laboratories in the three years he'd been the doctor's personal laborant. That was why he was helping Kurt Stoltz, the last of the four, set up the new oil of vitriol facility in Halle. Remembering Kurt stopped Michael's train of thought in its tracks. He grinned. "Doctor, I think I might know of someone suitable as a temporary replacement for Hans. He's a hard worker here at the spirits of hartshorn facility. He has steady hands, and he lived in England for a few years and has been living and working in Grantville for nearly two years, so he has a good command of both written and spoken English."

Phillip looked interested. "English is good. Frau Mittelhausen has been unable to find anyone suitable who can comprehend the up-time material. But is your man literate?"

"Of course. I wouldn't suggest him if he wasn't fluent in Latin."

"So, who is this paragon?"

Michael grinned. "Kurt Stoltz."

"What? But Kurt is running the Halle operation. He can't be...oh! Another Kurt Stoltz?"

"Yes, Doctor."

Michael watched Dr. Gribbleflotz worry his goatee and then polish his spectacles. Both well-known signs that he was deep in thought.

"Would he be willing to move to Jena?" Phillip asked.

Michael nearly burst out laughing. His Kurt Stoltz had been bothering him for months about a transfer to head office. To actually work as the personal assistant to his hero, even just for a few months until Hans returned, would be more than he could ever have hoped for. "There should be no trouble persuading my Kurt to move to Jena as your temporary personal laborant, Doctor. He has read everything you've written about your exploration of the invigoration of the Quinta Essentia of the humors using your special pyramid."

"He is interested in the invigoration of the Quinta Essentia of the human humors?"

Michael wasn't surprised by Dr. Gribbleflotz's reaction. The doctor was well aware that a number of his senior laborants were nonbelievers. Kurt Stoltz the Second though, he was as close to a true believer as Michael could believe existed. Apparently he had been a follower of Johann Valentin Andreae, and was into spiritual alchemy. "He is most interested in your work, Doctor."

Michael returned from seeing Dr. Gribbleflotz out of the office and glared at his sister. "Are you happy now?"

"It won't be too bad, Michael. Lettie and Celeste have done all the hard work. All you have to do is take their production methods and increase the volume. Your biggest problem will probably be making the Kirlian Imager, and I can ask Magdalena to help if you like."

Michael thought for a few seconds about Magdalena, the younger girl his sister was supporting while she studied for her electrical trades certificate. He glanced down at the drawings. He wasn't sure what was happening, but there was no way he was going to ask a fifteen-year-old girl for help. "It doesn't look too hard," he lied. "I'll get Kurt to help. If he knows something about the apparatus, he'll be more useful to the doctor."

"And with an expert right there in Jena, Dr. Gribbleflotz won't need to ask you to travel to Jena to help every time something goes wrong," Maria Anna suggested.

Michael grinned at his sister. She knew him so well. "The thought never crossed my mind."

A *few weeks later*

Michael looked down at the finished prototype Kirlian Imager. Things had not gone smoothly in its construction. First, he'd been unable to procure a suitable transformer, so he'd been forced to improvise. That had resulted in a decision to build a Wimshurst generator like the Kubiaks had built for Dr. Gribbleflotz, only much bigger. That decision had produced its own problems. The main one being that they didn't have any of the special discs large enough for the task. Fortunately, one of the laborants at the fuel tablet division had been experimenting with some of the surplus waters of formalin. Georg Heinz had been able to reproduce an up-time material with useful properties by using a cheat sheet and chemicals from the gas works. He'd been making "bakelite" insulators for several weeks now. Learning how to make suitable bakelite discs had taken over two weeks of expensive experimentation. However, the imager was finally ready for testing.

"Kurt, switch over to the safe light, please."

With just the red safe light to see by, Michael took a sheet of photosensitive paper out of its light-proof envelope and placed it on the thin sheet of rubber that covered the small sheet of copper that was the main electrode. Then he attached an earth to the specimen to be examined and placed it on the photosensitive paper.

"All right, you can start the generator now."

While Kurt pumped away at the treadle of the Wimshurst generator Michael counted the sparks snapping across the air gap until he thought there had been enough discharge to make an image. "Stop! That's enough." If the theory was right and the Kirlian Imager was properly constructed, the photosensitive paper should now contain an image of the aura of the object on the paper. Michael removed the coin and took the paper next door where a simple photographic laboratory had been set up. He could feel Kurt breathing over his shoulder as they watched the images appear.

Michael didn't see the fascination the Kirlian image had for Kurt. It was just a simple photograph of a coin. The books had much better pictures. Maybe it was the fact that he'd helped make the image.

Kurt looked up. "Could we try making a Kirlian image of a human hand?"

Michael had a quick look at his pocket watch. There was time. "Sure. I assume you're willing to donate the use of your hand?"

Kurt smiled and rolled up his sleeves. "Which one would you like? Or, better, why not both?"

❖   ❖   ❖

Michael looked at the images of Kurt's fingertips. They were, to put it mildly, disappointing.

Kurt sighed heavily. "It doesn't look as good as the images in the up-time books."

Michael nodded. They didn't look very good. That was probably due to a lot of things. "The paper probably isn't sensitive enough."

"The books say an earthed subject's image is stronger. Maybe if we were to earth me?"

"Kurt, the books also say that you shouldn't earth a live subject."

"But, Herr Siebenhorn, I am willing to take the risk. What harm can it do? You have said yourself that you have been stung by the lightning from Dr. Gribbleflotz's Wimshurst generator with no ill effect."

Michael bit his lip. He didn't like going against safety warnings, but Kurt was right. Most of the laborants had been stung by sparks when playing with the doctor's Wimshurst generator, with no ill effect. However, the new machine was significantly larger. It generated more electricity with a higher voltage, and could make much longer sparks. Further, it had a huge capacitor. It was entirely possible they could electrocute someone. Michael thought about the description of the up-timer Benjamin Franklin killing a turkey with a similar device. "Very well." He quietly adjusted the spark gap to make it smaller. The zaps, while more frequent, would be less dangerous.

Zap!

"Ouch!" Kurt jerked his hand off the imager.

Michael stopped spinning the generator and removed the wasted photosensitive paper. "Kurt, are you sure you want to do this?"

Kurt nodded. "It was just the surprise, Herr Siebenhorn. I'll be ready for it next time."

Michael sighed. He wasn't sure this was a good idea. He made a minor adjustment to the spark gap and drew another sheet of photosensitive paper from the light-proof envelope. "Right, let's try again."

When Kurt put his hand on the paper Michael started the generator spinning. He could see Kurt twitching as the current hit him again and again. "For God's sake, Kurt! Hold still or we'll never get an auroral image. The coin didn't move. Neither should you."

Kurt was still rubbing his hand as he examined the damp photograph. "It looks much clearer."

"Yes, it does. Would you like to try the left hand now?"

Kurt nodded. "Yes, Herr Siebenhorn. Herr Siebenhorn, could I please keep the images of my hands?"

Michael suppressed a sigh, Kurt, for all his experience with English, didn't seem to understand the concept of the rhetorical question. "Of course, Kurt."

A few weeks later, HDG Laboratories, Jena

Kurt still couldn't quite believe he was actually working as his hero's personal laborant. Even if it was just until his regular laborant returned from an important job. When Herr Siebenhorn made the offer, Kurt had been overcome with emotion.

He gave the safety glass of the fume cupboard a final polish to remove the last speck of dust and stood back to admire his handiwork. The fume cupboard was sparkling clean. Now to collect the various items for Dr. Gribbleflotz's next experimental session. Kurt's eyes lit up as he read the requirements sheet. *Another experiment with the Kirlian Imager.*

Phillip walked into the small laboratory and nodded in Kurt's general direction. "Are we all ready to proceed, Beta?"

With two Kurt Stoltzes being employed by the company in important positions there had been several instances of confusion. Phillip had solved the problem by telling Kurt that, as the latecomer, he was to no longer respond to the name Kurt Stoltz. Instead, he should only respond to Kurt Stoltz Beta or Kurt Beta. Or, as it turned out, just "Beta."

Kurt had no problem with this. If learning not to respond to the name Stoltz and answer to Beta was what it took to remain as Dr. Gribbleflotz's personal laborant, he was willing to adapt.

"Yes, Dr. Gribbleflotz. The envelope of the big sheets is in the top drawer under the table. The trays in the darkroom have been filled with chemicals and are at the correct temperature. All is ready for your experiments."

Several weeks later, the public seminar room, HDG Laboratories, Jena

Phillip held the static-charged rod close to the stream of water. There was an "oh" of astonishment from the audience as the stream of water bent away from the rod. Phillip started recharging the rod on the handful of wool in his other hand and smiled at his audience. He really enjoyed it when he got that reaction of amazement. "That was a demonstration of the repelling force of an electrical field. It is interesting to note that the same charged rod can also attract." Phillip passed the recharged rod above some small pieces of paper on his demonstration table. The paper leapt up to the rod.

The audience applauded the demonstration. "You have seen me use inanimate materials to make my electric fields, but did you know your own body also generates electricity?" He looked around his audience sympathetically. "I see a number of heads shaking. Yes, it is true. And now, using the wonders of the up-timer science of Kirlian photography, I shall prove it."

Phillip nodded to Kurt that he was ready. While Kurt made preparations, Phillip returned to his audience. "A gifted up-time philosopher, Semyon Kirlian, continuing the work of the great Nikola Tesla, discovered that he could photograph the life force, or aura, which surrounds all living beings, as I shall now demonstrate. Could I have a volunteer from the audience, please?"

Phillip stood back while Kurt hung the wet prints to dry. Each was carefully labeled with the volunteer's name so that they could take their own Kirlian image home with them, and they were crowding Kurt so they could see the images.

Once the images were hung up, Kurt opened the heavy blackout curtains and turned out the red safe light. Phillip waited for his audience to return to their seats.

"As you can see, the Kirlian Imager can detect forces

invisible to the human eye. Proving the existence of a field around our bodies..."

"Yes, but what use does it have, or is it just another useless party trick?"

Phillip froze. Was someone suggesting his Candles of the Essence of Light demonstrations were nothing but a "party trick"? He stared at the speaker. Could he be an agent from the university sent to try to discredit him? There was a gentle cough from his assistant. Phillip looked over at Beta. It appeared he had something he wanted to say. Well, Beta had spent a lot of his own time experimenting with the Kirlian Imager. Maybe he could silence the critic. "Would you like to explain, Beta?"

Kurt nodded enthusiastically. "Yes, and I have a number of Kirlian images that I would like to show everyone."

Phillip turned to his audience. "My assistant has made a personal study of the uses of the Kirlian Imager. If you will wait patiently for a few moments while he gathers some materials from the laboratory, he will attempt to answer your question."

Kurt approached the rostrum with his folder of notes and Kirlian images. This was his opportunity to impress his hero with his level of scientific knowledge and comprehension. He coughed gently into his hand to clear his throat and looked around at the curious faces and took a last steadying breath before starting his very first public presentation.

He held up an image of a modern coin so everyone could see it before passing it around the audience. "In this image of a coin we can see how the Kirlian image of the corona is regular and symmetrical. The life force follows the curvature of the coin." He passed out a second image. "This is the image from the same coin a week later. Notice how the 'flames,' those fine short lines radiating out from the edge of the coin, are the same."

He held up a new image. "And this is a Kirlian image of an old, well-used and abused coin. Notice how the corona is not symmetrical, showing the damage inflicted on the coin. Again, although I don't have the image available to show you, I can assure you that the corona from this coin didn't change when a second image was recorded a week later.

"However, when we examine a living being, things are different." Kurt passed around some images of his own hands. "Look at the coronas around each finger. Compare the same finger on different images. Notice the variation. That is evidence of the life force interacting with the world. We as human beings have the greatest variation in our Kirlian images, clearly demonstrating the greater complexity of the human spirit.

"It has been my privilege to investigate many Kirlian images. In the course of my investigations, I have determined that no two images, even of the same person, are ever the same. I have found that the variation is due to several things. First, just like the stream of water can be moved by the charged rod in Dr. Gribbleflotz's demonstration, other life forces can influence your aura. Second, what you eat, drink, or even wear, can influence your aura.

"My investigations suggest that the flames of the corona should be symmetrical around the surface being photographed. This would indicate a spirit in its ideal state. By carefully analyzing the placement and the ratios between various lengths of the flames of the aura, one can determine what is required to transform an individual's aura to its ideal state. Not, of course, that it is possible to actually achieve a true ideal state, not as long as there are other life forces able to wield influence. But my investigations have shown that one can 'manipulate' the forces acting on one's aura to arrive as closely as possible to the ideal state, where one is truly in balance with the universe, even by such simple things as changing the color of the clothes one wears on a given day."

Kurt held up his left hand so the audience could see the chased copper bracelet he was wearing. "Of course, sometimes a little more effort is necessary to bring a person's aura into balance. But since I have been manipulating my aura towards the ideal state I have improved not only my health, but my prospects. Clearly, an unbalanced aura is an indicator of poor health and vitality."

Kurt could feel that he had his audience in the palm of his hand. So this was why Dr. Gribbleflotz continued to give his seminars. The feeling of euphoria as everyone listens attentively to one's every word. "Of course, just looking at the fingertips doesn't tell us a lot about how our life force interacts with the world. Fortunately, Herr Dr. Gribbleflotz has a special Kirlian Imager that can record much larger images." Kurt unrolled a large Kirlian image and stuck it to the seminar backboard using magnets. With Dr. Gribbleflotz's pointer in hand he stepped aside so everyone could see.

"This is a Kirlian image of my head." He ran the tip of the pointer around the corona surrounding his head. "We can clearly see the 'halo' which is present around all of us. Obviously the head is not round, so the flames are not symmetrical, however, by analyzing the ratios of the length and density of the flames we can draw some conclusions as to what the individual must do to move their aura to the ideal state."

Kurt wasn't sure where the words were coming from, but he let them continue to flow. Anything to maintain the interest of his audience and the feeling of euphoria.

Phillip wasn't sure what to think. Beta had made a most enthusiastically received presentation. Even that dissenting voice was currently begging Kurt to interpret his Kirlian image and explain what he had to do to return his life force toward its ideal state. He shrugged. It seemed Beta had things well in hand. Meanwhile, he had papers to read and write. So Phillip left Beta to deal with the people crowding around him.

Later that day

Kurt knocked diffidently on the door. He had a request that he hoped the doctor would approve.

"Enter."

Kurt pushed the door open and stepped into Dr. Gribbleflotz's personal office. He passed an envious gaze at the shelves of books that lined one wall.

"Ah, Beta, a most impressive presentation."

Kurt flushed with pride. Dr. Gribbleflotz had been impressed. "Thank you, sir."

The doctor gestured toward an easy chair. "Please sit. What is it I can do for you?"

Kurt gingerly lowered himself into the soft easy chair. Previously he'd only been invited to sit on one of the hard wooden seats. He must have really done well. Maybe Dr. Gribbleflotz would be receptive to his request. "After the seminar today, sir, several of the attendees asked if I could take Kirlian images of their halos, and then interpret them so they could move their auras towards the ideal state. I was wondering if you would permit me to use your large Kirlian Imager to take the required photographs, and also allow me the time to interpret the images."

"The photosensitive paper isn't exactly cheap, Beta."

Kurt nodded his head rapidly. "I realize that, Herr Doctor. I expect to charge people a small fee."

"For the image and the interpretation?"

"If it is permitted, Dr. Gribbleflotz."

"Well, the Kirlian Imager isn't giving me the results I hoped for, so I don't see a problem letting you use it. However, I still need a personal laborant until Hans returns, so I can't really spare you."

"I wasn't thinking of performing the imaging when I should be working for you, Dr. Gribbleflotz!"

"You weren't? Very well. Make arrangements with Frau Mittelhausen."

"Thank you, Herr Dr. Gribbleflotz."

October 1634, Grantville

It was Michael's first visit to the explosives factory and he was curious. He paused at the door of his sister's office to look around. It was crowded with filing cabinets and wall charts. There was a good up-time typewriter on the desk and—wonder of wonders—a computer. Maria Anna was currently engrossed with the computer screen. "How come you rate your own computer, Sis?"

"Michael! Long time no see. I get the computer because I handle the books. What can I do for you?"

Michael had been so busy over the last couple of months he hadn't been able to spend much time with his sister. "I've got an order from Jena for some more Kirlian Imagers and photographic chemicals, and I was wondering if Celeste's daughter and her friends can get me some more milkweed latex."

"You could have phoned."

"Sure. But then I couldn't have shown you this." Michael tossed a booklet and covering letter over to Maria Anna. He was interested in how she reacted. He'd nearly fallen over laughing himself. "Kurt's calling himself Beta these days. Dr. Gribbleflotz was having too much trouble with two Kurt Stoltzes on the payroll."

Maria Anna gingerly picked up the booklet and looked at it. Her head shot up. "'How to Manage Your Aura for Personal Health and Gain.' By Kurt Beta. What the hell is happening in Jena?"

Michael winced at the blasphemy. "Such language, Maria Anna."

"You try working with the Hart brothers day after day and see what happens to your language," Maria Anna muttered. "Just answer the question."

"Read the letter. It explains everything."

Maria Anna dropped the booklet and opened Kurt's letter. "He's been teaching others to interpret the life forces made visible by the wonders of Kirlian photography. Is he for real?"

Michael shrugged. "I think so. That's why he needs

the additional imagers. He needs them for his students. Frau Mittelhausen has authorized the order."

Maria Anna grimaced. "Kurt's students? What's he trying to do?"

"Franchise auroral interpretation, of course."

"Franchise what? He's selling snake oil."

Michael shook his head. "No, snake oil is a total fraud. What Kurt Beta is doing is merely pseudo-science, like the doctor and his pyramid. Frau Mittelhausen says people in Jena are lapping it up."

"You know what I think of the doctor's pyramid."

"Sure, but it's harmless. Think of what Kurt's doing as being Feng Shui for the soul."

"What the hell is Fung Shway?"

Michael paused to consider an answer. Feng Shui wasn't one of those things that were easy to explain. "I think I need to lend you the book I read."

December 1634, office of micro lender
Boots Bank, Jena

Marguerite Lobstein called over to her partner. "Johann Diefenthaler wants a loan to take the new photographer course in Grantville and to buy a camera obscura photographer equipage. What do you think?"

Catherine Mutschler looked at the photographs of her and Marguerite's family displayed around the room. "Where does Johann hope to operate?"

"He wants to operate in Bamberg. There hasn't been anybody else saying they want to work there. Most of them want to operate in Magdeburg."

Catherine chewed on a lock of hair while she read

the detailed loan application. "He's got a reasonable business plan. I think we can make the loan to do the Certificate in Photography at Brennerei und Chemiefabrik Schwarza's school in Grantville easily enough. Tell him the rest is dependent on his passing the course."

"Right." Marguerite made a note on Johann's folder and tossed it into the yes basket. Then she pulled out another folder. "Oh, dear!"

Catherine took in the grimace of distaste on Marguerite's face. "What's the matter?"

"Another Kirlian Imager application."

"Just because you don't believe in the interpretation of the human spirit doesn't mean it isn't a sound business proposition."

"Are you suggesting that you believe in that mumbo-jumbo?"

Catherine shook her head. "No. Of course I don't believe it, but I know there are lots of people who do. If your applicant has completed Herr Beta's course and has a good business plan there is no more reason to deny the application than there was to deny Johann Diefenthaler's. Remember, the only criteria we use to determine whether or not to make a loan is whether or not they can pay it back."

Marguerite tossed the application across to Catherine. "Very well, you sign off on the loan. I don't want to touch the thing."

January 1635, HDG Laboratories, Jena

Ursula Mittelhausen smiled at the photograph her sister had sent her. It wasn't as good as the one she had sent to Margarethe, but her portrait had been taken by Frau Sebastian using a proper up-time camera, not one of the new manual exposure Camera Obscura Photographer machines that the traveling photographers were using.

Phillip shook Kurt Beta's hand. "Are you sure you have to leave, Beta? There's plenty a man with your talents can achieve here at HDG Laboratories."

Kurt shook his head. "Thank you for the offer, Dr. Gribbleflotz. But my time as your personal laborant has opened my eyes to a world of new opportunities. I intend spreading the science of interpreting Kirlian images. I already have a number of lectures scheduled in Magdeburg, and I have to see my publisher about my new book."

"Your new book?" Phillip asked.

"Yes. *Feng Shui for the Soul*. Herr Siebenhorn gave me the idea for the title. I had previously missed the obvious connection between the ancient Chinese science of Feng Shui and the new art of interpreting Kirlian images, but as soon as Herr Siebenhorn made the comparison, the relationship was obvious."

Kurt paused to consider just why he'd missed such an obvious connection. The Censors had been hard at work indeed. They'd hidden the truth with careful use of misdirection, surrounding the truths of Feng Shui with claims only the gullible could believe. It had taken him considerable time and effort to sort through all the up-timer material to discover the truth, but now he knew and it was going to make him rich.

Chapter 16

Dr. Phil's Distraction

April 1635, the rectory, St. Martin's in the Fields, south of Rudolstadt

Yesterday I helped Stepmama turn Papa's old Geneva gown. We unpicked the seams, darned threads to reinforce the worst worn spots and re-dyed the fabric beforehand sewing it back together, with what was formerly the inside now out. With a new detachable linen clerical collar, Papa will be set for another year or two.

Today I walked to the stationery store to purchase school supplies for tomorrow. When I got to the dress shop, I stopped to have a look at the dresses displayed in the window. There was one there, my favorite. Ever since it first appeared in the window I had stopped to admire it. If nobody was looking, I would position myself so my reflection appeared as if I was wearing it. I would have loved to buy it, but with eight children, including me, still dependent on poor Papa, there is not the money for such fripperies.

My new dress would be something made over from what Stepmama could find in the poor box.

Today, though, I suffered a shock. My beautiful dress was being taken from the window. I watched through the window in horror. Elisabeth Schwentzel, a girl my age, tried it on. It didn't suit her at all. But she bought it just the same.

Struggling to hold back the tears, I walked away. It wasn't fair. Why should Elisabeth have my dress? She was nothing more than a maid in one of Rudolstadt's hotels, and her father a laborer at the sawmill. But he earns more than Papa, even with all of Papa's learning. And the banns have been read for Elisabeth's upcoming marriage to a young man working at the steel mill.

Things haven't been the same since Andrea ran off to marry her up-timer. Before my sister eloped, we at least had each other when we taught the young boys and girls at Countess Katharina's, the parish school. It's been a year since Andrea eloped with Tony Chabert. In that time the parish hasn't found a replacement for her. They are too tight with their money. Andrea hadn't been paid any more than I am, of course. Daughters are considered a benefit of employing a parish pastor. Now I face eighty-three five- and six-year-old children every day on my own and I will continue to do so until I marry—if I ever do. Today in school I caught myself sighing heavily over my situation, before turning my attention back to what the children were doing. I don't think I'll ever get married. Who would have a woman of few looks and little dowry? Even Papa has given up on me, and he's the man who found up-timer husbands for seven of his congregation in less than twelve months.

❖   ❖   ❖

Dr. Phillip Theophrastus Gribbleflotz gave the image in the mirror a final searching look. A final brush with the clothes brush, a hat to cover his head, and he was ready. Briefcase in hand, Phillip walked to the hotel where a conference room had been booked for this meeting. It wasn't that he expected any problems with the women from Kubiak Country Industries, but with the up-timer females it helped to be prepared.

When he first started working with the Kubiak Country ladies, Phillip thought, he had been too timid. He hadn't been used to being around women, especially not forceful up-timer women. He had let them talk him into all sorts of irrelevant distractions from his research. But this time he intended to be firm. At last it appeared he would be able to start on his greatest project, his investigation into the invigoration of the Quinta Essentia of the human humors. The stumbling block had been the aluminum members for the pyramid. Faceted gems had been easy in comparison. But a couple of charming men had come visiting. They had obviously attended one of his seminars and knew of his interest in aluminum. They were offering preferential access to the new metal when they started producing it. However, they needed to raise money before they could extract the necessary ores. Phillip hoped to convince the Kubiak Country ladies to invest in the company they were planning to set up.

Phillip was reasonably happy with the way the meeting had gone. The ladies hadn't even had some new recipe for a product they just had to have. They had listened intently when he had described the aluminum company and how he wanted to invest in it. Just like properly behaved women they had promised to come back after they talked with their husbands.

There was a bookshop he just had to visit, and his favorite glass blower had sent him a letter advising him that he had some new scientific glassware to demonstrate. Phillip walked down the main street, a bounce to his step. All was well with his world.

Tasha Kubiak stalked around the room. "I don't like it. Does anybody know anything about making aluminum?"

"Well, I don't. And I reckon that's what these con artists are banking on. Their story sounds convincing, and the prospectus looks pretty with all of the color pictures and all those pretty graphs and tables. I think the whole thing stinks." Belle looked around the conference room to see if any of the other Kubiak Country ladies disagreed.

Tracy Kubiak stood up. As the driving force behind the formation of Kubiak Country Industries, what she said carried a lot of weight, so she had to be careful what she said. "We have a problem." The other ladies dutifully nodded their heads. That, they agreed with. "On the one hand, we don't want to alienate Dr. Phil. We can't just say 'no you can't invest in this aluminum company.' On the other hand, we don't want to commit funds if it is a fraud. It might be a perfectly legitimate company. The proprietors may be able to deliver what they claim."

"But you don't believe it, Mama?"

Tracy smiled at her adopted daughter. At nineteen, barely a dozen years her junior, Richelle and her daughter, Lenya, had been living with Tracy and her husband for the better part of four years. In that time Richelle had become her second in command in both Grantville Canvas and Outdoor and Kubiak Country Industries. "No. I don't believe it. It sounds too good. It targets Dr. Phil too well. And the prospectus is too much flash without enough substance."

"Is there anything we can do to distract Dr. Phil?"

Mary Rose Onofrio's question was met by the silence it deserved. Dr. Gribbleflotz had been talking about his aluminum pyramid every chance he got for the better part of three years. In that time his dream of an aluminum pyramid with its strategically placed faceted gems had survived dozens of alternative lines of research. What could possibly distract the man from the greatness he expected to realize through investigating the Quinta Essentia of the human humors?

He couldn't be sure how it happened. One moment he was walking around a peasant woman with funny white marks on the back of her drab skirt and bodice. The next, he was sent sprawling. He suddenly found himself on the ground; his arms wrapped around the woman, the contents of her basket scattered around them. There was the sound of laughter and running feet. For a moment Phillip's mind was blank. It felt so natural, the warm body wrapped in his arms. With a start he realized what was happening. This was a young woman, and he steered clear of young women. Or more precisely, they seemed to steer clear of him. Phillip couldn't remember the last time he had cuddled or been cuddled by anyone. Hastily he released her. He couldn't meet her eyes and turned to look elsewhere. Loose papers being scattered by a gentle breeze caught his attention.

"Oh!"

It was the sound of suppressed horror. Phillip had made similar utterances after dropping precious books and paper. Scrambling around on his hands and knees, he started to collect papers before they scattered too far. He turned to pass the papers he had collected to the woman. Their heads crashed together. Stunned, he jerked back. She also had reared back from the contact. A moment later Phillip turned away from her gaze and hastened to his feet.

He helped her to her feet. "Are you all right, miss?"

"Yes, thank you, sir. Those children, someone should teach them better manners. Oh dear."

Phillip watched the young woman reach down for a waxed paper parcel that had been ground into the pavement by someone's boots. When she opened it he could see the squashed remains of what had probably been intended as her midday meal. At the thought of food, Phillip realized it had been a while since he last ate.

"It would please me if you would join me over lunch." The young woman appeared on the point of refusing when he heard deep rumblings. Phillip had known hunger, and he understood pride; besides, he was curious about her. He had noticed the books and papers he had helped retrieve. Judging by the quality of the penmanship on the papers, she was an educated woman.

"It appears I am responsible for destroying your meal. Please allow me to make recompense. A simple meal in the public restaurant of your choice."

"Good sir, I couldn't. It was carelessness on my part. My meal is still fit to eat. A little squashed but the wrapping protected it." Maria Blandina backed away, then turned and ran.

Intrigued Phillip followed. Soon he was able to observe her running into the Countess Katharina the Heroic School next to the Lutheran church of St. Martin's. Things were becoming clear. Obviously the young woman was a teacher at Countess Katharina's. That explained the penmanship. A teacher had to be well educated. As for the plain clothes, Dr. Gribbleflotz wasn't much of a Lutheran, but he knew enough to understand how the church worked. Most likely the woman was a daughter of the pastor.

Settling down behind my desk at Countess Katharina's, I gave thanks to God for the fine weather of the last few days. The dry conditions meant none of the books or papers had taken any harm. The loud rumbling from my stomach reminded me I hadn't eaten yet. Pulling the waxed paper packet from my basket I peeled the paper away from what was supposed to have been my lunch. I looked at the sorry-looking meal, almost unrecognizable after some passerby had stood on it in his heavy boots.

It looked completely unappetizing, but beggars can't be choosers, and I was hungry. I had never been so embarrassed as when my stomach rumbled so loudly just as I refused the nice gentleman's offer of lunch in a restaurant. I can't remember when I last ate in one, and would have loved to accept his invitation. However, if Stepmama ever heard that Pastor Kastenmayer's younger daughter had been seen eating in a public restaurant with a strange man...It had been bad enough a year ago when Andrea had a meal in a public restaurant with the up-timer she later married.

He seemed a nice man. Not too old, and although the colors and style of his clothes didn't really suit him, they were well made. I have to blush when I remember the feel of his arms around me. It felt so comfortable, even for just a moment.

Phillip was unable to settle down that night. Every time he started to drop off to sleep a pair of sparkling eyes greeted him. The next day, while getting dressed, he thought about what he had to do. Somehow he would make time to see the young woman.

His eyes dropped to the knees of his trousers and his gleaming shoes. Last night the valet had had to clean them. He was proud of the way he dressed, and to have been walking around Rudolstadt with soiled knees and dirty shoes would normally have made him ill with embarrassment. He was surprised at his feeling of contentment.

He pulled out his pocket watch and checked the time. Yes, he should have plenty of time to get to the school before she arrived.

He stood on the corner, waiting. A rowdy mob of young children had assembled outside Countess Katharina the Heroic School. Then, the moment he had been waiting for. The teacher, the young woman of the previous day, arrived. Phillip let his eyes feast on her. She was ordering the mass of young children into lines. Phillip expected the other teachers to assist her, but they went straight into the rooms where the older children were waiting, leaving her to manage all of the youngsters on her own. Phillip was simply amazed. The redoubtable Frau Mittelhausen was complaining bitterly about dealing with a few young apprentices at HDG Laboratories back in Jena. Maybe she should take lessons from this teacher. An idea bubbled to the surface. Maybe he could offer the young woman a job helping Frau Mittelhausen run the household. Surely the pay and conditions would be much better than what she was receiving.

Phillip was ready and waiting when the children poured out of the school. Picnic basket in hand, he approached the young teacher. "You left so suddenly yesterday that we failed to introduce ourselves. I am Phillip Theophrastus Gribbleflotz, an alchemist at HDG Laboratories in Jena, and I would like to invite you to join me in sampling the delicacies my hotel prepared." He lifted the basket and stood waiting expectantly, the cloth covering the food pulled away to let her see inside it.

Maria Blandina stared at Phillip. Already the smells emerging from the basket were pulling at her senses. After a quick look around to see who might be watching, and to check that Stepmama wasn't one of them, she introduced herself. "I am Maria Blandina Kastenmayer, a teacher at Countess Katharina the Heroic School, and I would be delighted to share the contents of your basket."

I had to hurry back to class. The time had passed so quickly. Phillip asked if he could walk me home after school ended for the day. I told him yes. We had talked a little about each other. I now knew he was in Rudolstadt on business for the company that employed him. The company made products aimed at the up-timer market. I'd been forced to smother my laughter at the way Phillip proudly named some of the products, Gribbleflotz this and Gribbleflotz that. It was as if he felt, because he had the same name as their inventor, that he had some sort of reflected glory. And maybe there was, because most people find jobs for their relatives. It's a harmless conceit, a bit like the way Papa always manages to insert into conversations that Mama, his first wife, had been a Selfisch, a sister to the Selfisch of the respected Rudolstadt law firm of Hardegg, Selfisch, and Krapp.

Phillip was distracted, his mind concentrating on his recent luncheon date rather than where he was going. Maria Blandina Kastenmayer, such a pretty name. And she seemed to actually like him. He had arranged to walk her to work the next day. He still wanted to take her back Jena. But what if she said no to working for him? He would be too embarrassed to continue seeing her.

Sunday, after church lunch, Drahuta property

Belle Drahuta tapped the aluminum company prospectus. "What are we going to do about Dr. Phil?"

Erin Zaleski lowered her coffee cup. "About the only thing we can do is find something to distract him while our husbands scare off these con men."

Tracy Kubiak laughed. "Erin, the only thing I can

see distracting Dr. Phil from those tricksters and their aluminum mine is an improved way of investigating his Quinta Essentia of the human humors." She looked around the room. "Does anybody here know anything that might work?"

Belle shook her head. "I wouldn't know a Quinta Essentia of the human humors if it stood up and bit me, Tracy. But are you sure that they are con men?"

"Ted and Jonathan's father aren't sure if it's a con or wishful thinking. They are willing to give them the benefit of the doubt when they claim they will be mining aluminum ore. A lot of potential investors might get confused if you talked about mining bauxite to make aluminum. But they picked up on the problems of processing the ore. The prospectus implies that it's a simple matter of extracting the ore from the ground, isolating the aluminum and melting it to form ingots. Apparently it isn't that easy. It needs some pretty exotic chemicals to process the ore, and it really burns through electricity."

Hidden in a corner, snuggling up together were Jonathan Fortney and Tracy's adopted daughter, Richelle. Normally the self-satisfied smiles on their faces would be aimed at each other, but this time they were looking at the women grouped around the kitchen table. They were listening in on the discussion. Tracy pointed an accusing finger at them. "Okay, you two. Fess up. What do you know that we don't?"

All eyes turned to Jonathan and Richelle. "It appears that Dr. Phil has been a little distracted of late, Mama." Richelle had to use her elbow when Jonathan started to laugh.

Belle glared at Jonathan. "What's so funny about Dr. Phil being distracted?"

Imprisoning Richelle's arms so she couldn't strike him again, Jonathan dropped a kiss on her forehead before answering. "Dr. Phil is in love."

"In love? With who? What kind of woman is the geek interested in? Some half-naked, painted tart, all tits and no brain, I suppose. It would be just like the man. And what does she see in him? Money bags?"

Richelle waited for Tante Tasha to finish her diatribe. It was a little more extreme than the one she had addressed to Jonathan when he told her that Dr. Phil was seeing a young woman. Who could have imagined Dr. Phil being struck by Cupid's arrow at his age? Listening to him talk about the lady had established two things in her mind. First, that she was a very respectable young lady. Pastor's daughters charged with teaching the congregation's young had to be. And second, Dr. Phil was very unsure of his reception. His lack of confidence around women was crippling the progress of the romance.

"Dr. Phil says she is the sweetest, kindest, most enchanting young woman he has ever met, Tante Tasha."

"That wouldn't surprise me at all. How many women would be interested in him? What do we know about her? Who is she? Who is her family? Does she bring a dowry?"

"Dr. Phil says Maria Blandina Kastenmayer is the daughter of the pastor at St. Martin's in the Field, just outside the Ring of Fire. And I doubt they are talking dowry, or even marriage. Dr. Phil is so lacking in confidence around her he doesn't know how to behave."

"Have either of you two met this young woman?" Tracy asked.

"Jonathan has."

"Well?" Tracy turned her best stare of interrogation, perfected during her time as a NCO with the U.S. Army back up-time, onto Jonathan.

"I managed to get a good look after Dr. Phil pointed her out one day. She's a small thing. Youngish, passable-looking, but the clothes she wears drain her face of any color and do absolutely nothing for her. She moves gracefully when she walks. And she looked a little worn. But Dr. Phil reckons she's teaching something like eighty young kids at Countess Katharina the Heroic School, so that's not surprising."

There was disbelief at that. Who could possibly teach that many children in a single classroom? If true, then she must be a very special young woman indeed. Surely even the redoubtable Veronica Dreeson would tremble at the thought of taking charge of that classroom day after day.

Tracy thought a moment. "I want you both to meet this Maria Blandina. I want anything you can find out about her. This might be our best hope for distracting Dr. Gribbleflotz from the aluminum mine, but we don't want him jumping out of the frying pan into the fire."

"How do you suggest we find out about her, Mrs. Kubiak?" Jonathan asked.

Tracy threw up her arms. "Do I have to do everything for you, Jonathan? Think. Start with Frau Gundelfinger. She usually knows something about everything. Now get, go, get a move on. The pair of you should be outside in the sun."

Belle watched as the young couple walked out of the room arm in arm. "When are those two getting married?"

"Soon. Very soon. In fact tomorrow wouldn't be soon enough." Tracy gently shook her head at young love. "They're only waiting for Jonathan's term with the Army to finish."

"When's that, a couple of months' time?" Belle asked. Tracy nodded. "Can they afford to marry? I know you still have Ted's parents' house they can have, and Richelle virtually runs Grantville Canvas and Outdoor these days. But Jonathan can't have saved much on a soldier's salary, can he?"

Tracy had to smile at the family's concerns. Her gaze followed the couple as they gathered up Richelle's daughter, Lenya, and her own children, Justin and Terrie, and took them outside. She waited until they were out of sight. "I doubt it'll be a problem. The moment he's out of the army he'll start working full time for his father's consulting company, and that's doing quite well."

Several days later

"Maria Blandina, there is gossip about you seeing some young man on the sly. What do you have to say for yourself? You know it reflects badly on your papa. Especially after what happened with your sister. Who is he? Where does he work? Is he Lutheran?"

I waited patiently for Stepmama to finish before answering. "His name is Phillip Theophrastus Gribbleflotz. He has a responsible job with an up-timer firm based in Jena. I don't know if he is Lutheran. We haven't talked about religion. But I expect he is, since he works in Jena and almost everyone in Jena is Lutheran. It isn't like Grantville."

"What? My information is you have been seeing this man every day for more than a week. How can he have a responsible job in Jena and what is this 'responsible job' that allows him so much time in Rudolstadt?"

"He is an alchemist working in the laboratories at HDG Laboratories in Jena."

"An alchemist! A charlatan more like. He's probably a laborer barely making a living, and wasting what he does earn on his clothes from what I hear. I hope you haven't visited him in whatever shady boarding house he is staying."

I bravely weathered the hard stare from Stepmama. Phillip had taken me to lunch at the small private hotel where he was staying. It was little more than a boarding house, but not the sort Stepmama was suggesting. The lunch had been respectable, shared with friends of Phillip, a young couple engaged to be married. "He is on vacation, Stepmama. They allow their employees several weeks paid 'vacation' every year." *Unlike you and Papa, who expect me to teach and help you every day.* "And he is not a charlatan. He does have a respectable job. I have met a young couple who know him and they talked easily about what he was doing in Jena."

"And when, Marina Blandina, were you planning on introducing us to this man? Apparently you have been seeing him for a whole week, and still you haven't chosen to introduce him to your mama and papa. You didn't even let your papa and me know you were walking out with someone. I had to hear of it from Christiana Selfisch."

I started a little at that. That was definitely bad

news. Tante Christiana and Stepmama didn't get on at all. I didn't want to know just what was said, but it was bound to reflect badly on Stepmama.

"Your Tante Christiana was very happy to see you walking out with a young man." Stepmama stared unblinkingly straight into my eyes. "She asked when the banns would be read." I had to swallow at that. Marriage was a topic we hadn't touched on. I wasn't really sure that Phillip could afford a wife.

"Are we to expect this man to come calling to ask your papa for your hand?"

I'm afraid to say I panicked. I said the first thing that entered my head. "Yes."

It was pleasant to see Stepmama at a loss for words, but I was soon punished for my momentary pleasure. "Then bring him around for dinner tomorrow night. If you are going to marry the man, your papa and I had better meet him."

I stuttered an acknowledgement and ran from the room. What to do? I was going to have to say something to Phillip.

Dr. Gribbleflotz smiled at his guests. Jonathan Fortney, a close friend of several years, was watching his fiancée, Richelle Kubiak, playing with her daughter. Phillip recognized the look in his eyes. He had been seeing that same look in the mirror these last couple of days. The quiet contentment and air of rightness between the three settled it for Phillip.

"I intend asking Frau Kastenmayer to marry me." He carefully watched to see the reaction of the young couple. He didn't go unrewarded.

Richelle turned and smiled at Jonathan and then

at Phillip. "That's very nice, Dr. Gribbleflotz. She is a delightful young woman, and not without connections."

Jonathan snorted at Richelle's response. It was considerably different from what Richelle and the Kubiak Country ladies had originally thought.

"But, Salome dear, it really is time Maria Blandina married. We can't expect her to stay unmarried and teaching at Countess Katharina the Heroic School forever. And it reflects badly on me that I have been able to find husbands for seven dowerless young women of the parish, but failed to find a husband for my own daughter," Pastor Ludwig Kastenmayer said to his wife.

"Husband, if Maria Blandina marries, who is going to teach the children of Countess Katharina the Heroic?" Salome Piscatora, Ludwig's second wife and the mother of seven of his surviving sons, said. "The parish will be forced to pay a teacher. No, two teachers. The parish will never find another teacher willing to teach such a big class. Although Maria Blandina managed quite well on her own."

"Dear, that is a problem for the parish. They cannot have expected Maria Blandina to stay unmarried. And besides, her prospective husband works in Jena, you say?" At Salome's nod, Ludwig continued. "But, that is wonderful. Just think. Maria Blandina will have a house in Jena. Her brothers will be able to stay with her while they attend the university at Jena. The savings on room and board will be enough to ensure the education of all our children."

Salome was silenced. She had worried endlessly about how they were to support and educate her boys on a parish pastor's salary. Things had been extremely tight even with just the three eldest at the university in Jena. What they would be like as the other four grew didn't bear thinking about. If Maria Blandina and her husband could provide room and board for her brothers, things would be a lot easier.

Phillip waited nervously for Maria Blandina outside Countess Katharina's. When she followed the children out of the school, his heart started racing. She came out in a rush, throwing herself into his arms. "Oh Phillip. I'm so sorry. I'm so sorry."

Startled, but pleasantly surprised and heartened at the unexpected display of affection, Phillip wrapped his arms around her in an attempt to comfort her. "What's the matter, my dearest?"

"I'm so sorry, Phillip. But Stepmama heard that I've been seeing you, and demanded to know if you were going to ask Papa for permission to marry me. I panicked and said yes. Stepmama said I was to bring you to dinner tonight so you could ask Papa's permission." Maria Blandina had tears in her eyes. It sounded like she was begging his forgiveness.

Phillip looked down into the tear-filled eyes. "Would it be so hard to marry me, Maria Blandina?"

"Oh no! I would love to be your wife. But it is so soon. And can you afford a wife?"

Phillip crushed her against his chest. "I am sure I can afford a wife, Maria Blandina." He put his hands on her shoulders and pushed her far enough away that he could see her face. "Maria Blandina Kastenmayer, would you do me the honor of being my wife?"

"Oh, Phillip."

❖   ❖   ❖

Phillip Theophrastus Gribbleflotz, pretender to the title of doctor, dried his clammy hands on his trousers before entering Pastor Kastenmayer's study. Once there, he was confronted by the collar and vestments of the church he had avoided on all but the most compulsory of occasions for a quarter of a century. He felt a bit guilty when he passed over the character references the Kubiak Country folks had obtained. There was one from the management of HDG Laboratories and one from Hardegg, Selfisch and Krapp. Between them, they established the important facts. That Phillip Theophrastus Gribbleflotz had held a position of responsibility with the company for nearly four years, that he could afford a wife and family, and that he had no significant outstanding debts. While Pastor Kastenmayer read the references, Phillip thought a little bit about the fur coat he had ordered. The furrier would have to wait on his next dividend from the company before he could pay for that. Then he smiled, imagining the reactions when he and Maria Blandina attended important events wearing matching fur coats. Yes. He was sure the furrier would be happy to accept such an order.

He had been happy to see that there was no mention of a doctorate in the references. A learned man such as Pastor Kastenmayer would have been sure to ask embarrassing questions. He tried to remember what Jonathan Fortney had said when, panicking over meeting Maria Blandina's father, he had asked the up-timer for advice. "Keep your answers simple. Don't exaggerate, don't lie, and most of all, remember to say how much you love Maria Blandina." It had worked for Jonathan. Surely the same rules should work for him.

❖   ❖   ❖

"So, Herr Gribbleflotz. You wish to marry my beautiful daughter?" At Phillip's nod, Ludwig Kastenmayer continued. "I am sorry to say that she has little in the way of a dowry. It's been a struggle to make ends meet and educate all my boys on a pastor's salary."

"I assure you a dowry isn't necessary, Pastor Kastenmayer. As I am sure you have read from my references, I earn more than sufficient to provide for a wife and family, and the company provides me with an apartment close to my laboratory."

Ludwig scanned the references. The letterhead of Hardegg, Selfisch, and Krapp leaped out at him. A quick glance at the bottom identified the writer of the document. If Johann Georg Selfisch said Phillip Theophrastus Gribbleflotz was able to support his deceased sister's younger daughter, then Ludwig Kastenmayer had no doubt that Herr Gribbleflotz could. His eyes drifting from the references, Ludwig's attention fell on a short note from his wife. Looking up from the list of instructions, he posed the first of a set of important questions. "Very good. Err, Herr Gribbleflotz, what is it exactly that you do for HDG Laboratories?"

"There are a lot of processes that need utmost attention to detail. I have responsibility for seeing that the apprentices are properly trained and perform their tasks correctly."

"Is there much chance for your advancement with the company?"

Phillip paused in thought. Advancement? To what? He was already in charge! But he remembered Jonathan's advice and answered directly and simply. "No.

I don't believe I will advance any higher within the company. I am happy where I am, supervising the apprentices and working in my laboratory."

Ludwig stifled his disappointment. It appeared Herr Gribbleflotz had risen as high as he was ever likely to do in the company. Maybe Maria Blandina could give him the necessary motivation to improve his situation. "Herr Gribbleflotz, I currently have three sons attending the university in Jena. They are a constant drain on my slender pocket, and I have another four young sons to educate still. I was wondering..." He stumbled to a halt as he wondered how to word a request that his soon to be son-in-law provide room and board for three young men he had never met. Not that he wouldn't contribute to their keep, but family didn't charge commercial rates.

"Why, Pastor Kastenmayer. There is an obvious solution. Let your sons stay with Maria Blandina and myself. There are so many apprentices living in the company dormitories that three more won't be noticed. And, as educated men, they will be a good influence on the apprentices."

Ludwig was a little overcome at the response to his unasked request. It was beyond his wildest dreams that such an offer would be made.

A month later, St. Martin's in the Fields

Salome Piscatora verh. Kastenmayerin, Maria Blandina's stepmama, had been shocked when she was introduced to Herr Gribbleflotz's witnesses at the small, family-only ceremony in which Maria Blandina Kastenmayer became Maria Blandina Kastenmayerin, verh. Gribbleflotz.

It wasn't the fact that Richelle Kubiak had an illegitimate child that shocked her. Salome had been living in a war-ridden land for the past fifteen years and had seen too many women with children of unknown paternity. No, what had shocked her was that the young woman was a Catholic, and not only was she intending to marry a semi-Calvinistic heretic, she and her fiancé were still willing to show up as witnesses for a Lutheran wedding.

After the wedding trip, HDG Laboratories, Jena

I couldn't help but notice the large number of young men and women walking idly around the compound when our carriage trundled through the gate and onward toward what I could only imagine would be my new home.

Finally, the hired carriage ground to a halt. There was a mature woman waiting at the door. "Frau Mittelhausen." Phillip pointed her out. I had heard that she was responsible for the apprentices Phillip supervised. I hoped my marriage wouldn't be putting her out of a job.

We had one last kiss before Phillip stepped out of the carriage and then helped me out. The people were all staring. Obviously they knew I was Phillip's new wife. I smiled and waved to them. I was sincerely glad that I had let Richelle make me a couple of beautiful new dresses.

Phillip had just carried me over the threshold of the apartment building when two men, important men judging by their dress, approached us.

"A thousand apologies, *gnaedige Frau*, Herr Dr. Gribbleflotz. But there are important documents that need your signature. If we could have but a moment, so that they may catch the late post."

I was stunned. They had called him Herr Dr. Gribbleflotz. Phillip was a doctor. I stood staring at Phillip. He apologized for the interruption, a look of beseeching appeal in his eyes, a flush rising in his face. He passed me into Frau Mittelhausen's capable hands before going off with the two men. Shocked, I stood and watched the two men lead Phillip off.

"This way, Frau Kastenmayerin." Frau Mittelhausen led me into the building.

I struggled to understand. Looking back I could see the sign over the gate. HDG Laboratories. Suddenly it had new meaning. HDG, Herr Dr. Gribbleflotz. My Phillip was Herr Dr. Gribbleflotz. The man behind Gribbleflotz's Aeolian Transformers, Gribbleflotz Sal Vin Betula, Gribbleflotz Vin Sal Aer Fixus, Gribbleflotz Sal Aer Fixus and the Gribbleflotz Amazing Lightning Crystal. My Phillip was almost famous. He must be rich. And he had chosen to marry me.

Chapter 17

The Creamed Madonna

May 1635, HDG Laboratories, Jena

Newlywed Dr. Phillip Gribbleflotz was at a bit of a loose end. He'd finally concluded that there was something fundamentally wrong with the theory that pyramid power could be used to invigorate the Quinta Essentia of the human humors, and had regretfully given up on that line of research. He desperately needed something new to work on. Something interesting. Something impressive. Something that would prove to the world that he was in fact the World's Greatest Alchemist.

He sat back in his chair and surveyed his office, looking for inspiration. There was the large portrait photograph of his beautiful young wife, Dina Kastenmayerin, in pride of place over the fireplace. That was certainly inspiring, but not in any direction that would impress the academics at Jena University. On either side of the fireplace were bookshelves. It looked like he was going to have to do a lot more reading to get what Jonathan Fortney would call the "killer application" that would forever cement his place in history.

Phillip looked up hopefully when the door opened. He was hoping it would be Dina, but it was only his secretary with the mail. "Anything interesting?"

Frau Beier placed one envelope on his desk. "This one was marked personal and confidential, so I didn't open it. The rest are just the usual begging letters, inquiries about licensing agreements, and requests for you to endorse various products. I have prepared the usual responses."

Phillip sighed. Advertising was the curse of the new business environment. He reached for the envelope. The first thing he noticed was the excessive use of scent. He rubbed his nose and looked up at Frau Beier.

"I assume it is from a 'lady.'" The emphasis she put on the word indicated she thought the author no such thing.

Phillip read the sender's address. "Do we know a Velma Hardesty, in Haarlem, the Netherlands?"

Frau Beier shook her head. "No, but with a name like that I assume it is one of the up-timer females. Though what she has to say that could be both private and confidential, I can't imagine."

Phillip had had much the same thought. He'd received a few letters from up-timers before, but never one claiming to be personal and confidential. Oh well. There was surely one way to find out what Velma Hardesty wanted. If he could read the overly curly penmanship.

A few days later, Cora's Café, Grantville

Priscilla Fortney put down her cup of coffee, looked around to see who might be listening, and leaned closer to her fellow members of the Red Cross Sanitation Squad seated around the table. "You'll never guess what I overheard at the library this morning."

"No, we'll never guess. What did you overhear that you weren't supposed to hear, Prissy?" Minnie Frost asked.

Prissy sniffed delicately. That was Minnie, always trying to act like she didn't listen to gossip. "Dr. Gribbleflotz is going to make... well, you know. That sex pill. Via-something."

"Wow! Viagra? Are you sure?" Evelyn Paxton asked. "My Lacy's husband could sure use some."

"I heard Clara offer the job to the freelance researchers myself," Prissy said.

"Oh! So it's still in the research phase?" Evelyn asked.

"Well, yes. But this is Dr. Gribbleflotz we're talking about. The Aspirin King himself."

Richard Somers put his finger to his lips, signaling Carl Duvall to hush so he could listen in. The conversation from the other table was interesting. If he could get in on the ground floor of one of Dr. Gribbleflotz's inventions he could make a fortune. He was still cursing the fact that he missed the early days of the aspirin rush. And as for the Kirlian image interpretation industry, he'd dismissed that as a foolish fad until it was too late. This time he was going to get in on the ground floor.

After a few minutes he gave up on listening to the

old women and returned to his discussions with his old partner in crime. Not that they were discussing anything important. One visited Cora's to overhear the gossip, not to be overheard. He could ask Carl what he knew about this business later.

June 1635, HDG Laboratories, Jena

"Well?" Dina asked. "What does it say?"

Phillip passed the letter from the State Library over to his wife. "The whole synthesis is much too complex for my current capabilities. I've never made anything like the heterogeneous polycyclic structure I can see in the diagram, and I know I can't make the piperazine yet."

Dina tapped the folded letter against her teeth. Nice well-proportioned white teeth. She certainly didn't need the dubious benefit of a visit to the American dentists. He returned his attention to the letter. "I'm afraid I can't help Frau Hardesty with her little problem."

"Well, we tried. I'll write a letter saying we're sorry that she mistook the advertising for Gribbleflotz Sal Vin Betula as little blue pills of happiness to mean you were making the up-time kind of little blue pills."

Phillip broke the seal of the next letter. Moments later he looked up. "Would you believe it, Dear? Some American claims to have overheard that I was going to be making sex pills, and please could he place his order now, to get in before the rush."

"Pass it over. I'll write a letter saying you aren't going to be making any sex pills."

Phillip shook his head and picked up the next

letter. "Here's another one," he said moments later. He passed that letter to Dina and paused to look at the rest of the day's mail sitting in his in-basket. Many more than normal seemed to have originated in Grantville. "Dina, I think you might want to wait before starting on those letters. There might be a few more."

"Why? Why is everyone so interested in buying those pills?"

Phillip just raised his eyebrows. Even he knew why there was so much interest in what a certain up-time little blue pill offered.

"Yes, yes. I understand men having difficulty performing their husbandly duties might be interested, but why do they think you're making it?"

"I can only imagine that someone heard about my making inquiries and they assume that I can make it."

"Are you sure you can't?"

The obvious belief in Dina's voice forced Phillip to reconsider the problem. After some thought he shook his head. "You saw its insane molecular structure. Certainly I could learn how to make it, if I could afford to spend years working on nothing else and I had as many trained laborants as this 'Pfizer Laboratories' put on the task helping me. But you don't see the Great Stoner everyone fawns over wasting time on something like this. No, he has better things to do than waste time on a drug of such limited utility, and so do we."

Dina nodded. "Pity. Oh well, I'll send an announcement to the newspapers telling them you aren't working on it. Maybe it will stop these silly letters."

"Thank you, dear."

Two days later, Grantville

Carl Duvall passed the newspaper across to Richard Somers, his finger pointing to a column. "It says here that Dr. Gribbleflotz is not working on producing sex pills."

"An announcement placed by the good doctor himself," Richard said. "But then, he'd say that even if he was working on it, wouldn't he?"

Carl smiled. He'd thought exactly that when he saw the advertisement. Clearly Dr. Gribbleflotz was trying to divert attention from his latest project. "So what are we going to do about it?"

"Um. Talk to someone in his lab?" Richard suggested.

Carl grimaced. "Impossible. I can't imagine what he did to create such personal loyalty, but none of his laborants will do anything to hurt him."

"What about inserting our own man?"

"We can try," Carl answered.

A few days later, HDG Laboratories, Jena

Phillip looked at the letters still cascading out of the mail sack Frau Beier was emptying over his work table. He picked up the first one. It was from Erfurt. *I wonder what they want.*

A few minutes later Phillip was at the end of his rope. Erfurt, Halle, Magdeburg, even Leipzig. Letters from all over and the authors all wanted the same thing. *There must be over a hundred of these letters!* He stuffed them into a basket and went hunting for Dina.

✧   ✧   ✧

"Dina, that announcement didn't have the effect we expected."

"What announcement?"

"The one where we said I wasn't making sex pills," Phillip said as he offered her the basket. "It seems that nobody believes us."

Dina took the basket and started sorting through the letters. "This is ridiculous. What can we do?"

"I don't know. I guess I could do some more research. Maybe there are alternatives."

A *few days later, State Library, Grantville*

There were a lot of books on sex in the library and, surprisingly enough, very few of them mentioned Viagra. Dina compiled a list of everything that was supposed to help, from special compounds such as ground rhinoceros horn, to special diets and exercises. Maybe she could prepare a suitable pamphlet. Certainly, given all the interest shown in those letters, there was obviously a demand for information on how to reduce the incidence of erectile dysfunction. Dina grinned at the term, so American in its wishy-washy manner of describing *impotentia coeundi*.

She paused to consider some drawings of different positions. Then, with a smile, she made copies to show Phillip. Some of them looked ... interesting.

Phillip was also busy in the library. It seemed a bit wrong that *relaxation* of the muscles in the target area was what was needed, but that's what his research was telling him. It was the relaxation that allowed a greater inflow of blood, and thus an erection. Nitrous oxide reacted in the blood chambers, the muscle relaxed, and *poof,* there you were. Of course, there was also an off switch or...well, walking around that way all the time would be a bit uncomfortable. The up-time little blue pill worked by turning off the off-switch.

Well, if he couldn't produce the inhibitor, he could surely increase the amount of nitrous oxide available, couldn't he? Of course, he'd have to make nitrous oxide, and he wasn't overly entranced with one of the methods described to produce the gas. Any method that warned of the potential for explosions wasn't going to be amongst his favorite processes. There were other options, but they seemed to have their own problems. Maybe Hans, his personal laborant, could be enticed into making nitrous oxide.

Early June 1635, HDG Laboratories, Jena

Phillip ran Hans to ground in the high security area of HDG laboratories. It wasn't secure because of the value of anything in the rooms, but rather because of the potential danger of the experiments being undertaken there. "Hans, a moment of your time if you have it to spare."

"Of course, Doctor. I just need to add one last data point."

Phillip walked over to the large graph Hans was updating and considered what it indicated with interest. "I see the yield seems to be increasing as the pressure is increased."

"Yes," Hans agreed. "Just like Le Chatelier's principle suggests."

"How soon do you think before you can commence industrial-scale production of spirits of hartshorn from air?"

Hans shook his head and gave Phillip a wry smile. "A while yet, Doctor. It took Carl Bosch over a year to turn Fritz Haber's bench top experiments into a viable industrial process, and we haven't even finished duplicating Herr Haber's experiments. There is so much we don't understand. Have you heard anything from Herr Trainer? He would be of immense value to our research program."

Phillip shook his head. "I'm sorry, but I haven't heard anything yet."

"I understand, Dr. Gribbleflotz. Now, you wanted to talk to me? You have a new project?"

"Yes. If you'd like to join me in my office, I'll go over what I want you to do."

With Hans in charge of making the nitrous oxide, Phillip set out to investigate ways to introduce it into the human body. The experiment Hans was running in the secure laboratory had given him an idea. The experimental apparatus combined gases under pressure to force the production of spirits of hartshorn. What if he used nitrous oxide under pressure? Could that increase the production of the chemical responsible for the relaxation of the smooth muscle? But how to introduce it? Phillip turned to his books.

The article on diving suggested a pressure vessel large enough for a married couple might do the trick. It was certainly worth trying...not that he and Dina needed it. But, as a special service for couples having marital difficulties, it offered promise.

The real problem with a hypobaric chamber of sufficient size was that it would be beyond the pocket of all but the most wealthy. What was needed was something everyone could afford.

Phillip made a few notes and wrote a memo to look into the economics of building a suitable chamber before returning to the diving article. He could try making a pressure suit. Something like the new hard-hat rubberized diving suits, only without the helmet. The pressure the suit could be safely inflated to couldn't be high however, otherwise it would burst like a . . .

Phillip grabbed his pen and made a note before he forgot this idea. A balloon. A rubber balloon, just like the ones he used in some of his demonstrations. Surely he could make a special balloon. Something like a pair of rubber pants that could be inflated with nitrous oxide.

Dina Kastenmayerin chewed on the metal cap of her fountain pen. Frau Hardesty's request for the other type of blue pill of happiness had opened her eyes to a problem she hadn't really thought about. One heard about men finding it difficult to perform their husbandly duties, but it wasn't the kind of thing wives talked about in the presence of the unmarried daughter of their pastor.

She wrote a short memo to remind her to talk to Stepmama. She would surely have had to counsel wives whose husbands were unable to perform their duties properly. What was really needed was a pamphlet. Something that any wife could easily access for help. But what to put into it?

She wrote down a heading. *What Wives Should Know About Marital Health and Vigor*. Then she proceeded to construct a list of all the things she thought should be included.

Several days later

Dina had a good fire going to take the chill off the air and was kneeling in front of it, powdering the rubber pants with talc. Beside her was the cylinder of nitrous oxide.

"Are you nearly finished, Dina?" Phillip asked.

She looked up, a look of happy anticipation on her face. "Just about."

There were traces of white talcum powder in her hair and on her face. She looked delightful. Right then Phillip didn't think he needed any additional nitrous oxide, but a true scientist must complete his experiments.

The now well-powdered rubber pants had been made to a carefully considered design, with strong waist and leg bands to stop the pressurized gas escaping when they were inflated. This was the moment of truth. Phillip started to put them on. There was a stifled giggle from Dina. She'd obviously noticed how little he needed any extra help.

The gas-tight leg and waist bands made it difficult to pull the pants on, but finally, with sweat starting to bead on his body, he got them on. He sniffed delicately at the amused look on Dina's face. "Connect me to the gas, please."

Dina connected the short rubber umbilical cord

from the pants to the gas cylinder. Phillip took a deep breath. Time to test his theory. "All right, dear. Open the valve."

Cold didn't begin to describe the sensation. Phillip screamed.

Pop! The pants burst, sending a cloud of talcum powder around the room.

"The gas . . . turn it off," Phillip cried.

Dina scrambled to shut the valve, then looked up. She fell backward, laughing like a maniac.

Phillip ignored his wife's laughter. He had more important things to worry about. He disconnected the umbilical cord and made a dash for his dressing room.

He was a sight to behold. He was still wearing the rubber pants, but the front had blown out, revealing all his shrunken glory. The nitrous oxide gas had had a definite effect all right, but it wasn't the effect he had been looking for. He'd forgotten that gas stored under pressure would be extremely cold when it was released.

It seemed fair to say that the experiment had been a complete failure. The details of the write-up of this experiment would require considerable thought, if not outright creativity. There were some things the world's greatest alchemist did not want recorded for prosperity.

Next day, an apartment in Jena

"He's running late," Richard complained.

Carl checked the time on his wristwatch. "It's only just after five, Richard. Give Thomas a chance. He's said before that he doesn't finish before five, and sometimes has to stay late."

"Gribbleflotz is supposed to be a good employer, and very strict about overtime."

Carl nodded. "Yes, but Thomas is working with a research group, and you know you can't stop an experiment just because a clock says it's time to knock off."

Richard did know this. For a while there, a little over a year ago, he'd thought he'd had it made, siphoning off some of the production at the new explosives factory. But that damned female the down-time shareholders installed to run the business had instituted "quality control" testing and the Hart brothers had discovered the machine that cut the explosive into pound blocks was giving short measures. Worse still, over a year later, they were still checking the weight of the blocks regularly, so he and Carl hadn't been able to reset the cutters back to the short measure. That had been a nice little earner, and it could have made him and Carl rich. But no longer, more's the pity.

Thomas Brückner dawdled as he made his way to the meeting with the two men from Grantville. Initially it had seemed like a good idea to take money from them to spy on Dr. Gribbleflotz while also drawing a wage working for the good doctor. Now he wasn't so sure. He was the one taking all the risks while they took none.

He walked up the stairs and used the special knock that meant it was him at the door.

"You took your time. Have you any idea how long we've been waiting?" Richard demanded.

"I am most sorry. I got here as fast as I could, but

I had to wait for Dr. Gribbleflotz to leave before I could check his journal entries for the day."

"You have access to his journals?"

"It is very risky. I have to sneak into his personal library to access them, but yes, I have been able to read some of his journals." Most of what he'd just said was a lie. He hadn't had to sneak into Dr. Gribbleflotz's study to access the doctor's journals. All he'd had to do was ask permission to look at them, but the more risks the men thought he had to take, the more they paid him.

"So how is the old fraud planning on pulling this off?" Carl asked.

"The doctor is not trying to make the up-time drug. The chemistry is too complex for him to duplicate at this time. However, he believes that he can achieve the same result by increasing the availability of nitrous oxide to the body. His latest experiments are based around wearing a specially made pair of rubber 'pants' into which nitrous oxide is injected."

Carl started laughing. Thomas stared at the up-timer. "What is so funny? Last night the doctor was scheduled to test his new rubber pants."

"And did they work?" Carl asked.

"Dr. Gribbleflotz has not yet written up the results of the experiment, but Frau Kastenmayerin was walking around all day with a very broad smile on her face."

"She's probably just remembering what her husband looked like all tricked out in his rubber pants. Either that or she caught a good snort of laughing gas."

"Laughing gas?" Richard asked.

"It's another name for nitrous oxide. I think the old fraud has outdone himself this time. There is no way nitrous oxide can help sexual performance. Heck, the dentists use it as an anesthetic."

"So you don't think Dr. Gribbleflotz is going to be able to sell nitrous oxide as a sex aid?" Richard asked.

Carl shook his head. "No. There is absolutely no way he can sell nitrous oxide as a sex aid."

"That's a pity," Richard muttered. "I guess it's back to Grantville and the explosives factory."

HDG Laboratories, Jena

Phillip was still trying very hard to convince himself that Dina's broad smile and giggles were a consequence of her inhaling a quantity of nitrous oxide. It was a losing proposition, though. The effects of the gas surely couldn't last this long. He was going to have to admit that she was still laughing at the image of him standing in their bedroom with a ... well, thinking about it wasn't going to help him forget the experience. Fortunately there was only one witness and he could trust her not to spread the story.

The sound of the dinner gong dragged Phillip out of his retrospection. He hastily finished the entry he was making in his journal and put it away. When Frau Mittelhausen sounded the dinner gong that meant dinner would be served in five minutes, and she got upset when people were late. He'd have a terrible time finding another housekeeper of her quality, so he tried not to upset her.

After dinner Phillip followed Hans back to the secure laboratories, not that he needed to check up on Hans, but rather to get away from that smile on Dina's face. He left the dining room with the image of Dina talking to a couple of female laborants while gesturing in his direction burned in his brain. He was pretty sure she wouldn't talk about last night. Surely she wouldn't. Would she?

"How is the research on the spirits of hartshorn from air process going, Hans?" he asked.

"Pretty well, Doctor. If you like we can check the graph in my office."

"Thank you. I would like to see your progress."

"Of course, Doctor. And how's your nitrous oxide research progressing?"

That question had sounded much too innocent. Had Dina been talking about last night? "Not very well," Phillip admitted.

"That's too bad. Did you have troubles with the rubber pants last night?"

Now Phillip was sure Dina had been talking. "They didn't work. The nitrous oxide was too cold, and the pants over-inflated and burst. Are you happy now?" he snapped.

Hans nearly jumped back into the wall. "I'm sorry, Doctor. You were so hopeful, too. Will you try again?"

"No. There must be an easier way." To himself Phillip added, *and less embarrassing*. "I am going to the library."

Thomas Brückner shot to his feet, nearly spilling the glass at his side when Phillip burst into the library.

Phillip stared at the laborant for a moment as he processed faces and names. "Thomas. Thomas Brückner, the new laborant working with Hans?"

"Yes, Dr. Gribbleflotz. Do you want me to leave, Doctor?"

"What? Leave? No, stay where you are. What's that you're reading?"

"One of your old journals, Doctor. From when you first made the Sal Aer Fixus."

"Why are you wasting your time with that old stuff? The newer journals make better use of the new chemistry."

"I've just finished reading about your investigations into pyramid power."

"Ah! Not one of my better moments."

"But the research led you to the Gribbleflotz Kirlian Imager and the creation of the Kirlian image interpretation industry, Doctor."

"I suppose some good came of it." Phillip sighed. He wasn't particularly proud that his name was being used in connection with the pseudoscience of Kurt Beta's Kirlian image interpretation business, but the profits the business was making were not to be sneezed at. Still, he'd much rather have found evidence to support his theory of pyramid power. His eyes drifted to the glass Thomas was holding. He could see streams of tiny little bubbles forming on the bottom of the glass and rising to the top in a constant stream. "What's that you're drinking?"

Thomas held up his glass. "This? It's one of the new soda drinks, Sparkling Lemon. Would you like to try it?"

"If you have it to spare."

Thomas pulled a bottle from the floor, used something to open it and poured some into a glass. "Here you go, Doctor."

"Thank you." Phillip lifted the glass, then hesitated. "Why is it bubbling?"

"They call it soda pop, Doctor. I believe they force air into the liquid under pressure, and when the bottle is opened the gas is able to escape, causing the bubbles."

Phillip studied his drink. What was the gas? Could nitrous oxide be forced into solution? A vague memory from that diving article flashed though his mind. Something about nitrogen entering the blood and bubbling out if the diver returned to the surface too quickly. "Could I have a look at the bottle, please?"

Thomas passed the bottle over and Phillip searched the label for the name of the manufacturer. If they could replace the air they forced into solution with nitrous oxide, then a simple drink could be used to increase the nitrous oxide in a patient's body. It was, even if he said so himself, a quite brilliant idea. But first he needed a name, and there it was, "The Saalfeld Bottling Company." With the bottle still in hand he left the library calling out for Hans.

Thomas was left behind, wondering what had the doctor so excited.

Several weeks later, Grantville

Carl Duvall wasn't sure he believed what he was seeing. "'Gribbleflotz Revitalizing Tonic—for the restoration of the Vital Humors.' Does that mean what I think it means, Richard?"

"Does what mean what you think it means?" Richard Somers asked.

"Vital humors. Does that mean what I think it means?"

"That Gribbleflotz has managed to produce some kind of sex aid? Yes, that's what it means. Do you want to go in and ask for some?"

"No. But I wonder what it is."

Richard shrugged. "Wait here then. I'll go in and ask."

A few minutes later Richard returned with a pamphlet.

"Well?" Carl asked.

"Gribbleflotz Revitalizing Tonic is part of a complete program of diet and exercise aimed at restoring the Vital Humors," Richard read from the pamphlet. "Our special tonic contains nitrous oxide, a chemical identified by up-timer science as being important for successful sexual congress. Used in conjunction with a proper diet and exercise program Gribbleflotz Revitalizing Tonic will restore waning vital humors." Richard looked up. "It appears that the good doctor has found a way to sell nitrous oxide as a sex aid."

"What? Give me that. Nitrous oxide shouldn't have any effect on sexual performance." Carl grabbed the pamphlet out of Richard's hands and started reading. "Oh, the sneaky bastard. Whoever wrote this must have written copy for infomercials. The loopholes are big enough to sail an aircraft carrier through."

"You mean it's all a fraud?" Richard asked.

"You bet it is."

"How can you be so sure, Carl?"

"Follow me home and I'll show you."

Carl searched around in his chest of drawers before finally finding the small cardboard box he was looking for. He pulled out a folded sheet of paper. "I told you Gribbleflotz was a fraud, and here's the proof. It says right there under 'Clinical Pharmacology' that the important chemical is *nitric* oxide. *Nitrous* oxide is a completely different thing."

"Who is Pfizer Labs?"

"They're the up-time company that made Viagra."

"Oh! Um . . . ah . . . Carl, why do you have this pamphlet?"

Carl blushed. Something he couldn't remember doing since he was a pimple-faced teenager. "Well, ah . . . I ordered some when I heard about it. Not that I needed it, but there was a lot of talk about the effects back then."

"Of course you didn't need it, Carl."

Carl glared. That agreement lacked a little in the way of belief.

"Maybe the doctor means nitric oxide?"

"Why are you trying to give Gribbleflotz a break, Richard? It's a fraud, pure and simple. There's no way it can work."

"But people are buying it."

"Of course people are buying it. It gives hope, and depending on what their problem is, maybe a change of diet and a bit of exercise will do them some good."

"So it's not a complete fraud?"

Carl sighed. "Okay, it's probably not a complete fraud. Are you happy now?"

"Not yet. If it's not a fraud then I'm not going to be happy until I have my share of Dr. Gribbleflotz's latest Big Thing. I missed out on the Kirlian Imager craze, I don't intend missing out on the revitalizing tonic craze."

Dr. Shipley's office, Grantville

Dr. Susannah Shipley removed the blood pressure cuff from around Lacy Brumfield's arm and made a notation in her notes. "And how are things with Rick, Lacy?"

"Things couldn't be better since I started him on

Dr. Gribbleflotz's Revitalizing Tonic, Dr. Shipley. These days he's always raring to go."

Susannah contemplated telling Lacy that there was no scientific reason Dr. Gribbleflotz's Revitalizing Tonic should have any effect, but no, something had put that contented look on Lacy's face. Sometimes a patient's belief was more important than being properly informed. However, she might as well make sure Lacy and Rick got the maximum benefit from those beliefs. "I hope you're both following the diet and exercise program Dr. Gribbleflotz recommends. The revitalizing tonic won't work nearly as well if the program isn't followed."

"I'll be sure to tell Rick that, Dr. Shipley."

Dr. Shipley followed Lacy out of her consulting room and headed over to Dr. Jeff Adams' room. "You got a moment, Jeff?"

"Sure, Suz. What's up?"

"Rick Brumfield, apparently. Lacy says they've been having success using the new Gribbleflotz Revitalizing Tonic."

Jeff nodded. "I've had a few patients saying the same thing."

"So you don't think we should go public saying it has no foundation in scientific fact?"

"Hell, no. It's not like the tonic is dangerous, or even expensive, and it does seem to be doing some good. I say we don't rock the boat."

"Well, we agree on that. What I can't figure out is where on earth Dr. Gribbleflotz got the idea he should be using nitrous oxide."

Jeff gave Susannah a wry smile. "You didn't get

many guys asking about Viagra before the Ring of Fire, did you?"

"No. For some reason guys didn't come asking me to prescribe it. Why?"

Jeff pulled a folder out of a filing cabinet and handed it over. "You've probably only read the trade literature then. Take a look at some of the newspaper and magazine clippings in that folder."

Susannah picked up the first article, skimmed through it. She paused at one point and looked up at Jeff—he was smiling—then she returned to skimming through the articles. "What? The first one talked of nitric and nitrous oxide as if the terms are interchangeable, but this one only mentions nitrous oxide."

Jeff grinned. "Yep. There's a lot of poor information in the newspapers and magazines. Anybody looking at those clippings would have concluded that they meant nitrous oxide. Mind, there is one silver lining."

"And what's that?"

"We're not going to have a shortage of medical grade laughing gas, that's for sure."

Cora's Café, Grantville

Minnie Frost passed the bank statement around the rest of the group. "We're going to have to do another fund-raiser."

"Not another one," Evelyn Paxton complained.

"Yes, Evelyn, another one. And this time it might be nice if you actually turned up at the sausage sizzle."

"I was sick in bed, Minnie, as well you know."

Minnie snorted her disbelief.

"We really need something a bit better than a sausage sizzle, though, Minnie. I mean, we only raised two hundred dollars last time," Prissy Fortney said.

"Well, I'm open to suggestions."

A deep silence followed Minnie's statement. Then Prissy pointed through the window. "Evelyn, isn't that your Lacy's Rick over there?"

"Yes, that's Rick. I wonder where he's been."

"Judging by the fact he's holding a Nobili's Pharmacy bag, I can make a fair guess," Minnie said. "And if I was a betting woman, I'd be willing to bet five dollars I know what he's got in that bag."

"How can you know from here?" Prissy asked.

"Nobili's only uses their paper bags when the customers ask them to. And there's only one thing they sell that a guy is going to buy that needs a bag that big."

"Gribbleflotz Revitalizing Tonic," the three of them chorused.

"My Lacy swears by it, you know. Rick's a changed man since she started him on the Gribbleflotz treatment."

"Now that's what we need for a fund-raiser. Something like Gribbleflotz's tonic," Minnie said.

"Trouble is, Nobili's have the local market sewn up," Evelyn said.

"Yes, so it's another sausage sizzle, same time, same place, next Saturday."

"Yes, Minnie," Prissy and Evelyn mumbled.

Evelyn was a little fed up with Minnie and the incessant need to run fund-raisers to raise enough money to enable the Red Cross Sanitation Squad to continue their good works. What they needed was a real moneymaker. Something, anything, that could take the place of endless hours sizzling sausages.

She found her husband lying back on the sofa listening to a record with his eyes closed, a dreamy look on his face. He looked so happy and relaxed... which didn't sit well with her current mood. So she turned off the stereo.

"What the hell?" Charlie muttered. "Why did you do that?"

"Minnie says we have to hold another fund-raiser for the Red Cross Sanitation Squad next Saturday."

Charlie walked over to the stereo, removed the record from the turntable and examined it carefully. "Well there's no need to do that. You could have damaged my record."

Evelyn snorted. There was every reason to "do that." She wanted a fight to relieve her frustrations, but Charlie wasn't cooperating. Instead he was dusting the record and putting it back into its protective sleeve.

"Hold it!" Evelyn cried.

Charlie stopped, the record part way back into its slot. "What's wrong now?"

"That record. Let me see it."

Charlie shrugged and passed it over. "What's the problem? You've seen the cover often enough before. You've even laughed about it."

"Shush, I'm thinking." Evelyn stared at the cover. "Yes, I've seen it before, but not right after talking to the girls about Gribbleflotz Revitalizing Tonic."

"What're you thinking about now, Evelyn?"

Evelyn handed the record back to a bemused Charlie and went hunting in the pantry. "Charlie, do we have any gas cartridges for this? Doesn't it use nitrous oxide? Seems like I remember that." She held up a whipped cream maker.

"For what? Oh, the creamer. Yeah, I think so. Why?"

"Because I want to try something. Where are they?"

"In the garage somewhere." She gave him a look, so Charlie asked, "Do you want me to find them?"

Evelyn's foot was tapping a mile a minute. "Yes, dear, I do want you to go and find them."

"Okay, okay, I'll go. But why are you suddenly so all fire interested in making some whipped cream?"

"Just find them, Charlie, and all will be revealed."

Next evening, the Paxton residence

"Girls, I've got a brilliant idea for the fund-raiser to end all fund-raisers," Evelyn said. "Not only will it make the sanitation squad some real money, it's also sure to offend our children and grandchildren."

"An offensive fund-raiser?" Prissy asked.

Evelyn grinned. "I thought that would get your attention. Yes. Offensive to the delicate morals of our children and grandchildren, and a sure-fire fund-raiser."

"If it makes money I doubt *my* family will find it offensive," Minnie Frost said.

"Just wait and see," Evelyn said.

August 1635, Magdeburg

Milana Frost tugged on her mother's hand and pointed. "Look, Mommy. That woman's not wearing any clothes."

Richelle Frost swung around to look where her daughter was pointing, and released a sigh of relief. She'd feared a naked woman might be sitting in a shop window, not that that sort of thing was supposed to happen in this area of Magdeburg. Still, you could never be too sure.

"What's revitalizing cream do, Mommy? And why is the woman covered in whipped cream?"

Richelle tugged at Milana's hand. "Come on, dear. It's just an advertising poster."

"What is it they're advertising?"

"I have no idea, dear," Richelle lied. With the come hither look in the model's eyes, the finger licking the cream, and the close proximity to advertisements for Gribbleflotz Revitalizing Tonic, it didn't take a genius to detect the double entendre in the product being advertised. Revitalizing Cream, indeed.

"Is it advertising whipped cream, Mommy?"

"Yes, dear, it is advertising whipped cream."

"I like whipped cream, Mommy. Can we get some?"

"I'll buy some cream and make some when we get home. Now, come on."

"But it's a fund-raiser, Mommy, for Grandma's Red Cross Sanitation Squad."

"What?" Richelle all but roared.

Milana pointed. "It says so at the bottom of the poster, Mommy. 'A proportion of profits go to the Grantville Red Cross Sanitation Squad.'"

Richelle gulped. That was just like her mother-in-law. She desperately hoped none of the parents who sent their children to her branch of St. Veronica's Academy ever made the connection.

❖   ❖   ❖

Christian Köppe slipped discreetly into the shop. A peek through the window only revealed an American woman trying to control her daughter. He approached the man serving at the counter. "That poster in the window. Can I buy it from you?"

"The 'Creamed Madonna'? I'm afraid I need to keep that for advertising, sir."

Christian glanced back at the poster in all its colored glory. He had to have it. He pulled out his wallet. "I'll make it worth your while."

The shop assistant glanced around the shop, and then leaned closer and whispered. "There's a spare in the storeroom I might be able to let you have for a small consideration."

"It's the same poster?"

"Yes, the very same. Paxton's sent a few just in case they got damaged in transit."

Christian put down some money; when the shop assistant failed to move he added some more. Several bank notes later, the assistant scooped them up and slipped into the back room, returning a few seconds later with a large sheet of paper.

"I really shouldn't be doing this you know," the shop assistant said as he handed over the poster.

Christian accepted the poster, and after gazing at it for a few seconds rolled it up. "It can be our little secret."

Richard Somers watched the man walk out of the shop with his copy of the Creamed Madonna poster. His new shop was doing well supplying the revitalizing products craze. He didn't even need the boost that Paxton's Revitalizing Cream gave his business, and as for those posters... That reminded him. He slipped into the storeroom and ran a thumb through the stack of posters. Barely two dozen left. He'd better add a request for another hundred or so to his next order from Paxton's.

Gribbleflotz residence, the HDG laboratories facility, Jena

Dina scooped some of the cream onto her finger and licked it. Then she scooped up some more and offered her finger to Phillip.

"I can feel the nitrous oxide starting to work already."

"I noticed."

Phillip felt Dina shiver, and looked into her eyes. Starting the revitalizing products craze might not be the killer application he needed to be remembered as the world's greatest alchemist... but it did have its compensations.

Chapter 18

Dr. Phil's Family

*August 1635, Dr. Gribbleflotz's office,
HDG Laboratories, Jena*

Phillip took the next letter from his inbox. It was marked personal, and checking the back, he could see it was from his good friend, Jonathan Fortney. He broke the seal and started reading. He had to smile. Jonathan could be quite droll. The suggestion that his new wife might want to spend all his money on fine jewelry was clearly a joke. His Dina wasn't like that. *Hmmm, instructions on making synthetic rubies and sapphires attached.* Always interested in the American cheat sheets, he checked through the bundle of pages until he came across the notes.

There were several pages, so he checked the time. *Plenty of time for a quick glance before lunch.*

"...Corundum, a mineral consisting of aluminum oxide, Al2O3..."

"What?" Phillip stared hard at the paper in his hands. "Ruby and sapphire are a form of aluminum?"

He turned to look up at his model of the aluminum pyramid with the strategically placed faceted gems. Gems that included rubies and sapphires.

He slammed a fist down on his desk. It felt so good he did it again, and again.

A slightly worried Maria Blandina poked her head through the doorway. She could see her husband standing over his desk, and it looked as if he'd been pounding it with his fist. "Are you all right, Phillip? I heard some banging."

"Yes, Dina. Everything's all right. I have just realized why my special pyramid doesn't work. It's not the members that are supposed to be aluminum. It is the faceted gems. Of course it didn't work. With both the faceted gems and the structure itself made of aluminum, there was no balance."

Dina relaxed. It was just a problem with his aluminum pyramid. Not that she understood Phillip's fascination with pyramids, but if her brilliant husband was interested in them, they had to be important. "That's very nice, Phillip," and just to prove she had been listening, she asked a question. "What should the structure be made of?"

Phillip sighed. "I don't know. I'll have to research various materials until I find the one that gives balance." He stopped speaking and looked at Dina with some concern. "Darling, you're looking a bit pale. Do you feel unwell?"

Dina didn't feel all that well, in fact. "Perhaps it's a bit warm in here."

It had been Dina's American friend, Gerry Stone, who was attending the university in Jena, who started it. Phillip had been teaching a group of laborants the new science when Gerry disagreed with something he said. The laborants had been aghast and horrified that someone should disagree with him. If it had been anybody but the Frau Kastenmayerin's friend, Gerry Stone, of the House of Stone, Phillip was sure blood might have flowed. But Gerry had raised some interesting questions. They had entered into a lively debate, moving into the seminar room so Gerry could use the blackboard to explain his interpretation of the new science. Soon senior laborants joined in. Then, hesitantly at first, the junior laborants had started asking questions.

After that, Phillip's teaching seminars had turned into in-house seminars where anybody could stand up and talk about what they were doing or hoped to do. The lively discussions had forced Phillip to work even harder on his reading of the American text books so that he could answer the laborants' questions.

The gentle hubbub of conversation petered to a halt as Phillip, notes in hand, made his way to the podium. Today's seminar was about the current status of his exploration of the invigoration of the Quinta Essentia of the human humors.

Phillip knew that some of his laborants didn't believe that he would ever be able to invigorate the Quinta Essentia of the human humors, but one day he hoped to prove them wrong. Until then, any idea was a useful teaching tool. He had to prepare himself for any possible question the audience might ask, and the laborants had to understand the new science well enough to ask intelligent questions.

✧ ✧ ✧

While Phillip stood behind the podium checking his notes, Hans Saltzman and another laborant erected the stand holding the book of flip sheets he had prepared for this presentation. He waited patiently for the laborant to return to his seat and for Hans to place a cloth-covered stand beside the podium. When Hans indicated he was ready Phillip turned to his expectant audience.

"Good afternoon everyone, and thank you for coming for this seminar. As almost all of you know, for a number of years I have been investigating the invigoration of the Quinta Essentia of the human humors. I have high hopes for my research, but, as I'm sure you are all aware, there have been problems." He answered the many grins and smiles with a smile of his own.

"My scale model pyramid," he waited while Hans pulled away the dust cloth to reveal the scale model aluminum pyramid, "failed to invigorate the Quinta Essentia of the humors in selected laboratory animals. My first thought was that the framework of my pyramid," he ran a finger along the metal frame of his model, "was constructed of impure aluminum. The Americans confirmed this. Of course I immediately demanded that they provide me with pure aluminum." Phillip waited for the light laughter to settle. He doubted anybody believed he had demanded anything. His views on dominating American females were well known. "They in turn told me that they were currently unable to produce pure aluminum. Which reminds me," he searched his audience for a familiar face. "Kurt, what progress are you making with the aluminum project?"

Kurt Stoltz answered from where he was seated at

the back of the seminar room. "Slowly, Dr. Gribble-flotz. We've successfully produced some aluminum on the bench rig, However, to turn it into an industrial process we'll have to make larger batches of hydroflu-oric acid, and well, we're still experiencing difficulties producing suitable vessels that the acid won't dissolve. You'll remember what happened to Jochim Fritsch."

Phillip swallowed. He'd been forced to amputate Jochim's right arm below the elbow after a container of hydrofluoric acid disintegrated in his hand. It had been a very high price to pay for a moment's care-lessness, and the accident only reinforced his belief that he wanted nothing to do with the stuff. "How is Jochim?"

"The stump has healed well, Doctor. And he is becoming amazingly dexterous with his hook."

"Very good, Kurt. I'd like you to continue work-ing towards turning your bench rig into an industrial process, just be extremely careful. Now, where was I?"

"Pure aluminum for the framework of your pyramid, Herr Doctor," Hans Saltzman, his personal assistant, volunteered.

"Thank you, Hans. Right, pure aluminum." Phillip found his place in his notes. "Lacking pure aluminum, I was forced to shelve the project until such time as it became available. However," He paused dramati-cally. "There has been a new development. Recently, my good friend Jonathan Fortney sent me a 'cheat sheet' on the production of rubies and sapphires." Phillip smiled at the sudden shifting of bodies on seats. "Yes, that is correct. The Americans know how to make gems. But that wasn't the most important aspect. No. What I found interesting was the identity of the major components of the gems—Corundum, also known as aluminum oxide."

There were noisy intakes of breath as various members of the audience realized the significance of this discovery. "Yes," Phillip agreed. "If both the gems and the structural members were aluminum, then the pyramid was out of balance." He shook his head in disgust. "All that time and effort wasted because of a lack of such basic knowledge." He gave his audience a searching stare. "And let that be a lesson to you all. Make sure you know the composition of everything you intend using before you commence your experiment. It will save you considerable disappointment. I speak from experience." Phillip gave his model pyramid a gentle pat before indicating to Hans that he should cover it again.

"This brings me to the current state of my research into the invigoration of the Quinta Essentia. Obviously the members cannot be formed of aluminum. Which begs the question, what should the members be made of?" He nodded for Hans to reveal the first page of the flip book.

"The human spirit is embodied within the mind, even if the spirit itself is not physically *of* the mind. But as the various experiments of the various scientists have proven, as my own extensive electrical experimentation has shown, the mind, and therefore the spirit embodied within the mind is affected by electrics."

Phillip walked around his electrical demonstrations. "The external *gross* electrics of the sparks of the Wimshurst machine ..." He patted the machine before moving to the batteries. "... the more subtle electrics of the various batteries ..." He flicked a switch completing a circuit, turning on a weak light.

"...all have their effects on the spirit, but the electrical nature of the mind, and of the spirit actually happens at far too minute, far too small a level for these gross manipulations to affect with the subtlety that is needed to perfect the union of mind and spirit. This happens at a microscopic, or as the learned ones of the future said, a *quantum* level."

Phillip, now well into the swing of things, indicated that Hans should show the next page. "Now, as Oerstaed proved, electric is linked to magnetic." After a moment to check that his audience was following, he moved over to the large chart of the elements the Americans called the Periodic Table. "Free flowing electrons found in electric metals such as, nickel, copper, silver and gold, platinum, cadmium and cobalt..." He tapped each element with his pointer as he named them. "...will be strongly influenced by the magnetic potentials. But in all things, *balance* is the most needed. The metals with poor electric potentials like zinken and tin are too difficult to affect so as to provide the balance needed by the body. Similarly, the freely electric metals like copper and gold and yes, even aluminum, do not provide *enough* resistance to the electrons. Only in the middle do we find the needed balance, and that balance is most favorably found in nickel."

Hans flipped the next sheet revealing the important facts about nickel. "A framework of nickel can intercept the grosser variations of the magnetic influences, while allowing penetration, and indeed, *influence* of the *geomagnetic* forces which link our spirits to the world."

Phillip let his eyes roam over his audience. Everyone appeared to be deeply interested. "One might think that iron would be preferred, since iron is so often thought of as magnetic." He shook his head. "But one would be wrong. A *balance* is required. Iron is *too* magnetic for the Quinta Essentia humanum to be distilled. Aluminum, for all its other virtues is utterly *transparent* to the grosser magnetism. No, it is in *nickel* that we find the balance of free electrons *and* magnetic potentials which provide the shielding from those grosser variations while allowing the quantum development of the magnetic vector potentials which influence the human body at the quantum level. With this, we can look for behaviors, expressions, dreams, or fantasies, which express the true nature of this elimination of the quantum distortion."

Phillip smiled at his audience. "Nickel is a new metal, but not unknown. It should be easy to obtain a supply of the required ore. In fact, I have already sent an order to Annaberg for ore for research purposes."

He held up his hands to silence the sudden noisy intakes of breath before they could turn into groans. It was obvious that many in the audience well remembered what happened the last time he'd ordered ore for research purposes. "Do not panic. I learned my lesson with the sphalerite. That mistake will not be repeated. I placed the order with Ostermann Transport using the new scientific unit of kilograms."

"What ore are we talking about, Herr Dr. Gribbleflotz?" a voice called out.

Phillip located the source of the question, one of the laborants from the Halle oil of vitriol facility. "Kupfernickel." He nodded at the shocked looks he received. "Yes, that's right. The miners in Annaberg are dumping nickel ore. The price I was offered was," Phillip exchanged grins with Hans Saltzman, "extremely attractive. I am approaching completion of my calculations, and hope to soon begin the effort to produce the needed nickel members. Now, are there any questions?"

Michael Siebenhorn, Kurt Stoltz, and Hans Saltzman walked out of the seminar room together. "So, Hans, what does Dr. Gribbleflotz know about making gems? Will he be trying to do it himself?"

Hans squinted at the sun, then adjusted his pale blue Gribbleflotz "gimme" cap. "I don't think so, Kurt. He's intensely interested in making his nickel pyramid. He feels he's very close to proving his theory."

"I've spoken to several Americans about his investigations, Hans," Kurt said. "Most of them laughed. None of them believe such a thing is possible."

"I've heard the same," Hans said, "but that's no reason not to support his researches. The Americans said you couldn't make fuel tablets without using benzene rings, but Dr. Gribbleflotz proved them wrong. Maybe he'll prove them wrong again. We won't know until the doctor runs his experiments."

"In the meantime, Hans, what can you tell us about kupfernickel?" Michael asked.

A few days later, outside St. Martin's in the Fields

Phillip was worried about how he would be received by Dina's parents. It had come as a shock, but a pleasant shock, to discover that Dina had had no idea that he was a wealthy man. It was nice to know she had married him for the man he was and not what he could offer. However, her friend Gerry Stone had indicated that Dina's parents had heard rumors that he was some kind of charlatan. Herr Stone had quickly assured him that they didn't believe these rumors. This news should have reassured Phillip. And maybe it would have, if Herr Stone hadn't expressed an interest in seeing his doctorate.

Phillip had a guilty secret that he had even kept from Dina. He wasn't really entitled to use the title of Doctor. He'd never passed an examination for a doctorate. He'd never even completed a bachelor's degree. The impressive piece of parchment he had displayed in his office was a fake. Well, maybe not a fake. There were lawyers' letters confirming its validity. He knew he deserved to hold a doctorate degree, but since he'd been kicked out of Padua for being insufficiently scholarly after his mentor, Professor Casseri, died, he'd never again attempted to matriculate at another university. As for using the title of doctor, he'd sort of drifted into using that when he was in Basel a dozen years ago.

While he had been a relatively insignificant alchemist financing his research doing assays and producing acids for others, the university faculty had been prepared to overlook his use of the title, especially while he had Casparus Menius as his patron. However, Casparus had died suddenly, leaving Phillip in dire financial straits. That had left him vulnerable to the Kubiak Female, and she'd taken full advantage.

In only a matter of weeks Phillip had gone from someone the university faculty could ignore to someone they had to deal with. There had been a rumor that he would soon be run out of Jena in disgrace and he had rashly taken up the offer made by the

Frau Kubiak to do something about his little problem. That, of course, had happened before he met Dina.

The rectory of St. Martin's in the Fields was in sight when he finally came to a halt. "Dina, there is something I have to tell you."

Dina turned her shining eyes to him. "Yes, Phillip?"

He froze for a moment. Those honest, trusting eyes. He had to be strong. She had to know the truth before he confronted her parents. "I'm..." He stumbled to a halt. How to explain he had lived a lie. A lie that could reflect badly on his dearest Dina and her family. He swallowed. "I'm not a doctor. I've never earned a doctorate degree." He looked down into her eyes, silently pleading that she'd forgive him.

Dina reached for his hands and squeezed them gently. "I know, Phillip. Your friend Jonathan and his betrothed told me the whole story."

Phillip was shocked. "You knew?"

She burrowed into his chest. "Yes." Then she looked up and gave him the sweetest of little self-satisfied smiles. "They described how you have put one over the self-important professors at the university."

"But it's a lie, Dina. I haven't completed the requirements. I've never passed any exams. It's an empty title backed up by a worthless piece of parchment."

"No, Phillip. It isn't an empty title. You might not practice medicine, but you are a doctor in the true sense of the word. You are a teacher. You earned your right to the title with your research into the new sciences and teaching others about the new sciences."

Phillip purred. He gathered his wife into his arms. "I love you, Dina."

✧   ✧   ✧

Dina spared the streets a quick glance to check who might be watching. There was only the barrow boy with the cart loaded with gifts for her family. So she stood on tip toes and gave Phillip a quick peck on the cheek. "I love you too, Phillip."

She gazed into his eyes for a moment more before slowly slipping out of his embrace. She tucked her hand over his arm and led him towards the rectory. "Now don't worry about Papa and Stepmama, Phillip. Let me handle them. Gerry warned me that Stepmama and Papa are worried about the boys." She turned and gave Phillip a brilliant smile. "The fact that their studies are progressing so much better since they moved in with us will right many a wrong in Stepmama's eyes."

When Pastor Kastenmayer opened the rectory door, Maria Blandina threw herself at him. "Papa!"

"Dina!" Ludwig opened his arms for his daughter to rush into them. "You're looking well." Looking up, Ludwig smiled apologetically at Phillip. "Hello, Phillip. I apologize for my daughter. Anybody would think we hadn't seen each other for years."

"Dina misses her family, sir."

"What? With three of her brothers living in the same house, she can miss her family?"

Dina giggled. "Even then, Papa. How is everyone?"

The approaching thunder of bare feet on floor boards had Ludwig gently releasing Dina. "Brace yourself, I think you're about to find out."

The hall door burst open and a mass of arms and legs charged towards Dina.

"Dina, Dina, Dina. We've missed you so much.

Have you come back home?" Dina's youngest half-brother asked.

Dina knelt down and reached out to hug four-year-old Thomas. "No, Thomas. Phillip and I have just come to visit. I live in Jena now."

Thomas pouted. "It's not fair. Phillip, Salomon and Joseph get you all the time. Can I come and live with you? Please?"

"No, Thomas. You have to stay with Mama and Papa. I'll visit whenever I can, and maybe you can visit me in Jena sometime."

Dina greeted her other brothers before she stood to greet her stepmother. She offered her hands. "Step-mama. How are you?"

"I am well, thank you." Salome looked around. "I think it would be best if we all went inside."

Dina looked around guiltily. She'd been so happy to see her family that she'd forgotten about being out on the street. She waved to the locals who had stopped to watch the strange sight, and then gestured to the barrow boy to follow, before taking her husband's hand and following her family into their home.

The soccer ball had been such a hit with the boys that they had pleaded to be allowed outside to try it out. Salome and Dina waited at the window until they could see the men folk and boys kicking the new soccer ball around. Then Dina started unwrapping the remaining parcels.

"Oh!" It was a cry of pleasure. Salome ran her hands over the roll of quilted border suitable for attaching to the bottoms of petticoats and drawers. Hand-quilting those borders was very time-consuming, but they kept a person's ankles warm and toasty in cold weather. She looked up at her stepdaughter. "A sewing machine?"

Dina grinned. "You know me so well."

Salome returned the grin. Yes, she knew all about Maria Blandina Kastenmayerin and sewing. "But what would an alchemist want with a sewing machine?"

"I believe he bought it to make laboratory coats after the American fashion to protect his workers' clothes." Dina shook her head, an amused smile on her face. "He thinks like a man. It took his housekeeper to think of a better use."

Salome looked down at the precise stitching on the quilting. "What I wouldn't do for a sewing machine. What with the boys growing and your father..." She stopped for a moment, then looked closely at Dina. "Child, are you well?" She touched a hand to Dina's head. "You seem very pale. Have you been ill?"

Dina shook her head.

Salome dropped a hand to Dina's breast. "What about here? Do you feel tender?"

Dina jerked a bit with the contact, then nodded. "Yes, just a bit. There's nothing wrong is there?"

Salome reached out and hugged Dina. "You poor thing. How long have you been married?"

Dina looked up at her stepmother. "You know how long I've been married. It's been nearly three months since we...oh!"

Salome smiled at Dina's excited face. "It's really too soon to tell, but if you are, I suggest you see one of the American doctors about a delivery in the Leahy Medical Center. Take the word of someone who knows, anesthesia during childbirth is the only way to go."

Dina touched her breasts, then her belly. "Phillip. Oh, I have to tell Phillip. He'll be so pleased."

Salome reached out to stop Dina. "No, not yet." She led Dina to a chair and sat her down before sitting beside her. "Don't raise your hopes just yet. Many times I thought I was pregnant when I wasn't."

Dina sighed. Then she nodded. "Yes, I'll wait until I'm sure." Her gaze switched from her stepmother to the quilted cloth on the table. "Phillip gives me a generous allowance, and it would please me to give you something you want. Please, let me buy you one of the new sewing machines."

Salome swallowed. Her vision was all blurry. Wiping the tears from her eyes, she nodded. "Thank you, Dina."

Hearing her brothers' pet name for her on her stepmother's lips reduced Maria Blandina to tears. She walked up to Salome and wrapped her arms around her. "Mama, if there's ever anything you need, please, just ask."

Salome choked back tears. "You called me Mama..."

Salome watched her stepdaughter join her husband and son-in-law out in the courtyard. Phillip Gribbleflotz was no longer the monument to bad taste he had been. That was probably due to Dina's influence. He still wore expensive clothes, but now they were better coordinated and less gaudy. Dina, she noted, had succumbed to some of the American fashions. The colors, Salome was forced to admit, suited her. They gave her a glow that hadn't been there before. Mind, Salome thought, watching the affectionate way Dina's husband slipped an arm around her, maybe the glow had another source.

She moved away from the window and took in the rolls of fabric and clothes Dina had given her. Most of it was the sort of hard-wearing material that she would buy herself, just never so much at one time. She picked up the fine linen shift Dina had made for her and just stood there admiring it for several minutes before finally wrapping it in its paper. Then she returned her attention to the fabric on the table. If Dina did buy her a sewing machine...She gave a contented sigh. That would cut out the endless tedium of stitching together clothes and leave her with a little time for herself.

Salome gave the little bundle of knitting and crochet needles Dina and Phillip had given her a contented look before calling for the servant she was training to help put things away.

Ludwig Kastenmayer sat back in his armchair. "It was very nice of Dina and Phillip to bring the presents for the boys, wasn't it, Salome?"

"Yes, Ludwig." She hesitated a moment. "What do you think of Dina's husband?"

Ludwig pursed his lips. That was a difficult question. Phillip could support Dina. That was good. They seemed very happy together. That was always nice. It didn't appear that his wealth was pushing him on the slippery slide to damnation. And with Dina as his wife, that was even less likely now. There was the matter of the mysterious doctorate to still be considered, but Phillip had assured him that he had legal proof that he held a Doctorate of Medicine from the University of Amsterdam. And finally, there were the letters from the University of Jena commenting on how well the boys were progressing in their studies since they had moved in with Dina. Professor Hofmann had been particularly generous in his appreciation of the help young Phillip Kastenmayer had been with the new physics and mathematics.

"I think we did much better than we imagined marrying Dina to Phillip Gribbleflotz."

A few days later, the Fortney residence, Grantville

Phillip stopped to examine the two-storied, white, timber house. There were, he noticed, a lot of windows. But no more than most other houses in Grantville. He shook his head at the wastefulness of the Americans, walked up the path, and rapped on the front door. He didn't have to wait long before he could hear footsteps from within the house. There was a rattle of bolts and the door opened a few inches to show a chain across the door. A young face stared at him through the gap.

"Yes?" the woman asked.

"Is this the Fortney residence?" She nodded. "Herr Dr. Gribbleflotz." Phillip passed the woman one of his business cards. "Is Jonathan Fortney available?"

The woman looked at the card, then up at Phillip. "I'm sorry, Herr Dr. Gribbleflotz. Herr Fortney junior is not available, but Herr Fortney senior is at home if you would like to see him."

Phillip hesitated, surprisingly enough, for all the years he'd known Jonathan, he'd never actually met the rest of his family. "Yes, I'll see Herr Fortney."

The woman smiled. "If you'll just go round the

back, you can't miss him." Then she shut and bolted the door.

Phillip looked at the closed door for a moment, then shrugged and followed the woman's instructions.

Round the back of the house he immediately understood what she had meant about not missing Jonathan's father. A section of sail had been strung up to provide shade while he worked on a small motor vehicle.

"Herr Fortney."

A man in a soiled blue coverall turned at the sound. He pulled a rag from a pocket and wiped his hands clean before approaching and offering his hand. "Hi. Caleb Fortney. How can I help you?"

Phillip reached out and grasped Caleb's hand. The hand shake was firm, but he was thankful that Jonathan's father didn't attempt to show off his physical strength as so many of the Americans tended to do. "Dr. Phillip Gribbleflotz. I really wanted to see Jonathan about some information he sent me recently."

"Yeah, Jonathan's spoken of you. Which information are we talking about?"

"It's for making gems. Some of the senior laborants have voiced an interest in the process, so I was wondering if Jonathan could talk to them."

"Ah, the gemstones. Well, you're in luck. I've actually made some rubies. I wanted to make a ruby laser, so I made a furnace to make the ruby. If you'll wait a moment, I'll see if I can dig it out."

"No, Herr Fortney." Phillip reached out an arm to restrain Caleb. "There's no need for you stop what you're doing. Would you be willing to talk to some of my laborants about the process?"

"Sure. Where and when?"

"Anytime you're free. Normally our seminars are held at HDG Laboratories in Jena, but we have a facility here in Grantville that we can use if that is more convenient for you, Herr Fortney. We'll gladly pay you for your time."

"Hey, you don't have to pay me. And enough of this Herr Fortney crap. Call me Caleb."

It hadn't come easily, but four years of contact with up-timers, especially Ted and Tracy Kubiak and Caleb's son Jonathan, had weakened his natural aversion to such casualness, at least when dealing with up-timers. "Please, call me Phillip. And I really do insist that we pay for your time. You have no idea of how much preparation you'll need to do, Caleb. These seminars are a teaching exercise and the laborants are encouraged to ask questions. Some of the questions can be surprisingly acute."

Caleb raised his eyebrows. "That the voice of experience I hear?"

Phillip nodded. He'd only been caught out a couple of times. "Fortunately I was able to draw on my long experience with the subject in question both times. But after two close shaves I decided to never go into the seminar room unprepared again."

"In that case, I'll be happy to accept a fee." Caleb nodded towards the car he'd been working on. "I'm just about to go for a test drive. Is there anywhere I can drop you off?"

"Drop me off? You mean, travel in your car?"

"Yeah. Where're you staying?"

"The Higgins. If it's not too much trouble."

Caleb led Phillip over to the passenger side and opened the door. "You sure you wouldn't like to go a bit further afield? The Higgins is only a few minutes away."

"Dina is visiting her family."

Caleb grinned. "At the rectory at St. Martin's? That's more like it. Come on, hop in. I'll just tell the housekeeper where we're going."

Well, at least that explained who the woman was. Phillip looked down at the car. It was a small four-door car. Compared to most of the American cars he'd seen it was a very small car. He slid in and sat down. It was very different from the buses he had traveled in before. To his left he could see the steering wheel, the device by which the vehicle was steered. But other than the speedometer, that was all he recognized. He looked in the back. There was a bench seat that could take two or three people, and that was about all there was to it. A moment later Caleb returned and climbed into the driver's seat.

"Right. Shut your door and we'll be off."

Phillip copied Caleb's action of grabbing the handle on the door and pulling it closed. Then he sat still while Caleb did something under the steering wheel. There was a whirring noise, then the gentle rumble of an internal combustion engine. Caleb did something with the lever to his right and the car started moving.

Phillip sat back to enjoy the trip. He'd been on the Grantville buses often enough that the car's speed didn't bother him. But he was curious to know how fast they were going, so he leaned over a bit to read the speedometer. "Twenty-five miles per hour? It seems faster than that."

Caleb darted a look at Phillip before turning his eyes back to the road ahead. "You ever traveled in a car before?"

"No." Phillip shook his head. "Just the bus."

"That explains it. It's a perception thing. The closer you are to the ground, the faster you think you're going. If you were in something really low, like Trent Haygood's buggy, you'd really think you were motoring."

Phillip tried to visualize what Caleb was talking about. He couldn't. "Could you explain how this 'perception' works?"

Caleb shook his head. "No, it's just something I know."

"Well, if you ever find an explanation, I'm sure we can schedule a seminar."

"Maybe you'd be better off getting someone else. I wouldn't know where to start looking."

Phillip enjoyed the run out to the rectory. He felt very important being driven in a private car, and waved to anybody who stopped to stare. "Caleb, how is it that you can run a car? I thought there wasn't enough fuel."

"You're thinking of gasoline. This car's a diesel. That means we can run it on just about anything that'll burn. If your nose is sensitive enough you'll be able to smell the rapeseed oil. It's not cheap, but if we keep the speed down we should average over fifty miles to the gallon."

"Speed?" Phillip gave the car another look. "How fast can this car go?"

"The book on it says ninety-two-and-a-bit miles per hour, but I've never had the old girl up to more than eighty-five."

"Eighty-five miles per hour?" Phillip had thought he was traveling fast at twenty-five. What would that kind of speed be like? Was it even safe? "Surely traveling that fast can't be safe."

Caleb grinned. "It's not the speed that kills you, Phillip. It's the coming to a sudden stop."

Phillip checked his watch. The car trip had been exciting. It had also brought him back to the rectory well ahead of schedule. But for Caleb's kindness, he'd still be waiting for his bus. Phillip dropped his watch back into its pocket and entered the rectory.

He could hear voices coming from the kitchen. It sounded as if Dina was sharing confidences with her stepmother. That pleased him. He set off for the kitchen.

". . . said I was pregnant."

Phillip froze at the door. That was Dina talking. Did that mean she was with child? Phillip took a deep breath. It was, after all, a perfectly normal thing for a married woman to have a child. A couple of the older women he employed in Jena were married with children. Only, he'd never thought of being a father. But now that the possibility existed, he quite liked the idea. He could almost picture a pretty little girl who would take after her mother or a boy to share his interests in alchemy. A broad smile on his face, he pushed open the kitchen door.

"Phillip!" Dina flew into his arms. "Such news. Dr. Shipley says I'm with child."

Phillip wrapped his arms around her. "That's marvelous, Dina. We must see about reducing your work load back home."

Dina pushed her way out of Phillip's arms. "I'm not ill, Phillip. I'm pregnant. It's a perfectly natural condition."

Phillip glanced hopefully at Dina's stepmother. The self-satisfied look on her face told him there would be no support coming from that quarter. He struggled to think. What would Jonathan tell him to do? Then he smiled. When women start to gang up on you, there is only one way to survive. Abject surrender. "Yes, dear." He reached out to Dina. She smiled and burrowed into his chest.

Salome snorted and left them alone in the kitchen.

Later that evening, the Higgins Hotel, Grantville

Phillip sat on the bed beside Dina. She lay there with her hands on her belly and her head in his lap. Phillip gently caressed her neck and shoulders.

"Phillip, Mama suggests I should have the baby in Grantville to take advantage of the medical services."

"Of course, Dina."

"With the train service, I can stay at home until almost the last minute, and still have our baby at the Grantville hospital."

Phillip stilled. He didn't have much experience of children, and even less experience of babies. But he was pretty sure of one thing. "Dina, I don't think even your baby will decide to come to fit the train schedule. It'd be much better if you moved in with your family, or we rent an apartment in Grantville when you near your time."

"What? Leave home for a couple of weeks? But who will teach the children?"

"I'm sorry, Dina. But if you want to have the baby in Grantville, then you'll have to move here before you're due. Hans and your brothers can take your classes while you're away."

Dina grabbed Phillip's hand. "No. You're just trying to cut back my work load."

"No I'm not."

"Prove it."

"Be reasonable, Dina. You can't rely on the train service to get you to the hospital in time. What you need is a personal ambulance..." Suddenly, Phillip scrambled to his feet. "Don't go away. I have to make a telephone call."

"A phone call?"

He dipped down and kissed Dina on the tip of the nose. "Yes. I want to call a man about an ambulance."

Call a man about an ambulance? Surely that wasn't possible. Dina shook her head. If anybody could solve the problem of getting her from Jena to Grantville when the time came, it was Phillip.

She lay back on the bed and started to daydream about the child she carried. It would be a boy, with the intelligence of her husband and who would follow in his footsteps.

Downstairs at the Higgins Hotel

Phillip waited impatiently for his call to be put through. Eventually someone answered.

"Fortney Consulting. Caleb Fortney speaking."

"Hello, Herr Fortney. This is Phillip Gribbleflotz. We met earlier in the day."

"Hey, hi, Phillip. What can I do for you?"

Phillip hesitated. How to ask? Obviously the Jonathan way was best. Just come straight out and state what you want. "I was wondering about that car you were driving earlier. Could you teach me to drive?"

"Yeah, well. Sure I could teach you. But I'm not the greatest teacher. I don't have enough patience. Just ask my daughter. I think Dick Clelland, the Driver's Ed teacher at the high school, would be your best bet."

"Thank you, Caleb. How do I go about making arrangements?"

"Just call the high school and ask the secretary to make an appointment. Mind, you'll need to provide your own car. Do you have one?"

"I was wondering if you could help me there. Do you know where I might buy something like the car we traveled in earlier today?"

"You can have that one if you like. It belongs to my daughter, Lynette. She married Kevin Fritz late last year and, well, they could use the money."

Phillip beamed. This was better than he had hoped for. The little car would be perfect on the narrow streets of Jena. Not that he intended to drive through them very often. Maybe just once or twice, right past the university, every other week or so. "Thank you, Caleb. I'll let Frau Kubiak negotiate a fair price."

"Rightyo, and thanks. Lynette and Kevin will appreciate a quick sale. Reading between the lines, I think they're expecting my first grandchild."

"Thank you, Caleb, and congratulations on becoming a grandfather."

"It's not a sure thing yet, Phillip. The wife might be jumping to conclusions, but there must be a good reason why they suddenly asked if I could get the car ready for sale."

A few weeks later, Grantville

Phillip waved goodbye to Trent Haygood, engaged gear, and drove off. After a month of his commuting to Grantville for driving lessons, Dick Clelland had declared himself satisfied with Phillip's driving. However, Jonathan had suggested that Phillip might benefit from some lessons from a real driver. He shuddered when he remembered that first trip as a passenger in Trent's vehicle. Caleb had been right. That close to the ground you really did think you were traveling very fast. Of course, Trent had driven fast—over eighty miles per hour. It had been an interesting few hours, but now Phillip considered himself sufficiently skilled to safely drive Dina between Jena and Grantville. Thanks to Caleb, he even had some idea how to maintain the car and its engine.

Phillip stopped just outside the Leahy Medical Center. He zeroed the trip meter, took note of the time and started the stopwatch function on his pocket watch. Then he set off for home.

It was a gentle drive along the road connecting Grantville to Rudolstadt and Jena. He kept the speed down for several reasons. First, fuel economy and preserving the tires. The other reason was the fancy new road could be damaged if he traveled too fast.

He was happy to find that he had no difficulties with other road users. Not even when passing through Rudolstadt and the villages on his route. Apparently the locals and their animals were used to the American vehicles, although a number of dogs had attempted to give chase.

Pulling up outside the door of his apartments at

HDG Laboratories, Phillip stopped the stopwatch—one hour eight minutes and four point three-four seconds. Not bad for a run of, he checked the trip meter, of twenty-six and three-tenths miles. It was certainly much quicker than going by train, and it was door to door.

Phillip undid the seatbelt, a safety measure Trent had recommended he use, and reached for the door latch. That was when he realized he'd attracted a crowd. Pushing the door open he set about showing off his new car.

November 1635, HDG Laboratories, Jena

Dina knocked on the door of Phillip's laboratory and poked her head in. "Phillip. You haven't forgotten that I have an appointment to see Dr. Shipley this afternoon?"

"Of course not, Dina. If you're ready, I'll come now."

Dina suppressed a sigh. She had used to think Phillip was perfect. She now knew that he wasn't. But she had to admit, he tried, although sometimes he was just "trying." Like right now, when it should be obvious that she was ready to go. "I'm ready, dear."

Phillip knew how to take a hint. He marked his place and put the book he'd been reading into his shoulder bag. He could read some more while Dina was with the doctor. He called over to his assistant. "Hans, you know the drill."

Hans nodded.

"Right, Dina, I'm all yours." Phillip slung the shoulder bag over his shoulder and escorted Dina out of his office and set off for the garage.

The garage was a work of art. There was plenty of room for the car, and anybody working on it. It was heated by a radiator, because Caleb had suggested that there might be problems with the fuel jelling in cold weather. The car itself was covered by a heavy quilt custom made for the job.

A couple of laborants removed and folded the cover while Phillip led Dina to the passenger door and helped her in. After making sure she was comfortable and was wearing her seatbelt, he walked around to the driver's side, stopping a couple of times to polish specks off the metal work and the rear window. Before entering the car he checked the windshield for blemishes. Finally he got in.

"You think more of this car than you do of me," Dina accused.

Phillip was shocked. "No I don't, Dina. Whatever gave you that idea?"

"You certainly pamper it more than you pamper me."

"But dear, the car is temperamental and needs delicate handling..." Phillip bit his tongue. In the mood she was in right now, Dina was bound to take that the wrong way.

"I am not temperamental."

Phillip wilted under his wife's glare. *Yes. Definitely a big mistake.* "Of course you aren't temperamental, Dina." Before Dina could start an argument Phillip started the car and reversed out of the garage. To fill the silence he inserted a tape into the car's tape deck. To the strains of Elgar's "Pomp and Circumstance," they set off for Grantville.

The Higgins Hotel

Phillip frowned. What the book on pyramid power said didn't agree with his findings. That meant either there was something wrong with the author's theory, or there was something wrong with Phillip's pyramid. He slumped back in the easy chair and contemplated the possibility that the author's theory was wrong. It wasn't an attractive thought. If the theory of pyramid power was wrong, then all of his efforts to use it to invigorate the Quinta Essentia of the human humors had been wasted. Alternatively, Phillip couldn't imagine what he could have done wrong with his pyramid. He had even obtained pure nickel for the structural members, and Michael and Kurt had made some new gems from aluminum oxide which he'd had faceted by a local jeweler. What Phillip needed was access to a computer so he could check his calculations. At least, Gerry Stone had suggested he run his calculations through a computer spreadsheet just in case the problem was accumulated rounding errors. Dina's friend Ronella Koch taught mathematics at the Grantville high school and she had arranged for Ronella to check the numbers for him.

Phillip looked up at the clock. Dina had said that Ronella wouldn't be free to run the calculations until after school, but it was now well past six. He sighed. He had always heard that when women got together to gossip, they could forget about time. And he wanted those calculations. He wasn't sure if he wanted his calculations to be right though, because that would mean he had wasted nearly four years on a pipe dream. Maybe he wasn't destined to be remembered in the same breath as his great grandfather, the great Paracelsus.

Phillip took another sip of wine. Now that he had Dina, he could live with not being as famous as Great-grandfather Paracelsus. He knew he would be remembered through his children. Right now, that was much more important than fame. And he was scared. What did he know about raising children? And then there was the bombshell Dr. Shipley had delivered earlier in the day. Twins. His Dina was carrying two babies. Of course Frau Mittelhausen would be there, but maybe Dina would like a nursery maid to help. Maybe he should see Dina's stepmother about hiring one. Phillip froze at the thought. That was probably the wrong way to go about it. Maybe a better bet would be to ask Dina if she wanted help first. He nodded. Surely Dina wouldn't bite his head off if he suggested employing a nursery maid, especially as it would leave her more time for her teaching.

Proud of his logic, Phillip closed his pyramid power book, placed it on the occasional table beside his chair, and picked up the first of the books on babies and child rearing Frau Kubiak had found for him.

Dina entered the suite first. Together she and Ronella looked around the room. The light was on, so Phillip should be in the suite. "Phillip," Dina called.

There was no response. Both women started to walk around the room. Then Ronella stopped and gestured for Dina to come over.

"He looks kinda cute, doesn't he?" Ronella asked, pointing to the sleeping Phillip.

Dina nodded. Yes, Phillip did look cute sleeping slumped in his chair. He must have dozed off while he waited for her. There was an open book on the floor that must have slipped from his grasp when he fell asleep. *I wonder what he was reading?* She bent to pick it up, and almost burst out laughing. She showed Ronella the book.

"*The Expectant Father*." Ronella grinned. "What else has he been reading?"

Dina looked through the mountain of books beside Phillip. All but the book on pyramid power were about pregnancy. Reading the titles, she started to get worried. *What to Expect When You're Expecting*, *What to Eat When You're Expecting*, *Pregnancy for Dummies*, *Fit Pregnancy for Dummies*, *Dr. Spock's Baby and Child Care*. Even one titled *The Womanly Art of Breastfeeding*. Then there were the ones on raising twins. *Raising Multiple Birth Children: A Parents' Survival Guide*. Ouch. Dina wasn't sure she liked the idea of needing a survival guide. Even worse was the idea that Phillip had read, or intended to read, these books, and maybe try to implement the ideas put forward. Heck, look at the effort he'd put into his research into pyramid power. Dina wasn't sure she wanted Phillip that focused on her babies.

Ronella looked up after looking at the titles. "Girl, you've got problems. Whoever gave Phillip these is either too well meaning for words, or they have it in for you."

Dina didn't get to respond, because just then Phillip jerked awake.

"Dina, where have you been? I expected you home hours ago."

Dina flushed. "I'm sorry, Phillip. We got talking and just forgot the time."

"Well, you're home now." He turned to Ronella.

"Thank you for seeing my wife safely home. Can I escort you to your home?"

Ronella turned expectantly to Dina. She took the hint. "Phillip, the reason I'm so late is we got talking about the chemical engineer you said you wanted. You know Jerry Trainer?"

"What?" Phillip was suddenly all attentive. "Herr Jerry Trainer? He is willing to work for us?"

"No, Phillip." Dina shook her head. "But he has an apprentice he's been training for the last few years. Lori Drahuta. Mrs. Penzey thinks she might be interested."

February 29, 1636, 1:00 am, HDG Laboratories, Jena

Phillip had thought he was prepared, but right now, he was on the verge of panicking. He'd woken up when Dina jerked and cried out. At least her waters hadn't broken yet. There was still time to get to Grantville if they hurried. "I have to get you to the hospital, Dina." Phillip slipped out of bed and made for the bell pull. He pulled it and could hear the distant ringing of a bell. He grabbed some clothes and made for the dressing room door. "Don't go away, I'll be right back."

Frau Mittelhausen bustled into the bedroom. She could see immediately that the doctor had grabbed some clothes and made for his dressing room. She spared the mess he'd made a single sigh before turning her attention to the mistress. After helping her out of bed, she helped Dina into a fresh nightdress and started to wrap her in a dressing gown and coat to keep out the cold. "How do you feel, Frau Gribble-flotz? I've sent Hans out to get the car ready. Would you like anything to eat or drink?"

Dina shook her head and let Frau Mittelhausen take charge.

Dina let Phillip help her into the car. "I'm all right, Phillip. Are you sure it's safe to drive to Grantville at night?"

"Of course it's safe, Dina. Jonathan and his father fitted the extra lights just in case we had to make a night run. It'll be just like driving during the day, but without the traffic."

Dina nodded. That sounded safe. She tried to make herself comfortable in the car seat. The seat belt wasn't very comfortable, but Phillip insisted she wear it, so she made the best of it.

It was a still winter's morning. The moon was high in the sky; moonlight illuminated the countryside. Phillip, she could see, was fiddling with the radio-cassette player. Then he started the car moving forward. He was driving a little faster than normal, but as he had said, the road was clear of other traffic. Dina tried to relax. Suddenly she jerked. Another contraction. She didn't need Phillip's watch to know they were getting closer together.

Dina noticed Phillip flicking a switch. She thought nothing had happened until she looked up at the road ahead. It was well illuminated for hundreds of paces ahead. She could see the beam hitting the windows of the neighbors. She sighed. She'd have to placate them when she got back from Grantville.

"We'll soon be out of Jena, Dina. Then I'll be able to go a bit faster."

"That'll be nice, Phillip." Dina snuggled deeper into her heavy fur coat. Phillip had one just like it. Sable, if she remembered what the furrier said—a special delivery from Russia. Whatever, it was very warm.

Dina jerked awake. She tried to work out where they were, but she wasn't used to seeing the countryside by moonlight. She turned to ask Phillip, but stopped at the sight of him concentrating on the road ahead. She looked out the side window, and rapidly turned back to face the front. Surely the landscape was going past overly fast. She edged over so she could see the speedometer, and immediately wished she hadn't. She sat back firmly in her seat, with both hands gripping it firmly.

"You're awake, Dina? Don't worry, we'll soon be in Grantville."

Dina swallowed. Surely Phillip shouldn't be looking at her when he was driving. "Keep your eyes on the road, Phillip."

"Of course dear, but there's nothing to worry about. I know this road well."

There was a screeching of brakes and the car fishtailed for a few seconds.

"Whoops! Sorry about that. Went around that curve a little fast. Nothing to worry about. There was nothing coming the other way. We'll soon be there, Dina. Rudolstadt should be just around this next curve."

Dina could feel her nails digging into the upholstery. *When will this nightmare trip end?*

She could hear the muted roar of the car engine

reverberating back off the buildings as they sped through Rudolstadt. And Dina was sure they were speeding. Everything was whizzing past so much quicker than when Phillip normally drove through Rudolstadt. Even the sound of tires on cobblestones suggested excessive speed.

Before she'd realized, they were through Rudolstadt. The hospital was only a few miles away.

Leahy Medical Center

Phillip screeched to a halt outside the admissions area at the Leahy Medical Center. He leaped out of the car and ran around to the passenger door. Even before he got to Dina, medical orderlies were approaching with a gurney. "It's my wife. She's about to have a baby. Two of them!"

The orderlies carefully lifted Dina onto the padded gurney and set off for the medical center. Phillip ran alongside, holding Dina's hand. She was wheeled into a delivery room and transferred to a hospital bed. Dr. Shipley arrived and immediately suggested Phillip might like to wait outside.

Dina looked tired but happy. Dr. Shipley had claimed that it had been a remarkably easy labor. Phillip wasn't so sure. If that had been an easy delivery, he wasn't sure he wanted his Dina going through a difficult one. He'd already talked to Dr. Shipley about that. She had suggested that there was a simple medical procedure that could prevent him fathering another child. She had suggested he talk to Dina about the option. Phillip had been terrified for Dina. The way she screamed and yelled, she must have been in extreme pain. And the blood. He, a man who'd performed amputations time and again in the past, had almost fainted at the sight of so much blood. But after the nurse had given her the two wrapped bundles, Dina had been all smiles. It was as if the pain had never occurred.

He looked over at his children. A boy and a girl. He smiled. That meant there was one each. Not that a parent should place a claim on a child. But he was sure his daughter would take after her mother. His son, maybe he would have the look of his mother, too. That was all for the good. They'd have to think of names. Dina had suggested Salome Blandina for a girl, after her mother and stepmother. She had asked Phillip if the boy should be called Theophrastus, but he'd managed to dissuade her. Anyway, there was plenty of time to worry about names. Dina and the children were healthy. That was what was important.

A week later, HDG Laboratories, Jena

The car drew to a halt just outside their apartment in Jena. Dina waited for Phillip to open the door and help her out. That was when she saw the two women. One of them was a young American. That was probably Lori Drahuta. She'd indicated interest in finding out more about what the position at HDG entailed, and been invited to visit. The other woman looked much the same age. She had rich black hair and an unlined porcelain white face. Her clothes left little to the imagination. *Who is this woman?*

Dina watched silently as the female approached a clearly embarrassed Phillip. She looked over at Frau Mittelhausen. The housekeeper looked embarrassed that the homecoming had been disrupted, but she wasn't looking at Phillip with condemnation. It struck Dina that Frau Mittelhausen's look was more one of pity.

Dina looked back at the woman. There was something unnatural about her. Dina stepped closer.

Makeup. That explained it. This female, whoever she was, gave the lie to the American claim that lead-based cosmetics were unhealthy. She had seen the sales records for the new oxide of zinken, and there was no indication that anybody was buying it in the quantities this female was using. She must be applying her makeup with a trowel. Dina was sure of one thing now. This female was not someone she wished to associate with. Her friend Ronella had pointed out an American woman dressed up and made up to appear much younger. She would have used the same expression, "mutton dressed as lamb" to describe this female. Obviously she was much older than she appeared. Just how much older was impossible to tell. Dina stepped up beside Phillip. One of his hands shot out and latched onto her hand.

"Theophrastus. Aren't you pleased to see me?" the female asked.

Dina felt the tension in Phillip. He gave her a beseeching look before returning his gaze to the female. "Hello, Mother."

Part Four

Prague
1636

Chapter 19

Dr. Phil for President

January 1634, Grantville

Phillip "Lips" Kastenmayer stood despondently in front
of the window, gazing at the unobtainable fashions on
display. The mannequin that most drew his attention
was dressed in T-shirt, leather jacket, blue jeans, and
black leather boots—just like the hero in the movie
he'd just seen. There was no price displayed, but
then there wouldn't be, because those clothes were
authentic up-time fashions, and if you had to ask, you
couldn't afford them.

He stepped back so he could see his reflection in
the window. Anything less like what was on display was
hard to imagine. He was dressed in the uniform Mama
believed suitable for the student son of a Lutheran
pastor. It was drab, uninspiring, but long-lasting. So
long-lasting that he expected to still be wearing it
when he graduated from university.

He thrust his thumbs through his belt—how much

he'd love to be able to thrust them into the pockets of his own pair of jeans or leather jacket—but that was just a dream. Papa could barely afford to send him and his brothers to university, let alone splash out on expensive up-time fashions. With a final sad glance at the fashions in the window, he set off on the five mile walk home.

May, 1635, the rectory, St. Martin's in the Field, south of Rudolstadt

Lips was happy that his sister was getting married, but he wasn't happy that he had to dress up just because she was getting married.

"Stand still," Salome Piscatora, his mama, demanded as she tried to straighten his collar.

Lips did as he was told while Mama dusted down his freshly starched collar—he could already feel it starting to itch. Then he felt her pulling a brush through his hair. Eventually he was tidy enough, and she sent him off to stand in a corner with his younger brother.

"What's the guy Dina's marrying like?" He asked Ernst, who'd at least met the man Dina was marrying.

Ernst shrugged. "He's old, and he's got the weirdest taste in clothes, but Dina seems happy."

That didn't sound good. Lips knew the man had agreed to board him and his brothers while they attended university in Jena, and he worried that Dina was selling herself to support the family.

"Here he comes now."

Lips followed Ernst's gaze, and just about died of shock. He'd been given the impression that Dina's betrothed was an employee at HDG Laboratories. "What did you say he did in Jena?"

"Papa said he's in charge of training and supervising the laborants." Ernst grinned. "Papa's hoping Dina might encourage Phillip to seek promotion from his wealthy relative."

"Yeah, right," Lips muttered as he watched the man approach.

"Phillip, this is my son Phillip, although we usually call him Lips," Ludwig Kastenmayer said.

Lips hastily put out his hand to shake the one being offered. "A pleasure to meet you, Phillip."

"Joseph, have you met Dina's betrothed?" Lips asked when he ran his older brother to ground, in the library, reading some boring law text.

"He seems a good enough man. No interest in the law, of course."

"But don't you know who he is?"

"Papa told you who he is, or weren't you listening, as usual?"

"You don't understand. Dina is marrying Dr. Gribbleflotz."

"Oh, does Phillip have a doctorate? Do you know where from?"

Lips bared his teeth at his brother. How could he not understand? "Joseph, Dina's betrothed is *the* Dr. Gribbleflotz. He doesn't just work at HDG Laboratories. He *is* HDG Laboratories." The stunned look on his brother's face told Lips that he'd finally made his point.

"*The* Dr. Gribbleflotz is marrying our Dina?" Joseph managed to splutter.

"Not only is she marrying Dr. Gribbleflotz, but nobody in the family seems to know who he is."

"Uncle Arnold vouches for him," Joseph said.

"Well, that's someone who knows who Dina's marrying."

"Why would someone as rich as Dr. Gribbleflotz want to marry Dina?"

That question stumped Lips. It wasn't that Dina was ugly, or stupid, or even too old. It was the fact that although money didn't always marry money, it certainly didn't marry the dowerless daughter of a poor pastor. "You don't suppose he fell in love with Dina?"

"Dina's very..." Joseph screwed up his nose and shrugged.

Lips felt exactly the same. Dina was a great sister, but what did she have to attract the attention of a wealthy man like Dr. Gribbleflotz?

Lips remained doubtful about his sister's marrying Dr. Gribbleflotz right up to the minute, soon after the exchange of vows, when she launched herself into her husband's arms. There was a sparkle in her eyes he hadn't seen for years, and she was glowing. Her new husband looked just as happy.

November 1635, HDG Laboratories, Jena

"Lips, you have to save me," Dina implored the moment she got home from the recent trip to Grantville for a medical checkup.

Lips shot out of his chair and rushed over to his sister. "What's the matter?"

"Someone's given Phillip books on bringing up babies."

Lips whistled. That could be serious. He glanced through the window and saw Phillip putting away his car. "Has he said anything?"

"Not yet, but you know what Phillip's like, and I don't want him making a project out of my babies."

"Babies?" Lips knew Dina was pregnant, but that seemed to suggest more than one.

Dina smiled and ran a hand over her belly. "Yes, Dr. Shipley says I'm carrying twins. She let me listen to their heartbeats."

Lips ignored the dreamy look on his sister's face and concentrated on dealing with her problem. "What is it you want me to do?"

"I need you to approach Phillip and pretend an interest in alchemy. Maybe teaching you what he knows will stop him concentrating on me and the babies." She slumped. "Why did he have to pick now to decide that there was something wrong with the pyramid power thing?"

Lips hugged his sister. He'd always been interested in the new science, and now, instead of sneaking into the laboratories and seminars, he could do it openly, firm in the knowledge that Dina would support him if Mama and Papa asked questions.

A couple of days later, Jena

Lips stared at the poster of a young woman wearing nothing but strategically placed whipped cream, and wondered, *how did they do it?* It was definitely a photograph. He'd seen several, including photographs from Dina and Phillip's wedding, so he knew what cameras could do. Except that the poster was in color, and realistic color at that. He went in search of the gatekeeper to up-time knowledge.

He found him in his office, with Frau Mittelhausen, Frau Beier, and Dina. "Oh, I'm sorry," Lips said as he hastily backed out of the room.

"What is it, Lips," Dina asked.

"I just wanted to ask Phillip something, but it can wait."

"We aren't doing anything important, just reviewing the new advertising campaign for Sal Vin Betula."

Lips struggled to stop the grin that statement elicited from turning into a smirk. It had been Phillip's Sal Vin Betula, better known in the market as Dr. Gribbleflotz's Little Blue Pills of Happiness, that had got him into selling revitalizing fluid. Some up-timer had mistaken his blue aspirin pills for some up-time sex drug. "Maybe you should try something like Paxton's poster."

"What poster would that be?" Phillip asked.

"Are you talking about the poster of the female wearing nothing but revitalizing cream?" Frau Mittelhausen asked.

"That's the one," Lips said. "Phillip, do you know how they did it?"

"Did what?"

"You haven't seen the poster?"

Phillip shook his head.

"Well, it's a color poster, but it's not block color like most posters are. The color is so realistic; it's like a photograph out of an up-time book."

"That certainly bears looking at. Where is this poster?"

"In the front window of Vorkeuffer's," Lips said, naming a local store that had been nothing much more than a common grocery store four years ago, and was now the largest general store in Jena, all on the back of selling the products of HDG Laboratories.

Phillip pushed back his chair. "If you will all excuse me, I must have a look at this poster Lips is so excited about."

"I'm coming too," Dina insisted, as she too pushed back her chair.

November 1635, Prague, capital of Bohemia

"I was invited in to record the king's aura yesterday," Zacharias Held told his colleague. Well, more bragged, really, but serving the king was surely something to brag about.

Johann Dent whistled. "How did you manage that?"

"Talent, Johann, pure talent."

Johann snorted. "More likely you found out who to pay. So, is the king as ill as we hear?"

Zacharias nodded. "I think he's in a very bad way, but that dragon guarding him refused to let me take a Kirlian image of his head. How does she expect me to know how to rebalance his aura if I can't see it properly?"

"So you only got a hand?"

"And just the left one at that."

"You can't tell much from the weaker hand. Didn't you explain?"

"In front of the king? With his dragon glaring at me? Of course I didn't." Zacharias pulled out a Kirlian photograph and passed it over to Johann. "Have a look at that. I think he definitely needs an aluminum bracelet to balance the aura, but it also needs a red gemstone in a number three cut."

"Oh, dear. You do have a problem."

Zacharias ignored the smug smile on Johann's face. He was merely jealous that he hadn't been invited to examine the king. However, Johann did have a point. Both of them knew, from Aural Balance 101, that you didn't mix aluminum metal with gems containing aluminum.

"You can't use glass for the king."

"No," Zacharias agreed. One didn't use glass for the king, not even if you were adding gold to it to make a lovely ruby red.

"And rubies are just aluminum oxide, after all. Spinels and tourmaline are out, too. But what about a carbuncle?"

"No. All red garnets have aluminum in the B location, all the ones with something else are green or black."

"Then I guess you need see if Roth's can suggest anything," Johann said.

December 1635, HDG Laboratories, Jena

Lips helped his brother-in-law set up his latest creation—a three-color camera obscura. Not that Phillip was laying claim to the idea for the machine. That had been someone at Schmucker and Schwentzel, in Rudolstadt. After seeing the poster for Paxton's Revitalizing Cream, Phillip had been as interested as Lips in learning how it was done. And Lips had learned just how powerful his brother-in-law was, although to be fair, Phillip didn't seem to be aware of his power.

No sooner had Phillip asked Paxton's how the poster had been produced, than he'd been directed to Schmucker and Schwentzel. The fact that Paxton's Revitalizing Cream was riding on the coattails of Phillip's revitalizing fluid probably had something to do with their friendly response to his inquiries.

The printers hadn't been as obeisant when Phillip and Lips turned up to ask questions, but they'd been more than willing to describe their technique—maybe the fact the film and photographic chemicals they were using all came from one of the HDG facilities had something to do with it. Not that Lips was feeling cynical.

The visit had seen the commissioning of a smaller version of Schmucker and Schwentzel's camera. The camera for Phillip had been treated as a rush job, and been delivered just yesterday. Lips, again not feeling particularly cynical, wondered how much Phillip was going to be charged, because none of the people they dealt with that day had mentioned anything as common as price. He made a mental note to ask Frau Mittelhausen how much everything had cost.

"It would be so much easier if we had color film," Lips said. Certainly Phillip's black and white camera was nowhere near as finicky to set up.

"It would, but there have been difficulties replicating the *Autochrome* process."

The Autochrome process used starch grains dyed in red, green and blue, randomly distributed over a photosensitive emulsion. Or at least that's what the instructions in the eleventh edition of the *Encyclopedia Britannica* said. "Do you know what is wrong?" Lips asked.

"It's obvious that there is some step, some additional

chemical or process, missing from the published directions, so we will do what we always do."

"And that is?" Lips asked.

"Revert to basic principles. Take what we know, and try adding things to the known until we discover the unknown."

That didn't fit with the basic principles of chemistry he'd picked up in the few up-time science classes he'd managed to sneak into back in Grantville. Those had suggested a much more theoretical approach. "Does that work?"

"It is how I discovered how to make the Amazing Essence of Fire Tablets the up-time chemists claimed couldn't be made." Phillip pulled the camera's blackout cloth over his head.

Yes, well, Lips knew all about those fire tablets. If you knew what you were doing, and Hans Saltzman, Phillip's trusted personal laborant of nearly five years, certainly did know, you could turn those fire tablets into high explosive. It had been interesting watching Hans make up some of the explosive and then detonate it on a farm outside Jena's walls. For such a small amount of explosive, it had made a very big hole. But it was the first time he'd heard that the up-timers hadn't believed it was possible to make the precursor. Maybe there was something to Phillip's approach to research that was better than the up-timer science.

Phillip reappeared from under the blackout cloth and closed the shutter before opening the slides on the film cassettes. "Everything is ready. If you would like to set the experiment in motion."

Lips took the hint and turned off the lights before initiating the flame test. Moments later the spectral lines were visible on the detector. Phillip opened the shutter, and Lips ensured the flame had a steady supply of prepared loops for the twenty-second exposure.

Lips sat beside Phillip as he studied the color image projected onto the screen. The use of colored filters meant that the sets of black and white photographs taken by the three-color camera could be projected onto a screen to form a single color image. On the screen in front of him was a nearly perfect record of the spectral lines produced in the flame test.

"Well, that seems to have worked," Phillip said.

"You sound surprised," Lips said. "Surely you expected it to work?"

"Of course I'm surprised, Lips. It's been my experience that nothing ever works as it should the first time."

"But Schmucker and Schwentzel's camera worked, so why shouldn't yours?"

Phillip looked up and shook his head. "The voice of someone who has not yet run into the great Murphy." He looked Lips directly in the eyes. "If anything can go wrong, it will. Remember that, Lips. Remember that."

January 1636, Prague

There was a hubbub of conversation in the meeting room of the Prague chapter of the Society of Aural Investigators, the professional body responsible for maintaining the standards of the profession. Zacharias carried his steaming mug of Tincture of Cacao—the beverage the society had virtually made its own—to the table where Johann was sitting. "Sorry I'm late, but some fool forgot to refill the Wetmore's reservoir, and it ran out of water in the middle of a calculation. I had to refill the reservoir and bleed the whole thing before I could do anything."

"Another reading for the king?" Johann asked.

"Yes." Zacharias was proud of himself. He hadn't come across as overly smug. As aural investigator to the king, he was *someone*—and the increase in business from people who wanted the king's aural investigator to read their aura didn't hurt.

"Did you manage to find yourself a red gemstone for the bracelet?"

"Yes, Roth's had the perfect red gemstone—a Mexican opal. I had them cut and set it in the bracelet."

"Did it work?"

"It was the calculations based on the bracelet that kept me so long." He took out a notebook, opened it to the right page, and passed it to Johann. "Have a look. The king should be highly impressed when I tell him how much closer to the ideal state his aura is."

Johann skimmed over the numbers before handing the notebook back. "Of course, it would be a lot better if you could record the aura in color."

"Of course it would be better, but nobody is doing color..." Zacharias stopped because Johann was shaking his head. "Someone is?"

"If you'd been here earlier you would have heard Zänkel reading from the latest issue of the *Proceedings of the HDG Laboratories*. It has a centerfold of color photographs from one of the doctor's experiments."

"What?" Zacharias was horrified that he'd missed such news. He stood and searched the tables for a copy of the *Proceedings*. Sighting one, he hastened over and picked it up. He knew he had the right issue as soon as he opened it. There was a centerfold in high-quality white paper with color images of spectral lines from flame tests. He hastened back to Johann and sat down. "Does he say how he does it?"

"Would you?" Johann asked.

"No." Of course he wouldn't give away information like that. It'd be worth a fortune. He hastily skimmed through the articles in the journal, looking for anything that might cast light on the question of how it was done, and more importantly, how long it would be before the technique was available for everyday use.

"You can stop hunting. Everyone has already looked, and there is nothing about the method in that issue."

Zacharias quickly checked the publication date— January, 1636. The *Proceedings* were published three times a year, so that meant the next issue wouldn't be out until May. "A letter to the doctor asking about the technique's application to Kirlian imaging is definitely indicated."

"Already decided while you were playing with the aqualator," Johann said. "Martin Zänkel has been told to write a letter on behalf of the chapter."

"We won't be the only chapter writing, you know," Zacharias pointed out.

"Of course not. But if we don't send a letter the doctor won't know we're interested in knowing the answer. I expect he'll put together a form letter and send it out to anybody who inquires."

February 1636, Jena

Lips was happily sitting in the sun in a protected corner of the compound reading one of Phillip's uptime science textbooks when his light was suddenly cut off. He looked up to see the looming shapes of Fraus Beier and Mittelhausen, and Hans Saltzman blocking out the sun.

"See, he's perfect for the job," Hans said.

"Just because he reads the doctor's books doesn't mean he understands them," Frau Beier said.

Lips used a bookmark to mark where he was and shut the book. "What job?"

"The doctor is distracted by Frau Kastenmayerin's pregnancy, and is not giving his correspondence the attention it needs," Frau Beier said.

"You want me to go through Phillip's mail?"

"Only the letters that raise scientific concerns," Ursula Mittelhausen said. "I will continue to manage the business correspondence."

"But why me? Why not Hans? He knows much more about the new science than I do."

"Because someone has to run the laboratories while the doctor is distracted, and besides, your Latin is much better than mine."

"What is it I'm supposed to do?"

"It is a very difficult task," Ursula said. "Frau Beier or I would have sent Frau Hardesty a polite letter when she mistook the Sal Vin Betula for an up-time treatment for *impotentia coeundi*. The doctor saw an opportunity. You must take the doctor's place looking for opportunities."

"But how am I supposed to do that? How does

Phillip decide whether or not something is an opportunity or not?" Lips got three matching shrugs in reply.

"Now you see why I don't want the job," Hans said.

Lips had thought the letters asking about color Kirlian photography lacked any possible opportunity for the company, but he had passed them onto Phillip anyway. There had been a feeling, coming mostly from Dina, that anything that could distract Phillip had to be tried.

Phillip's reaction hadn't been what Lips had expected. Instead of intensifying the efforts to succeed with Autochrome, Phillip had decided to try to photograph Kirlian images with his special camera.

Lips had provided the hand for the image, and it was still stinging as he sat down in the projection room to see what the Kirlian image looked like.

It was a major disappointment. The screen was almost black. The only light showing on the screen was from scratches on the negatives. Phillip walked up to the image for a closer look. "Nothing! If we believed this image, we would be forced to conclude that your hand completely lacks an aura."

"Perhaps the camera was too far away to detect the discharges?"

Phillip studied the projected image for a few moments before shaking his head. "No, it seems my brilliant idea of using the three-color camera to record a Kirlian image has failed. We need to try something different."

Lips moved to the windows and pulled open the heavy drapes. "What about replacing the paper with the film?" he said over his shoulder.

"Well, the paper we left in the usual place to produce a Kirlian image for comparison purposes certainly recorded an image. But the film is just black and white, and we are trying to produce a color image."

"What if we used filters?"

"We have three filters, unless you are hoping to combine plates from three separate Kirlian images . . ."

Lips realized Phillip was thinking of registering problems. Unless the photos exactly overlapped, the image just wouldn't work, and layering the filters would just stop light getting through to the lower plates.

"No, Lips, what we need is plates sensitive to one or other of the primary colors."

"Isn't that what we're trying to do with the Autochrome?"

"Not quite. With the Autochrome, we are trying to make a single plate sensitive to each of the primary colors, whereas what I'm thinking is we sensitize three plates, each to a different color."

They tried it with glass negatives first, because that's what they had for the camera. But that hadn't worked. The glass was acting as an insulator, and only the top plate registered anything. That had meant an urgent order had to be sent out for some cellulose acetate sheet-film. Fortunately, there had been a photographer in Jena who had some.

Phillip held the last of the three still dripping negatives up to the red safe light, and smiled. "We have an image on all three sheets. Now all we have to do is sensitize each sheet of film to a different color."

"How are you planning on doing that?" Lips asked.

"We send an order to Michael for some sheet cellulose acetate that we can apply our own, custom, emulsions onto. And we experiment until we have three dyed plates that give us a color image."

March 1636, Jena

Lips arrived home from lectures to a surprise. The up-timer chemical engineer Phillip had been waiting for had finally arrived.

"Lips, this is Lori Drahuta, she'll be staying in the apartment while she decides whether or not she wants to work at HDG Laboratories," Hans said.

Lips looked enviously at the young woman. She was wearing fancy leather boots, blue jeans, a T-shirt with a fancy design on it, and a denim jacket. "Nice T-shirt.".

Lori looked down at the image of St. George defeating a wild dog on her T-shirt. "It's my own design."

"How do you get the image onto the material? Did you paint it?"

"You can, but this is silk-screen. I produced a number of them as a fund-raiser for the rabies awareness program."

That word sent a shiver through Lips. Rabies was a disease to be feared, even if the up-timers did have a treatment for it. "Is it the same as wood-block printing?"

"No. If you're interested, I can show you how it's done."

"Yes, please." Lips was definitely interested. He had visions of printing a T-shirt with the image of his hero. If he couldn't afford the jeans and jacket, he could at least afford a printed T-shirt.

✧   ✧   ✧

Lips had expected to dine alone, again. His brother was visiting friends, while Phillip was in Grantville with Dina, who'd given birth to a boy and a girl in the early hours of the twenty-ninth of February, and they were spending a few days in Grantville. Instead, he found the new girl sitting at the table. There was a moment of shock, then he remembered his duties as host. "Good evening, Frau Drahuta."

"Please, make it Lori. And what do I call you?"

"My name is Phillip, but family call me Lips, Lori."

"And I'm family?"

"We certainly hope you will join the family here at HDG Laboratories."

"Well, I hope I can fit in, although I was expecting to see Dr. Phil. Whoops!" Lori clapped her hands over her mouth. "Sorry, that just slipped out."

"I haven't heard that name for Phillip before. Where did you hear it?"

"Ted and Tracy Kubiak. Apparently Ted started it. But it's not a sign of disrespect, honest. It's just the American tendency to give people nicknames, and well, back up-time there was some guy on TV who went by the moniker of Dr. Phil."

"Dr. Phil." Lips tried it on his tongue. It came naturally. Almost more naturally than Phillip, and certainly much easier than Dr. Gribbleflotz, which, with his experience of up-timers, they would have found a bit of a tongue twister. "Why haven't I heard it before?"

"I think it's just a pet name for Dr. Gribbleflotz within a tight group in the Kubiak clan."

"Well, I think Phillip would be happy for you to call him Dr. Phil."

"I think I'll stick to Dr. Gribbleflotz until I get to know him better."

Late March 1636, Jena

Phillip, Dina, and the babies, Jon and Salome, had arrived back in Jena to a hideous surprise. Phillip's mother, recently widowed—again—had turned up. And she wasn't a very nice person. Lips had tried to send a message before Phillip left Grantville, but he'd just missed him. What should have been a joyous homecoming had been ruined by Maria Elisabeth Bombast von Neuburg.

Lips heard the heavy footsteps of Phillip's mother ringing through the apartment and tried to find somewhere to hide. Maria Elisabeth was an equal opportunity critic, and everybody was a legitimate target. Except for Lori Drahuta, who was an up-timer, and thus almost a noble.

Maria Elisabeth burst into the room in all her painted glory. Dressed in age-inappropriate colors and styles, and with enough white-lead on her face to sink one of the new ironclads, she was a sight to terrify even the bravest. Lips backed farther into the corner he'd found when Phillip's mother burst in. She looked angry, again.

"I don't know how I'm going to hold up my head," she said as she waved a letter under Phillip's nose. "Margaretha's Friedrich, such a hard working and successful boy, is now the personal alchemist to Ulrich of Ostfriesland." She glared at Phillip. "Why can't you have a noble patron?" she demanded. "Every great man needs a great patron, but not you, Theophrastus; you don't even have a patron. You are *self-employed*."

"I might be self-employed, but I am still a successful alchemist. And I am much more successful than Friedrich Weiser."

Lips nodded. That was telling her. The Great Stoner was probably the only alchemist in the world anywhere near as successful as Phillip.

"Friedrich Weiser is a graduate of Tübingen. He not only has a Baccalaureus Artium, but he also has his Magister Artium. What do you have? Nothing, that's what you have!"

"I have a doctorate," Phillip spat out.

Maria Elisabeth was not impressed. "A doctorate from some university in the United Provinces nobody has heard of does not compare with degrees from Tübingen. Why, Tübingen has Johannes Kepler and Wilhelm Schickard amongst their alumni. Who does your university have?"

Lips knew the answer to that one. Nobody. The institution awarding Phillip's degree hadn't existed until 1632.

"Kepler believed in astrology."

There was outrage in Phillip's voice. Although his great-grandfather, Paracelsus, had believed in astrology; Lips had heard him on the topic many times. Apparently the failure of astrologers to predict the arrival of Grantville had been enough for him to turn his back on something his great-grandfather had believed strongly in.

"He was imperial mathematician to Emperor Rudolph II, and if he was still living, would have the king of Bohemia as his patron." Suddenly Maria slapped Phillip.

It was no love tap; Phillip was knocked off balance. "You are a grave disappointment, Theophrastus. What would Grandfather think?"

Lips winced, not so much at the slap, but at the last bit of spleen Phillip's mother had vented before she stalked out. That had been a low blow. Paracelsus was Phillip's hero; to be a disappointment to Paracelsus . . . Lips hurried out to get Dina. Phillip needed serious comforting.

"Something has to be done about that . . ." Words failed Lips.

"Witch, bitch, cow," Lori suggested.

Lips smiled. You could always trust Lori to lighten the mood. "Take your pick, but something has to be done. She's making Phillip miserable."

"And she is upsetting Frau Kastenmayerin," Frau Mittelhausen said.

Lips hadn't noticed any conflict between Dina and Phillip's mother, but he wasn't surprised. The daughter of a poor pastor wasn't something she could boast about to her friends back in Neuburg.

"What about poison? I'm sure there are plenty of possibilities," Lori suggested.

"It's something to dream about, but it probably wouldn't work. I mean, lead oxide is supposed to be toxic, but you've seen how much she puts on."

"That's lead oxide? I thought it was zinc oxide. Maybe she hasn't been using it for long," Lori suggested.

"Phillip says she was painting her face with white lead even before he left to train in Augsburg," Lips said.

"Painting? She's putting the stuff on with a trowel by the looks of it. But you're right. If she hasn't gone down with lead poisoning after all this time, what chance is there for success with anything else?"

Christoph Seidel stood outside the HDG Laboratories facility just outside Jena and wondered just how he was supposed to persuade Dr. Gribbleflotz, the owner of the facility before him, to move to Prague to serve as King Venceslas V Adalbertus of Bohemia's personal aural investigator. Normally, such a question wouldn't arise. The social cachet of anyone treating the king would result in the rich and powerful beating a way to that practitioner's door, but Dr. Gribbleflotz wasn't normal. Money alone was not going to entice him to make the move; he had more than enough of it already.

To make a poor case even worse, neither the Catholic courtiers nor the Calvinist courtiers were likely to show much enthusiasm for the king introducing a close personal adviser of the Lutheran persuasion into the court. Again, normally that would be a minor problem, just as long as the doctor wasn't overly enthusiastic in his religion. However, Dr. Gribbleflotz had married a Lutheran pastor's daughter, and was therefore undoubtedly personally deeply religious.

"Run that past me again," Phillip told his visitor. "You are asking me to move to Prague to act as the King of Bohemia's aural investigator? Why me? Surely there are plenty of aural investigators already in Prague?"

Lips was busy holding on to his chair to stop himself jumping up and down. Here was the perfect opportunity for Phillip to finally silence his harping mother. He couldn't believe the polite boredom in Phillip's expression. He should be dancing on the table and swinging from the rafters, but no, he was just sitting there listening with polite disinterest.

"But none of them are able to do color." Christoph raised a hand and snapped his fingers. One of the servants who'd accompanied him stepped forward and opened a large leather bag before stepping back. Christoph started to stack bundles of USE paper money on the table. "One month's stipend in advance." Then he started on another pile. "And enough to cover your removal expenses."

Lips had virtually no experience of handling money, and certainly no experience with the quantities the man had just placed on Phillip's desk. However, he had learned how to estimate the mass of objects based on their size and composition. Each pile looked like half a kilogram of paper, and if the rest of the bills in the piles were the same denomination as those on the top, then each bundle represented fifty thousand dollars. He licked his suddenly dry lips. Even a small part of one of those piles would be enough to buy the clothes of his dreams.

"I must consult my wife," Phillip said.

Lips wasn't the only shocked face in the room when Phillip walked out. There was a hundred thousand dollars on that desk and Phillip had completely ignored it. Well, Lips knew his job as host in Phillip's absence. "Would you like some refreshments while we await Dr. Gribbleflotz's return?"

"I don't understand," Lori protested. "I thought Dr. Phil didn't believe in Kirlian image interpretation."

Lips glanced over at Hans, who'd been sticking to the up-timer like glue. He'd jerked back, making protection from evil hand-signs. Lips settled for gently shaking his head and looking very disappointed, very much like one of his teachers when he'd failed to grasp a concept.

"Well, that's what he told me," Lori said, gesturing to Hans. "And now you're saying he's planning to drop everything he's got going here in Jena and high-tail it to Prague to be the personal aural investigator to some king. How can he do that if he doesn't believe in it?"

"HDG Laboratories will continue to operate. Hans will still be here, and my brother Martin will take over Frau Mittelhausen's job of running the commercial side of the business."

"Still," Lori said, "why would he want to give all this up to move to Prague?"

"Frau Bombast," Hans said.

Lips nodded. "That's right, Phillip's mother. It's especially attractive because the king who is employing Phillip used to employ Johannes Kepler. And more importantly, when he employed Kepler he was only a general, but now, of course, he is a king."

"What's so important about working for a king?" Lori asked.

"Herr Weiser's patron is merely a graf," Hans said.

"Oh, one-upmanship and social climbing, I wouldn't have thought Dr. Phil was overly interested in doing that."

"And you'd be right," Lips said. "However, his mother is. All will be forgiven if her son has a king for a patron, and more importantly, Frau Bombast will return home a happy woman," Lips said.

"It seems a bit extreme just to get rid of one woman," Lori said.

"Frau Bombast is no ordinary woman. Almost anything is to be considered when the reward is getting rid of that female," Hans said.

"How long do you think it'll take before she finds out?" Lori asked.

"Not very long," Hans said. "Someone, who shall remain nameless, but is in this room, escorted Herr Seidel's party to the inn where Frau Bombast is residing."

Lips modestly burnished his nails. That had been a brainwave. No doubt the men would talk about their purpose in Jena. "The story should be all around the city by morning."

"Well, if it is, you'd better be ready to reassure all the people who depend on Dr. Phil," Lori said. "They'll probably worry that the business will shut down if he isn't here."

That was something Lips hadn't thought of. He rose from the table. "I'd better have a few words with Frau Mittelhausen. She'll probably send a few of the girls shopping."

"How does sending some of the girls shopping reassure anybody?" Lori demanded.

"Women gossip," Lips said, before hastily leaving the room.

Next day

Lips made sure he had a prime spot when Frau Bombast, as expected, stormed in on the family without knocking. Fortunately, her heavy-footed stride gave them some warning.

"What is this I hear?" Maria Elisabeth Bombast demanded in her most strident voice.

Phillip appeared calm as he finished chewing the food in his mouth, took a sip of herbal tea, and finally smiled at his mama as he lowered his cup. "What is it you've heard, Mama Dearest?"

"I wish you wouldn't call me that, Theophrastus. You know I don't like it."

"Of course, Mama Dearest. Now, what is it that brings you visiting at such an early hour?"

But Maria Elisabeth had been distracted. She pointed an accusing finger at Dina. "Why is she suckling that child? The wife of a king's advisor should have a wet nurse."

"I haven't signed the contract yet."

Maria Elisabeth turned, aghast. "Not signed it yet? You can't be thinking of refusing to enter a king's service? You wouldn't do that to your poor mama. How will I be able to hold up my head when I return home?"

Success, she was going home. "I'm sure Phillip has every intention of signing, Frau Bombast," Lips said. "However, it is only sensible to have a lawyer check the contract first."

A *few days later*

Lips stared at the money being counted out in front of him. "What is that for?" he asked.

"It is your pay for handling Dr. Gribbleflotz's correspondence," Frau Mittelhausen said.

He licked his lips and carefully counted the USE bank bills for himself to reassure himself just how much was there. In his mind's eye he could see a shop in Grantville, with blue jeans, T-shirt, and a leather jacket.

"Don't spend it all at once, Lips. That has to last you until next month," Frau Mittelhausen warned.

That did surprise Lips. He hadn't expected to get paid for doing Phillip's correspondence, and now that Phillip was no longer distracted by Dina's pregnancy, surely he wouldn't continue to do it. "I won't."

"But I bet he knows what he wants to spend some of it on," Lori said.

A smile twitched at Lips' lips. "I want some blue jeans, and a leather jacket, and . . ." memory failed him. He couldn't remember everything his screen hero had worn in that movie.

"If you want to buy jeans, I might be able to help."

"I don't want girl's jeans," Lips protested.

"Don't worry. I wasn't going to offer you any of mine, but there's bound to be someone in my family about your size who could use the money. Do you have any particular style in mind?"

Lips hadn't realized jeans came in different styles. He shrugged.

"Well, you must have an idea. Where did you see the ones you like?"

"It was in a movie," Lips admitted.

Lori shook her head. "It's like pulling teeth. What movie?"

"Rebel without a Cause."

"Ahhhh! You see yourself as James Dean." Lori nodded. "You'll need a haircut. I don't suppose anybody is making hair cream, are they?"

"Hair cream?"

April 1636, Prague

Phillip burst into the kitchen still in dishabille, brandishing a collar. "I can't wear this. I'm supposed to be meeting the king."

"What is wrong with the collar, Doctor?" Frau Mittelhausen asked.

"The starch is showing." Phillip showed where white particles of starch showed up against the brilliant lime-green fabric. "I can't wear that to see the king. Why hasn't the laundry been using dyed starch?"

"Let me see what I can do." Frau Mittelhausen grabbed the collar and disappeared.

Lips studied Phillip. His brother-in-law was resplendent in a doublet and knee breeches, with silk stockings and short boots. That was basically the standard garb for meeting important people, however, Phillip had gone to town in his choice of colors. The doublet was an interesting shade of red, with an under-shirt in lime green visible through the slashed sleeves. The stockings were a pale pink, and the boots, well, there was no single dominant color. Lori Drahuta would have broken down laughing at the sight, but Lips was already aware that the colors, if not Phillip's combinations, were starting to be seen around Prague.

Frau Mittelhausen arrived back with the repaired collar and fitted it around Phillip's neck. Seconds later they were left in peace.

"What is dyed starch?" Frau Mittelhausen asked.

"It's from the Autochrome experiments, Frau Mittelhausen. Phillip has been trying to rediscover how the up-timers made color photographs using dyed starch particles scattered randomly over a photographic plate." Suddenly Lips' thought process kicked him. "Frau Mittelhausen, is white starch on collars much of a problem?"

"Only on colored collars. Oh!"

Lips nodded. Frau Mittelhausen had reached the same conclusion he had. White starch on white collars wouldn't be a problem, but with people copying Phillip and buying colored collars, surely they too were having problems with the white starch ruining the desired effect. He rose from his chair. "If you need me, I'll be in the laboratory doing some research."

"I'll get you some old collars to experiment with."

May 1636, Prague

Lips sat watching Phillip pacing around his laboratory in the Mihulka Tower. He'd been acting strangely since he returned from his latest meeting with the king.

"What's bothering you, Phillip?" he asked.

"Dr. Stone agrees that the king's aura is blue," Phillip muttered.

"But that's impossible, isn't it?"

"I thought so. I thought that Kurt Beta's Kirlian image interpretation ideas were impossible, but if Dr. Stone says the king's aura is blue, just like the color Kirlian image suggests, then that means Kirlian image interpretation is a valid science." He paused to correct himself. "More correctly, it is a poor cousin to the real Science of *Chakras*."

"What are chakras?"

Phillip sent Lips a wry grin. "I'm not overly sure myself. It seems to be some technique that only

Dr. Stone and his assistant, Guptah Rai Singh, are familiar with."

"Are you going to ask him to speak about the chakras at one of your seminars?"

"In the fullness of time, when I have had a chance to learn more about them myself. But meanwhile, I have a problem. If aural investigating is valid science, then I may have given up on invigorating the Quinta Essentia of the human humors with pyramid power too soon."

"I wonder what Dr. Stone knows about pyramid power?" Lips asked.

"I can't ask the Great Stoner about pyramid power. No, I'll just have to recommence my research based on the new information."

Lips left Phillip to his ruminating and retired to the library, where he dug out the latest copy of the *Grantville Genealogy Club's Who's Who of Grantville Up-timers*, and spent a fruitless couple of hours looking for someone named Guptah Rai Singh.

A *few days later*

Lips was in the laboratory furthering his experiments with dyed starch and starched collars when Phillip walked in.

"What's that you've got there?"

"Dyed starch for collars, Phillip. Nobody in Prague has been doing any research on dyed starch, so I thought I'd try it."

"And does it work?"

"Oh, yes." Lips held up a dyed collar. "This is

just experimenting in different shades. Thomas has a production line going, and we're already selling it in the Dr. Gribbleflotz Emporium of Natural Wonders."

"I don't think the store was a good idea," Phillip muttered.

"But why not? It's doing amazing business."

"Because someone showed the king one of Paxton's posters."

"I hope he wasn't offended?"

"No, much worse," Phillip said. "The king would like me to develop color photography."

"Ouch, did you tell him about the problems we are having with Autochrome?"

"One does not tell one's patron more than he needs to know. Besides, a patron is never interested in problems; a patron is only ever interested in results."

Lips brushed Phillip's patronizing hand from the top of his head. "So we get back to work on Autochrome?"

"No, we have left Hans working hard on that problem back in Jena. If he, with the resources at his command, hasn't discovered the solution yet, then the two of us working together won't succeed. No, we need to think outside the box."

"What is it the king wants?"

"The king wants to be able to take a photograph of his son and hang it across from his bed."

"What about doing what Schmucker and Schwentzel do and just make printing plates?"

Phillip reached out a patronizing hand again, but Lips managed to avoid it. "Okay, what did I say wrong this time?" he asked.

"One pleases one's patron not by replicating what has already been done, but by creating new and different things that he can show off. The printing process Schmucker and Schwentzel use is well known, and so not sufficiently impressive. What we need is something completely different."

"But there are only so many ways to lay colors onto a surface to produce a color image."

"The king doesn't know that. We only have to have something sufficiently different from everything else that it has the appearance of being unique."

Lips chewed over what Phillip was saying. He fingered the T-shirt he was wearing, and suddenly had an idea. "Phillip, are you familiar with staining slides so that cells are more visible under a microscope?"

"I've read about it, but never done it."

"Well I have, in some classes in Grantville I sneaked into. You use dyes to stain the cells and various parts hold more or less dye so that you can see everything a lot better. Could I try something?"

"Of course."

Lips made up some gelatin and poured a little into several watch-glasses. Then he added a different dye to each watch glass. Finally, he painted a design on several blank glass photographic plates, using one color per plate. When they dried he stacked them and held them up against the light.

"Very nice, now how do you paint a photographic image onto the plates?" Phillip asked.

"We don't, we photo-transfer the images. Lori showed me how to do it when she taught me how to silk-screen print. What images do we have in three-color?"

"Just the spectral lines, but I'm sure Dina would be happy to have a photograph of her and the twins."

A *few days later*

Lips shivered as he paced around the room. Phillip had been gone for hours. Surely it didn't take this long to show the king the new Gribblechrome, as they'd decided to call their new process. He pulled his leather jacket closer round his body.

"You wouldn't be so cold if you changed into something more suitable," Dina said.

He glared at his sister. Yes, his blue jeans, T-shirt, and leather jacket weren't really warm enough in this room—why they couldn't have central heating like they had in Jena he didn't know—but what price comfort when he could look like James Dean? He ran a hand through his closely cropped locks. "Phillip should have been back ages ago."

"He's dealing with a king, Lips. Kings work to their own schedule. He might not even have seen Phillip yet."

"Frau Kastenmayerin," Frau Mittelhausen called as she burst into the room, "the doctor, they've just carried him home on a stretcher."

Dina erupted from her chair and ran off. Lips followed.

"Can you tell me what has happened?" Lips asked the man who'd accompanied the royal guardsmen who'd brought Phillip home.

"I'm not really sure myself, Herr Kastenmayer. You have to understand, I wasn't there when it happened. However, it seems Dr. Gribbleflotz has been putting his health at considerable risk caring for the king. Dr. Stone's assistant saved Dr. Gribbleflotz by performing emergency surgery to remove a *Mishawaka*."

Lips wanted to ask what a Mishawaka was, but there were more important questions to ask. "Is the doctor going to be all right?"

"Oh, yes, Dr. Stone was most definite. The emergency surgery has removed the problem, although Dr. Gribbleflotz should be allowed to rest for several days."

"How long will it be before the anesthesia wears off, do you know?" Lips asked, wondering what sort of pain Phillip was likely to be suffering.

"There was no anesthesia. Actually, although there was a lot of blood, there appears to be no wound. A most amazing piece of surgery."

Lips barely noticed when Christoph Seidel left. He was deep in thought, and his thoughts weren't pretty. Something was wrong here. He needed the opinion of an up-timer he knew and trusted. That meant writing Lori a letter.

A week later and Lips had a reply, and it reinforced his disquiet over what had happened in the king's chamber. Phillip hadn't been able to tell him much. He'd just shown the king the Gribblechrome of Dina and the babies when Dr. Stone and his assistant—the assistant who wasn't listed in the list of up-timers—had burst in saying something about his chakras fluctuating so dangerously the effect could be felt in the antechambers. Then there had been the surgery. Phillip had been adamant that Guptah Rai Singh had pulled something out of his body, even though there was no wound, or even a magically quickly healed scar.

Lori had called it "psychic surgery," and Lips had been left in no doubt she didn't approve. Corrupt fakery was amongst the more polite terms she had used to describe it. Which raised the question of why would Dr. Stone fake not only an illness—if fake surgery could cure a problem, surely the problem had to be fake—but also a cure?

Frau Mittelhausen appeared at the door to the office Lips was occupying. "A gentleman to see you."

Lips shot to his feet. He wasn't used to greeting anyone Frau Mittelhausen would class as a gentleman. The man who was guided in was a shock. Lips instantly recognized him as the king's private secretary—although he'd heard that Heinrich Niemann was the king's secretary the same as Frau Mittelhausen had been Phillip's housekeeper. The title didn't adequately describe just how much responsibility either of them had.

"Herr Niemann, how can I be of assistance?"

"I wish to convey the king's regrets for Dr. Gribbleflotz's illness and discuss a reward suitable for the risks Dr. Gribbleflotz has taken in caring for the king's health. I do hope the good doctor is recovering?"

"Yes, Dr. Gribbleflotz is almost fully recovered. Please, have a seat. Can I get anything for you? Tea, coffee?"

"Could I have a Tincture of Cacao?"

Behind Heinrich, Lips saw Frau Mittelhausen nod. "Yes, that will be possible. Could I have one too, please, Frau Mittelhausen?" Lips returned to his chair behind the desk. "Did the king like the Gribblechrome?"

"Yes, he was most impressed. And to get a result so quickly after making the request! Most impressive."

Lips clamped down on his tongue before he could say the first thing that entered his head. This was the client he was dealing with, not Phillip, or even one of the people who attended his seminars. Instead he smiled and shrugged. "Sometimes everything just comes together like that."

"The king wishes to know how long it will be before Dr. Gribbleflotz will be able to create a Gribblechrome of his wife and son?"

"If we don't ask too much of the doctor, I'm sure we could start the process any time His Majesty is ready. It will then take but three days to produce a finished Gribblechrome."

Heinrich nodded sagely. "Then there is just the matter of a suitable reward for Dr. Gribbleflotz. Before he took ill the doctor was talking about his Society for Improving Natural Knowledge by Experimentation, and how they swapped ideas about the new sciences."

Lips nodded. He knew all about Phillip's group of natural philosophers. They spent half their time arguing over the most insignificant detail in the methodology of experiments they demonstrated.

"His Majesty believes that it would be beneficial to have a group of scientists keeping abreast of the latest developments in science and technology, and has decided that he will become patron of Dr. Gribbleflotz's society, awarding it a royal charter. Funds and facilities will be provided to the society to conduct scientific experiments on anything the members wish, as long as the members are always available to advise the king on scientific matters. Do you feel Dr. Gribbleflotz would be interested in being the society's president?"

"I believe Dr. Gribbleflotz would be most happy with such an offer."

"Good, very good. And, of course, as Dr. Gribbleflotz would be the premier scientist in Bohemia, he will be awarded doctorates by the universities of Bohemia."

"Prague, and the new university funded by Herr Roth?"

Heinrich smiled. "Actually, I was thinking of Prague and Olmütz, but I'm sure Herr Roth would feel offended if his new university wasn't invited to similarly honor Dr. Gribbleflotz."

After an hour of discussion, Lips escorted Herr Niemann back to his portion of the palace. He stopped at a window and stared out on the street. Revenge was going to be sweet, even if Phillip never knew he was getting revenge. He wondered how Dr. Stone would react to receiving an invitation to present a seminar on the chakras to the Royal Academy of Science in Prague, signed by the academy's president for life, Dr. Phillip Theophrastus Gribbleflotz.

Chapter 20

Dr. Phil and the Philosopher Stone

May 1636, Prague, Bohemia

Phillip Theophrastus Gribbleflotz rose from his sick-bed after being confined to it for several days. He'd been extremely lucky that Herr Dr. Tom Stone and his associate, Herr Guptah Rai Singh, had been in the palace and able to perform emergency surgery to remove a *Mishawaka*. At least he thought it was a *Mishawaka* that had been removed. It might have been a *Sheboygan*. Phillip wasn't sure. He'd been in rather a distressed state at the time. According to Herr Singh, Phillip's chakras had been fluctuating extremely dangerously, life threateningly dangerously.

He lifted his nightshirt and carefully examined the area of his abdomen where Herr Singh had operated. There had been lots of blood at the time, but there was no detectable scar. Phillip dropped his nightshirt and reached for the pen and paper that were always within arm's reach. Then he tried to remember and record everything that had happened that fateful day.

He'd visited King Venceslas V Adalbertus, his royal patron, to show him the progress he was making in rediscovering the lost up-time art of color photography. He'd been showing Wallenstein an image he'd produced using the new Gribblechrome process. The king had been impressed, and had just been about to say something when the doors burst open and Herr Dr. Stone and Herr Singh had charged in, saying Phillip's life was in danger.

There had been a wand. Phillip was sure of that. Or maybe it'd been a medical flashlight—he'd seen one Frau Dr. Shipley used when she was examining Dina during her pregnancy. He made a note. Then there had been a crystal. Herr Dr. Stone had passed that over his body as if it was a detector of some description. Something in his abdomen had responded by glowing, and Herr Singh had operated using just his bare hands. Phillip wondered what had happened to whatever he'd pulled out of his body. He made a note to ask.

For someone who'd been so close to death, Phillip felt remarkably well. Whatever Herr Dr. Stone and Herr Singh had done had certainly healed the problem. He was a little shaky on his feet after so long confined to his bed, but he managed to get to the nightstand and pour enough water into the basin to wash before dressing.

"Phillip! You should be in bed," Dina Kastenmayerin cried when Phillip appeared at the kitchen door.

"I'm perfectly okay, Dina," he assured his wife as

he fell into a chair at the table and looked around hopefully. It was a kitchen, after all, and he was hungry. "Is there anything to eat?"

"I'll make some gruel," Dina offered.

"No!" Phillip cried out. "I need something more substantial. Meat, bread, fruit..." As he ran down the food groups Phillip was becoming more and more desperate to find something his wife would allow him to eat that wasn't gruel. "Vegetables?"

Frau Ursula Mittelhausen, Phillip's trusted housekeeper, came to his aid, and placed a plate laden with bread and cold meat before him.

"Ursula!" Dina protested.

"The doctor needs to rebuild his strength now he's well enough to leave his bed."

Phillip nodded his head in agreement as he chewed mightily on his first real food in days. He swallowed his current mouthful and tried to catch up on events. "Has anything interesting happened while I was ill?"

"The king has decided to create a Royal Academy of Science," Dina answered.

Phillip nodded. He wasn't surprised. "The king has been most interested in my Society for Improving Natural Knowledge by Experimentation, and talked of creating a similar organization of his own." Now he had been reminded about that discussion, he also remembered the king talking about funding for his new society. Phillip paused to think about what he could do with some of that money, and wondered who he'd have to sweet-talk to get some of it. "Who's he putting in charge?"

"Actually, Phillip." Dina paused to put a smile on her face. "The king wants you to be the president of his royal academy."

For a few seconds Phillip was entranced by the idea of being president of the king's royal academy, but then reality hit. A moment ago he'd been wondering who he'd have to sweet-talk into giving him some of the academy's funds. Now he had a mental image of a line of hopefuls awaiting their opportunity to sweet-talk him into funding their pet projects from the academy's coffers. He'd have no time for his own research. He'd have to delegate. He cast hopeful glances towards Dina and Ursula.

"Frau Mittelhausen, how would you like to handle the day-to-day business of the Royal Academy?"

Ursula shook her head. "I'm sorry, Doctor, but I already have too much to do with running the laboratory here in Prague."

"And I have the twins to look after," Dina said.

"Lips..." Phillip suggested, thinking of Dina's young half-brother who was doing so well in the business.

"Too young for most to accept, and besides, he has no reputation," Ursula said.

Dina had made a name for herself when she published her pamphlet "What Wives Should Know About Marital Health and Vigor" last year. And anyone who had ever dealt with HDG Laboratories would know Frau Mittelhausen's reputation for getting things done. Nobody outside the business knew the value of seventeen-year-old Lips' contributions to his various research projects. It had been Lips who'd developed the colored starch for collars, but it was sold as a Gribbleflotz product. For a moment Phillip felt guilty about gaining all the glory, but he quickly moved on to more important things.

"Who can we get to run the academy that everyone will accept?" Phillip asked.

"Maybe Martin knows of someone," Dina suggested.

Dina's brother, Martin Kastenmayer, had been left to run the HDG Laboratories facility in Jena and to supervise the various off-shoot facilities in Grantville and Halle. He was an educated young man, as all of the Kastenmayer boys were, and he had a number of useful contacts. "I will write him a letter," Phillip announced.

Jena, a few days later

Martin Kastenmayer finished reading the letter from Dr. Gribbleflotz aloud and tossed it onto the table, where it was immediately grabbed by Hans Saltzman, the twenty-one-year-old senior alchemist at the HDG Laboratories Jena facility. "Any suggestions?" Martin asked of the people around the table—Hans; the up-timer chemical engineer Lori Drahuta; and his wife, Hieronyma Ableidinger.

"Would the Ram know anybody?" Hans asked.

Martin winced and sent Hieronyma an apologetic smile for the insulting reference to her brother, the head of the Franconian Ram movement. "His name is Constantin," he told Hans. "But you're right. He does correspond with a large pool of people who might know of someone suitable."

"Is John Pell still teaching in Grantville?" Lori asked. "I understand he's someone big in the mathematics community. Maybe he knows someone."

"It won't hurt to write to both Constantin and John Pell," Martin said.

June 1636, Amsterdam

John Pell had known someone suitable and he'd immediately written back recommending his old principal from his days at the Chichester Academy.

In his lodgings in Amsterdam, Samuel Hartlib carefully placed the letter from Martin Kastenmayer on the dresser beside his bed and started to dress.

"It won't just go away if you ignore it, Samuel," his wife Marie said from the bed. "We can't go on living like this." She gestured around the room the whole family was packed into. "And your brothers and my family can't continue to subsidize us."

"If only the up-timer encyclopedias didn't link me to Cromwell we could return to London," Samuel complained.

"But they do, and it hasn't been safe for you to be in England since the up-timers broke Cromwell out of the Tower. And all for a mere one hundred pounds a year."

That one hundred pounds a year was the pension the encyclopedias said Cromwell was supposed to pay Samuel in appreciation for his efforts to improve agriculture. "A hundred pounds a year would be useful right now," Samuel muttered incautiously.

"And that's precisely why you should be jumping at the opportunity to become secretary of King Venceslas V Adalbertus' new Royal Academy of Science in Prague!" Marie snapped. "They are offering over two hundred pounds a year, and a house. You do remember what a house is, don't you?" she asked sarcastically. "We used to have one back in London. You know the sort of thing. A place with rooms for the children and us. A study for you, and a proper dining room..."

Once started Marie could go on complaining for hours. She was from well to do stock, and had married the son of a wealthy dye merchant. She didn't think she should have to live in a single room apartment. In an attempt to stop her before she was in full flow his returned to his great lament. "But I'd be subordinate to Dr. Phillip Theophrastus Gribbleflotz."

"The Aspirin King himself," Marie said. "What's so wrong with being subordinate to such a successful man?"

"But he's a..." Samuel tried to remember what his friend John Dury had heard about Dr. Gribbleflotz during his time in Thuringia five years ago. The words "fraud" and "charlatan" had been mentioned. There was even a rumor that he hadn't been a real doctor. "He wasn't entitled to call himself a doctor back in 1631," he said finally.

"But he was awarded a doctorate by the University of Amsterdam in early 1632. You've got your own copies of his dissertation and the proceedings of the debates."

"Yes, but..."

"He is now a doctor, with a doctorate from Amsterdam, agreed?" Samuel nodded glumly. "Right, so, forget your objections and think of the money. Think of what it would mean for the children to be brought up in a real house. And if that's not enough, think of what it would mean for your dream of founding an institution of investigation and learning. You won't have to found one. It's being handed to you on a silver platter."

Samuel winced. Everything Marie was saying was true, but... "Dr. Gribbleflotz believes in Kirlian aura interpretation," he said in a last ditch attempt to justify his ambivalence.

Marie snorted. "That's not the impression I got from his writings in the *Proceedings of the HDG Laboratories.*"

"But he is King Venceslas V Adalbertus' personal Kirlian aura interpreter."

"That doesn't mean he believes in it," Marie said. She cast a scornful look Samuel's way. "How many people get to have royal patronage? Do you think they all believe in what they are saying? Did Kepler really believe in astrology when he was imperial mathematician to Emperor Rudolph II? Or was supplying readings the price of the emperor's patronage?"

Samuel sighed. There were problems with having an educated wife. They had this horrible tendency to argue about things they shouldn't understand. "The planetary motions Kepler observed..."

"Have no correlation to predictions of personal events or actions. I'm sorry." She didn't sound sorry. "But Dr. Gribbleflotz wrote that he recreated the up-time process of Kirlian imaging in an attempt to detect activity in an experiment that was invisible to the human eye. He can't be held responsible for what other people do with it."

Samuel had been married to Marie for over seven years. He knew when to surrender, and about now would be a very good time to change the subject. "I think I need to talk to someone who has actually met Dr. Gribbleflotz."

Marie took the bait and nodded her head vigorously.

"Your friend, Nicolaes Tulp, the *Praelector Anatomiae* at the Amsterdam Guild of Surgeons, would surely have been present when Dr. Gribbleflotz presented his dissertation and debated it. Especially as it was the very first doctorate the new University of Amsterdam awarded."

Marie was left in the room to contemplate what they'd been reduced to. Once upon a time, when they were first married, they'd had a fine home, with fine friends. However, things had changed since the coming of the up-timers. London had ceased to be a safe place. First, there had been the efforts the king made to round up the people responsible for his execution up-time, but much worse had been the plague brought into the city by the mercenaries Charles filled the city with. Things had been bad for a while, and they'd only gotten worse after the queen was killed and the king injured in a carriage accident. In the winter of 1634-35 the family had hastily gathered what they could and taken passage to Amsterdam on a fishing boat out of Harwich. They had cleared the port just as a company of soldiers arrived.

She climbed out of bed and checked the children. Young Samuel was awake, and huddled up in a ball. Marie gently nudged Sam until he opened his eyes.

"I don't like it here. When can we go home, Mama?"

She sighed. How did one explain politics to a six-year-old? "Your Papa is looking to take a job in Prague. You'll like it there," she said hopefully. At least there shouldn't be the same risk of plague. "You'll be able to play outside again, and you'll have your own room." And she'd have people to talk to. Adult people,

people who had at least two thoughts to rub together, not like some of the women she was currently forced to associate with. She pulled Sam into her arms and started to sing to him.

Samuel was shown straight to Nicolaes' office when he called.

"How can I help you, my good friend?" Nicolaes asked as he guided Samuel into his office.

"I have been invited to apply for the position of secretary to the new Royal Academy of Science the king of Bohemia has chartered. However, the academy's president is to be none other than Dr. Phillip Theophrastus Gribbleflotz himself, and I would be working under him."

"A royal academy of science? In Bohemia? With Phillip in charge? Our Phillip to be president of a royal academy. I wonder how he managed that. Well, the Lord moves in mysterious ways, his wonders to achieve. And he wants you to work as his secretary? Congratulations," Nicolaes said.

"Phillip? You know him well enough to call him by his Christian name? Does that mean you have met him?"

"Ah, well. No, I've never met him," Nicolaes dissembled. "But I have corresponded with him, and the University of Amsterdam is proud to claim him as an alumnus, and as the recipient of the very first doctorate we awarded."

Samuel sighed. "I am trying to get the measure of the man and I had hoped that you might have met Dr. Gribbleflotz when he visited Amsterdam to present and debate his dissertation."

Nicolaes blushed. It was an honest to goodness blush. Samuel couldn't understand what he could have said to so embarrass his friend. "I don't suppose you could introduce me to any of the people who did debate the dissertation with Dr. Gribbleflotz?"

Nicolaes coughed several times. Way more than a normal man would need to clear his throat. "Unfortunately, none of the original debaters survived the siege," he said.

It sounded to Samuel like Nicolaes was apologizing for the unfortunate deaths of the debaters, but why would he do that? Surely the deaths weren't his fault. "That is most unfortunate, as I'd hoped to better understand the nature of the man by talking to someone who had met him."

"I'm sorry, but I can't help you. There is nobody I know of in Amsterdam who has visited Dr. Gribbleflotz in Jena. And of course, he was a relative nobody when he visited Amsterdam to present and debate his dissertation, so nobody would have particularly noticed him back then."

"Except for the people who he talked to at the university," Samuel suggested hopefully. Except that Nicolaes was shaking his head. "They're all dead?" he asked in disbelief.

"Dead or moved on," Nicolaes said. "Remember, Phillip's visit was before the siege, and thousands of people fled ahead of the invading Spanish, many of whom have yet to return. Your best bet might to be to visit Jena and ask around there, although I wouldn't expect to get an unbiased opinion from anybody at the university."

That wouldn't surprise Samuel. From something John

Dury had said he had the feeling there was bad blood between Dr. Gribbleflotz and the University of Jena.

July 1636, Jena

Samuel and Marie stood outside the gates of the HDG Laboratories facility just outside the walls of the city of Jena and stared openmouthed at the buildings.

"It must be as big as the university," Marie said.

"Bigger," Samuel said with some confidence, as he'd counted his paces as they walked from the corner to the central entry.

"Why do you think the facility has to be so large?"

"Ask me an easy question, Marie. Just a moment, there's someone approaching the gate. Maybe they can answer some questions."

The young man he'd spotted was dressed most peculiarly. He looked like a rat. A pale-blue rat. Samuel guided Marie through the open gate and called out to the man. "Excuse me, do you work here?"

Matthias Knupe stood up straight and puffed out his thin chest. "Yes, I am an HDG Laboratories apprentice laborant. How may I be of assistance?"

"I'm looking for Herr Kastenmayer."

"Which one?" Matthias asked. "We have several of the Frau Doctor's brothers living here."

Samuel pulled out his letter and consulted it. "Herr Martin Kastenmayer."

"The managing director." Matthias glanced up at the HDG Laboratories' clock tower. "He should still be in his office, if you would like to follow me."

"But weren't you heading somewhere?" Marie asked.

Matthias waved away the question. "Just the game, but there's plenty of time to escort you to the MD's office before they start."

Samuel took Marie's hand and they followed the youth. They had to be careful not to step on the rat-tail of the youth's costume.

Matthias poked his head into an office and called out. "A couple to see the MD."

"Do they have a name?" a voice called from within.

Matthias turned back to Samuel and Marie. "Who do I say is calling?"

Samuel shook his head at the outrageous behavior and advanced to the door. "Samuel and Marie Hartlib. It's about the job of secretary of the Royal Academy of Science in Prague."

There was a screech of wood on wood as a chair was pushed along a floor and Martin Kastenmayer appeared at the door. "Herr Hartlib, Frau Hartlib, please come in." He glanced at Matthias, frowned at him, then sent him on his way.

"Who was that strange youth?" Marie asked.

"That was Matthias Knupe, and he's not really that strange. He just happens to be the team mascot."

"You have a rat as a team mascot?" Samuel asked.

Martin nodded. "The team is the Jena Lab Rats, so naturally, the mascot has to be a rat. There's a female soccer team in Grantville that call themselves Brillo's Beauties, and . . ."

"They have someone dressed up as Brillo the ram," Marie suggested.

"Only when they can't persuade Frau Richards to let them borrow the real Brillo, which is any away game."

"Brillo, I've heard of the ram, and the woman with the merino sheep and angora rabbits. I'd like to talk with her about agricultural development."

"If you want to talk agriculture, you'll also want to talk to her husband, the chairman of the Department of Agriculture," Martin said. "I can arrange an introduction."

"Thank you, I'd appreciate that."

"Samuel," Marie muttered, "the job."

That brought Samuel down to earth. They weren't destitute, yet, but accommodation in Jena wasn't cheap, and a trip to Grantville was bound to be expensive. Samuel turned his attention to Martin. "About the job . . ."

"If you want it, it's yours. You come highly recommended, and I've read the encyclopedia articles about you. Samuel Hartlib, educational and agricultural reformer and tireless advocate of universal education. You sound perfect for the position. Do you have somewhere to stay while you're in Jena? If you like, the doctor's apartment is empty, and you're welcome to stay there until you're ready to leave for Prague."

Common courtesy demanded that Samuel didn't throw his arms around Martin and hug him for the offer that would save them a lot of money. Dignity demanded that he be polite, so he was only mildly enthusiastic in his acceptance of the offer. Marie, being a woman, didn't worry about her dignity. She did hug Martin, and her repeated uttering of "thank you, thank you" would have left the man in no doubt as to their financial situation.

"If you've read the articles about me, you'll have noticed that the pension Oliver Cromwell paid my alternative self was three hundred pounds," Samuel suggested hopefully.

Martin gently fought his way free of Marie. "Yes, but it was initially only one hundred pounds, and in later years, when it was increased to three hundred pounds, it seems to have fallen into arrears." He smiled to show he hadn't taken offense. "I believe the house being provided will make up for any deficiency between the remuneration offered by the academy and whatever Oliver Cromwell paid."

Prague

They spent just over a month in Thuringia, mostly because of the required waiting period after the family was vaccinated against smallpox, typhoid, and tetanus, but Samuel got to visit a lot of people involved in education and agriculture. Then they started the long journey to Prague. They stopped off for a couple of days in Halle so Samuel could examine the HDG Laboratories oil of vitriol facility, and spent a few days exploring Magdeburg before taking the steam ferry on the first leg of their journey to Prague.

Samuel was amazed at how he was received. The Doctor, Phillip Theophrastus Gribbleflotz himself, welcomed him into the palace. Samuel glanced over at Marie to see how she was taking the down-grade from a promised house to just a mere apartment in a distant wing of the royal palace. She appeared happy. Although part of that might be the group of women, including the doctor's wife, gathered around her and the children.

While Marie and the children were carried off, Samuel was led into Dr. Gribbleflotz's office. Well, study might be a better description, as it was clearly a place of study. There was a whole wall of books—more books than Samuel had seen in a private home before. There was also a small chemistry laboratory in one corner, with its very own fume hood. The only thing lacking was one of the latest aqualators.

Samuel unloaded the brochures he'd collected, or had thrust upon him by just about everyone he'd met from Grantville to Magdeburg. "I was given these to examine," he told Dr. Gribbleflotz and Lips, yet another of the Kastenmayer brothers, who seemed to be some kind of assistant to Dr. Gribbleflotz.

Lips grabbed the pile and skimmed through it, sorting the stack into several piles. He stopped with one brochure and looked up. "Phillip. You have to get one of these," he said, waving the brochure.

"What is it?" Phillip asked.

"The Wetmore 3S. It's a programmable scientific aqualator, with a card reader. The academy really has to have one." Lips turned towards Samuel. "Have you seen one?"

Samuel nodded. "I was invited to inspect the Wetmore factory in Magdeburg, where I was shown aqualators being made. I was also privileged enough to be shown the new aqualator they are working on." He leaned closer to whisper, "a proper computer."

"Oh! Wow! Now that would be great. Phillip, you really need to encourage research into fluidic computing."

"That will be up to Herr Hartlib, Lips. Now, Samuel—I may call you Samuel?" Samuel nodded. "Very good, and you must call me Phillip. We like to be on first name terms at HDG Laboratories. Anyway, I hope you are ready to take up your duties as secretary to the academy,

I'm finding the constant interruptions are distracting me from my own research."

"I will endeavor to take the load off your shoulders as soon as possible," Samuel said.

"Very good. Lips, will you guide Samuel back to his family?"

Samuel found himself outside Dr. Gribbleflotz's office seconds later. He glanced back to see the doctor already had his head buried into a journal. "What's he working on now?" he asked Lips.

"The recent visit by the up-timer Dr. Thomas Stone has forced Phillip to reevaluate some previous conclusions."

Samuel recognized the name. He was himself the son of a wealthy dye merchant and he'd found the dyes manufactured by Dr. Stone's Lothlorien Farbenwerk extremely interesting. The man was obviously a gifted scientist. "What conclusions is Dr. Gribbleflotz reevaluating?"

"The validity of Kirlian aura interpretation," Lips said.

"The what!" That certainly hadn't been what Samuel had expected to hear. "I was told by the up-timer woman at the Jena facility that Dr. Gribbleflotz didn't believe in aura interpretation."

Lips nodded. "And that's why Phillip has to reevaluate his position. You see, he developed a method of taking color Kirlian photographs, and well, the one he took of the king showed that his aura was blue."

"So?" Samuel asked.

"Dr. Stone, using his superior science of the chakras, agrees that the king's aura is indeed blue."

Samuel whistled. "And if Dr. Stone says the king's

aura is blue, not only is he saying auras exist, but that Kirlian photography can detect them..."

"And that's why Phillip is reevaluating his stance on Kirlian aura interpretation. If Kirlian photography can correctly determine an aura's color, what else can it do?"

Samuel could only nod in agreement. The information that Phillip was willing to reevaluate his position could only be seen in a good light. Some people, when confronted with evidence that goes against what they believe, would ignore it. Phillip's willingness to at least reassess the evidence indicated a proper scientific mind.

A month later Samuel was comfortably ensconced in his office admiring the view of the city while he sipped on a fine wine. Oh how he'd missed fine wines while he was stuck in Amsterdam. There was a clatter at his door, and Samuel cursed his procrastination over finding a secretary to guard his office. The door burst open.

Samuel recognized the man immediately. He fumbled his glass onto his desk and hurried forward to greet his friend. "Jan, Jan Amos Komenský, how long has it been?"

"Too long," Jan said. "I expected you to call as soon as you settled in Prague, but not a word have I heard from you since you took up your position as secretary of King Venceslas V Adalbertus' new royal academy, so having spoken with your fine wife, I decided to beard the lion in his den."

Jan had been rector of the new University of Prague for over two years, and knowing his old friend had such an important position in Prague had been one reason Samuel had hesitated over taking up the position of secretary of the Royal Academy. He'd felt that the connection with Dr. Gribbleflotz wouldn't reflect well. "I'm sorry, Jan, but I've been rushed off my feet establishing the royal academy."

"Rushed off your feet?" Jan stepped up to Samuel's desk and picked up the wine glass. He sniffed, and then tasted the wine. Licking his lips he looked back at Samuel. "Is this what you call being rushed off your feet? If only I could be rushed off my feet like you are." He shook his head in disappointment. "My friend is in my city for a month, and he can't find the time to even send me a note."

Samuel retreated back to his comfortable chair behind his desk. "It's an illusion. I was enjoying a glass of wine as a reward for my hard work. Just today I have had the Prague chapter of the Society of Aural Investigators begging me to invite Herr Dr. Stone, the great pharmaceuticals manufacturer from Grantville, to come to Prague to teach them the Science of the Chakras, and no sooner had I ushered them out of my office but who should arrive but a delegation from the Prague Guild of Surgeons wanting me to invite Herr Dr. Stone's associate, Herr Guptah Rai Singh, to teach them the surgical technique he used to treat Dr. Gribbleflotz."

"Two emissaries before four o'clock doesn't sound like hard work. Who did you have to bribe to get such an easy life?"

"Two emissaries from important organizations in Prague that took me several hours each to deal with."

"How do you take several hours to deal with emissaries? Surely you just have to agree to make inquiries."

"They want more than just inquiries. They want Herr Dr. Stone and Herr Singh to turn up and teach them what they want to learn. Most of my time was spent trying to convince them that Herr Dr. Stone is a very important man who might have other commitments. We have compromised. If they provide me with letters of invitation, I will forward them under the academy's letterhead."

August 1636, Lothlorien Farbenwerk, Grantville

Lori Drahuta didn't storm into Tom Stone's office, but it was a close run thing. The only reason she'd throttled down her emotions was the sure knowledge that Tom's employees would never have let her this close to their hero if they'd known how close to exploding she was.

She waited until Tom's secretary had left before closing the door firmly behind the man. Then she turned to Tom Stone and removed the mirror-finish sunglasses from her face, revealing the fire in her eyes. "Why did you do it?" she demanded.

Tom Stone reared back, pushing his wheeled chair backwards until he hit the wall behind him. "Do what?" he demanded.

"Why did you have to make a fool of Dr. Gribbleflotz?"

"But I didn't . . ."

"Guptah Rai Singh, psychic surgery. Am I starting to ring any bells?" Lori demanded as she approached Tom's desk and planted her palms on it.

"I needed to get close to King Venceslas to perform a medical examination," Tom insisted, standing up.

Lori stared straight into Tom's eyes. "It never occurred to you to simply ask Dr. Gribbleflotz for help?"

Tom shrugged uncomfortably. "Well, no," he said. "What help could he have been?"

"He's a doctor. What help do you think he could have been?" Lori shouted across the desk at Tom.

"He's not a real doctor, he's a fake," Tom protested, shouting back. "He's a charlatan, peddling cures that don't work, and trying to make gold out of base metals."

"Charlatan!" Lori roared right in Tom's face. "You're a fine one to talk with your chakras and psychic surgery. Well, I hope you're happy." She collected the attaché case she'd dropped to confront Tom and pulled out three letters on the finest quality writing paper and slid them across the desk to Tom.

He trapped them on the desktop and looked at Lori. "What are they?"

"They are your comeuppance," Lori said with considerable satisfaction. She glared at Tom one last time and stalked towards the door. She paused before opening it and looked over her shoulder. "I hope you enjoy your just deserts next time you visit Prague."

Lori hauled open the door, scattering the Lothlorien Farbenwerk workers who'd gathered outside Tom Stone's office. She glared at them, daring them to stop her, before putting on her mirrored shades and stalking through them.

"What's got Miss Drahuta all fired up?" Gerry Stone asked when he joined his father a few minutes later.

When he failed to get a reply he tried again. "Dad? I asked why you and Miss Drahuta had a shouting match that could be heard throughout the whole company."

Tom winced and lowered the letter he'd been reading. "Surely it wasn't that bad."

Gerry nodded vigorously, much to Tom's discomfort. He dropped the letter he was holding and it joined the other two lying discarded on his desk. "What did I ever do to deserve this?" he asked of the universe.

"What's the matter, Dad?" Gerry asked.

Tom gathered up the letters and sighed. "Where to start? How about a letter from Dr. Phillip Theophrastus Gribbleflotz, president for life of the Royal Academy of Science in Prague, inviting me to become a Fellow of the Royal Academy of Science?"

"What's wrong with that, Dad? Mr. Roth has already told you about the royal academy and that Dr. Gribbleflotz was the president."

"What's wrong is that Dr. Gribbleflotz is asking me to present seminars on the Science of the Chakras."

"Oh!"

Tom was happy to see Gerry had grasped the nature of the problem. He held up a second letter. "And as if that wasn't bad enough, the Prague Guild of Surgeons hopes that I might be able to persuade my colleague, Herr Guptah Rai Singh, to teach them his special surgical techniques."

"Whoops! Mr. Mundell isn't going to like that."

Tom stared hard at his youngest son. "George Mundell is not going to hear about this. Guptah Rai Singh is going to quietly disappear—we will inform the Guild of Surgeons that he has unfortunately been called home to deal with a domestic emergency."

"You've still got one letter left," Gerry noted.

Tom opened the last letter and reread it quietly. "Compared to the others, this is a bit of an anti-climax. Martin Zänkel, writing as the secretary of the Prague Chapter of the Society of Aural Investigators, hopes that I might consent to provide training on the Science of the Chakras to the membership."

"Why would they want that?"

Tom passed the letter across to Gerry, "Their clients have heard that Kirlian aura interpretation is a poor cousin to the Science of the Chakras, and are asking for readings using the superior science."

Roth's, Prague

Phillip was shown into a private room almost the moment he entered Roth's jewelry store.

"Please take a seat, Dr. Gribbleflotz. A jeweler will be with you shortly," the young woman from reception said. She waited for him to sit before continuing. "Would you like some refreshments? Something to eat or drink?" she asked.

"No, thank you," Phillip said as he gazed around the small room.

The moment the woman left him alone Phillip got to his feet and walked around the room. This was the first time he had been in one of the back rooms. Normally, when he prescribed gems to balance his patron's aura, he gave a palace functionary the necessary instructions. However, this was visit was personal. He was examining a drawing of the various ways gemstones could be cut when the hairs on the back of his head stood up. He turned around in time to see a man in his forties quietly shutting the door behind him.

"Herr Dr. Gribbleflotz, my name is Samuel Kohen. Sara informs me that you wish to be advised on a selection of gems you wish to commission," Samuel said as he walked around to the business side of a table placed in the middle of the room. "Please, take a seat."

"That's right," Phillip said as walked over to the well-padded client chair and gingerly lowered himself into it. He'd been warned about how client chairs were often designed to look comfortable, but be sufficiently uncomfortable that clients would want to get out of them as quickly as possible. He needn't have worried. This was one of the comfortable ones. He pulled a sheet of paper out of an inner jacket pocket. "I wish to commission a set of chakras gems."

"Ah, the new science that Herr Dr. Stone used to treat the king," Samuel said.

Phillip nodded. "I need seven colored stones. Red, orange, yellow, green, light blue, dark blue, and purple. And I want them to complement this white topaz." Phillip placed his lucky crystal on the table in front of him.

"May I examine the stone?" Samuel asked, gesturing at the white topaz.

Phillip nodded. He didn't like people handling his lucky topaz, but he knew enough about gems to know that the man had to examine it to determine how big a stone he could cut from it. He watched the man weigh the topaz with a set of jeweler's scales. And smiled at the raised brows Samuel sent his way. His lucky topaz was big.

"Three hundred and forty carats," Samuel said.

There was a noticeable tremor in Samuel's voice. "Is there something the matter?" Phillip asked.

"You say this is a white topaz," Samuel said, moistening his lips with his tongue.

"That's right," Phillip said. "I measured its specific gravity myself and got a value of three-point-five-two."

Samuel nodded. "That is certainly in the range one would expect to find for a topaz." He placed Phillip's lucky topaz on the table and got to his feet. "If you wouldn't mind waiting for a movement, I need to talk to someone more senior."

Phillip didn't have a chance to say if he minded or not, because Samuel scampered out of the room so quickly that the door actually slammed closed behind him. Phillip reached out and caressed his lucky topaz. "What have you done this time?" he asked.

A few minutes later the door opened again and Morris Roth himself walked in, with Samuel close behind him.

"Herr Dr. Gribbleflotz," Morris said, holding out his hand. "It is a pleasure to meet you. And Samuel says you have a most interesting stone."

Phillip held up the topaz. "My lucky topaz. We've been through a lot together."

Morris held out a hand for the egg-sized raw crystal. "And now you would like us to cut it as one of a set of chakras gems?"

"That's right," Phillip said, although, truth to tell, he was a bit ambivalent about breaking up his lucky piece.

Morris took out a jeweler's loupe and carefully examined the stone, even going so far as to place it on a piece of pristine white paper and using a combination of mirrors to direct sunlight onto it. Eventually he lowered the loupe, nodded to Samuel, and faced Phillip. "I have to tell you, Dr. Gribbleflotz, that this is not a white topaz."

"But of course it is," Phillip protested. "I measured

its specific gravity myself, and there are only two things it could possibly be. Topaz..."

"Or diamond," Morris said. "Catch him!"

Strong arms helped Phillip into the chair. "A diamond?" Phillip asked.

Morris nodded. "It's one of the best stones of any size Roth's has handled. But I can assure you that all care will be taken to maximize the cutting of the stone."

"I think I could cut a true flawless diamond of not less than three hundred carats from the raw stone," Samuel said.

Phillip stared blankly at Morris Roth. "A white diamond is useless for the chakras," he muttered.

"Oh." Morris handed the stone back to Phillip. "I'm sure Roth's will be able to provide you with a similar sized white topaz if that's what you wish."

Phillip tightened his hand around his lucky topaz. He smiled. Make that lucky diamond. The chief thought flowing through his mind was that he wasn't going to be cutting up his lucky crystal. He handed Morris the data sheet Lori Drahuta had sent him about chakras gems. "I will need eight gemstones now."

"Of course you will," Morris said as he passed the paper on to Samuel. "Meanwhile, I think we've all had a bit of a shock." He looked down at Phillip. "Your diamond is extremely valuable, Dr. Gribbleflotz, and I recommend that you improve your security. Alternatively, you can lodge the diamond with Roth's and we will store it for you."

Phillip tightened his hold on his lucky crystal and shook his head. "I like to have it close," he said as he got to his feet.

"Very good, Dr. Gribbleflotz. Samuel will assemble

a collection of stones for you to inspect and get back to you. Meanwhile, would you like someone to accompany you home?"

Phillip shook his head. "No, thank you. I'll be fine. It was just a bit of a shock."

"Of course it was," Morris said. He signaled to Samuel before leading Phillip out of his store.

Phillip walked back to his apartment in a daze, totally oblivious to the four-man security detail Morris Roth had set to see him home safely. He made for his study, where he returned his lucky crystal to its spot on the shelf above his desk and below the portrait of Dina. A silly smile appeared on his face as he admired both, before gently patting the diamond. His old friend was back to stay.

Chapter 21

The Mouser that Soared

May 1636, Prague, Bohemia

Dr. Phillip Gribbleflotz, president of the Royal Academy
of Science, was protesting every step of the way as
Samuel Hartlib dragged him from his private laboratory on the top floor of the Mihulka Tower.

"Why do I have to be there? Surely you, as the
secretary, are sufficient," Phillip protested.

"Because you are the president of the Royal Academy of Science," Samuel said as he jerked Phillip
along, "and it is the president's job to show up for the
publicity photographs whenever the Royal Academy
does something newsworthy."

Phillip muttered something about always knowing
it was going to be a problem.

"What was that, Phillip?"

"You were employed expressly so that I didn't have
to abandon my research to participate in things like
this."

"You have to be there when the contracts to build the radio tower are signed," Samuel said. "It's a very important occasion for the Royal Academy."

Phillip fell into step beside Samuel, but he wasn't going quietly. He continued protesting the interruption to his research all the way to the reception room where everything had been set up.

He hadn't been overly interested in the proposed broadcast radio transmitter—he'd had other, more important things to concern himself—so this was the first time he'd set eyes on the scale model of the proposed radio station. The radio station, complete with its lattice-work timber tower, was located on high ground south of Prague Castle. He tried to measure the distance between the castle and the radio station. It was just over his handspan. He was about to compare that measure with the castle to get an estimate of distance when someone called out.

"If you'd like to just hold your hand there, Dr. Gribbleflotz!"

Phillip most definitely didn't like. While he'd been looking at the model half a dozen photographers had set up their cameras and focused them on him. He knew enough about photography to know that the poor light in the reception room would require exposure times in the seconds, and that was just for the regular cameras obscura. There was one man using a new Gribblechrome camera, and he was probably going to need tens of seconds to get a good image.

A discreet cough reminded Phillip that Samuel was watching, so he put a smile on and held his pose until he was told he could release it.

The man giving the orders was the photographer with

the Gribblechrome, which made some kind of sense. Not only did he need the most time to take his photographs, but also, if he could afford a Gribblechrome camera, he was probably a portrait photographer to the wealthy and therefore the photographer the Royal Academy had commissioned to record this momentous occasion.

The photo session took another valuable forty minutes from Phillip's research time and he was eager to get away. He said his good-byes to Herr Fritz, the up-timer representing the company that had won the contract to build King Venceslas' broadcast radio station, and made his way to the door.

He was prevented from making a quick exit by the photographer with the Gribblechrome, who was struggling with the massive camera.

"I don't suppose you could make a smaller Gribblechrome camera, Herr Dr. Gribbleflotz?" the man asked.

Phillip shook his head. "The size of a Gribblechrome is a function of the negative size." That was the simple answer. It was actually a function of several things, of which negative size was one of the most important.

The photographer nodded. "I understand that, Herr Doctor, but surely there is a way to make it a little more manageable?"

Phillip was anxious to get back to his experiments, so he promised to look into it before escaping.

May 1636, Graduation day, Grantville High School

Daniel Pastorius delivered the valedictory, and after a few seconds' silence, probably to be sure that Daniel had finished, Marcus Wendell got the band playing. Magdalena

Rutilius was playing her theremin. Not the Moog Etherwave Theremin she'd been learning on for four years, but the one that she had made as her senior project.

While the band played, the graduates marched off, leaving the football ground in orderly files. Shortly after the last graduate filed off the field there was a huge shout and academic caps were thrown into the air. Magdalena smiled; that had been her yesterday, when she graduated with her Electrical Trades Certificate.

Unlike the high school diploma or the GED, the ETC was a professional qualification. Some of the graduates had already been head-hunted by choice employers such as the broadcast radio stations and Grantville's power station. Magdalena hadn't been one of the lucky ones. Instead, like the rest of the currently jobless graduates, she'd be attending the hiring fair tomorrow. Not that any of them would have difficulty finding jobs. She sighed. There had to be more to look forward to in life than running wires around buildings, which was what the future held for her if she accepted the standing offer she had from Kelly Construction. She finished packing away her theremin and went in search of her boyfriend.

She knew just where to look for Jason, at the front of the high school, where photographers had set up shop taking graduation photographs for posterity.

Naturally, everyone had the same idea, so there were some four hundred graduates and three or four times that number of family milling around the front of the high school waiting for a photographer to become free. Finding anyone in such a crowd would have been virtually impossible. Fortunately, Jason's mother had told her that they would be heading for Lettie Sebastian's tent.

Lettie was one of the mothers of down-time photography. Her up-time knowledge of photography combined with Celeste Frost's up-time chemistry training had combined to recreate photography downtime. They'd skipped several historical steps, missing wet-plate completely, and gone straight to dry-plate photography using a gelatin-based emulsion. They were making the technology available to the world through Brennerei und Chemiefabrik Schwarza.

Magdalena located the tent easily enough. The heavy green canvas roof was a clue, but not as much as the banner advertising Brennerei und Chemiefabrik Schwarza strung between the poles above the tent was. It took her a few minutes to wind her way through the crowd to get to the tent, where she found the Cheng family patiently waiting in line.

"You made it." Jason's mother, Jennie Lee Cheng, hugged her before looking her up and down. "It's good that you were with the band today." She ordered Jason to hold their place in the line before dragging her and Jason's sister towards the makeup stands Lettie had set out in front of the tent that doubled as her field darkroom. "Diana, see what you can do about her bare face."

"What?" Magdalena protested as she was planted in front of a mirror and Jason's sister got to work cleaning her face and then applying makeup.

"You want to be in Jason's graduation photographs, don't you?" Diana asked.

"Yes," Magdalena muttered around the lip pencil Diana was using to define the border of her lips.

"Then shut up and cooperate," Jennie Lee said. She scanned the crowd. "Jason, can you see your father?"

"No."

"Men," she muttered, "never where they're supposed to be when you need them."

"Dad said he saw someone he needed to have a few words with," Diana said as she stepped back to admire her handiwork before adding a few more finishing details.

"I can see Dad," Jason called.

The actual taking of the photographs took almost no time at all, so after barely five minutes in front of the camera they were all finished and free to go. Diana dashed off almost immediately, and Jason's mother and father paused just long enough to ensure that Magdalena was coming around for dinner before they too wandered off.

Jason held out a hand and Magdalena grabbed it. "Where to now?" he asked.

"Food," Magdalena suggested.

"Sure," Jason said. He sniffed a couple of times before pointing. "That way."

Magdalena giggled as she fell in beside him. Jason had a male teenager's unerring ability to find food. This time it turned out to be a hotdog stand. She waited while he braved the queue.

"Hey, Mags." the greeting from behind was accompanied by a pair of arms being thrown around Magdalena.

She had recognized the voice, now she got to recognize the smell of Kelli Fritz's favorite perfume. "Kelli."

Kelli loosened her hold on Magdalena and looked around. "Where's Jason?" she asked.

Magdalena pointed towards the line in front of the hotdog stand. "Getting us something to eat."

Kelli nodded. "You haven't got a job yet, have you?"

Magdalena shook her head. "I've got a standing offer from Kelly Construction, but I thought I might see if tomorrow's hiring fair has anything more interesting to offer."

"Whew!" Kelli released her breath. "That's good. I told Dad you'd be perfect, and it'd be a bit annoying if you weren't available."

"Available for what?" Magdalena asked, clamping down heavily on her excitement. Kelli's father was high up at the radio station in Magdeburg. "I thought Voice of Luther already had all the new workers they wanted." She finished with a scowl, because it hurt that they hadn't wanted her.

"Sorry about that," Kelli muttered.

Magdalena shrugged. "It's not your fault," she said, "and anyway, Markus and Dietrich did finish near the top of the class." Dietrich Bockelmann was a really nice guy and fully deserved such a plum job. She couldn't say the same about Markus. She certainly felt she would have been a better fit for the broadcaster.

"Anyway, Dad's got a new contract and he's looking for people who know about Alexanderson alternators and crystal sets."

Magdalena smiled. She had been making crystal radios for sale for years, and she'd built her own small Alexanderson alternator as the signal generator for the theremin she'd built as her senior project. "That's me!"

Kelli grinned back. "That's what I told him. Anyway, Dad's seeing Herr Trelli right now. If you hurry over, you might be able to catch him."

Magdalena was excited; but there was Jason to consider. "Do I have time to eat a hotdog?" she asked.

"Sure, but don't take too long. Dad wants to be

home before five." Kelli took a couple of steps away before turning. "And take your theremin." She smiled and dashed off.

"Here you are," Jason said a couple of minutes later. "What are you staring at?" he asked.

Magdalena smiled at Jason and accepted the hotdog he was holding out. "I was just talking to Kelli Fritz. She says that her father might be interested in employing me on a new job."

"Not Voice of Luther?"

Magdalena shook her head. "She says not." She took a bite of her hotdog, being careful not to drip mustard sauce all over her best outfit. "Herr Fritz is talking to Herr Trelli right now, and Kelli thinks I should wander over with my theremin and say hi."

"Then let's do that," Jason said. He stuffed the last couple of inches of his hotdog into his mouth and caught Magdalena's hand.

SoTF State Technical College, administration offices

Magdalena knocked on the door to Herr Trelli's office and waited.

Felix Trelli opened the door. "I'm busy at the moment, can you come back in," he paused to look at his watch, "twenty minutes?"

Magdalena was all ready to agree and walk off, but Jason butted in. "Mr. Trelli, Kelli Fritz said that her father was here talking to you and that Mags should drop by with her theremin."

"Theremin?" a muffled voice said from Felix's office. "Is that Magdalena Rutilius you're talking to?"

Felix smiled at Magdalena before calling over his shoulder. "Yes it is. Apparently Kelli sent them over."

"Them?" Vernon Fritz asked as he appeared at the door. "Oh, hi, Jason." He looked at the box Jason was carrying. "Is that the theremin I've heard so much about?"

Jason nodded and gently stood the box on the floor. Meanwhile Magdalena unslung the bag containing the legs and treadle components and lowered it to the floor.

Vernon approached. "It looks heavy," he said as he laid a hand gently on the highly polished wooden box.

Jason grinned. "That's why I'm here. It's way too heavy for Mags to carry around. If you want to chat with her in private, I can make myself scarce."

Vernon shook his head. "No, there's nothing secret about the job." He smiled at Magdalena. "Would you mind showing me how your theremin works?"

"Silly question," Jason muttered.

Magdalena dug an elbow into Jason's ribs while she smiled at Herr Fritz. "Where would you like me to set it up?" she asked.

"Inside Felix's office will do," Vernon said, standing clear of the door to let Magdalena and Jason in.

Jason carried the theremin into the office while Magdalena followed with the bag of accessories. It took her only a few minutes to screw in the four legs and attach the treadle system, then she stood back while Jason and Herr Fritz stood it on its legs.

"Do you want a demonstration, or do you just want to see the workings?" Magdalena asked.

"I'd like a quick demonstration," Vernon said.

Twenty minutes later Magdalena suggested that maybe Herr Fritz might want to check the internals.

Felix hastily stepped back from the theremin and sent her an apologetic smile. "It's a very interesting instrument," he said.

"It can be addictive," Magdalena agreed as she used an Allen key to unscrew the bolts that held the casing in place. "Careful," she said as Jason started to lift the top off.

"What's that?" Felix asked, crowding over Magdalena to have a look.

Vernon's gaze slid past the Alexanderson alternator to where Felix was pointing and his eyes lit up. He turned to Magdalena. "Are those the famous flame triodes I've heard about?"

Magdalena did her best to appear humble as she nodded that, yes, they were the flame triodes she'd made that had so impressed her examiners.

"That's a nice bit of innovation." Vernon patted the theremin's box. "You made everything yourself?"

"Yes," Magdalena said. Then she qualified the bald statement. "Except for the nuts and bolts." It was unnecessary to add the wire had also been bought. Nobody was going to make their own wire when they could buy it already drawn to the required size. However, she had insulated some of that wire herself, using the same cellulose acetate plastic that Brennerei und Chemiefabrik Schwarza used to make sheet and roll photographic film to coat the wire.

Vernon smiled. "I think we can forgive you the nuts and bolts." He patted the theremin. "Kelli was right. You may be just what I'm looking for."

"Just a minute," Felix said as he started flipping through some files on his desk, "Frau Rutilius' file should be in here somewhere."

"I'm probably near the bottom, Herr Trelli." Magdalena turned to Vernon. "I graduated near the bottom of the class," she said.

"Don't let that worry you, Frau Rutilius," Vernon said. "I'd rather have practical people who can do things than people who excel at regurgitating facts for tests," Vernon said.

"Mags also makes crystal radio sets," Jason added.

"Shush." Magdalena tugged at Jason's arm as the heat flooded her face. Herr Fritz was the person responsible for the crystal radio program. It was from one of his cheat sheets that she'd made her first crystal radio.

Vernon turned his attention back to Magdalena. "You do?" Suddenly his brows shot up and he looked at Jason. "Mags, as in MAGS crystal radios?"

Jason nodded.

"Those are pretty good crystal sets." Vernon turned back to Magdalena. "I like the way you use only the bare minimum of metal. Those wooden cat's whisker holders are sheer genius."

Magdalena blushed. "I had help designing them," she said, gazing up at Jason.

"But you make them, Mags. Me and Dad just helped design them, to your specifications."

"What specifications?" Vernon asked.

"As cheap and easy as possible to make while also doing the job," Jason said.

Vernon nodded. "Yes, well, Frau Rutilius, thanks for showing me your theremin. I'll read your file and I expect to see you at the hiring fair tomorrow."

"Thank you, Herr Fritz," Magdalena said as she and Jason started to disassemble her theremin.

"Mr. Fritz, just what is the job Mags is going to be applying for?" Jason asked.

The use of English surprised Magdalena, but so did Jason's question. How had she forgotten to ask about the job?

"Radio Prague," Vernon answered. He looked from Jason to Magdalena. "Still interested?"

A hand with a handkerchief arrived at her mouth and gently patted her lips. She reacted to the implication that she was drooling at the offer by swinging an elbow into Jason's ribs. She glared at him as he backed off, holding his ribs as if she'd done real damage and snorted her contempt for his acting. She was five foot one and could, on a good day, weigh in at nearly eighty pounds. Jason was quite literally twice her size—five foot nine and a hundred and sixty pounds.

"I'll take that as a yes," Vernon said. He offered his hand to Magdalena. "Until tomorrow."

Magdalena walked out of Felix Trelli's office in a bit of a daze. Fortunately, she had Jason to guide her.

"So you've got another job offer," Jason said.

"Herr Fritz hasn't read my file yet," she said.

"Come off it, Mags. There's nothing in your file to put Kelli's father off employing you."

Magdalena desperately wanted to believe Jason. Then a stray thought occurred and she laughed.

"What's tickled your funny bone?" Jason asked.

"Markus is going to have a fit," she said.

"Is it going to be a problem working with him?" Jason asked.

Magdalena chewed on her lip while she considered how to answer that question. Finally she shook her head. "He'll be with Voice of Luther in Magdeburg."

"And you'll be in Prague," Jason said.

Magdalena nodded. "I'll miss you," she said as she wound her arms around Jason.

Jason kissed the top of her head. "It's too good an opportunity to turn down. Besides, I'm sure KCE will be involved, and who better to send out to Prague than someone who knows about Alexanderson alternators?"

Magdalena tilted her head back so she could kiss Jason. "I love you," she said. She was sure he was just putting the best possible spin on the job offer. Sure Kitt and Cheng Engineering, the company he was about to start an engineering apprenticeship with, was likely to win some of the contracts to build components for the new broadcast radio transmitter, but she didn't see them sending him to Prague anytime soon.

"Love you too. Just don't fall in love with anyone else while you're in Prague."

"We could get married before I go," Magdalena said.

"Mom and Dad would never go for it."

"We could ask," she said hopefully.

Jason nodded. "Sure, and we will, but I bet they'll tell us to wait until you get back, just in case absence doesn't make the heart grow fonder."

Magdalena sighed. She knew Jason was right, but she was afraid that his parents would use the separation to break up their relationship. It wasn't anything they'd said, but Magdalena wasn't stupid. Wealthy families didn't really want their sons marrying nobodies like her.

July 1636, Prague

Magdalena was tired and exhausted. The last few weeks had been a whirl of activity as she helped make the components for the new transmitter. It had been a rush job with a monumental amount of overtime. She'd made the mistake of saying out loud that the rig the people building the Alexanderson alternator were using to cut the slots in the rotor was just like the one she'd used to cut the slots in the rotor of her theremin, only bigger. That had resulted in her being allocated to the team building the alternator, and she'd spent most of her time in Magdeburg working on the rotor disc. It had been extremely tiring work. Not only did each slot have to be precisely positioned, it also had to be precisely cut. And there had been thousands of slots to be cut, cleaned, and filled with nonconducting filler. Then everything had to be smoothed out so that the rotor had a clean aerodynamic surface.

The steamer trip from Magdeburg had seemed like an ideal way to reduce some of her sleep deficit, but she'd been awake for hours. They'd set out that morning at first light, and were just arriving in Prague now, some fourteen hours later. It had turned out to be a long and boring trip. She said as much to Dietrich.

A recumbent Dietrich Bockelmann raised a single eyelid a fraction. "You don't know how lucky you are," he said.

"I bet you're going to tell me that when you were a soldier you had to walk the route," Magdalena said. Throughout their time at college Dietrich had kept the class amused with stories of his time as a soldier. He never spoke about the fighting though. It was always the silly little day to day things.

"Fourteen days on the march, through mud, all our stuff on our backs. Everything we owned soaking wet. Poor food. Never enough to drink..."

"Soldiers always complain about not having enough to drink," Magdalena said.

Dietrich opened both eyes. "Who's telling this story?" he demanded.

Magdalena grinned. "You are."

Dietrich nodded and closed his eyes again. "Where was I?"

"Never enough to drink," Magdalena said.

Dietrich nodded. "Because we were thirsty we'd scoop water from puddles to drink as we marched."

"That's not healthy."

"You don't worry about things like that when you're dying of thirst," Dietrich said.

"You could have drunk from the river," Magdalena said.

Dietrich shook his head. "That would have meant breaking ranks, and the captain would never have stood for that."

It seemed silly to Magdalena not to let soldiers drink from the river when they were thirsty, but then, what did she know about the military? "I admit that you probably had it hard in the good old days."

"So stop complaining," Dietrich said.

Magdalena sighed. "I suppose I should be thankful that Markus isn't here."

A hint of a smile bubbled through as Dietrich held back a snigger. "You're really on his shit list now."

Magdalena could only agree. Markus had been

seriously upset to discover that she was working on the Radio Prague project while he was stuck in Magdeburg. "I think I'll survive," she said.

The steamboat bumped against the dock and the crew and men on the dock swung into action.

"You two get your things," Vernon Fritz called out as he went in search of the rest of his team.

Magdalena sent Dietrich her most winning smile as she collected her knapsack and cat carrier and stood beside her other luggage. There was a large steamer trunk and her theremin, with the legs and treadle packed into the trunk. She could only barely carry the rest of her things and the theremin, but there was no way she could carry the trunk as well. Dietrich on the other hand, was six three and two hundred and forty pounds of lean muscle. Just then the man in question stood and stretched. Magdalena wasn't the only female who enjoyed the sight.

Dietrich smiled at her. "Your boyfriend wouldn't approve," he said as he tipped his trunk up on its end so he could grab a handle.

"Window shopping is permitted," Magdalena said. She gestured towards her luggage. "Could you please give me a hand?"

"You want me to help get your trunk up on your shoulder?"

"Ha ha, very funny," Magdalena said. "No, I'd like you to carry my trunk for me."

Dietrich dragged his trunk over beside Magdalena's and crouched down to pull one onto each shoulder. "The accommodation you arranged had better be as good as you promised," he said as he got to his feet.

"You'll find it a vast improvement over your previous

lodgings," Magdalena said. She giggled at Dietrich's scowl. It wouldn't take much to be an improvement over the cockroach infested clapboard shed he'd shared with five others back in Grantville. "I sent a letter to Frau Mittelhausen telling her how big you are, so your bed should be long enough."

They followed Vernon and the rest of his team off the steamer. On shore Vernon turned to Magdalena and Dietrich. "You sure you don't want to stay with the rest of us?" he asked.

Magdalena and Dietrich both shook her heads. The rest of the team had taken rooms at a local inn, but then, they were all on higher pay than Dietrich and her.

"Okay, go and settle in. We'll meet at the Blue Lion tomorrow at first light."

A short time later, the Gribbleflotz facility, Prague

"What is that?" Ursula Mittelhausen demanded.

Magdalena was in no doubt what *that* was. She put on her best winning smile and held up the cat carrier so Frau Mittelhausen could admire her cat. "This is Liova, isn't he beautiful?"

"You didn't say you were bringing a pet," Ursula accused.

"He's very well behaved," Magdalena said.

Ursula snorted. "Cats should not be kept in the house, they make their messes everywhere."

"But Liova won't do that," Magdalena said. "He's fully house trained and he's undergone surgical behavioral modification."

Ursula planted her hands on her hips and glared at Magdalena. "He's undergone what?"

Dietrich sniggered. "That's up-time animal doctor speak, Frau Mittelhausen. It just means that the cat's been gelded. Just like with a horse, gelding improves a cat's behavior."

Magdalena knew just the way to win over Frau Mittelhausen. She carefully opened the cat carrier and picked up Liova. Then she turned and faced Frau Mittelhausen with Liova held against her chest and started to scratch his ear. It didn't take long before he was purring loudly. Then she walked closer to Frau Mittelhausen, and Liova, being his usual self-important attention-seeking self, reached out to her.

Frau Mittelhausen took the bait and reached out to stroke the beautiful long-haired gray tabby. Almost immediately his purr leapt in volume.

Ursula was smiling when she finally stopped stroking Liova. "You're responsible for cleaning up any mess your cat makes," she warned.

Magdalena nodded.

"And if anybody complains about the noise he makes, he'll have to leave," Ursula added.

Magdalena smiled. Surely no one could complain about a cat purring?

"Right then, let's get you settled." Ursula swung around and called to a youth. "Lips, show Dietrich to his room."

Dietrich picked up his trunk and followed Lips Kastenmayer. He stopped at the door to call over his shoulder. "I'll be right back to help you with your trunk, Mags."

Ursula watched the two men, Dietrich in his late

twenties and Lips in his late teens, leave before turning back to Magdalena. "What's your relationship with Herr Bockelmann?" she asked.

"We're just friends, Frau Mittelhausen."

"Yet he calls you Mags?"

Magdalena nodded. "It's just a nickname, Frau Mittelhausen. It's short for Magdalena. I like it better than Mouse."

"Why would anyone call you Mouse?" Ursula asked as she guided Magdalena to the female laborant dormitory.

Magdalena gave her a wry smile. "An electrician's mouse is a small weight that you tie a lead-line to and lower down wall cavities so someone at the other end can use the lead-line to pull cables."

"And do they lower you down wall cavities so they can pull cables?" Ursula asked.

"Not very often," Magdalena said, "but when I first started, any time we had to pull cable through confined spaces they used to call out for 'the Mouse' to take a lead-line through."

Ursula gazed back in the direction Dietrich and Lips had gone. "I imagine your friend would have difficulty passing through some spaces."

"That's one reason why he specialized in generators," Magdalena said. "He's hoping that if he does well with this job he might have a chance at working on the hydroelectricity development at Glomfjord."

Ursula nodded. "I'll keep your friend in mind."

Magdalena jerked round. "The doctor's involved with the power station they're building at Glomfjord?"

"No, but he has plans for an aluminum smelter there to take advantage of the extra electricity stage two will produce. I'm sure the people working on the power station will listen to a recommendation from the doctor."

Magdalena had seen what a recommendation from Dr. Gribbleflotz could do. It was how her friend Maria Anna had got a job at Brennerei und Chemiefabrik Schwarza more than four years ago. "Thank you, Frau Mittelhausen. Dietrich will appreciate that."

"He'll have to prove himself," Ursula warned.

Magdalena just nodded. That was nothing new for Dietrich. His life was littered with occasions when he'd had to prove himself.

Liova was lying on a bed washing himself while Magdalena set out his essential services on the floor when Dietrich turned up with her trunk.

"Where do you want it?" Dietrich asked as he shuffled into the room carrying the trunk by a handle attached to one end and using a foot under it to make lifting easier.

"At the foot of the bed please," Magdalena said as she poured kitty litter into Liova's litter box.

"You carried that stuff?" Dietrich demanded as he pushed the trunk into position. "I thought you said you only carried the essentials in your knapsack."

Magdalena added a sprinkling of Sal Aer Fixus over the litter and mixed it in. "Liova considers his litter box essential," she said.

"He's just a cat," Dietrich said.

Magdalena glared at Dietrich. "Wash your mouth out." She turned to Liova and picked him up. "Ignore the horrible man," she said as she gently stroked him.

"Meowwwww," Liova said.

"Yes, I know. You're hungry," Magdalena said, putting

Liova down on the bed. She dug a couple of enameled metal bowls out of her knapsack and placed them on the floor. Liova immediately jumped down to investigate, and then protested because they were empty.

"Give me a chance," she told him as she pushed his head aside so she could put a couple of handfuls of dry food into a bowl. While Liova set to eating she poured a little boiled water into the other bowl. She set the plastic bottle of water and plastic food container down on the trunk and got to her feet. "Shall we see what they have to offer for dinner?" she asked Dietrich as she collected a small bottle of hand sanitizer and squeezed a little onto her hand before slipping the little plastic squeeze bottle into her skort pocket and started to rub the liquid all over her hands. She wasn't a complete fanatic about cleanliness, but she always sanitized her hands after handling Liova's litter box, even if she was going to wash her hands with soap and water a few minutes later, as she expected she would do before sitting down for dinner— one never knew what she might touch in between.

"You're singing my song," Dietrich said. "Lead the way."

That evening

Magdalena and Dietrich trailed behind Lips as he guided them around their new home. Liova walked with them, twining his way between their legs whenever they stopped.

They left the spiraling staircase and entered a cavernous room in the Mihulka Tower. Early evening sunlight streamed in through several of the recessed windows.

"What is this place?" she asked.

"Originally it was built as a cannon bastion, but it was being used as a powder store right up until we arrived." Lips shrugged. "I guess someone decided that it was a good place to put Dr. Gribbleflotz."

"Why do you say that?" Dietrich asked.

"Well," Lips said, "in the time of Emperor Rudolph II, it was used as a laboratory for his alchemists." He grinned. "They managed to convince him that they could turn lead into gold."

"What happened to them when they failed to deliver?" Dietrich asked.

Again Lips grinned. "The story I heard is that at least one of them died in prison."

"Then I hope Dr. Gribbleflotz doesn't claim to be able to make gold from lead," Dietrich said.

"Oh, the doctor wouldn't claim anything as outlandish as that." Lips said with conviction.

While Lips had been talking, Liova had been exploring, and he was now walking up another staircase.

"Hey, no, you can't go up there," Lips shouted as he ran after Liova. Naturally this just made Liova climb the stairs faster.

"What's up there?" Magdalena called out as she and Dietrich chased after Lips.

"These stairs lead to Dr. Gribbleflotz's personal study and laboratory," Lips said. "I hope the door wasn't left open," he muttered half to himself.

"I told you that cat was going to be trouble," Dietrich said.

Magdalena poked her tongue out at Dietrich and set off after Lips and Liova.

"Oh, heck!" Lips said.

Magdalena didn't have to ask what the problem was. It was as obvious as the open door right in front of them. "Liova's in there?" she asked.

Lips nodded as he pushed the door open further and stepped into another cavernous room. The central space was occupied by several heavy wooden benches, each with at least one experiment set up on it. Against the walls were more benches and a fume cupboard. On the south wall there was a large portrait of Dina Kastenmayerin, Dr. Gribbleflotz's wife. Below the portrait was a writing desk surrounded by multiple nooks for papers and things to be stored. On either side of the desk were bookshelves.

Unlike the previous rooms they'd explored, this room had a flat ceiling, probably because it didn't have to support any great weight. As with the lower rooms, there were several deep nooks carved into the thick walls, each ending in a window that had originally been a gun loop for shooting at attackers. Now they were just windows. Open windows.

"Oh, dear," Magdalena said. She'd spotted Liova, and he'd spotted a couple of birds who were pecking at something on a bench top. "No, Liova," she called just as her cat jumped onto the bench and scampered after the birds, sending papers cascading over the floor.

The birds were able to take to the air and escape, but that didn't stop Liova trying to catch them. He launched himself at one that flew close enough to encourage him. He missed, reoriented himself as he fell and landed softly on his feet. He then proceeded to walk across the room as if that was what he'd intended to do.

"That was weird," Lips said as he bent to pick up some of the papers that had fallen onto the floor.

"What was weird?" Dietrich asked as he got down on the floor to help.

"The way he contorted himself in midair," Lips said.

"Cats do that naturally," Magdalena said as she started to pick up papers. "They're supposed to be able to right themselves so they can land on their feet if they have a fall."

Lips stopped picking up papers to stare at Magdalena. "How do you know that?" he asked, "experimentation?"

"Of course not," Magdalena said. She'd never do a thing like that to Liova. "I asked a veterinarian the first time Liova fell out of a tree," Magdalena said. "Dr. Blocker said that cats like heights and evolution favored those that could survive falls. Liova has something he called a righting reflex."

"That's nice to know, but can you please do something about catching your cat before he does any more damage?" Lips said as he started sorting the papers they had picked up. "Otherwise he might find himself demonstrating that righting reflex out of a tower window."

Magdalena was pretty sure that was an empty threat, but she realized she had to get Liova out of Dr. Gribbleflotz's study. She pulled a stuffed cloth drawstring purse the size of a mouse, a long ribbon, and a zipper-locked plastic bag from her shoulder bag. She selected a leaf from the plastic bag, bruised it, and put it into the cloth bag. She then drew the drawstrings tight, looped the ribbon through the drawstrings, and tossed the bag towards the nook where Liova was hiding. Liova failed to respond, so she pulled it back and tried again. It took several attempts before Liova suddenly dived on the bag and started playing with it.

"What's in the bag?" Lips asked.

"Catnip," Magdalena said. "Cats go wild for it," she said as she picked up an ecstatic Liova. "Shall we go?" she asked pointedly.

Lips nodded. "And you need to make sure he doesn't come in here again."

A couple of weeks later, the Dr. Gribbleflotz Emporium of Natural Wonders

Lips was amusing himself playing Magdalena's theremin in a side room in the Gribbleflotz shop, where he was supposed to be working. He raised his right hand and spread the fingers to produce a new effect; his eyes were on his hand, but a movement beyond it drew his attention, and he realized he'd attracted an audience. Six members of the Prague Chapter of the Society of Aural Investigators were staring at him and the instrument he was playing. He stepped back from the theremin, allowing the music to die as the rotor of the Alexanderson alternator inside the theremin slowed. "Can I help you?"

"What is that?" Zacharias Held asked, pointing at the theremin.

Lips was a little slow answering, which gave Martin Zänkel an opportunity to misidentify the theremin.

"Surely it's obvious!" he told his colleagues. "Dr. Gribbleflotz has built a machine that can detect a person's aura." He turned to Lips. "What happens when you modify a person's aura by adding gems and colored clothes?"

Lips could have corrected Martin, but a mischievous streak had him playing along to see what happened.

He stepped into the electromagnetic field again and worked the treadle, speeding up the rotor, which caused the theremin to emit a tone. "Why don't you try it," he suggested to Martin.

Martin studied Lips for a few seconds before removing a copper bracelet with several sapphires mounted around the rim from his left wrist. He reached out to place it around Lips' left wrist, changing the pitch the theremin generated as his hands entered the electromagnetic field. He pulled his hands back immediately, and the theremin's pitch returned to what it had been. Martin nodded as if this was very significant and held out the bracelet to Lips. "Put this on your right wrist and let your arms hang by your side."

Lips slipped the bracelet on and dropped his arms. As his arms moved, the tone the theremin made changed, remaining steady at a new tone when his arms were back by his sides.

"Oh, this is wonderful," Martin said. "I have to have it," he told Lips. "How much do you want for it?"

Lips tried to say that he didn't have the right to sell the theremin, but Martin and his colleagues just treated that as a bargaining tool. Before he knew it Lips was in the middle of a bidding war as the other members of the group indicated that they too wanted the new Gribbleflotz aura detector.

Meanwhile, the Gribbleflotz residence

The Gribbleflotz residence wasn't actually in the Mihulka Tower. That was reserved for Dr. Gribbleflotz's study and the work rooms. No, the place where they all lived was right next door, and occupied part of what had once been Rudolph II's foundry. There was a door connecting it to the Mihulka Tower while another opened out onto the old foundry courtyard. It was this door Ursula Mittelhausen dashed through, calling out to Dina Kastenmayerin that she had to pick something up from the market.

She was thinking more about what she had to buy than where she was going and she slipped on the steps leading down to the cobbled courtyard. Ursula wasn't as young as she used to be and her reflexes were slow. She also wasn't helped by the wicker basket she was holding. When she slipped it impeded her attempts to catch the hand rail as she fell. She didn't fall far—no more than five or six steps, but they were stone steps leading to a cobbled courtyard.

She regained consciousness surrounded by a crowd of curious bystanders and Dina. "Help me," she said as she struggled to stand up.

Eager hands grabbed her hands and pulled, until Ursula screamed out in pain. Then she was dropped, resulting in a squeal as a stabbing pain ran through her chest.

A little tentative touching revealed a problem with her ribs. This was in addition to the more obvious grazes and cuts on her arms, legs, and head.

Dina started giving orders and Ursula was gently helped to her feet. Fortunately, she could walk, even if it did hurt to the point Ursula was clenching her teeth. Eventually she was settled on her bed and Dina sent out an urgent request for her husband's professional services.

Meanwhile, the Radio mast, Radio Prague

Magdalena passed her tool bag down to Vernon Fritz before scrambling the last few feet down onto the observation deck of the new transmission tower. Safe on the deck she wiped the sweat from her face before unclipping her safety line. She turned to Vernon Fritz, who'd been waiting impatiently for her to finish the repair. "All fixed," she said with some satisfaction at a job well done, and relief at having a floor under her feet again.

"Thanks, Mags. Sorry to send you up like that, but..." He handed back her tool bag.

"I understand, Herr Fritz," Magdalena said as she slung the bag over her shoulder, "you needed someone small enough to get at the problem, otherwise you'd have had to dismantle the whole thing, bring it down to fix it, then put it back."

"Which would have cost us three days," Vernon said.

"That's why you hired me," Magdalena said.

Vernon grinned. "Actually it isn't. But having someone small, strong, and not afraid of heights has been a real boon for this build."

Magdalena just smiled. Herr Fritz was only right on two of those. She was actually pretty terrified of heights.

"Have you started making crystal radios for sale yet?" Vernon asked as he led the way down from the observation deck.

"I've got Dietrich teaching some of Dr. Gribbleflotz's laborants how to make cat's whisker holders."

"What about making the boxes?" Vernon asked.

Magdalena answered that question and several others

as they climbed down the aerial tower. Finally they got to the ground.

"You're safe on the ground again," Vernon said.

Only then did Magdalena realize Herr Fritz had been asking about her crystal radio production arrangements to distract her from her fear of heights, which she'd thought she'd managed to hide from him. She gave him a bright smile. "Thank you, Herr Fritz."

Vernon smiled back. "You're welcome, and I did want to know how you were getting on making radios. There'll be a lot of people wanting them when Radio Prague goes on the air. Do you have an outlet set up?"

Magdalena nodded. "Frau Mittelhausen has offered to sell them in the Dr. Gribbleflotz Emporium of Natural Wonders."

"That sounds good. I hope they aren't taking too much in commission."

"We're still negotiating. I plan to ask Jason what he thinks next time I talk to him."

Vernon nodded. "You still have the eight o'clock slot on Friday night."

Magdalena smiled. "I can't thank you enough for letting me use your radio to chat with Jason." Herr Fritz was an amateur radio enthusiast and he'd brought his up-time transceiver with him to Prague so that he could stay in touch with his family. He also allowed members of the team to use it to call home. Not that Jason or anyone in his family were amateur radio enthusiasts, but they had arranged with Siler Hastings, who'd come out of retirement to teach radio technology at the State Technical College in Grantville, to allow Jason to chat with Magdalena using his transceiver.

✧   ✧   ✧

Magdalena walked home tired and hungry after a long day's work. She was looking forward to her dinner, which would be ready shortly after she got home. Frau Mittelhausen had it timed so that she had time for a hot shower before dinner.

Things were not as she expected when she arrived home. Dietrich, Lips, and the laborants were all sitting around the table talking. "What's happened? Why hasn't the table been set?" As she asked the questions she realized there was no sound of activity coming from the kitchen. She confirmed her worst fears by dashing into the room. Food was on the preparation surfaces, but nothing had been done about cooking it. She returned to the dining area.

"Where's Frau Mittelhausen? Why hasn't she started dinner?" Her stomach picked that moment to protest the lack of sustenance.

"Frau Mittelhausen suffered a bad fall," Lips said. "Dina's been looking after her."

Magdalena passed her eyes over the six young males seated around the table. "And none of you thought to start dinner?"

They all turned defensive and looked expectantly at Lips.

"If you say cooking is woman's work..." Magdalena warned.

"It's like this," Dietrich said. "None of us know how to cook."

"None of you?" Magdalena demanded. She received nothing but shaking heads in return. "That's great," she muttered. "All right you lot, into the kitchen. This is your chance to learn how to cook."

"But we don't know what to do," Lips said.

"I do," Magdalena said. "I'll tell you what to do, and supervise."

It took over twenty minutes before Magdalena had everything on the stove or in the oven. She could have done everything in a fraction of the time on her own, but that would have set a bad precedent, and anyway, it wasn't every day a girl got the chance to order six guys around. She made a final inspection, giving instructions for pots to be stirred while she was away, before slipping off to check on Frau Mittelhausen.

She found Ursula sitting up in her bed with Lips' sister in attendance. Dina wasn't paying her patient as much attention as she should, because in the next room one of the twins was crying. "Why don't you go and check on your children, Frau Kastenmayerin," Magdalena said. "I can check in on Frau Mittelhausen while I supervise dinner."

"Dinner!" Ursula said, adding a sharp intake of breath as she tried to sit up.

"Stay down, Ursula," Dina said.

"It's all right, Frau Mittelhausen. I've got the boys preparing dinner," Magdalena said.

"But none of them can cook to save their lives," Ursula said.

"But I do know how to cook," Magdalena said. "I took my turn at the house on Grays Run along with everyone else."

Ursula relaxed back onto the pile of pillows behind her. "You're a good girl, Magdalena."

Magdalena smiled smugly. Coming from Frau Mittelhausen, that was a big compliment. "What's wrong with you?" she asked Ursula.

"The doctor says I cracked a few ribs when I fell down the outside steps."

Magdalena winced. Still, she knew something that might help. "I'll be right back," she said before disappearing.

She returned a couple of minutes later carrying Liova. She carried him over to Ursula's bed and laid him down on it. "The up-timers believe a cat's purr has medicinal properties," she explained as she stroked Liova until he settled.

"Really?" Dina asked.

"Yes," Magdalena told Dr. Gribbleflotz's wife. "I know some people who are studying veterinary medicine and they say that cats heal faster than dogs, and if there are cats in the animal hospital, all the animals heal faster than they do if there are no cats."

She glanced to the bed to see how Frau Mittelhausen was reacting. She had to smile at the sight of the older woman gently stroking Liova, who was enjoying every bit of the attention he was getting. Naturally, he was purring. "I need to check on the guys, to make sure they haven't burnt anything."

Phillip's knock on the door to Frau Mittelhausen's room was answered by his wife. They kissed. "Sorry I was so long," Phillip said, "but I had to wait on the king." He glanced at the bed. "How's the patient?"

"Sleeping," Dina said.

That surprised Phillip. "How much laudanum have you given her?"

"Just the rest of the dose you prepared before you were called away," Dina said.

"I wouldn't have thought that would be enough to

let Frau Mittelhausen sleep. Are you sure you didn't give her more laudanum?"

Dina nodded. "I'm sure, Phillip. I think Magdalena's cat has helped Ursula fall asleep."

"Cat?" Phillip demanded as he glanced at the bed and wondered how he'd missed the animal curled up beside Frau Mittelhausen.

"Magdalena says that according to the up-timers, the purr of a cat has healing properties."

"Healing properties?" Phillip's mind latched onto that phrase. "The purr of a cat can invigorate the Quinta Essentia of the human humors? Nothing I've read has suggested anything like that."

Dina gently tugged Phillip until he started following her out of Ursula's room. "Maybe you should talk to Magdalena," she suggested as she gently led him away from the sleeping Frau Mittelhausen.

Magdalena was wiping the cooking surfaces down when Dr. Gribbleflotz and his wife walked into the kitchen. The boys had done a reasonable job cleaning up, but Magdalena didn't consider reasonable to be good enough and was giving everything a proper clean.

"Magdalena, could you tell Phillip more about how Liova's purr has healing properties?" Dina said.

"Sure," Magdalena said as she hung up the cloth she'd been using and gestured for Dr. Gribbleflotz and Frau Kastenmayerin to sit down.

Dina shook her head. "No, I'd better check on Salome and Jon. Poor Eva has had them all afternoon while I've cared for Ursula."

Eva Schroeter was the twin's nursery maid, and Magdalena thought she had it easy. There was no climbing several hundred feet above the ground for her. All she had to do was look after two babies, who spent most of their time sleeping. She didn't even have to feed them; their mother took care of that.

Magdalena served Dr. Gribbleflotz a glass of small beer before joining him at the kitchen table. "What would you like to know, Dr. Gribbleflotz?"

Phillip took a sip of his small beer before answering. "Dina says you think your cat has healing properties."

Magdalena nodded. "It's the purr, Dr. Gribbleflotz. There is something about the frequency of the purr that encourages natural healing."

"Sound has healing properties?" Phillip asked.

Magdalena nodded. "I think it's the vibration rather than the sound. I'd have to check with Jason's sister's friends in the veterinarian program to be sure." She suddenly grinned at Dr. Gribbleflotz. "Have you ever held Liova when he's purring?" she asked.

"No." Phillip shook his head. "I can't say that I've ever held a cat, let alone held one while it was purring."

Magdalena nodded knowingly. "You should try it some time."

"I will," Phillip said. "But why, if it has healing properties, have I seen nothing about this in the up-time books?"

Magdalena thought about that. "I think it's more anecdotal than proven scientific fact," she said. "Once, when Liova fell out of a tree and hurt himself, I was confused by the fact he was purring even though he was in pain. I took him to Dr. Blocker, one of the up-time veterinarians. He said that cats used their purr to encourage healing, and that as long as Liova was purring, I shouldn't worry."

Dr. Gribbleflotz was nodding. "But you claim that your cat's purring can help Frau Mittelhausen heal?"

"Yes," Magdalena agreed. "Dr. Blocker said that animals in the hospital always healed faster when there were cats in there as well."

Dr. Gribbleflotz fell silent for a while. He cleaned his spectacles, twice—a sure sign that he was thinking. Finally he put them back on and looked at Magdalena. "So if I could capture a number of cats and have them in a ward, then the patients should recover faster, because the purring invigorates the Quinta Essentia of the human humors."

Magdalena winced at the image that produced. "I don't think you could get the cats to stay on the beds," she said.

Phillip nodded. "Yes, that might be a problem. Maybe if we kept them in cages..." He got to his feet and wandered out of the kitchen, leaving a very bemused Magdalena sitting watching him disappear.

Friday

Magdalena was excited as she hurried home from work. She needed to shower and eat before heading to the Blue Lion in time to make her scheduled radio slot.

Lips was saying something in the common room that seemed to have the other guys in stitches. Magdalena interrupted her mad dash for the showers to find out what was so funny. "Hi, guys," she said. "What's so funny?"

Lips was laughing his head off, and the laborants weren't much better, so Dietrich tried to explain. "Dr.

Gribbleflotz brought several cages of cats into one of the wards today."

"What's so funny about that?" Magdalena asked.

Lips managed to control himself long enough to explain. Magdalena couldn't help herself. She too started laughing.

The laughter was interrupted by the dinner bell. Magdalena sent Dietrich an inquiring look.

"New cook," Dietrich answered.

"Tell her I'll be as quick as I can," Magdalena said before speeding off.

Later that evening at the Blue Lion

There was laughter on both sides as Magdalena related the story of Dr. Gribbleflotz and the cats to Jason. Vernon Fritz at her end had tears running down his face. On Jason's end she could hear someone in the background laughing. "Who's with you?" she asked.

"That's just Siler," Jason answered. "Hang on. Wait a moment."

The radio went dead as Jason stopped transmitting. Magdalena glanced at Herr Fritz, who just shrugged.

A couple of minutes later Jason was back transmitting. "Siler says that if you need vibrations for healing, maybe you should try vibrating beds." That was followed by a peculiar sound from Jason's end.

"What's that noise?" Magdalena asked.

"Just Siler laughing his head off. Anyway, what he said makes sense. I'll have a word with Dad and see what he thinks."

"Thanks." After that Magdalena and Jason switched

to Chinese. Even after four years of irregular lessons she didn't have a very big vocabulary, but she knew all the words she needed for the personal things they wanted to say that they didn't want broadcast to the world.

"Time's up," Vernon said.

Magdalena said her final farewells before switching to German to sign off. She passed the handset to Vernon. "Thank you, Herr Fritz."

"You're welcome, Mags." Vernon grinned at her. "Was that story about Dr. Gribbleflotz and the cats true?"

Magdalena got to her feet and collected the papers she'd spread over the desk. "I wasn't there," she said, "but Lips was. He might have exaggerated what happened."

Vernon grinned. "Either way, it was a good story. Please send the next person in as you leave."

August 1636, Prague

Phillip was happily ensconced in his top floor study-cum-laboratory reading material on the beneficial effects of cats' purrs that Magdalena had passed onto him when there was a knock at the door. "Get that please, Lips."

Lips laid down the papers he'd been reading and hurried across the room to open the heavy door. With Liova thinking he owned the tower and having a cat's natural affinity to high places it had become necessary to keep the door closed. Lips opened it and stepped back to allow Samuel Hartlib, the secretary of the Royal Academy of Science to enter. He was closely followed by the secretary of the Prague Chapter of the Society of Aural Investigators, Martin Zänkel.

Phillip looked up and recognized his guests. "Samuel, how can I help you?" he asked. "I hope you don't have more papers I have to sign."

"No, Herr President Dr. Gribbleflotz," Samuel said. "Herr Zänkel is here on behalf of the Society of Aural Investigators."

Phillip was immediately on alert. Something was up. Samuel only used the presidential title when it was Academy business, or when he, Phillip, had managed to do something to upset Samuel. Judging by the look in his eye, Phillip was inclined to think that this time Samuel was inspired by a bit of both.

Martin stepped forward. "Yes, Herr President Dr. Gribbleflotz, I must protest, on behalf of the Prague Chapter of the Society of Aural Investigators, at the unfair professional advantage the sale of the prototype Gribbleflotz Magneto-Etheric Aural Aura Detector has given to Zacharias Held. I must insist, on behalf of the Society, that additional Gribbleflotz Magneto-Etheric Theremins be made available to the other members of the Society."

Phillip had absolutely no idea what Martin was talking about, but the guilty look that had flashed across Lips' face gave him a clue as to whom he could ask. "Of course, Herr Zänkel. I'll get onto it right away."

Martin nodded in a self-satisfied manner. "Thank you, Herr President Dr. Gribbleflotz. The Society applauds your commitment to fair play."

Samuel waited for Martin to leave before turning a condemning glare onto Phillip. "Herr President, I am deeply upset that you didn't think to tell me about the Gribbleflotz Magneto-Etheric Theremin. I really must insist that I be kept properly informed of developments in future."

"I'm sorry, Samuel, but this is the first I've heard of a Gribbleflotz theremin. The only theremin I know of is a musical instrument one of the junior electricians boarding with us brought with her from Grantville."

"A musical instrument?" Samuel shook his head. "Why would members of the Society of Aural Investigators be interested in a musical instrument?"

Phillip shot Lips another glance. If there had ever been any doubt of his guilt, his flushed face would have settled it. "Is there something you need to tell us, Lips?" he asked.

Lips' face was a fiery red. "It was an accident, Phillip. I was playing Mags' theremin when Herr Held and some other members of the Society of Aural Investigators turned up." He paused to steady his breathing. "Herr Held asked what it was, and before I could explain that it was a musical instrument, Herr Zänkel jumped in, claiming that it was obviously a machine to detect a person's aura, and well . . ." Lips broke eye contact and looked towards the floor while kicking his toe into the ground. "I might have sort of kind of let them believe it."

"You what?" Phillip demanded. "Why would you do a thing like that?"

Lips looked up. "You had to have been there, Phillip," he said, dropping any pretense of formality. "There were six members of the Prague Chapter of the Society of Aural Investigators who absolutely believed that a musical instrument could detect auras!" He shot Phillip a hopeful smile. "It was just a bit of harmless fun."

Phillip managed to suppress his urge to laugh. He could well imagine the urge to enjoy a joke at the expense of members of the Society of Aural Investigators, but there was still a problem. "You do realize that the moment the king hears about this he's going to insist on me doing a reading of his aura using the... what did you call it?"

"A Gribbleflotz Magneto-Etheric Theremin. The Society members referred to it as an Aural Aura Detector."

"Right, a Gribbleflotz Magneto-Etheric Theremin," Phillip said. He folded his arms and glared at Lips. "So what do you suggest I do when King Venceslas asks me to perform an aura reading with the latest thing in aura detectors?"

Lips' face blanched. "The king?" he whispered.

"Yes, the king," Phillip confirmed. "If you remember, I am his personal aura interpreter."

Lips lowered his head and shuffled his feet.

"I'm waiting, Lips," Phillip said.

Lips lifted his head a fraction. "Magdalena made her theremin. I suppose we could ask her to make another one," he suggested hopefully.

"Perfect." Phillip clapped his hands together. "Go and find her and tell her I need a Gribbleflotz Magneto-Etheric Theremin. Oh, and tell her I'll probably need it soon."

Lips swallowed convulsively and gave Phillip and Samuel harassed looks before running out of Phillip's office.

"I would have expected you to administer some kind of punishment for his thoughtless actions," Samuel told Phillip.

Phillip just grinned. "Oh, Lips is going to be punished," he said.

"What? All I've seen you do is tell him to inform Frau Rutilius that you would like her to make you a Gribbleflotz Magneto-Etheric Theremin. Where's the punishment in that?" he asked. "She'll know you'll pay her handsomely for it."

"What you say is true, Samuel. However," Phillip said, "I would be surprised if Frau Rutilius knows that Lips sold her theremin."

Samuel whistled. "You mean he..."

Phillip nodded.

Lips walked down the stairs from Phillip's office like a condemned man making his way to the scaffold. He rubbed a hand around his neck just to confirm that there wasn't a noose looped around it. Well, he told himself, there was no getting out of it. He was going to have to tell Mags that he'd sold her theremin. There was one thing that might save him. He stopped by his room to collect the purse.

Magdalena launched herself at Lips, kicking him and hammering at him with her fists. "How could you sell my theremin?" she demanded.

Lips was sufficiently bigger than Magdalena that he was easily able to catch her wrists and hold her off. He also managed to plant his feet firmly on Magdalena's boots so she couldn't kick him. "They made me do it," he said.

"Made you do it?" Magdalena parroted. "What did they do, twist your arm?" She stared pointedly at the arms currently holding her at bay.

"They used something much more powerful than that," Lips said. "If you promise to stop trying to hit me I'll show you."

Magdalena glanced over at Dietrich. "Make him let me go," she insisted.

Dietrich shook his head. "No way! I'm staying well out of this scrap. Why don't you promise to stop trying to hit him and listen? You can always attack him later."

Lips glared at Dietrich. "Thank you, Mister Reasonable."

That made Magdalena smile and she relaxed her fists. "Okay, I promise not to hit you if you let me go, unless I don't like your excuse."

"Oh, you'll like this one," Lips said as he gingerly let Magdalena go.

They stared at each other for a few seconds before Magdalena backed up a few steps. "Okay, what's this powerful reason you're going to show me?"

Lips pulled a drawstring purse from a pocket in his jeans. "Hold out your hands," he told her. When she did he emptied the contents of the purse into them.

The moment she realized it was silver coins Lips was pouring into her hands she opened them, letting the coins fall to the floor. Dietrich showed unusual levels of energy scampering after them.

"I found thirty, how many were there?" he asked Lips a few minutes later.

"That's all of them," Lips said. "I sold your theremin for thirty newly minted Venceslasthaler."

"How fitting," Magdalena said scornfully. "Well, you can take your thirty pieces of silver and . . ." She was too angry to continue stringing coherent sentences together. She turned and stormed out of the room.

"Well," Lips said, "that went remarkably well."

Dietrich laughed. "You think *that* was something going well?"

Lips nodded. "She didn't try to kill me."

Dietrich grinned. "Well, if you look at it that way, I guess it did go remarkably well. Mind, I'd recommend you sleep with one eye open for the foreseeable future."

Lips sighed. "I really expected Mags to jump at the money I got for her theremin. After all, didn't she say she owed her friend back in Grantville thousands?"

"She did," Dietrich agreed. "However, she's hoping to earn enough from the sale of her crystal radios to pay off all her debts."

Lips limped over to a chair—Magdalena had got in a few well-delivered kicks to his shins with her industrial safety boots—and slumped into it. "I'm in a bit of a bind," he admitted.

Dietrich gave a sign of resignation. "What haven't you told us?"

"I desperately need to get a new theremin for Dr. Gribbleflotz."

"Why would he want one?" Dietrich asked.

Lips sighed. "I sold Mags' theremin to Zacharias Held of the Prague Chapter of the Society of Aural Investigators, and he's been doing something of a roaring trade with his new interactive aura tuning device. Dr. Gribbleflotz thinks it's only a matter of time before King Venceslas asks him to do a reading using one of the new Gribbleflotz Magneto-Etheric Theremins."

"Ouch!" Dietrich said with feeling.

Lips nodded. "I don't know what not having the

latest machine will do to Dr. Gribbleflotz's position with the king."

"Why didn't you say you needed a theremin for the doctor?" Magdalena asked from the door.

Lips' head shot up and he looked hopefully at the young woman currently propping up the doorjamb. "Because you didn't give me a chance," he said. "Can you make another one?"

"Sure," Magdalena said, "but it'll cost you."

Lips perked up. "Don't worry. The doctor will pay well for a new theremin."

"Don't you mean a Gribbleflotz Magneto-Etheric Theremin?" Magdalena asked.

"One small problem, Lips," Dietrich said.

Lips turned questioning eyes onto Dietrich. "What's the problem? You and Mags have both said that she made her theremin as her senior year project, and Mags just said she could make another one."

"That's all true, Lips, but the important part of a senior year project is that you complete it during your senior year."

Lips eyes opened wide as his jaw dropped in horror. He turned to Magdalena. "It takes a year to build a theremin?"

"Yes," Dietrich said.

Lips started cursing.

Magdalena listened to Lips' curses and wondered where he'd learned them. She recognized a few of them from her on-the-job training stints with Kelly Construction and the power station, but she couldn't image how a Lutheran pastor's son would learn them. She was enjoying Lips' discomfort, but it was time to put him out of his misery. "That's not entirely true, Dietrich."

"What's not true?" Dietrich demanded. "I was there when you were struggling to get your theremin working before the deadline."

"You're forgetting who Jason's father is, Dietrich."

Lips' head swung back and forth between Dietrich and Magdalena. "What's your boyfriend's father got to do with anything?" he asked.

"Yeah, Mags, what's Jason's father got to do with it not taking you a year to build a new theremin?" Dietrich asked.

"You do know that Jason's father is a highly qualified mechanical engineer?"

"You might have said something along those lines once or twice," Dietrich said.

Magdalena grinned. She was pretty sure she'd bragged about her boyfriend's father a lot more often than that. "Engineers are by their very nature heavily into being precise. Well, the holes in the rotor of an Alexanderson alternator need to be placed with extreme precision; otherwise the frequency of the signal it generates can vary throughout each rotation of the rotor." She smiled. "Jason's father takes being precise to a whole new level. He insisted that the only way I could reliably make all the cuts I needed to make in the rotor was to build a custom cutting machine that can automatically rotate the rotor just the right amount between slits so that all the slits on the rotor are an equal distance apart."

"You made a smaller version of the rig they used to form the rotor of the Alexanderson alternator for the Radio Prague transmitter?" Dietrich asked.

Magdalena nodded. "KCE were involved in making the one for Voice of Luther, so Jason's father and

Herr Kitt already had the drawings. They just had to scale them down for me.

"I spent over half my senior year just building that cutting machine." She smiled. A lot of that time had been spent alone with Jason in his father's workshop, and not all of it had been spent working.

"Does that mean it wouldn't take you long to make a new theremin?" Lips asked hopefully.

"If I had my tools, the right materials, and my notes, I could build a new one in a month."

"A month?" Lips muttered. "I need it sooner than that."

"That's not my problem," she said. "I have a day job."

Lips let his hopes rise. "So you could build one in much less than a month?" he asked. "Dr. Gribbleflotz really needs it as soon as possible," he said, not giving Magdalena a chance to reply. "Don't you owe it to him to do everything you can to help him?"

Magdalena stared hard at Lips. This was emotional blackmail, and they both knew it. Still, blackmail or not, Lips did have a point. When Frau Mittelhausen first recruited her she'd been a small twelve-year-old orphan. The best she could have hoped for was employment as a junior maid in some household. Instead she'd been taken in by the doctor and looked after. She might have only stayed with Dr. Gribbleflotz for a year, but that year had given her options. Without the doctor she would never have trained to be an electrician. She wouldn't have Liova, and of course, she'd never have met Jason. She sighed. "It'll mean working late, and I'll need help."

"We'll both help you," Lips said, volunteering Dietrich as well.

"You'll be able to contract out some of the work," Dietrich said. "The woodwork can be done by a proper cabinet maker for a start."

Magdalena planted her fist on her hips and glared up at Dietrich. "Are you suggesting there was something wrong with the quality of the woodwork of my theremin?" she demanded.

"No," Dietrich said. "Just that it took you over a month to make something a good cabinet maker could put together in a few days."

Magdalena wanted to continue arguing, but Dietrich was right. "I'll need to go over the drawings and work out what can be contracted out."

"That's good," Lips said. "So when can you start?"

"I need to get a message to Jason asking him to send me my stuff," she said.

Lips smiled. "That's not a problem. If you can write out a list of what you need, I can take it to the radiograph station and Jason can have the message tonight."

"There's also the matter of paying for everything to be delivered." Magdalena licked her lips. "There's rather a lot of stuff I'll need."

"I can get a payment authority from Frau Mittelhausen to cover transport and send that in the same message," Lips said.

A few days later, Prague

Dr. Gribbleflotz was an old hand at handling patrons. He understood that if you couldn't give them what they wanted you had to give them an alternative, and he didn't think Frau Rutilius would be able to build a new theremin before the king heard about Zacharias Held's new Gribbleflotz Magneto-Etheric Theremin. He knew it wouldn't be long before the king was asking him to read his aura using one of the new machines. He could ask Zacharias if he could borrow his, but that would only encourage the man's pretensions to grandeur. What he needed was something new, and he didn't mean something new in the mold of a vibrating bed such as was described in the information Frau Rutilius had passed on.

No, what was needed was something sufficiently new that would appeal to his patron. Phillip knew just the thing. He walked up to the niche below the portrait of Dina and picked up his lucky crystal. He'd measured the crystal's specific gravity and come to the conclusion that it was something called a white topaz. That was quite significant, because, according to his reading about the chakras, white topaz made for a good "Master Crystal" in Dr. Stone's Science of the Chakras.

He wasn't really looking forward to having his lucky crystal cut up, but he needed to have something to placate his patron. He pocketed it and set out for Roth's the jewelers.

Meanwhile

Magdalena stared at the pile of boxes on the floor of the bottom room of the Mihulka Tower. "I know I asked him to send everything, but this is ridiculous," she muttered to herself.

"What is all this stuff?" Lips asked.

"Everything I had stored at Jason's home." Seeing

everything sitting on the floor of the tower was very upsetting. It was as if Jason's parents were trying to send a message, and that message was that they didn't want her associating with their son. She swallowed her disappointment and started sorting things out, directing Lips and a couple of the laborants to move things to various parts of the room. It only took three hours to get everything set up to her satisfaction. Now all she had to do was take her notes to the various contractors she'd lined up. Fortunately she'd had the thirty Venceslasthaler Lips had got for her theremin. Craftsmen listened to teenage girls a lot better when they could show them the money.

Later that day

Phillip carefully laid his lucky crystal, or maybe that should be his lucky diamond, back in its niche. He patted it affectionately and stepped back. It looked at home where it lay, and for now it could stay there. He'd been surprised when Herr Roth told him that his lucky crystal was a diamond. Obviously he'd known it could be a diamond—both gems having much the same specific gravity, but he'd immediately discounted that possibility and decided it had to be a white topaz. It was just too big, and surely no one in their right mind would give away a diamond the size of an egg. Unless of course the Dutch officer who'd given it to him hadn't known what he had? Phillip shrugged. It didn't matter. He now knew his lucky crystal was a diamond, and it was back where it belonged, sitting in its niche just below his wife's portrait. Nothing else mattered.

It was going to be a few days at least before Roth's could assemble a suitable selection of gems to be cut for his set of chakras crystals, so he thought he might as well get on with his latest line of research. He picked up the file he was compiling on the efficacy of a cat's purr as a tool for invigorating the Quinta Essentia of the human humors and set off to check on the progress of his test subjects at the hospital.

Meanwhile

There was the usual hubbub of conversation in the meeting room of the Prague Chapter of the Society of Aural Investigators when Johann Dent walked in, full of news. He waved for one of the waiters to bring him a mug of Tincture of Cacao and headed for the fireplace.

There was no fire lit of course, it being a warm August day, but the sofas and easy chairs arranged around it were where the senior members of the society tended to congregate when they weren't working.

"You look full of news, Johann," Zacharias Held said from one of the well-padded easy chairs.

"I've just been checking out the stock at Roth's, and you'll never believe what I heard."

"Try us," Martin Zänkel suggested.

Johann quickly scanned the room before dragging a chair close to Martin and Zacharias. "Dr. Gribbleflotz was in Roth's asking about having a set of chakras crystals cut to complement a diamond he had."

"So?" Zacharias asked.

"So the diamond he had was four hundred and thirty carats." Johann might have misheard the actual weight of the diamond, but he was in no doubt as to its size. "That's right, a diamond the size of an egg."

Martin whistled, and then he vocalized the question all three were thinking. "I wonder how he made it."

Johann was about to respond when Merckel Meisel coughed discreetly, and presented him with his Tincture of Cacao. He took the mug from the waiter's tray and turned back to Zacharias and Martin. "Wasn't there an article in an issue of the *Proceedings of the HDG Laboratories* where Dr. Gribbleflotz described a method of making synthetic rubies and sapphires?" Johann asked. He nodded. "Yes, I'm sure of it."

Zacharias and Martin nodded. "I remember reading that. It needs a lot of heat," Zacharias said.

"Electric arc furnaces are supposed to get very hot," Martin said. "Do you think Dr. Gribbleflotz might have made it in the annex to the new power plant?" Martin asked.

"It's possible," Zacharias said. "Maybe we should ask him."

That evening, Golden Lane, Prague Castle

Abraham Lieblitz waited for his son Isaac to return after showing out the waiter from the chapter house of the Prague chapter of the Society of Aural Investigators. While he waited he checked his notes, not that there were many.

"Four hundred and thirty carats," Isaac said when he returned. "That's a pretty big diamond."

Abraham gestured for his son to sit down. "Yes it is, but a diamond of that size is too big to fence."

"We could cut it up," Isaac suggested.

Abraham glared at his son. "Who do you suggest we ask to cut it, Roth's?"

Isaac winced. "They'd know it was Dr. Gribbleflotz's diamond immediately."

"As would every other jeweler in the world, a diamond of that size would be noticed and talked about."

"So we don't go after the diamond?" Isaac asked.

"No. Unfortunately it's too big for us to handle."

"What about the story that Dr. Gribbleflotz made the diamond?" Isaac asked. "Surely if he made a big one he also made some smaller ones?"

"If he made a big one," Abraham said.

"This is Dr. Gribbleflotz we're talking about, Father, the kingdom's preeminent scientist."

"That doesn't mean he can make diamonds. However, if he has made smaller ones, we might be interested."

"I'll start making inquiries," Isaac said.

An hour later, somewhere in Prague

Ascher Meisel backhanded his youngest brother, knocking him to the floor. "You silly fool," he yelled at him. "You overhear that Dr. Gribbleflotz has a diamond the size of an egg and the first thing you do is take the information to the Lieblitzes."

Merckel could taste the blood in his mouth. He ran his tongue over his teeth, and was relieved to find none of them broken. "They pay well for the information I sell them from the Society."

"Do you have any idea how much such a diamond might be worth?" Ascher demanded.

Merckel nodded. As a waiter at the Society of Aural Investigators he often heard the members talking about the prices of various gemstones.

Ascher spat at Merckel. "And now they're going to get it all."

"Who'll get it all?" Jakob Meisel asked.

Ascher turned to glare at his younger brother. "The Lieblitzes of course. They're probably already planning how they can steal the diamond."

"We don't even know where he keeps it hidden," Jakob said.

"It's a diamond. It'll be kept where all diamonds are kept, in his wife's jewelry safe," Ascher said.

Merckel pulled himself up enough to rest his back against a wall. "Not this diamond. Dr. Gribbleflotz will keep it for himself."

"What haven't you told me?" Ascher demanded.

Merckel didn't like the look in his brother's eyes and tried to back right into the wall. "Dr. Gribbleflotz is having a set of chakras gems made to the same size and cut of the diamond. That means it'll be one of the set. He won't keep his chakras gems with his wife's jewelry."

"So where will he keep it?" Jakob asked.

"In his study," Merckel suggested.

Jakob whistled. "But that's in the Mihulka Tower. We'll never find it in there."

"His study is on the top floor," Merckel said.

"And how do you know that?" Ascher asked, with menace.

Merckel tried to slide against the wall to get away from his approaching brother. "I overheard it mentioned at the Society."

Ascher stopped and stared at Merckel. He nodded. "You will find a way to get into Dr. Gribbleflotz's study so we can search it."

"Yes, of course," Merckel said. He was prepared to agree to anything, just so long as his brother didn't hit him again.

A *few days later*

Vernon Fritz turned round at the sound of something hitting the floor and saw Magdalena Rutilius staring vacantly at a screwdriver rolling on the floor. He skipped over and picked it up. "What's the matter, Mags?" he asked as he offered the screwdriver to her.

Magdalena blinked a few times. "Huh!"

Vernon released a heavy sigh. He wrapped her hand around the screwdriver before picking her up and carrying her over to a packing crate, where he sat her down. "Are you sick? Have you been eating properly?" Anorexia wasn't the problem it had been up-time, but while Mags had always seemed skinny, he was sure she'd lost weight. "Are you missing your boyfriend?"

"Yes."

Vernon had to smile. That answer could apply to any of the questions he'd just rattled off. "What have you been doing to yourself, Mags?"

Magdalena lowered her head. "I'm sorry, Herr Fritz."

Vernon tilted her head up so he could make eye contact. "I don't want apologies. I want to know what's going on." He noticed the dark circles around her eyes. "Have you been burning the candle at both ends?"

"I was building a theremin for Dr. Gribbleflotz after work."

"And you had to work yourself to the point of exhaustion to do that?"

She nodded. "Dr. Gribbleflotz needed it urgently, Herr Fritz. He might be asked to use it to investigate the king's aura at any moment."

"And you've run yourself into the ground just so Dr. Gribbleflotz has a new toy with which to entertain the king?" He shook his head. "I can't afford to have you exhausted on the job."

"Am I fired?" Magdalena asked in a small voice.

"No, of course not," Vernon said. "But I want you to go home and catch up on your sleep. You can come back at the usual time tomorrow."

Magdalena slid off the packing case, grabbing it to steady herself as she landed. "Thank you, Herr Fritz."

Vernon laid a fatherly hand on Magdalena's shoulder. "And I want you to stop working all hours on Dr. Gribbleflotz's theremin."

Magdalena broke into a smile. "It's finished," she said. "That's why I'm so tired. I worked right through last night to finish it."

"That's good, but I don't want you to start working all hours to make another one."

"That won't happen, Herr Fritz."

"Good. Well, off you go."

Vernon watched Magdalena collect her things and head off toward home. She seemed steady enough on her feet that he decided not to send someone after her to see that she got home safely. A few good nights' sleep was all she needed. The moment she disappeared out of sight he turned back to the job at hand, and realized he hadn't been the only person watching. "Don't you all have work you should be doing?"

That was enough to disperse the work crew. They were a good group, and he was sure they wouldn't tease Mags too much when she came back to work tomorrow.

Magdalena was so exhausted by the time she got home she didn't even announce to anyone that she was home. Instead she made her way to the female dormitory, where she was still the only occupant, and after dropping her work bag and boiled leather hardhat on one of the empty beds, crawled onto her bed, boots and all, and pulled a blanket over her. She was still vaguely awake when Liova burrowed his way under the blanket and head-butted her a few times. She stroked him before falling asleep to the sound of his purr.

Magdalena woke with a start. The first thing she realized was that she was still fully dressed. Frau Mittelhausen wouldn't have approved, especially not of her wearing her work boots to bed.

She sat up. Sunlight was streaming onto her bed. That meant it was about five o'clock in the afternoon. She was confused as to what she was doing at home at that time, but then she started to remember. She was blushing as she swung her feet to the floor. What did the other workers think of her? she wondered as she stood up. Then she looked around for Liova. He'd deserted her, probably for a handout in the kitchen or some sunny spot to sleep. She smiled at the thought of her cat and set out in search of him.

Meanwhile, in the Mihulka Tower

"Quiet!" Ascher ordered in a loud whisper as Jakob's wooden clog clomped onto the step.

"There's no one in the tower to hear," Jakob said. "Dr. Gribbleflotz and his assistant are attending to the king and we counted out all the laborants as they left."

"But they're just next door," Ascher said.

"This is a castle, Ascher," Jakob said as he gently slapped the stone wall. "We could be tearing the place apart and they wouldn't hear us."

Ascher glared at his brother, but his next step wasn't as carefully placed or as quiet as the previous one. Nothing happened, so he increased his speed. There were a lot of stairs to negotiate before they got to Dr. Gribbleflotz's study.

Behind them, in the shadows, Liova followed.

The old foundry, next door to the Mihulka Tower

Frau Mittelhausen wasn't well enough to do any heavy work yet, but she could give directions. She was sitting at the kitchen table ordering the laborants about when Magdalena poked her head into the room. "Has anyone seen Liova?" she asked.

Frau Mittelhausen shook her head. "I haven't seen him." She paused for a moment. "Now that you mention it, he's usually smooching about in here about this time."

"Thank you," she said. She knew Liova visited the kitchen when meals were being prepared in the hope of being fed. That was why she'd started her search there. She conducted a quick search of his usual haunts in the old foundry before conceding that Liova was probably somewhere he shouldn't be. She hurried back to her room and collected her catnip kit. She primed the little drawstring bag with fresh catnip and looped the long ribbon through the drawstrings as she made for the stairs in the Mihulka Tower. Hopefully no one had left the door to Dr. Gribbleflotz's study open.

She heard the first indication that the door to Dr. Gribbleflotz's study was open halfway up the last flight of stairs. The crash and tinkle of breaking glass had her rushing up the last few steps, any tiredness she might have felt forgotten.

She was almost at the door when she heard the man speak out. It wasn't Dr. Gribbleflotz, nor was it Lips. That left Dietrich, who should still be at work as the only unaccounted-for male who had any business even being in the tower. She edged up to the door and peeped around it. In the light of a lantern she could see a man searching amongst Dr. Gribbleflotz's books.

"What about this? Is this it?" another man called out.

Magdalena crept further into the room and saw two men were standing by the portrait of Dina Kastenmayer. One of them had something shiny in his hand. Neither of them was Dietrich, so whoever they were, they had no right being here.

"Does it look like a diamond to you?" Ascher demanded before knocking the item from Jakob's hand.

Magdalena saw something shiny skittle across the stone floor. She couldn't be sure, but she thought it might be Dr. Gribbleflotz's lucky crystal.

She thought of running for help, but she knew that crystal was important to Dr. Gribbleflotz. Her tongue ran over her dry lips. She'd never forgive herself if these men decided to take it and escaped. Besides, the room was full of shadowy places to hide. It shouldn't be too hard for her to slip in unnoticed.

She glanced towards the two men to see what they were doing. They'd moved on to Dr. Gribbleflotz's fume cupboard. She winced as one of them tore the glazed sliding hatch out of its rails and threw it carelessly onto the floor.

While they proceeded to tear the fume cupboard apart Magdalena used the shadows to hide in as she made her way over to where she thought the crystal might have ended up. She found it in one of the cannon niches, and Liova found her. He smooched around the hand holding his catnip toy.

"Meooooowwwww!"

"Hey, who're you?" Jakob called out.

Magdalena looked up to see both men were staring at her from across the room.

"Catch her," Ascher said.

There were heavy wooden tables with various experiments laid out on them between Magdalena and the two men. She was small and fast, but she wasn't small and fast enough to escape from two men. Liova, on the other hand, was a past master at escaping, especially in a room so full of potential hiding places. She slipped Dr. Gribbleflotz's crystal into the catnip toy and used the long ribbon she usually used as a lead to tie it around Liova's neck before diving under one of the tables. Meanwhile Liova protested the indignity of having something tied around his neck and tried to paw it off.

"She's tied something to the cat. What's the bet it's the diamond?" Ascher said as he dashed for the door, slamming it shut.

There was a hazel wood and twig broom in the corner. Ascher grabbed that and started towards Magdalena and Liova. Magdalena smiled as she dived under one of the tables. Her cat loved this game. He ran straight at the man, only to dodge at the last moment as the broom swung through where he would have been.

Liova wasn't a gracious winner. He leapt up onto one of Dr. Gribbleflotz's work tables and sat and licked a front paw. Frau Mittelhausen had always complained that he looked as if he was laughing at her when he did that. The man with the broom obviously felt the same and charged the table, slamming the broom down.

Liova wasn't there when the broom hit the table, sending alchemical glassware flying. He had jumped off the table once Ascher was committed to his blow and was now bounding towards the door. Unfortunately, it was shut.

"We've got you now," Ascher said as he Jakob approached Liova from opposite sides.

Liova took off, charging right past Ascher. He scampered across the floor under one of the tables and into one of the cannon niches. A moment later he was up on the window sill and through the open window.

Ascher charged after Liova while Jakob grabbed an unsuspecting Magdalena by the ankle. She'd been so entranced with Liova's antics that she'd forgotten the other man.

Jakob hauled her out from under the table before grabbing her by the collar of her industrial strength coveralls and spun her around to face him. Magdalena kicked out, landing a couple of good blows against her assailant's shins with her steel capped work boots. Unfortunately, the man retaliated with his wooden clogs. Magdalena screamed in pain.

"You don't like it when it's done to you, do you?" Jakob said. He tightened his grip on Magdalena's collar. "What was in the bag you tied to the cat?" he demanded.

Magdalena had a belt knife, and tried to stab him with it, but the leather jerkin he was wearing easily turned her ineffective thrust.

The man used both hands to twist her wrist until she screamed and dropped her knife. "That wasn't very nice," Jakob said as he grabbed her by the jaw with his right hand and thrust her up against the wall, easily lifting her from her feet. "What did you hang around the cat?" he demanded. He punched her in the gut. "Well, the cat got your tongue?" He sniggered at his own joke.

Magdalena was really panicking now. Her head was ringing from the impact with the wall, her gut was sore from the punches, and her right hand was numb with pain. She felt around her pockets with her other hand hoping that maybe she'd left something in a pocket that could be used as a weapon.

Her hand felt something. She'd hoped for a screwdriver, but maybe this was better. She pulled out the plastic squeeze bottle of hand sanitizer, popped open the top.

An electrician usually builds up a lot of grip strength in their hands. It came from gripping wires while pulling them. People who were paranoid of falling also tended to develop a lot of grip strength. Magdalena was both of those, and when you added the adrenaline of a flight or fight moment even using her left hand the contents of the bottle of sanitizer didn't stand a chance.

Before Jakob could react to the threat, she squirted almost a hundred milliliters of sanitizer—eighty-plus percent ethyl alcohol by volume—right into both of his eyes. He screamed and let her go, rubbing vigorously at his eyes.

Magdalena landed awkwardly, dropping the squeeze bottle and hurting her wrist when she tried to use her right hand to keep her balance. She ran for cover, looking for Liova as she ran. She couldn't see him, but she could see the man with the broom trying to hit something on the ledge beyond the open window.

Reoooooowwwwwl!

The man with the broom stepped back from the window. "Forget about the girl, Jakob. The cat's escaped. We need to catch it before someone else finds it and our diamond."

Magdalena realized the noise had been Liova reacting to being knocked off the ledge. "Liova!" she screamed as she ran for the door, everything else forgotten in her fear for her pet's safety.

She didn't make it. A panicking Ascher ran straight into her. Eighty pounds of girl hit a hundred and eighty pounds of fully grown man and came off second best. Ascher was barely slowed by the impact. The same couldn't be said for Magdalena. She was sent flying into a stone wall. She tried to break her fall, but too much weight went onto her left hand and something cracked, then the rest of her hit the stone floor, knocking her out.

❖   ❖   ❖

"What happened to you?" Ascher demanded of his brother as he grabbed him and got him moving towards the door.

Tears were running down Jakob's cheeks as his eyes blinked continually in an attempt to neutralize the alcohol that had got into both his eyes. "That bitch sprayed something in my eyes," he said. He all but tripped over the unconscious Magdalena and broke free of his brother's hold.

"What're you doing?" Ascher said as he grabbed at Jakob's hand.

Jakob fended off Ascher's hand long enough to plant a couple of kicks into the unconscious Magdalena. "Bitch!"

"Come on," Ascher insisted as he pulled Jakob away from Magdalena, "we need to get out of here. People are bound to have noticed a cat go flying out of a window."

Unlike Magdalena, Dietrich hadn't been up most of the night finishing and testing the Gribbleflotz Magneto-Etheric Theremin, so he'd managed to put in a full day's work. Still, he was a little tired when he finally stepped into the courtyard of the old foundry. He'd barely taken two steps when he heard Liova cry out. He looked up in surprise, and saw Liova falling off the ledge of one of the highest windows on the Mihulka Tower.

Dietrich watched the last few feet of Liova's fall with dread. He wasn't looking forward to telling Magdalena that her cat had been badly hurt in a fall, but he was in for a surprise. Liova landed on his feet and took off. Dietrich knew that didn't necessarily mean he wasn't hurt, but at least he didn't have to describe

Liova pancaking onto the cobblestones. He watched Liova disappear around a corner before entering the old foundry.

Sounds emanating from the kitchen attracted him, and he looked in to see Frau Mittelhausen firmly in charge of the laborants as they prepared dinner.

"Hello, Dietrich," Frau Mittelhausen said. "Why don't you catch up with Magdalena and tell her to wash her hands if she wants to eat."

"Mags is already home from work?" Dietrich asked in surprise. He usually beat her home. "Where is she?"

"She came in looking for Liova a few minutes ago."

Dietrich stared at Frau Mittelhausen while he digested this information. Liova had been in Dr. Gribbleflotz's study, a place where he shouldn't be. "Is Dr. Gribbleflotz about?" he asked.

Frau Mittelhausen shook her head. "He and Lips are attending the king with the Gribbleflotz Magneto-Etheric Theremin Magdalena finished last night."

Dietrich started moving. "I'll find Mags," he called back as he hurried towards the door to the Mihulka Tower. It was possible that Dr. Gribbleflotz had forgotten to shut the door to his study when he went out, but it was very unlikely. And as Lips had gone out with him, there was nobody with any legitimate business in Dr. Gribbleflotz's study. "Mags, are you up there?" he called. There was no reply. He drew the heavy up-time revolver he'd been given by the Chengs before he and Magdalena left Jena and started climbing the stairs.

He ran into Ascher and Jakob on the third level. He exited the spiral staircase going up while they entered the room coming down from Dr. Gribbleflotz's study.

Both parties froze on first sight of the other before Ascher charged Dietrich, pulling Jakob along with him.

Dietrich had been a farm laborer and then a soldier before becoming a student. Until he'd started his compulsory militia service in Grantville, he'd never held, let alone fired a gun. During his career as a soldier he'd been a simple spearman. As such, shooting wasn't a standard reaction to a threat, so he didn't try to fire at either of the two men—at such close range he probably wouldn't have had a chance to aim before the two men were on top of him anyway. Instead he reverted to instinct and learned behavior, and used the revolver in his right hand as a cudgel.

In cricket, a top-of-the-line fast bowler can send the hard five-and-a-half-ounce ball toward the opposition batsman at speeds of up to a hundred miles per hour. A hit to the body at those speeds can break bones. People have died from being hit in the head by a cricket ball.

Dietrich didn't achieve a hand-speed of anything like a hundred miles per hour, peaking at no more than eighty-five miles per hour. However, the six-inch Colt Python he was swinging had over seven times the mass of a cricket ball. He struck Ascher's skull with more than enough energy to break bones, and then his two hundred and forty pounds provided momentum for the follow-through.

There was a sickening crunch when the gun hit Ascher before he was thrown farther into the third-level room, falling in a sprawling heap on the floor. Dietrich stared at the body, sure in his mind that he'd just killed a man. It was enough of a distraction for Jakob to run past him, into the spiral staircase.

Dietrich thought of following, but there was still Magdalena to worry about. He paused long enough to confirm the man he'd hit was dead before charging up the last flight of stairs, calling out her name as he ran. The door into Dr. Gribbleflotz's study was wide open, and Dietrich could see the carnage the two men had wreaked. With the Colt Python held out in front of him he started to search the room. Then he saw the crumpled heap that was Magdalena. He holstered the revolver as he ran over to her, careless of the glass and chemicals all over the floor.

That evening, the hospital in Prague

Magdalena was lying down in bed feeling sorry for herself when Nurse Kaufmann twitched back the curtain. "You have visitors. Isn't that nice?"

She perked up. "Liova?" she asked.

Gertraud Kaufmann frowned. "No, it's just Herr Kastenmayer and Herr Bockelmann. Now let's sit you up a bit." She easily lifted Magdalena forward so she could pile pillows behind her before standing back to admire her handiwork. "I'll just go and get your visitors."

A couple of minutes later Lips and Dietrich were led into the curtained cubicle.

"How're you feeling?" Lips asked.

Magdalena ignored the question, going instead to something much more important. "Liova?"

"We haven't seen him since he flew out the window," Dietrich said. "He managed to run off after he landed, but he might have hurt himself."

"But everyone is looking for him," Lips said. "Even Phillip."

It was so unusual for Lips to use the doctor's Christian name outside the family. "Is something the matter?"

"One of the thieves got away with his lucky crystal. Dina thought helping find your cat would take his mind off his loss."

"One of the thieves?" Magdalena asked. "What happened to the other one?"

"So there were only the two of them?" Dietrich asked.

Magdalena attempted to nod, but the bruising around her neck hurt too much. "Just the two," she said.

"Dietrich killed the other one," Lips said. "You should have seen the mess he made of him."

Magdalena caught sight of Dietrich's eyes. He seemed uncomfortable with Lips' enthusiasm, so she tried to divert him, but nothing could stop Lips.

"He had this up-time revolver and he smashed in the man's skull with it."

"Up-time revolver?" Magdalena asked. How could Dietrich afford such a thing?

"That's right." Lips turned to Dietrich. "Go on, show her your gun."

Magdalena could see that there would be no peace until Dietrich showed her his revolver. It became obvious that Dietrich had reached the same conclusion when he slowly pulled a large revolver from a waist holster.

"Where did you get that?" she demanded with enough force to have her wincing with pain. She could see, because it had its name engraved on the barrel, that it was a Colt Python .357 magnum. That made it one of the most expensive up-time handguns available, and way outside anything Dietrich should have been able to afford.

"I was given it," Dietrich said.

"Who would give you a Colt Python?" she asked.

"The Chengs."

"What?" Magdalena demanded. "Why would they give you an expensive handgun?"

Dietrich broke into the first smile she'd seen from him since he arrived. "They asked me to look out for you. Frau Cheng said that after spending the last four years turning you into a suitable wife for their son, they didn't want to see it going to waste." He shot her a wry smile. "Fat lot of good I was as a bodyguard."

Magdalena felt tears forming in her eyes. She started to lift her hands to wipe them, but the heavy plaster casts stopped her.

"Hey, Mags, don't cry," Dietrich said. He reached forward and used the bedsheet to mop up her eyes. "If I'd known it'd upset you, I wouldn't have said anything."

That just set Magdalena off even worse. All she could think of was that she'd been misreading the signs. Jason's parents might think they were too young to marry, but from what Dietrich had just said, she knew they didn't object to her becoming his wife. Meanwhile Lips and Dietrich got to their feet, intent on deserting her to her tears.

"Where do you think you're going with that animal, Dr. Gribbleflotz?"

The roar from beyond the curtain belonged to

Nurse Kaufmann and was piercing enough to bring Magdalena back to the present. An animal in the ward, could it be . . .

"This isn't an animal," Dr. Gribbleflotz could be heard to say. "This is Liova, Frau Rutilius' cat."

"I remember what happened last time you brought cats into the ward, Dr. Gribbleflotz."

Magdalena turned pleading eyes onto Dietrich. He smiled and pulled the curtain open to reveal Dr. Gribbleflotz, his wife, and one of his laborants, but she only had eyes for the cat being carried in his carrier by the laborant. "Liova," she called.

Young Hans, the laborant, lowered Liova onto the bed. Magdalena tried to stick a finger between the bars of the cat carrier, but she lacked the strength and motor control.

"How are you feeling?" Dina asked.

"Better for having Liova back. How did you find him?" she asked.

Dina took one of the seats vacated by Lips and Dietrich. "Hans found him. Someone had tied something around his back, and he'd got his leg caught in it."

Hans pulled a tangled mass of ribbon and catnip toy out of a pocket. "I hope it wasn't valuable," he said, "but I had to cut the ribbon. It was the only way I could free his leg. I tried to undo the knots, but your cat wouldn't let me."

Magdalena winced when she saw how heavily his hands had been painted with iodine antiseptic lotion. "I'm sorry you were so badly hurt."

Hans blushed. "It was nothing. I'd do the same for any animal caught up like that." He held out the catnip toy and tangle of ribbon.

With both hands in casts Magdalena couldn't take the catnip toy and ribbon. This started to dawn on Hans, but before he could blush again Dietrich stepped in. "I'll take that for Mags," he said.

Even before his hand closed around the bundle Dietrich was looking inquiringly at Magdalena. That gave hope to her that today could end happily for more than just her. "Open it," she told Dietrich.

Dietrich opened the drawstrings and started to squeeze out whatever was in the bag. A clear crystal started to immerge.

"My lucky crystal!" Dr. Gribbleflotz said, reaching a hand towards Dietrich.

Dietrich squeezed the crystal out into Dr. Gribbleflotz's waiting hand, and he immediately started stroking it, rather like Magdalena would stroke Liova. He turned to Magdalena. "I can't thank you enough for saving my lucky crystal," Dr. Gribbleflotz said, still stroking the crystal. "I thought I'd lost it."

"I don't think they were really interested in it, Dr. Gribbleflotz. They were looking for a diamond, and it doesn't look anything like a diamond."

Dr. Gribbleflotz smiled at Magdalena, a twinkle in his eye. "But what is a diamond supposed to look like?"

Dr. Gribbleflotz gave Magdalena a barely detectable wink before making his excuses and leaving with Hans and Dina. Lips and Dietrich soon followed. That left Magdalena alone in her bed with Liova, and Nurse Kaufmann watching her from just outside the curtained off cubical.

"So that's the Liova you've been calling out for," she said.

Magdalena nodded. She was distracted, slowly

absorbing the importance of what Dr. Gribbleflotz had been suggesting before he left.

"I hope he isn't going to make any messes in my ward."

Magdalena was drawn back from the dawning realization that Dr. Gribbleflotz's lucky crystal was the diamond the thieves had been looking for to answer Nurse Kaufmann's question. "Did anyone bring in Liova's litter box and his food bowls?"

Nurse Kaufmann shook her head.

"Then someone is going to have to take him back to the tower tonight."

Phillip stood at the door to his study and surveyed the devastation with the aid of an up-time design lantern. Even in the yellow light of a single lantern he could see that the intruders had made a mess of his study. The one bright spot in the whole catastrophe was that, thanks to Magdalena, he still had his lucky crystal.

He stepped into his study and, being careful where he put his feet so that he didn't stand on any broken glass or step into any of the puddles of acids or chemicals lying on the stone floor, he made his way across the room to his writing desk. Once there he pulled his lucky crystal out of his pocket and carefully set it back in its niche. He stroked it a couple of times before stepping back, and almost tripped over some of the books the intruders had dropped on the floor.

Phillip stared at the books littering the floor. Such treatment of books was sacrilege. He muttered curses at the intruders as he hooked the lantern up above his desk and got down on his knees to carefully put them back where they belonged.

With the books taken care of he stood and brushed at the dirt on the knees of his trousers. He'd promised Dina that he would only put his lucky crystal back where it belonged before returning, but he was sure that she'd understand about the books.

It was time for him to leave. He unhooked his lantern and set out on a slow loop of his laboratory, checking on the damage.

It was obvious where most of mess on the floor had come from. Before he left to attend to the king he'd had three experiments set up on the tables—two of them waiting for him to start them, and the third one he'd had to shut down and abandon at short notice when he was summoned to attend the king. Now those same experiments were scattered all over the place. He sighed. Someone was going to have to clean up the mess.

In addition to the debris from his experiment, there were also the shattered remains of his fume cupboard. That was even worse than what'd happened to the experiments set up on the benches. At least those used easily procured chemicals and glassware. The fume cupboard was different. Most of it could be rebuilt by a good carpenter or cabinet maker, but the shattered safety glass front hatch was something else altogether. It had been a piece of irreplaceable up-time automotive safety glass. He was going to have to order a new piece, and it was going to take a while for a suitable piece to be procured and shipped.

With the happy thought that he wasn't going to be able to use his fume cupboard for a minimum of a week, if he was lucky, Phillip continued the depressing survey of the damage. He walked around, crouching every now and again to pick up a piece of glassware. He was hoping to discover something that hadn't been broken, but he wasn't having much luck—stone floors were particularly unforgiving of glass items falling onto them from not less than three feet.

Phillip rounded a corner and the light of his lantern fell on a beaker that seemed unbroken. He didn't exactly pounce on it, but he got to it quickly. He picked it up, and only then did he realize that the beaker had been shattered.

He held it up to his lantern and examined it. Something inside the flask was holding the glass fragments together. He stared at it for a while, until a light started to dawn. He'd been experimenting with turning cellulose acetate into a thermo-plastic when he'd been summoned to attend the king. He'd needed Lips to come along with him to provide power for the Gribbleflotz Magneto-Etheric Theremin, so there had been no one to clean up the abandoned experiment,

He'd made up a batch of cellulose acetate in the beaker. After he poured the freshly made plastic into the mincer he'd placed the used beaker back on the bench. In the time between him doing that and the beaker being knocked off the table, the cellulose acetate sticking to the sides of the beaker had set.

Phillip was still staring at the shattered beaker when Dina appeared at the door to his study. "I thought you said you were only going to be a couple of minutes," she said.

Phillip guiltily put the beaker on the bench. "I'm sorry, dear, but those horrible men scattered my books over the floor. I just had to pick them up and put them away."

"Just as long as you're not thinking about cleaning up the rest of the mess tonight."

"I'm not," Phillip said as he picked his way across the room to join his wife.

When he got to the door he started to close it, pausing for a moment just before it was fully closed to have a final look at the shattered beaker on the bench. He couldn't actually see it, but he knew it was there, and he knew what it represented.

The shattered glass of the beaker looked just like the shattered safety glass of his fume cupboard. He'd read the articles in the encyclopedias. He knew laminated safety glass could be made using cellulose nitrate or polyvinyl butyral. The first was a form of guncotton, and therefore not something he wanted to use in a fume cupboard, while the later was a plastic he currently had no idea how to make. He hadn't realized that cellulose acetate could be used, at least until now.

He firmly closed the door and joined his wife. Arm in arm they made their way back to their apartment. Dina talked about Frau Rutilius while Phillip thought about using his new discovery to get his fume cupboard back in to operation as quickly as possible. Only this time, instead of having only a small glass window, he'd glaze the whole thing with safety glass.

Afterword

Dr. Phil was created on a Saturday afternoon in 2003 in Mannington, West Virginia, the town that is the model for Grantville.

The first three 1632 minicons were held there. We were meeting upstairs in the boardroom of Mannington Main Street, the local chamber of commerce. After lunch Virginia DeMarce voiced the opinion that the southern women of Grantville would never be satisfied after they ran out of baking powder for biscuits. A discussion ensued that went over all the other important chemistry that was in the way of biscuits becoming a priority. Eventually, Virginia turned to me and said, "Couldn't you write out a cheat sheet for a downtimer alchemist?"

Dr. Phil, Phillip Theophrastus Gribbleflotz, the world's greatest alchemist, great-grandson of the great Paracelsus (he was a Bombast on his mother's side) rose up from the depths of my mind and invaded it. I wrote up a description of the character—who he was, where he came from, his personality, etc.—and an outline of the cheat sheet to make baking soda, and

I posted it in the 1632 forums on Baen's bar. At the time, I thought that was the end of it. I had gotten Dr. Phil down onto bytes and he was out of my mind.

Then, Kerryn Offord decided to combine Dr. Phil with his characters, the Kubiaks, and "Calling Dr. Phil" came into being. After that, it became an annual event. At the 1632 minicon Virginia would make some mild, innocuous sounding request, and Dr. Phil would roar out of the depths of my mind, and I would end up channeling him until I had the science parts of the story worked out. The most difficult of these was when Virginia explained that Phil's wife Dina would have written her guide to Marital Health, and someone else reminded us of Herb Albert's album, *Creamed Madonna*. Story by story, the setting would go to Kerryn, who would turn it into a real story with characters and people and everything.

This book adds to the chronicles with new stories dated after the most recent from the *Grantville Gazette*, plus the first third of the book explaining Phil's backstory. I hope you enjoy it.

I'm sure this isn't the end of Kerryn's and my collaboration with Dr. Phil. Doubtless Virginia has a mild, innocuous question to be asked with a smile and a tilt of her head, which will pull Phil out of his resting place once again. I hope you enjoy it when it happens.

Rick Boatright
Topeka, Kansas
August 2015

MERCEDES LACKEY:
MISTRESS OF FANTASY

BARDIC VOICES
The Lark and the Wren
The Robin and the Kestrel
The Eagle and the Nightingales
The Free Bards
Four & Twenty Blackbirds
Bardic Choices: A Cast of Corbies (with Josepha Sherman)

URBAN FANTASIES WITH ROSEMARY EDGHILL
Beyond World's End
Spirits White as Lightning
Mad Maudlin
Bedlam's Edge(ed.)
Music to My Sorrow

This Scepter'd Isle (with Roberta Gellis)
Ill Met by Moonlight (with Roberta Gellis)
And Less Than Kind (with Roberta Gellis)
By Slanderous Tongues (with Roberta Gellis)
Knight of Ghosts and Shadows (with Ellen Guon)
Born to Run (with Larry Dixon)
Wheels of Fire (with Mark Shepherd)
Chrome Circle (with Larry Dixon)
The Chrome Borne (with Larry Dixon)
The Otherworld (with Larry Dixon & Mark Shepherd)

AND MORE!
Werehunter
Fiddler Fair
The Fire Rose
The Wizard of Karres (with Eric Flint & Dave Freer)
The Shadow of the Lion (with Eric Flint & Dave Freer)
This Rough Magic (with Eric Flint & Dave Freer)
Brain Ships (with Anne McCaffrey & Margaret Ball)
The Sword of Knowledge (with C.J. Cherryh Leslie Fish,
& Nancy Asire)